# HORNET FLIGHT
# &
# PAPER MONEY

**Ken Follett** was twenty-seven when he wrote *Eye of the Needle*, an award-winning thriller that became an international bestseller. After writing more successful thrillers he surprised everyone with *The Pillars of the Earth*, about the building of a cathedral in the Middle Ages, which continues to captivate millions of readers all over the world. His last book was the long-awaited sequel, *World Without End*, a number-one bestseller in the United States, Great Britain, Germany, Italy, Spain and France.

www.ken-follett.com

# KEN FOLLETT

## HORNET FLIGHT

&

## PAPER MONEY

PAN BOOKS

*Hornet Flight* first published 2002 by Macmillan
First published by Pan Books 2003
*Paper Money* first published 1977 by William Collins Sons & Co.
First published by Pan Books 1996

This edition published 2011 by Pan Books
an imprint of Pan Macmillan, a division of Macmillan Publishers Limited
Pan Macmillan, 20 New Wharf Road, London N1 9RR
Basingstoke and Oxford
Associated companies throughout the world
www.panmacmillan.com

ISBN 978-0-330-54553-2

3 5 7 9 8 6 4 2

A CIP catalogue record for this book is available from
the British Library.

Printed and bound by CPI Group (UK) Ltd, Croydon, CR0 4YY

# HORNET FLIGHT

Some of what follows really happened.

# PROLOGUE

A man with a wooden leg walked along a hospital corridor.

He was a short, vigorous type with an athletic build, thirty years old, dressed in a plain charcoal grey suit and black toecapped shoes. He walked briskly, but you could tell he was lame by the slight irregularity in his step: tap-*tap*, tap-*tap*. His face was fixed in a grim expression, as if he were suppressing some profound emotion.

He reached the end of the corridor and stopped at the nurse's desk. 'Flight Lieutenant Hoare?' he said.

The nurse looked up from a register. She was a pretty girl with black hair, and she spoke with the soft accent of County Cork. 'You'll be a relation, I'm thinking,' she said with a friendly smile.

Her charm had no effect. 'Brother,' said the visitor. 'Which bed?'

'Last on the left.'

He turned on his heel and strode along the aisle to the end of the ward. In a chair beside the bed, a figure in a brown dressing-gown sat with his back to the room, looking out of the window, smoking.

The visitor hesitated. 'Bart?'

The man in the chair stood up and turned around. There was a bandage on his head and his left arm was in a sling, but he was smiling. He was a younger, taller version of the visitor. 'Hello, Digby.'

Digby put his arms around his brother and hugged him hard. 'I thought you were dead,' he said.

Then he began to cry.

\* \* \*

'I was flying a Whitley,' Bart said. The Armstrong Whitworth Whitley was a cumbersome long-tailed bomber that flew in an odd nose-down attitude. In the spring of 1941, Bomber Command had a hundred of them, out of a total strength of about seven hundred aircraft. 'A Messerschmitt fired on us and we took several hits,' Bart continued. 'But he must have been running out of fuel, because he peeled off without finishing us. I thought it was my lucky day. Then we started to lose altitude. The Messerschmitt must have damaged both engines. We chucked out everything that wasn't bolted down, to reduce our weight, but it was no good, and I realized we'd have to ditch in the North Sea.'

Digby sat on the edge of the hospital bed, dry-eyed now, watching his brother's face, seeing the thousand-yard-stare as Bart remembered.

'I told the crew to jettison the rear hatch then get into ditching position, braced against the bulkhead.' The Whitley had a crew of five, Digby recalled. 'When we reached zero altitude I heaved back on the stick and opened the throttles, but the aircraft refused to level out, and we hit the water with a terrific smash. I was knocked out.'

They were step-brothers, eight years apart. Digby's mother had died when he was thirteen, and his father had married a widow with a boy of her own. From the start, Digby had looked after his little brother, protecting him from bullies and helping him with his school work. They had both been mad about aeroplanes, and dreamed of being pilots. Digby lost his right leg in a motorcycle accident, studied engineering, and went into aircraft design; but Bart lived the dream.

'When I came to, I could smell smoke. The aircraft was floating and the starboard wing was on fire. The night was dark as the grave, but I could see by the light of the flames. I crawled along the fuselage and found the dinghy pack. I bunged it through the hatch and jumped. Jesus, that water was cold.'

His voice was low and calm, but he took hard pulls on his cigarette, drawing the smoke deep into his lungs and blowing it out between tight-pursed lips in a long jet. 'I was wearing a life jacket and I came to the surface like a cork. There was quite a swell, and I was going up and down like a tart's knickers. Luckily, the dinghy pack was right in front of my nose. I pulled the string and it inflated itself but I couldn't get in. I didn't have the strength to heave myself out of the water. I couldn't understand it – didn't realize I had a dislocated shoulder and a broken wrist and three cracked ribs and all that. So I just stayed there, holding on, freezing to death.'

There had been a time, Digby recalled, when he thought Bart had been the lucky one.

'Eventually Jones and Croft appeared. They'd held on to the tail until it went down. Neither could swim, but their Mae Wests saved them, and they managed to scramble into the dinghy and pull me in.' He lit a fresh cigarette. 'I never saw Pickering. I don't know what happened to him, but I assume he's at the bottom of the sea.'

He fell silent. There was one crew member unaccounted for, Digby realized. After a pause, he said: 'What about the fifth man?'

'John Rowley, the bomb-aimer, was alive. We heard him call out. I was in a bit of a daze, but Jones and Croft tried to row towards the voice.' He shook his head in a gesture of hopelessness. 'You can't imagine how difficult it was. The swell must have been three or four feet, the flames were dying down so we couldn't see much, and the wind was howling like a bloody banshee. Jones yelled, and he's got a strong voice. Rowley would shout back, then the dinghy would go up one side of a wave and down the other and spin around at the same time, and when he called out again his voice seemed to come from a completely different direction. I don't know how long it went on. Rowley kept shouting, but his voice became weaker as the cold got to him.' Bart's face stiffened. 'He started to sound a bit pathetic, calling to God and his mother and that sort of rot. Eventually he went quiet.'

Digby found he was holding his breath, as if the

mere sound of breathing would be an intrusion on such a dreadful memory.

'We were found soon after dawn, by a destroyer on U-boat patrol. They dropped a cutter and hauled us in.' Bart looked out of the window, blind to the green Hertfordshire landscape, seeing a different scene, far away. 'Bloody lucky, really,' he said.

\* \* \*

They sat in silence for a while, then Bart said: 'Was the raid a success? No one will tell me how many came home.'

'Disastrous,' Digby said.

'What about my squadron?'

'Sergeant Jenkins and his crew got back safely.' Digby drew a slip of paper from his pocket. 'So did Pilot Officer Arasaratnam. Where's he from?'

'Ceylon.'

'And Sergeant Riley's aircraft took a hit but made it back.'

'Luck of the Irish,' said Bart. 'What about the rest?'

Digby just shook his head.

'But there were six aircraft from my squadron on that raid!' Bart protested.

'I know. As well as you, two more were shot down. No apparent survivors.'

'So Creighton-Smith is dead. And Billy Shaw. And . . . oh, God.' He turned away.

'I'm sorry.'

Bart's mood changed from despair to anger. 'It's

not enough to be sorry,' he said. 'We're being sent out there to die!'

'I know.'

'For Christ's sake, Digby, you're part of the bloody government.'

'I work for the prime minister, yes.' Churchill liked to bring people from private industry into the government and Digby, a successful aircraft designer before the war, was one of his troubleshooters.

'Then this is your fault as much as anyone's. You shouldn't be wasting your time visiting the sick. Get the hell out of here and do something about it.'

'I am doing something,' Digby said calmly. 'I've been given the task of finding out why this is happening. We lost fifty per cent of the aircraft on that raid.'

'Bloody treachery at the top, I suspect. Or some fool air marshal boasting in his club about tomorrow's raid, and a Nazi barman taking notes behind the beer pumps.'

'That's one possibility.'

Bart sighed. 'I'm sorry, Diggers,' he said, using a childhood nickname. 'It's not your fault, I'm just blowing my top.'

'Seriously, have you any idea why so many are being shot down? You've flown more than a dozen missions. What's your hunch?'

Bart looked thoughtful. 'I wasn't just sounding off about spies. When we get to Germany, they're ready for us. *They know we're coming.*'

'What makes you say that?'

'Their fighters are in the air, waiting for us. You know how difficult it is for defensive forces to time that right. The fighter squadron has to be scrambled at just the right moment, they must navigate from their airfield to the area where they think we might be, then they have to climb above our ceiling, and when they've done all that they have to find us in the moonlight. The whole process takes so much time that we should be able to drop our ordnance and get clear before they catch us. But it isn't happening that way.'

Digby nodded. Bart's experience matched that of other pilots he had questioned. He was about to say so when Bart looked up and smiled over Digby's shoulder. Digby turned to see a Negro in the uniform of a squadron leader. Like Bart, he was young for his rank, and Digby guessed he had received the automatic promotions that came with combat experience – flight lieutenant after twelve sorties, squadron leader after fifteen.

Bart said: 'Hello, Charles.'

'You had us all worried, Bartlett. How are you?' The newcomer's accent was Caribbean overlaid with an Oxbridge drawl.

'I may live, they say.'

With a fingertip, Charles touched the back of Bart's hand where it emerged from his sling. It was a curiously affectionate gesture, Digby thought. 'I'm jolly glad to hear it,' Charles said.

'Charles, meet my brother Digby. Digby, this is Charles Ford. We were together at Trinity until we left to join the air force.'

'It was the only way to avoid taking our exams,' Charles said, shaking Digby's hand.

Bart said: 'How are the Africans treating you?'

Charles smiled and explained to Digby: 'There's a squadron of Rhodesians at our airfield. First class flyers, but they find it difficult to deal with an officer of my colour. We call them the Africans, which seems to irritate them slightly. I can't think why.'

Digby said: 'Obviously you're not letting it get you down.'

'I believe that with patience and improved education we may eventually be able to civilize such people, primitive though they seem now.' Charles looked away, and Digby caught a glimpse of the anger beneath his good humour.

'I was just asking Bart why he thinks we're losing so many bombers,' Digby said. 'What's your opinion?'

'I wasn't on this raid,' Charles said. 'By all accounts, I was lucky to miss it. But other recent operations have been pretty bad. I get the feeling the Luftwaffe can follow us through cloud. Might they have some kind of equipment on board that enables them to locate us even when we're not visible?'

Digby shook his head. 'Every crashed enemy aircraft is minutely examined, and we've never seen anything like what you're talking about. We're working hard to invent that kind of device, and I'm sure the enemy are too, but we're a long way from success, and we're pretty sure they're well behind us. I don't think that's it.'

'Well, that's what it feels like.'

'I still think there are spies,' Bart said.

'Interesting.' Digby stood up. 'I have to get back to Whitehall. Thanks for your opinions. It helps to talk to the men at the sharp end.' He shook hands with Charles and squeezed Bart's uninjured shoulder. 'Sit still and get well.'

'They say I'll be flying again in a few weeks.'

'I can't say I'm glad.'

As Digby turned to go, Charles said: 'May I ask you a question?'

'Of course.'

'On a raid like this one, the cost to us of replacing lost aircraft must be more than the cost to the enemy of repairing the damage done by our bombs.'

'Undoubtedly.'

'Then . . .' Charles spread his arms in a sign of incomprehension. 'Why do we do it? What's the point of bombing?'

'Yes,' Bart said. 'I'd like to know that.'

'What else can we do?' Digby said. 'The Nazis control Europe: Austria, Czechoslovakia, Holland, Belgium, France, Denmark, Norway. Italy is an ally, Spain is sympathetic, Sweden is neutral, and they have a pact with the Soviet Union. We have no military forces on the Continent. We have no other way of fighting back.'

Charles nodded. 'So we're all you've got.'

'Exactly,' Digby said. 'If the bombing stops, the war is over – and Hitler has won.'

* * *

The prime minister was watching *The Maltese Falcon*. A private cinema had recently been built in the old kitchens of Admiralty House. It had fifty or sixty plush seats and a red velvet curtain, but it was usually used to show film of bombing raids and to screen propaganda pieces before they were shown to the public.

Late at night, after all the memoranda had been dictated, the cables sent, the reports annotated, and the minutes initialled, when he was too worried and angry and tense to sleep, Churchill would sit in one of the large VIP seats in the front row with a glass of brandy and lose himself in the latest enchantment from Hollywood.

As Digby walked in, Humphrey Bogart was explaining to Mary Astor that when a man's partner is killed he's supposed to do something about it. The air was thick with cigar smoke. Churchill pointed to a seat. Digby sat down and watched the last few minutes of the movie. As the credits appeared over the statuette of a black falcon, Digby told his boss that the Luftwaffe seemed to have advance notice when Bomber Command was coming.

When he had finished, Churchill stared at the screen for a few moments, as if he were waiting to find out who had played Bryan. There were times when he was charming, with an engaging smile and a twinkle in his blue eyes, but tonight he seemed sunk in gloom. At last he said: 'What does the RAF think?'

'They blame poor formation flying. In theory, if

the bombers fly in close formation, their armament should cover the entire sky, so any enemy fighter that appears should be shot down immediately.'

'And what do you say to that?'

'Rubbish. Formation flying has never worked. Some new factor has entered the equation.'

'I agree. But what?'

'My brother blames spies.'

'All the spies we've caught have been amateurish – but that's why they were caught, of course. It may be that the competent ones have slipped through the net.'

'Perhaps the Germans have made a technical breakthrough.'

'The Secret Intelligence Service tell me the enemy are far behind us in the development of radar.'

'Do you trust their judgement?'

'No.' The ceiling lights came on. Churchill was in evening dress. He always looked dapper, but his face was lined with weariness. He took from his waistcoat pocket a folded sheet of flimsy paper. 'Here's a clue,' he said, and he handed it to Digby.

Digby studied the sheet. It appeared to be a decrypt of a Luftwaffe radio signal, in German and English. It said that the Luftwaffe's new strategy of dark night-fighting – *Dunkel Nachtjagd* – had scored a great triumph, thanks to the excellent information from Freya. Digby read the message in English then again in German. 'Freya' was not a word in either language. 'What does this mean?' he said.

'That's what I want you to find out.' Churchill stood up and shrugged into his jacket. 'Walk back with me,' he said. As he left, he called out: 'Thank you!'

A voice from the projectionist's booth replied: 'My pleasure, sir.'

As they passed through the building, two men fell in behind them: Inspector Thompson from Scotland Yard, and Churchill's private bodyguard. They emerged on the parade ground, passed a team operating a barrage balloon, and went through a gate in the barbed-wire fence to the street. London was blacked out, but a crescent moon gave enough light for them to find their way.

They walked side by side a few yards along Horse Guards Parade to Number One Storey's Gate. A bomb had damaged the rear of Number Ten Downing Street, the traditional residence of the prime minister, so Churchill was living at the nearby annexe over the Cabinet War Rooms. The entrance was protected by a bombproof wall. The barrel of a machine gun poked through a hole in the wall.

Digby said: 'Goodnight, sir.'

'It can't go on,' said Churchill. 'At this rate, Bomber Command will be finished by Christmas. I need to know who or what Freya is.'

'I'll find out.'

'Do so with the utmost despatch.'

'Yes, sir.'

'Goodnight,' said the prime minister, and he went inside.

# PART ONE

PART ONE

# ONE

On the last day of May 1941, a strange vehicle was seen on the streets of Morlunde, a city on the west coast of Denmark.

It was a Danish-made Nimbus motorcycle with a sidecar. That in itself was an unusual sight, because there was no petrol for anyone except doctors and the police and, of course, the German troops occupying the country. But this Nimbus had been modified. The four-cylinder petrol engine had been replaced by a steam engine taken from a scrapped river launch. The seat had been removed from the sidecar to make room for a boiler, firebox and chimney stack. The substitute engine was low in power, and the bike had a top speed of about twenty-two miles per hour. Instead of the customary roar of a motorcycle exhaust, there was only the gentle hiss of steam. The eery quiet and the slow pace gave the vehicle a stately air.

In the saddle was Harald Olufsen, a tall youth of eighteen, with clear skin and fair hair brushed back from a high forehead. He looked like a Viking in a school blazer. He had saved for a year to buy the Nimbus, which had cost him six hundred crowns –

then, the day after he got it, the Germans had imposed the petrol restrictions.

Harald had been furious. What right did they have? But he had been brought up to act rather than complain.

It had taken him another year to modify the bike, working in school holidays, fitting it in with revision for his university entrance exams. Today, home from his boarding school for the Whitsun break, he had spent the morning memorizing physics equations and the afternoon attaching a sprocket from a rusted lawn mower to the back wheel. Now, with the motorcycle working perfectly, he was heading for a bar where he hoped to hear some jazz and perhaps even meet some girls.

He loved jazz. After physics, it was the most interesting thing that had ever happened to him. The American musicians were the best, of course, but even their Danish imitators were worth listening to. You could sometimes hear good jazz in Morlunde, perhaps because it was an international port, visited by sailors from all over the world.

But when Harald drove up outside the Club Hot, in the heart of the dockside district, its door was closed and its windows shuttered.

He was mystified. It was eight o'clock on a Saturday evening, and this was one of the most popular spots in town. It should be swinging.

As he sat staring at the silent building, a passer-by stopped and looked at his vehicle. 'What's that contraption?'

'A Nimbus with a steam engine. Do you know anything about this club?'

'I own it. What does the bike use for fuel?'

'Anything that burns. I use peat.' He pointed to the pile in the back of the sidecar.

'*Peat?*' The man laughed.

'Why are the doors shut?'

'The Nazis closed me down.'

Harald was dismayed. 'Why?'

'Employing Negro musicians.'

Harald had never seen a coloured musician in the flesh, but he knew from records that they were the best. 'The Nazis are ignorant swine,' he said angrily. His evening had been ruined.

The club owner looked up and down the street to make sure no one had heard. The occupying power ruled Denmark with a light hand, but all the same few people openly insulted the Nazis. However, there was no one else in sight. He returned his gaze to the motorcycle. 'Does it work?'

'Of course it does.'

'Who converted it for you?'

'I did it myself.'

The man's amusement was turning to admiration. 'That's pretty clever.'

'Thank you.' Harald opened the tap that admitted steam into the engine. 'I'm sorry about your club.'

'I'm hoping they'll let me open again in a few weeks. But I'll have to promise to employ white musicians.'

'Jazz without Negroes?' Harald shook his head

in disgust. 'It's like banning French cooks from restaurants.' He took his foot off the brake and the bike moved slowly away.

He thought of heading for the town centre, to see if there was anyone he knew in the cafés and bars around the square, but he felt so disappointed about the jazz club that he decided it would be depressing to hang around. He steered for the harbour.

His father was pastor of the church on Sande, a small island a couple of miles offshore. The little ferry that shuttled to and from the island was in dock, and he drove straight on to it. It was crowded with people, most of whom he knew. There was a merry gang of fishermen who had been to a football match and had a few drinks afterwards; two well-off women in hats and gloves with a pony and trap and a stack of shopping; and a family of five who had been visiting relations in town. A well-dressed couple he did not recognize were probably going to dine at the island's hotel, which had a high-class restaurant. His motorcycle attracted everyone's interest, and he had to explain the steam engine again.

At the last minute a German-built Ford sedan drove on. Harald knew the car: it belonged to Axel Flemming, owner of the hotel. The Flemmings were hostile to Harald's family. Axel Flemming felt he was the natural leader of the island community, a role which Pastor Olufsen believed to be his own, and the friction between the rival patriarchs affected all other family members. Harald wondered how Flemming had managed to get petrol for his car. He supposed anything was possible to the rich.

The sea was choppy and there were dark clouds in the western sky. A storm was coming in, but the fishermen said they would be home before it arrived, just. Harald took out a newspaper he had picked up in the town. Entitled *Reality*, it was an illegal publication, printed in defiance of the occupying power and given away free. The Danish police had not attempted to suppress it and the Germans seemed to regard it as beneath contempt. In Copenhagen, people read it openly on trains and streetcars. Here people were more discreet, and Harald folded it to hide the masthead while he read a report about the shortage of butter. Denmark produced millions of pounds of butter every year, but almost all of it was now sent to Germany, and Danes had trouble getting any. It was the kind of story that never appeared in the censored legitimate press.

The familiar flat shape of the island came closer. It was twelve miles long and a mile wide, with a village at each end. The fishermen's cottages, and the church with its parsonage, constituted the older village at the south end. Also at the south end, a school of navigation, long disused, had been taken over by the Germans and turned into a military base. The hotel and the larger homes were at the north end. In between, the island was mostly sand dunes and scrub with a few trees and no hills, but all along the seaward side was a magnificent ten-mile beach.

Harald felt a few drops of rain as the ferry approached its dock at the north end of the island. The hotel's horse-drawn taxi was waiting for the well-dressed couple. The fishermen were met by the wife of one of them driving a horse and cart. Harald decided to cross the island and drive home along the beach, which had hard-packed sand – in fact it had been used for speed trials of racing cars.

He was half way from the dock to the hotel when he ran out of steam.

He was using the bike's petrol tank as a water reserve, and he realized now that it was not big enough. He would have to get a five-gallon oil drum and put it in the sidecar. Meanwhile, he needed water to get him home.

There was only one house within sight, and unfortunately it was Axel Flemming's. Despite their rivalry, the Olufsens and the Flemmings were on speaking terms: all members of the Flemming family came to church every Sunday and sat together at the front. Indeed, Axel was a deacon. All the same, Harald did not relish the thought of asking the antagonistic Flemmings for help. He considered walking a quarter of a mile to the next nearest house, then decided that would be foolish. With a sigh, he set off up the long drive.

Rather than knock at the front door, he went around the side of the house to the stables. He was pleased to see a manservant putting the Ford in the garage. 'Hello, Gunnar,' said Harald. 'Can I have some water?'

The man was friendly. 'Help yourself,' he said. 'There's a tap in the yard.'

Harald found a bucket beside the tap and filled it. He went back to the road and poured the water into the tank. It looked as if he might manage to avoid meeting any of the family. But when he returned the bucket to the yard, Peter Flemming was there.

A tall, haughty man of thirty in a well-cut suit of oatmeal tweed, Peter was Axel's son. Before the quarrel between the families, he had been best friends with Harald's brother Arne, and in their teens they had been known as ladykillers, Arne seducing girls with his wicked charm and Peter by his cool sophistication. Peter now lived in Copenhagen but had come home for the holiday weekend, Harald assumed.

Peter was reading *Reality*. He looked up from the paper to see Harald. 'What are you doing here?' he said.

'Hello, Peter, I came to get some water.'

'I suppose this rag is yours?'

Harald touched his pocket and realized with consternation that the newspaper must have fallen out when he reached down for the bucket.

Peter saw the movement and understood its meaning. 'Obviously it is,' he said. 'Are you aware that you could go to jail just for having it in your possession?'

The talk of jail was not an empty threat: Peter was a police detective. Harald said, 'Everyone reads it in the city.' He made himself sound defiant, but in fact he was a little scared: Peter was mean enough to arrest him.

'This is not Copenhagen,' Peter intoned solemnly.

Harald knew that Peter would love the chance to disgrace an Olufsen. Yet he was hesitating. Harald thought he knew why. 'You'll look a fool if you arrest a schoolboy on Sande for doing something half the population does openly. Especially when everyone finds out you've got a grudge against my father.'

Peter was visibly torn between the desire to humiliate Harald and the fear of being laughed at. 'No one is entitled to break the law,' he said.

'Whose law – ours, or the Germans'?'

'The law is the law.'

Harald felt more confident. Peter would not be arguing so defensively if he intended to make an arrest. 'You only say that because your father makes so much money giving Nazis a good time at his hotel.'

That hit home. The hotel was popular with German officers, who had more to spend than the Danes. Peter flushed with anger. 'While your father gives inflammatory sermons,' he retorted. It was true: the pastor had preached against the Nazis, his theme being 'Jesus was a Jew'. Peter continued: 'Does he realize how much trouble will be caused if he stirs people up?'

'I'm sure he does. The founder of the Christian religion was something of a troublemaker himself.'

'Don't talk to me about religion. I have to keep order down here on earth.'

'To hell with order, we've been invaded!' Harald's

frustration over his blighted evening out boiled over. 'What right have the Nazis got to tell us what to do? We should kick the whole evil pack of them out of our country!'

'You mustn't hate the Germans, they're our friends,' Peter said with an air of pious self-righteousness that maddened Harald.

'I don't hate Germans, you damn fool, I've got German cousins.' The pastor's sister had married a successful young Hamburg dentist who came to Sande on holiday, back in the twenties. Their daughter Monika was the first girl Harald had kissed. 'They've suffered more from the Nazis than we have,' Harald added. Uncle Joachim was Jewish and, although he was a baptized Christian and an elder of his church, the Nazis had ruled that he could only treat Jews, thereby ruining his practice. A year ago he had been arrested on suspicion of hoarding gold and sent to a special kind of prison, called a *Konzentrazionslager*, in the small Bavarian town of Dachau.

'People bring trouble on themselves,' Peter said with a worldly-wise air. 'Your father should never have allowed his sister to marry a Jew.' He threw the newspaper to the ground and walked away.

At first Harald was too taken aback to reply. He bent and picked up the newspaper. Then he said to Peter's retreating back: 'You're starting to sound like a Nazi yourself.'

Ignoring him, Peter went in by a kitchen entrance and slammed the door.

Harald felt he had lost the argument, which was

infuriating, because he knew that what Peter had said was outrageous.

It started to rain heavily as he headed back toward the road. When he returned to his bike, he found that the fire under the boiler had gone out.

He tried to relight it. He crumpled up his copy of *Reality* for kindling, and he had a box of good quality wood matches in his pocket, but he had not brought with him the bellows he had used to start the fire earlier in the day. After twenty frustrating minutes bent over the firebox in the rain, he gave up. He would have to walk home.

He turned up the collar of his blazer.

He pushed the bike half a mile to the hotel and left it in the small car park, then set off along the beach. At this time of year, three weeks from the summer solstice, the Scandinavian evenings lasted until eleven o'clock; but tonight clouds darkened the sky and the pouring rain further restricted visibility. Harald followed the edge of dunes, finding his way by the feel of the ground underfoot and the sound of the sea in his right ear. Before long, his clothes were so soaked that he could have swum home without getting any wetter.

He was a strong young man, and as fit as a greyhound, but two hours later he was tired, cold and miserable when he came up against the fence around the new German base and realized he would have to walk two miles around it in order to reach his home a few hundred yards away.

If the tide had been out, he would have continued

along the beach for, although that stretch of sand was officially off limits, the guards would not have been able to see him in this weather. However, the tide was in, and the fence reached into the water. It crossed his mind to swim the last stretch, but he dismissed the idea immediately. Like everyone in this fishing community, Harald had a wary respect for the sea, and it would be dangerous to swim at night in this weather when he was already exhausted.

But he could climb the fence.

The rain had eased, and a quarter moon showed fitfully through racing clouds, intermittently shedding an uncertain light over the drenched landscape. Harald could see the chicken-wire fence six feet high with two strands of barbed wire at the top, formidable enough but no great obstacle to a determined person in good physical shape. Fifty yards inland, it passed through a copse of scrubby trees and bushes that hid it from view. That would be the place to get over.

He knew what lay beyond the fence. Last summer he had worked as a labourer on the building site. At that time, he had not known it was destined to be a military base. The builders, a Copenhagen firm, had told everyone it was to be a new coastguard station. They might have had trouble recruiting staff if they had told the truth – Harald for one would not knowingly have worked for the Nazis. Then, when the buildings were up and the fence had been completed, all the Danes had been sent away, and Germans had been brought in to instal the equipment. But Harald knew the layout. The disused navigation school had been refurbished, and two new buildings put up either side of it. All the buildings were set back from the beach, so he could cross the base without going near them. In addition, much of the ground at this end of the site was covered with low bushes that would help conceal him. He would just have to keep an eye out for patrolling guards.

He found his way to the copse, climbed the fence, eased himself gingerly over the barbed wire at the top, and jumped down the other side, landing softly on the wet dunes. He looked around, peering through the gloom, seeing only the vague shapes of trees. The buildings were out of sight, but he could hear distant music and an occasional shout of laughter. It was Saturday night: perhaps the soldiers were having a few beers while their officers dined at Axel Flemming's hotel.

He headed across the base, moving as fast as he dared in the shifting moonlight, staying close to bushes when he could, orienting himself by the waves on his right and the faint music to the left. He passed a tall structure and recognized it, in the dimness, as a searchlight tower. The whole area could be lit up in an emergency, but otherwise the base was blacked out.

A sudden burst of sound to his left startled him, and he crouched down, his heart beating faster. He looked over toward the buildings. A door stood open, spilling light. As he watched, a soldier came out and ran across the compound; then another door opened in a different building, and the soldier ran in.

Harald's heartbeat eased.

He passed through a stand of conifers and went down into a dip. As he came to the bottom of the declivity, he saw a structure of some kind looming up in the murk. He could not make it out clearly, but he did not recall anything being built in this location. Coming closer, he saw a curved concrete wall about as high as his head. Above the wall something moved, and he heard a low hum, like an electric motor.

This must have been erected by the Germans after the local workers had been laid off. He wondered why he had never seen the structure from outside the fence, then realized that the trees and the dip in the ground would hide it from most viewpoints, except perhaps the beach – which was out of bounds where it passed the base.

When he looked up and tried to make out the details, rain drove into his face, stinging his eyes. But he was too curious to pass by. The moon shone bright for a moment. Squinting, he looked again. Above the circular wall he made out a grid of metal or wire like an oversize mattress, twelve feet on a side. The whole contraption was rotating like a merry-go-round, completing a revolution every few seconds.

Harald was fascinated. It was a machine of a kind he had never seen before, and the engineer in him was spellbound. What did it do? Why did it revolve? The sound told him little – that was just the motor that turned the thing. He felt sure it was not a gun, at least not the conventional kind, for there was no barrel. His best guess was that it was something to do with radio.

Nearby, someone coughed.

Harald reacted instinctively. He jumped, got his arms over the edge of the wall, and hauled himself up. He lay for a second on the narrow top, feeling dangerously conspicuous, then eased himself down on the inside. He worried that his feet might encounter moving machinery, but he felt almost sure there would be a walkway around the mechanism to allow engineers to service it, and after a tense moment he touched a concrete floor. The hum was louder, and he could smell engine oil. On his tongue was the peculiar taste of static electricity.

Who had coughed? He presumed a sentry was passing by. The man's footsteps must have been lost in the wind and rain. Fortunately, the same noises had muffled the sound Harald made scrambling over the wall. But had the sentry seen him?

He flattened himself against the curved inside of the wall, breathing hard, waiting for the beam of a powerful flashlight to betray him. He wondered what would happen if he were caught. The Germans were amiable, out here in the countryside: most of them did not strut around like conquerors, but seemed almost embarrassed at being in charge. They would probably hand him over to the Danish police. He was not sure what line the cops would take. If Peter Flemming were part of the local force, he would make sure Harald suffered as much as possible; but he was based in Copenhagen, fortunately. What Harald dreaded, more than any official punishment, was his father's anger. He could already hear the pastor's sarcastic interrogation: 'You climbed the fence? And entered the secret military compound? At night? And used it as a short cut home? Because it was *raining*?'

But no light shone on Harald. He waited, and stared at the dark bulk of the apparatus in front of him. He thought he could see heavy cables coming from the lower edge of the grid and disappearing into the gloom on the far side of the pit. This had to be a means of sending radio signals, or receiving them, he thought.

When a few slow minutes had passed, he felt sure the guard had moved on. He clambered to the top of the wall and tried to see through the rain. On either side of the structure he could make out two smaller dark shapes, but they were static, and he decided they must be part of the machinery. No sentry was visible. He slid down the outside of the wall and set off once again across the dunes.

In a dark moment, when the moon was behind a thick cloud, he walked smack into a wooden wall. Shocked and momentarily scared, he let out a muffled curse. A second later he realized he had run into an old boathouse that had been used by the navigation school. It was derelict, and the Germans had not repaired it, apparently having no use for it. He stood still for a moment, listening, but all he could hear was his heart pounding. He walked on.

He reached the far fence without further incident. He scrambled over and headed for his home.

He came first to the church. Light glowed from the long row of small, square windows in its seaward wall.

Surprised that anyone should be in the building at this hour on a Saturday night, he looked inside.

The church was long and low-roofed. On special occasions it could hold the island's resident population of four hundred, but only just. Rows of seats faced a wooden lectern. There was no altar. The walls were bare except for some framed texts.

Danes were undogmatic about religion, and most of the nation subscribed to Evangelical Lutheranism. However, the fishing folk of Sande had been converted, a hundred years ago, to a harsher creed. For the last thirty years Harald's father had kept their faith alight, setting an example of uncompromising puritanism in his own life, stiffening the resolve of his congregation in weekly brimstone sermons, and confronting backsliders personally with the irresistible holiness of his blue-eyed gaze. Despite the example of this blazing conviction, his son was not a believer. Harald went to services whenever he was at home, not wanting to hurt his father's feelings, but in his heart he dissented. He had not yet made up his mind about religion in general, but he knew he did not believe in a god of petty rules and vengeful punishments.

As he looked through the window he heard music. His brother Arne was at the piano, playing a jazz tune with a delicate touch. Harald smiled with pleasure. Arne had come home for the holiday. He was amusing and sophisticated, and he would enliven the long weekend at the parsonage.

Harald walked to the entrance and stepped inside. Without looking around, Arne changed the music seamlessly to a hymn tune. Harald grinned. Arne had heard the door open and thought their father might be coming in. The pastor disapproved of jazz and certainly would not permit it to be played in his church. 'It's only me,' Harald said.

Arne turned around. He was wearing his brown army uniform. Ten years older than Harald, he was a flying instructor with the army aviation troops, based at the flying school near Copenhagen. The Germans had halted all Danish military activity, and the aircraft were grounded most of the time, but the instructors were allowed to give lessons in gliders.

'Seeing you out of the corner of my eye, I thought you were the old man.' Arne looked Harald up and down fondly. 'You look more and more like him.'

'Does that mean I'll go bald?'

'Probably.'

'And you?'

'I don't think so. I take after Mother.'

It was true. Arne had their mother's thick dark hair and hazel eyes. Harald was fair, like their father, and had also inherited the penetrating blue-eyed stare with which the pastor intimidated his flock. Both Harald and their father were formidably tall, making Arne seem short at an inch under six feet.

'I've got something to play you,' Harald said. Arne got off the stool and Harald sat at the piano. 'I learned this from a record someone brought to school. You know Mads Kirke?'

'Cousin of my colleague Poul.'

'Right. He discovered this American pianist called

Clarence Pine Top Smith.' Harald hesitated. 'What's the old man doing at this moment?'

'Writing tomorrow's sermon.'

'Good.' The piano could not be heard from the parsonage, fifty yards away, and it was unlikely that the pastor would interrupt his preparation to take an idle stroll across to the church, especially in this weather. Harald began to play *Pine Top's Boogie-Woogie*, and the room filled with the sexy harmonies of the American south. He was an enthusiastic pianist, though his mother said he had a heavy hand. He could not sit still to play, so he stood up, kicking the stool back, knocking it over, and played standing, bending his long frame over the keyboard. He made more mistakes this way, but they did not seem to matter as long as he kept up the compulsive rhythm. He banged out the last chord and said in English: 'That's what I'm talkin' about!' just as Pine Top did on the record.

Arne laughed. 'Not bad!'

'You should hear the original.'

'Come and stand in the porch. I want to smoke.'

Harald stood up. 'The old man won't like that.'

'I'm twenty-eight,' Arne said. 'I'm too old to be told what to do by my father.'

'I agree – but does he?'

'Are you afraid of him?'

'Of course. So is Mother, and just about every other person on this island – even you.'

Arne grinned. 'All right, maybe just a little bit.'

They stood outside the church door, sheltered from the rain by a little porch. On the far side of a patch of sandy ground they could see the dark shape of the parsonage. Light shone through the diamond-shaped window set into the kitchen door. Arne took out his cigarettes.

'Have you heard from Hermia?' Harald asked him. Arne was engaged to an English girl whom he had not seen for more than a year, since the Germans had occupied Denmark.

Arne shook his head. 'I tried to write to her. I found an address for the British Consulate in Gothenburg.' Danes were allowed to send letters to Sweden, which was neutral. 'I addressed it to her at that house, not mentioning the consulate on the envelope. I thought I'd been quite clever, but the censors aren't so easily fooled. My commanding officer brought the letter back to me and said that if I ever tried anything like that again I'd be court-martialled.'

Harald liked Hermia. Some of Arne's girlfriends had been, well, dumb blondes, but Hermia had brains and guts. She was a little scary on first acquaintance, with her dramatic dark looks and her direct manner of speech; but she had endeared herself to Harald by treating him like a man, not just someone's kid brother. And she was sensationally voluptuous in a swimsuit. 'Do you still want to marry her?'

'God, yes – if she's alive. She might have been killed by a bomb in London.'

'It must be hard, not knowing.'

Arne nodded, then said: 'How about you? Any action?'

Harald shrugged. 'Girls my age aren't interested in schoolboys.' He said it lightly, but he was hiding real resentment. He had suffered a couple of wounding rejections.

'I suppose they want to date a guy who can spend some money on them.'

'Exactly. And younger girls . . . I met a girl at Easter, Birgit Claussen.'

'Claussen? The boatbuilding family in Morlunde?'

'Yes. She's pretty, but she's only sixteen, and she was so boring to talk to.'

'It's just as well. The family are Catholics. The old man wouldn't approve.'

'I know.' Harald frowned. 'He's strange, though. At Easter he preached about tolerance.'

'He's about as tolerant as Vlad the Impaler.' Arne threw away the stub of his cigarette. 'Let's go and talk to the old tyrant.'

'Before we go in . . .'

'What?'

'How are things in the army?'

'Grim. We can't defend our country, and most of the time I'm not allowed to fly.'

'How long can this go on?'

'Who knows? Maybe for ever. The Nazis have won everything. There's no opposition left but the British, and they're hanging on by a thread.'

Harald lowered his voice, although there was no

one to listen. 'Surely someone in Copenhagen must be starting a Resistance movement?'

Arne shrugged. 'If they were, and I knew about it, I couldn't tell you, could I?' Then, before Harald could say more, Arne dashed through the rain toward the light shining from the kitchen.

# TWO

Hermia Mount looked with dismay at her lunch – two charred sausages, a dollop of runny mashed potato, and a mound of overcooked cabbage – and she thought with longing of a bar on the Copenhagen waterfront that served three kinds of herring with salad, pickles, warm bread and lager beer.

She had been brought up in Denmark. Her father had been a British diplomat who spent most of his career in Scandinavian countries. Hermia had worked in the British Embassy in Copenhagen, first as a secretary, later as assistant to a naval attaché who was in fact with MI6, the secret intelligence service. When her father died, and her mother returned to London, Hermia stayed on, partly because of her job, but mainly because she was engaged to a Danish pilot, Arne Olufsen.

Then, on 9 April 1940, Hitler invaded Denmark. Four anxious days later, Hermia and a group of British officials had left in a special diplomatic train that brought them through Germany to the Dutch frontier, from where they travelled through neutral Holland and on to London.

Now, at the age of thirty, Hermia was an

intelligence analyst in charge of MI6's Denmark desk. Along with most of the service, she had been evacuated from its London headquarters at 54 Broadway, near Buckingham Palace, to Bletchley Park, a large country house on the edge of a village fifty miles north of the capital.

A Nissen hut hastily erected in the grounds served as a canteen. Hermia was glad to be escaping the Blitz, but she wished that by some miracle they could also have evacuated one of London's charming little Italian or French restaurants, so that she would have something to eat. She forked a little mash into her mouth and forced herself to swallow.

To take her mind off the taste of the food, she put that day's *Daily Express* beside her plate. The British had just lost the Mediterranean island of Crete. The *Express* tried to put a brave face on it, claiming the battle had cost Hitler 18,000 men, but the depressing truth was that this was another in a long line of triumphs for the Nazis.

Glancing up, she saw a short man of about her own age coming towards her, carrying a cup of tea, walking briskly but with a noticeable limp. 'May I join you?' he said cheerfully, and sat opposite her without waiting for an answer. 'I'm Digby Hoare. I know who you are.'

She raised an eyebrow and said: 'Make yourself at home.'

The note of irony in her voice made no apparent impact. He just said: 'Thanks.'

She had seen him around once or twice. He had an energetic air, despite his limp. He was no matinée idol, with his unruly dark hair, but he had nice blue eyes, and his features were pleasantly craggy in a Humphrey Bogart way. She asked him: 'What department are you with?'

'I work in London, actually.'

That was not an answer to her question, she noted. She pushed her plate aside.

He said: 'You don't like the food?'

'Do you?'

'I'll tell you something. I've debriefed pilots who have been shot down over France and made their way home. We think we're experiencing austerity, but we don't know the meaning of the word. The Frogs are starving to death. After hearing those stories, everything tastes good to me.'

'Austerity is no excuse for vile cooking,' Hermia said crisply.

He grinned. 'They told me you were a bit waspish.'

'What else did they tell you?'

'That you're bilingual in English and Danish – which is why you're head of the Denmark desk, I presume.'

'No. The war is the reason for that. Before, no woman ever rose above the level of secretary-assistant in MI6. We didn't have analytical minds, you see. We were more suited to home-making and child-rearing. But since war broke out, women's brains have undergone a remarkable change, and we have become capable of work that previously could only be accomplished by the masculine mentality.'

He took her sarcasm with easy good humour. 'I've noticed that, too,' he said. 'Wonders never cease.'

'Why have you been checking up on me?'

'Two reasons. First, because you're the most beautiful woman I've ever seen.' This time he was not grinning.

He had succeeded in surprising her. Men did not often say she was beautiful. Handsome, perhaps; striking, sometimes; imposing, often. Her face was a long oval, perfectly regular, but with severe dark hair, hooded eyes, and a nose too big to be pretty. She could not think of a witty rejoinder. 'What's the other reason?'

He glanced sideways. Two older women were sharing their table, and although they were chatting to one another, they were probably also half-listening to Digby and Hermia. 'I'll tell you in a minute,' he said. 'Would you like to go out on the tiles?'

He had surprised her again. 'What?'

'Will you go out with me?'

'Certainly not.'

For a moment he seemed nonplussed. Then his grin returned, and he said: 'Don't sugar the pill, give it to me straight.'

She could not help smiling.

'We could go to the pictures,' he persisted. 'Or to the Shoulder of Mutton pub in Old Bletchley. Or both.'

She shook her head. 'No, thank you,' she said firmly.

'Oh.' He seemed crestfallen.

Did he think she was turning him down because of his disability? She hastened to put that right. 'I'm engaged,' she said. She showed him the ring on her left hand.

'I didn't notice.'

'Men never do.'

'Who's the lucky fellow?'

'A pilot in the Danish army.'

'Over there, I presume.'

'As far as I know. I haven't heard from him for a year.'

The two ladies left the table, and Digby's manner changed. His face turned serious and his voice became quiet but urgent. 'Take a look at this, please.' He drew from his pocket a sheet of flimsy paper and handed it to her.

She had seen such flimsy sheets before, here at Bletchley Park. As she expected, it was a decrypt of an enemy radio signal.

'I imagine I've no need to tell you how desperately secret this is,' Digby said.

'No need.'

'I believe you speak German as well as Danish.'

She nodded. 'In Denmark, all school children learn German, and English and Latin as well.' She studied the signal for a moment. 'Information from Freya?'

'That's what's puzzling us. It's not a word in German. I thought it might mean something in one of the Scandinavian languages.'

'It does, in a way,' she said. 'Freya is a Norse goddess – in fact she's the Viking Venus, the goddess of love.'

'Ah!' Digby looked thoughtful. 'Well, that's something, but it doesn't get us far.'

'What's this all about?'

'We're losing too many bombers.'

Hermia frowned. 'I read about the last big raid in the newspapers – they said it was a great success.'

Digby just looked at her.

'Oh, I see,' she said. 'You don't tell the newspapers the truth.'

He remained silent.

'In fact, my entire picture of the bombing campaign is mere propaganda,' she went on. 'The truth is that it's a complete disaster.' To her dismay, he still did not contradict her. 'For heaven's sake, how many aircraft did we lose?'

'Fifty per cent.'

'Dear God.' Hermia looked away. Some of those pilots had fiancées, she thought. 'But if this goes on . . .'

'Exactly.'

She looked again at the decrypt. 'Is Freya a spy?'

'It's my job to find out.'

'What can I do?'

'Tell me more about the goddess.'

Hermia dug back into her memory. She had learned the Norse myths at school, but that was a long time ago. 'Freya has a gold necklace that is very precious. It was given to her by four dwarves. It's guarded by the watchman of the gods . . . Heimdal, I think his name is.'

'A watchman. That makes sense.'

'Freya could be a spy with access to advance information about air raids.'

'She could also be a machine for detecting approaching aircraft before they come within sight.'

'I've heard that we have such machines, but I've no idea how they work.'

'Three possible ways: infra-red, lidar, and radar. Infra-red detectors would pick up the rays emitted by a hot aircraft engine, or possibly its exhaust. Lidar is a system of optical pulses sent out by the detection apparatus and reflected back off the aircraft. Radar is the same thing with radio pulses.'

'I've just remembered something else. Heimdal can see for a hundred miles by day or night.'

'That makes it sound more like a machine.'

'That's what I was thinking.'

Digby finished his tea and stood up. 'If you have any more thoughts, will you let me know?'

'Of course. Where do I find you?'

'Number Ten, Downing Street.'

'Oh!' She was impressed.

'Goodbye.'

'Goodbye,' she said, and watched him walk away.

She sat there for a few moments. It had been an interesting conversation in more ways than one. Digby Hoare was very high-powered: the prime minister himself must be worried about the loss of bombers.

Was the use of the codename Freya mere coincidence, or was there a Scandinavian connection?

She had enjoyed Digby's asking her out. Although she was not interested in dating another man, it was nice to be asked.

After a while, the sight of her uneaten lunch began to get her down. She took her tray to the slops table and scraped her plate into the pigbin. Then she went to the ladies' room.

While she was in a cubicle, she heard a group of young women come in, chattering animatedly. She was about to emerge when one of them said: 'That Digby Hoare doesn't waste time – talk about a fast worker.'

Hermia froze with her hand on the door knob.

'I saw him move in on Miss Mount,' said an older voice. 'He must be a tit man.'

The others giggled. In the cubicle, Hermia frowned at this reference to her generous figure.

'I think she gave him the brush-off, though,' said the first girl.

'Wouldn't you? I couldn't fancy a man with a wooden leg.'

A third girl spoke with a Scots accent. 'I wonder if he takes it off when he shags you,' she said, and they all laughed.

Hermia had heard enough. She opened the door, stepped out, and said: 'If I find out, I'll let you know.'

The three girls were shocked into silence, and Hermia left before they had time to recover.

She stepped out of the wooden building. The wide

green lawn, with its cedar trees and swan pond, had been disfigured by huts thrown up in haste to accommodate the hundreds of staff from London. She crossed the park to the house, an ornate Victorian mansion built of red brick.

She passed through the grand porch and made her way to her office in the old servants' quarters, a tiny L-shaped space that had probably been the boot room. It had one small window too high to see out of, so she worked with the light on all day. There was a phone on her desk and a typewriter on a side table. Her predecessor had had a secretary, but women were expected to do their own typing. On her desk, she found a package from Copenhagen.

After Hitler's invasion of Poland, she had laid the foundations of a small spy network in Denmark. Its leader was her fiancé's friend, Poul Kirke. He had put together a group of young men who believed that their small country was going to be overrun by its larger neighbour, and the only way to fight for freedom was to cooperate with the British. Poul had declared that the group, who called themselves the Nightwatchmen, would not be saboteurs or assassins, but would pass military information to British Intelligence. This achievement by Hermia – unique for a woman – had won her promotion to head of the Denmark desk.

The package contained some of the fruits of her foresight. There was a batch of reports, already decrypted for her by the code room, on German military dispositions in Denmark: army bases on the central island of Fyn; naval traffic in the Kattegat, the sea that separated Denmark from Sweden; and the names of senior German officers in Copenhagen.

Also in the package was a copy of an underground newspaper called *Reality*. The underground press was, so far, the only sign of resistance to the Nazis in Denmark. She glanced through it, reading an indignant article which claimed there was a shortage of butter because all of it was sent to Germany.

The package had been smuggled out of Denmark to a go-between in Sweden, who passed it to the MI6 man at the British legation in Stockholm. With the package was a note from the go-between saying he had also passed a copy of *Reality* to the Reuters wire service in Stockholm. Hermia frowned at that. On the surface, it seemed a good idea to publicize news of conditions under the occupation, but she did not like agents mixing espionage with other work. Resistance action could attract the attention of the authorities to a spy who might otherwise work unnoticed for years.

Thinking about the Nightwatchmen reminded her painfully of her fiancé. Arne was not one of the group. His character was all wrong. She loved him for his careless *joie de vivre*. He made her relax, especially in bed. But a happy-go-lucky man with no head for mundane detail was not the type for secret work. In her more honest moments, she admitted to herself that she was not sure he had the courage. He was a daredevil on the ski slopes – they had met on a Norwegian mountain, where Arne had been the only skier more proficient than Hermia – but she was not sure how he would face the more subtle terrors of undercover operations.

She had considered trying to send him a message via the Nightwatchmen. Poul Kirke worked at the flying school, and if Arne was still there they must see one another every day. It would have been shamefully unprofessional to use the spy network for a personal communication, but that was not what stopped her. She would have been found out for sure, because her messages had to be encrypted by the code room, but even that might not have deterred her. It was the danger to Arne that held her back. Secret messages could fall into enemy hands. The ciphers used by MI6 were unsophisticated poem codes left over from peacetime, and could be broken easily. If Arne's name appeared in a message from British intelligence to Danish spies, he would probably lose his life. Hermia's inquiry about him could turn into his death warrant. So she sat in her boot room with acid anxiety burning inside her.

She composed a message to the Swedish go-between, telling him to keep out of the propaganda war and stick to his job as courier. Then she typed a report to her boss containing all the military information in the package, with carbon copies to other departments.

At four o'clock she left. She had more work to do, and she would return for a couple of hours this evening, but now she had to meet her mother for tea.

Margaret Mount lived in a small house in Pimlico. After Hermia's father had died of cancer in his late forties, her mother had set up home with an unmarried school friend, Elizabeth. They called one another Mags and Bets, their adolescent nicknames. Today the two had come by train to Bletchley to inspect Hermia's lodgings.

She walked quickly through the village to the street where she rented a room. She found Mags and Bets in the parlour talking to her landlady, Mrs Bevan. Hermia's mother was wearing her ambulance driver's uniform, with trousers and a cap. Bets was a pretty woman of fifty in a flowered dress with short sleeves. Hermia hugged her mother and gave Bets a kiss on the cheek. She and Bets had never become friends, and Hermia sometimes suspected Bets was jealous of her closeness to her mother.

Hermia took them upstairs. Bets looked askance at the drab little room with its single bed, but Hermia's mother said heartily: 'Well, this isn't bad, for wartime.'

'I don't spend much time here,' Hermia lied. In fact she spent long, lonely evenings reading and listening to the radio.

She lit the gas ring to make tea and sliced up a small cake she had bought for the occasion.

Mother said: 'I don't suppose you've heard from Arne?'

'No. I wrote to him via the British legation in Stockholm, and they forwarded the letter, but I never heard back, so I don't know whether he got it.'

'Oh, dear.'

Bets said: 'I wish I'd met him. What's he like?'

Falling in love with Arne had been like skiing

downhill, Hermia thought: a little push to get started, a sudden increase in speed, and then, before she was quite ready, the exhilarating feeling of hurtling down the piste at a breakneck pace, unable to stop. But how to explain that? 'He looks like a movie star, he's a wonderful athlete, and he has the charm of an Irishman, but that's not it,' Hermia said. 'It's just so easy to be with him. Whatever happens, he just laughs. I get angry sometimes – though never at him – and he smiles at me and says: "There's no one like you, Hermia, I swear." Dear God, I do miss him.' She fought back tears.

Her mother said briskly: 'Plenty of men have fallen in love with you, but there aren't many who can put up with you.' Mags's conversational style was as unadorned as Hermia's own. 'You should have nailed his foot to the floor while you had the chance.'

Hermia changed the subject and asked them about the Blitz. Bets spent air raids under the kitchen table, but Mags drove her ambulance through the bombs. Hermia's mother had always been a formidable woman, somewhat too direct and tactless for a diplomat's wife, but war had brought out her strength and courage, just as a secret service suddenly short of men had allowed Hermia to flourish. 'The Luftwaffe can't keep this up indefinitely,' said Mags. 'They don't have an unending supply of aircraft and pilots. If our bombers keep pounding German industry, it must have an effect eventually.'

Bets said: 'Meanwhile, innocent German women and children are suffering just as we do.'

'I know, but that's what war is about,' said Mags.

Hermia recalled her conversation with Digby Hoare. People like Mags and Bets imagined that the British bombing campaign was undermining the Nazis. It was a good thing they had no inkling that half the bombers were being shot down. If people knew the truth they might give up.

Mags began to tell a long story about rescuing a dog from a burning building, and Hermia listened with half an ear, thinking about Digby. If Freya was a machine, and the Germans were using it to defend their borders, it might well be in Denmark. Was there anything she could do to investigate? Digby had said the machine might emit some kind of beam, either optical pulses or radio waves. Such emissions ought to be detectable. Perhaps her Nightwatchmen could do something.

She began to feel excited about the idea. She could send a message to the Nightwatchmen. But first, she needed more information. She would start work on it tonight, she decided, as soon as she had seen Mags and Bets back on to their train.

She began to feel impatient for them to go. 'More cake, Mother?' she said.

# THREE

Jansborg Skole was three hundred years old, and proud of it.

Originally the school had consisted of a church and one house where the boys ate, slept and had lessons. Now it was a complex of old and new red-brick buildings. The library, at one time the finest in Denmark, was a separate building as large as the church. There were science laboratories, modern dormitories, an infirmary, and a gym in a converted barn.

Harald Olufsen was walking from the refectory to the gym. It was twelve noon, and the boys had just finished lunch – a make-it-yourself open sandwich with cold pork and pickles, the same meal that had been served every Wednesday throughout the seven years he had attended the school.

He thought it was stupid to be proud that the institution was old. When teachers spoke reverently of the school's history, he was reminded of old fishermen's wives on Sande who liked to say: 'I'm over seventy, now,' with a coy smile, as if it were some kind of achievement.

As he passed the headmaster's house, the head's

wife came out and smiled at him. 'Good morning, Mia,' he said politely. The head was always called Heis, the Ancient Greek word for the number one, so his wife was Mia, the feminine form of the same Greek word. The school had stopped teaching Greek five years ago, but traditions died hard.

'Any news, Harald?' she asked.

Harald had a home-made radio that could pick up the BBC. 'The Iraqi rebels have been defeated,' he said. 'The British have entered Baghdad.'

'A British victory,' she said. 'That makes a change.'

Mia was a plain woman with a homely face and lifeless brown hair, always dressed in shapeless clothes, but she was one of only two women at the school, and the boys constantly speculated about what she looked like naked. Harald wondered if he would ever stop being obsessed with sex. Theoretically, he believed that after sleeping with your wife every night for years you must get used to it, and even become bored, but he just could not imagine it.

The next lesson should have been two hours of maths, but today there was a visitor. He was Svend Agger, an old boy of the school who now represented his home town in the Rigsdag, the nation's parliament. The entire school was to hear him speak in the gym, the only room big enough to hold all one hundred and twenty boys. Harald would have preferred to do maths.

He could not remember the precise moment when school work had become interesting. As a small boy, he had regarded every lesson as an infuriating distraction from important business such as damming streams and building tree houses. Around the age of fourteen, almost without noticing it, he had begun to find physics and chemistry more exciting than playing in the woods. He had been thrilled to discover that the inventor of quantum physics was a Danish scientist, Niels Bohr. Bohr's interpretation of the periodic table of the elements, explaining chemical reactions by the atomic structure of the elements involved, seemed to Harald a divine revelation, a fundamental and deeply satisfying account of what the universe was made of. He worshipped Bohr the way other boys adored Kaj Hansen – 'Little Kaj' – the soccer hero who played inside forward for the team known as B93 København. Harald had applied to study physics at the University of Copenhagen, where Bohr was director of the Institute of Theoretical Physics.

Education cost money. Fortunately Harald's grandfather, seeing his own son enter a profession that would keep him poor all his life, had provided for his grandsons. His legacy had paid for Arne and Harald to go to Jansborg Skole. It would also finance Harald's time at university.

He entered the gym. The younger boys had put out benches in neat rows. Harald sat at the back, next to Josef Duchwitz. Josef was very small, and his surname sounded like the English word 'duck', so he had been nicknamed Anaticula, the Latin word for a duckling. Over the years it had got shortened to Tik. The two boys had very different backgrounds – Tik was from a wealthy Jewish family – yet they had been close friends all through school.

A few moments later, Mads Kirke sat next to Harald. Mads was in the same year. He came from a distinguished military family: his grandfather a general, his late father a defence minister in the thirties. His cousin Poul was a pilot with Arne at the flying school.

The three friends were science students. They were usually together, and they looked comically different – Harald tall and blond, Tik small and dark, Mads a freckled redhead – so that when a witty English master had referred to them as the Three Stooges, the nickname had stuck.

Heis, the head teacher, came in with the visitor, and the boys stood up politely. Heis was tall and thin with glasses perched on the bridge of a beaky nose. He had spent ten years in the army, but it was easy to see why he had switched to schoolteaching. A mild-mannered man, he seemed apologetic about being in authority. He was liked rather than feared. The boys obeyed him because they did not want to hurt his feelings.

When they had sat down again, Heis introduced the parliamentary deputy, a small man so unimpressive that anyone would have thought he was the schoolteacher and Heis the distinguished guest. Agger began to talk about the German occupation.

Harald remembered the day it had begun, fourteen months before. He had been woken up in the middle of the night by aircraft roaring overhead. The Three Stooges had gone up on the roof of the dormitory to watch but, after a dozen or so aircraft had passed over, nothing else happened, so they went back to bed.

He had learned no more until morning. He had been brushing his teeth in the communal bathroom when a teacher had rushed in and said: 'The Germans have landed!' After breakfast, at eight o'clock when the boys assembled in the gym for the morning song and announcements, the head had told them the news. 'Go to your rooms and destroy anything that might indicate opposition to the Nazis or sympathy with Britain,' he had said. Harald had taken down his favourite poster, a picture of a Tiger Moth biplane with RAF roundels on its wings.

Later that day – a Tuesday – the older boys had been detailed to fill sandbags and carry them to the church to cover the priceless ancient carvings and sarcophagi. Behind the altar was the tomb of the school's founder, his stone likeness lying in state, dressed in medieval armour with an eye-catchingly large codpiece. Harald had caused great amusement by mounting a sandbag end-up on the protrusion. Heis had not appreciated the joke, and Harald's punishment had been to spend the afternoon moving paintings to the crypt for safety.

All the precautions had been unnecessary. The school was in a village outside Copenhagen, and it was a year before they saw any Germans. There had never been any bombing or even gunfire.

Denmark had surrendered within twenty-four hours. 'Subsequent events have shown the wisdom of that decision,' said the speaker with irritating smugness, and there was a susurration of dissent as the boys shifted uncomfortably in their seats and muttered comments.

'Our king continues on his throne,' Agger went on. Next to Harald, Mads grunted disgustedly. Harald shared Mads's annoyance. King Christian X rode out on horseback most days, showing himself to the people on the streets of Copenhagen, but it seemed an empty gesture.

'The German presence has been on the whole benign,' the speaker went on. 'Denmark has proved that a partial loss of independence, due to the exigencies of war, need not necessarily lead to undue hardship and strife. The lesson, for boys such as yourselves, is that there may be more honour in submission and obedience than in ill-considered rebellion.' He sat down.

Heis clapped politely, and the boys followed suit, though without enthusiasm. If the head had been a shrewder judge of an audience's mood, he would have ended the session then; but instead he smiled and said: 'Well, boys, any questions for our guest?'

Mads was on his feet in an instant. 'Sir, Norway was invaded on the same day as Denmark, but the Norwegians fought for two months. Doesn't that make us cowards?' His tone was scrupulously polite, but the question was challenging, and there was a rumble of agreement from the boys.

'A naive view,' Agger said. His dismissive tone angered Harald.

Heis intervened. 'Norway is a land of mountains and fjords, difficult to conquer,' he said, bringing his military expertise to bear. 'Denmark is a flat country with a good road system – impossible to defend against a large motorized army.'

Agger added: 'To put up a fight would have caused unnecessary bloodshed, and the end result would have been no different.'

Mads said rudely: 'Except that we would have been able to walk around with our heads held high, instead of hanging them in shame.' It sounded to Harald like something he might have heard at home from his military relations.

Agger coloured. 'The better part of valour is discretion, as Shakespeare wrote.'

Mads said: 'In fact, sir, that was said by Falstaff, the most famous coward in world literature.' The boys laughed and clapped.

'Now, now, Kirke,' said Heis mildly. 'I know you feel strongly about this, but there's no need for discourtesy.' He looked around the room and pointed to one of the younger boys. 'Yes, Borr.'

'Sir, don't you think Herr Hitler's philosophy of national pride and racial purity could be beneficial if adopted here in Denmark?' Woldemar Borr was the son of a prominent Danish Nazi.

'Elements of it, perhaps,' Agger said. 'But Germany and Denmark are different countries.' That was plain prevarication, Harald thought angrily. Couldn't the man find the guts to say that racial persecution was wrong?

Heis said plaintively: 'Would any boy like to ask Mr Agger about his everyday work as a member of the Rigsdag, perhaps?'

Tik stood up. Agger's self-satisfied tone had irritated him, too. 'Don't you feel like a puppet?' he said. 'After all, it's the Germans who really rule us. You're just pretending.'

'Our nation continues to be governed by our Danish parliament,' Agger replied.

Tik muttered: 'Yes, so you get to keep your job.' The boys nearby heard him and laughed.

'The political parties remain – even the Communists,' Agger went on. 'We have our own police, and our armed forces.'

'But the minute the Rigsdag does something the Germans disapprove of, it will be closed down, and the police and the military will be disarmed,' Tik argued. 'So you're acting in a farce.'

Heis began to look annoyed. 'Remember your manners, please, Duchwitz,' he said peevishly.

'That's all right, Heis,' said Agger. 'I like a lively discussion. If Duchwitz thinks our parliament is useless, he should compare our circumstances with those prevailing in France. Because of our policy of cooperation with the Germans, life is a great deal better, for ordinary Danish people, than it might be.'

Harald had heard enough. He stood up and spoke

without waiting for permission from Heis. 'And what if the Nazis come for Duchwitz?' he said. 'Will you advise friendly cooperation then?'

'And why should they come for Duchwitz?'

'The same reason they came for my uncle in Hamburg – because he's a Jew.'

Some of the boys looked around with interest. They probably had not realized Tik was Jewish. The Duchwitz family was not religious, and Tik went along to services in the ancient redbrick church just like everyone else.

Agger showed irritation for the first time. 'The occupying forces have demonstrated complete tolerance towards Danish Jews.'

'So far,' Harald argued. 'But what if they change their minds? Suppose they decide that Tik is just as Jewish as my Uncle Joachim? What is your advice to us then? Shall we stand aside while they march in and seize him? Or should we now be organizing a Resistance movement in preparation for that day?'

'Your best plan is to make sure you are never faced with such a decision, by supporting the policy of cooperation with the occupying power.'

The smooth evasiveness of the answer maddened Harald. 'But what if that doesn't work?' he persisted. 'Why won't you answer the question? What do we do when the Nazis come for our friends?'

Heis put in: 'You're asking what's called a hypothetical question, Olufsen,' he said. 'Men in public life prefer not to meet trouble half way.'

'The question is how far his policy of cooperation

will go,' Harald said hotly. 'And there won't be time for debate when they bang on your door in the middle of the night, Heis.'

For a moment, Heis looked ready to reprimand Harald for rudeness, but in the end he answered mildly. 'You've made an interesting point, and Mr Agger has answered it quite thoroughly,' he said. 'Now, I think we've had a good discussion, and it's time to go back to our lessons. But first, let's thank our guest for taking the time out of his busy life to come and visit us.' He raised his hands to lead a round of applause.

Harald stopped him. 'Make him answer the question!' he shouted. 'Should we have a Resistance movement, or will we let the Nazis do anything they like? For God's sake, what lessons could be more important than this?'

The room went quiet. Arguing with the staff was permitted, within reason, but Harald had crossed the line into defiance.

'I think you'd better leave us,' Heis said. 'Off you go, and I'll see you afterwards.'

This made Harald furious. Boiling with frustration, he stood up. The room remained silent as all the boys watched him walk to the door. He knew he should leave quietly, but he could not bring himself to do it. He turned at the door and pointed an accusing finger at Heis. 'You won't be able to tell the Gestapo to leave the damn room!' he said.

Then he went out and slammed the door.

# FOUR

Peter Flemming's alarm clock went off at half past five in the morning. He silenced it, turned on the light, and sat upright in bed. Inge was lying on her back, eyes open, staring at the ceiling, as expressionless as a corpse. He looked at her for a moment, then got up.

He went into the little kitchen of their Copenhagen apartment and turned on the radio. A Danish reporter was reading a sentimental statement by the Germans about the death of Admiral Luetjens, who had gone down with the Bismarck ten days ago. Peter put a small pot of oatmeal on the cooker, then laid a tray. He buttered a slice of rye bread and made ersatz coffee.

He felt optimistic, and after a moment he recalled why. Yesterday there had been a break in the case he was working on.

He was a detective-inspector in the security unit, a section of the Copenhagen criminal investigation department whose job was to keep tabs on union organizers, Communists, foreigners and other potential troublemakers. His boss, the head of the department, was superintendent Frederik Juel, clever but lazy. Educated at the famous Jansborg Skole, Juel was fond of the Latin proverb *Quieta non movere,* Let sleeping dogs lie. He was descended from a hero of Danish naval history, but the aggression had long been bred out of his line.

In the past fourteen months their work had expanded, as opponents of German rule had been added to the department's watch list.

So far the only outward sign of resistance had been the appearance of underground newspapers such as *Reality,* the one the Olufsen boy had dropped. Juel believed the illegal newspapers were harmless, if not actually beneficial as a safety valve, and refused to pursue the publishers. This attitude infuriated Peter. Leaving criminals at large, to continue their offences, seemed madness to him.

The Germans did not really like Juel's *laissez-faire* attitude, but so far they had not pushed the matter to a confrontation. Juel's liaison with the occupying power was General Walter Braun, a career soldier who had lost a lung in the battle of France. Braun's aim was to keep Denmark tranquil at all costs. He would not overrule Juel unless forced to.

Recently Peter had learned that copies of *Reality* were being smuggled to Sweden. Until now, he had been obliged to abide by his boss's hands-off rule, but he hoped Juel's complacency would be shaken by the news that the papers were finding their way out of the country. Last night, a Swedish detective who was a personal friend of Peter's had called to say he thought the paper was being carried on a Lufthansa flight from Berlin to Stockholm that stopped at

Copenhagen. That was the breakthrough that accounted for Peter's feeling of excitement when he woke up. He could be on the brink of a triumph.

When the oatmeal was ready, he added milk and sugar then took the tray into the bedroom.

He helped Inge sit upright. He tasted the oatmeal to make sure it was not too hot, then began to feed her with a spoon.

A year ago, just before petrol restrictions came in, Peter and Inge had been driving to the beach when a young man in a new sports car had crashed into them. Peter had broken both his legs and recovered rapidly. Inge had smashed her skull, and she would never be the same.

The other driver, Finn Jonk, the son of a well-known university professor, had been thrown clear and landed in a bush, unharmed.

He had no driving licence – it had been taken from him by the courts after a previous accident – and he had been drunk. But the Jonk family had hired a top lawyer who had succeeded in delaying the trial for a year, so Finn still had not been punished for destroying Inge's mind. The personal tragedy, for Inge and Peter, was also an example of the disgraceful way crimes could go unpunished in modern society. Whatever you might say against the Nazis, they were gratifyingly tough on criminals.

When Inge had eaten her breakfast, Peter took her to the toilet, then bathed her. She had always been scrupulously neat and clean. It was one of the things he had loved about her. She was especially clean about sex, always washing carefully afterwards – something he appreciated. Not all girls were like that. One woman he had slept with, a nightclub singer he had met during a raid and had a brief affair with, had objected to his washing himself after sex, saying it was unromantic.

Inge showed no reaction as he bathed her. He had learned to be equally unmoved, even when he touched the most intimate parts of her body. He dried her soft skin with a big towel, then dressed her. The most difficult part was putting her stockings on. First he rolled the stocking, leaving only the toe sticking out. Then he carefully eased it over her foot and unrolled it up her calf and over her knee, finally fastening the top to the clips of the garter belt. When he started doing this he had laddered them every time, but he was a persistent man, and could be very patient when he had his mind set on achieving something; and now he was expert.

He helped her into a cheerful yellow cotton dress, then added a gold wristwatch and bracelet. She could not tell the time, but he sometimes thought she came near to smiling when she saw jewellery glinting on her wrists.

When he had brushed her hair, they both looked at her reflection in the mirror. She was a pretty, pale blonde, and before the accident she had had a flirtatious smile and a coy way of fluttering her eyelashes. Now her face was blank.

On their Whitsun visit to Sande, Peter's father had tried to persuade him to put Inge into a private nursing home. Peter could not afford the fees, but Axel was willing to pay. He said he wanted Peter to be free, though the truth was he was desperate for a grandson to bear his name. However, Peter felt it was his duty to take care of his wife. For him, duty was the most important of a man's obligations. If he shirked it, he would lose his self-respect.

He took Inge to the living room and sat her by the window. He left the radio playing music at low volume, then returned to the bathroom.

The face in his shaving mirror was regular and well-proportioned. Inge had used to say he looked like a film star. Since the accident he had noticed a few grey hairs in his red morning stubble, and there were lines of weariness around the orange-brown eyes. But there was a proud look in the set of his head, and an immovable rectitude in the straight line of his lips.

When he had shaved he tied his tie and strapped on his shoulder holster with the standard issue Walther 7.65mm pistol, the smaller seven-round 'PPK' version designed as a concealed weapon for detectives. Then he stood in the kitchen and ate three slices of dry bread, saving the scarce butter for Inge.

The nurse was supposed to come at eight o'clock.

Between eight and five past Peter's mood changed. He began to pace up and down the little hallway of the apartment. He lit a cigarette then crushed it out impatiently. He looked at his wristwatch every few seconds.

Between five and ten past he became angry. Did he not have enough to cope with? He combined caring for his helpless wife with a taxing and highly responsible job as a police detective. The nurse had no *right* to let him down.

When she rang the doorbell at eight fifteen, he threw open the door and shouted: 'How dare you be late?'

She was a plump girl of nineteen, wearing a carefully pressed uniform, her hair neatly arranged under her nurse's cap, her round face lightly made up. She was shocked by his anger. 'I'm sorry,' she said.

He stood aside to let her in. He felt a strong temptation to strike her, and she obviously sensed this, for she hurried past him nervously.

He followed her into the living room. 'You had time to do your hair and make-up,' he said angrily.

'I said I'm sorry.'

'Don't you realize that I have a very demanding job? You've got nothing on your mind more important than walking with boys in the Tivoli Garden – yet you can't even get to work on time!'

She looked nervously at his gun in the shoulder holster, as if she was afraid he was going to shoot her. 'The bus was late,' she said in a shaky voice.

'Get an earlier bus, you lazy cow!'

'Oh!' She looked about to cry.

Peter turned away, fighting an urge to slap her fat face. If she walked out, he would be in worse trouble. He put on his jacket and went to the door. 'Don't you ever be late again!' he shouted. Then he left the apartment.

Outside the building he jumped on to a tram

heading for the city centre. He lit a cigarette and smoked in rapid puffs, trying to calm himself. He was still angry when he got off outside the Politigaarden, the daringly modern police headquarters, but the sight of the building soothed him: its squat shape gave a reassuring impression of strength, its blindingly white stone spoke of purity, and its rows of identical windows symbolized order and the predictability of justice. He passed through the dark vestibule. Hidden in the centre of the building was a large open courtyard, circular, with a ring of double pillars marking a sheltered walkway like the cloisters of a monastery. Peter crossed the courtyard and entered his section.

He was greeted by detective constable Tilde Jespersen, one of a handful of women in the Copenhagen force. The young widow of a policeman, she was as tough and smart as any cop in the department. Peter often used her for surveillance work, a role in which a woman was less likely to arouse suspicion. She was rather attractive, with blue eyes and fair curly hair and the kind of small, curvy figure that women would call too fat but men thought just right. 'Bus delayed?' she said sympathetically.

'No. Inge's nurse turned up a quarter of an hour late. Empty-headed flibbertigibbet.'

'Oh, dear.'

'Anything happening?'

'I'm afraid so. General Braun is with Juel. They want to see you as soon as you get here.'

That was bad luck: a visit from Braun on the day

Peter was late. 'Damn nurse,' he muttered, and headed for Juel's office.

Juel's upright carriage and piercing blue eyes would have suited his naval namesake. He spoke German as a courtesy to Braun. All educated Danes could get by in German, and English as well. 'Where have you been, Flemming?' he said to Peter. 'We are waiting.'

'I apologize,' Peter replied in the same language. He did not give the reason for his lateness: excuses were undignified.

General Braun was in his forties. He had probably been handsome once, but the explosion that destroyed his lung had also taken away part of his jaw, and the right side of his face was deformed. Perhaps because of his damaged appearance, he always wore an immaculate field service uniform, complete with high boots and holstered pistol.

He was courteous and reasonable in conversation. His voice was a soft near-whisper. 'Take a look at this, if you would, Inspector Flemming,' he said. He had spread several newspapers on Peter's desk, all folded open to show a particular report. It was the same story in each newspaper, Peter saw: an account of the butter shortage in Denmark, blaming the Germans for taking it all. The newspapers were the *Toronto Globe*, the *Washington Post* and the *Los Angeles Times*. Also on the table was the Danish underground newspaper *Reality*, badly printed and amateur-looking beside the legitimate publications, but containing the original story the others had copied. It was a small triumph of propaganda.

Juel said: 'We know most of the people who produce these home-made newspapers.' He spoke in a tone of languid assurance that irritated Peter. You might imagine, from his manner, that it was he, not his famous ancestor, who had defeated the Swedish navy at the battle of Koge Bay. 'We could pick them all up, of course. But I'd rather leave them alone and keep an eye on them. Then, if they do something serious like blowing up a bridge, we'll know who to arrest.'

Peter thought that was stupid. They should be arrested now, to *stop* them blowing up bridges. But he had had this argument with Juel before, so he clamped his teeth together and said nothing.

Braun said: 'That might have been acceptable when their activities were confined to Denmark. But this story has gone all over the world! Berlin is furious. And the last thing we need is a clampdown. We'll have the damned Gestapo stamping all over town in their jackboots, stirring up trouble and throwing people in jail, and God knows where it will end.'

Peter was gratified. The news was having the effect he wanted. 'I'm already working on this,' he said. 'All these American newspapers got the story from the Reuters wire service, which picked it up in Stockholm. I believe the *Reality* newspaper is being smuggled out to Sweden.'

'Good work!' said Braun.

Peter stole a glance at Juel, who looked angry. So he should. Peter was a better detective than his boss, and incidents such as this proved it. Two years ago, when the post of head of the security unit had fallen vacant, Peter had applied for the job, but Juel had got it. Peter was a few years younger than Juel, but had more successful cases to his credit. However, Juel belonged to a smug metropolitan élite who had all gone to the same schools, and Peter was sure they conspired to keep the best jobs for themselves and hold back talented outsiders.

Now Juel said: 'But how could the newspaper be smuggled out? All packages are inspected by the censors.'

Peter hesitated. He had wanted to get confirmation before revealing what he suspected. His information from Sweden could be wrong. However, Braun was right here in front of him, pawing the earth and champing at the bit, and this was not the moment to equivocate. 'I've had a tip. Last night I spoke to a detective friend in Stockholm who has been discreetly asking questions at the wire service office. He thinks the newspaper comes on the Lufthansa flight from Berlin to Stockholm that stops here.'

Braun nodded excitedly. 'So if we search every passenger boarding the flight here in Copenhagen, we should find the latest edition.'

'Yes.'

'Does the flight go today?'

Peter's heart sank. This was not the way he worked. He preferred to verify information before rushing into a raid. But he was grateful for Braun's aggressive attitude – a pleasing contrast with Juel's laziness and caution. Anyway, he could not hold back the avalanche of Braun's eagerness. 'Yes, in a few hours,' he said, hiding his misgivings.

'Then let's get moving!'

Haste could ruin everything. Peter could not let Braun take charge of the operation. 'May I make a suggestion, General?'

'Of course.'

'We must act discreetly, to avoid forewarning our culprit. Let's assemble a team of detectives and German officers, but keep them here at headquarters until the last minute. Allow the passengers to assemble for the flight before we move in. I'll go alone to Kastrup aerodrome to make arrangements quietly. When the passengers have checked their baggage, the aircraft has landed and refuelled, and they're about to board, it will be too late for anyone to slip away unnoticed – and then we can pounce.'

Braun smiled knowingly. 'You're afraid that a lot of Germans marching around would give the game away.'

'Not at all, sir,' Peter said with a straight face. When the occupiers made fun of themselves it was not wise to join in. 'It will be important for you and your men to accompany us, in case there is any need to question German citizens.'

Braun's face stiffened, his self-deprecating sally rebuffed. 'Quite so,' he said. He went to the door. 'Call me at my office when your team is ready to depart.' He left.

Peter was relieved. At least he had regained control.

His only worry was that Braun's enthusiasm might have forced him to move too soon.

'Well done, for tracing the smuggling route,' Juel said condescendingly. 'Good detective work. But it would have been tactful to tell me before you told Braun.'

'I'm sorry, sir,' Peter said. In fact it would not have been possible: Juel had already left for the day when the Swedish detective had called last night. But Peter did not make the excuse.

'All right,' Juel said. 'Put together a squad and send them to me for briefing. Then go to the aerodrome and phone me when the passengers are ready to board.'

Peter left Juel's room and returned to Tilde's desk in the main office. She was wearing a jacket, blouse and skirt in different shades of light blue, like a girl in a French painting. 'How did it go?' she asked.

'I was late, but I made up for it.'

'Good.'

'There's a raid on at the aerodrome this morning,' he told her. He knew which detectives he wanted with him. 'I'll take Bent Conrad, Peder Dresler and Knut Ellegard.' Detective sergeant Conrad was enthusiastically pro-German. Detective constables Dresler and Ellegard had no strong political or patriotic feelings, but were conscientious policemen who took orders and did a thorough job. 'And I'd like you to come along, too, if you would, in case there are female suspects to be searched.'

73

'Of course.'

'Juel will brief you all. I'm going ahead to Kastrup.' Peter went to the door, then turned back. 'How's little Stig?' Tilde had a son six years old, looked after by his grandmother during the working day.

She smiled. 'He's fine. His reading is coming along fast.'

'He'll be chief of police one day.'

Her face darkened. 'I don't want him to be a cop.'

Peter nodded. Tilde's husband had been killed in a shootout with a gang of smugglers. 'I understand.'

She added defensively: 'Would you want your son to do this job?'

He shrugged. 'I don't have any children, and I'm not likely to.'

She gave him an enigmatic look. 'You don't know what the future holds.'

'True.' He turned away. He did not want to start that discussion on a busy day. 'I'll call in.'

'OK.'

Peter took one of the police department's unmarked black Buicks, recently equipped with two-way radio. He drove out of the city and across a bridge to the island of Amager, where Kastrup Aerodrome was located. It was a sunny day, and from the road he could see people on the beach.

He looked like a businessman or lawyer in his conservative chalk-stripe suit and discreetly patterned tie. He did not have a briefcase, but for verisimilitude he had brought with him a file folder, filled with papers taken from a waste basket.

He felt anxious as he approached the aerodrome. If he could have had another day or two, he might have been able to establish whether every flight carried illegal packages, or only some. There was a maddening possibility that today he might find nothing, but his raid would alert the subversive group, and they might change to a different route. Then he would have to start again.

The aerodrome was a scatter of low buildings on one side of a single runway. It was heavily guarded by German troops, but civilian flights continued to be operated by the Danish airline, DDL, and the Swedish ABA, as well as Lufthansa.

Peter parked outside the office of the airport controller. He told the secretary he was from the government's Aviation Safety Department, and was admitted instantly. The controller, Christian Varde, was a small man with a salesman's ready smile. Peter showed his police card. 'There will be a special security check on the Lufthansa flight to Stockholm today,' he said. 'It has been authorized by General Braun, who will be arriving shortly. We must get everything ready.'

A frightened look came over the face of the manager. He reached for the phone on his desk, but Peter covered the instrument with his own hand. 'No,' he said. 'Please do not forewarn anyone. Do you have a list of passengers expected to board the flight here?'

'My secretary does.'

'Ask her to bring it in.'

Varde called his secretary and she brought a sheet of paper. He gave it to Peter.

Peter said: 'Is the flight coming in on time from Berlin?'

'Yes.' Varde checked his watch. 'It should land in forty-five minutes.'

That was enough time, just.

It would simplify Peter's task if he had to search only those passengers joining the flight in Denmark. 'I want you to call the pilot and say that no one will be permitted to deplane at Kastrup today. That includes passengers and crew.'

'Very good.'

He looked at the list the secretary had brought. There were four names: two Danish men, a Danish woman and a German man. 'Where are the passengers now?'

'They should be checking in.'

'Take their baggage, but do not load it on to the aircraft until it has been searched by my men.'

'Very well.'

'The passengers, too, will be searched before they board. Is anything else loaded here, in addition to passengers and their luggage?'

'Coffee and sandwiches for the flight, and a bag of mail. And the fuel, of course.'

'The food and drink must be examined, and the mailbag. One of my men will observe the refuelling.'

'Fine.'

'Go now and send the message to the pilot. When

all the passengers have checked in, come and find me in the departure lounge. But please – try to give the impression that nothing special is happening.'

Varde went out.

Peter made his way to the departure area, racking his brains to make sure he had thought of everything. He sat in the lounge and discreetly studied the other passengers, wondering which of them would end up in jail today instead of on a plane. This morning there were scheduled flights to Berlin, Hamburg, the Norwegian capital of Oslo, the southern Swedish city of Malmo, and the Danish holiday island of Bornholm, so he could not be sure which of the passengers were destined for Stockholm.

There were only two women in the room: a young mother with two children, and a beautifully dressed older woman with white hair. The older woman could be the smuggler, Peter thought: her appearance might be intended to allay suspicion.

Three of the passengers wore German uniforms. Peter checked his list: his man was a Colonel von Schwarzkopf. Only one of the soldiers was a colonel. But it was wildly unlikely that a German officer would smuggle Danish underground newspapers.

All the others were men just like Peter, wearing suits and ties, holding their hats in their laps.

Trying to appear bored but patient, as if waiting for a flight, he watched everyone carefully, alert for signs that someone had sensed the imminent security check. Some passengers looked nervous, but that could just be fear of flying. Peter was most concerned to make sure no one tried to throw away a package, or conceal papers somewhere in the lounge.

Varde reappeared. Beaming as if delighted to see Peter again, he said: 'All four passengers have checked in.'

'Good.' It was time to begin. 'Tell them that Lufthansa would like to offer them some special hospitality, then take them to your office. I'll follow.'

Varde nodded and went to the Lufthansa desk. While he was asking the Stockholm passengers to come forward, Peter went to a pay phone, called Tilde, and told her all was ready for the raid. Varde led the group of four passengers away, and Peter tagged on to the little procession.

When they were assembled in Varde's office, Peter revealed his identity. He showed his police badge to the German colonel. 'I'm acting under orders from General Braun,' he said to forestall protests. 'He is on his way here and will explain everything.'

The colonel looked annoyed, but sat down without comment, and the other three passengers – the white-haired lady and two Danish businessmen – did the same. Peter leaned against the wall, watching them, alert for guilty behaviour. Each had a bag of some kind: the old lady a large handbag, the officer a slim document case, the businessmen briefcases. Any of them could be carrying copies of an illegal newspaper.

Varde said brightly: 'May I offer you tea or coffee while you're waiting?'

Peter checked his watch. The flight from Berlin was

due now. He looked out of Varde's window and saw it coming in to land. The aircraft was a Junkers Ju-52 trimotor – an ugly machine, he thought: its surface was corrugated, like a shed roof, and the third engine, protruding from the nose, looked like the snout of a pig. But it approached at a remarkably low speed for such a heavy aircraft, and the effect was quite majestic. It touched down and taxied to the terminal. The door opened, and the crew threw down the chocks that secured the wheels when the aircraft was parked.

Braun and Juel arrived, with the four detectives Peter had chosen, while the waiting passengers were drinking the airport's ersatz coffee.

Peter watched keenly while his detectives emptied out the men's briefcases and the white-haired lady's handbag. It was quite possible the spy would have the illegal newspaper in hand baggage, he thought. Then the traitor could claim he had brought it to read on the plane. Not that it would do him any good.

But the contents of the bags were innocent.

Tilde took the lady into another room to be searched, while the three male suspects removed their outer clothing. Braun patted down the colonel, and Sergeant Conrad did the Danes. Nothing was found.

Peter was disappointed, but he told himself it was much more likely that the contraband would be in checked baggage.

The passengers were allowed to return to the lounge, but not to board the aircraft. Their luggage was lined up on the apron outside the terminal building: two new-looking crocodile cases that undoubtedly belonged to the old lady, a duffle bag that was probably the colonel's, a tan leather suitcase and a cheap cardboard one.

Peter felt confident he would find a copy of *Reality* in one of them.

Bent Conrad got the keys from the passengers. 'I bet it's the old woman,' he murmured to Peter. 'She looks like a Jew to me.'

'Just unlock the luggage,' Peter said.

Conrad opened all the bags and Peter began to search them, with Juel and Braun looking over his shoulders, and a crowd of people watching through the window of the departure lounge. He imagined the moment when he would triumphantly produce the newspaper and flourish it in front of everyone.

The crocodile cases were stuffed with expensive old-fashioned clothing, which he dumped on the ground. The duffle bag contained shaving tackle, a change of underwear, and a perfectly pressed uniform shirt. The businessman's tan leather case held papers as well as clothing, and Peter looked through them all carefully, but there were no newspapers nor anything suspicious.

He had left the cheap cardboard suitcase until last, figuring the less affluent businessman was the likeliest of the four passengers to be a spy.

The case was half empty. It held a white shirt and a black tie, supporting the man's story that he was going to a funeral. There was also a well-worn black Bible. But no newspaper.

Peter began to wonder despairingly if his fears had been well founded, and this was the wrong day for the raid. He felt angry that he had let himself be pushed into acting prematurely. He controlled his fury. He was not finished yet.

He took a penknife from his pocket. He pushed its point into the lining of the old lady's expensive luggage and tore a ragged gash in the white silk. He heard Juel grunt with surprise at the sudden violence of the gesture. Peter ran his hand beneath the ripped lining. To his dismay, nothing was hidden there.

He did the same to the businessman's leather case, with the same result. The second businessman's cardboard suitcase had no lining, and Peter could see nothing in its structure that might serve as a hiding place.

Feeling his face redden with frustration and embarrassment, he cut the stitching on the leather base of the colonel's canvas duffle and felt inside for concealed papers. There was nothing.

He looked up to see Braun, Juel, and the detectives staring at him. Their faces showed fascination and a hint of fear. His behaviour was beginning to look a little crazy, he realized.

To hell with that.

Juel said languidly: 'Perhaps your information was wrong, Flemming.'

And wouldn't that please you, Peter thought resentfully. But he was not finished yet.

He saw Varde watching from the departure lounge,

and beckoned him. The man's smile looked strained as he contemplated the wreckage of his customers' luggage. 'Where is the mailbag?' Peter said.

'In the baggage office.'

'Well, what are you waiting for? Bring it here, idiot!'

Varde went off. Peter pointed at the luggage with a disgusted gesture and said to his detectives: 'Get rid of this stuff.'

Dresler and Ellegard repacked the suitcases roughly. A baggage handler came to take them to the Junkers. 'Wait,' Peter said as the man began to pick up the cases. 'Search him, sergeant.' Conrad searched the man and found nothing.

Varde brought the mailbag and Peter emptied the letters on the ground. They all bore the stamp of the censor. There were two envelopes large enough to hold a newspaper, one white and one brown. He ripped open the white one. It held six copies of a legal document, some kind of contract. The brown envelope contained the catalogue of a Copenhagen glassware factory. Peter cursed aloud.

A trolley bearing a tray of sandwiches and several coffee pots was wheeled out for Peter's inspection. This was Peter's last hope. He opened each pot and poured the coffee out on the ground. Juel muttered something about this being unnecessary, but Peter was too desperate to care. He pulled away the linen napkins covering the tray and poked about among the sandwiches. To his horror, there was nothing. In a rage, he picked up the tray and dumped the sandwiches on the ground, hoping to find a newspaper underneath, but there was only another linen napkin.

He realized he was going to be completely humiliated, and that made him madder.

'Begin refuelling,' he said. 'I'll watch.'

A tanker was driven out to the Junkers. The detectives put out their cigarettes and looked on as aviation fuel was pumped into the wings of the aircraft. Peter knew this was useless, but he persevered stubbornly, wearing a wooden expression, because he could not think what else to do. Passengers watched curiously through the rectangular windows of the Junkers, no doubt wondering why a German general and six civilians needed to observe the refuelling.

The tanks were filled and the caps closed.

Peter could not think of any way to delay the take-off. He had been wrong, and now he looked a fool.

'Let the passengers board,' he said with suppressed fury.

He returned to the departure lounge, his humiliation complete. He wanted to strangle someone. He had made a complete mess of things in front of General Braun as well as Superintendent Juel. The appointments board would feel justified in having picked Juel instead of Peter for the top job. Juel might even use this fiasco as an excuse for having Peter shunted sideways to some low-profile department such as Traffic.

He stopped in the lounge to watch the take-off. Juel, Braun and the detectives waited with him. Varde was standing nearby, trying hard to look as if nothing out of the ordinary had happened. They watched while the four angry passengers boarded. The chocks were removed from the wheels by the ground crew and thrown on board, then the door was closed.

As the aircraft moved off its stand, Peter was struck by inspiration. 'Stop the plane,' he said to Varde.

Juel said: 'For God's sake . . .'

Varde looked as if he might cry. He turned to General Braun. 'Sir, my passengers . . .'

'Stop the plane!' Peter repeated.

Varde continued to look pleadingly at Braun. After a moment, Braun nodded. 'Do as he says.'

Varde picked up a phone.

Juel said: 'My God, Flemming, this had better be good.'

The aircraft rolled on to the runway, turned a full circle, and came back to its stand. The door opened, and the chocks were thrown down to the ground crew.

Peter led the rest of the detectives out on to the apron. The propellers slowed and stopped. Two men in overalls were wedging the chocks in front of the main wheels. Peter addressed one of them. 'Hand me that chock.'

The man looked scared, but did as he was told.

Peter took the chock from him. It was a simple triangular block of wood about a foot high – dirty, heavy, and solid.

'And the other one,' Peter said.

Ducking under the fuselage, the mechanic picked up the other and handed it over.

It looked the same, but felt lighter. Turning it over

in his hands, Peter found that one face was a sliding lid. He opened it. Inside was a package carefully wrapped in oilcloth.

Peter gave a sigh of profound satisfaction.

The mechanic turned and ran.

'Stop him!' Peter cried, but it was unnecessary. The man veered away from the men and tried to run past Tilde, no doubt imagining he could easily push her aside. She turned like a dancer, letting him pass, then stuck out a foot and tripped him. He went flying.

Dresler jumped on him, hauled him to his feet, and twisted his arm behind his back.

Peter nodded to Ellegard. 'Arrest the other mechanic. He must have known what was going on.'

Peter turned his attention to the package. He unwrapped the oilcloth. Inside were two copies of *Reality*. He handed them to Juel.

Juel looked at the papers, then up at Peter.

Peter stared at him expectantly, saying nothing, waiting.

Juel said reluctantly: 'Well done, Flemming.'

Peter smiled. 'Just doing my job, sir.'

Juel turned away.

Peter said to his detectives: 'Handcuff both mechanics and take them to headquarters for questioning.'

There was something else in the package. Peter pulled out a sheaf of papers clipped together. They were covered with typed characters in five-letter groups that made no sense. He stared at them in puzzlement for a moment. Then enlightenment dawned, and he realized this was a triumph greater than he had dreamed.

The papers he was holding bore a message in code.

Peter handed the papers to Braun. 'I think we have uncovered a spy ring, General.'

Braun looked at the papers and paled. 'My God, you're right.'

'Perhaps the German military has a department that specializes in breaking enemy ciphers?'

'It certainly does.'

'Good,' said Peter.

# FIVE

An old-fashioned carriage drawn by two horses picked up Harald Olufsen and Tik Duchwitz at the railway station in Tik's home village of Kirstenslot. Tik explained that the carriage had been rotting in a barn for years, then had been resurrected when the Germans imposed petrol restrictions. The coachwork gleamed with fresh paint, but the team was a pair of ordinary carthorses borrowed from a farm. The coachman looked as if he might have been more comfortable behind a plough.

Harald was not sure why Tik had invited him for the weekend. The Three Stooges had never visited each other's homes, even though they had been close friends at school for seven years. Perhaps the invitation was a consequence of Harald's anti-Nazi outburst in class. Maybe Tik's parents were curious to meet the pastor's son who was so concerned about the persecution of Jews.

They drove from the station through a small village with a church and a tavern. At the far edge of the village they turned off the road and passed between a pair of massive stone lions. At the far end of a half-mile drive Harald saw a fairy-tale castle with battlements and turrets.

There were hundreds of castles in Denmark. Harald sometimes took comfort from that fact. Although it was a small country, it had not always surrendered abjectly to its belligerent neighbours. There might be something of the Viking spirit left.

Some castles were historic monuments, maintained as museums and visited by tourists. Many were little more than country manor houses occupied by prosperous farming families. In between were a number of spectacular homes owned by the wealthiest people in the land. Kirstenslot – the house had the same name as the village – was one of those.

Harald was intimidated. He had known the Duchwitz family were wealthy – Tik's father and uncle were bankers – but he was not prepared for this. He wondered anxiously if he would know the right ways to behave. Nothing about life at the parsonage had prepared him for a place such as this.

It was late on Saturday afternoon when the carriage dropped them at the cathedral-like front entrance. Harald walked in, carrying his small suitcase. The marbled hall was crammed with antique furniture, decorated vases, small statues and large oil paintings. Harald's family was inclined to take literally the Second Commandment, which forbade the making of a likeness of anything in heaven or on earth, so there were no pictures in the parsonage (though Harald knew that he and Arne had been secretly photographed as babies, for he had found the pictures hidden in his mother's stocking drawer). The wealth of art in the Duchwitz home made him mildly uncomfortable.

Tik led him up a grand staircase into a bedroom. 'This is my room,' he said. There were no old masters or Chinese vases here, just the kind of stuff an eighteen-year-old collected: a football, a picture of Marlene Dietrich looking sultry, a clarinet, and a framed advertisement for a Lancia Aprilla sports car designed by Pininfarina.

Harald picked up a framed photo. It showed Tik about four years before with a girl about the same age. 'Who's the girlfriend?'

'My twin sister, Karen.'

'Oh.' Harald knew, vaguely, that Tik had a twin. She was taller than Tik in the picture. It was a black-and-white photo, but she seemed to have lighter colouring. 'Obviously not an identical twin, she's too good-looking.'

'Identical twins have to be the same sex, idiot.'

'Where does she go to school?'

'The Danish Royal Ballet.'

'I didn't know they ran a school.'

'If you want to be in the corps you have to go to the school. Some girls start at the age of five. They do all the usual lessons, and dancing as well.'

'Does she like it?'

Tik shrugged. 'It's hard work, she says.' He opened a door and went along a short corridor to a bathroom and a second, smaller bedroom. Harald followed him. 'You'll be in here, if it's all right,' Tik said. 'We'll share the bathroom.'

'Great,' said Harald, dropping his case on the bed.

'You could have a grander room, but you'd be miles away.'

'This is better.'

'Come and say hello to my mother.'

Harald followed Tik along the main first-floor corridor. Tik tapped on a door, opened it a little, and said: 'Are you receiving gentlemen callers, Mother?'

A voice replied: 'Come in, Josef.'

Harald followed Tik into Mrs Duchwitz's boudoir, a pretty room with framed photographs on every level surface. Tik's mother looked like him. She was very short, though dumpy where Tik was slim, and she had the same dark eyes. She was about forty, but her black hair was already touched with grey.

Tik presented Harald, who shook her hand with a little bow. Mrs Duchwitz made them sit down and asked them about school. She was amiable and easy to talk to, and Harald began to feel less apprehensive about the weekend.

After a while she said: 'Go along and get ready for dinner, now.' The boys returned to Tik's room. Harald said anxiously: 'You don't wear anything special for dinner, do you?'

'Your blazer and tie are fine.'

It was all Harald had. The school blazer, trousers, overcoat, and cap, plus sports kit, were a major expense for the Olufsen family, and they had to be replaced constantly as he grew a couple of inches every year. He had no other clothes, apart from sweaters for the winter and shorts for the summer. 'What are you going to wear?' he asked Tik.

'A black jacket and grey flannels.'

Harald was glad he had brought a clean white shirt.

'Would you like to bathe first?' Tik said.

'Sure.' The idea that you had to have a bath before dinner seemed odd to Harald, but he told himself he was learning the ways of the rich.

He washed his hair in the bath, and Tik shaved at the same time. 'You don't shave twice a day at school,' Harald said.

'Mother's so fussy. And my beard is dark. She says I look like a coal miner if I don't shave in the evening.'

Harald put on his clean shirt and school trousers, then went into the bedroom to comb his damp hair in the mirror over the dressing table. While he was doing so, a girl walked in without knocking. 'Hello,' she said. 'You must be Harald.'

It was the girl in the photograph, but the monochrome picture had not done her justice. She had white skin and green eyes, and her curly hair was a vivid shade of coppery red. A tall figure in a long dark-green dress, she glided across the room like a ghost. With the easy strength of an athlete, she picked up a heavy chair by its back and turned it around to sit on it. She crossed her long legs and said: 'Well? Are you Harald?'

He managed to speak. 'Yes, I am.' He felt conscious of his bare feet. 'You're Tik's sister.'

'Tik?'

'That's what we call Josef at school.'

'Well, I'm Karen, and I don't have a nickname. I heard about your eruption at school. I think you're absolutely right. I hate the Nazis – who do they think they are?'

Tik emerged from the bathroom wrapped in a towel. 'Have you no regard for a gentleman's privacy?' he said.

'No, I don't,' she retorted. 'I want a cocktail, and they won't serve them until there's at least one male in the room. I believe servants make up these rules themselves, you know.'

'Well, just look the other way for a minute,' Tik said, and to Harald's surprise he dropped the towel.

Karen was unperturbed by her brother's nakedness and did not bother to look away. 'How are you, anyway, you black-eyed dwarf?' she said amiably as he pulled on clean white undershorts.

'I'm fine, though I'll be finer when the exams are over.'

'What will you do if you fail?'

'I suppose I'll work at the bank. Father will probably make me start at the bottom, filling the inkwells of the junior clerks.'

Harald said to Karen: 'He won't fail the exams.'

She replied: 'I suppose you're clever, like Josef.'

Tik said: 'Much cleverer, actually.'

Harald could not honestly deny it. Feeling bashful, he asked: 'What's it like at ballet school?'

'A cross between serving in the army and being in jail.'

Harald stared at Karen in fascination. He did not know whether to regard her as one of the boys or one of the gods. She bantered with her brother like a kid. Nevertheless she was extraordinarily graceful. Just sitting in the chair, waving an arm or pointing or resting her chin on her hand, she seemed to be dancing. All her movements were harmonious. Yet her poise did not restrain her, and Harald watched the changing expressions of her face like one mesmerized. She had a full-lipped mouth and a wide smile that was slightly lopsided. In fact her whole face was a little irregular – her nose was not quite straight and her chin was uneven – but the overall effect was beautiful. In fact, he thought, she was the most beautiful girl he had ever met.

'You'd better put some shoes on,' Tik said to Harald.

Harald retreated to his room and finished dressing. When he returned, Tik was looking spiffy in a black jacket, white shirt and plain dark tie. Harald felt very much the schoolboy in his blazer.

Karen led the way downstairs. They entered a long, untidy room with several large sofas, a grand piano, and an elderly dog on a rug in front of the fireplace. The relaxed air contrasted with the stuffy formality of the hall, although here, too, the walls were crowded with oil paintings.

A young woman in a black dress and a white apron

asked Harald what he would like to drink. 'Whatever Josef is having,' he replied. There was no alcohol at the parsonage. At school, in the final year, the boys were allowed to drink one glass of beer each at the Friday night get-together. Harald had never drunk a cocktail and was not quite sure what one was.

To give himself something to do, he bent down and patted the dog. It was a long, lean red setter with a sprinkling of grey in its gingery fur. It opened an eye and wagged its tail once in polite acknowledgement of Harald's attentions.

Karen said: 'That's Thor.'

'The god of thunder,' Harald said with a smile.

'Silly, I agree, but Josef named him.'

Tik protested: 'You wanted to call him Buttercup!'

'I was only eight years old at the time.'

'So was I. Besides, Thor isn't so silly. He sounds like thunder when he farts.'

At that moment Tik's father came in, and he looked so like the dog that Harald almost laughed. A tall, thin man, he was elegantly dressed in a velvet jacket and a black bow tie, and his curly red hair was turning grey. Harald stood up and shook hands.

Mr Duchwitz addressed him with the same languid courtesy the dog had shown. 'I'm so glad to meet you,' he said in a lazy drawl. 'Josef is always talking about you.'

Tik said: 'So now you know the whole family.'

Mr Duchwitz said to Harald: 'How are things at school, after your outburst?'

'I wasn't punished, oddly enough,' Harald

answered. 'In the past, I've had to cut the grass with nail scissors just for saying "Rubbish" when some teacher made a stupid statement. I was much ruder than that to Mr Agger. But Heis, that's the head, just gave me a quiet lecture about how much more effectively I would have made my point if I had kept my temper.'

'Setting an example himself by not being angry with you,' Mr Duchwitz said with a smile, and Harald realized that was exactly what Heis had been doing.

Karen said: 'I think Heis is wrong. Sometimes you have to make a stink to get people to listen.'

That struck Harald as true, and he wished he had thought to say it to Heis. Karen was shrewd as well as beautiful. But he had a question for Mr Duchwitz and had been looking forward to the chance of asking it. 'Sir, aren't you worried about what the Nazis might do to you? We know how badly Jews are treated in Germany and Poland.'

'I do worry. But Denmark is not Germany, and the Germans seem to regard us as Danes first and Jews second.'

'So far, anyway,' Tik put in.

'True. But then there's the question of what options are open to us. I suppose I could make a business trip to Sweden, then apply for a visa to the United States. Getting the whole family out would be more difficult. And think what we would be leaving behind: a business that was started by my great-grandfather, this house where my children were born, a collection of paintings it has taken me a lifetime to put together . . . When you look at it that way, it seems simplest to sit tight and hope for the best.'

'Anyway, it's not as if we're shopkeepers, for heaven's sake,' Karen said airily. 'I hate the Nazis, but what are they going to do to the family that owns the largest bank in the country?'

Harald thought that was stupid. 'The Nazis can do anything they like, you should know that by now,' he said scornfully.

'Oh, should I?' Karen said coldly, and he realized he had offended her. He was about to explain how Uncle Joachim had been persecuted but, at that moment, Mrs Duchwitz joined them, and they started talking about the Royal Danish Ballet's current production, which was *Les Sylphides*.

'I love the music,' Harald said. He had heard it on the radio and could play snatches of it on the piano.

'Have you seen the ballet?' Mrs Duchwitz asked him.

'No.' He felt the urge to give the impression that he had seen many ballets, but had happened to miss this one. Then he realized just how risky it would be to fake it in front of this highly knowledgeable family. 'To be honest, I've never been to the theatre,' he confessed.

'How dreadful,' Karen said with a supercilious air.

Mrs Duchwitz shot her a look of disapproval. 'Then Karen must take you,' she said.

'Mother, I'm terribly busy,' Karen protested. 'I'm understudying a principal role!'

Harald felt hurt by her rejection, but guessed he

was being punished for speaking dismissively to her about the Nazis.

He drained his glass. He had enjoyed the bittersweet taste of the cocktail, and it had given him a relaxed sense of wellbeing, but perhaps it had also made him careless of what he said. He regretted affronting Karen. Now that she had suddenly cooled, he realized how much he had come to like her.

The maid who had been serving drinks announced that dinner was ready, and opened a pair of doors that led to the dining room. They walked through and sat at one end of a long table. The maid offered wine, but Harald declined.

They had vegetable soup, cod in white sauce, and lamb chops with gravy. There was plenty of food, despite rationing, and Mrs Duchwitz explained that much of what they ate came from the estate.

Throughout the meal, Karen said nothing directly to Harald, but addressed her conversation to the company in general. Even when he asked her a question, she looked at the others as she answered. Harald was dismayed. She was the most enchanting girl he had ever met, and he had got on the wrong side of her within a couple of hours.

Afterwards, they returned to the drawing room and had real coffee. Harald wondered where Mrs Duchwitz had bought it. Coffee was like gold dust, and she certainly had not grown it in a Danish garden.

Karen went out on to the terrace for a cigarette, and Tik explained that their old-fashioned parents did not like to see girls smoking. Harald was awestruck at the sophistication of a girl who drank cocktails *and* smoked.

When Karen came back in, Mr Duchwitz sat at the piano and began turning over the pages on the music stand. Mrs Duchwitz stood behind him. 'Beethoven?' he said, and she nodded. He played a few notes, and she began to sing a song in German. Harald was impressed, and at the end he applauded.

Tik said: 'Sing another one, Mother.'

'All right,' she said. 'But then you have to play something.'

The parents performed another song, then Tik fetched his clarinet and played a simple Mozart lullaby. Mr Duchwitz returned to the piano and played a Chopin waltz, from *Les Sylphides*, and Karen kicked off her shoes and showed them one of the dances she was understudying.

Then they all looked expectantly at Harald.

He realized he was supposed to perform. He could not sing, except for roaring out Danish folk songs, so he would have to play. 'I'm not very good at classical music,' he said.

'Rubbish,' Tik said. 'You play the piano in your father's church, you told me.'

Harald sat at the keyboard. He really could not inflict inspirational Lutheran hymns on a cultured Jewish family. He hesitated, then began to play *Pine Top's Boogie-Woogie*. It started with a melodic trill played by the right hand. Then the left hand began the insistently rhythmic bass pattern, and the right played the blues discords that were so seductive. After a few moments, he lost his self-consciousness and began to feel the music. He played louder and more emphatically, calling out in English at the high points: 'Everybody, boogie-woogie!' just like Pine Top. The tune came to its climax and he said: 'That's what I'm talkin' about!'

When he finished, there was silence in the room. Mr Duchwitz wore the pained expression of a man who has accidentally swallowed something rotten. Even Tik looked embarrassed. Mrs Duchwitz said: 'Well, I must say, I don't think anything quite like that has ever been heard in this room.'

Harald realized he had made a mistake. The highbrow Duchwitz family disapproved of jazz as much as his own parents. They were cultured, but that did not make them open-minded. 'Oh, dear,' he said. 'I see that was not the right sort of thing.'

'Indeed not,' said Mr Duchwitz.

From behind the sofa, Karen caught Harald's eye. He expected to see a supercilious smile on her face but, to his surprise and delight, she gave him a broad wink.

That made it worthwhile.

* * *

On Sunday morning, he woke up thinking about Karen.

He hoped she might come into the boys' room to chat, as she had yesterday, but they did not see her.

She did not appear at breakfast. Trying hard to sound casual, Harald asked Tik where she was. Uninterested, Tik said she was probably doing her exercises.

After breakfast, Harald and Tik did two hours of exam revision. They both expected to pass easily, but they were not taking any chances, as the results would decide whether they could go to university. At eleven o'clock they went for a walk around the estate.

Near the end of the long drive, partly hidden from view by a stand of trees, was a ruined monastery. 'It was taken over by the king after the Reformation, and used as a home for a hundred years,' Tik said. 'Then Kirstenslot was built, and the old place fell into disuse.'

They explored the cloisters where the monks had walked. The cells were now storerooms for garden equipment. 'Some of this stuff hasn't been looked at for decades,' Tik said, poking a rusty iron wheel with the toe of his shoe. He opened a door into a large, well-lit room. There was no glass in the narrow windows, but the place was clean and dry. 'This used to be the dormitory,' Tik said. 'It's still used in summer, by seasonal workers on the farm.'

They entered the disused church, now a junk room. There was a musty smell. A thin black-and-white cat stared at them as if to ask what right they had to walk in like that, then it escaped through a glassless window.

Harald lifted a canvas sheet to reveal a gleaming Rolls-Royce sedan mounted on blocks. 'Your father's?' Harald said.

'Yes – put away until petrol goes on sale again.'

There was a scarred wooden work bench with a vice, and a collection of tools that had presumably been used to maintain the car when it was running. In the corner was a wash basin with a single tap. Up against the wall were stacks of wooden boxes that had once held soap and oranges. Harald looked inside one and found a jumble of toy cars made of painted tin. He picked one up. A driver was depicted on the windows, in profile on the side window, full face on the windscreen. He remembered when such toys had been infinitely desirable to him. He put the car back carefully.

In the far corner was a single-engined aeroplane with no wings.

Harald looked at it with interest. 'What's this?'

'A Hornet Moth, made by de Havilland, the English company. Father bought it five years ago, but he never learned to fly it.'

'Have you been up in it?'

'Oh, yes, we had great rides when it was new.'

Harald touched the great propeller, at least six feet long. The mathematically precise curves made it a work of art in his eyes. The aircraft leaned slightly to one side, and he saw that the undercarriage was damaged and one tyre was flat.

He felt the fuselage and was surprised to find it was made of some kind of fabric, stretched taut over a frame, with small rips and wrinkles in places. It was painted light blue with a black coachline edged in white, but the paintwork that might once have been cheerful was now dull, dusty and streaked with oil. It did have wings, he now saw – biplane wings, painted silver – but they were hinged, and had been swung around to point backwards.

He looked through the side window into the cabin. It was much like the front of a car. There were two seats side by side and a varnished wooden instrument panel with an assortment of dials. The upholstery of one seat had burst, and the stuffing was coming out. It looked as if mice had nested there.

He found the door handle and clambered inside, ignoring the soft scuttling sounds he heard. He sat on the one intact seat. The controls appeared simple. In the middle was a Y-shaped joystick that could be operated from either seat. He put his hand on the stick and his feet on the pedals. He thought flying would be even more thrilling than driving a motorcycle. He imagined himself soaring over the castle like a giant bird, with the roar of the engine in his ears.

'Did you ever fly it yourself?' he asked Tik.

'No. Karen took lessons, though.'

'Did she?'

'She wasn't old enough to qualify, but she was very good.'

Harald experimented with the controls. He saw a pair of 'On–Off' switches and flicked them both, but nothing happened. The stick and the pedals seemed loose, as if they were not connected to anything. Seeing what he was doing, Tik said: 'Some of the cables were taken out last year – they were needed to repair one of the farm machines. Let's go.'

Harald could have spent another hour fiddling with the aircraft, but Tik was impatient, so he climbed out.

They left from the back of the monastery and followed a cart track through a wood. Attached to Kirstenslot was a large farm. 'It's been rented to the Nielsen family since before I was born,' Tik said. 'They raise pigs for bacon, they keep a dairy herd that wins prizes, and they have several hundred acres under cereal crops.'

They tramped around a broad wheat field, crossed a pasture full of black-and-white cows, and smelled the pigs from a distance. On the dirt road leading to the farmhouse, they came across a tractor and trailer. A young man in overalls was peering at the engine. Tik shook hands with the man and said: 'Hello, Frederik, what's wrong?'

'Engine died on me in the middle of the road. I was taking Mr Nielsen and the family to church in the trailer.' Harald looked again at the trailer and saw that it contained two benches. 'Now the grown-ups are walking to church and the kiddies have been took home.'

'My friend Harald here is a wizard with all kinds of engines.'

'I wouldn't mind if he'd take a look.'

The tractor was an up-to-date model, with a diesel engine, and rubber tyres rather than steel wheels. Harald bent down to study the innards. 'What happens when you turn her over?'

'I'll show you.' Frederik pulled a handle. The starter motor whined, but the engine would not catch.

'She needs a new fuel pump, I think.' Frederik shook his head despairingly. 'We can't get spare parts for none of our machines.'

Harald frowned sceptically. He could smell fuel, which suggested to him that the pump was working, but the diesel was not reaching the cylinders. 'Would you try the starter once more?'

Frederik pulled the handle. Harald thought he saw the fuel filter outlet pipe move. Looking more closely, he saw that diesel was leaking from the release valve. He reached in and wiggled the nut. The entire valve assembly came away from the filter. 'There's the problem,' he said. 'The screw thread inside this nut has worn down, for some reason, and it's letting the fuel escape. Have you got a piece of wire?'

Frederik reached into the pockets of his tweed trousers. 'I've got a stout bit of string here.'

'That will do temporarily.' Harald put the valve back in position and tied it to the filter with the string so that it could not wobble. 'Try the starter now.'

Frederik pulled the handle, and the engine started. 'Well, I'm damned,' he said. 'You've mended it.'

'When you get a chance, replace the string with wire. Then you won't need a spare part.'

'I don't suppose you're going to be here for a week or two?' Frederik said. 'This farm has got broken machinery all over the place.'

'No, sorry – I have to go back to school.'

'Well, good luck.' Frederik climbed on his tractor. 'I can get to the church in time to bring the Nielsens back home, anyhow, thanks to you.' He drove off.

Harald and Tik strolled back towards the castle. 'That was impressive,' Tik said.

Harald shrugged. For as long as he could remember, he had been able to fix machines.

'Old Nielsen is keen on all the latest inventions,' Tik added. 'Machines for sowing, reaping, even milking.'

'Can he get fuel for them?'

'Yes. You can if it's for food production. But no one can find spare parts for anything.'

Harald checked his watch: he was looking forward to seeing Karen at lunch. He would ask her about her flying lessons.

In the village they stopped at the tavern. Tik bought two glasses of beer and they sat outside to enjoy the sunshine. Across the street, people were coming out of the small red-brick church. Frederik drove by on the tractor and waved. Seated in the trailer behind him were five people. The big man with white hair and a ruddy outdoor face must be Farmer Nielsen, Harald thought.

A man in black police uniform came out with a mousy woman and two small children. He gave Tik a hostile glare as he approached.

One of the children, a girl of about seven, said in a loud voice: 'Why don't they go to church, Daddy?'

'Because they're Jews,' the man said. 'They don't believe in Our Lord.'

Harald looked at Tik.

'The village policeman, Per Hansen,' Tik said

quietly. 'And local representative of the Danish National Socialist Workers Party.'

Harald nodded. The Danish Nazis were a weak party. In the last general election, two years ago, they had won only three seats in the Rigsdag. But the occupation had raised their hopes and, sure enough, the Germans had pressed the Danish government to give a ministerial post to the Nazi leader, Fritz Clausen. However, King Christian had dug in his heels and blocked the move, and the Germans had backed off. Party members such as Hansen were disappointed, but appeared to be waiting for a change of mood. They seemed confident that their time would come. Harald was afraid they might be right.

Tik drained his glass. 'Time for lunch.'

They returned to the castle. In the front courtyard Harald was surprised to see Poul Kirke, the cousin of their classmate Mads and friend of Harald's brother Arne. Poul was wearing shorts, and a bicycle was propped against the grand brick portico. Harald had met him several times, and now he stopped to talk while Tik went inside.

'Are you working here?' Poul asked him.

'No, visiting. School isn't over yet.'

'The farm hires students for the harvest, I know. What are you planning to do this summer?'

'I'm not sure. Last year I worked as a labourer at a building site on Sande.' He grimaced. 'Turned out to be a German base, although they didn't say so until later.'

Poul seemed interested 'Oh? What sort of base?'

'Some kind of radio station, I think. They fired all the Danes before they installed the equipment. I'll probably work on the fishing boats this summer, and do the preliminary reading for my university course. I'm hoping to study physics under Niels Bohr.'

'Good for you. Mads always says you're a genius.'

Harald was about to ask what Poul was doing here at Kirstenslot, when the answer became obvious. Karen came around the side of the house pushing a bicycle.

She looked ravishing in khaki shorts that showed off her long legs.

'Good morning, Harald,' she said. She went up to Poul and kissed him. Harald noted enviously that it was a kiss on the lips, though a brief one. 'Hi,' she said.

Harald was dismayed. He had been counting on an hour with Karen at the lunch table. But she was off on a bicycle ride with Poul, who was obviously her boyfriend, even though he was ten years older. Harald now saw, for the first time, that Poul was very good looking, with regular features and a movie-star smile that showed perfect teeth.

Poul held Karen's hands and looked her up and down. 'You are completely delectable,' he said. 'I wish I had a photo of you like this.'

She smiled graciously. 'Thank you.'

'Ready to go?'

'All set.'

They climbed on their bikes.

Harald felt sick. He watched them set off side by side down the half-mile drive in the sunshine. 'Have a nice ride!' he called.

Karen waved without turning around.

# SIX

Hermia Mount was about to get the sack.

This had never happened to her before. She was bright and conscientious, and her employers had always regarded her as a treasure, despite her sharp tongue. But her current boss, Herbert Woodie, was going to tell her she was fired, as soon as he worked up the courage.

Two Danes working for MI6 had been arrested at Kastrup aerodrome. They were now in custody and undoubtedly being interrogated. It was a bad blow to the Nightwatchmen network. Woodie was a peacetime MI6 man, a long-serving bureaucrat. He needed someone to blame, and Hermia was a suitable candidate.

Hermia understood this. She had worked for the British civil service for a decade, and she knew its ways. If Woodie were forced to accept that the blame lay with his department, he would pin it on the most junior person available. Woodie had never been comfortable working with a woman anyway, and he would be happy to see her replaced by a man.

At first Hermia was inclined to offer herself up as the sacrificial victim. She had never met the two aircraft mechanics – they had been recruited by Poul Kirke – but the network was her creation and she was responsible for the fate of the arrested men. She was as upset as if they had already died, and she did not want to go on.

After all, she thought, how much had she actually done to help the war effort? She was just accumulating information. None of it had ever been used. Men were risking their lives to send her photographs of Copenhagen harbour with nothing much happening. It seemed foolish.

But in fact she knew the importance of this laborious routine work. At some future date, a reconnaissance plane would photograph the harbour full of ships, and military planners would need to know whether this represented normal traffic or the sudden build-up of an invasion force – and at that point Hermia's photographs would become crucial.

Furthermore, the visit of Digby Hoare had given an immediate urgency to her work. The Germans' aircraft detection system could be the weapon that would win the war. The more she thought about it, the more likely it seemed that the key to the problem could lie in Denmark. The Danish west coast seemed the ideal location for a warning station designed to detect bombers approaching Germany.

And there was no one else in MI6 who had her ground-level knowledge of Denmark. She knew Poul Kirke personally and he trusted her. It could be disastrous if a stranger took over. She had to keep her job. And that meant outwitting her boss.

'This is bad news,' Woodie said sententiously as she stood in front of his desk.

His office was a bedroom in the old house of Bletchley Park. Flowered wallpaper and silk-shaded wall lights suggested it had been occupied by a lady before the war. Now it had filing cabinets instead of wardrobes full of dresses, and a steel map table where once there might have been a dressing table with spindly legs and a triple mirror. And instead of a glamorous woman in a priceless silk negligee, the room was occupied by a small, self-important man in a grey suit and glasses.

Hermia faked the appearance of calm. 'There's always danger when an operative is interrogated, of course,' she said. 'However—' She thought of the two brave men being interrogated and tortured, and her breath caught in her throat for a moment. Then she recovered. 'However, in this case I feel the risk is slight.'

Woodie grunted sceptically. 'We may need to set up an inquiry.'

Her heart sank. An inquiry meant an investigator from outside the department. He would have to come up with a scapegoat, and she was the obvious choice. She began the defence she had prepared. 'The two men arrested don't have any secrets to betray,' she said. 'They were ground crew at the aerodrome. One of the Nightwatchmen would give them papers to be smuggled out, and they would stow the contraband in a hollow wheel chock.' Even so, she knew, they might reveal apparently innocent details about how they were recruited and run, details which a clever spycatcher could use to track down other agents.

'Who passed them the papers?'

'Matthies Hertz, a lieutenant in the army. He's gone into hiding. And the mechanics don't know anyone else in the network.'

'So our tight security has limited the damage to the organization.'

Hermia guessed that Woodie was rehearsing a line he might speak to his superiors, and she forced herself to flatter him. 'Exactly, sir, that's a good way of putting it.'

'But how did the Danish police get to your people in the first place?'

Hermia had anticipated this question, and her answer was carefully prepared. 'I think the problem is at the Swedish end.'

'Ah.' Woodie brightened. Sweden, being a neutral country, was not under his control. He would welcome the chance of shifting the blame to another department. 'Take a seat, Miss Mount.'

'Thank you.' Hermia felt encouraged: Woodie was reacting as she had hoped. She crossed her legs and went on: 'I think the Swedish go-between has been passing copies of the illegal newspapers to Reuters in Stockholm, and this may have alerted the Germans. You have always had a strict rule that our agents stick to information gathering, and avoid ancillary activities such as propaganda work.' This was more flattery: she had never heard Woodie say any such thing, though it was a general rule in espionage.

However, he nodded sagely. 'Indeed.'

'I reminded the Swedes of your ruling as soon as I found out what was happening, but I fear the damage had been done.'

Woodie looked thoughtful. He would be happy if he could claim that his advice had been ignored. He did not really like people to do as he suggested, because when things went well they just took the credit themselves. He preferred it if they ignored his counsel and things went wrong. Then he could say: 'I told you so.'

Hermia said: 'Shall I do you a memo, mentioning your rule and quoting my signal to the Swedish legation?'

'Good idea.' Woodie liked this even better. He would not be allocating blame himself, merely quoting an underling who would incidentally be giving him credit for sounding the alarm.

'Then we'll need a new way of getting information out of Denmark. We can't use radio for this kind of material, it takes too long to broadcast.'

Woodie had no idea how to organize an alternative smuggling route. 'Ah, that's a problem,' he said with a touch of panic.

'Fortunately we have set up a fallback option, using the boat train that crosses from Elsinore in Denmark to Helsingborg in Sweden.'

Woodie was relieved. 'Splendid,' he said.

'Perhaps I should say in my memo that you've authorized me to action that.'

'Fine.'

She hesitated. 'And . . . the inquiry?'

'You know, I'm not sure that will be necessary. Your memo should serve to answer any questions.'

She concealed her relief. She was not going to be fired after all.

She knew she should quit while she was ahead. But there was another problem she was desperate to raise with him. This seemed like an ideal opportunity. 'There is one thing we could do that would improve our security enormously, sir.'

'Indeed?' Woodie's expression said that if there were such a procedure he would already have thought of it.

'We could use more sophisticated codes.'

'What's wrong with our poem and book codes? Agents of MI6 have been using them for years.'

'I fear the Germans may have figured out how to break them.'

Woodie smiled knowingly. 'I don't think so, my dear.'

Hermia decided to take the risk of contradicting him. 'May I show you what I mean?' Without waiting for his answer, she went on: 'Take a look at this coded message.' She quickly scribbled on her pad:

*gsff cffs jo uif dbouffo*

She said: 'The commonest letter is *f*.'

'Obviously.'

'In the English language, the letter used most commonly is *e*, so the first thing a codebreaker would do is assume that *f* stands for *e*, which gives you this.'

*gsEE cEEs jo uiE dbouEEo*

'It could still mean anything,' Woodie said.

'Not quite. How many four-letter words are there ending in double *e*?'

'I'm sure I've no idea.'

'Only a few common ones: *flee, free, glee, thee,* and *tree.* Now look at the second group.'

'Miss Mount, I don't really have time—'

'Just another few seconds, sir. There are many four-letter words with a double *e* in the middle. What could the first letter be? Not *a*, certainly, but it could be *b*. So think of words beginning *bee* that might logically come next. *Flee been* makes no sense, *free bees* sounds odd, although *tree bees* might be right—'

Woodie interrupted. 'Free beer!' he said triumphantly.

'Let's try that. The next group is two letters, and there aren't many two-letter words: *an, at, in, if, it, on, of, or,* and *up* are the commonest. The fourth group is a three-letter word ending in *e*, of which there are many, but the commonest is *the.*'

Woodie was getting interested despite himself. 'Free beer at the something.'

'Or in the something. And that something is a seven-letter word with a double *e* in it, so it ends *eed, eef, eek, eel, eem, een, eep*—'

'Free beer in the canteen!' said Woodie triumphantly.

'Yes,' Hermia said. She sat in silence, looking at Woodie, letting the implications of what had just happened sink in. After a few moments she said: 'That's how easy our codes are to break, sir.' She looked at her watch. 'It took you three minutes.'

He grunted. 'A good party trick, Miss Mount, but the old hands at MI6 know more about this sort of thing than you, take it from me.'

It was no good, she thought despairingly. He would not be moved on this today. She would have to try again later. She forced herself to give in gracefully. 'Very good, sir.'

'Concentrate on your own responsibilities. What are the rest of your Nightwatchmen up to?'

'I'm about to ask them to keep their eyes open for any indications that the Germans have developed long-distance aircraft detection.'

'Good Lord, don't do that!'

'Why not?'

'If the enemy finds out we're asking that question, he'll guess we've got it!'

'But, sir – what if he does have it?'

'He doesn't. You can rest assured.'

'The gentleman who came here from Downing Street last week seemed to think otherwise.'

'In strict confidence, Miss Mount, an MI6 committee looked into the whole radar question quite recently, and concluded that it would be another eighteen months before the enemy developed such a system.'

So, Hermia thought, it was called radar. She smiled. 'That's so reassuring,' she lied. 'I expect you were on the committee yourself, sir?'

Woodie nodded. 'In fact I chaired it.'

'Thank you for setting my mind at rest. I'll get on with that memo.'

'Jolly good.'

Hermia went out. Her face ached with smiling and she was exhausted by the effort of constantly deferring to Woodie. She had saved her job, and she permitted herself a moment of satisfaction as she walked back to her own office. But she had failed with the codes. She had found out the name of the long-distance aircraft detection system – radar – but it was clear Woodie would not let her investigate whether the Germans had such a system in Denmark.

She longed to do something of immediate value to the war effort. All this routine work made her impatient and frustrated. It would be so satisfying to see some real results. And it might even justify what had happened to those two poor aircraft mechanics at Kastrup.

She could investigate enemy radar without Woodie's permission, of course. He might find out, but she was willing to take that risk. However, she did not know what to tell her Nightwatchmen. What should they be looking for, and where? She needed more information before she could brief Poul Kirke. And Woodie was not going to give it to her.

But he was not her only hope.

She sat down at her desk, picked up the phone, and said: 'Please connect me with Number Ten, Downing Street.'

\* \* \*

She met Digby Hoare in Trafalgar Square. She stood at the foot of Nelson's Column and watched him cross the road from Whitehall. She smiled at the energetic, lopsided stride that already seemed to her characteristic of him. They shook hands, then walked towards Soho.

It was a warm summer evening, and the West End of London was busy, its pavements thronged with people heading for theatres, cinemas, bars and restaurants. The happy scene was marred only by bomb damage, the occasional blackened ruin in a row of buildings standing out like a rotten tooth in a smile.

She had thought they were going for a drink in a pub, but Digby led her to a small French restaurant. The tables either side of them were empty, so they could talk without being overheard.

Digby was wearing the same dark grey suit, but this evening he had on a light blue shirt that set off his blue eyes. Hermia was pleased she had decided to wear her favourite piece of jewellery, a panther brooch with emerald eyes.

She was keen to get down to business. She had refused to go on a date with Digby and she did not want him to get the idea that she might have changed her mind. As soon as they had ordered, she said: 'I want to use my agents in Denmark to find out whether the Germans have radar.'

He looked at her through narrowed eyes. 'The question is more complicated than that. It's now beyond doubt that they have radar, as we do. But theirs is more effective than ours – devastatingly so.'

'Oh.' She was taken aback. 'Woodie told me . . . never mind.'

'We're desperate to find out why their system is so good. Either they have invented something better than we've got, or they've devised a way of using it more effectively – or both.'

'All right.' She rapidly readjusted her ideas in the light of this new information. 'Just the same, it seems likely that some of this machinery is in Denmark.'

'It would be a logical place – and the codename "Freya" suggests Scandinavia.'

'So what are my people looking for?'

'That's difficult.' He frowned. 'We don't know what their machinery looks like – that's the point, isn't it?'

'I presume it gives out radio waves.'

'Yes, of course.'

'And presumably the signals travel a good distance – otherwise the warning wouldn't be early enough.'

'Yes. It would be useless unless the signals travelled at least, say, fifty miles. Probably more.'

'Could we listen for them?'

He raised his eyebrows in surprise. 'Yes, with a radio receiver. Clever notion – I don't know why no one else thought of it.'

'Can the signals be distinguished from other transmissions, such as normal broadcasts, the news and so on?'

He nodded. 'You'd be listening for a series of pulses, probably very rapid, say a thousand per second. You'd hear it as a continuous musical note. So you'd know it wasn't the BBC. And it would be quite different from the dots and dashes of military traffic.'

'You're an engineer. Could you put together a radio receiver suitable for picking up such signals?'

He looked thoughtful. 'It's got to be portable, presumably.'

'It should pack into a suitcase.'

'And work off a battery, so it can be used anywhere.'

'Yes.'

'It might be possible. There's a team of boffins in Welwyn who do this stuff all day.' Welwyn was a small town between Bletchley and London. 'Exploding turnips, radio transmitters concealed in bricks, that sort of thing. They could probably cobble something together.'

Their food came. Hermia had ordered a tomato salad. It came with a sprinkling of chopped onion and a sprig of mint, and she wondered why British cooks could not produce food that was simple and delicious like this, instead of tinned sardines and boiled cabbage.

'What made you set up the Nightwatchmen?' Digby asked her.

She was not sure what he meant. 'It seemed like a good idea.'

'Still, not an idea that would occur to the average young woman, if I may say so.'

She thought back, remembering the struggle she had had with another bureaucratic boss, and asked herself why she had persisted. 'I wanted to strike a blow against the Nazis. There's something about them that I find absolutely loathsome.'

'Fascism blames problems on a false cause – people of other races.'

'I know, but it's not that. It's the uniforms, the strutting and posturing, and the way they howl out those hateful speeches. It just makes me sick.'

'When did you experience all this? There aren't many Nazis in Denmark.'

'I spent a year in Berlin in the thirties. I watched them marching and saluting and spitting on people and smashing the windows of Jewish shopkeepers. I remember thinking: these people have to be stopped before they spoil the whole world. I still think so. I'm more sure of that than anything.'

He smiled. 'Me, too.'

Hermia had a seafood fricassee, and once again she was struck by what a French cook could do with common ingredients, despite rationing. The dish contained sliced eel, some of the winkles beloved of Londoners, and flaked cod, but it was all fresh and well seasoned, and she tucked in with relish.

Every now and again she caught Digby's eye, and he always had the same look, a mixture of adoration and lust. It alarmed her. If he fell in love with her, it could only lead to trouble and heartbreak. But it was pleasing, as well as embarrassing, to have a man so obviously desire her. At one point she felt herself flush, and put her hand to her throat to hide her blushes.

She deliberately turned her thoughts to Arne. The first time she talked to him, in the bar of a ski hotel in Norway, she knew she had found what was missing in her life. 'Now I understand why I've never had a satisfactory relationship with a man,' she had written to her mother. 'It's because I hadn't met Arne.' When he proposed to her, she had said: 'If I'd known there were men like you, I'd have married one years ago.'

She said yes to everything he suggested. She was normally so intent on having her own way that she had never been able to share an apartment with a girlfriend, but with Arne she lost her will power. Every time he asked her to go out with him she accepted; when he kissed her, she kissed him back; when he stroked her breasts under her ski sweater she just sighed with pleasure; and when he knocked on the door of her hotel room at midnight she said: 'I'm so glad you're here.'

Thinking of Arne helped her to feel cooler towards Digby, and as they finished their meal she turned the conversation to the war. An Allied army including British, Commonwealth and Free French forces had invaded Syria. It was a skirmish on the far fringes, and they both found it hard to see the outcome as important. The conflict in Europe was all that really counted. And here it was a war of bombers.

When they left the restaurant it was dark, but there was a full moon. They walked south, heading for her mother's house in Pimlico, where Hermia was going to spend the night. As they were crossing St James's

Park the moon went behind a cloud, and Digby turned to her and kissed her.

She could not help admiring the swift sureness of his moves. His lips were on hers before she could turn away. With a strong hand he pulled her body to his, and her breasts pressed against his chest. She knew she should be indignant, but to her consternation she found herself responding. She suddenly remembered what it was like to feel a man's hard body and hot skin, and in a rush of desire she opened her mouth to him.

They kissed hungrily for a minute, then his hand went to her breast, and that broke the spell. She was too old and respectable to be groped in a park. She broke the clinch.

The thought of taking him home crossed her mind. She imagined the pained disapproval of Mags and Bets, and the picture made her laugh.

'What is it?' he said.

She saw that he looked hurt. He probably imagined her laughter had to do with his disability. I must remember how vulnerable he might be to mockery, she thought. She hastened to explain. 'My mother is a widow who lives with a middle-aged spinster. I just thought how they would react if I told them I wanted to bring a man home for the night.'

The hurt look went away. 'I like your thinking,' he said, and he tried to kiss her again.

She was tempted, but thought of Arne, and put a resisting hand on Digby's chest. 'No more,' she said firmly. 'Walk me home.'

They left the park. The momentary euphoria left her, and she began to feel troubled. How could she enjoy kissing Digby when she loved Arne? As they passed Big Ben and Westminster Abbey, an air-raid warning put all such thoughts out of her mind.

Digby said: 'Do you want to find a shelter?'

Many Londoners no longer took cover during air raids. Fed up with sleepless nights, some had decided it was worth risking the bombs. Others had become fatalistic, saying that a bomb either had your number on it or not, and there was nothing you could do either way. Hermia was not quite so blasé, but on the other hand she had no intention of spending the night in an air-raid shelter with the amorous Digby. She nervously twisted the engagement ring on her left hand. 'We're only a few minutes away,' she replied. 'Do you mind if we keep going?'

'I may be forced to spend the night at your mother's house after all.'

'At least I'll be chaperoned.'

They hurried through Westminster into Pimlico. Searchlights probed the scattered clouds, then they heard the sinister low drone of heavy aircraft, like a large beast growling hungrily, deep in its throat. An anti-aircraft gun boomed somewhere, and flak burst in the sky like fireworks. Hermia wondered whether her mother was out driving her ambulance tonight.

To Hermia's horror, bombs started to fall nearby, although it was normally the industrial East End that was hardest hit. There was a deafening crump that seemed to come from the next street. A minute later, a fire engine roared by. Hermia walked on as fast as she could.

Digby said: 'You're so cool – aren't you scared?'

'Of course I'm scared,' she said impatiently. 'I'm just not panicking.'

They turned a corner and saw a blazing building. The fire engine was outside and the men were unrolling hoses.

'How much farther?' Digby asked.

'Next street,' Hermia said, panting.

When they rounded the next corner, they saw another fire engine at the far end of the street, near Mags's house. 'Oh, God,' Hermia said, and she broke into a run. Her heart pounded with fear as she dashed along the pavement. There was an ambulance, she saw, and at least one house in her mother's section had been hit. 'No, please,' she said aloud.

Coming closer, she was perplexed that she could not identify her mother's house, though she saw clearly that the house next door was on fire. She stopped and stared, trying to understand what she was looking at. Then, at last, she realized that her mother's house was gone. Nothing was left of it but a gap in the terrace and a pile of debris. She groaned in despair.

Digby said: 'Is that the house?'

Hermia nodded, unable to speak.

Digby called to a fireman in an authoritative voice. 'You!' he said. 'Any sign of the occupants of this building?'

'Yes, sir,' said the fireman. 'One person was blown clear by the blast.' He pointed to the small front yard of the undamaged house on the far side. There was a body on a stretcher lying on the ground. The face was covered.

Hermia felt Digby take her arm. Together they entered the yard.

Hermia knelt down and Digby uncovered the face.

'It's Bets,' Hermia said, with a sickeningly guilty feeling of relief.

Digby was looking around. 'Who's that, sitting on the wall?'

Hermia looked up, and her heart lurched as she recognized the figure of her mother, dressed in her ambulance uniform and tin hat, slumped on the low wall as if all the life had gone out of her. 'Mother?' she said.

Her mother looked up, and Hermia saw that tears were streaming down her face.

Hermia went to her and put her arms around her.

'Bets is dead,' her mother said.

'I'm sorry, Mother.'

'She loved me so much,' her mother sobbed.

'I know.'

'Do you? Do you know? She waited all her life for me. Did you realize that? All her life.'

Hermia hugged her mother hard. 'I'm so sorry,' she said.

*　*　*

There had been about two hundred Danish ships at sea on the morning of 9 April 1940, when Hitler invaded Denmark. All that day, Danish-language broadcasts by the BBC appealed to sailors to head for Allied ports rather than return home to a conquered country. In total, about five thousand men accepted the offer of refuge. Most sought harbour on the east coast of England, hoisted the Union Jack, and continued to sail throughout the war under the British flag. Consequently, by the middle of the following year small communities of Danes had settled in several English ports.

Hermia decided to go to the fishing town of Stokeby. She had visited the place twice previously to talk to the Danes there. On this occasion she told her boss, Herbert Woodie, that her mission was to check her somewhat out-of-date plans of the main Danish ports and make any alterations necessary.

He believed her.

She had a different story for Digby Hoare.

Digby came to Bletchley, two days after the bomb destroyed her mother's house, with a radio receiver and direction finder neatly packed into a used-looking tan leather suitcase. As he showed her how to use the equipment, she thought guiltily of the kiss in the park, and how much she had enjoyed it, and wondered uneasily how she would be able to look Arne in the eye.

Her original plan had been to attempt to smuggle the radio receiver to the Nightwatchmen, but she had since thought of something simpler. The signals from the radar apparatus could probably be picked up at sea just as easily as on land. She told Digby she was going to pass the suitcase to the captain of a fishing boat and teach him how to use it. Digby approved.

That plan might well have worked, but in truth she did not want to hand such an important job over to someone else. So she intended to go herself.

In the North Sea, between England and Denmark, there was a large sandbank known as Dogger Bank, where the sea was as shallow as fifty feet in places, and the fishing was good. Both British and Danish ships trawled there. Strictly speaking, Denmark-based vessels were banned from venturing so far from their coast, but Germany needed herrings, so the ban was irregularly enforced and constantly defied. For some time, Hermia had had it in the back of her mind that messages – or even people – might travel between the two countries on fishing boats, transferring from Danish to British or vice versa in the middle. Now, however, she had a better idea. The far end of the Dogger Bank was only a hundred miles from the Danish coast. If all her guesswork turned out to be right, the signals from the Freya machine should be detectable from the fishing ground.

She took a train on Friday afternoon. She was dressed for the sea in trousers, boots, and a loose sweater, with her hair pushed under a man's checked cap. As the train rolled through the flat fen country of eastern England, she worried whether her plan would work. Would she find a ship willing to take her? Would she pick up the signals she was expecting? Or was the whole thing a waste of time?

After a while her mind turned to her mother. Mags had been under control again yesterday at Bets's funeral, appearing calmly sorrowful rather than stricken by grief, and today she had gone to Cornwall to stay with her sister, Hermia's Aunt Bella. But on the night of the bomb her soul had been laid bare.

The two women had been devoted friends, but it was clearly more than that. Hermia did not really want to think what else could be involved, but she could not help being intrigued. Setting aside the embarrassing thought of what physical relation there might have been between Mags and Bets, Hermia was shocked that her mother had nourished a passionate lifelong attachment that had remained carefully disguised, all those years, from Hermia herself and presumably from Mags's husband, Hermia's father.

She arrived in Stokeby at eight o'clock on a mild summer evening and went from the railway station straight to the Shipwright's Arms pub on the dockside. It took her only a few minutes of asking around to learn that Sten Munch, a Danish captain she had met on her last visit here, was due to sail in the morning in his vessel *Morganmand*, which meant 'early riser'. She found Sten at his house on the hillside, clipping the hedge in his front garden like a born Englishman. He invited her in.

He was a widower and lived with his son, Lars, who had been on the boat with him on 9 April 1940. Lars had since married a local girl, Carol. When Hermia went inside, Carol was nursing a tiny baby a few days old. Lars made tea. They all spoke English for Carol's sake.

Hermia explained that she needed to get as close as possible to the Danish coast in an attempt to listen to a German wireless transmission – she did not say what kind. Sten did not question her story. 'Of course!' he said expansively. 'Anything to help defeat the Nazis! But my boat is not really suitable.'

'Why not?'

'It's very small – only thirty-five feet – and we'll be away for about three days.'

Hermia had been expecting this. She had told Woodie she needed to get her mother settled in new accommodation and would be back some time next week. 'That's all right,' she told Sten. 'I've got time.'

'My boat has only three berths. We sleep in shifts. It's not designed for ladies. You should go in a larger vessel.'

'Is there one leaving in the morning?'

Sten looked at Lars, who said: 'No. Three set off yesterday, won't return until next week. Peter Gorning should be back tomorrow. He'll go out again about Wednesday.'

She shook her head. 'Too late.'

Carol looked up from her baby. 'They sleep in their clothes, you know. That's why they stink when they get home. It's worse than the smell of the fish.'

Hermia immediately liked her for her down-to-earth directness. 'I'll be fine,' she said. 'I can sleep in my clothes, in a bed still warm from the previous occupant. It won't kill me.'

Sten said: 'You know I want to help. But the sea is not for women. You were made for the gracious things in life.'

Carol snorted scornfully. 'Like giving birth?'

Hermia smiled, grateful to have Carol as an ally. 'Exactly. We can put up with discomfort.'

Carol nodded vigorously. 'Think of what Charlie's going through in the desert.' She explained to Hermia: 'My brother Charlie's in the army somewhere in North Africa.'

Sten looked cornered. He did not want to take Hermia, but he was reluctant to say so, wanting to appear patriotic and brave. 'We leave at three o'clock in the morning.'

'I'll be there.'

Carol said: 'You might as well stay here, now. We've got a spare room.' She looked at her father-in-law. 'If that's all right with you, Pa.'

He had run out of excuses. 'Of course!' he said.

'Thank you,' said Hermia. 'You're very kind.'

They went to bed early. Hermia did not undress, but sat up in her room with the light on. She was afraid that, if she overslept, Sten would leave without her. The Munch family were not great readers, and the only book she could find was the Bible in Danish, but it kept her awake. At two o'clock she went to the bathroom and washed quickly, then tiptoed downstairs and put the kettle on. Sten appeared at half past two. When he saw Hermia in the kitchen he looked surprised and disappointed. She poured tea into a big cup and he took it gratefully enough.

Hermia, Sten and Lars walked down the hill to the quay a few minutes before three o'clock. Two more Danish men were waiting at the dockside. The *Morganmand* was very small. Thirty-five feet was about the length of a London bus. The vessel was made of wood, and had one mast and a diesel engine. On deck was a small wheelhouse and a series of hatches over the hold. From the wheelhouse, a companionway led down to the living quarters. At the stern end were the massive spars and the winding gear for the nets.

Dawn was breaking as the little vessel threaded its way through the defensive minefield at the mouth of the harbour. The weather was fine, but they encountered a swell of five or six feet as soon as they left the shelter of the land. Fortunately, Hermia was never seasick.

Throughout the day, she tried to make herself useful around the boat. She knew no seamanship, so she kept the galley clean. The men were used to preparing food for themselves, but she washed their dishes and the frying pan in which they cooked almost everything they ate. She made sure she talked to the two crewmen, speaking Danish, getting on terms of respectful friendliness with each of them. When she had nothing else to do, she sat on the deck and enjoyed the sunshine.

Towards midday they reached the Outer Silver Pit, on the south-east corner of the Dogger Bank, and began to trawl. The boat reduced speed and headed north-east. At first they could not find the fish, and the nets came up almost empty. Then, towards the end of the afternoon, the fish started running.

At nightfall, Hermia went below and lay on a bunk. She thought she would not sleep, but she had been up for thirty-six hours, and tiredness got the better of tension. She dropped off within minutes.

During the night she was awakened, briefly, by the volcanic rumble of a flight of bombers overhead. She wondered vaguely whether it was the RAF heading for Germany or the Luftwaffe going the other way, then drifted off to sleep again.

The next thing she knew, Lars was shaking her. 'We're approaching our nearest point to Denmark,' he said. 'We're about a hundred and twenty miles off Morlunde.'

Hermia took her suitcase receiver up on deck. It was already full daylight. The men were hauling in a net full of flapping fish, mainly herrings and mackerel, and tipping them into the hold. Hermia found it a gruesome sight, and looked away.

She connected the battery to the radio and was relieved to see the dials flicker. She fixed the aerial to the mast with a length of wire thoughtfully provided by Digby. She let the set warm up, then put on the headphones.

As the boat motored north-east, Hermia roamed up and down the wireless frequencies. As well as the BBC's broadcasts in English, she picked up French, Dutch, German and Danish radio programmes, plus a host of Morse transmissions which she presumed were military signals from both sides. At the first pass up and down, she heard nothing that might have been radar.

She repeated the exercise more slowly, making sure she missed nothing. She had plenty of time. But once again she did not hear what she was listening for.

She kept trying.

After two hours she noticed that the men had stopped fishing and were watching her. She caught the eye of Lars, who said: 'Any luck?'

She pulled off the headphones. 'I'm not picking up the signal I was expecting,' she said in Danish.

Sten replied in the same language. 'The fish were running all night. We've done well – our hold is full. We're ready to go home.'

'Would you motor north for a while? I must try to find this signal – it's really important.'

Sten looked doubtful, but his son said: 'We can afford it, we've had a good night.'

Sten was reluctant. 'What if a German spotter plane flies overhead?'

Hermia said: 'You could throw out nets and pretend to be fishing.'

'There are no fishing grounds where you want to go.'

'German pilots don't know that.'

One of the crew put in: 'If it's to help free Denmark . . .'

The other hand nodded vigorously.

Once again, Hermia was saved by Sten's reluctance

to appear cowardly in front of others. 'All right,' he said. 'We'll head north.'

'Keep a hundred miles off the coast,' Hermia said as she put the headphones back on.

She continued to scan the frequencies. As time went by, she became less hopeful. The likeliest place for a radar station was at the southern end of Denmark's coast, near the border with Germany. She had thought she would pick up the broadcast early. But her hopes fell by the hour as the boat headed north.

She was not willing to leave the set alone for more than a minute or two, so the fishermen brought her tea at intervals, and a bowl of canned stew at supper time. While listening, she gazed east. She could not see Denmark, but she knew Arne was there somewhere, and she enjoyed feeling closer to him.

Towards nightfall, Sten knelt on the deck beside her to talk, and she took off the headphones. 'We're off the northern point of the Jutland peninsula,' he said. 'We have to turn back.'

In desperation she said: 'Could we go closer? Maybe a hundred miles offshore is too far away to pick up the signal.'

'We need to head for home.'

'Could we follow the coast southward, retracing our course, but fifty miles closer to land?'

'Too dangerous.'

'It's almost dark. There are no spotter planes at night.'

'I don't like it.'

'Please. It's very important.' She shot an appealing look at Lars, who was standing nearby, listening. He was bolder than his father, perhaps because he saw his future in Britain, with his English wife.

As she was hoping, Lars joined in. 'How about seventy-five miles offshore?'

'That would be great.'

Lars looked at his father. 'We have to go south anyway. It won't add more than a few hours to our voyage.'

Sten said angrily: 'We'll be putting our crew in danger!'

Lars replied mildly: 'Think of Carol's brother in Africa. He's put himself in danger. This is our chance to do something to help.'

'All right, you take the wheel,' Sten said sulkily. 'I'm going to sleep.' He stepped into the wheelhouse and flung himself down the companionway.

Hermia smiled at Lars. 'Thanks.'

'We should thank you.'

Lars turned the boat around and Hermia continued to scan the airwaves. Night fell. They sailed without lights, but the sky was clear and there was a three-quarter moon, which made Hermia feel that the boat must be conspicuous. However, they saw no aircraft and no other shipping. Periodically, Lars checked their position with a sextant.

Her mind drifted back to the air raid she and Digby had been in a few days ago. It was the first time she had been caught out of doors during a raid. She had managed to remain calm, but it had been a terrifying scene: the drone of the aircraft, the searchlights and the flak, the crump of falling bombs and the hellish light of burning houses. Yet here she was doing her best to help the RAF inflict the same horrors on German families. It seemed mad – but the only alternative was to let the Nazis take over the world.

It was a short midsummer night, and dawn broke early. The sea was unusually calm. A morning mist rose from the surface, reducing visibility and making Hermia feel safer. As the boat continued south, she became more anxious. She must pick up the signal soon – unless she and Digby were wrong, and Herbert Woodie right.

Sten came on deck with a mug of tea in one hand and a bacon sandwich in the other. 'Well?' he said. 'Have you got what you wanted?'

'It's most likely to come from the south of Denmark,' she said.

'Or nowhere at all.'

She nodded despondently. 'I'm beginning to think you're right.' Then she heard something. 'Wait!' She had been scanning upwards through the frequencies, and thought she had heard a musical note. She reversed the knob and went down, searching for the spot. She got a lot of static, then the note again – a pure machine-like tone about an octave above middle C. 'I think this could be it!' she said joyfully. The wavelength was 2.4 metres. She made a note in the little book Digby had tucked into the suitcase.

Now she had to determine the direction.

Incorporated into the receiver was a dial graduated from one to three hundred and sixty with a needle pointing to the source of the signal. Digby had emphasized that the dial had to be aligned precisely with the centre line of the boat. Then the direction of the signal could be calculated from the heading of the boat and the needle on the dial. 'Lars!' she called. 'What's our heading?'

'East south-east,' he said.

'No, exactly.'

'Well . . .' Although the weather was fine and the sea was calm, nevertheless the boat was moving all the time, and the compass was never still.

'As best you can,' she said.

'One hundred and twenty degrees.'

The needle on her dial pointed to 340. Adding 120 to that brought the direction around to 100. Hermia made a note. 'And what is our position?'

'Wait a minute. When I shot the stars, we were crossing the fifty-sixth parallel.' He looked at the log, checked his wristwatch, and called out their latitude and longitude. Hermia wrote down the numbers, knowing they were only an estimate.

Sten said: 'Are you satisfied now? Can we go home?'

'I need another reading so that I can triangulate the source of the broadcast.'

He grunted in disgust and walked away.

Lars winked at her.

She kept the receiver tuned to the note as they motored south. The needle on the direction finder moved imperceptibly. After half an hour she again asked Lars for the boat's heading.

'Still one-twenty.'

The needle on her dial now pointed to 335. The direction of the signal was therefore 095. She asked him to estimate their position again, and wrote the numbers down.

'Home?' he said.

'Yes. And thank you.'

He turned the wheel.

Hermia was triumphant, but she could not wait to find out where the signal was coming from. She went into the wheelhouse and found a large-scale chart. With Lars's help she marked the two positions she had noted and drew lines for the bearing of the signal from each position, correcting for True North. The lines intersected off the coast, near the island of Sande.

'My God,' Hermia said. 'That's where my fiancé comes from.'

'Sande? I know it – I went to watch the racing car speed trials there a few years back.'

She was jubilant. Her guess had been right and her method had worked. The signal she had been expecting was coming from the most logical place.

Now she needed to send Poul Kirke, or one of his team, to Sande to look around. As soon as she returned to Bletchley she would send a coded message.

A few minutes later, she took another heading. The

signal was weak now, but the third line on the map made a triangle with the other two, and the island of Sande lay mainly within that triangle. All the calculations were approximate, but the conclusion seemed clear. The radio signal was coming from the island.

She could hardly wait to tell Digby.

# SEVEN

Harald thought the Tiger Moth was the most beautiful machine he had ever seen. It looked like a butterfly poised for flight, its upper and lower wings spread wide, its toy-car wheels resting lightly on the grass, its long tail tapering behind. The weather was fine with gentle breezes, and the little aircraft trembled in the wind, as if eager to take off. It had a single engine in the nose, driving the big cream-painted propeller. Behind the engine were two open cockpits, one in front of the other.

It was cousin to the dilapidated Hornet Moth he had seen in the ruined monastery at Kirstenslot, and the two aircraft were mechanically similar, except that the Hornet Moth had an enclosed cabin with seats side by side. However, the Hornet Moth had looked sorry for itself, leaning to one side on its broken undercarriage, its fabric torn and oil-stained, its upholstery bursting. By contrast, the Tiger Moth had a sprightly look, with new paint bright on its fuselage and the sun glinting off its windscreen. Its tail rested on the ground and its nose pointed up, as if it were sniffing the air.

'You'll notice that the wings are flat underneath

but curved above,' said Harald's brother, Arne Olufsen. 'When the aircraft is moving, the air travelling over the top of the wing is forced to move faster than the air passing underneath.' He gave the engaging grin that made people forgive him anything. 'For reasons I have never understood, this lifts the aircraft off the ground.'

'It creates a pressure difference,' Harald said.

'Indeed,' Arne replied drily.

The senior class at Jansborg Skole were spending the day at the Army Aviation School at Vodal. They were being shown around by Arne and his friend Poul Kirke. It was a recruiting exercise by the army, who were having trouble persuading bright young men to join a military force that had nothing to do. Heis, with his army background, liked Jansborg to send one or two pupils into the military each year. For the boys, the visit was a welcome break from exam revision.

'The hinged surfaces on the lower wings are called ailerons,' Arne told them. 'They are connected by cables to the control column, which is sometimes called the joystick, for reasons you are too young to understand.' He grinned again. 'When the stick is moved to the left, the left aileron moves up and the right one down. This causes the aircraft to tilt and turn left. We call it banking.'

Harald was fascinated, but he wanted to get in and fly.

'You'll observe that the rear half of the tailplane is also hinged,' Arne said. 'This is called the elevator, and it points the aircraft up or down. Pull back on the stick and the elevator tilts up, depressing the tail, so that the aircraft climbs.'

Harald noticed that the upright part of the tail also had a flap. 'What's that for?' he asked, pointing at it.

'This is the rudder, controlled by a pair of pedals in the footwell of the cockpit. It works in the same way as the rudder of a boat.'

Mads put in: 'Why do you need a rudder? You use the ailerons to change direction.'

'Good point!' Arne said. 'Shows that you're listening. But can't you figure it out? Why would we need a rudder as well as ailerons to steer the aircraft?'

Harald guessed. 'You can't use the ailerons when you're on the runway.'

'Because . . .?'

'The wings would hit the ground.'

'Correct. We use the rudder while taxiing, when we can't tilt the wings because they would hit the ground. We also use the rudder in the air, to control unwanted sideways movement of the aircraft, which is called yaw.'

The fifteen boys had toured the air base, sat through a lecture – on opportunities, pay and training in the army – and had lunch with a group of young pupil pilots. Now they were eager for the individual flying lesson which had been promised to each of them as the climax of the day. Five Tiger Moths were lined up on the grass. Danish military aircraft had been officially grounded since the beginning of the occupation, but there were exceptions. The flying school was allowed to give lessons in gliders, and special permission had been granted for today's exercise in Tiger Moths. Just in case anyone had the idea of flying a Tiger Moth all the way to Sweden, two Messerschmitt Me-109 fighter aircraft stood on the runway, ready to give chase and shoot down anyone who tried to escape.

Poul Kirke took over the commentary from Arne. 'I want you to look into the cockpit, one at a time,' he said. 'Stand on the black walkway on the lower wing. Don't step anywhere else or your foot will go through the fabric and you won't be able to fly.'

Tik Duchwitz went first. Poul said: 'On the left side you see a silver-coloured throttle lever, which controls the speed of the engine, and lower down a green trim lever which applies a spring loading to the elevator control. If the trim is correctly set when cruising, the aircraft should fly level when you take your hand off the stick.'

Harald went last. He could not help being interested, despite his resentment of the smoothly arrogant way Poul had swept Karen Duchwitz off on her bicycle.

As he stepped down, Poul said: 'So, what do you think, Harald?'

Harald shrugged. 'It seems straightforward.'

'Then you can go first,' Poul said with a grin.

The others laughed, but Harald was pleased.

'Let's all get kitted up,' Poul said.

They returned to the hangar and put on flying suits – step-in overalls that buttoned in front. Helmets and goggles were also given out. To Harald's annoyance, Poul made a point of helping him.

'Last time we met was at Kirstenslot,' Poul said as he adjusted Harald's goggles.

Harald nodded curtly, not wishing to be reminded. Still, he could not help wondering exactly what Poul's relationship with Karen was. Were they just dating, or something more? Did she kiss him passionately and let him touch her body? Did they talk of getting married? Had they had sexual intercourse? He did not want to think about these things, but he could not help it.

When they were ready, the first five students returned to the field, each with a pilot. Harald would have liked to go up with his brother, but once again Poul chose Harald. It was almost as if he wanted to get to know Harald better.

An airman in oily overalls was refuelling the aircraft, standing with one foot in a toehold in the fuselage. The tank was in the centre of the upper wing where it passed above the front seat – a worrying position, Harald felt. Would he be able to forget the gallons of inflammable fluid over his head?

'First, the pre-flight inspection,' Poul said. He leaned into the cockpit. 'We check that the magneto switches are off and the throttle is closed.' He looked at the wheels. 'Chocks in place.' He kicked the tyres and wiggled the ailerons. 'You mentioned that you had worked on the new German base at Sande,' he said casually.

'Yes.'

'What sort of work?'

'Just general labouring – digging holes, mixing concrete, carrying bricks.'

Poul moved to the back of the aircraft and checked the movement of the elevators. 'Did you find out what the place is for?'

'Not then, no. As soon as the basic construction work was done, the Danish workers were dismissed, and the Germans took over. But I'm pretty sure it's a radio station of some kind.'

'I think you mentioned that last time. But how do you know?'

'I've seen the equipment.'

Poul looked at him sharply, and Harald realized this was no casual inquiry. 'Is it visible from outside?'

'No. The place is fenced and guarded, and the radio equipment is screened by trees, except on the side facing the sea, and that part of the beach is off limits.'

'So how come you saw it?'

'I was in a hurry to get home, so I took a short cut across the base.'

Poul crouched down behind the rudder and checked the tail skid shoe. 'So,' he said, 'what did you see?'

'A large aerial, the biggest I've ever come across, maybe twelve feet square, on a rotating base.'

The airman who had been refuelling the aircraft interrupted the conversation. 'Ready when you are, sir.'

Poul said to Harald: 'Ready to fly?'

'Front or back?'

'The trainee always sits in the back.'

Harald climbed in. He had to stand on the bucket seat then ease himself down. The cockpit was narrow, and he wondered how fat pilots managed, then he realized there were no fat pilots.

Because of the nose-up angle at which the aircraft sat on the grass, he could see nothing in front of him but the clear blue sky. He had to lean out to one side to see the ground ahead.

He put his feet on the rudder pedals and his right hand on the control stick. Experimentally, he moved the stick from side to side and saw the ailerons move up and down at his command. With his left hand he touched the throttle and trim lever.

On the fuselage just outside his cockpit were two small knobs which he assumed were the twin magneto switches.

Poul leaned in to adjust Harald's safety harness. 'These aircraft were designed for training, so they have dual controls,' he said. 'While I'm flying, rest your hands and feet lightly on the controls and feel how I'm moving them. I'll tell you when to take over.'

'How will we talk?'

Poul pointed to a Y-shaped rubber pipe like a doctor's stethoscope. 'This works like the speaking tube on a ship.' He showed Harald how to fix the ends to earpieces in his flying helmet. The foot of the Y was plugged into an aluminium pipe which undoubtedly led to the front cockpit. Another tube with a mouthpiece was used for speaking.

Poul climbed into the front seat. A moment later Harald heard his voice through the speaking tube. 'Can you hear me?'

'Loud and clear.'

The airman stood by at the left front of the aircraft, and a shouted dialogue ensued, with the airman asking questions and Poul answering.

'Ready to start, sir?'

'Ready to start.'

'Fuel on, switches off, throttle closed?'

'Fuel is on, switches are off, throttle is closed.'

Harald expected the airman to turn the propeller at that point, but instead he moved to the right side of the aircraft, opened the cowling panel in the fuselage, and fiddled with the engine – priming it, Harald assumed. Then he closed the panel and returned to the nose of the aircraft.

'Sucking in, sir,' he said, then he reached up and pulled the propeller blade down. He repeated the action three times, and Harald guessed this procedure drew fuel into the cylinders.

The airman reached over the lower wing and flicked the two little switches just outside Harald's cockpit. 'Throttle set?'

Harald felt the throttle lever move forward half an inch under his hand, then heard Poul say: 'Throttle set.'

'Contact.'

Poul reached out and flicked the switches forward of his cockpit.

Once again the airman swung the propeller, this time stepping back smartly immediately afterwards. The engine fired and the propeller turned. There was a roar, and the little aircraft trembled. Harald had a sudden vivid sense of how light and frail it was, and remembered with a sense of shock that it was made, not of metal, but of wood and linen. The vibration was not like that of a car or even a motorcycle, which felt solid and firmly grounded by comparison. This was more like climbing a young tree and feeling the wind shake its slender branches.

Harald heard Poul's voice over the speaking tube. 'We have to let the engine warm up. It takes a few minutes.'

Harald thought about Poul's questions on the subject of the base at Sande. This was not idle curiosity, he felt sure. Poul had a purpose. He wanted to know the strategic importance of the base. Why? Was Poul part of some secret Resistance movement? What else could it be?

The engine note rose, and Poul reached out and turned magneto switches off and on again in turn – performing yet another safety check, Harald assumed. Then the note declined to idling pitch, and at last Poul signalled to the airman to remove the wheel chocks. Harald felt a lurch, and the aircraft moved forward.

The pedals at his feet moved as Poul used the

rudder to steer the aircraft across the grass. They taxied to the runway, which was marked by little flags, and turned into the wind, then they stopped, and Poul said: 'A few more checks before we take off.'

For the first time, it occurred to Harald that what he was about to do was dangerous. His brother had been flying for years without an accident, but other pilots had crashed, and some had died. He told himself that people died in cars, on motorcycles, and aboard boats – but somehow this felt different. He made himself stop thinking about the dangers. He was not about to panic and disgrace himself in front of the class.

Suddenly the throttle lever beneath his hand moved smoothly forward, the engine roared louder, and the Tiger Moth eagerly moved along the runway. After only a few seconds, the control stick eased away from Harald's knees, and he felt himself tip forward slightly as the tail lifted behind him. The little aircraft gathered speed, rattling and shaking over the grass. Harald's blood seemed to thrill with excitement. Then the stick eased back under his hand, the aircraft seemed to jump from the ground, and they were airborne.

It was exhilarating. They climbed steadily. To one side, Harald could see a small village. In crowded Denmark, there were not many places from which you could not see a village. Poul banked right. Feeling himself tipped sideways, Harald fought the panicky notion that he was going to fall out of the cockpit.

To calm himself, he looked at the instruments. The

rev counter showed two thousand rpm, and their speed was sixty miles per hour. They were at an altitude of one thousand feet already. The needle on the turn-and-slip indicator pointed straight up.

The aircraft straightened out and levelled off. The throttle lever moved back, the engine note dipped, and the revs slipped back to nineteen hundred. Poul said: 'Are you holding the stick?'

'Yes.'

'Check the line of the horizon. It probably goes through my head.'

'In one ear and out the other.'

'When I release the controls, I want you to simply keep the wings level and the horizon in the same place relative to my ears.'

Feeling nervous, Harald said: 'OK.'

'You have control.'

Harald felt the aircraft come alive in his hands, as every slight movement he made affected its flight. The line of the horizon fell to Poul's shoulders, showing that the nose had lifted, and he realized that a barely conscious fear of diving to the ground was making him pull back on the stick. He pushed it forward infinitesimally, and had the satisfaction of seeing the horizon line slowly rise to Poul's ears.

The aircraft lurched sideways and banked. Harald felt he had lost control and they were about to fall out of the sky. 'What was that?' he cried.

'Just a gust of wind. Correct for it, but not too much.'

Fighting back panic, Harald moved the stick against

the direction of bank. The aircraft lurched in the other direction, but at least he felt he was controlling it, and he corrected again with another small movement. Then he saw that he was climbing again, and brought the nose down. He found he had to concentrate fiercely on responding to the aircraft's slightest motion just to keep a steady course. He felt that a mistake could send him crashing to the ground.

When Poul spoke, Harald resented the interruption. 'That's very good,' Poul said. 'You're getting the hang of it.'

Harald felt he just needed to practise for another year or two.

'Now press lightly on the rudder pedals with both feet,' Poul said.

Harald had not thought about his feet for a while. 'All right,' he said brusquely.

'Look at the turn-and-slip indicator.'

Harald wanted to say *For God's sake, how can I do that and fly the aircraft at the same time?* He forced himself to take his eyes off the horizon for a second and look at the instrument panel. The needle was still in the twelve noon position. He looked back at the horizon and found that he had lifted the nose again. He corrected.

'When I take my feet off the rudder, you'll find the nose will yaw left and right with the turbulence. In case you're not sure, check the indicator. When the aircraft yaws left, the needle will move to the right, telling you to press down with your right foot to correct.'

'All right.'

Harald felt no sideways movement but a few moments later, when he managed to steal a glance at the dial, he saw he was yawing left. He pressed down on the rudder pedal with his right foot. The needle did not move. He pressed harder. Slowly, the pointer edged back to the central position. He looked up and saw that he was diving slightly. He pulled the stick back. He checked the turn-and-slip indicator again. The needle was steady.

It would have seemed simple and easy if he had not been fifteen hundred feet up in the air.

Poul said: 'Now let's try a turn.'

'Oh, shit,' said Harald.

'First, look left to see if there's anything in the way.'

Harald glanced to the left. In the far distance he could see another Tiger Moth, presumably with one of his classmates aboard, doing the same as he. That was reassuring. 'Nothing nearby,' he said.

'Ease the stick to the left.'

Harald did so. The aircraft banked left and he again experienced the sickening feeling that he was going to fall out. But the aircraft began to swing around to the left, and Harald felt a surge of excitement as he realized he was actually steering the Tiger Moth.

'In a turn, the nose tends to dip,' Poul said. Harald saw that indeed the aircraft was heading downwards, and he pulled back on the stick.

'Watch that turn-and-slip indicator,' Poul said. 'You're doing the equivalent of a skid.'

Harald checked the dial and saw that the needle had

moved to the right. He pressed the rudder pedal with his right foot. Once again, it responded only slowly.

The aircraft had turned through ninety degrees, and Harald was eager to straighten up and feel safe again, but Poul seemed to read his mind – or perhaps all pupils felt the same way at this point – and said: 'Keep turning, you're doing fine.'

The angle of bank seemed dangerously steep to Harald but he held the turn, keeping the nose up, checking the slip indicator every few seconds. Out of the corner of his eye he noticed a bus driving along the road below, just as if nothing in the least dramatic was happening in the sky, and there was no danger of a Jansborg schoolboy dropping out of the heavens to his death on its roof.

He had turned through three-quarters of a circle before Poul at last said: 'Straighten up.'

With relief, Harald eased the stick right, and the aircraft straightened.

'Watch that slip indicator.'

The needle had moved left. Harald pressed the rudder pedal with his left foot.

'Can you see the airfield?'

At first Harald could not. The countryside beneath him was a meaningless pattern of fields dotted with buildings. He had no idea what the air base would look like from above.

Poul helped him out. 'A row of long white buildings beside a bright green field. Look to the left of the propeller.'

'I see it.'

'Head that way, keeping the airfield on the left of our nose.'

Until now, Harald had not thought about the course they were following. It had been all he could manage to keep the aircraft steady. Now he had to do all the things he had previously learned and at the same time head for home. There was always one thing too many to think about.

'You're climbing,' Poul said. 'Throttle back an inch and bring us down to a thousand feet as we approach the buildings.'

Harald checked the altimeter and saw that the aircraft was indeed at two thousand feet. It had been fifteen hundred last time he looked. He throttled back and eased the stick forward.

'Dip the nose a bit more,' said Poul.

Harald felt the aircraft was in danger of diving vertically to the ground, but he forced himself to push the stick farther forward.

'Good,' said Poul.

By the time they were at a thousand feet, the base was below them.

'Turn left around the far side of that lake and bring us in line with the runway,' Poul ordered.

Harald levelled out and checked the slip indicator.

As he drew parallel with the end of the lake, he moved the stick left. This time, the feeling that he was going to fall out was not so bad.

'Watch that slip indicator.'

He had forgotten. Correcting with his foot, he brought the aircraft around.

'Throttle back an inch.'

Harald brought the lever back, and the engine note dipped sharply.

'Too much.'

Harald eased it forward again.

'Dip the nose.'

Harald pushed the control stick forward.

'That's it. But try to keep heading for the runway.'

Harald saw that he had wandered off course and was headed for the hangars. He put the aircraft into a shallow turn, correcting with the rudder, then lined it up with the runway again. But now he could see that he was too high.

'I'll take over from here,' Poul said.

Harald had thought Poul might talk him through a landing, but clearly he had not gained sufficient control for that. He felt disappointed.

Poul closed the throttle. The engine note fell abruptly, giving Harald the worrying feeling that there was nothing to keep the aircraft from falling straight down, but in fact it glided gradually to the runway. A few seconds before touchdown, Poul eased the stick back. The aircraft seemed to float along a few inches above the earth. Harald felt the footwell pedals moving constantly, and realized Poul was steering with the rudder now they were too close to the ground to dip a wing. At last there was a bump as the wheels and the tailskid touched earth.

Poul turned off the runway and taxied towards their parking space. Harald was thrilled. It had been even more exciting than he had imagined. He was also exhausted from concentrating so hard. It had only been a short time, he thought, then he glanced at his watch, and saw to his astonishment that they had been airborne for forty-five minutes. It had felt like five.

Poul shut down the engine and climbed out. Harald pushed back his goggles, took off his helmet, fumbled with his safety harness, and struggled out of his seat. He stepped on to the reinforced strip on the wing and jumped to the ground.

'You did very well,' said Poul. 'Showed quite a talent for it, in fact – just like your brother.'

'I'm sorry I couldn't bring it in to the runway.'

'I doubt if any of the other boys will even be allowed to try. Let's go and get changed.'

When Harald had got out of his flying suit, Poul said: 'Come to my office for a minute.' Harald went with him to a door marked 'Chief Flying Instructor' and entered a small room with a filing cabinet, a desk and a couple of chairs.

'Would you mind making a drawing of that radio equipment you were describing to me earlier?' Poul's tone was casual, but his body was stiff with tension.

Harald had wondered whether that subject would come up again. 'Sure.'

'It's quite important. I won't go into the reasons why.'

'That's all right.'

'Sit at the desk. There's a box of pencils and some paper in the drawer. Take your time. Do it over until you're satisfied.'

'OK.'

'How long do you think you might need?'

'Maybe a quarter of an hour. It was dark so I can't draw details. But I have a clear outline in my head.'

'I'll leave you alone so you don't feel pressured. I'll come back in fifteen minutes.'

Poul left and Harald began to draw. He cast his mind back to that Saturday night in the pouring rain. There had been a circular concrete wall, he recalled, about six feet high. The aerial had been a grid of wires looking like bedsprings. Its rotating base was inside the circular wall, and cables had run from the back of the aerial into a duct.

First he drew the wall with the aerial above. He vaguely recalled that there had been one or two similar structures nearby, so he sketched them in lightly. Then he drew the machinery as if the wall were not there, showing its base and the cables. He was no artist but he could render machinery accurately, probably because he liked it.

When he had finished, he turned the sheet of paper over and made a plan of the island of Sande, showing the position of the base and the restricted area of beach.

Poul came back after fifteen minutes. He studied the drawings intently, then said: 'This is excellent – thank you.'

'You're welcome.'

He pointed to the ancillary structures Harald had sketched. 'What are these?'

'I really don't know. I didn't look closely. But I thought I should put them in.'

'Quite right. One more question. This grid of wires, which is presumably an aerial. Is it flat, or dished?'

Harald racked his brains, but could not remember. 'I'm not sure,' he said. 'Sorry.'

'That's all right.' Poul opened the filing cabinet. All the files were labelled with names, presumably of past and present pupils at the school. He selected one marked 'Andersen, H.C.' It was not an unusual name, but Hans Christian Andersen was Denmark's most famous writer, and Harald guessed the file might be a hiding place. Sure enough, Poul put the drawings in the folder and returned the file to its place.

'Let's go back to the others,' he said. He went to the door. Stopping with his hand on the doorknob, he said: 'Making drawings of German military installations is a crime, technically. It would be best not to mention this to anyone – not even Arne.'

Harald felt a pang of dismay. His brother was not involved in this. Even Arne's best friend did not think he had the nerve.

Harald nodded. 'I'll agree to that – on one condition.'

Poul was surprised. 'Condition? What?'

'That you tell me something honestly.'

He shrugged. 'All right, I'll try.'

'There is a Resistance movement, isn't there?'

'Yes,' Poul said, looking serious. After a moment's pause, he added: 'And now you're in it.'

# EIGHT

Tilde Jespersen wore a light, flowery perfume that wafted across the pavement table and teased Peter Flemming's nostrils, never quite strong enough for him to identify it, like an elusive memory. He imagined how the fragrance would rise from her warm skin as he slipped off her blouse, her skirt, and her underwear.

'What are you thinking about?' she said.

He was tempted to tell her. She would pretend shock, but secretly be pleased. He could tell when a woman was ready for that kind of talk, and he knew how to do it: lightly, with a self-deprecating smile, but an underlying tone of sincerity.

Then he thought of his wife, and held back. He took his marital vows seriously. Other people might think he had a good excuse for breaking them, but he set himself higher standards.

So he said: 'I was thinking about you tripping up the runaway mechanic at the aerodrome. You showed great presence of mind.'

'I didn't even think about it, just stuck out my foot.'

'You have good instincts. I was never in favour of

women police and, to tell you the truth, I still have my doubts – but no one could deny you're a first class cop.'

She shrugged. 'I have doubts myself. Maybe women ought to stay home and look after babies. But after Oskar died . . .' Oskar had been her husband, a Copenhagen detective and friend of Peter's. 'I had to work, and law enforcement is the only life I know anything about. My father was a customs officer, my older brother is a military police officer, and my younger brother a uniformed policeman in Aarhus.'

'I'll tell you the great thing about you, Tilde – you never try to get men to do your work by playing the helpless female.'

He intended his remark as a compliment, but she did not look as pleased as he had hoped. 'I never ask for help at all,' she said crisply.

'Probably a good policy.'

She gave him a look he could not read. Puzzling over the sudden chill in the atmosphere, he wondered whether she might be afraid to ask for assistance in case she was immediately classed as a helpless female. He could see how she might resent that. After all, men asked one another for help all the time.

She said: 'But why are you a cop? Your father has a successful business – don't you want to take it over, one day?'

He shook his head ruefully. 'I used to work at the hotel in the school holidays. I hated the guests, with their demands and complaints: this beef is overcooked, my mattress is lumpy, I've been waiting twenty minutes for a cup of coffee. I couldn't stand it.'

The waiter came. Peter resisted the temptation to have herrings and onions on his smorrebrod, thinking, vaguely, that he might get close enough to Tilde for her to smell his breath, so he ordered soft cheese and cucumbers instead. They handed their ration cards to the waiter.

Tilde said: 'Any progress in the spy case?'

'Not really. The two men we arrested at the aerodrome told us nothing. They were sent to Hamburg for what the Gestapo calls "deep interrogation", and they gave the name of their contact – Matthies Hertz, an army officer. But he has disappeared.'

'A dead end, then.'

'Yes.' The phrase made him think of another dead end he had run into. 'Do you know any Jews?'

She looked surprised. 'One or two, I should think. None in the police force. Why?'

'I'm making a list.'

'A list of Jews?'

'Yes.'

'Where, in Copenhagen?'

'In Denmark.'

'Why?'

'The usual reason. It's my job to keep tabs on troublemakers.'

'And Jews are troublemakers?'

'The Germans think so.'

'You can see why *they* might have problems with Jews – but do we?'

He was taken aback. He had expected her to see this from his point of view. 'It's as well to be prepared. We have lists of union organizers, communists, foreign nationals, and members of the Danish Nazi Party.'

'And you think that's the same thing?'

'It's all information. Now, it's easy to identify new Jewish immigrants, who've come here in the last fifty years. They dress funny, they speak with a peculiar accent, and most of them live in the same few Copenhagen streets. But there are also Jews whose families have been Danish for centuries. *They* look and talk the same as everyone else. Most of them eat roast pork and go to work on Saturday mornings. If we ever need to find them, we could have trouble. So I'm making a list.'

'How? You can't just go round asking people if they know any Jews.'

'It's a problem. I have two junior detectives going through the phone book, and one or two other lists, making notes of Jewish-sounding names.'

'That's not very reliable. There are lots of people called Isaksen who aren't Jewish.'

'And lots of Jews with names like Jan Christiansen. What I'd really like to do is raid the synagogue. They probably have a membership list.'

To his surprise, she was looking disapproving, but she said: 'Why don't you?'

'Juel won't allow it.'

'I think he's right.'

'Really? Why?'

'Peter, can't you see? What use might your list be put to in the future?'

'Isn't it obvious?' Peter said irritably. 'If Jewish groups start to organize resistance to the Germans, we'll know where to look for suspects.'

'And what if the Nazis just decide to round up all the Jews and send them to those concentration camps they have in Germany? They'll use your list!'

'But why would they send the Jews to camps?'

'Because Nazis hate Jews. But we're not Nazis, we're police officers. We arrest people because they've committed crimes, not because we hate them.'

'I know that,' Peter said angrily. He was astonished to be attacked from this angle. Tilde should know that his motive was to uphold the law, not subvert it. 'There's always a risk that information will be misused.'

'So wouldn't it be better not to make the damn list?'

How could she be so stupid? It maddened him to be opposed by someone he thought of as a comrade in the war against lawbreakers. 'No!' he shouted. He lowered his voice with an effort. 'If we thought that way, we wouldn't have a security department at all!'

Tilde shook her head. 'Look, Peter, the Nazis have done a lot of good things, we both know that. They're on the side of the police, basically. They've clamped down on subversion, they maintain law and order, they've reduced unemployment, and so on. But on the subject of Jews, they're insane.'

'Maybe, but they're making the rules now.'

'Just look at the Danish Jews – they're law-abiding, hard-working, they send their children to school . . . It's ludicrous to make a list of their names and addresses as if they were all part of some Communist conspiracy.'

He sat back and said accusingly: 'So, you'd refuse to work on this with me?'

It was her turn to be offended. 'How can you say that? I'm a professional police officer, and you're my boss. I'll do what you say. You ought to know that.'

'Do you mean it?'

'Look, if you wanted to make a complete list of witches in Denmark, I'd tell you I didn't think witches were criminals or subversives – but I'd help you make the list.'

Their food arrived. There was an awkward silence as they began to eat. After a few minutes, Tilde said: 'How are things at home?'

Peter had a sudden memory of himself and Inge, a few days before the accident, walking to church on Sunday morning, two healthy, happy young people in their best clothes. With all the scum and riff-raff in the world, why did it have to be his wife whose mind was destroyed by that drunken boy in his sports car? 'Inge is the same,' he said.

'No improvement?'

'When the brain is damaged that badly, it doesn't mend. There will never be any improvement.'

'It must be hard for you.'

'I'm fortunate to have a generous father. I couldn't afford a nurse on police wages – Inge would have to go into an asylum.'

Once again Tilde gave him a look that was hard to read. It was almost as if she felt the asylum might not be a bad solution. 'What about the driver of the sports car?'

'Finn Jonk. His trial started yesterday. It should be over in a day or two.'

'At last! What do you think will happen?'

'He's pleading guilty. I assume he'll be jailed for five or ten years.'

'It doesn't seem enough.'

'For destroying someone's mind? What would be enough?'

After lunch, when they were walking back to the Politigaarden, Tilde put her arm through Peter's. It was an affectionate gesture, and he felt she was telling him that she liked him despite their disagreement. As they approached the ultramodern police headquarters building, he said: 'I'm sorry you disapprove of my Jewish list.'

She stopped and turned to him. 'You're not a bad man, Peter.' To his surprise, she seemed to be on the edge of tears. 'Your sense of duty is your great strength. But doing your duty isn't the only law.'

'I don't really understand what you mean.'

'I know.' She turned away and went into the building alone.

Making his way to his office, he tried to see the

issue from her point of view. If the Nazis imprisoned law-abiding Jews, that would be a crime, and his list would help the criminals. But you could say that about a gun, or even a car: the fact that something might be used by criminals did not mean it was wrong to have it.

As he was crossing the open central courtyard, he was hailed by his boss, Frederik Juel. 'Come with me,' Juel said briskly. 'We've been summoned by General Braun.' He marched ahead, his military bearing giving an impression of decisiveness and efficiency that Peter knew to be quite false.

It was a short walk from the Politigaarden to the town square, where the Germans had taken over a building called the Dagmarhus. It was surrounded by barbed wire and had cannons and anti-aircraft guns on the flat roof. They were shown to Walter Braun's office, a corner room overlooking the square, comfortably furnished with an antique desk and a leather couch. There was a rather small picture of the Fuehrer on the wall and a framed photograph on the desk of two small boys in school uniform. Braun wore his pistol even here, Peter noted, as if to say that although he had a cosy office, nevertheless he meant business.

Braun was looking pleased with himself. 'Our people have decoded the message you found in the hollow aeroplane chock,' he said in his habitual near-whisper.

Peter was elated.

'Very impressive,' Juel murmured.

'Apparently it was not difficult,' Braun went on. 'The British use simple codes, often based on a poem or famous passage of prose. Once our cryptanalysts get a few words, a professor of English can usually fill in the rest. I have never before known the study of English literature to serve any useful purpose.' He laughed at his own wit.

Peter said impatiently: 'What was in the message?'

Braun opened a file on his desk. 'It comes from a group calling themselves the Nightwatchmen.' Although they were speaking German, he used the Danish word *natvaegterne*. 'Does that mean anything to you?'

Peter was taken by surprise. 'I'll check the files, of course, but I'm pretty sure we haven't come across this name before.' He frowned, considering. 'Real-life nightwatchmen are usually police or soldiers, aren't they?'

Juel bridled. 'I hardly think that Danish police officers—'

'I didn't say they were Danish,' Peter interrupted. 'The spies could be German traitors.' He shrugged. 'Or they may just aspire to military status.' He looked at Braun. 'What's the content of the message, General?'

'Details of our military dispositions in Denmark. Take a look.' He passed a sheaf of papers across the desk. 'Locations of anti-aircraft batteries in and around Copenhagen. German naval vessels in the harbour during the last month. Regiments stationed in Aarhus, Odense and Morlunde.'

'Is the information accurate?'

Braun hesitated. 'Not precisely. Close to the truth, but not exact.'

Peter nodded. 'Then the spies probably are not Germans with inside information, for such people would be able to get correct details from the files. More likely, they are Danes who are careful observers making educated estimates.'

Braun nodded. 'A shrewd deduction. But can you find these people?'

'I certainly hope so.'

Braun's focus of attention had switched entirely to Peter, as if Juel were not there, or just an underling in attendance rather than the senior officer. 'Do you think the same people are putting out the illegal newspapers?'

Peter was pleased that Braun recognized his expertise, but frustrated that Juel was nevertheless the boss. He hoped that Braun himself had noted this irony. He shook his head. 'We know the underground editors and we keep an eye on their activities. If they had been making meticulous observations of German military dispositions, we would have noticed. No – I believe this is a new organization we haven't encountered.'

'Then how will you catch them?'

'There is one group of potential subversives whom we have never properly investigated – the Jews.'

Peter heard a sharp intake of breath from Juel.

Braun said: 'You had better take a look at them.'

'It's not always easy to know who the Jews are, in this country.'

'Then go to the synagogue!'

'Good idea,' Peter said. 'They may have a membership list. That would be a start.'

Juel gave Peter a thunderous look, but said nothing.

Braun said: 'My superiors in Berlin are impressed with the loyalty and efficiency of the Danish police in intercepting this message to British intelligence. Nevertheless, they were keen to send in a team of Gestapo investigators. I have dissuaded them, by promising that you will vigorously investigate the spy ring and bring the traitors to justice.' It was a long speech for a man with one lung, and it left him breathless. He paused, looking from Peter to Juel and back again. When he had caught his breath, he finished: 'For your own sakes, and for the good of everyone in Denmark, you'd better succeed.'

Juel and Peter stood up, and Juel said tightly: 'We will do everything possible.'

They left. As soon as they were outside the building, Juel rounded on Peter with a blazing blue-eyed stare. 'You know perfectly well this has nothing to do with the synagogue, damn you.'

'I know nothing of the kind.'

'You're just toadying to the Nazis, you disgusting creep.'

'Why shouldn't we help them? They represent the law, now.'

'You think they'll help your career.'

'And why not?' Peter said, stung to retaliate. 'The

Copenhagen élite are prejudiced against men from the provinces – but the Germans may be more fair-minded.'

Juel was incredulous. 'Is *that* what you believe?'

'At least they're not blind to the abilities of boys who did not go to Jansborg Skole.'

'So you think you were passed over because of your background? Idiot – you didn't get the job because you're too extreme! You've got no sense of proportion. You'd wipe crime out by arresting everyone who looked suspicious!' He made a disgusted sound. 'If I have anything to do with it, you'll never get another promotion. Now get out of my sight.' He walked away.

Peter burned with resentment. Who did Juel think he was? Having a famous ancestor did not make him better than anyone else. He was a cop, just like Peter, and he had no right to talk as if he were a higher life form.

But Peter had got his way. He had defeated Juel. He had permission to raid the synagogue.

Juel would hate him for ever for that. But did it matter? Braun, not Juel, was the power now. Better to be Braun's favourite and Juel's enemy than the other way around.

Back at headquarters, Peter swiftly assembled his team, choosing the same detectives he had used at Kastrup: Conrad, Dresler, and Ellegard. He said to Tilde Jespersen: 'I'd like to take you along, if you don't object.'

'Why would I object?' she said testily.

'After our conversation over lunch . . .'

'Please! I'm a professional. I told you that.'

'Good enough,' he said.

They drove to a street called Krystalgade. The yellow-brick synagogue stood side-on to the street, as if hunching a shoulder against a hostile world. Peter stationed Ellegard at the gate to make sure no one could sneak out.

An elderly man in a yarmulke appeared from the Jewish old people's home next door. 'May I help you?' he said politely.

'We're police officers,' Peter said. 'Who are you?'

The man's face took on a look of such abject fear that Peter almost felt sorry for him. 'Gorm Rasmussen, I'm the day manager of the home,' he said in a shaky voice.

'You have keys to the synagogue?'

'Yes.'

'Let us in.'

The man took a bunch of keys from his pocket and opened a door.

Most of the building was taken up by the main hall, a richly decorated room with gilded Egyptian columns supporting galleries over the side aisles. 'These Jews have plenty of money,' Conrad muttered.

Peter said to Rasmussen: 'Show me your membership list.'

'Membership? What do you mean?'

'You must have the names and addresses of your congregation.'

'No – all Jews are welcome.'

Peter's instinct told him the man was telling the truth, but he would search the place anyway. 'Are there any offices here?'

'No. Just small robing rooms for the rabbi and other officials, and a cloakroom for the congregation to hang their coats.'

Peter nodded to Dresler and Conrad. 'Check them out.' He walked up the centre of the room to the pulpit end and climbed a short flight of steps to a raised dais. Behind a curtain he found a concealed niche. 'What have we here?'

'The Torah scrolls,' said Rasmussen.

There were six large, heavy-looking scrolls lovingly wrapped in velvet cloth, providing perfect hiding-places for secret documents. 'Unwrap them all,' he said. 'Spread them out on the floor so I can see there's nothing else inside.'

'Yes, right away.'

While Rasmussen was doing his bidding, Peter walked a short distance away with Tilde, and talked to her while keeping a suspicious eye on the manager. 'Are you OK?'

'I told you.'

'If we find something, will you admit I was right?'

She smiled. 'If we don't, will you admit you were wrong?'

He nodded, pleased that she was not angry with him.

Rasmussen spread out the scrolls, covered with Hebrew script. Peter saw nothing suspicious. He supposed it was possible they had no register of members. More likely, they used to have one but destroyed it as a precaution the day the Germans invaded. He felt frustrated. He had gone to a lot of trouble for this raid, and had made himself even more unpopular with his boss. It would be maddening if it came to nothing.

Dresler and Conrad returned from opposite ends of the building. Dresler was empty-handed, but Conrad was carrying a copy of the newspaper *Reality*.

Peter took the newspaper and showed it to Rasmussen. 'This is illegal.'

'I'm sorry,' the man said. He looked as if he might cry. 'They push them through the letter box.'

The people who printed the newspaper were not being sought by the police, so those who merely read it were in no danger at all – but Rasmussen did not know that, and Peter pushed his moral advantage. 'You must write to your people sometimes,' he said.

'Well, of course, to leading members of the Jewish community. But we don't have a list. We know who they are.' He tried a weak smile. 'So do you, I imagine.'

It was true. Peter knew the names of a dozen or more prominent Jews: a couple of bankers, a judge, several professors at the university, some political figures, a painter. They were not who he was after: they were too well known to be spies. Such people could not stand at the dockside counting ships without being noticed. 'Don't you send letters to the ordinary people, asking them to donate to charities, telling them of events you're organizing, celebrations, picnics, concerts?'

'No,' said the man. 'We just put up a notice at the community centre.'

'Ah,' said Peter with a satisfied smile. 'The community centre. And where is that?'

'Near Christiansborg, in Ny Kongensgade.'

It was about a mile away. 'Dresler,' said Peter. 'Keep this guy here for fifteen minutes and make sure he doesn't warn anyone.'

They drove to the street called Ny Kongensgade. The Jewish community centre was a large eighteenth-century building with an internal courtyard and an elegant staircase, though it needed redecorating. The cafeteria was closed, and there was no one playing ping-pong in the basement. A well-dressed young man with a disdainful air was in charge of the office. He said they had no list of names and addresses, but the detectives searched the place anyway.

The young man's name was Ingemar Gammel, and something about him made Peter thoughtful. What was it? Unlike Rasmussen, Gammel was not frightened; but whereas Peter had felt Rasmussen was scared but innocent, Gammel gave him the opposite impression.

Gammel sat at a desk, wearing a waistcoat with a watch chain, and looked on coolly while his office was ransacked. His clothes seemed expensive. Why was a wealthy young man acting as secretary here? This kind of work was normally done by underpaid girls, or middle-class housewives whose children had flown the nest.

'I think this is what we're looking for, boss,' said Conrad, passing Peter a black ringbinder. 'A list of rat holes.'

Peter looked inside and saw page after page of names and addresses, several hundred of them. 'Bang,' he said. 'Well done.' But instinct told him there was more to find here. 'Keep looking, everyone, in case something else turns up.'

He flicked through the pages, looking for anything odd, or familiar, or ... something. He had that dissatisfied feeling. But nothing caught his eye.

Gammel's jacket hung from a hook behind the door. Peter read the tailor's label. The suit had been made by Anderson & Sheppard of Savile Row, London, in 1938. Peter was jealous. He bought his clothes from the best shops in Copenhagen, but he could never afford an English suit. There was a silk handkerchief in the outside breast pocket. He found a well-stuffed money clip in the left side pocket. In the right pocket was a train ticket to Aarhus, return, with a neat hole made by a ticket inspector's punch. 'Why did you go to Aarhus?'

'To visit friends.'

The decoded message had included the name of the German regiment stationed at Aarhus, Peter recalled. However, Aarhus was Denmark's largest town after Copenhagen, and hundreds of people travelled between the two cities every day.

In the inside pocket of the jacket was a slim diary. Peter opened it.

Gammel said with contempt: 'Do you enjoy your work?'

Peter looked up with a smile. He did enjoy infuriating pompous rich men who thought they were superior to ordinary people. But what he said was: 'Like a plumber, I see a lot of shit.' He pointedly returned his gaze to Gammel's diary.

Gammel's handwriting was stylish, like his suit, with big capitals and full loops. The entries in the diary all looked normal: lunch dates, theatre, Mother's birthday, phone Jorgen about Wilder. 'Who is Jorgen?' Peter asked.

'My cousin, Jorgen Lumpe. We exchange books.'

'And Wilder?'

'Thornton Wilder.'

'And he is . . .?'

'The American writer. *The Bridge of San Luis Rey*. You must have read it.'

There was a sneer in that, an implication that policemen were not sufficiently cultured to read foreign novels, but Peter ignored it and turned to the back of the diary. As he expected, he found a list of names and addresses, some with phone numbers. He glanced up at Gammel, and thought he saw the hint of a flush on his clean-shaven cheeks. That was promising. He scrutinized the address list with care.

He picked a name at random. 'Hilde Bjergager – who is she?'

'A lady friend,' Gammel answered coolly.

Peter tried another. 'Bertil Bruun?'

Gammel remained unflustered. 'We play tennis.'

'Fred Eskildsen.'

'My bank manager.'

The other detectives had stopped searching and fallen silent, sensing the tension.

'Poul Kirke?'

'Old friend.'

'Preben Klausen.'

'Picture dealer.'

For the first time, Gammel showed a hint of emotion, but it was relief, rather than guilt. Why? Did he think he had got away with something? What was the significance of the picture dealer Klausen? Or was the previous name the important one? Had Gammel shown relief because Peter had *moved on* to Klausen?

'Poul Kirke is an old friend?'

'We were at university together.' Gammel's voice was even, but there was just the suggestion of fear in his eyes.

Peter glanced at Tilde, and she gave a slight nod. She, too, had seen something in Gammel's reaction.

Peter looked again at the diary. There was no address for Kirke, but beside the phone number was a capital 'N', written uncharacteristically small. 'What does this mean – the letter N?' Peter said.

'Naestved. It's his number at Naestved.'

'What's his other number?'

'He doesn't have another.'

'So why do you need the annotation?'

'To tell you the truth, I don't remember,' Gammel said, showing irritation.

It might have been true. On the other hand, 'N' might stand for 'Nightwatchman'.

Peter said: 'What does he do for a living?'

'Pilot.'

'With whom?'

'The army.'

'Ah.' Peter had speculated that the Nightwatchmen might be army people, because of their name and because they were accurate observers of military details. 'At which base?'

'Vodal.'

'I thought you said he was at Naestved.'

'It's nearby.'

'It's twenty miles away.'

'Well, that's how I remember it.'

Peter nodded thoughtfully, then said to Conrad: 'Arrest this lying prick.'

* * *

The search of Ingemar Gammel's apartment was disappointing. Peter found nothing of interest: no code book, no subversive literature, no weapons. He concluded that Gammel must be a minor figure in the spy ring, one whose role was simply to make observations and report them to a central contact. That key man would compile the messages and send them to England. But who was the pivotal figure? Peter hoped it might be Poul Kirke.

Before driving the fifty miles to the flying school at Vodal where Poul Kirke was stationed, Peter spent an hour at home with his wife, Inge. As he fed her apple-

and-honey sandwiches in tiny squares, he found himself daydreaming about domestic life with Tilde Jespersen. He imagined himself watching Tilde getting ready to go out in the evening – washing her hair and drying it vigorously with a towel, sitting at the dressing-table in her underwear polishing her nails, looking in the mirror as she tied a silk scarf around her neck. He realized he was yearning to be with a woman who could do things for herself.

He had to stop thinking this way. He was a married man. The fact that a man's wife was sick did not provide an excuse for adultery. Tilde was a colleague and a friend, and she should never be any more to him than that.

Feeling restless and discontented, he turned on the radio and listened to the news while he waited for the evening nurse to arrive. The British had launched a new attack in North Africa, crossing the Egyptian border into Libya with a tank division in an attempt to relieve the besieged city of Tobruk. It sounded like a major operation, though the censored Danish radio station naturally predicted that German antitank guns would decimate the British forces.

The phone rang, and Peter crossed the room to pick it up.

'Allan Forslund here, Traffic Division.' Forslund was the officer dealing with Finn Jonk, the drunk driver who had crashed into Peter's car. 'The trial has just ended.'

'What happened?'

'Jonk got six months.'

'Six *months*?'

'I'm sorry—'

Peter's vision blurred. He felt he was going to fall over, and he put a hand on the wall to steady himself. 'For destroying my wife's mind and ruining my life? Six months?'

'The judge said he had already suffered torment and he would have to live with the guilt for the rest of his life.'

'That's shit!'

'I know.'

'I thought the prosecution was going to ask for a severe sentence.'

'We did. But Jonk's lawyer was very persuasive. Said the boy has stopped drinking, rides around on a bicycle, is studying to be an architect—'

'Anyone can say that.'

'I know.'

'I don't accept this! I refuse to accept it!'

'Nothing we can do—'

'Like hell there isn't.'

'Peter, don't take any hasty action.'

Peter tried to calm himself. 'Of course I won't.'

'Are you alone?'

'I'm going back to work in a few minutes.'

'So long as you have someone to talk to.'

'Yes. Thanks for calling, Allan.'

'I'm very sorry we didn't do better.'

'Not your fault. A slick lawyer and a stupid judge. We've seen that before.' Peter hung up. He had forced himself to sound calm, but he was boiling. If

Jonk had been at large he might have sought him out
and killed him – but the kid was safe in jail, if only for
a few months. He thought of finding the lawyer,
arresting him on a pretext, and beating the shit out of
him; but he knew he would not do it. The lawyer had
not broken any laws.

He looked at Inge. She was sitting where he had
left her, watching him blank-faced, waiting for him to
continue feeding her. He noticed that some of the
chewed apple had dribbled from her mouth on to the
bodice of her dress. She was not normally a messy
eater, despite her condition. Before the accident
she had been extraordinarily fastidious about her
appearance. Seeing her with food on her chin and
stains on her clothing suddenly made him want to
weep.

He was saved by the doorbell. He pulled himself
together rapidly and answered it. The nurse had
arrived at the same time as Bent Conrad, who had
come to pick him up for the journey to Vodal. He
shrugged on his jacket and left the nurse to clean
Inge up.

They went in two cars, standard black police Buicks.
Peter thought the army might put obstacles in his way,
so he had asked General Braun to detail a German
officer to impose authority if necessary, and a Major
Schwarz from Braun's staff was in the lead car.

The journey took an hour and a half. Schwarz
smoked a large cigar, filling the car with fumes. Peter
tried not to think about the outrageously light
sentence on Finn Jonk. He might need his wits about

him at the air base, and he did not want his judgement to be skewed by rage. He tried to smother his blazing fury, but it smouldered on under a blanket of false calm, stinging his eyes with its smoke, like Schwarz's cigar.

Vodal was a grass airfield with a scatter of low buildings along one side. Security was light – it was only a training school, so nothing remotely secret went on here – and a single guard at the gate casually waved them through without asking their business. Half a dozen Tiger Moths were parked in a line, like birds on a fence. There were also some gliders and two Messerschmitt Me109s.

As Peter got out of the car, he saw Arne Olufsen, his boyhood rival from Sande, sauntering across the car park in his smart brown army uniform. The sour taste of resentment came into Peter's mouth.

Peter and Arne had been friends, all through childhood, until the quarrel between their families twelve years before. It had started when Axel Flemming, Peter's father, had been accused of tax fraud. Axel felt the prosecution was outrageous: he had only done what everyone else did, and understated his profits by inflating his costs. He had been convicted, and had to pay a hefty fine on top of all the back tax.

He had persuaded his friends and neighbours to see the case as an argument about an accounting technicality, rather than an accusation of dishonesty. Then Pastor Olufsen had intervened.

There was a church rule that any member who

committed a crime should be 'read out', or expelled from the congregation. The offender could rejoin the following Sunday, if he wished, but for one week he was an outsider. The procedure was not invoked for trivial crimes such as speeding, and Axel had argued that his transgression fell into that category. Pastor Olufsen thought otherwise.

This humiliation had been much worse for Axel than the fine with which the court had punished him. His name had been read to the congregation, he had been obliged to leave his place and sit at the back of the church throughout the service, and to complete his mortification the pastor had preached a sermon on the text: 'Render unto Caesar that which is Caesar's.'

Peter winced every time he remembered it. Axel was proud of his position as a successful businessman and community leader, and there could be no greater punishment for him than to lose the respect of his neighbours. It had been torture to Peter to see his father publicly reprimanded by a pompous, self-righteous prig like Olufsen. He believed his father had deserved the fine, but not the humiliation in church. He had sworn then that if any member of the Olufsen family ever transgressed, there would be no mercy.

He hardly dared to hope that Arne was involved in the spy ring. That would be a sweet revenge.

Arne caught his eye. 'Peter!' He looked surprised, but not afraid.

'Is this where you work?' Peter said.

'When there's any work to do.' Arne was as

debonair and relaxed as ever. If he had anything to feel guilty about, he was concealing it well.

'Of course, you're a pilot.'

'This is a training school, but we don't have many pupils. More to the point, what are you doing here?' Arne glanced at the major in German uniform standing behind Peter. 'Is there a dangerous outbreak of littering? Or has someone been cycling after dark without lights?'

Peter did not find Arne's raillery very funny. 'Routine investigation,' he replied shortly. 'Where will I find your commanding officer?'

Arne pointed to one of the low buildings. 'Base headquarters. You need Squadron Leader Renthe.'

Peter left him and went into the building. Renthe was a lanky man with a bristly moustache and a sour expression. Peter introduced himself and said: 'I'm here to interview one of your men, a Flight Lieutenant Poul Kirke.'

The squadron leader looked pointedly at Major Schwarz and said: 'What's the problem?'

The reply 'None of your damn business' sprang to Peter's lips, but he was resolved to be calm, so he told a polite lie. 'He's been dealing in stolen property.'

'When military personnel are *suspected* of crimes, we prefer to investigate the matter ourselves.'

'Of course you do. However . . .' He moved a hand in the direction of Schwarz. 'Our German friends want the police to deal with it, so your *preferences* are irrelevant. Is Kirke on the base at this moment?'

'He happens to be flying.'

Peter raised his eyebrows. 'I thought your planes were grounded.'

'As a rule, yes, but there are exceptions. We're expecting a visit from a Luftwaffe group tomorrow, and they want to be taken up in our training aircraft, so we have permission to do test flights today to make sure the aircraft are in readiness. Kirke should land in a few minutes.'

'I'll search his quarters meanwhile. Where does he bed down?'

Renthe hesitated, then answered reluctantly. 'Dormitory A, at the far end of the runway.'

'Does he have an office, or a locker, or anywhere else he might keep things?'

'He has a small office three doors along this corridor.'

'I'll start there. Tilde, come with me. Conrad, go out to the airfield to meet Kirke when he comes back – I don't want him to slip away. Dresler and Ellegard, search Dormitory A. Squadron Leader, thank you for your help . . .' Peter saw the commander's eyes stray to the phone on the desk, and added: 'Don't make any phone calls for the next few minutes. If you were to warn anyone that we're on our way, that would constitute obstruction of justice. I'd have to throw you in jail, and that wouldn't do the army's reputation much good, would it?'

Renthe made no reply.

Peter, Tilde and Schwarz went along the corridor to a door marked 'Chief Flying Instructor'. A desk and a filing cabinet were squeezed into a small room with no windows. Peter and Tilde began to search and Schwarz lit another cigar. The filing cabinet contained pupil records. Peter and Tilde patiently looked at every sheet of paper. The little room was airless, and Tilde's elusive perfume was lost in Schwarz's cigar smoke.

After fifteen minutes, Tilde made a surprised noise and said: 'This is odd.'

Peter looked up from the exam results of a student called Keld Hansen who had failed his navigation test.

Tilde handed him a sheet of paper. Peter studied it, frowning. It bore a careful sketch of a piece of apparatus that Peter did not recognize: a large square aerial on a stand, surrounded by a wall. A second drawing of the same apparatus without the wall showed more details of the stand, which looked as if it might revolve.

Tilde looked over his shoulder. 'What do you think it can be?'

He was intensely aware of how close she was. 'I've never seen anything like it, but I'd bet the farm it's secret. Anything else in the file?'

'No.' She showed him a folder marked 'Andersen, H.C.'

Peter grunted. 'Hans Christian Andersen – that's suspicious in itself.' He turned the sheet over. On its reverse was a sketch map of an island whose long, thin shape was as familiar to Peter as the map of Denmark itself. 'This is Sande, where my father lives!' he said.

Looking more closely, he saw that the map showed the new German base and the area of the beach that was off limits.

'Bang,' he said softly.

Tilde's blue eyes were shining with excitement. 'We've caught a spy, haven't we?'

'Not yet,' Peter said. 'But we're about to.'

They went outside, followed by the silent Schwarz. The sun had set, but they could see clearly in the soft twilight of the long Scandinavian summer evening.

They walked on to the airfield and stood beside Conrad, near where the planes were parked. The aircraft were being put away for the night. One was being wheeled into the hangar, two airmen pushing its wings and a third lifting its tail off the ground.

Conrad pointed to an incoming aircraft downwind of the airfield and said: 'I think this must be our man.'

It was another Tiger Moth. As it descended in a textbook circuit and turned into the wind for landing, Peter reflected that there was no doubt Poul Kirke was a spy. The evidence found in the filing cabinet would be enough to hang him. But before that happened, Peter had a lot of questions to ask him. Was he simply a reporter, like Ingemar Gammel? Had Kirke travelled to Sande himself to check out the air base and sketch the mystery apparatus? Or did he play the more important role of coordinator, assembling information and transmitting it to England in coded messages? If Kirke was the central contact, who had gone to Sande and made the sketch? Could it have been Arne

Olufsen? That was possible, but Arne had shown no sign of guilt an hour ago when Peter had arrived unexpectedly at the base. Still, it might be worthwhile to put Arne under surveillance.

As the aircraft touched down and bumped along the grass, one of the police Buicks came from the upwind end of the runway in a tearing hurry. It skidded to a stop, and Dresler jumped out, carrying something bright yellow.

Peter threw him a nervous look. He did not want a kerfuffle that might forewarn Poul Kirke. Glancing around, he realized that he had relaxed his guard for a moment, and failed to notice that the group at the edge of the runway appeared somewhat out of place: himself in a dark suit, Schwarz in German uniform smoking a cigar, a woman, and now a man jumping out of a car in an obvious hurry. They looked like a reception committee, and the setup might ring alarm bells in Kirke's mind.

Dresler came up to him excitedly waving the yellow object, a book with a brightly coloured dust jacket. 'This is his code book!' he said.

That meant Kirke *was* the key man. Peter looked at the little aircraft, which had turned off the runway before drawing level with the waiting group, and was now taxiing past them to the parking area. 'Put the book under your coat, you damn fool,' he said to Dresler. 'If he sees you waving that about, he'll know we're on to him!'

He looked again at the Tiger Moth. He could see

Kirke in the open cockpit, but could not read the man's expression behind the goggles, scarf and helmet.

However, there was no room to misinterpret what happened next.

The engine suddenly roared louder as the throttle was opened wide. The aircraft swung around, turning into the wind but also heading straight for the little group around Peter. 'Damn, he's going to run for it!' Peter cried.

The plane picked up speed and came directly at them.

Peter drew his pistol.

He wanted to take Kirke alive, and interrogate him – but he would rather have him dead than let him get away. Holding the gun with both hands, he pointed it at the oncoming aircraft. It was virtually impossible to shoot down a plane with a handgun, but perhaps he might hit the pilot with a lucky shot.

The Tiger Moth's tail came up off the ground, levelling the fuselage and bringing Kirke's head and shoulders into view. Peter took careful aim at the flying helmet and pulled the trigger. The aircraft lifted off the ground, and Peter raised his aim, emptying the seven-shot magazine of the Walther PPK. He saw with bitter disappointment that he had shot too high, for a series of small holes like ink blots appeared in the fuel tank over the pilot's head, and petrol was spurting into the cockpit in small jets. The aircraft did not falter.

The others threw themselves flat.

A suicidal rage seized Peter as the spinning propeller approached him at sixty miles per hour. At the controls with Poul Kirke were all the criminals who had ever escaped justice, including Finn Jonk, the driver who had injured Inge. Peter was going to stop Kirke getting away if it killed him.

Out of the corner of his eye, he saw Major Schwarz's cigar smouldering on the grass, and he was seized by inspiration.

As the biplane swept lethally towards him he stooped, picked up the burning cigar, and threw it at the pilot.

Then he flung himself sideways.

He felt the rush of wind as the lower wing passed within inches of his head.

He hit the ground, rolled over and looked up.

The Tiger Moth was climbing. The bullets and the lighted cigar seemed to have had no effect. Peter had failed.

Would Kirke get away? The Luftwaffe would scramble the two Messerschmitts to chase him, but that would take a few minutes, by which time the Tiger Moth would be out of sight. Kirke's fuel tank was damaged, but the holes might not be at the lowest point of the tank, in which case he might retain sufficient petrol to get him across the water to Sweden, which was only twenty miles away. And darkness was falling.

Kirke had a chance, Peter concluded bitterly.

Then there was the whoosh of a sudden fire, and a single big flame rose from the cockpit.

It spread with ghastly speed all over the visible head and shoulders of the pilot, whose clothing must have been soaked with petrol. The flames licked back along the fuselage, rapidly consuming the linen fabric.

For a few seconds the aircraft continued to climb, although the head of the pilot had turned to a charred stump. Then Kirke's body slumped, apparently pushing the control stick forward, and the Tiger Moth turned nose-down and dived the short distance to earth, plunging like an arrow into the ground. The fuselage crumpled like a concertina.

There was a horrified silence. The flames continued to lick around the wings and the tail, stripping the fabric, eating into the wooden wing spars, and revealing the square steel tubes of the fuselage like the skeleton of a burned martyr.

Tilde said: 'My God, how dreadful – the poor man.' She was shaking.

Peter put his arms around her. 'Yes,' he said. 'And the worst of it is, now he can't answer questions.'

# PART TWO

PART TWO

# NINE

The sign outside the building read 'Danish Institute of Folk Song and Country Dancing', but that was just to fool the authorities. Down the steps, through the double curtain that served as a light trap, and inside the windowless basement, there was a jazz club.

The room was small and dim. The damp concrete floor was littered with cigarette ends, and sticky with spilled beer. There were a few rickety tables and some wooden chairs, but most of the audience was standing. There were sailors and dockers shoulder to shoulder with well dressed young people and a sprinkling of German soldiers.

On the tiny stage, a young woman sat at the piano, crooning ballads into a microphone. Perhaps it was jazz, but it was not the music Harald was passionate about. He was waiting for Memphis Johnny Madison, who was coloured, even though he had lived most of his life in Copenhagen and had probably never seen Memphis.

It was two o'clock in the morning. Earlier this evening, after lights out at school, the Three Stooges – Harald, Mads and Tik – had put their clothes back on, sneaked out of the dormitory building, and caught the last train into the city. It was risky – they would be in deep trouble if they were found out – but it would be worth it to see Memphis Johnny.

The aquavit Harald was drinking with draft beer chasers was making him even more euphoric.

In the back of his mind was the thrilling memory of his conversation with Poul Kirke, and the frightening fact that he was now in the Resistance. He hardly dared to think about it, for it was something he could not share even with Mads and Tik. He had passed secret military information to a spy.

After Poul had admitted that there was a secret organization, Harald had said he would do anything else he could to help. Poul had promised to use Harald as one of his observers. His task would be to collect information on the occupying forces and give it to Poul for onward transmission to Britain. He was proud of himself, and eager for his first assignment. He was also frightened, but he tried not to think about what might happen if he were caught.

He still hated Poul for dating Karen Duchwitz. He had the sour taste of jealousy in the pit of his stomach every time he thought about it. But he suppressed the feeling for the sake of the Resistance.

He wished Karen were here now. She would appreciate the music.

Just as he was thinking that female company was lacking, he noticed a new arrival: a woman with curly dark hair, wearing a red dress, sitting on a stool at the bar. He could not see her too clearly – the air was smoky, or perhaps there was something wrong with his vision – but she seemed to be alone. 'Hey, look,' he said to the others.

'Nice, if you like older women,' said Mads.

Harald peered at her, trying to focus better. 'Why, how old is she?'

'She's got to be thirty at least.'

Harald shrugged. 'That's not really *old*. I wonder if she'd like someone to talk to?'

Tik, who was not as drunk as the other two, said: 'She'll talk to you.'

Harald was not sure why Tik was grinning like a fool. Ignoring him, Harald stood up and headed for the bar. As he got closer, he saw that the woman was quite plump, and her round face was heavily made up. 'Hello, schoolboy,' she said, but her smile was friendly.

'I noticed that you were alone.'

'For the moment.'

'I thought you might want someone to talk to.'

'That's not really what I'm here for.'

'Ah – you prefer to listen to the music. I'm a great jazz fan, have been for years. What do you think of the singer? She's not American, of course, but—'

'I hate the music.'

Harald was nonplussed. 'Then why—'

'I'm a working girl.'

She seemed to think that explained everything, but he was mystified. She continued to smile warmly at him, but he had the sense they were talking at cross-purposes. 'A working girl,' he repeated.

'Yes. What did you think I was?'

He was inclined to be nice to her, so he said: 'You look like a princess to me.'

She laughed.

He asked her: 'What's your name?'

'Betsy.'

It was an unlikely name for a working-class Danish girl, and Harald guessed it was assumed.

A man appeared at Harald's elbow. Harald was taken aback by the newcomer's appearance: he was unshaven, he had rotten teeth, and one eye was half closed by a big bruise. He wore a stained tuxedo and a collarless shirt. Despite being short and skinny, he looked intimidating. He said: 'Come on, sonny, make up your mind.'

Betsy said to Harald: 'This is Luther. Leave the boy alone, Lou, he's not doing anything wrong.'

'He's driving other customers away.'

Harald realized he had no idea what was going on, and he decided he must be drunker than he had imagined.

Luther said: 'Well – do you want to fuck her, or not?'

Harald was astonished. 'I don't even know her!'

Betsy burst out laughing.

'It's ten crowns, you can pay me,' Luther said.

Enlightenment dawned. Harald turned to her and said in a voice loud with astonishment: 'Are you a prostitute?'

'All right, don't shout,' she said with annoyance.

Luther grabbed Harald by the shirt front and

pulled him forwards. His grip was strong, and Harald staggered. 'I know you educated types,' Luther spat. 'You think this kind of thing is funny.'

Harald smelled the man's bad breath. 'Don't get upset,' he said. 'I just wanted to talk to her.'

A barman with a rag around his head leaned over the bar and said: 'No trouble, please, Lou. The lad means no harm.'

'Doesn't he? I think he's laughing at me.'

Harald was beginning to wonder anxiously whether Luther had a knife, when the club manager picked up the microphone and announced Memphis Johnny Madison, and there was a burst of applause.

Luther pushed Harald away. 'Get out of my sight, before I slit your fool throat,' he said.

Harald went back to the others. He knew he had been humiliated, but he was too drunk to care. 'I made an error of etiquette,' he said.

Memphis Johnny walked on stage, and Harald instantly forgot Luther.

Johnny sat at the piano and leaned towards the microphone. Speaking perfect Danish with no trace of an accent, he said: 'Thank you. I'd like to open with a composition by the greatest boogie-woogie pianist of them all, Clarence Pine Top Smith.'

There was renewed applause, and Harald shouted in English: 'Play it, Johnny!'

Some kind of disturbance broke out near the door, but Harald took no notice. Johnny played four bars of introduction then stopped abruptly and said into the microphone: 'Heil Hitler, baby.'

A German officer walked on stage.

Harald looked around, bewildered. A group of military police had come into the club. They were arresting the German soldiers, but not the Danish civilians.

The officer snatched the microphone from Johnny and said in Danish: 'Entertainers of inferior race are not permitted. This club is closed.'

'No!' cried Harald in dismay. 'You can't do that, you Nazi peasant!'

Fortunately, his voice was drowned in the general hubbub of protest.

'Let's get out before you make any more errors of etiquette,' said Tik. He took Harald's arm.

Harald resisted. 'Come on!' he yelled. 'Let Johnny play!'

The officer handcuffed Johnny and walked him out.

Harald was heartbroken. It had been his first chance to hear a real boogie pianist, and the Nazis had stopped the show after a few bars. 'They have no right!' he shouted.

'Of course not,' Tik said soothingly, and steered him to the door.

The three young men made their way up the steps to the street. It was midsummer, and the short Scandinavian night was already over. Dawn had broken. The club was on the waterfront, and the broad channel of water gleamed in the half light. Sleeping ships floated motionless at their moorings. A cool, salty breeze blew in from the sea. Harald breathed deeply then felt momentarily dizzy.

'We might as well go to the railway station and wait for the first train home,' Tik said. Their plan was to be in bed, pretending to sleep, before anyone at school got up.

They headed for the town centre. At the main intersections, the Germans had erected concrete guard posts, octagonal in plan and about four feet high, with room in the middle for a soldier to stand, visible from the chest up. They were not manned at night. Harald was still furious about the closure of the club, and he was further enraged by these ugly symbols of Nazi domination. Passing one, he gave it a futile kick.

Mads said: 'They say the sentries at these posts wear lederhosen, because no one can see their legs.' Harald and Tik laughed.

A moment later, they passed a pile of builder's rubble outside a shop that had been newly refitted, and Harald happened to notice a cluster of paint cans on top of the pile – whereupon he was struck by an idea. He leaned across the rubbish and picked up a can.

'What the hell are you doing?' Tik said.

There was a little black paint left in the bottom, still liquid. From among the odd bits of timber on the pile, Harald selected a piece of wooden slat an inch wide that would serve as a brush.

Ignoring bemused questions from Tik and Mads, he walked back to the guard post. He knelt in front of it with the paint and the stick. He heard Tik say something in a warning voice, but ignored him. With great care, he wrote in black paint on the concrete wall:

THIS NAZI
HAS NO
TROUSERS
ON

He stepped back to admire his work. The letters were large and the words could be read at a distance. Later this morning, thousands of Copenhageners on their way to work would see the joke and smile.

'What do you think of that?' he said. He looked around. Tik and Mads were nowhere to be seen, but two uniformed Danish policemen stood immediately behind him.

'Very amusing,' said one of them. 'You're under arrest.'

* * *

He spent the rest of the night in the Politigaarden, in the drunk tank with an old man who had urinated in his trousers and a boy his own age who vomited on the floor. He was too disgusted with them and himself to sleep. As the hours went by, he developed a headache and a raging thirst.

But the hangover and the filth were not his worst worries. He was more concerned about being interrogated about the Resistance. What if he were turned over to the Gestapo and tortured? He did not know how much pain he could stand. Eventually he might betray Poul Kirke. And all for a stupid joke! He could not believe how childish he had been. He was bitterly ashamed.

At eight o'clock in the morning, a uniformed policeman brought a tray with three mugs of ersatz tea and a plate of black bread, thinly smeared with a butter substitute. Harald ignored the bread – he could not eat in a place like a toilet – but he drank the tea greedily.

Shortly afterwards, he was taken from the cell to an interview room. He waited a few minutes, then a sergeant came in carrying a folder and a typed sheet of paper. 'Stand up!' the sergeant barked, and Harald leaped to his feet.

The sergeant sat at the table and read the report. 'A Jansborg schoolboy, eh?' he said.

'Yes, sir.'

'You ought to know better, lad.'

'Yes, sir.'

'Where did you get the liquor?'

'At a jazz club.'

He looked up from the typed sheet. 'The Danish Institute?'

'Yes.'

'You must have been there when the Krauts closed it down.'

'Yes.' Harald was confused by his use of the mildly

derogatory slang word 'Kraut' for 'German'. It jarred with his formal tone.

'Do you often get drunk?'

'No, sir. First time.'

'And then you saw the guard post, and you happened to come across a pot of paint . . .'

'I'm very sorry.'

The cop grinned suddenly. 'Well, don't be too sorry. I thought it was pretty funny, myself. No trousers!' He laughed.

Harald was bewildered. The man had seemed hostile, but now he was enjoying the joke. Harald said: 'What's going to happen to me?'

'Nothing. We're the police, not the joke patrol.' The sergeant tore the report in half and dropped it in the waste-paper basket.

Harald could hardly believe his luck. Was he really going to be let off? 'What . . . what should I do?'

'Go back to Jansborg.'

'Thank you!' Harald wondered if he could sneak back into school unnoticed, even at this late stage. He would have some time, on the train, to think of a story. Perhaps no one need ever find out about this.

The sergeant stood up. 'But take a word of advice. Keep off the booze.'

'I will,' Harald said fervently. If he could get out of this scrape, he would never drink alcohol again.

The sergeant opened the door, and Harald suffered a dreadful shock.

Standing outside was Peter Flemming.

Harald and Peter stared at one another for a long moment.

The sergeant said: 'Can I help you, Inspector?'

Peter ignored him and spoke to Harald. 'Well, well,' he said in the satisfied tone of a man who has been proved right at last. 'I wondered, when I saw the name on the overnight arrest list. Could Harald Olufsen, graffiti writer and drunk, be Harald Olufsen, son of the pastor of Sande? Lo and behold, they are one and the same.'

Harald was dismayed. Just when he had started to hope that this dreadful incident could be kept secret, the truth had been discovered by one who had a grudge against his whole family.

Peter turned to the sergeant and said dismissively: 'All right, I'll deal with it now.'

The sergeant looked resentful. 'There are to be no charges, sir, the superintendent has decided.'

'We'll see about that.'

Harald felt he could weep. He had been on the point of getting away with it. This seemed so unfair.

The sergeant hesitated, seeming disposed to argue, and Peter said firmly: 'That will be all.'

'Very good, sir.' He left.

Peter stared at Harald, saying nothing, until at last Harald said: 'What are you going to do?'

Peter smiled, then said: 'I think I'll take you back to school.'

\* \* \*

They entered the grounds of Jansborg Skole in a police Buick driven by a uniformed officer, with Harald in the back like a prisoner.

The sun was shining on the old red-brick buildings and the lawns, and Harald felt a stab of regret for the simple, safe life he had lived here over the past seven years. Whatever happened now, this reassuringly familiar place was not going to be a home to him much longer.

The sight aroused different feelings in Peter Flemming, who muttered sourly to the driver: 'This is where they breed our future rulers.'

'Yes, sir,' the driver said neutrally.

It was the time of the mid-morning sandwich, and the boys were eating outside, so most of the school was watching as the car drove up to the main office and Harald got out.

Peter showed his police badge to the school secretary, and he and Harald were immediately taken to Heis's study.

Harald did not know what to think. It seemed Peter was not going to hand him over to the Gestapo, his worst fear. He was reluctant to let his hopes rise too soon, but all the signs were that Peter regarded him as a mischievous schoolboy, not a member of the Danish Resistance. For once he was grateful to be treated as a child rather than a man.

But in that case, what *was* Peter up to?

As they walked in, Heis unwound his lanky frame from behind his desk and stared at them, with vague concern, through the glasses perched on his beaky nose. His voice was kindly, but a tremor betrayed his nervousness. 'Olufsen? What's all this?'

Peter did not give Harald the chance to answer the question. Jerking a thumb in his direction, he said to Heis in a grating tone: 'Is this one of yours?'

The gentle Heis flinched as if he had been struck. 'Olufsen is a pupil here, yes.'

'He was arrested last night for defacing a German military installation.'

Harald realized that Peter was enjoying the humiliation of Heis, and was determined to make the most of it.

Heis looked mortified. 'I'm very sorry to hear that.'

'He was also drunk.'

'Oh, dear.'

'The police have to decide what to do about it.'

'I'm not sure I—'

'Frankly, we'd rather not prosecute a schoolboy for a childish prank.'

'Well, I'm glad to hear that . . .'

'On the other hand, he can't go unpunished.'

'Indeed not.'

'Apart from anything else, our German friends will want to know that the perpetrator has been dealt with firmly.'

'Of course, of course.'

Harald felt sorry for Heis, but at the same time wished he were not such a weakling. So far, he had done nothing but agree with the bullying Peter.

Peter went on: 'So the outcome depends on you.'

'Oh? In what way?'

'If we let him go, will you expel him from school?'

Harald immediately saw what Peter was up to. He just wanted to be sure that Harald's transgression would become public knowledge. He was only interested in the embarrassment of the Olufsen family.

The arrest of a Jansborg schoolboy would make headlines. The shame of Heis would be exceeded only by that of Harald's parents. His father would be volcanic and his mother suicidal.

But, Harald realized, Peter's enmity towards the Olufsen family had blunted his policeman's instincts. He was so happy to have caught an Olufsen drunk that he had overlooked a greater crime. He had not even considered whether Harald's dislike of the Nazis went beyond slogan-daubing to espionage. Peter's malice had saved Harald's skin.

Heis showed the first sign of opposition. 'Expulsion seems a bit harsh—'

'Not as harsh as a prosecution and possible jail sentence.'

'No, indeed.'

Harald did not enter the argument himself, because he could see no way out of this that would enable him to keep the incident secret. He consoled himself with the thought that he had escaped the Gestapo. Any other punishment would seem minor.

Heis said: 'It's almost the end of the academic year. He wouldn't miss much schooling if he were expelled now.'

'Then it will not permit him to avoid much work.'

'Something of a technicality, considering that he is only a couple of weeks away from leaving.'

'But it will satisfy the Germans.'

'Will it? That's important, of course.'

'If you can assure me that he will be expelled, I can release him from custody. Otherwise, I'll have to take him back to the Politigaarden.'

Heis threw a guilty look at Harald. 'It does seem as if the school has no real choice in the matter, doesn't it?'

'Yes, sir.'

Heis looked at Peter. 'Very well, then. I will expel him.'

Peter gave a satisfied smile. 'I'm glad we've resolved this so sensibly.' He stood up. 'Try to keep out of trouble in future, young Harald,' he said pompously.

Harald looked away.

Peter shook hands with Heis. 'Well, thank you, Inspector,' Heis said.

'Pleased to help.' Peter went out.

Harald felt all his muscles relax. He had got away with it. There would be hell to pay at home, of course, but the important thing was that his foolishness had not compromised Poul Kirke and the Resistance.

Heis said: 'A dreadful thing has happened, Olufsen.'

'I know I've done wrong—'

'No, not that. I think you know Mads Kirke's cousin.'

'Poul, yes.' Harald tensed again. Now what? Had

Heis somehow found out about Harald's involvement with the Resistance? 'What about Poul?'

'He has been in a plane crash.'

'My God! I was flying with him a few days ago!'

'It happened last night at the flying school.' Heis hesitated.

'What . . .?'

'I'm sorry to have to tell you that Poul Kirke is dead.'

# TEN

'Dead?' said Herbert Woodie with a squeak in his voice. 'How can he be dead?'

'They're saying he crashed his Tiger Moth,' Hermia replied. She was angry and distraught.

'The damn fool,' Woodie said callously. 'This could ruin everything.'

Hermia stared at him in disgust. She would have liked to slap his stupid face.

They were in Woodie's office at Bletchley Park with Digby Hoare. Hermia had sent a message to Poul Kirke, instructing him to get an eyewitness description of the radar installation on the island of Sande. 'The reply came from Jens Toksvig, one of Poul's helpers,' she said, making an effort to be calm and factual. 'It was sent via the British legation in Stockholm, as usual, but it wasn't even enciphered – Jens obviously doesn't know the code. He said the crash was being passed off as an accident, but in fact Poul was trying to escape from the police and they shot at the aircraft.'

'The poor man,' said Digby.

'The message came in this morning,' Hermia added. 'I was about to come and tell you, Mr Woodie, when you sent for me.' In fact she had been in tears.

She did not cry often, but her heart was touched by the death of Poul, so young, handsome, and full of energy. She knew, too, that she was responsible for his being killed. It was she who had asked him to spy for Britain, and his courageous assent had led directly to his death. She thought of his parents, and his cousin Mads, and she had wept for them, too. Most of all, she longed to finish the job he had started, so that his killers would not prevail in the end.

'I'm so sorry,' Digby said, and he put his arm around Hermia's shoulders in a sympathetic squeeze. 'Lots of men are dying, but it hurts when it's someone you know.'

She nodded. His words were simple and obvious, but she was grateful for the thought. What a good man he was. She felt a surge of affection for him, then remembered her fiancé and felt guilty. She wished she could see Arne again. Talking to him and touching him would reinforce her love and make her immune to the appeal of Digby.

'But where does that leave us?' Woodie asked.

Hermia collected her thoughts rapidly. 'According to Jens, the Nightwatchmen have decided to lie low, at least for a while, and see how far the police carry their investigation. So, to answer your question, it leaves us without any sources of information in Denmark.'

'Makes us appear damned incompetent,' Woodie said.

'Never mind that,' Digby said crisply. 'The Nazis

have found a war-winning weapon. We thought we were years ahead with radar – now we learn that they have it too, and theirs is better than ours! I don't give a fuck about how you appear. The only question is how we find out more.'

Woodie looked outraged but said nothing. Hermia asked: 'What about other sources of intelligence?'

'We're trying them all, of course. And we've picked up one more clue: the word *himmelbett* has appeared in Luftwaffe decrypts.'

Woodie said: '*Himmelbett*? That means heaven bed. What does it signify?'

'It's their word for a four-poster bed,' Hermia told him.

'Makes no sense,' Woodie said grumpily, as if it were her fault.

She asked Digby: 'Any context?'

'Not really. It seems that their radar operates in a *himmelbett*. We can't figure it out.'

Hermia reached a decision. 'I'll have to go to Denmark myself,' she said.

'Don't be ridiculous,' Woodie said.

'We have no agents in the country, so someone has to be infiltrated,' she said. 'I know the ground better than anyone else in MI6, that's why I'm chief of the Denmark desk. And I speak the language like a native. I've got to go.'

'We don't send women on missions like that,' Woodie said dismissively.

Digby said: 'Yes, we do.' He turned to Hermia.

'You'll leave for Stockholm tonight. I'll come with you.'

* * *

'Why did you say that?' Hermia asked Digby the following day, as they walked through the Golden Room in the Stadhuset, Stockholm's famous City Hall.

Digby paused to study a wall mosaic. 'I knew the prime minister would want me to keep the closest possible watch on such an important mission.'

'I see.'

'And I wanted the chance to have you to myself. This is the next best thing to a slow boat to China.'

'But you know I have to get in touch with my fiancé. He's the only person I can trust to help us.'

'Yes.'

'And I'll probably see him all the sooner in consequence.'

'That suits me fine. I can't compete with a man who is trapped in a country hundreds of miles away, heroically silent and unseen, holding on to your affection by invisible cords of loyalty and guilt. I'd rather have a flesh-and-blood rival with human failings, someone who gets grumpy with you and has dandruff on his collar and scratches his bum.'

'This isn't a contest,' she said with exasperation. 'I love Arne. I'm going to marry him.'

'But you're not married yet.'

Hermia shook her head as if to detach herself from this irrelevant talk. Previously, she had enjoyed Digby's romantic interest in her – albeit guiltily – but now it was a distraction. She was here for a rendezvous. She and Digby were only pretending to be tourists with time to kill.

They left the Golden Room and went down the broad marble staircase and out into the cobbled courtyard. They crossed an arcade of pink granite pillars and found themselves in a garden overlooking the grey water of Lake Malaren. Turning to look up at the three-hundred-foot tower that rose over the red-brick building, Hermia checked that their shadow was with them.

A bored-looking man in a grey suit and well-worn shoes, he made little effort to conceal his presence. As Digby and Hermia had pulled away from the British legation, in a chauffeur-driven Volvo limousine that had been adapted to run on charcoal, they had been followed by two men in a black Mercedes 230. When they stopped outside the Stadhuset, the man in the grey suit had followed them inside.

According to the British air attaché, a group of German agents kept all British citizens in Sweden under constant surveillance. They could be shaken off, but it was unwise. Losing your tail was taken as proof of guilt. Men who evaded surveillance had been arrested and accused of espionage, and the Swedish authorities had been pressured to expel them.

Therefore, Hermia had to escape without the shadow realizing it.

Following a prearranged plan, Hermia and Digby wandered across the garden and turned around the corner of the building to look at the cenotaph of the city's founder, Birger Jarl. The gilded sarcophagus lay in a canopied tomb with stone pillars at each corner. 'Like a *himmelbett*,' Hermia said.

Concealed from view on the far side of the cenotaph was a Swedish woman of the same height and build as Hermia, with similar dark hair.

Hermia looked inquiringly at the woman, who nodded decisively.

Hermia suffered an instant of fear. Until now she had done nothing illegal. Her visit to Sweden had been as innocent as it seemed. From this moment on, she would be on the wrong side of the law, for the first time in her life.

'Quickly,' the woman said in English.

Hermia slipped off her light summer raincoat and red beret, and the other woman put them on. Hermia took from her pocket a dull brown scarf and tied it around her head, covering her distinctive hair and partly concealing her face.

The Swedish woman took Digby's arm, and the two of them moved away from the cenotaph and sauntered back into the garden in full view.

Hermia waited a few moments, pretending to study the elaborate wrought-iron railing around the monument, fearful that the tail would be suspicious and come to check. But nothing happened.

She moved out from behind the cenotaph, half-expecting him to be lying in wait, but there was no one nearby. Pulling the scarf a little farther over her face, she walked around the corner into the garden.

She saw Digby and the decoy heading for the gate

at the far end. The shadow was following them. The plan was working.

Hermia went in the same direction, tailing the tail. As arranged, Digby and the woman went straight to their car, which was waiting in the square. Hermia saw them get into the Volvo and drive away. The tail followed in the Mercedes. They would lead him all the way back to the legation, and he would report that the two visitors from Britain had spent the afternoon as innocent tourists.

And Hermia was free.

She crossed the Stadhusbron bridge and headed for Gustav Adolf Square, the centre of the city, walking fast, eager to get on with her task.

Everything had happened with bewildering rapidity in the last twenty-four hours. Hermia had been given only a few minutes to throw a few clothes into a suitcase, then she and Digby had been driven in a fast car to Dundee, in Scotland, where they checked into a hotel a few minutes after midnight. That morning at dawn they had been taken to Leuchars Aerodrome, on the Fife coast, and an RAF crew wearing civilian British Overseas Airways Corporation uniforms had flown them to Stockholm, a three-hour journey. They had had lunch at the British legation then put into operation the plan they had devised in the car between Bletchley and Dundee.

As Sweden was neutral, it was possible to phone or write from here to people in Denmark. Hermia was going to try to call her fiancé, Arne. At the Danish end, calls were monitored and letters opened by the censors, so she would have to be extraordinarily careful in what she said. She had to mount a deception that would sound innocent to an eavesdropper yet bring Arne into the Resistance.

Back in 1939, when she had set up the Nightwatchmen, she had deliberately excluded Arne. It was not because of his convictions: he was as anti-Nazi as she was, albeit in a less passionate way – he thought they were stupid clowns in silly uniforms who wanted to stop people having fun. No, the problem was his careless nature. He was too open and friendly for clandestine work. Perhaps also she had been unwilling to put him in danger, although Poul had agreed with her about Arne's unsuitability. But now she was desperate. Arne was as happy-go-lucky as ever, but she had no one else.

Besides, everyone felt differently about danger today from at the outbreak of war. Thousands of fine young men had given their lives already. Arne was a military officer: he was supposed to take risks for his country.

All the same, her heart felt cold at the thought of what she was going to ask him to do.

She turned into the Vasagatan, a busy street in which there were several hotels, the central railway station, and the main post office. Here in Sweden, telephone services had always been separate from the mail, and there were special public phone bureaus. Hermia was heading for the one in the railway station.

She could have telephoned from the British legation, but that would almost certainly have aroused suspicion. At the phone bureau, there would be nothing unusual about a woman who spoke hesitant Swedish with a Danish accent coming in to phone home.

She and Digby had talked about whether the phone call would be listened to by the authorities. In every telephone exchange in Denmark there was at least one young German woman in uniform listening in. They could not possibly eavesdrop on every phone call, of course. However, they were more likely to pay attention to international calls, and calls to military bases, so there was a strong chance that Hermia's conversation with Arne would be monitored. She would have to communicate in hints and doubletalk. But that should be possible. She and Arne had been lovers, so she ought to be able to make him understand without being explicit.

The station was built like a French château. The grand entrance lobby had a coffered ceiling and chandeliers. She found the phone bureau and stood in line.

When she got to the counter, she told the clerk that she wanted to make a person-to-person call to Arne Olufsen, and gave the number of the flying school. She waited impatiently, full of apprehension, while the operator tried to get Arne on the line. She did not even know whether he was at Vodal today. He might be flying, or away from the base for the afternoon, or on leave. He might have been transferred to another base or have resigned from the army.

But she would try to track him down, wherever he was. She could speak to his commanding officer and ask where he had gone, she could call his parents on Sande, and she had numbers for some of his friends in Copenhagen. She had all afternoon to spend, and plenty of money for phone calls.

It would be strange to talk to him after more than a year. She was thrilled but anxious. The mission was the important thing, but she could not help fretting about how Arne would feel about her. Perhaps he no longer loved her as he once had. What if he were cold to her? It would break her heart. But he might have met someone else. After all, she had enjoyed a flirtation with Digby. How much more easily might a man find his heart straying?

She remembered skiing with him, racing down a sunlit slope, the two of them leaning to one side then the other in perfect rhythm, perspiring in the icy air, laughing with the sheer joy of being alive. Would those days ever come back?

She was called to a booth.

She picked up the phone and said: 'Hello?'

Arne said: 'Who is it?'

She had forgotten his voice. It was low and warm and sounded as if it might break into laughter at any minute. He spoke educated Danish, with a precise diction he had learned in the military and the hint of a Jutland accent left over from his childhood.

She had planned her first sentence. She intended to use the pet names they had for each other, hoping this would alert Arne to the need to speak discreetly.

But for a moment she could not speak at all.

'Hello?' he said. 'Is anyone there?'

She swallowed and found her voice. 'Hello, Toothbrush, this is your black cat.' She called him 'Toothbrush' because that was what his moustache felt like when he kissed her. Her nickname came from the colour of her hair.

It was his turn to be dumbstruck. There was a silence.

Hermia said: 'How are you?'

'I'm OK,' he said at last. 'My God, is it really you?'

'Yes.'

'Are you all right?'

'Yes.' Suddenly she could not stand any more small talk. Abruptly she said: 'Do you still love me?'

He did not answer immediately. That made her think his feelings had changed. He would not say so directly, she thought; he would equivocate, and say they needed to reassess their relationship after all this time, but she would know—

'I love you,' he said.

'Do you?'

'More than ever. I've missed you terribly.'

She closed her eyes. Feeling dizzy, she leaned against the wall.

'I'm so glad you're still alive,' he said. 'I'm so happy to be talking to you.'

'I love you, too,' she said.

'What's been happening? How are you? Where are you calling from?'

She pulled herself together. 'I'm not far away.'

He noticed her guarded manner and responded in a similar tone. 'OK, I understand.'

She had prepared the next part. 'Do you remember the castle?' There were many castles in Denmark, but one was special to them.

'You mean the ruins? How could I forget?'

'Could you meet me there?'

'How could you get there – Never mind. Do you mean it?'

'Yes.'

'It's a long way.'

'It's really very important.'

'I'd go a lot farther to see you. I'm just figuring out how. I'll ask for leave, but if it's a problem I'll just go AWOL—'

'Don't do that.' She did not want the military police looking for him. 'When's your next day off?'

'Saturday.'

The operator came on the line to tell them they had ten seconds.

Hastily, Hermia said: 'I'll be there on Saturday – I hope. If you don't make it, I'll come back every day for as long as I can.'

'I'll do the same.'

'Be careful. I love you.'

'I love you—'

The line went dead.

Hermia kept the receiver pressed to her ear, as if she could hold on to him a little longer that way. Then the operator asked her if she wanted to make another call, and she declined and hung up.

She paid at the counter then went out, dazed with happiness. She stood in the station concourse, under the high curved roof, with people hurrying past her in all directions. He still loved her. In two days' time she would see him. Someone bumped into her, and she got out of the crowd into a café where she slumped in a chair. Two days.

The ruined castle to which they had both enigmatically referred was Hammershus, a tourist attraction on the Danish holiday island of Bornholm, in the Baltic Sea. They had spent a week on the island in 1939, posing as man and wife, and had made love among the ruins one warm summer evening. Arne would take the ferry from Copenhagen, a trip of seven or eight hours, or fly from Kastrup, which took about an hour. The island was a hundred miles from mainland Denmark, but only twenty miles from the south coast of Sweden. Hermia would have to find a fishing boat to take her across that short stretch of water illegally.

But it was the danger to Arne, not herself, that she kept thinking about. He was going to meet secretly with an agent of the British secret service. She would ask him to become a spy.

If he were caught, the punishment would be death.

# ELEVEN

On the second day after his arrest, Harald returned home.

Heis had allowed him to stay at school another two days to take the last of his exams. He would be permitted to graduate, though not to attend the ceremony, which was a week away. But the important thing was that his university place was safe. He would study physics under Niels Bohr – if he lived that long.

During those two days he had learned, from Mads Kirke, that the death of Poul had not been a straightforward crash. The army was refusing to reveal details, saying they were still investigating, but other pilots had told the family that the police had been on the base at the time, and shots had been fired. Harald was sure, though he could not say this to Mads, that Poul had been killed because of his Resistance work.

Nevertheless, he was more afraid of his father than of the police as he made his way home. It was a tediously familiar journey across the width of Denmark from Jansborg, in the east, to Sande, off the west coast. He knew every small-town railway station and fish-smelling ferry dock and all the flat green landscape in between. The journey took the whole day, because of multiple train delays, but he wished it could be longer.

He spent the time anticipating his father's wrath. He composed indignant speeches of self-justification which even he found unconvincing. He tried out a variety of more or less grovelling apologies, unable to find a formula that was sincere but not abject. He wondered whether to tell his parents to be grateful he was alive, when he might have met the same fate as Poul Kirke; but that seemed to make cheap use of a heroic death.

When he reached Sande, he further postponed his arrival by walking home along the beach. The tide was out, and the sea was barely visible a mile away, a narrow strip of dark blue touched with inconstant smears of white surf, sandwiched between the bright blue of the sky and the buff-coloured sand. It was evening, and the sun was low. A few holidaymakers strolled through the dunes, and a group of boys around twelve or thirteen years old were playing football. It would have been a happy scene, but for the new grey concrete bunkers at intervals of a mile along the high-tide mark, bristling with artillery and manned by steel-helmeted soldiers.

He came to the new military base and left the beach to follow the long diversion around it, welcoming the additional delay. He wondered whether Poul had managed to send off his sketch of the radio equipment to the British. If not, the police must have found it. Would they wonder who had drawn it? Fortunately there was nothing to connect it with Harald. All the same, the thought was frightening. The police still did not know he was a criminal, but now they knew about his crime.

At last he came within sight of his home. Like the church, the parsonage was built in the local style, with red-painted bricks and a thatched roof that swept low over the windows, like a hat pulled over the eyes to keep out the rain. The lintel over the front door was painted in slanting stripes of black, white and green, a local tradition.

Harald went to the back and looked through the diamond-shaped pane of glass in the kitchen door. His mother was alone. He studied her for a moment, wondering what she had been like when she was his age. Ever since he could remember, she had looked tired; but she must have been pretty, once.

According to family legend Harald's father, Bruno, had been thought by everyone to be a confirmed bachelor at the age of thirty-seven, wholly dedicated to the work of his little sect. Then he had met Lisbeth, ten years younger, and lost his heart. So madly in love was he that he had worn a coloured tie to church in an attempt to appear romantic, and the deacons had been obliged to reprimand him for inappropriate attire.

Watching his mother as she bent over the sink, scrubbing a pot, Harald tried to imagine the tired grey hair as it had once been, jet black and gleaming, and the hazel eyes twinkling with humour; the lines of the face smoothed away, and the weary body full of energy. She must have been irresistibly sexy, Harald supposed, to have turned his father's remorselessly holy thoughts to the lusts of the flesh. It was hard to imagine.

He went in, put down his suitcase, and kissed his mother.

'Your father's out,' she said.

'Where has he gone?'

'Ove Borking is sick.' Ove was an elderly fisherman and faithful member of the congregation.

Harald was relieved. Any postponement of the confrontation was a reprieve.

His mother looked solemn and tearful. Her expression touched his heart. He said: 'I'm sorry to have caused you distress, Mother.'

'Your father is mortified,' she said. 'Axel Flemming has called an emergency meeting of the Board of Deacons to discuss the matter.'

Harald nodded. He had anticipated that the Flemmings would make the most of this.

'But why did you do it?' his mother asked plaintively.

He had no answer.

She made him a ham sandwich for his supper. 'Is there any news of Uncle Joachim?' he asked.

'Nothing. We get no answers to our letters.'

Harald's own troubles seemed nothing when he thought about his cousin Monika, penniless and persecuted, not even knowing whether her father was dead or alive. While Harald was growing up, the annual visit of the Goldstein cousins had been the highlight of the year. For two weeks the monastic atmosphere of the parsonage was transformed, and the place was full of people and noise. The pastor had for his sister and her family an indulgent fondness that he showed no one else, certainly not his own children, and he would smile benignly as they committed transgressions, such as buying ice-cream on a Sunday, for which he would have punished Harald and Arne. For Harald, the sound of the German language meant laughter and pranks and fun. Now he wondered if the Goldsteins would ever laugh again.

He turned on the radio to hear the war news. It was bad. The British assault in North Africa had been abandoned, a catastrophic failure, half their tanks lost, either crippled in the desert by mechanical failures or destroyed by experienced German antitank gunners. The Axis grip on North Africa was unshaken. Danish radio and the BBC told essentially the same story.

At midnight a flight of bombers crossed overhead. Harald looked out and saw they were heading east. That meant they were British. The bombers were all the British had, now.

When he went back inside, his mother said: 'Your father could be out all night. You'd better go to bed.'

He lay awake for a long time. He asked himself why he was scared. He was too big to be beaten. His father's wrath was formidable, but how bad could a tongue-lashing be? Harald was not easily intimidated. Rather the reverse: he was inclined to resent authority and defy it out of sheer rebelliousness.

The short night came to an end, and a rectangle of

grey dawn light appeared around the curtain at his window like a picture frame. He drifted into sleep. His last thought was that perhaps what he really feared was not some hurt to himself, but his father's suffering.

He was awakened brusquely an hour later.

The door burst open, the light came on, and the pastor stood beside the bed, fully dressed, hands on his hips, chin thrust forward. 'How could you do it?' he shouted.

Harald sat up, blinking at his father, tall, bald, dressed in black, staring at Harald with the blue-eyed glare that terrified his congregation.

'What were you thinking of?' his father raged. 'What possessed you?'

Harald did not want to cower in his bed like a child. He threw off the sheet and stood up. Because the weather was warm, he had slept in his undershorts.

'Cover yourself, boy,' his father said. 'You're practically naked.'

The unreasonableness of this criticism stung Harald into a rejoinder. 'If underwear offends you, don't enter bedrooms without knocking.'

'Knocking? Don't tell me to knock on doors in my own house!'

Harald suffered the familiar feeling that his father had an answer for everything. 'Very well,' he said sulkily.

'What devil took hold of you? How could you bring such disgrace upon yourself, your family, your school and your church?'

Harald pulled on his trousers and turned to face his father.

'Well?' the pastor raged. 'Are you going to answer me?'

'I'm sorry, I thought you were asking rhetorical questions.' Harald was surprised by his own cool sarcasm.

His father was infuriated. 'Don't try to use your education to fence with me – I went to Jansborg too.'

'I'm not fencing. I'm asking whether there's any chance you'll listen to anything I say.'

The pastor raised his hand as if to strike. It would have been a relief, Harald thought as his father hesitated. Whether he took the blow passively, or hit back, violence would have been some kind of resolution.

But his father was not going to make it that easy. He dropped his hand and said: 'Well, I'm listening. What have you got to say for yourself?'

Harald gathered his thoughts. On the train he had rehearsed many versions of this speech, some of them most eloquent, but now he forgot all his oratorical flourishes. 'I'm sorry I daubed the guard post, because it was an empty gesture, a childish act of defiance.'

'At the least!'

For a moment he considered whether to tell his father about his connection with the Resistance, but he quickly decided not to risk further ridicule. Besides, now that Poul was dead, the Resistance might no longer exist.

Instead, he concentrated on the personal. 'I'm sorry to have brought disgrace on the school, because Heis is a kindly man. I'm sorry I got drunk, because it made me feel dreadful the next morning. Most of all, I'm sorry to have caused my mother distress.'

'And your father?'

Harald shook his head. 'You're upset because Axel Flemming knows all about this and he's going to rub your nose in it. Your pride has been hurt, but I'm not sure you're worried about me at all.'

'Pride?' his father roared. 'What has pride to do with anything? I've tried to bring up my sons to be decent, sober, God-fearing men – and you've let me down.'

Harald felt exasperated. 'Look, it's not that much of a disgrace. Most men get drunk—'

'Not my sons!'

'—once in their lives, at least.'

'But you were *arrested*.'

'That was bad luck.'

'It was bad *behaviour*—'

'And I wasn't charged – the police sergeant actually thought that what I did was funny. "We're not the joke patrol," he said. I wouldn't even have been expelled from school if Peter Flemming hadn't threatened Heis.'

'Don't you dare try to minimize this. No member of this family has ever been to jail for any reason. You've dragged us into the gutter.' The pastor's face changed suddenly. For the first time, he showed sadness rather than anger. 'And it would be shocking and tragic even if no one in the world knew of it but me.'

Harald saw that his father was sincere in this, and the realization threw him off balance. It was true that the old man's pride was wounded, but that was not all. He genuinely feared for his son's spiritual welfare. Harald was sorry he had been sarcastic.

But his father gave him no chance to be conciliatory. 'There remains the question of what is to be done with you.'

Harald was not sure what this meant. 'I've only missed a few days of school,' he said. 'I can do the preliminary reading for my university course here at home.'

'No,' his father said. 'You're not getting off so lightly.'

Harald had a dreadful foreboding. 'What do you mean? What are you planning?'

'You're not going to university.'

'What are you talking about? Of course I am.' Suddenly Harald felt very afraid.

'I'm not going to send you to Copenhagen to pollute your soul with strong drink and jazz music. You've proved you aren't mature enough for the city. You'll stay here, where I can supervise your spiritual development.'

'But you can't phone the university and say: "Don't teach this boy." They've given me a place.'

'They haven't given you any money, though.'

Harald was shocked. 'My grandfather bequeathed money for my education.'

'But he left it to me to dispense. And I'm not going to give it to you to spend in nightclubs.'

'It's not your money – you don't have the right!'

'I most certainly do. I'm your father.'

Harald was stunned. He had not dreamed of this. It was the only punishment that could really hurt him. Bewildered, he said: 'But you've always told me that education was so important.'

'Education is not the same as godliness.'

'Even so . . .'

His father saw that he was genuinely shocked, and his attitude softened a little. 'An hour ago, Ove Borking died. He had no education worth speaking of – he could barely write his name. He spent his life working on other men's boats, and never made enough to buy a carpet for his wife to put on the parlour floor. But he raised three God-fearing children, and every week he gave a tenth of his meagre wages to the church. That's what God considers a good life.'

Harald knew and liked Ove, and was sorry he had died. 'He was a simple man.'

'Nothing wrong with simplicity.'

'Yet if all men were like Ove, we'd still be fishing from dugout canoes.'

'Perhaps. But you're going to learn to emulate him before you do anything else.'

'And what does that mean?'

'Get dressed. Put on your school clothes and a clean shirt. You're going to work.' He left the room.

Harald stared at the closed door. What next?

He washed and shaved in a daze. He could hardly believe what was happening.

He might go to university without his father's help, of course. He would have to get a job to support himself, and he would not be able to afford the private tuition that most people considered essential to supplement the free lectures. But could he achieve all he wanted in those circumstances? He did not want merely to pass his exams. He wanted to be a great physicist, the successor to Niels Bohr. How could he do that if he did not have the money to buy books?

He needed time to think. And while he was thinking, he had to go along with whatever his father was planning.

He went downstairs and ate without tasting the porridge his mother had made.

His father saddled the horse, Major, a broad-backed Irish gelding strong enough to carry them both. The pastor mounted, and Harald got up behind.

They rode the length of the island. The journey took Major more than an hour. When they reached the dock, they watered the horse at the quayside trough and waited for the ferry. The pastor still had not told Harald where they were going.

When the boat docked, the ferryman touched his cap to the pastor, who said: 'Ove Borking was called home early this morning.'

'I expected as much,' said the ferryman.

'He was a good man.'

'Rest his soul.'

'Amen.'

They crossed to the mainland and rode up the hill to the town square. The stores were not yet open, but the pastor knocked at the door of the haberdashery. It was opened by the owner, Otto Sejr, a deacon of the Sande church. He seemed to be expecting them.

They stepped inside, and Harald looked around. Glass cases displayed balls of coloured wool. The shelves were stacked with lengths of material, wool cloth and printed cotton and a few silks. Below the shelves were drawers, each neatly marked.

*Ribbon – white*

*Ribbon – fancy*

*Elastic*

*Buttons – shirt*

*Buttons – horn*

*Pins*

*Knitting needles*

There was a dusty smell of mothballs and lavender, like an old lady's wardrobe. The odour brought to Harald's mind a childhood memory, suddenly vivid: standing here as a small boy while his mother bought black satin for his father's clerical shirts.

The shop had a run-down air now, probably because of wartime austerity. The higher shelves were empty, and it seemed to him there was not the astonishing variety of colours of knitting wool he recalled from his childhood.

But what was he doing here today?

His father soon answered the question. 'Brother Sejr has kindly agreed to give you a job,' he said. 'You'll be helping in the shop, serving customers and doing anything else you can to make yourself useful.'

He stared at his father, speechless.

'Mrs Sejr is in poor health, and can't work any longer, and their daughter has recently married and gone to live in Odense, so he needs an assistant,' the pastor went on, as if that were what needed explaining.

Sejr was a small man, bald with a little moustache. Harald had known him all his life. He was pompous, mean and sly. He wagged a fat finger and said: 'Work hard, pay attention, and be obedient, and you may learn a valuable trade, young Harald.'

Harald was flabbergasted. He had been thinking for two days about how his father would respond to his crime, but nothing he anticipated had come close to this. It was a life sentence.

His father shook hands with Sejr and thanked him, then said to Harald in parting: 'You'll take your lunch with the family here, and come straight home when you finish work. I'll see you tonight.' He waited a moment as if expecting an answer, but when Harald said nothing he went out.

'Right,' said Sejr. 'There's just time to sweep the floor before we open. You'll find a broom in the cupboard. Start at the back, sweep towards the front, and push the dust out through the door.'

Harald began his task. Seeing him brush one-handed, Sejr snapped: 'Put both hands on that broom, boy!'

Harald obeyed.

At nine o'clock, Sejr put the 'Open' sign in the door. 'When I want you to deal with a customer, I'll say: "Forward," and you step forward,' he said. 'You say: "Good morning, how may I serve you?" But watch me with one or two customers first.'

Harald watched Sejr sell six needles on a card to an old woman who counted out her coins as carefully as if they were pieces of gold. Next was a smartly dressed woman of about forty who bought two yards of black braid. Then it was Harald's turn to serve. The third customer was a thin-lipped woman who looked familiar. She asked for a reel of white cotton thread.

Sejr snapped: 'On your left, top drawer.'

Harald found the cotton. The price was marked in pencil on the wooden end of the reel. He took the money and made change.

Then the woman said: 'So, Harald Olufsen, you've been in the fleshpots of Babylon, I hear.'

Harald flushed. He had not prepared himself for this. Did the whole town know what he had done? He was not going to defend himself to gossip-mongers. He made no reply.

Sejr said: 'Young Harald will come under a more steady influence here, Mrs Jensen.'

'I'm sure it will do him good.'

They were thoroughly enjoying his humiliation, Harald realized. He said: 'Will there be anything else, then?'

'Oh, no thank you,' said Mrs Jensen, but she made no move to leave. 'So you won't be going to the university?'

Harald turned away and said: 'Where's the toilet, Mr Sejr?'

'Through the back and upstairs.'

As he left, he heard Sejr say apologetically: 'He's embarrassed, of course.'

'And no wonder,' the woman replied.

Harald climbed the stairs to the apartment over the shop. Mrs Sejr was in the kitchen, dressed in a pink quilted housecoat, washing breakfast cups at the sink. 'I've only got a few herrings for lunch,' she said. 'I hope you don't eat much.'

He lingered in the bathroom, and when he returned to the shop he was relieved to see that Mrs Jensen had gone. Sejr said: 'People are bound to be curious – you must be polite, whatever they say.'

'My life is none of Mrs Jensen's business,' he replied angrily.

'But she's a customer, and the customer is always right.'

The morning wore on with painful slowness. Sejr checked stock, wrote orders, did his books, and dealt with phone calls, but Harald was expected to stand waiting, ready for the next person to come through the door. It left him plenty of time to ponder. Was he really going to spend his life selling reels of cotton to housewives? It was unthinkable.

By midmorning, when Mrs Sejr brought him and

Sejr a cup of tea, he had decided he could not even spend the rest of the summer working here.

By lunch time he knew he was not going to last the day.

As Sejr flipped the 'Closed' sign, Harald said: 'I'm going for a walk.'

Sejr was startled. 'But Mrs Sejr has prepared lunch.'

'She told me she doesn't have enough food.' Harald opened the door.

'You've only got an hour,' Sejr called after him. 'Don't be late!'

Harald walked down the hill and got on the ferry.

He crossed to Sande and walked along the beach towards the parsonage. He felt a strange, tight sensation in his chest when he looked at the dunes, the miles of damp sand, and the endless sea. The view was as familiar as his own face in the mirror, yet now it gave him an aching sense of loss. He almost felt like crying, and after a while he realized why.

He was going to leave this place today.

The rationale came after the realization. He did not have to do the job selected for him – but he could not continue to live in the house after defying his father. He would have to go.

The thought of disobeying his father was no longer frightening, he realized as he strode along the sand. The drama had gone out of it. When had this change taken place? It was when the pastor had said he would withhold the money grandpa had left, Harald decided. That had been a shocking betrayal which could not possibly leave their relationship intact. At that moment, Harald had understood that he could no longer trust his father to have his best interests at heart. He had to look after himself now.

The conclusion was strangely anticlimactic. Of course he had to take responsibility for his own life. It was like realizing that the Bible was not infallible: he found it hard to imagine how he had formerly been so trusting.

When he reached the parsonage, the horse was not in the paddock. Harald guessed his father had returned to the Borking house to make arrangements for Ove's funeral. He went in by the kitchen door. His mother was at the table peeling potatoes. She looked frightened when she saw him. He kissed her, but gave no explanations.

He went to his room and packed his case as if he were going to school. His mother came to the bedroom door and stood watching him, wiping her hands in a towel. He saw her face, lined and sad, and he looked quickly away. After a while, she said: 'Where will you go?'

'I don't know.'

He thought of his brother. He went into his father's study, picked up the telephone, and placed a call to the flying school. After a few minutes, Arne came on the line. Harald told him what had happened.

'The old man overplayed his hand,' Arne commented. 'If he'd put you into a tough job, like cleaning fish at the canning plant, you'd have stuck it out just to prove your manhood.'

'I suppose I might.'

'But you were never going to stay long working in a damn shop. Our father can be a fool, sometimes. Where will you go now?'

Harald had not decided until this moment, but now he had a flash of inspiration. 'Kirstenslot,' he said. 'Tik Duchwitz's place. But don't tell Father. I don't want him coming after me.'

'Old man Duchwitz might tell him.'

That was a good point, Harald reflected. Tik's respectable father would have little sympathy for a boogie-playing, slogan-daubing runaway. But the ruined monastery was used as a dormitory by seasonal workers on the farm. 'I'll sleep in the old monastery,' he said. 'Tik's father won't even know I'm there.'

'How will you eat?'

'I may be able to get a job on the farm. They employ students in summer.'

'Tik is still at school, I presume.'

'But his sister might help me.'

'I know her, she went out with Poul a couple of times. Karen.'

'Only a couple of times?'

'Yes. Why – are you interested in her?'

'She's out of my league.'

'I suppose she is.'

'What happened to Poul . . . exactly?'

'It was Peter Flemming.'

'Peter!' Mads Kirke had not known that detail.

'He came with a car full of cops, looking for Poul.

Poul tried to escape in his Tiger Moth, and Peter shot at him. The aircraft crashed and burned.'

'Good God! Did you see it?'

'No, but one of my airmen did.'

'Mads told me some of this, but he didn't know it all. So Peter Flemming killed Poul. That's terrible.'

'Don't talk about it too much, you might get into trouble. They're trying to pass it off as an accident.'

'All right.' Harald noticed that Arne was not saying *why* the police had come after Poul. And Arne must have noticed that Harald did not ask.

'Let me know how you get on at Kirstenslot. Phone if you need anything.'

'Thanks.'

'Good luck, kid.'

As Harald hung up, his father walked in. 'And what do you think you're doing?'

Harald stood up. 'If you want money for the phone call, ask Sejr for my morning's wages.'

'I don't want money, I want to know why you're not at the shop.'

'It's not my destiny to be a haberdasher.'

'You don't know what your destiny is.'

'Perhaps not.' Harald left the room.

He went outside to the workshop and lit the boiler of his motorcycle. While he waited for it to build up steam, he stacked peat in the sidecar. He did not know how much he would need to get him to Kirstenslot, so he took it all. He returned to the house and picked up his suitcase.

His father waylaid him in the kitchen. 'Where do you think you're going?'

'I'd rather not say.'

'I forbid you to leave.'

'You can't really forbid things any more, Father,' Harald said quietly. 'You're no longer willing to support me. You're doing your best to sabotage my education. I'm afraid you've forfeited the right to tell me what to do.'

The pastor looked stunned. 'You have to tell me where you're going.'

'No.'

'Why not?'

'If you don't know where I am, you can't interfere with my plans.'

The pastor looked mortally wounded. Harald felt regret like a sudden pain. He had no desire for revenge, and it gave him no satisfaction to see his father's distress; but he was afraid that if he showed remorse he would lose his strength of purpose, and allow himself to be bullied into staying. So he turned his face away and walked outside.

He strapped his suitcase to the back of the bike and drove it out of the workshop.

His mother came running across the yard and thrust a bundle into his hands. 'Food,' she said. She was crying.

He stowed the food in the sidecar with the peat.

She threw her arms around him as he sat on the bike. 'Your father loves you, Harald. Do you understand that?'

'Yes, Mother, I think I do.'

She kissed him. 'Let me know that you're all right. Telephone, or send a postcard.'

'OK.'

'Promise.'

'I promise.'

She released him, and he drove away.

# TWELVE

Peter Flemming undressed his wife.

She stood passively in front of the mirror, a warm-blooded statue of a pale, beautiful woman. He took off her wristwatch and necklace, then patiently undid the hooks and eyes of her dress, his blunt fingers expert from months of practice. There was a smear on the side, he noticed with a disapproving frown, as if she touched something sticky then wiped her hand on her hip. She was not normally dirty. He pulled the dress over her head, careful not to disarrange her hair.

Inge was as lovely today as she had been the first time he had seen her in her underwear. But then she had been smiling, speaking fond words, her expression showing eagerness and a trace of apprehension. Today her face was blank.

He hung her dress in the wardrobe then took off her brassiere. Her breasts were full and round, the nipples so light in colour they were almost invisible. He swallowed hard and tried not to look at them. He made her sit on the dressing-table stool, then removed her shoes, unfastened her stockings and rolled them down, and took off her garter belt. He stood her up

again to pull down her underpants. Desire rose in him
as he uncovered the blonde curls between her legs.
He felt disgusted with himself.

He knew he could have sexual intercourse with her
if he wished. She would lie still and accept it with
blank impassivity, as she took everything that
happened to her. But he could not bring himself to
do it. He had tried, one time, not long after she came
home from the hospital, telling himself that perhaps
this would rekindle in her the spark of awareness; but
he had been revolted by himself, and had stopped
after a few seconds. Now the desire came back, and he
had to fight it off even though he knew that giving in
would bring no relief.

He threw her underwear into the linen basket with
an angry gesture. She did not move as he opened a
drawer and took out a white cotton nightdress
embroidered with small flowers, a gift to Inge from
his mother. She was innocent in her nakedness, and
to desire her seemed as wrong as to desire a child. He
drew the nightdress over her head, put her arms into
it, and smoothed it down her back. He looked over
her shoulder into the mirror. The flower pattern
suited her, and she looked pretty. He thought he saw
a faint smile touch her lips, but it was probably his
imagination.

He took her to the bathroom then put her to bed.
As he undressed himself, he looked at his own body
in the mirror. There was a long scar across his belly,
souvenir of a Saturday-night street brawl he had

broken up as a young policeman. He no longer had the athletic physique of his youth, but he was still fit. He wondered how long it would be before a woman touched his skin with hungry hands.

He put on pyjamas, but he did not feel sleepy. He decided to return to the living room and smoke another cigarette. He looked at Inge. She lay still with her eyes open. He would hear her if she moved. He generally knew when she needed something. She would simply stand up, and wait, as if she could not figure out what to do next; and he would have to guess what she wanted: a drink of water, the toilet, a shawl to keep her warm, or something more complicated. Occasionally she would move about the apartment, apparently at random, but she would soon come to a halt, perhaps at a window, or staring helplessly at a closed door, or just in the middle of the room.

He left the bedroom and crossed the little hallway to the living room, leaving both doors open. He found his cigarettes then, on impulse, took a half-empty bottle of aquavit from a cupboard and poured some into a glass. Sipping his drink and smoking, he thought about the week past.

It had started well and finished badly. He had begun by catching two spies, Ingemar Gammel and Poul Kirke. Better still, they were not like his usual targets, union organizers who intimidated strike-breakers, or Communists who sent coded letters to Moscow saying that Jutland was ripe for revolution.

No, Gammel and Kirke were real spies, and the sketches Tilde Jespersen had found in Kirke's office constituted important military intelligence.

Peter's star seemed in the ascendant. Some of his colleagues had begun to act coolly towards him, disapproving of his enthusiastic cooperation with the German occupiers, but they hardly mattered. General Braun had called him in to say that he thought Peter should be head of the security department. He did not say what would happen to Frederik Juel. But he had made it clear that the job was Peter's if he could wrap this case up.

It was a pity Poul Kirke had died. Alive, he might have revealed who his collaborators were, where his orders came from, and how he sent information to the British. Gammel was still alive, and had been handed over to the Gestapo for 'deep interrogation', but he had revealed nothing further, probably because he did not know any more.

Peter had pursued the investigation with his usual energy and determination. He had questioned Poul's commanding officer, the supercilious Squadron Leader Renthe. He had interviewed Poul's parents, his friends, and even his cousin Mads, and had got nothing from any of them. He had detectives tailing Poul's girlfriend, Karen Duchwitz, but so far she appeared to be no more than a hard-working student at the ballet school. Peter also had Poul's best friend, Arne Olufsen, under surveillance. Arne was the best prospect, for he could easily have drawn the sketches of the military base on Sande. But Arne had spent the week blamelessly going about his duties. Tonight, Friday, he had taken the train into Copenhagen, but there was nothing unusual about that.

After a brilliant start, the case seemed to have dead-ended.

The week's minor triumph had been the humiliation of Arne's brother, Harald. However, Peter felt sure Harald was not involved in espionage. A man who was risking his life as a spy did not daub silly slogans.

Peter was wondering where to go next with the investigation when there was a knock at the door.

He glanced at the clock on the mantelpiece. It was ten-thirty, not outrageously late but still an unusual time for an unexpected visit. The caller certainly could not be surprised to find him in pyjamas. He stepped into the hallway and opened the door. Tilde Jespersen stood there, a sky-blue beret perched on her fair curly hair.

'There's been a development,' she said. 'I thought we should discuss it.'

'Of course. Come in. You'll have to excuse my appearance.'

She glanced at the pattern on his pyjamas with a grin. 'Elephants,' she said as she walked into the living room. 'I wouldn't have guessed.'

He felt embarrassed and wished he had put on a robe, although it was too warm.

Tilde sat down. 'Where's Inge?'

'In bed. Would you like some aquavit?'

'Thank you.'

He got a fresh glass and poured for both of them.

She crossed her legs. Her knees were round and her calves plump, quite different from Inge's slender legs. She said: 'Arne Olufsen bought a ticket for tomorrow's ferry to Bornholm.'

Peter froze with the glass half way to his lips. 'Bornholm,' he said softly. The Danish holiday island was tantalizingly close to the Swedish coast. Could this be the break he was waiting for?

She took out a cigarette and he lit it. Blowing out smoke, she said: 'Of course, he might simply be due for some leave, and have decided to take a vacation . . .'

'Quite so. On the other hand, he may be planning to escape to Sweden.'

'That's what I thought.'

Peter swallowed his drink with a satisfying gulp. 'Who's with him now?'

'Dresler. He relieved me fifteen minutes ago. I came straight here.'

Peter forced himself to be sceptical. It was too easy, in an investigation, to let wishful thinking mislead you. 'Why would Olufsen want to leave the country?'

'He might have been scared by what happened to Poul Kirke.'

'He hasn't been acting scared. Until today he's been doing his job, apparently happily.'

'Maybe he's just noticed the surveillance.'

Peter nodded. 'They always do, sooner or later.'

'Alternatively, he might be going to Bornholm to spy. The British could have ordered him there.'

Peter made a doubtful face. 'What's on Bornholm?'

Tilde shrugged. 'Maybe that's the question they want answered. Or perhaps it's a rendezvous. Remember, if he can get from Bornholm to Sweden, the journey the other way is probably just as easy.'

'Good point.' Tilde was very clear-thinking, he reflected. She kept all possibilities in view. He looked at her intelligent face and clear blue eyes. He watched her mouth as she spoke.

She seemed unaware of his scrutiny. 'The death of Kirke probably broke their normal line of communication. This could be an emergency fall-back plan.'

'I'm not convinced – but there's only one way to find out.'

'Continue to shadow Olufsen?'

'Yes. Tell Dresler to get on the ferry with him.'

'Olufsen has a bicycle with him. Shall I tell Dresler to take one?'

'Yes. Then book yourself and me on tomorrow's flight to Bornholm. We'll get there first.'

Tilde stubbed out her cigarette and stood up. 'Right.'

Peter did not want her to go. The aquavit was warm in his belly, he felt relaxed, and he was enjoying having an attractive woman to talk to. But he could not think of an excuse to detain her.

He followed her into the hallway. She said: 'I'll see you at the airport.'

'Yes.' He put his hand on the doorknob but did not open it. 'Tilde . . .'

She looked at him with a neutral expression. 'Yes?'

'Thanks for this. Good work.'

She touched his cheek. 'Sleep well,' she said, but she did not move away.

He looked at her. The trace of a smile touched the corners of her mouth, but he could not tell whether it was inviting or mocking. He leaned forward, and suddenly he was kissing her.

She kissed him back with fierce passion. He was taken by surprise. She pulled his head to hers, thrust her tongue into his mouth. After a moment of shock he responded. He grabbed her soft breast and squeezed roughly. She made a noise deep in her throat, and thrust her hips against his body.

He saw a movement out of the corner of his eye. He broke the kiss and turned his head.

Inge stood in the bedroom doorway, like a ghost in her pale nightdress. Her face wore its perpetual blank expression, but she was looking straight at them. Peter heard himself make a sound like a sob.

Tilde slipped from his embrace. He turned to speak to her, but no words came. She opened the apartment door and stepped outside. She was gone in a breath.

The door slammed shut.

\* \* \*

The daily flight from Copenhagen to Bornholm was operated by the Danish airline, DDL. It departed at nine a.m. and took an hour. The plane landed at an airstrip a mile or so outside Bornholm's main town, Ronne. Peter and Tilde were met by the local police chief, who gave them the loan of a car as if entrusting them with royal jewels.

They drove into the town. It was a sleepy place, with more horses than cars. The half-timbered houses were painted in striking deep colours: dark mustard, terracotta pink, forest green, and rust red. Two German soldiers stood in the central square, smoking and chatting to passers-by. From the square, a cobbled street led downhill to the harbour. There was a Kriegsmarine torpedo boat in the dock, with a group of small boys clustered on the quayside staring at it. Peter located the ferry port, across from the brick custom house, the largest building in town.

Peter and Tilde drove around to familiarize themselves with the streets, then returned to the port in the afternoon to meet the ferry. Neither mentioned last night's kiss, but Peter was intensely aware of her physical presence: that elusive flowery perfume, her alert blue eyes, the mouth that had kissed him with such urgent passion. At the same time, he kept remembering Inge standing in the bedroom doorway, her expressionless white face a reproach more agonizing than any explicit accusation.

As the ship came into the harbour, Tilde said: 'I hope we're right, and Arne is a spy.'

'You haven't lost your enthusiasm for this work?'

Her reply was sharp. 'Whatever makes you say that?'

'Our discussion about Jews.'

'Oh, that.' She shrugged it off. 'You were right, weren't you? You proved it. We raided the synagogue and it led us to Gammel.'

'Then, I wondered if the death of Kirke might have been too gruesome . . .'

'My husband died,' she said crisply. 'I don't mind seeing criminals die.'

She was even tougher than he had thought. He hid a pleased smile. 'So you'll stay in the police.'

'I don't see any other future. Besides, I might be the first woman to get promotion to sergeant.'

Peter doubted that would ever happen. It would involve men taking orders from a woman, and that seemed beyond the bounds of possibility. But he did not say so. 'Braun virtually promised me promotion if I can round up this spy ring.'

'Promotion to what?'

'Head of the department. Juel's job.' And a man who was head of the security department at thirty could well end up chief of the entire Copenhagen police, he thought. His heart beat faster as he envisioned the crackdown he would impose, with the backing of the Nazis.

Tilde smiled warmly. Putting a hand on his arm, she said: 'Then we'd better make sure we catch them all.'

The ship docked and the passengers began to disembark. As they watched, Tilde said: 'You've known Arne since childhood – is he the type for espionage?'

'I'd have to say no,' Peter replied thoughtfully. 'He's too happy-go-lucky.'

'Oh.' Tilde looked glum.

'In fact, I might have dismissed him as a suspect, but for his English fiancée.'

She brightened. 'That puts him right in the frame.'

'I don't know whether they're still engaged. She went back to England hot-foot when the Germans came. But the possibility is enough.'

A hundred or so passengers got off, some on foot, a handful in cars, many with bicycles. The island was only twenty miles from end to end, and cycling was the easiest way to get around.

'There,' said Tilde, pointing.

Peter saw Arne Olufsen disembarking, wearing his army uniform, pushing his bicycle. 'But where's Dresler?'

'Four people behind.'

'I see him.' Peter put on sunglasses and pulled his hat low, then started the engine. Arne cycled up the cobbled street toward the town centre, and Dresler did the same. Peter and Tilde followed slowly in the car.

Arne headed out of town to the north. Peter began to feel conspicuous. There were few other cars on the roads, and he had to drive slowly to stay with the bikes. Soon he was obliged to fall behind and drop out of sight for fear of being noticed. After a few minutes, he speeded up until he caught sight of Dresler, then slowed again. Two German soldiers on a motorcycle with a sidecar passed them, and Peter wished he had borrowed a motorbike instead of a car.

A few miles out of town, they were the only people on the road. 'This is impossible,' Tilde said in a high, anxious voice. 'He's bound to spot us.'

Peter nodded. She was right, but now a new

thought occurred to him. 'And when he does, his reaction will be highly revealing.'

She gave him an inquiring look, but he did not explain.

He increased speed. Rounding a bend, he saw Dresler crouching in the woods at the side of the road and, a hundred yards ahead, Arne sitting on a wall, smoking a cigarette. Peter had no option but to drive past. He continued another mile then reversed down a farm track.

'Was he checking on us, or just taking a rest?' Tilde said.

Peter shrugged.

A few minutes later Arne cycled past, followed by Dresler. Peter pulled on to the road again.

The daylight was fading. Three miles farther on, they came to a crossroads. Dresler had stopped there and was looking perplexed.

There was no sign of Arne.

Dresler came up to the car window, looking distraught. 'I'm sorry, boss. He put on a burst of speed and got ahead of me. I lost sight of him, and I don't know which way he went at this crossroads.'

Tilde said: 'Hell. He must have planned it. He obviously knows the road.'

'I'm sorry,' Dresler said again.

Tilde said quietly: 'There goes your promotion – and mine.'

'Don't be so gloomy,' Peter said. 'This is good news.'

Tilde was bewildered. 'What do you mean?'

'If an innocent man thinks he's being followed, what does he do? He stops, turns around, and says: "Who the hell do you think you are, following me around?" Only a guilty man deliberately shakes off a surveillance team. Don't you see? This means we were right: Arne Olufsen is a spy.'

'But we've lost him.'

'Oh, don't worry. We'll find him again.'

\* \* \*

They spent the night at a seaside hotel with a bathroom at the end of each corridor. At midnight, Peter put a robe over his pyjamas and knocked on the door of Tilde's room. She called: 'Come in.'

He stepped inside. She was sitting up in the single bed, wearing a light blue silk nightdress, reading an American novel called *Gone with the Wind*. He said: 'You didn't ask who it was at the door.'

'I knew.'

His detective's mind noticed that she wore lipstick, her hair was carefully brushed, and the flowery perfume was in the air, as if she had dressed for a date. He kissed her lips, and she stroked the back of his head. After a moment he looked back to the door, to make sure he had closed it.

'She's not there,' Tilde said.

'Who?'

'Inge.'

He kissed her again, but after a few moments he realized he was not getting excited. He broke the kiss and sat on the edge of the bed.

'It's the same for me,' Tilde said.

'What?'

'I keep thinking about Oskar.'

'He's dead.'

'Inge might as well be.'

He winced.

She said: 'I'm sorry. But it's true. I'm thinking about my husband, and you're thinking about your wife, and neither of them cares.'

'It wasn't like this last night, at my apartment.'

'We didn't give ourselves time to think then.'

This was ridiculous, he thought. In his youth he had been a confident seducer, able to persuade many women to yield to him, and leaving most of them well satisfied. Was he just out of practice?

He shrugged off his robe and slipped into bed beside her. She was warm and welcoming, and her round body under the nightdress was soft to his touch. She turned off the light. He kissed her, but he could not rekindle last night's passion.

They lay side by side in the dark. 'It's all right,' she said. 'You have to leave the past behind. It's difficult for you.'

He kissed her again, briefly, then he got up and returned to his own room.

# THIRTEEN

Harald's life was in ruins. All his plans were cancelled and he had no future. Yet, instead of agonizing over his fate, he was looking forward to renewing his acquaintance with Karen Duchwitz. He recalled her white skin and vivid red hair, and the way she walked across the room as if she were dancing, and nothing seemed as important as seeing her again.

Denmark was a small, pretty country, but at twenty miles per hour it seemed like the endless desert. Harald's peat-burning motorcycle took a day and a half to get from his home on Sande across the width of the country to Kirstenslot.

The bike's progress over the monotonous undulating landscape was further slowed by breakdowns. He suffered a puncture before he was thirty miles from home. Next, on the long bridge that linked the Jutland peninsula with the central island of Fyn, his chain broke. The Nimbus motorcycle originally had a shaft drive, but that was difficult to connect to a steam engine, so Harald had taken a chain and sprockets from an old lawn mower. Now he had to push the bike miles to a garage and have a new link inserted. By the time he had crossed Fyn, he had missed the last ferry to the main island of Zealand. He parked the bike, ate the food his mother had given him – three thick slices of ham and a slab of cake – and spent a chill night waiting on the dockside. When he relit the boiler the next morning, the safety valve had developed a leak, but he managed to plug it with chewing gum and sticking plaster.

He arrived at Kirstenslot late on Saturday afternoon. Although he was impatient to see Karen, he did not go immediately to the castle. He drove past the ruined monastery and the entrance to the castle grounds, passed through the village with its church and tavern and railway station, and found the farm he had visited with Tik. He was confident he could get a job here. It was the right time of year, and he was young and strong.

There was a large farmhouse in a neat yard. As he parked the bike, he was watched by two little girls – granddaughters, he imagined, of Farmer Nielsen, the white-haired man he had seen driving away from the church.

He found the farmer at the rear of the house, dressed in muddy corduroys and a collarless shirt, leaning on a fence and smoking a pipe. 'Good evening, Mr Nielsen,' he said.

'Hello, young man,' Nielsen said guardedly. 'What can I do for you?'

'My name is Harald Olufsen. I need a job, and Josef Duchwitz told me you hire summer labourers.'

'Not this year, son.'

Harald was dismayed. He had not even considered the possibility of refusal. 'I'm a hard worker—'

'I don't doubt it, and you look strong enough, but I'm not hiring.'

'Why not?'

Nielsen raised an eyebrow. 'I might say it's none of your business, my lad, but I was a brash young man myself, once, so I'll tell you that times are hard, the Germans buy most of what I produce at a price decided by them, and there's no cash to pay casual labourers.'

'I'll work for food,' Harald said desperately. He could not return to Sande.

Nielsen gave him a penetrating look. 'You sound as if you're in some kind of trouble. But I can't hire you on those terms. I'd have trouble with the union.'

It seemed hopeless. Harald cast about for an alternative. He might find work in Copenhagen, but then where would he live? He could not even go to his brother, who lived on a military base where overnight guests were not permitted.

Nielsen saw his distress and said: 'Sorry, son.' He knocked his pipe out against the top rail of the fence. 'Come on, I'll see you off the premises.'

The farmer probably thought he was desperate enough to steal, Harald thought. The two of them walked around the house to the front yard.

'What the hell's that?' said Nielsen when he saw the bike, with its boiler gently puffing steam.

'It's just an ordinary motorcycle, but I've rigged it to run on peat.'

'How far have you come on it?'

'From Morlunde.'

'Good God! It looks ready to blow up any minute.'

Harald felt offended. 'It's perfectly safe,' he said indignantly. 'I know about engines. In fact, I mended one of your tractors, a few weeks ago.' For a moment, Harald wondered whether Nielsen might hire him out of gratitude, but then he told himself not to be foolish. Gratitude would not pay wages. 'You had a leak in the fuel supply.'

Nielsen frowned. 'What do you mean?'

Harald threw another slab of peat into the firebox. 'I was staying at Kirstenslot for the weekend. Josef and I came across one of your men, Frederik, trying to start a tractor.'

'I remember. So you're that lad?'

'Yes.' He climbed on the bike.

'Wait a minute. Maybe I can hire you.'

Harald looked at him, hardly daring to hope.

'I can't afford labourers, but a mechanic is a different matter. Do you know about all kinds of machinery?'

This was no time for modesty, Harald decided. 'I can usually fix anything with an engine.'

'I've got half a dozen machines lying idle for lack of spares. Do you think you could make them work?'

'Yes.'

Nielsen looked at the motorcycle. 'If you can do this, maybe you can repair my seed drill.'

'I don't see why not.'

'All right,' the farmer said decisively. 'I'll give you a trial.'

'Thank you, Mr Nielsen!'

'Tomorrow's Sunday, so come here on Monday morning at six o'clock. We farmers start early.'

'I'll be here.'

'Don't be late.'

Harald opened the regulator to let steam into the cylinder and drove off before Nielsen could change his mind.

As soon as he was out of earshot, he let out a triumphant yell. He had a job – one much more interesting than serving customers in a haberdashery – and he had done it himself. He felt full of confidence. He was on his own, but he was young and strong and smart. He was going to be all right.

Daylight was fading as he drove back through the village. He almost failed to see a man in police uniform who stepped into the road and waved him down. He braked hard at the last minute, and the boiler sighed a cloud of steam through the safety valve. He recognized the policeman as Per Hansen, the local Nazi.

'What the hell is this?' Hansen said, pointing to the bike.

'It's a Nimbus motorcycle, converted to steam power,' Harald told him.

'It looks dangerous to me.'

Harald had little patience with this kind of officious busybody, but he forced himself to answer politely. 'I assure you, officer, it's perfectly safe. Are you making official inquiries, or just indulging your curiosity?'

'Never mind the cheek, lad. I've seen you before, haven't I?'

Harald told himself not to get on the wrong side of the law. He had already spent one night in jail this week. 'My name is Harald Olufsen.'

'You're a friend of the Jews at the castle.'

Harald lost his temper. 'It's none of your damn business who my friends are.'

'Oho! Is it not?' Hansen looked satisfied, as if he had the result he wanted. 'I've got the measure of you, young man,' he said maliciously. 'I shall keep a close eye on you. Off you go, now.'

Harald pulled away. He cursed his short temper. He had now made an enemy of the local policeman, just because of a throwaway remark about Jews. When would he learn to keep out of trouble?

A quarter of a mile from the gates of Kirstenslot, he turned off the road on to the cart track that led through the wood to the back of the monastery. He could not be seen from the house, and he was betting no one would be working in the garden on a Saturday evening.

He stopped the bike at the west front of the disused church, then walked through the cloisters and entered the church by a side door. At first he could see only ghostly shapes in the dim evening light coming through the high windows. As his eyesight adjusted, he made out the long Rolls-Royce car under its tarpaulin, the boxes of old toys, and the Hornet Moth biplane with its folded wings. He had the feeling that no one had entered the church since last time he was here.

He opened the large main door, drove his bike inside, and closed the door.

He permitted himself a moment of satisfaction as he shut down the steam engine. He had crossed the country on his improvised motorcycle, got himself a job, and found a place to stay. Unless he was unlucky, his father could not find out where he was; but if there should be any important family news, his brother knew how to get in touch with him. Best of all, there was a good chance he would see Karen Duchwitz. He recalled that she liked to smoke a cigarette on the terrace after dinner. He decided to go and look out for her. It was risky – he might be seen by Mr Duchwitz – but he felt lucky today.

In a corner of the church, next to the workbench and tool rack, was a sink with a cold water tap. Harald had not washed for two days. He stripped off his shirt and got cleaned up as best he could without soap. He rinsed out the shirt, hung it on a nail to dry, and put on the spare one from his bag.

An arrow-straight drive half a mile long led from the main gates to the castle, but it was too exposed, and Harald took a roundabout route to approach the place through the wood. He passed the stables, crossed the kitchen garden, and studied the back of the house from the shelter of a cedar tree. He was able to identify the drawing room by its French windows, which were open to the terrace. Next to it was the dining room, he recalled. The blackout curtains were not yet drawn, for the electric lights had not yet been switched on, although he saw the flicker of a candle.

He guessed the family was having dinner. Tik would be at school – Jansborg boys were allowed home once a fortnight, and this was a school weekend – so the dinner party would consist of Karen and her parents, unless there were guests. He decided to risk a closer look.

He crossed the lawn and crept up to the house. He heard the sound of a BBC announcer saying that Vichy French forces had abandoned Damascus to an army of British, Commonwealth and Free French. It made a pleasant change to hear of a British victory, but he found it hard to see how good news from Syria was going to help his cousin Monika in Hamburg. Peeping in through the dining room window, he saw that dinner was over, and a maid was clearing the table.

A moment later, a voice behind him said: 'What do you think you're doing?'

He spun around.

Karen was walking along the terrace towards him. Her pale skin was luminous in the evening light. She wore a long silk dress in a watery shade of blue-green. Her dancer's carriage made it seem as if she were gliding. She looked like a ghost.

'Hush!' he said.

She did not recognize him in the fading light. 'Hush?' she said indignantly. There was nothing ghostly about her challenging tone. 'I find an intruder peering through a window into my house and he tells me to *hush*?' There was a bark from inside.

Harald could not decide whether Karen was genuinely outraged or just amused. 'I don't want your father to know I'm here!' he said in a low, urgent voice.

'You should worry about the police, not my father.'

The old red setter, Thor, came bounding out, ready to savage a burglar, but he recognized Harald and licked his hand.

'I'm Harald Olufsen, I was here two weeks ago.'

'Oh – the boogie-woogie boy! What are you doing skulking on the terrace? Have you come back to rob the place?'

To Harald's dismay, Mr Duchwitz came to the French window and looked out. 'Karen?' he said. 'Is someone there?'

Harald held his breath. If Karen betrayed him now, she could spoil everything.

After a moment, she said: 'It's all right, Daddy – just a friend.'

Mr Duchwitz peered at Harald in the gloom, but did not seem to recognize him, and after a moment he grunted and went back inside.

'Thanks,' Harald breathed.

Karen sat on a low wall and lit a cigarette. 'You're welcome, but you have to tell me what this is all about.' The dress matched her green eyes, which shone out of her face as if lit from within.

He sat on the wall facing her. 'I quarrelled with my father and left home.'

'Why did you come here?'

Karen herself was half the reason, but he decided not to say so. 'I've got a job with Farmer Nielsen, repairing his tractors and machines.'

'You are enterprising. Where are you living?'

'Um . . . in the old monastery.'

'Presumptuous, too.'

'I know.'

'I assume you brought blankets and things.'

'Actually, no.'

'It may be chilly at night.'

'I'll survive.'

'Hmm.' She smoked in silence for a while, watching darkness fall like a mist over the garden. Harald studied her, mesmerized by the twilight on the shapes of her face, the wide mouth and the slightly crooked nose and the mass of wiry hair that somehow combined to be bewitchingly lovely. He watched her full lips as she blew out smoke. Eventually she threw her cigarette into a flower bed, stood up, and said: 'Well, good luck.' Then she went back into the house and closed the French window behind her.

That was abrupt, Harald thought. He felt deflated. He stayed where he was for a minute. He would have been happy to talk to her all night, but she had got bored with him in five minutes. He remembered, now, that she had made him feel alternately welcomed and rejected during his weekend visit. Perhaps it was a game she played. Or maybe it reflected her own vacillating feelings. He liked the thought that she might have feelings about him, even if they were unstable.

He walked back to the monastery. The night air was already cooling. Karen was right, it would be chilly. The church had a tiled floor that looked cold. He wished he had thought to bring a blanket from home.

He looked around for a bed. The starlight that came through the windows faintly illuminated the interior of the church. The east end had a curved wall that had once enclosed the altar. To one side, a broad ledge was incorporated into the wall. A tiled canopy stood over it, and Harald guessed it had once framed some object of veneration – a holy relic, a jewelled chalice, a painting of the Virgin. Now, however, it looked more like a bed than anything else he could see, and he lay down on the ledge.

Through a glassless window he could see the tops of trees and a scatter of stars against a midnight-blue sky. He thought about Karen. He imagined her touching his hair with a fond gesture, brushing his lips with hers, putting her arms around him and hugging him. These images were different from the scenes he had imagined with Birgit Claussen, the Morlunde girl he had dated at Easter. When Birgit starred in his fantasies, she was always taking off her brassiere, or rolling on a bed, or ripping his shirt in her haste to get at him. Karen played a subtler part, more loving than lustful, although there was always the promise of sex deep in her eyes.

He was cold. He got up. Maybe he could sleep in

the aeroplane. Fumbling in the dark, he found the door handle. But when he opened it he heard scuttling sounds, and recalled that mice had nested in the upholstery. He was not afraid of scuttling creatures, but he could not quite bring himself to bed down with them.

He considered the Rolls-Royce. He could curl up on the back seat. It would be roomier than the Hornet Moth. Taking the canvas cover off, in the dark, might take a while, but perhaps it would be worth it. He wondered if the car doors were locked.

He was fumbling with the cover, looking for some kind of fastening that he could undo, when he heard light footsteps. He froze. A moment later, the beam of an electric torch swept past the window. Did the Duchwitzes have a security patrol at night?

He looked through the door that led to the cloisters. The torch was approaching. He stood with his back to the wall, trying not to breathe. Then he heard a voice. 'Harald?'

His heart leaped with pleasure. 'Karen.'

'Where are you?'

'In the church.'

Her beam found him, then she pointed it upward to shed a general light. He saw that she was carrying a bundle. 'I brought you some blankets.'

He smiled. He would be grateful for the warmth, but he was even more happy that she cared. 'I was just thinking of sleeping in the car.'

'You're too tall.'

When he unfolded the blankets he found something inside.

'I thought you might be hungry,' she explained.

In the light of her torch he saw half a loaf of bread, a small basket of strawberries, and a length of sausage. There was also a flask. He unscrewed the lid and smelled fresh coffee.

He realized he was ravenous. He fell on the food, trying not to eat like a starved jackal. He heard a mew, and a cat came into the circle of light. It was the skinny black-and-white tom he had seen the first time he entered the church. He dropped a piece of sausage on the ground. The cat sniffed it, turned it over with a paw, then began to eat it daintily. 'What's the cat called?' Harald asked Karen.

'I don't think it has a name. It's a stray.'

At the back of its head it had a tuft of hair like a pyramid. 'I think I'll call him Pinetop,' Harald said. 'After my favourite pianist.'

'Good name.'

He ate everything. 'Boy, that was great. Thank you.'

'I should have brought more. When was the last time you ate?'

'Yesterday.'

'How did you get here?'

'Motorcycle.' He pointed across the church to where he had parked the bike. 'But it's slow, because it runs on peat, so I took two days to get here from Sande.'

'You're a determined character, Harald Olufsen.'

'Am I?' He was not sure whether this was a compliment.

'Yes. In fact, I've never met anyone quite like you.'

On balance, he thought this was good. 'Well, to tell the truth, I feel the same about you.'

'Oh, come on. The world is full of spoiled rich girls who want to be ballet dancers, but how many people have crossed Denmark on a peat-burning motorcycle?'

He laughed, pleased. They were quiet for a minute. 'I was very sorry about Poul,' Harald said eventually. 'It must have been a terrible shock for you.'

'It was completely devastating. I cried all day.'

'Were you very close?'

'We only had three dates, and I wasn't in love with him, but all the same it was dreadful.' Tears came to her eyes, and she sniffed and swallowed.

Harald was shamefully pleased to learn that she had not been in love with Poul. 'It's very sad,' he said, and felt hypocritical.

'I was heartbroken when my grandma died, but somehow this was worse. Gran was old and sick, but Poul was so full of energy and fun, so good-looking and fit.'

'Do you know how it happened?' Harald said tentatively.

'No – the army has been ridiculously secretive about it,' she said, her voice becoming angry. 'They just say he crashed his plane, and the details are classified.'

'Perhaps they're covering something up.'

'Such as what?' she said sharply.

Harald realized he could not tell her what he thought without revealing his own connection to the Resistance. 'Their own incompetence?' he improvised. 'Perhaps the aircraft wasn't properly serviced.'

'They couldn't use the excuse of military secrecy to hide something like that.'

'Of course they could. Who would know?'

'I don't believe our officers would be so dishonourable,' she said stiffly.

Harald realized he had offended her, as he had when he first met her – and in the same way, by being scornful about her credulity. 'I expect you're right,' he said hastily. That was insincere: he felt sure she was wrong. But he did not want to quarrel with her.

Karen stood up. 'I must get back before they lock up.' Her voice was cold.

'Thanks for the food and blankets – you're an angel of mercy.'

'Not my usual role,' she said, softening a little.

'Perhaps I'll see you tomorrow?'

'Maybe. Goodnight.'

'Goodnight.'

Then she was gone.

# FOURTEEN

Hermia slept badly. She had a dream in which she was talking to a Danish policeman. The conversation was amiable, though she was anxious not to give herself away; but she realized, after a while, that they were speaking English. The man continued to talk as if nothing had happened, while she trembled and waited for him to arrest her.

She woke up to find herself on a narrow bed in a lodging-house on the island of Bornholm. She was relieved to find that the conversation with the policeman had been a dream – but there was nothing unreal about the danger that faced her now that she had woken up. She was in occupied territory, carrying forged papers, pretending to be a secretary on vacation, and if she were found out, she would be hanged as a spy.

Back in Stockholm, she and Digby had again deceived their German followers with substitutes and, having shaken them off, had taken a train to the south coast. In the tiny fishing village of Kalvsby they had found a boatman willing to take her across the twenty miles or so of sea to Bornholm. She had said goodbye to Digby – who could not possibly pass for Danish –

and climbed aboard. He was going to London for a day to report to Churchill, but he would fly back immediately and be waiting for her on the jetty in Kalvsby when she returned – if she returned.

The fisherman had put her ashore, with her bicycle, on a lonely beach at dawn yesterday. The man had promised to return to the same spot four days later at the same hour. To make sure of him, Hermia had promised him double the fee for the return journey.

She had cycled to Hammershus, the ruined castle that was her rendezvous with Arne, and had waited there for him all day. He had not come.

She told herself not to be surprised. Arne had been working the previous day, and she guessed he had not been able to get away early enough to catch the evening ferry. He had probably taken the Saturday morning boat and arrived on Bornholm too late to reach Hammershus before dark. In those circumstances, he would find somewhere to spend the night, and come to the rendezvous first thing in the morning.

That was what she believed in her more cheerful moments. But at the back of her mind was the constant thought that he might have been arrested. It was useless to ask herself what he could have been arrested for, or to argue that he had not yet committed a crime, for that only led her to imagine fanciful scenarios in which he confided in a treacherous friend, or wrote everything in a diary, or confessed to a priest.

Late in the day, she had given up on Arne and

cycled to the nearest village. In summer many of the islanders offered bed and breakfast to tourists, and she found a place to stay without difficulty. She fell into bed anxious and hungry, and had bad dreams.

Getting dressed, she recalled the holiday she and Arne had spent on this island, registering at their hotel as Mr and Mrs Olufsen. That was when she had felt most intimate with him. He loved to gamble, and he would make bets with her for sexual favours: 'If the red boat gets into harbour first, you have to go around with no panties all day tomorrow, and if the blue boat wins, you can be on top tonight.' You can have anything you want, my love, she thought, if you just show up today.

She decided to have breakfast that morning before cycling back to Hammershus. She might be waiting all day again, and she did not want to faint from hunger. She dressed in the cheap new clothes she had bought in Stockholm – English clothes might have given her away – and went downstairs.

She felt nervous as she walked into the family dining room. It was more than a year since she had been in the habit of speaking Danish daily. After landing yesterday she had had only a few brief exchanges of words. Now she would have to make small talk.

There was one other guest in the room, a middle-aged man with a friendly smile who said: 'Good morning. I'm Sven Fromer.'

Hermia forced herself to relax. 'Agnes Ricks,' she said, using the name on her false papers. 'It's a beautiful day.' She had nothing to fear, she told herself. She spoke Danish with the accent of the metropolitan bourgeoisie, and Danes never knew she was English until she told them. She helped herself to porridge, poured cold milk over it, and began to eat. The tension she felt made it difficult for her to swallow.

Sven smiled at her and said: 'English style.'

She stared at him, appalled. How had he found her out so fast? 'What do you mean?'

'The way you eat porridge.'

He had his milk in a glass, and took sips from it between mouthfuls of porridge. That was how Danes ate porridge, she knew perfectly well. She cursed her carelessness and tried to bluff it out. 'I prefer it this way,' she said as casually as she could. 'The milk cools the porridge and you can eat it faster.'

'A girl in a hurry. Where are you from?'

'Copenhagen.'

'Me, too.'

Hermia did not want to get into a conversation about exactly where in Copenhagen they both lived. That could too easily lead her into more errors. Her safest plan would be to ask him questions. She had never met a man who did not like to talk about himself. 'Are you on holiday?'

'Unfortunately not. I'm a surveyor, working for the government. However, the job is done, and I don't have to be home until tomorrow, so I'm going to spend today driving around, and catch the overnight ferry this evening.'

'You have a car?'

'I need one for my work.'

The landlady brought bacon and black bread. When she had left the room, Sven said: 'If you're on your own, I'd be happy to take you around.'

'I'm engaged to be married,' Hermia said firmly.

He smiled ruefully. 'Your fiancé is a lucky man. I'd still be glad of your company.'

'Please don't be offended, but I want to be alone.'

'I quite understand. I hope you don't mind my asking.'

She gave him her most charming smile. 'On the contrary, I'm flattered.'

He poured himself another cup of ersatz coffee, and seemed inclined to linger. Hermia began to relax. So far she had aroused no suspicion.

Another guest came in, a man of about Hermia's age, neatly dressed in a suit. He bowed stiffly to them and spoke Danish with a German accent. 'Good morning. I am Helmut Mueller.'

Hermia's heart raced. 'Good morning,' she said. 'Agnes Ricks.'

Mueller turned expectantly to Sven, who stood up, pointedly ignoring the newcomer, and stalked out of the room.

Mueller sat down, looking hurt. 'Thank you for your courtesy,' he said to Hermia.

Hermia tried to behave normally. She pressed her hands together to stop their shaking. 'Where are you from, Herr Mueller?'

'I was born in Luebeck.'

She asked herself what a friendly Dane might say to a German by way of small talk. 'You speak our language well.'

'When I was a boy, my family came often here to Bornholm for holidays.'

He was not suspicious, Hermia saw, and she felt emboldened to ask a less superficial question. 'Tell me, do many people refuse to speak to you?'

'Such rudeness as our fellow guest has just displayed is unusual. In the present circumstances, Germans and Danes have to live together, and most Danes are polite.' He gave her a look of curiosity. 'But you must have observed this – unless you have from another country recently arrived.'

She realized she had made another slip. 'No, no,' she said hastily, covering up. 'I'm from Copenhagen where, as you say, we live together as best we can. I just wondered if things were different here on Bornholm.'

'No, much the same.'

All conversation was dangerous, she realized. She stood up. 'Well, I hope you enjoy your breakfast.'

'Thank you.'

'And have a pleasant day here in our country.'

'I wish you the same.'

She left the room, wondering if she had been too nice. Over-friendliness might arouse suspicion as easily as hostility. But he had shown no sign of mistrust.

As she was leaving on her bicycle, she saw Sven putting his luggage in his car. It was a slope-backed Volvo PV444, a popular Swedish car often seen in

Denmark. She saw that the rear seat had been removed to make room for his equipment, tripods and a theodolite and other gear, some in an assortment of leather cases, some wrapped in blankets for protection. 'I apologize for creating a scene,' he said. 'I didn't wish to be rude to you.'

'That's all right.' She could see that he was still angry. 'You obviously feel strongly.'

'I come from a military family. It's difficult for me to accept that we surrendered so quickly. I believe we should have fought. We should be fighting now!' He made a gesture of frustration, as if throwing something away. 'I shouldn't speak this way. I'm embarrassing you.'

She touched his arm. 'You have nothing to apologize for.'

'Thank you.'

She rode off.

* * *

Churchill was pacing the croquet lawn at Chequers, the official country residence of the British prime minister. He was writing a speech in his head: Digby knew the signs. His weekend guests were the American ambassador, John Winant, and the foreign secretary, Anthony Eden, with their wives; but none of them were to be seen. Digby sensed there was some crisis, but no one had told him what. Churchill's private secretary, Mr Colville, gestured towards the brooding premier. Digby approached Churchill across the smooth grass.

The prime minister lifted his bent head. 'Ah, Hoare,' he said. He stopped walking. 'Hitler has invaded the Soviet Union.'

'Christ!' said Digby Hoare. He wanted to sit down but there were no chairs. 'Christ!' he repeated. Yesterday, Hitler and Stalin had been allies, their friendship cemented by the Nazi–Soviet pact of 1939. Today they were at war. 'When did that happen?'

'This morning,' Churchill said grimly. 'General Dill has just been here to give me the details.' Sir John Dill was chief of the Imperial General Staff, therefore the most senior man in the military. 'Early intelligence estimates put the size of the invading army at three million men.'

'Three *million*?'

'They have attacked along a two-thousand-mile front. There is a northern group heading for Leningrad, a central one making for Moscow, and a southern force on its way to the Ukraine.'

Digby was dazed. 'Oh, my God. Is this the end, sir?'

Churchill drew on his cigar. 'It may be. Most people believe the Russians can't win. They will be slow to mobilize. With heavy air support from the Luftwaffe, Hitler's tanks could wipe out the Red Army in a few weeks.'

Digby had never seen his boss look so defeated. In the face of bad news Churchill normally became even more pugnacious, always wanting to respond to defeat by going on the attack. But today he looked worn down. 'Is there any hope?' Digby asked.

'Yes. If the Reds can survive until the end of

summer, it may be a different story. The Russian winter defeated Napoleon and it might yet undo Hitler. The next three or four months will be decisive.'

'What are you going to do?'

'I shall go on the BBC tonight at nine.'

'And say . . .?'

'That we must give whatever help we can to Russia and the Russian people.'

Digby raised his eyebrows. 'A hard thing for a passionate anti-Communist to propose.'

'My dear Hoare, if Hitler invaded Hell, I would at least make a favourable reference to the Devil in the House of Commons.'

Digby smiled, wondering whether that line was being considered for inclusion in tonight's speech. 'But is there any help we *can* give?'

'Stalin has asked me to step up the bombing campaign against Germany. He hopes it will force Hitler to bring aircraft home to defend the Fatherland. That would weaken the invading army and might give the Russians an even chance.'

'Are you going to do it?'

'I have no choice. I've ordered a bombing raid for the next full moon. It will be the largest air operation of the war so far, which means the largest in the history of mankind. There will be more than five hundred bombers, over half our entire strength.'

Digby wondered if his brother would be on the raid. 'But if they suffer the kind of losses we've been experiencing . . .'

'We will be crippled. That's why I've called you in. Do you have an answer for me?'

'Yesterday I infiltrated an agent into Denmark. Her orders are to get photographs of the radar installation on Sande. That will answer the question.'

'It had better. The bombing raid is scheduled in sixteen days' time. When do you hope to have the photographs in your hands?'

'Within a week.'

'Good,' Churchill said dismissively.

'Thank you, prime minister.' Digby turned away.

'Don't fail me,' said Churchill.

\* \* \*

Hammershus was on the northern tip of Bornholm. The castle stood on a hill that looked across the sea to Sweden, and had once guarded the island against invasion by its neighbour. Hermia wheeled her bicycle along the winding path up the rocky slopes, wondering if today would be as fruitless as yesterday. The sun was shining, and she was warm from the effort of cycling.

The castle had been built of mixed brick and stone. Solitary walls remained, their features forlornly suggestive of family life: large sooty fireplaces exposed to the sky, cold stone cellars for storing apples and ale, broken staircases that led nowhere, narrow windows through which thoughtful children must once have stared at the sea.

Hermia was early, and the place was deserted.

Judging by yesterday's experience, she would have it to herself for another hour or more. What would it be like if Arne did turn up today, she wondered as she pushed her bike through ruined archways and across grass-grown floors.

In Copenhagen before the invasion she and Arne had been a glamorous couple, the centre of a social set of young officers and pretty girls with government connections, always having parties and picnics, going dancing and playing sports, sailing and riding horses and driving to the beach. Now that those days were over, would she seem to Arne like part of his past? On the phone, he had said he still loved her – but he had not seen her for more than a year. Would he find her the same, or changed? Would he still like the smell of her hair and the taste of her mouth? She began to feel nervous.

She had spent all day yesterday looking at the ruins, and they held no more interest for her. She walked to the seaward side, leaned her bike against a low stone wall, and looked down at the beach far below.

A familiar voice said: 'Hello, Hermia.'

She whirled around and saw Arne walking towards her, smiling, his arms spread wide. He had been waiting behind a tower. Her nervousness vanished. She ran into his arms and hugged him hard enough to hurt.

'What's the matter?' he said. 'Why are you weeping?'

She realized she was crying, her chest heaving with

sobs, tears running down her face. 'I'm so happy,' she said.

He kissed her wet cheeks. She held his face in both hands, feeling his bones with her fingertips to prove to herself that he was real, this was not one of the imaginary reunion scenes she had dreamed so often. She nuzzled his neck, breathing in the smell of him, army soap and brilliantine and aeroplane fuel. There were no smells in her dreams.

She was overwhelmed by emotion, but the feeling slowly changed from excitement and happiness to something else. Their tender kisses turned searching and hungry, their gentle caresses became urgently demanding. When her knees felt weak she sank to the grass, pulling him down with her. She licked his neck, sucked his lip, and bit his earlobe. His erection pressed against her thigh. She fumbled with the buttons of his uniform trousers, opening the fly so that she could feel him properly. He pushed up the skirt of her dress and slid his hand beneath the elastic of her underwear. She suffered a moment of coy embarrassment at how wet she was, then it was forgotten in a wave of pleasure. Impatiently, she broke the embrace long enough to take off her panties and throw them aside, then pulled him on top of her. It occurred to her that they were in full view of any early tourists coming to see the ruins, but she did not care. She knew that later, when the madness had left her, she would shudder with horror at the risk she had taken, but she could not hold back. She gasped as he entered her, then clung to him with her arms and legs, pressing his belly to hers, his chest to her breasts, his face into her neck, insatiably hungry for the touch of his body. Then that, too, passed as she focused on a node of intense pleasure that began small and hot, like a distant star, and grew steadily, seeming to possess more and more of her body, until it exploded.

They lay still for a while. She enjoyed the weight of his body on her, the breathless feeling it gave her, his slow detumescence. Then a shadow fell on them. It was only a cloud passing over the sun, but it reminded her that the ruins were open to the public, and someone could come along at any time. 'Are we still alone?' she murmured.

He lifted his head and looked around. 'Yes.'

'We'd better get up before the tourists arrive.'

'OK.'

She grabbed him as he pulled away. 'One more kiss.'

He kissed her softly, then stood up.

She found her underpants and pulled them on quickly, then stood up and brushed grass off her dress. Now that she was decent the sense of urgency left her, and all the muscles of her body felt pleasantly lassitudinous, as they sometimes did when she lay in bed on Sunday morning, dozing and listening to church bells.

She leaned on the wall, looking at the sea, and Arne put his arm around her. It was hard to wrench her mind back to war, deception and secrecy.

'I'm working for British Intelligence,' she said abruptly.

He nodded. 'I was afraid of that.'

'Afraid? Why?'

'It means you're in even more danger than if you had come here just to see me.'

She was pleased that his first thought was of the peril to her. He really did love her. But she brought trouble. 'Now you're at risk, too, just because you're with me.'

'You'd better explain.'

She sat on the wall and gathered her thoughts. She had failed to think of a censored version of the story that included only what he absolutely had to know. No matter how she chopped it up, half the truth made no sense, so she had to tell him everything. She was going to ask him to risk his life, and he needed to know why.

She told him about the Nightwatchmen, the arrests at Kastrup aerodrome, the devastating rate of bomber losses, the radar installation on his home island of Sande, the *himmelbett* clue, and the involvement of Poul Kirke. As she talked, his face changed. The merriment went from his eyes, and his perennial smile was replaced by a look of anxiety. She wondered whether he would accept the mission.

If he were a coward, surely he would not have chosen to fly the flimsy wood-and-linen machines of the Army Aviation Troops? On the other hand, being a pilot was part of his dashing image. And he often put pleasure before work. It was one of the reasons she loved him: she was too serious, and he made her enjoy herself. Which was the real Arne – the hedonist or the airman? Until now he had never been put to the test.

'I've come to ask you to do what Poul would have done, if he had lived: go to Sande, get into the base, and examine the radar installation.'

Arne nodded, looking solemn.

'We need photographs, good ones.' She leaned across to her bicycle, opened the saddlebag, and took out a small 35mm camera, a German-made Leica IIIa. She had considered a miniature Minox Riga, which was easier to conceal, but in the end had preferred the precision of the Leica's lens. 'This is probably the most important job you'll ever be asked to do. When we understand their radar system, we will be able to devise ways to defeat it, and that will save the lives of thousands of airmen.'

'I can see that.'

'But if you're caught, you'll be executed – shot or hanged – for spying.' She held out the camera.

She half wanted him to refuse the mission, for she could hardly bear the thought of the danger he would be in if he accepted. But, if he refused, could she ever respect him?

He did not take the camera. 'Poul was the head of your Nightwatchmen.'

She nodded.

'I suppose most of our friends were in it.'

'Better that you don't know—'

'Just about everyone except me.'

She nodded. She feared what was coming.

'You think I'm a coward.'

'It didn't seem like your kind of thing—'

'Because I like parties, and I make jokes, and flirt with girls, you thought I didn't have the guts for secret work.' She said nothing, but he was insistent. 'Answer me.'

She nodded miserably.

'In that case, I'll have to prove you wrong.' He took the camera.

She did not know whether to be happy or sad. 'Thank you,' she said, fighting back tears. 'You'll be careful, won't you?'

'Yes. But there's a problem. I was followed to Bornholm.'

'Oh, hell.' This was something she had not anticipated. 'Are you sure?'

'Yes. I noticed a couple of people hanging around the base, a man and a young woman. She was on the train to Copenhagen with me, then he was on the ferry. When I got here, he followed me on a bicycle, and there was a car behind. I shook them off a few miles outside Ronne.'

'They must suspect you of working with Poul.'

'Ironically, as I wasn't.'

'Who do you think they are?'

'Danish police, acting under orders from the Germans.'

'Now that you've given them the slip, they undoubtedly feel sure you're guilty. They must still be looking for you.'

'They can't search every house in Bornholm.'

'No, but they'll have people watching the ferry port and the aerodrome.'

'I hadn't thought of that. So how am I going to get back to Copenhagen?'

He was not yet thinking like a spy, Hermia noted. 'We'll have to smuggle you on to the ferry somehow.'

'And then where would I go? I can't return to the flying school – it's the first place they'll look.'

'You'll have to stay with Jens Toksvig.'

Arne's face darkened. 'So he's one of the Nightwatchmen.'

'Yes. His address—'

'I know where he lives,' Arne snapped. 'He was my friend before he was a Nightwatchman.'

'He may be jumpy, because of what happened to Poul—'

'He won't turn me away.'

Hermia pretended not to notice Arne's anger. 'Let's assume you get tonight's ferry. How long will it take you to get to Sande?'

'First I'll talk to my brother, Harald. He worked as a labourer on the site when they were building the base, so he can give me the layout. Then you have to allow a full day to get to Jutland, because the trains are always delayed. I could get there late on Tuesday, sneak into the base on Wednesday, and return to

Copenhagen on Thursday. Then how do I get in touch with you?'

'Come back here next Friday. If the police are still watching the ferry, you'll have to find some way of disguising yourself. I'll meet you right here. We'll cross to Sweden with the fisherman who brought me. Then we'll get you false papers at the British legation and fly you to England.'

He nodded grimly.

She said: 'If this works out, we could be together again, and free, in a week's time.'

He smiled. 'It seems too much to hope for.'

He did love her, she decided, even though he was still feeling wounded at having been left out of the Nightwatchmen. And still, in her heart of hearts, she was not sure he had the nerve for this work. But she was undoubtedly going to find out.

While they had been talking, the first few tourists had arrived, and a handful of people were now strolling around the ruins, peering into cellars and touching the ancient stones. 'Let's get out of here,' Hermia said. 'Did you come on a bicycle?'

'It's behind that tower.'

Arne fetched his bike and they left the castle, Arne wearing sunglasses and a cap to make him hard to recognize. The disguise would not pass a careful check of passengers boarding a ferry, but might protect him if he chanced to meet his pursuers on the road.

Hermia considered the problem of escape as they freewheeled down the hillside. Could she devise a better disguise for Arne? She had no wigs or costumes, nor any make-up other than the minimal lipstick and powder she used herself. He had to look like a different person, and for that he needed professional help. He could surely find it in Copenhagen, but not here.

At the foot of the hill she spotted her fellow guest at the boarding house, Sven Fromer, getting out of his Volvo. She did not want him to see Arne, and she hoped to ride past without his noticing her, but she was unlucky. He caught her eye, waved, and stood expectantly beside the path. It would have been conspicuously rude to ignore him, so she felt obliged to stop.

'We meet again,' he said. 'This must be your fiancé.'

She was not in any danger from Sven, she told herself. There was nothing suspicious about what she was doing, and anyway Sven was anti-German. 'This is Oluf Arnesen,' she said, reversing Arne's name. 'Oluf, meet Sven Fromer. He stayed at the same place as me last night.'

The two men shook hands. Arne said conversationally: 'Have you been here long?'

'A week. I leave tonight.'

Hermia was struck by a thought. 'Sven,' she said. 'This morning you told me we should be fighting the Germans.'

'I talk too much. I ought to be more circumspect.'

'If I gave you a chance to help the British, would you take a risk?'

He stared at her. 'You?' he said. 'But how . . . Do you mean to say that you are—'

'Would you be willing?' she pressed him.

'This isn't some kind of trick, is it?'

'You'll have to trust me. Yes or no?'

'Yes,' he said. 'What do you want me to do?'

'Could a man hide in the back of your car?'

'Sure. I could conceal him behind my equipment. He wouldn't be comfortable, but there's room.'

'Would you be willing to smuggle someone on the ferry tonight?'

Sven looked at his car, then at Arne. 'You?'

Arne nodded.

Sven smiled. 'Hell, yes,' he said.

# FIFTEEN

Harald's first day working at the Nielsen farm was more successful than he had dared to hope. Old Nielsen had a small workshop with enough equipment for Harald to repair just about anything. He had patched the water pump on a steam plough, welded a hinge on a caterpillar track, and found the short circuit that caused the farmhouse lights to fuse every night. He had eaten a hearty lunch of herrings and potatoes with the farmhands.

In the evening he had spent a couple of hours at the village tavern with Karl, the farmer's youngest son – although he had drunk only two small glasses of beer, remembering what a fool he had made of himself with liquor a week before. Everyone was talking about Hitler's invasion of the Soviet Union. The news was bad. The Luftwaffe claimed to have destroyed 1,800 Soviet aircraft on the ground in lightning raids. In the tavern, everyone thought Moscow would fall before winter, except the local Communist, and even he seemed worried.

Harald left early because Karen had said she might see him after dinner. He felt weary but pleased with himself as he walked back to the old monastery. When he entered the ruined building, he was astonished to find his brother in the church, staring at the derelict aircraft. 'A Hornet Moth,' Arne said. 'The gentleman's aerial carriage.'

'It's a wreck,' Harald said.

'Not really. The undercarriage is a bit bent.'

'How do you think it happened?'

'On landing. The back end of a Hornet tends to swing out of control, because the main wheels are too far forward. But the axle tubes aren't designed to withstand sideways pressure, so when you swerve violently they can buckle.'

Arne looked terrible, Harald saw. Instead of his army uniform, he wore what seemed to be someone else's old clothes, a worn tweed jacket and faded corduroy trousers. He had shaved off his moustache, and a greasy cap covered his curly hair. In his hands he held a small, neat 35mm camera. There was a strained expression on his face instead of his usual insouciant smile. 'What happened to you?' Harald said anxiously.

'I'm in trouble. Have you got anything to eat?'

'Not a thing. We can go to the tavern—'

'I can't show my face. I'm a wanted man.' Arne tried a wry grin, but it finished up as a grimace. 'Every policeman in Denmark has my description, and there are posters of me all over Copenhagen. I was chased by a cop all along the Stroget and only just got away.'

'Are you in the Resistance?'

Arne hesitated, shrugged, then said: 'Yes.'

Harald was thrilled. He sat on the ledge he used as

a bed and Arne sat next to him. Pinetop the cat appeared and rubbed his head against Harald's leg. 'So you were working with them when I asked you, at home, three weeks ago?'

'No, not then. I was left out at first. Apparently they thought I wasn't suitable for secret work. By Christ, they were right. But now they're desperate, so I'm in it. I have to take pictures of some machinery at the military base on Sande.'

Harald nodded. 'I drew a sketch of it for Poul.'

'Even you were in it before me,' Arne said bitterly. 'Well, well.'

'Poul told me not to tell you.'

'Apparently everyone thought I was a coward.'

'I could redraw my sketches . . . although they were only from memory.'

Arne shook his head. 'They need accurate photos. I came to ask you if there's a way to sneak inside.'

Harald found this talk of espionage exciting, but it bothered him that Arne did not seem to have a well thought out plan. 'There's a place where the fence is concealed by trees, yes – but how are you going to get to Sande if the police are looking for you?'

'I've changed my appearance.'

'Not much. What papers are you carrying?'

'Only my own – how would I get any others?'

'So if you're stopped by the police for any reason, it will take them about ten seconds to establish that you're the man they're all looking for.'

'That's about it.'

Harald shook his head. 'It's crazy.'

'It has to be done. This equipment enables the Germans to detect bombers when they're still miles away – in time to scramble their fighters.'

'It must use radio waves,' Harald said excitedly.

'The British have a similar system, but the Germans seem to have refined it, and they're shooting down as many as half the aircraft on a raid. The RAF is desperate to figure out how they're doing it. It's worth risking my life.'

'Not pointlessly. If you're caught, you won't be able to pass the information to the British.'

'I have to try.'

Harald took a deep breath. 'Why don't I go?'

'I knew you were going to say that.'

'No one's looking for me. I know the site. I've already been over the fence – I took a short cut one night. And I know more about radio than you, so I'll have a better idea of what to photograph.' Harald thought the logic of his argument irresistible.

'If you're caught, you'll be shot as a spy.'

'Same applies to you – only you're virtually certain to be caught, whereas I'll probably get away with it.'

'The police may have found your sketches when they came for Poul. If so, the Germans must know that someone's interested in the base on Sande, and they will have improved their security as a result. Getting over the fence may not be as easy as it was.'

'I still have a better chance than you.'

'I can't send you into danger. What if you're caught – what will I say to Mother?'

'You'll say that I died fighting for freedom. I've as

much right as you to take the risk. Give me the damn camera.'

Before Arne could reply, Karen came in.

She walked softly and appeared without warning, so Arne had no chance to hide, although reflexively he made a move to get up, then stopped himself.

'Who are you?' Karen said with her customary directness. 'Oh! Hello, Arne. You've shaved off your moustache – I suppose that's because of all the posters I saw in Copenhagen today. Why are you an outlaw?' She sat on the covered bonnet of the Rolls-Royce, crossing her long legs like a fashion model.

Arne hesitated, then said: 'I can't tell you.'

Karen's mind raced ahead, drawing inferences with impressive speed. 'My God, you're in the Resistance! Was Poul in it too? Is that why he died?'

Arne nodded. 'He didn't crash his aircraft. He was trying to escape from the police, and they shot at him.'

'Poor Poul.' She looked away for a moment. 'So you've taken up where he left off. But now the police are on to you. Someone must be sheltering you – probably Jens Toksvig, he was Poul's closest friend after you.'

Arne shrugged and nodded.

'But you can't move around without risking arrest, so . . .' She looked at Harald, and her voice went quiet. 'You're in it now, Harald.'

To Harald's surprise, she looked concerned, as if she were afraid for him. He was pleased that she cared.

He looked at Arne. 'Well? Am I in it?'

Arne sighed and gave him the camera.

\*   \*   \*

Harald arrived in Morlunde late the following day. He left the steam bike in a car park next to the ferry dock, feeling it would be too conspicuous on Sande. He had nothing with which to cover it, and no way of locking it, but he trusted that a casual thief would be unable to figure out how to make it go.

He was in time for the last ferry of the day. As he waited on the dockside, the evening slowly dimmed, and stars appeared like the lights of distant ships on a dark sea. A drunk islander came staggering along the quay, peered rudely at Harald, muttered: 'Ah, young Olufsen,' then sat on a capstan some distance away and tried to light a pipe.

The boat docked and a handful of people got off. To Harald's surprise, a Danish policeman and a German soldier stood at the head of the gangway. As the drunk boarded, they checked his identity card. Harald's heartbeat seemed to falter. He hesitated, scared, unsure whether to board. Had they simply stepped up security after finding his sketches, as Arne had forecast? Or were they looking for Arne himself? Would they know Harald was the brother of the wanted man? Olufsen was a common name – but they might have been briefed on the family. He had an expensive camera in his satchel. It was a popular German make, but all the same it could arouse suspicion.

He tried to calm his mind and consider his options. There were other ways of getting to Sande. He was not sure he could swim two miles in the open sea, but he might be able to borrow or steal a small boat. However, if he were seen beaching the boat on Sande he would be sure to be questioned. He might do better to act innocent.

He boarded the ferry.

The policeman asked him: 'What is your reason for wanting to travel to Sande?'

Harald suppressed his indignation that anyone should presume to ask such a question. 'I live there,' he said. 'With my parents.'

The policeman looked at his face. 'I don't remember seeing you before, and I've been doing this for four days.'

'I've been away at school.'

'Tuesday is a strange day to come home.'

'It's the end of term.'

The policeman grunted, apparently satisfied. He checked the address on Harald's card and showed it to the soldier, who nodded and let Harald on board.

He went to the far end of the boat and stood looking out to sea, waiting for his heart to stop racing. He was relieved to have passed the checkpoint, but furious that he had to justify himself to a policeman when moving around his own country. It seemed a silly reaction, when he thought about it logically, but he could not help feeling outraged.

At midnight the boat left the dock.

There was no moon. In the starlight, the flat island

of Sande was a dark swell like another wave on the horizon. Harald had not expected to return so soon. In fact, when he left on Friday he had wondered if he would ever see the place again. Now he was back as a spy, with a camera in his bag and a mission to photograph the Nazis' secret weapon. He vaguely recalled thinking what a thrill it would be to become part of the Resistance. In reality, it was no fun at all. On the contrary, he was sick with fear.

He felt worse as he disembarked on the familiar quay and looked across the road to the post office and the grocery store that had not changed since he could remember. His life had been secure and stable for the first eighteen years. Now he felt he would never be safe again.

He made his way to the beach and began to tramp south. The wet sand gleamed silver in the starlight. He heard a girlish giggle from an unseen source in the dunes, and he felt a pang of jealousy. Would he ever make Karen giggle like that?

It was near dawn when he came within sight of the base. He could make out the fence posts. The trees and bushes inside the site showed as dark patches on the dunes. If he could see, so could the guards, he realized. He dropped to his knees and began to crawl forward.

A minute later he was glad of his caution. He spotted two guards patrolling inside the fence, side by side, with a dog.

That was new. They had not patrolled in pairs before, and there had been no dogs.

He dropped flat. The two men did not seem especially alert. They were strolling, not marching. The one holding the dog was talking animatedly while the other smoked. As they came nearer, Harald could hear the voice over the sound of the waves breaking on the beach. He had learned German in school, like all Danish children. The man was telling a boastful story about a woman called Margareta.

Harald was fifty yards from the fence. As the guards approached the nearest point to him, the dog sniffed the air. It could probably smell Harald, but did not know where he was. It barked uncertainly. The guard holding the lead was not as well trained as the dog, and he told the animal to shut up, then carried on explaining how he got Margareta to meet him in the wood shed. Harald lay completely still. The dog barked again, and one of the guards turned on a powerful flashlight. Harald hid his face in the sand. The beam of the torch played along the dunes but passed over him without stopping.

The guard said: 'Then she said all right, but you'll have to pull it out at the last minute.' They walked on, and the dog became quiet again.

Harald lay still until they were out of sight. Then he turned inland and approached the section of the fence that was concealed by vegetation. He feared the soldiers might have cut down the trees, but the copse was still there. He crawled through the bushes, reached the fence, and stood up.

He hesitated. He could back out at this point, and he would have broken no law. He could return to

Kirstenslot and concentrate on his new job, spending his evenings in the tavern and his nights dreaming of Karen. He could take the attitude that war and politics were none of his concern, as many Danes did. But even as he contemplated that line, he was revolted. He imagined himself explaining his decision to Arne and Karen, or Uncle Joachim and cousin Monika, and he felt ashamed just for thinking about it.

The fence was unchanged, six feet of chicken wire topped by two strands of barbed wire. Harald swung his satchel around to his back, to keep it out of the way, then climbed the fence, stepped gingerly over the barbed wire, and jumped down the other side.

Now he was committed. He was inside a military base with a camera. If they caught him, they would kill him.

He walked quickly forward, treading softly, keeping close to bushes and trees, looking around constantly. He passed the searchlight tower, and thought with trepidation how utterly exposed he would be if someone decided to switch on the powerful beams. He listened hard for patrolling footsteps, but heard only the constant hushing urged by the waves. After a few minutes he descended a gentle slope and entered a stand of conifers which provided him with good cover. He wondered for a moment why the soldiers had not thought of chopping down the trees, for better security, then he realized that they served to conceal the secret radio equipment from prying eyes.

A moment later he reached his destination. Now that he knew what he was looking for, he could see quite clearly the circular wall and the big rectangular grid rising from its hollow core, the aerial slowly rotating, like a mechanical eye scanning the dark horizon. He heard again the low hum of the electric motor. On either side of the structure he could make out the two smaller shapes, and now in the starlight he saw that they were miniature versions of the big rotating aerial.

So there were three machines. He wondered why. Might that somehow explain the remarkable superiority of German radar? Looking more closely at the smaller aerials, he thought they were constructed differently. He would need to look again in daylight, but it seemed to him they might tilt as well as rotate. Why would that be? He must make sure to get good photographs of all three pieces of apparatus.

The first time he was here, he had jumped over the circular wall in a fright, after hearing a guard cough nearby. Now that he had time to think, he felt sure there must be an easier way in. The walls were needed to protect the equipment from accidental damage, but engineers surely needed to get inside for maintenance. He walked around the circle, peering at the brickwork in the dim light, and came across a wooden door. It was not locked, and he passed through, quietly closing it behind him.

He felt a little safer. No one could see him from outside. Engineers would not do maintenance at this time of night except in an emergency. If someone did come in, he might just have time to leap over the wall before he was spotted.

He looked up at the great revolving grid. It must pick up radio beams reflected off aircraft, he guessed. The aerial must act like a lens, focusing the signals received. The cable protruding from the base carried the data back to the new buildings Harald had helped to construct last summer. There, presumably, monitors displayed the results, and operators stood ready to alert the Luftwaffe.

In the half dark, with the humming machinery looming over him and the ozone smell of electricity in his nostrils, he felt he was inside the beating heart of the war machine. The struggle between the scientists and engineers on both sides could be as important as the battlefield clash of tanks and machine guns. And he had become part of it.

He heard an aircraft. There was no moon, so it was not likely to be a bomber. It might be a German fighter on a local flight, or a civilian transport that had got lost. He wondered if the big aerial had detected its approach an hour ago. He wondered whether the smaller aerials were pointed at it. He decided to step outside and take a look.

One of the smaller aerials faced the sea, in the direction from which the aircraft was approaching. The other pointed inland. Both were tilted at angles different from previously, he thought. As the aircraft roared closer, he noticed the first aerial tilt more, as if following it. The other continued to move, though in response to what he could not figure.

The aircraft crossed Sande and headed inland, the aerial dish continuing to follow it until after its sound died away to nothing. Harald returned to his hiding place inside the circular wall, musing on what he had seen.

The sky was turning from black to grey. At this time of year, dawn broke before three o'clock. In another hour, the sun would rise.

He took the camera out of his satchel. Arne had shown him how to use it. As daylight strengthened, he moved quietly around inside the wall, figuring out the best angles for photographs that would reveal every detail of the machinery.

He and Arne had agreed he would take the shots at about a quarter to five. The sun would be up, but it would not be shining over the wall into the installation. Sunshine was not necessary – the film in the camera was sensitive enough to record details without it.

As time went by, Harald's thoughts turned anxiously to escape. He had arrived at night, and entered the base cloaked by darkness, but he could not wait until tomorrow night before leaving. It was almost certain that an engineer would routinely inspect the equipment at least once during the course of a day, even if nothing went wrong. So Harald had to get away as soon as he had taken the photos – when it would be full daylight. His departure would be a lot more dangerous than his arrival.

He considered which way to go. To the south of where he was, in the direction of his parents' home, the fence was only a couple of hundred yards away, but the route lay across open dunes without trees or bushes. Going north, retracing his steps, under cover of vegetation much of the way, would take longer but might be safer.

He wondered how he would face a firing squad. Would he be calm and proud, keeping his terror under control, or would he break and turn into a gibbering fool, pleading for mercy and wetting himself?

He forced himself to wait calmly. The light grew stronger and the minute hand crawled around the face of his watch. He heard no new sounds from outside. A soldier's day started early, but he was hoping there would not be much activity before six o'clock – by which time he would be gone.

At last it was time to take the pictures. The sky was cloudless and there was a clear morning light. He could see every rivet and terminal of the complex piece of machinery in front of him. Focusing the lens carefully, he photographed the revolving base of the apparatus, the cables, and the grid of the aerial. He unfolded a yard rule from the monastery tool rack and placed it in some of the pictures to show scale – his own bright idea.

Next he had to go outside the wall.

He hesitated. In here he felt safe. But he had to have pictures of the two smaller aerials.

He cracked the door. All was still. He could tell, by the sound of the surf, that the tide was coming in. The base was bathed in the watery light of a seaside morning. There was no sign of life. It was the hour when men sleep heavily, and even dogs have dreams.

He took careful shots of the two smaller aerials, which were protected only by low walls. Thinking about their function, he realized that one of them had been tracking an aircraft that was within visual range. The whole point of this apparatus was to detect bombers *before* they came in sight, he had thought. Presumably the second small aerial was tracking another aircraft.

Snapping photographs, he turned the puzzle over in his mind. How could three devices work together to increase the kill rate of Luftwaffe fighters? Perhaps the large aerial gave advance warning of a bomber's approach and the smaller one tracked the bomber within German air space. But then what did the second smaller aerial do?

It occurred to him that there would be another aircraft in the sky – the fighter that had been scrambled to attack the bomber. Could the second aerial be used by the Luftwaffe to track *their own aircraft?* It seemed crazy, but as he stepped back to photograph the three aerials together, showing their placement relative to one another, he realized it made perfect sense. If a Luftwaffe controller knew the positions of the bomber and the fighter, he could direct the fighter by radio until it made contact with the bomber.

He began to see how the Luftwaffe might be working. The large aerial gave advance warning of a raid so that the fighters could be scrambled in time. One of the smaller aerials picked up a bomber as it came closer. The other tracked a fighter, enabling the controller to direct the pilot precisely to the bomber's location. After that, it was like shooting fish in a barrel.

That thought made Harald realize how exposed he was: standing upright, in full daylight, in the middle of a military base, photographing top secret equipment. Panic surged through his veins like poison. He tried to calm himself and take the last few photos he had planned, showing the three aerials from different angles, but he was too terrified. He had taken at least twenty shots. It must be enough, he told himself.

He thrust the camera into his satchel and started walking quickly away. Forgetting his resolution to take the longer but safer route north, he headed south, across the open dunes. In that direction the fence was visible, just beyond the old boathouse he had bumped into last time. Today he would pass it on the seaward side, and it would hide him from sight for a few paces.

As he approached it, a dog barked.

He looked around wildly but saw no soldiers and no dog. Then he realized the sound had come from the boathouse. The soldiers must be using the derelict building as a kennel. A second dog joined the barking.

Harald broke into a run.

The dogs excited one another, more joined in, and the noise became hysterically loud. Harald reached the building then turned seaward, trying to keep the boathouse between himself and the main buildings while he sprinted for the fence. Fear gave him speed. Every second he expected a shot to ring out.

He reached the fence, not knowing whether he had

been seen or not. He climbed it like a monkey and vaulted over the barbed wire at the top. He came down hard on the other side, splashing in shallow water. He scrambled to his feet and glanced back through the fence. Beyond the boathouse, partly obscured by trees and bushes, he could see the main buildings, but no soldiers were in view. He turned away and ran. He stayed in the shallow water for a hundred yards, so that the dogs could not follow his scent, then he turned inland. He left shallow footprints in the hard sand, but he knew the fast-moving tide would cover them in a minute or two. He reached the dunes, where he left no visible trace.

A few minutes later he came to the dirt road. He glanced back and saw no one following. Breathing hard, he headed for the parsonage. He ran past the church to the kitchen door.

It was open. His parents were always up early.

He stepped inside. His mother was at the stove, wearing a dressing gown, making tea. When she saw him she gave a cry of shock and dropped the earthenware teapot. It hit the tiled floor and the spout broke off. Harald picked up the two pieces. 'I'm sorry to startle you,' he said.

'Harald!'

He kissed her cheek and hugged her. 'Is my father at home?'

'In the church. There wasn't time to tidy up last night, so he's gone to straighten the chairs.'

'What happened last night?' There was no service on a Monday evening.

'The board of deacons met to discuss your case. They're going to read you out next Sunday.'

'The revenge of the Flemmings.' Harald found it strange that he had once thought that sort of thing important.

By now, guards would have gone to find out what had disturbed the dogs. If they were thorough, they might check nearby houses, and look for a fugitive in sheds and barns. 'Mother,' he said, 'if the soldiers come here, will you tell them I've been in bed all night?'

'Whatever has happened?' she said fearfully.

'I'll explain later.' It would be more natural if he were in bed, he thought. 'Tell them I'm still asleep – will you?'

'All right.'

He left the kitchen and went upstairs to his bedroom. He slung his satchel over the back of the chair. He took the camera out and put it in a drawer. He thought of hiding it, but there was no time, and a hidden camera was proof of guilt. He shed his clothes quickly, put on his pyjamas, and got into bed.

He heard his father's voice in the kitchen. He got out of bed and went to the top of the stairs to listen.

'What's he doing here?' the pastor said.

His mother replied: 'Hiding from the soldiers.'

'For goodness' sake, what has the boy got himself into now?'

'I don't know, but—'

His mother was interrupted by a loud knocking. A young man's voice said in German: 'Good morning.

We're looking for someone. Have you seen a stranger at any time in the last few hours?'

'No, nobody at all.' The nervousness in his mother's voice was so evident that the soldier must have noticed it – but perhaps he was used to people being frightened of him.

'How about you, sir?'

His father said firmly: 'No.'

'Is there anyone else here?'

Harald's mother replied: 'My son. He's still asleep.'

'I need to search the house.' The voice was polite, but it was making a statement, not asking permission.

'I'll show you around,' said the pastor.

Harald returned to his bed, heart thudding. He heard booted footsteps on the tiled floors downstairs, and doors opening and closing. Then the boots came up the wooden staircase. They entered his parents' bedroom, then Arne's old room and finally approached Harald's. He heard the handle of his door turn.

He closed his eyes, feigning sleep, and tried to make his breathing slow and even.

The German voice said quietly: 'Your son.'

'Yes.'

There was a pause.

'Has he been here all night?'

Harald held his breath. He had never known his father to tell even a white lie.

Then he heard: 'Yes. All night.'

He was flabbergasted. His father had lied for him. The hard-hearted, stiff-necked, self-righteous old tyrant had broken his own rules. He was human after all. Harald felt tears behind his closed eyelids.

The boots receded along the passage and down the stairs, and Harald heard the soldier take his leave. He got out of bed and went to the top of the stairs.

'You can come down now,' his father said. 'He's gone.'

He went down. His father looked solemn. 'Thank you for that, Father,' Harald said.

'I committed a sin,' his father said. For a moment, Harald thought he was going to be angry. Then the old face softened. 'However, I believe in a forgiving God.'

Harald realized the agony of conflict his father had been through in the last few minutes, but he did not know how to say that he understood. The only thing he could think of was to shake hands. He held out his hand.

His father looked at it, then took it. He drew Harald to him and put his left arm around Harald's shoulders. He closed his eyes, struggling to contain a profound emotion. When he spoke, the resonant boom of the preacher had gone from his voice, and his words came out in a murmur of anguish. 'I thought they would kill you,' he said. 'My dear son, I thought they would kill you.'

# SIXTEEN

Arne Olufsen had slipped through Peter Flemming's fingers.

Peter brooded over this as he boiled an egg for Inge's breakfast. After Arne shook off the surveillance on Bornholm, Peter had said blithely that they would soon pick him up again. Peter's confidence had been badly misplaced. He believed Arne was not cunning enough to get off the island unobserved – and he had been wrong. He did not yet know how Arne had managed it, but there was no doubt he had returned to Copenhagen, for a uniformed policeman had spotted him in the city centre. The patrolman had given chase, but Arne had outrun him – and vanished again.

Some kind of espionage was obviously still going on, as Peter's boss, Frederik Juel, had pointed out with icy scorn. 'Olufsen is apparently performing evasive manoeuvres,' he had said.

General Braun had been more blunt. 'The killing of Poul Kirke has clearly failed to disable the spy ring,' he had said. There had been no further talk of promoting Peter to head of department. 'I shall call in the Gestapo.'

It was so unfair, Peter thought angrily. He had uncovered this spy ring, found the secret message in the aeroplane chock, arrested the mechanics, raided the synagogue, arrested Ingemar Gammel, raided the flying school, killed Poul Kirke, and flushed out Arne Olufsen. Yet people such as Juel who had done nothing were able to denigrate his achievements and prevent his getting the recognition that was his due.

But he was not finished yet. 'I can find Arne Olufsen,' he had said to General Braun the night before. Juel had started to object, but Peter had overridden him. 'Give me twenty-four hours. If he's not in custody tomorrow night, call in the Gestapo.'

Braun had agreed.

Arne had not returned to barracks, nor was he with his parents on Sande, so he had to be hiding out at the home of a fellow spy. But they would all be lying low. However, one person who probably knew most of the spies was Karen Duchwitz. She had been Poul's girlfriend, and her brother was at school with Poul's cousin. She was not a spy, Peter felt sure, so she had no reason to lie low. She might lead Peter to Arne.

It was a long shot, but it was all he had.

He mashed the soft-boiled egg up with salt and a little butter, then took the tray into the bedroom. He sat Inge up and gave her a spoonful of egg. He got the feeling she did not much like it. He tasted it, and it was fine, so he gave her another spoonful. After a moment she pushed it out of her mouth, like a baby. The egg ran down her chin and on to the bodice of her nightdress.

Peter stared in despair. She had made a mess of herself several times in the past week or two. This was a new development. 'Inge would never have done that,' he said.

He put the tray down, left her and went to the phone. He dialled the hotel on Sande and asked for his father, who was always at work early. When he got through, he said: 'You were right. It's time to put Inge in a home.'

* * *

Peter studied the Royal Theatre, a domed nineteenth-century building of yellow stone. Its façade was carved with columns, pilasters, capitals, corbels, wreaths, shields, lyres, masks, cherubs, mermaids and angels. On the roof were urns, torchères, and four-legged creatures with wings and human breasts. 'It's a bit overdone,' he said. 'Even for a theatre.'

Tilde Jespersen laughed.

They were sitting on the verandah of the Hotel d'Angleterre. They had a good view across the Kongens Nytorv, the largest. square in Copenhagen. Inside the theatre, the students of the ballet school were watching a dress rehearsal of *Les Sylphides*, the current production. Peter and Tilde were waiting for Karen Duchwitz to come out.

Tilde was pretending to read today's newspaper. The front-page headline said: LENINGRAD AFLAME. Even the Nazis were surprised at how well the Russian campaign was going, saying their success 'baffled the imagination'.

Peter was talking to release tension. So far, his plan was a complete failure. Karen had been under surveillance all day and had done nothing but go to school. But fruitless anxiety was debilitating, and led to mistakes, so he tried to relax. He said: 'Do you think architects deliberately make theatres and opera houses intimidating, to discourage ordinary people from going in?'

'Do you consider yourself an ordinary person?'

'Of course.' The entrance was flanked by two green statues of sitting figures, larger than life-size. 'Who are those two?'

'Holberg and Oehlenschläger.'

He recognized the names. They were both great Danish playwrights. 'I don't much like drama – too many speeches. I'd rather see a movie, something to make me laugh, Buster Keaton or Laurel and Hardy. Did you see the one where these guys are whitewashing a room, and someone comes in carrying a plank on his shoulder?' He chuckled at the recollection. 'I nearly fell on the damn floor laughing.'

She gave him one of her enigmatic looks. 'Now you have surprised me. I wouldn't have put you down as a lover of slapstick.'

'What did you imagine I would like?'

'Western movies, where gunplay ensures that justice is triumphant.'

'You're right, I like those too. What about you? Do you enjoy theatre? Copenhageners approve of culture in theory, but most of them have never been inside that building.'

'I like opera – do you?'

'Well . . . the tunes are OK but the stories are silly.'

She smiled. 'I've never thought of it that way, but you're right. How about ballet?'

'I don't really see the point. And the costumes are peculiar. To tell the truth, I find the men's tights a bit embarrassing.'

She laughed again. 'Oh, Peter, you're so funny, but I like you all the same.'

He had not intended to be amusing, but he accepted the compliment cheerfully. He glanced down at the photograph in his hand. He had taken it from Poul Kirke's bedroom. It showed Poul sitting on a bicycle with Karen perched on the crossbar. They were both wearing shorts. Karen had wonderful long legs. They looked such a happy couple, full of energy and fun, that for a moment Peter felt sad that Poul had died. He had to remind himself sternly that Poul had chosen to be a spy and to flout the law.

The purpose of the photo was to help him identify Karen. She was attractive, with a big smile and masses of curly hair. She seemed the antithesis of Tilde, who had small, neat features in a round face. Some of the men said Tilde was frigid, because she repelled their advances – but I know better, Peter thought.

They had not talked about the fiasco in the hotel on Bornholm. Peter was too embarrassed to raise it. He was not going to apologize – that would just be further humiliation. But a plan was forming in his mind, something so dramatic he preferred to think about it only vaguely.

'Here she comes,' said Tilde.

Peter looked across the square and saw a group of young people emerging from the theatre. He picked out Karen immediately. She was wearing a straw boater at a jaunty angle and a mustard-yellow summer dress with a flared skirt that danced enticingly around her knees. The black-and-white photograph had not shown her white skin and flaming red hair, nor had it done justice to the spirited air that was obvious to Peter even at a distance. She looked as if she were making an entrance on the stage of the theatre, rather than merely walking down the steps outside.

She crossed the square and turned into the main drag, the Stroget.

Peter and Tilde stood up.

'Before we go,' Peter said.

'What?'

'Will you come to my apartment this evening?'

'Any special reason?'

'Yes, but I'd rather not explain.'

'All right.'

'Thanks.' He said no more, but hurried after Karen. Tilde followed him at a distance, by prearrangement.

The Stroget was a narrow street crowded with shoppers and buses, frequently blocked by illegally parked cars. Double the fines and ticket every car and the problem would go away, Peter felt sure. He kept Karen's straw hat in sight. He prayed she was not simply heading for home.

At the end of the Stroget was the town hall square. Here the group of students dispersed. Karen walked on with just one of the girls, chatting animatedly. Peter drew closer. They passed the Tivoli Garden and stopped, as if about to part company, but continued their conversation. They looked pretty and carefree in the afternoon sunshine. Peter wondered impatiently how much more two girls could have to say to one another after having spent all day together.

At last Karen's friend walked towards the main railway station and Karen went the opposite way. Peter's hopes rose. Did she have a rendezvous with one of the circle of spies? He followed her, but to his dismay she approached Vesterport, a suburban railway station from which she could catch a train to her home village of Kirstenslot.

This was no good. He had only a few hours left. Clearly she was not going to lead him to one of the circle. He would have to force the situation.

He caught up with her at the entrance to the station. 'Excuse me,' he said. 'I must speak to you.'

She gave him a level look and kept walking. 'What is it?' she said with cool politeness.

'Could we talk for just a minute?'

She passed through the entrance and started down the steps to the platform. 'We're talking.'

He pretended to be nervous. 'I'm taking a terrible risk just speaking to you.'

That got to her. She stopped on the platform and glanced around nervously. 'What's this about?'

She had wonderful eyes, he noticed: a striking clear green. 'It's about Arne Olufsen.' He saw fear in those eyes, and was gratified. His instinct had been right. She knew something.

'What about him?' She managed to keep her voice low and even.

'Aren't you a friend of his?'

'No. I've met him – I used to go out with a friend of his. But I don't really know him. Why are you asking me?'

'Do you know where he is?'

'No.'

She spoke firmly, and he thought with dismay that she looked as if she was telling the truth.

But he was not yet ready to give up. 'Could you get a message to him?'

She hesitated, and Peter's heart leaped with hope. He guessed she was wondering whether to lie or not. 'Possibly,' she said after a moment. 'I can't be sure. What sort of message?'

'I'm with the police.'

She took a frightened step back.

'It's all right, I'm on your side.' He could tell that she did not know whether to believe him. 'I'm nothing to do with the security department, I do road accidents. But our office is next to theirs, and sometimes I hear what's going on.'

'What have you heard?'

'Arne is in great danger. The security department know where he's hiding.'

'My God.'

Peter noted that she did not ask what the security

department was, nor what crime Arne was supposed to have committed, and she showed no surprise about his being in hiding. She must therefore know what Arne was up to, he concluded with a sense of triumph.

On that basis, he could arrest and interrogate her. But he had a better plan. He put a note of dramatic urgency into his voice. 'They're going to arrest him tonight.'

'Oh, no!'

'If you know how to reach Arne please, for God's sake, try to get a warning to him in the next hour.'

'I don't think—'

'I can't risk being seen with you. I have to go. I'm sorry. Do your best.' He turned and walked rapidly away.

At the top of the steps he passed Tilde, who was pretending to read a timetable. She did not look at him, but he knew she had seen him, and she would now follow Karen.

Across the street, a man in a leather apron was unloading crates of beer from a wagon drawn by two big horses. Peter stepped behind the cart. He took off his trilby hat, stuffed it inside his jacket, and replaced it with a peaked cap. He knew from experience that this simple switch effected a remarkable change in his appearance. It would not defy careful scrutiny, but at a casual glance he looked like a different person.

Standing half concealed by the wagon, he watched the station entrance. After a few moments, Karen came out.

Tilde was a few paces behind her.

Peter followed Tilde. They turned a corner and walked along the street that lay between the Tivoli and the main railway station. On the next block, Karen turned into the main post office, a grand classical building of red brick and grey stone. Tilde followed her in.

She was going to make a phone call, Peter thought with exhilaration. He ran to the staff entrance. He showed his police badge to the first person he met, a young woman, and said: 'Bring the duty manager, quick.'

A few moments later, a stooped man in a well-worn black suit appeared. 'How may I help you?'

'A young woman in a yellow dress has just entered the main hall,' Peter told him. 'I don't want her to see me, but I need to know what she does.'

The manager looked thrilled. This was probably the most exciting thing that had ever happened in the post office, Peter thought. 'My goodness,' said the man. 'You'd better come with me.'

He hurried along a corridor and opened a door. Peter could see a counter with a row of stools facing small windows. The manager stepped through the door. 'I think I see her,' he said. 'Curly red hair and a straw hat?'

'That's the one.'

'I'd never have guessed she was a criminal.'

'What is she doing?'

'Looking in the telephone directory. Amazing that someone so pretty—'

'If she makes a call, I need to listen.'

The manager hesitated.

Peter had no right to listen to private phone calls without a warrant – but he was hoping the manager would not know that. 'It's very important,' he said.

'I'm not sure I can—'

'Don't worry, I'll take responsibility.'

'She's putting the phone book down.'

Peter was not going to let Karen phone Arne without listening in. If necessary he would pull his gun and threaten this dozy post office clerk, he decided. 'I must insist.'

'We have rules here.'

'Nevertheless—'

'Ah!' said the manager. 'She's put the book down, but she's not coming to the counter.' His face cleared with relief. 'She's leaving!'

Peter cursed with frustration and ran for the exit.

He cracked the door and peeped out. He saw Karen crossing the road. He waited until Tilde emerged, following Karen. Then he tagged along.

He was disappointed, but not defeated. Karen knew the name of someone who could get in touch with Arne. She had looked that name up in the phone book. Why the hell had she not phoned the person? Perhaps she feared – rightly – that the conversation might be overheard by police or German security staff doing routine surveillance.

Still, if she had not wanted the phone number, she must have been looking for the address. And now, if Peter's luck was in, she was heading for that address.

He let Karen get out of sight but kept Tilde in view.

Walking behind Tilde was always a pleasure. It was good to have an excuse to watch her rounded rear. Did she know he was staring at her? Was she exaggerating the sway of her hips deliberately? He had no idea. Who could tell what was in a woman's mind?

They crossed to the small island of Christiansborg and followed the waterfront, with the harbour on their right and the ancient buildings of the government island on their left. The sun-warmed air of the city was refreshed here by a salty breeze from the Baltic Sea. The broad channel of water was lined by freighters, fishing boats, ferries, and ships of the Danish and German navies. Two young sailors fell in behind Tilde and cheerfully tried to pick her up, but she spoke sharply to them and they peeled off immediately.

Karen walked as far as the palace of Amalienborg, then turned inland. Following Tilde, Peter crossed the wide square formed by the four rococo mansions where the royal family lived. From there they headed into Nyboder, a neighbourhood of small houses originally built as cheap accommodation for sailors.

They entered a street called St Paul's Gade. Peter could see Karen in the distance, looking at a row of yellow houses with red roofs, apparently searching for a number. He had a strong, exciting feeling of being close to his quarry.

Karen paused and looked up and down the street, as if checking whether she was observed. It was far too late for that, of course, but she was an amateur. In any case, she did not appear to register Tilde, and Peter was too far away to be recognized.

She knocked on a door.

As Peter caught up with Tilde, the door opened. He could not see who was there. Karen said something and stepped inside, and the door closed. It was number fifty-three, Peter noted.

Tilde said: 'Do you think Arne is in there?'

'Either him, or someone who knows where he is.'

'What do you want to do?'

'Wait.' He looked up and down the street. On the opposite side was a corner shop. 'Over there.' They crossed the road and stood looking in the window. Peter lit a cigarette.

Tilde said: 'The shop probably has a phone. Should we call headquarters? We might as well go in in force. We don't know how many spies might be in there.'

Peter considered summoning reinforcements. 'Not yet,' he said. 'We're not sure what's happening. Let's see how this develops.'

Tilde nodded. She removed her sky-blue beret and put a nondescript patterned scarf over her head. Peter watched her tuck the curls of her fair hair under the scarf. She would look somewhat different when Karen came out of the house, so that Karen was less likely to notice her.

Tilde took the cigarette from Peter's fingers, put it to her own mouth, drew in smoke, and handed the cigarette back. It was an intimate gesture, and he felt almost as if she had kissed him. He sensed that he was blushing, and looked away, towards number fifty-three.

The door opened and Karen came out.

'Look,' he said, and Tilde followed his gaze.

The door closed behind Karen and she walked away alone.

'Damn,' Peter said.

'What do we do now?' Tilde asked.

Peter thought fast. Suppose Arne was inside the little yellow house. Then Peter needed to summon reinforcements, bust into the house and arrest him and anyone with him. On the other hand, Arne might be somewhere else, and Karen could be on her way there – in which case Peter needed to follow her.

Or she might have failed in her quest and decided to give up and go home.

He made a decision. 'We'll split up,' he told Tilde. 'You follow Karen. I'll call headquarters and raid that house.'

'OK.' Tilde hurried after Karen.

Peter went into the shop. It was a general store, selling vegetables and bread and household necessities such as soap and matches. There were cans of food on the shelves, and the floor was obstructed by bundles of firewood and sacks of potatoes. The place looked dirty but prosperous. He showed his police badge to a grey-haired woman in a stained apron. 'Do you have a phone?'

'I'll have to charge you.'

He fumbled in his pocket for change. 'Where is it?' he said impatiently.

She jerked her head towards a curtain at the back. 'Through there.'

He threw some coins on the counter and passed

into a small parlour that smelled of cats. He snatched up the phone, called the Politigaarden, and got Conrad. 'I think I may have found Arne's hideout. Number fifty-three St Paul's Gade. Get Dresler and Ellegaard and come here in a car as fast as you can.'

'Right away,' said Conrad.

Peter hung up and hurried outside. He had been less than a minute. If anyone had left the house during that time, they should still be visible on the street. He looked up and down. He saw an old man in a collarless shirt walking an arthritic dog, the two of them moving with painful slowness. A lively pony was drawing a flatbed cart carrying a sofa with holes in the leather upholstery. A group of boys was playing football in the road, using an old tennis ball worn bald with use. There was no sign of Arne. He crossed the street.

Indulging himself for a moment, he thought how satisfying it would be to arrest the elder son of the Olufsen family. What a revenge that would be for the humiliation of Axel Flemming all those years ago. Coming immediately after the expulsion from school of the younger son, the unmasking of Arne as a spy would surely mean the end of Pastor Olufsen's hegemony. How could he strut and preach when both his sons had gone wrong? He would have to resign.

Peter's father would be pleased.

The door of number fifty-three opened. Peter reached under his jacket and touched the grip of his gun in its shoulder holster as Arne stepped out of the house.

Peter was filled with elation. Arne had shaved off

his moustache and covered his black hair with a workman's cap, but Peter had known him all his life, and recognized him immediately.

After a moment, triumph was replaced by caution. There was often trouble when a lone officer tried to make an arrest. The possibility of escape looked tempting to the suspect who was up against only one cop. Being a plain-clothes detective, lacking the authority of a uniform, made it worse. If there was a fight, passers-by had no way of knowing that one of the two was an officer, and might even intervene on the wrong side.

Peter and Arne had fought once before, twelve years before, at the time of the quarrel between their families. Peter was bigger, but Arne was fit and strong from all the sports he did. There was no clear result. They had traded several blows then been separated. Today Peter had a gun. But perhaps Arne did too.

Arne slammed the house door and turned on to the street, walking towards Peter.

As they came closer, Arne avoided his eye, walking on the inside of the pavement, near the house walls, in the manner of a fugitive. Peter walked on the kerb side, furtively watching Arne's face.

When they were ten yards apart, Arne stole a glance at Peter's face. Peter met his eye, watching his expression. He saw a frown of puzzlement, then recognition, then shock, fear and panic.

Arne stopped, momentarily frozen.

'You're under arrest,' Peter said.

Arne partly recovered his composure, and for a

moment the familiar careless grin flickered across his face. 'Gingerbread Pete,' he said, using a childhood nickname.

Peter saw that Arne was about to make a run for it. He drew his gun. 'Lie on the ground face down with your hands behind your back.'

Arne looked worried rather than frightened. In a moment of insight, Peter saw that it was not the gun Arne was scared of, but something else.

Arne said in a challenging tone: 'Are you ready to shoot me?'

'If necessary,' Peter said. He levelled the gun threateningly, but in truth he was desperate to take Arne alive. Poul Kirke's death had dead-ended the investigation. He wanted to interrogate Arne, not kill him.

Arne smiled enigmatically, then turned and ran.

Peter held his gun arm straight and sighted along the barrel. He aimed at Arne's legs, but it was impossible to shoot accurately with a pistol, and he knew he might hit any part of Arne's body, or none. But Arne was getting farther away, and Peter's chances of stopping him were diminishing with every split second that passed.

Peter pulled the trigger.

Arne kept running.

Peter fired again repeatedly. After the fourth shot, Arne seemed to stagger. Peter fired again, and Arne fell, hitting the ground with the heavy thud of a dead weight, rolling on to his back.

'Oh, Christ, no, not again,' Peter said.

He ran forward, still pointing the gun at Arne.

The figure on the ground lay still.

Peter knelt beside it.

Arne opened his eyes. His face was white with pain. 'You stupid pig, you should have killed me,' he said.

* * *

Tilde came to Peter's apartment that evening. She was wearing a new pink blouse with flowers embroidered on the cuffs. Pink suited her, Peter thought. It brought out her femininity. The weather was warm, and she seemed to have nothing on under the blouse.

He showed her into the living room. The evening sun shone in, lighting the room with a weird glow, giving a fuzzy edge to the furniture and the pictures on the walls. Inge sat in a chair by the fireplace, gazing into the room with the expressionless look she always wore.

Peter drew Tilde to him and kissed her. She froze for a moment, surprised, then she kissed him back. He stroked her shoulders and her hips.

She pulled back and looked in his face. He could see desire in her eyes, but she was troubled. She glanced at Inge. 'Is this all right?' she said.

He touched her hair. 'Hush.' He kissed her again, hungrily. They became more passionate. Without breaking the kiss, he unbuttoned her blouse, exposing her soft breasts. He stroked the warm skin.

She pulled away again, breathing hard. Her breasts rose and fell as she panted. 'What about her?' she said. 'What about Inge?'

Peter looked at his wife. She was regarding the two of them with a blank stare, showing no emotion at all, as always. 'There's no one there,' he told Tilde. 'No one there at all.'

She looked into his eyes. Her face showed compassion and understanding mingled with curiosity and lust. 'All right,' she said. 'All right.'

He bent his head to her naked breasts.

# PART THREE

# SEVENTEEN

The quiet village of Jansborg was creepy by twilight. The villagers seemed to go to bed early, so the streets were deserted and the houses dark and still. Harald felt as if he were driving through a place where something dreadful had happened, and he was the only person who did not know about it.

He parked the motorcycle outside the railway station. It did not look as conspicuous as he had feared, for next to it was a gas-powered Opel Olympia cabriolet, with a wooden structure like a shed over its rear roof to house the giant fuel bag.

He left the bike and set off to walk to the school in the gathering darkness.

After his escape from the guards on Sande he had got back into his old bed and slept heavily until midday. His mother woke him, fed him a vast lunch of cold pork and potatoes, pushed money into his pocket, and pleaded with him to tell her where he was living. Weakened by her affection and his father's unexpected mellowing, he had told her he was staying in Kirstenslot. However, he had not mentioned the disused church, for fear she would worry about him sleeping rough, and he had left her with the impression he was a guest at the big house.

Then he had set out to drive across Denmark from west to east again. Now, in the evening of the following day, he was approaching his old school.

He had decided to develop the film before going to Copenhagen to hand it over to Arne, who was hiding out at Jens Toksvig's house in the Nyboder district. He needed to be sure that his photography had been successful, and there were clear images on the roll. Cameras could go wrong, and photographers made mistakes. He did not want Arne to risk his life travelling to England with a film that turned out to be blank. The school had its own darkroom, with all the chemicals necessary for processing. Tik Duchwitz was secretary of the Camera Club, and had a key.

Harald avoided the main gates and cut across the neighbouring farm to enter the school via the stables. It was ten o'clock. The younger boys were already in bed, and the middle school was getting undressed. Only the seniors were still about, and most of them were in their study-bedrooms. It was graduation day tomorrow, and they would be packing for home.

Threading through the familiar cluster of buildings, Harald fought the temptation to skulk furtively along walls and dash across open spaces. If he walked naturally and confidently he would appear, to the casual glance, to be a senior boy heading for his room. He was surprised at how difficult it was to fake an identity that had been genuinely his only ten days before.

He saw no one on his way to the Red House, the building where Tik and Mads had their rooms. There was no way he could conceal himself as he climbed the stairs to the top floor: if he met someone, he would be recognized instantly. But his luck held. The upper corridor was deserted. He hurried past the rooms of the housemaster, Mr Moller. He quietly opened Tik's door and stepped inside.

Tik was sitting on the lid of his suitcase, trying to close it. 'You!' he said. 'Good God!'

Harald sat beside him and helped him snap the catches closed. 'Looking forward to going home?'

'No such luck,' Tik said. 'I'm being exiled to Aarhus. I've got to spend the summer working in a branch of the family bank. It's my punishment for going to that jazz club with you.'

'Oh.' Harald had been looking forward to having Tik's company at Kirstenslot, but now he decided there was no need to mention that he was living there.

'What are you doing here?' Tik asked when they had the suitcase shut and strapped.

'I need your help.'

Tik grinned. 'What now?'

Harald took the small roll of thirty-five-millimetre film from his trousers pocket. 'I want to develop this.'

'Why can't you take it to a shop?'

'Because I would be arrested.'

Tik's grin faded and he became solemn. 'You're involved in a conspiracy against the Nazis.'

'Something like that.'

'You're in danger.'

337

'Yes.'

There was a tap at the door.

Harald dropped to the floor and slid under the bed.

Tik said: 'Yes?'

Harald heard the door opening, then Moller's voice saying: 'Lights out, please, Duchwitz.'

'Yes, sir.'

'Goodnight.'

'Goodnight, sir.'

The door closed, and Harald rolled out from under the bed.

They listened while Moller progressed along the corridor, saying goodnight to each boy. They heard his footsteps returning to his own rooms, then his door closing. They knew he would not reappear until morning, unless there should be an emergency.

Keeping his voice low, Harald said to Tik: 'Have you still got the key to the darkroom?'

'Yes, but first we'd have to get into the labs.' The science building was locked at night.

'We can break a window at the back.'

'When they see the smashed glass, they'll know someone broke in.'

'What do you care? You're leaving tomorrow!'

'All right.'

They took off their shoes and crept out into the corridor. They went down the stairs silently and put their shoes back on when they reached the door. Then they stepped outside.

It was now after eleven, and night had fallen. At

this hour, no one would normally be moving about the grounds, so they had to take care not to be seen from a window. Fortunately there was no moon. They hurried away from the Red House, their footsteps muffled by grass. As they reached the church Harald glanced back, and saw a light in one of the senior rooms. A figure crossed the window and paused. A split-second later, Harald and Tik had turned the corner of the church.

'I think we might have been seen,' Harald whispered. 'There's a light on in the Red House.'

'Staff bedrooms all look out on to the back,' Tik pointed out. 'If we were seen by someone, it must have been a boy. Nothing to worry about.'

Harald hoped he was right.

They circled the library and approached the science building from the rear. Although new, it had been designed to match the older structures around, so it had red brick walls and composite casement windows each made up of six panes of glass.

Harald took off a shoe and tapped a window with its heel. It seemed quite strong. 'When you're playing football, glass is so fragile,' he murmured. He put his hand inside the shoe and hit the pane hard. It broke with a noise like the last trump. The two boys stood still, aghast at how loud it had been; but silence descended as if nothing had happened. There was no one in the nearby buildings – the church, the library and the gymnasium – and, when Harald's heartbeat quietened, he realized that the smash had gone unheard.

He used his shoe to knock out the jagged edges from the frame. They fell inside on to a laboratory bench. He put his arm through and unlatched the window. Still using the shoe to protect his hand from cuts, he reached inside and swept the shards to one side. Then he climbed in.

Tik followed, and they closed the window behind them.

They were in the chemistry lab. Astringent smells of acids and ammonia stung Harald's nostrils. He could see almost nothing, but the room was familiar, and he made his way to the door without crashing into anything. He passed into the corridor and found the door to the darkroom.

Once they were both inside, Tik locked the door and switched on the light. Harald realized that, as no light could get into the darkroom, none could escape either.

Tik rolled up his sleeves and went to work. He ran warm water into a sink and busied himself with chemicals from a row of jars. He took the temperature of the water in the sink and added hot until he was satisfied. Harald understood the principles, but had never tried to do this himself, so he had to trust his friend.

What if something had gone wrong – the shutter had not operated properly, or the film had been fogged, or the image was blurred? The pictures would be useless. Did he have the nerve to try again? He would have to go back to Sande, climb that fence in the dark, sneak into the installation, wait for sunrise, take more pictures, then attempt to escape in daylight, all over again. He was not sure he could summon up the strength of will.

When all was ready, Tik set a timer and turned off the light. Harald sat patiently in the dark while Tik unrolled the exposed film and began the process that would develop the pictures – if there were any pictures. He explained that he was bathing the film first in pyrogallol, which would react with the silver salts to form a visible image. They sat and waited until the clockwork timer rang its bell, then Tik washed the film in acetic acid to stop the reaction. Finally he bathed it in hypo to fix the image.

At last he said: 'That should do it.'

Harald held his breath.

Tik turned on the light. Harald was dazzled for a few moments, and could not see anything. When his vision cleared, he peered at the length of greyish film in Tik's hands. Harald had risked his life for this. Tik held it up to the light. At first Harald could not make out any images, and he thought he would have to do it all again. Then he remembered he was looking at a negative, on which black appeared white and vice versa; and he began to make out the shapes. He saw a reverse image of the large rectangular aerial that had so intrigued him when he first saw it four weeks before.

He had succeeded.

He looked along the row of images and recognized each one: the rotating base, the clustered cables, the grid taken from several angles, the smaller machines with their tilting aerials, and finally the last picture, the general view of all three structures, taken when he was on the edge of panic. 'They came out!' he said triumphantly. 'They're great!'

Tik looked pale. 'What are these pictures of?' he said in a frightened voice.

'Some new machinery the Germans have invented for detecting approaching aircraft.'

'I wish I hadn't asked. Do you realize what the punishment is for what we're doing?'

'I took the pictures.'

'And I developed the film. God in heaven, I could be hanged.'

'I told you it was this kind of thing.'

'I know, but I didn't really think it through.'

'I'm sorry.'

Tik rolled the film and put it in its cylindrical container. 'Here, take it,' he said. 'I'm going back to bed to forget that this ever happened.'

Harald put the canister in his trousers pocket.

Then they heard voices.

Tik groaned.

Harald froze, listening. At first he could not make out the words, but he felt sure the sounds came from within the building, not outside. Then he heard the distinctive voice of Heis say: 'There doesn't seem to be anyone here.'

The next voice belonged to a boy. 'They definitely came this way, sir.'

Harald frowned at Tik. 'Who . . .?'

Tik whispered: 'It sounds like Woldemar Borr.'

'Of course,' Harald groaned. Borr was the school Nazi. It must have been he who saw them from the window. What bad luck – any other boy would have kept his mouth shut.

Then there was a third voice. 'Look, there's a broken pane in this window.' It was Mr Moller. 'This must be how they got in – whoever they are.'

'I'm sure Harald Olufsen was one of them, sir,' said Borr. He sounded pleased with himself.

Harald said to Tik: 'Let's get out of this darkroom. Maybe we can prevent their learning that we've been doing photography.' He flicked off the light, turned the key in the lock, and opened the door.

All the lights were on, and Heis was standing right outside.

'Oh, shit,' said Harald.

Heis was wearing a shirt without a collar: he had obviously been on his way to bed. He looked down his long nose. 'So it is you, Olufsen.'

'Yes, sir.'

Borr and Mr Moller appeared behind Heis.

'You're no longer a pupil at this school, you know,' Heis went on. 'It's my duty to call the police and have you arrested for burglary.'

Harald suffered a moment of panic. If the police found the film in his pocket, he would be finished.

'And Duchwitz is with you – I might have known,' Heis added, seeing Tik behind Harald. 'But what on earth are you doing?'

Harald had to persuade Heis not to call the police – but he could not explain in front of Borr. He said: 'Sir, if I could speak to you alone?'

Heis hesitated.

Harald decided that if Heis refused, and called the police, he would not surrender gracefully. He would make a run for it. But how far would he get? 'Please, sir,' he said. 'Give me a chance to explain.'

'Very well,' Heis said reluctantly. 'Borr, go back to bed. And you, Duchwitz. Mr Moller, perhaps you'd better see them to their rooms.' They all departed.

Heis walked into the chemistry lab, sat on a stool, and took out his pipe. 'All right, Olufsen,' he said. 'What is it this time?'

Harald wondered what to say. He could not think of a plausible lie, but he feared the truth would be more incredible than anything he might invent. In the end he simply took the little cylinder out of his pocket and gave it to Heis.

Heis took out the roll of film and held it up to the light. 'This looks like some kind of new-fangled radio installation,' he said. 'Is it military?'

'Yes, sir.'

'Do you know what it does?'

'It tracks aircraft by radio beams, I think.'

'So that's how they're doing it. The Luftwaffe claim they've been shooting down RAF bombers like flies. This explains it.'

'I believe they track the bomber and the fighter that has been sent to intercept it, so that the controller can direct the fighter precisely.'

Heis looked over his glasses. 'My God. Do you realize how important this is?'

'I think so.'

'There's only one way the British can help the Russians, and that's by forcing Hitler to bring aircraft back from the Russian front to defend Germany from air raids.'

Heis was ex-army, and military thinking came naturally to him. Harald said: 'I'm not sure I see what you're getting at.'

'Well, the strategy won't work while the Germans can shoot bombers down easily. But if the British find out how it's done, they can devise countermeasures.' Heis looked around. 'There must be an almanac here somewhere.'

Harald did not see why he needed an almanac, but he knew where it was. 'In the physics office.'

'Go and get it.' Heis put the film down on the laboratory bench and lit his pipe while Harald stepped into the next room, found the almanac on the bookshelf, and brought it back. Heis flipped through the pages. 'The next full moon is on the eighth of July. I'd bet there will be a big bombing raid that night. It's twelve days away. Can you get this film to England by then?'

'It's someone else's job.'

'Good luck to him. Olufsen, do you know how much danger you're in?'

'Yes.'

'The penalty for spying is death.'

'I know.'

'You always had guts, I'll give you that.' He handed back the film. 'Is there anything you need? Food, money, petrol?'

'No, thanks.'

Heis stood up. 'I'll see you off the premises.'

They went out by the main door. The night air cooled the perspiration on Harald's forehead. They walked side by side along the road to the gate. 'I don't know what I'm going to tell Moller,' said Heis.

'If I might make a suggestion?'

'By all means.'

'You could say we were developing dirty pictures.'

'Good idea. They'll all believe that.'

They reached the gate, and Heis shook Harald's hand. 'For God's sake, be careful, boy,' said the head.

'I will.'

'Good luck.'

'Goodbye.'

Harald walked away in the direction of the village.

When he reached the bend in the road, he looked back. Heis was still at the gate, watching him. Harald waved, and Heis waved back. Then Harald walked on.

\* \* \*

He crawled under a bush and slept until sunrise, then retrieved his motorcycle and drove into Copenhagen.

He felt good as he steered through the outskirts of the city in the morning sunshine. He had suffered some close shaves, but in the end he had done what he promised. He was going to enjoy handing over the film. Arne would be impressed. Then Harald's job would be done, and it would be up to Arne to get the pictures to Britain.

After seeing Arne, he would drive back to Kirstenslot. He would have to beg Farmer Nielsen for his job back. He had only worked one day before disappearing for the rest of the week. Nielsen would be annoyed – but he might need Harald's services badly enough to hire him again.

Being at Kirstenslot would mean seeing Karen. He looked forward eagerly to that. She was not interested in him romantically, and she never would be, but she seemed to like him. For his part, he was content to talk to her. The idea of kissing her was too remote even to wish for.

He made his way to Nyboder. Arne had given Harald the address of Jens Toksvig. St Paul's Gade was a narrow street of small terraced houses. There were no front gardens: the doors opened directly on to the pavement. Harald parked the bike outside fifty-three and knocked.

It was answered by a uniformed policeman.

For a moment, Harald was struck dumb. Where was Arne? He must have been arrested—

'What is it, lad?' the policeman said impatiently. He was a middle-aged man with a grey moustache and sergeant's stripes on his sleeve.

Harald was inspired. Displaying a panic that was all too real, he said: 'Where's the doctor, he must come right away, she's having the baby now!'

The policeman smiled. The terrified father-to-be was a perennial figure of comedy. 'There's no doctor here, lad.'

'But there must be!'

'Calm down, son. There were babies before there were doctors. Now, what address have you got?'

'Doctor Thorsen, fifty-three Fischer's Gade, he must be here!'

'Right number, wrong street. This is St Paul's Gade. Fischer's Gade is one block south.'

'Oh, my God, the wrong street!'Harald turned away and jumped on to the bike. 'Thank you!' he shouted. He opened the steam regulator and pulled away.

'All part of the job,' the policeman said.

Harald drove to the end of the street and turned the corner.

Very clever, he thought, but what the hell do I do now?

# EIGHTEEN

Hermia spent all Friday morning in the beautiful ruin of Hammershus castle, waiting for Arne to arrive with the vital film.

It was now even more important than it had been five days ago, when she had sent him on the mission. In the interim, the world had changed. The Nazis were set fair to conquer the Soviet Union. They had already taken the key fortress of Brest. Their total air superiority was devastating the Red Army.

Digby had told her, in a few grim sentences, of his conversation with Churchill. Bomber Command would commit every plane it could get off the ground to the biggest air raid of the war, in a desperate attempt to draw Luftwaffe strength away from the Russian front and give the Soviet soldiers a chance to fight back. That raid was now eleven days away.

Digby had also talked to his brother, Bartlett, who was fit again, back on active service, and certain to be piloting one of the bombers.

The raid would be a suicide mission, and Bomber Command would be fatally weakened, unless they could develop tactics for evading German radar in the next few days. And that depended on Arne.

Hermia had persuaded her Swedish fisherman to bring her across the water again – although he had warned her that this would be the last time, as he felt it dangerous to fall into a pattern. At dawn she had splashed through the shallows, carrying her bike, on to the beach below Hammershus. She had climbed the steep hill to the castle, where she stood on the ramparts, like a medieval queen, and watched the sun rise on a world that was increasingly ruled by the strutting, shouting, hate-filled Nazis she so loathed.

During the day she moved, every half hour or so, from one part of the ruins to another, or strolled through the woods, or descended to the beach, just so that it would not be obvious to tourists that she was waiting to meet someone. She suffered a combination of terrible tension and yawn-making boredom that she found strangely wearying.

She diverted herself by recalling their last meeting. The memory was sweet. She was shocked at herself for making love to Arne right there on the grass in broad daylight. But she did not regret it. She would remember that all her life.

She expected him on the overnight ferry. The distance from the harbour at Ronne to the castle of Hammershus was only about fifteen miles. Arne could bike it in an hour or walk it in three. However, he did not show up during the morning.

This made her anxious, but she told herself not to worry. The same thing had happened last time: he had missed the overnight boat and taken the morning sailing. She assumed he would arrive that evening.

Last time she had sat tight and waited for him, and he had not shown up until the following morning. Now she was too impatient for that. When she felt sure he could not have come on the overnight ferry, she decided to cycle to Ronne.

She felt increasingly nervous as she passed from the lonely country roads into the more populous streets of the little town. She told herself this was safer – she was more conspicuous in the countryside and could lose herself in the town – but it felt the opposite. She saw suspicion in everyone's eyes, not just policemen and soldiers but shopkeepers in their doorways, carters leading horses, old men smoking on benches, and dockers drinking tea on the quay. She walked around the town for a while, trying not to meet anyone's eye, then went into a hotel on the harbour and ate a sandwich. When the ferry docked, she stood with a small group of people waiting to meet passengers. As they disembarked she scrutinized every face, expecting Arne to be in some kind of disguise.

It took a few minutes for them all to come ashore. When the flow stopped, and passengers started boarding for the return journey, Hermia realized Arne was not on the boat.

She fretted over what to do next. There were a hundred possible explanations for his non-appearance, ranging from the trivial to the tragic. Had he lost his nerve and abandoned the mission? She felt ashamed of such a suspicion, but she had always doubted whether Arne was hero material. He might be dead, of course. But it was most likely he had been held up by something stupid like a delayed train. Unfortunately, he had no way of letting her know.

But, she realized, she might be able to contact him.

She had told him to hide out at Jens Toksvig's house in the Nyboder district of Copenhagen. Jens had a phone, and Hermia knew the number.

She hesitated. If the police were listening in on Jens's phone, for any reason, they could trace the call, and then they would know . . . what? That something might be going on on Bornholm. That would be bad, but not fatal. The alternative was for her to find overnight accommodation and wait to see whether Arne came in on the next ferry. She did not have the patience for that.

She returned to the hotel and placed the call.

As the operator was putting her through, she wished she had taken more time to plan what to say. Should she ask for Arne? If anyone happened to be listening in, that would give away his whereabouts. No, she would have to speak in riddles, as she had when calling from Stockholm. Jens would probably answer the phone. He would recognize her voice, she thought. If not, she would say: 'It's your friend from Bredgade, remember me?' Bredgade was the street where the British Embassy had been located when she worked there. That should be enough of a hint for him – though it might also be enough to alert a detective.

Before she had time to think it through, the phone was picked up, and a man's voice said: 'Hello?'

It certainly was not Arne. It might have been Jens, but she had not heard his voice for more than a year.

She said: 'Hello.'

'Who is that speaking?' The voice was that of an older man. Jens was twenty-nine.

She said: 'Let me speak to Jens Toksvig, please.'

'Who is calling?'

Who the hell was she speaking to? Jens lived alone. Maybe his father had come to stay. But she was not going to give her real name. 'It's Hilde.'

'Hilde who?'

'He'll know.'

'May I have your second name, please?'

This was ominous. She decided to try to bully him. 'Look, I don't know who the hell you are, but I didn't call to play stupid games, so just put Jens on the damn phone, will you?'

It did not work. 'I must have your surname.'

This was not someone playing games, she decided. 'Who are you?'

There was a long pause, then he replied. 'I am Sergeant Egill of the Copenhagen police.'

'Is Jens in trouble?'

'What is your full name, please?'

Hermia hung up.

She was shocked and frightened. This was as bad as it could be. Arne had taken refuge in Jens's house, and now the house was under police guard. It could only mean that they had found out that Arne was hiding there. They must have arrested Jens and perhaps Arne too. Hermia fought back tears. Would she ever see her lover again?

She walked out of the hotel and looked across the harbour towards Copenhagen, a hundred miles away in the direction of the setting sun. Arne was probably in jail there.

There was no way she was going to meet up with her fisherman and return to Sweden empty-handed. She would be letting down Digby Hoare and Winston Churchill and thousands of British airmen.

The ferry's horn sounded the all-aboard with a noise like a bereaved giant. Hermia jumped on her bicycle and cycled furiously to the dock. She had a complete set of forged papers, including identity card and ration book, so she could pass any checkpoint. She bought a ticket and hurried on board. She had to go to Copenhagen. She had to find out what had happened to Arne. She had to get his film, if he had taken any pictures. When she had done that, she would worry about how to escape from Denmark and get the film to England.

The ferry hooted mournfully again and moved slowly away from the dock.

# NINETEEN

Harald drove along the Copenhagen quayside at sundown. The dirty water of the harbour was an oily grey in daytime, but now it glowed with the reflection of the sunset, a red and yellow sky broken up, by the wavelets, into dabs of colour like strokes of a paint brush.

He stopped the motorcycle near a line of Daimler-Benz trucks partly loaded with timber from a Norwegian freighter. Then he saw two German soldiers guarding the cargo. The roll of film in his pocket suddenly felt burning hot against his leg. He put his hand in his pocket and told himself not to be panicky. No one suspected him of any wrongdoing – and the bike would be safe near the soldiers. He parked next to the trucks.

The last time he was here he had been drunk, and now he struggled to remember exactly where the jazz club was. He walked along the row of warehouses and taverns. The grimy buildings were transformed, like the dirty water of the harbour, by the romantic glow of the setting sun. Eventually he spotted the sign that read: 'Danish Institute of Folk Song and Country

Dancing.' He went down the steps to the cellar and pushed the door. It was open.

The time was ten o'clock, early for night clubs, and the place was half empty. No one was playing the beer-stained piano on the little stage. Harald crossed the room to the bar, scanning the faces. To his disappointment, he did not recognize anyone.

The barman wore a rag tied around his head like a gypsy. He nodded warily to Harald, who did not look like the usual type of customer.

'Have you seen Betsy today?' Harald asked.

The barman relaxed, apparently reassured that Harald was just another young man looking for a prostitute. 'She's around,' he said.

Harald sat on a stool. 'I'll wait.'

'Trude's over there,' the barman said helpfully.

Harald glanced in the direction he pointed and saw a blonde woman drinking from a lipstick-stained glass. He shook his head. 'I want Betsy.'

'These things are very personal,' said the barman sagely.

Harald suppressed a smile at the obviousness of this remark. What could be more personal than sexual intercourse? 'That's very true,' he said. Were tavern conversations always stupid?

'A drink while you're waiting for her?'

'Beer, please.'

'Chaser?'

'No, thanks.' The thought of aquavit still made Harald feel nauseated.

He sipped his beer thoughtfully. He had spent the

day brooding over his plight. The presence of police at Arne's hideout almost certainly meant that Arne had been found out. If by some miracle he had evaded arrest, the only place he might be hiding was the ruined monastery at Kirstenslot; so Harald had driven there and checked. He found the place empty.

He had sat on the floor of the church for several hours, alternately grieving at his brother's fate and trying to figure out what he should do next.

If he were to finish the job Arne had started, he had to get the film to London in the next eleven days. Arne must have had a plan for this, but Harald did not know what it was, and could not think of any way to find out. So he had to devise his own.

He considered simply putting the negatives in an envelope and mailing them to the British legation in Stockholm. However, he felt sure all mail for that address was routinely opened by the censors.

He did not have the luck to be acquainted with any of the small group of people who travelled legitimately between Denmark and Sweden. He could simply go to the ferry dock in Copenhagen, or the boat train station at Elsinore, and ask a passenger to take the envelope; but that seemed almost as risky as mailing it.

He had concluded, after a day of racking his brains, that he had to go himself.

He could not do so openly. He would not be given a permit to travel, now that his brother was known to be a spy. He would have to find a clandestine route. Danish ships went to and from Sweden every day.

There had to be a way to get on board one and slip off unnoticed on the other side. He could not get a job on a boat – sailors had special identity papers. But there was always underworld activity around docks: smuggling, theft, prostitution, drugs. So he needed to make contact with criminals and find someone willing to smuggle him to Sweden.

When the afternoon began to cool, and the tiled floor of the monastery became chilly, he had got back on his motorcycle and returned to the jazz club, in the hope of seeing the only criminal he had ever met.

He did not have to wait long for Betsy. He had drunk only half his beer when she arrived. She came down the rear staircase with a man whom, Harald presumed, she had just serviced in a bedroom upstairs. The client had pale, unhealthy skin and a brutally short haircut, and there was a cold sore on his left nostril. He was about seventeen. Harald guessed he was a sailor. He walked quickly across the room and out of the door, looking furtive.

Betsy came to the bar, saw Harald, and did a double-take. 'Hello, schoolboy,' she said amiably.

'Hello, princess.'

She tossed her head coquettishly, shaking her dark curls. 'Changed your mind? Want to have a go?'

The thought of having sex with her only minutes after the sailor was vile, but he answered with a joke. 'Not before we're married.'

She laughed. 'What would your mother say?'

He looked at her plump figure. 'That you need feeding up.'

She smiled. 'Flatterer. You're after something, aren't you? You didn't come back for the watery beer.'

'As a matter of fact, I need a word with your Luther.'

'Lou?' She looked disapproving. 'What do you want with him?'

'A little problem he may be able to help me with.'

'What?'

'I probably shouldn't tell you—'

'Don't be stupid. Are you in trouble?'

'Not exactly.'

She looked across at the door and said: 'Oh, shit.'

Following her gaze, Harald saw Luther come in. Tonight he was wearing a silk sports coat, very dirty, over an undershirt. With him was a man of about thirty who was so drunk he could hardly stand. Holding the man's arm, Luther steered him to Betsy. The man stood peering lustfully at her.

Betsy said to Luther: 'How much did you take off him?'

'Ten.'

'Lying turd.'

Luther handed her a five-crown note. 'Here's your half.'

She shrugged, pocketed the money, and took the man upstairs.

Harald said: 'Would you like a drink, Lou?'

'Aquavit.' His manners had not improved. 'What are you after, then?'

'You're a man with many contacts along the waterfront.'

'Don't bother to butter me up, son,' Luther interrupted. 'What do you want? A little boy with a nice bum? Cheap cigarettes? Dope?'

The barman filled a small glass with aquavit. Luther emptied it at a gulp. Harald paid and waited until the barman moved away. Lowering his voice, he said: 'I want to go to Sweden.'

Luther narrowed his eyes. 'Why?'

'Does it matter?'

'It might.'

'I've got a girlfriend in Stockholm. We want to get married.' Harald began to improvise. 'I can get a job in her father's factory. He makes leather goods, wallets and handbags and—'

'So apply to the authorities for a permit to go abroad.'

'I did. They turned me down.'

'Why?'

'They wouldn't say.'

Luther looked thoughtful. After a minute he said: 'Fair enough.'

'Can you get me on a ship?'

'Anything's possible. How much money have you got?'

Harald recalled Betsy's mistrust of Luther a minute ago. 'None,' he said. 'But I can get some. So, can you arrange something for me?'

'I know a man I can ask.'

'Great! Tonight?'

'Give me ten crowns.'

'What for?'

'For going to see this man. You think I'm a free public service, like the library?'

'I told you, I haven't got any money.'

Luther grinned, showing his rotten teeth. 'You paid for that drink with a twenty, and got a ten in your change. Give it to me.'

Harald hated to yield to a bully, but he seemed to have no choice. He handed over the note.

'Wait here,' said Luther, and he went out.

Harald waited, sipping his beer slowly to make it last. He wondered where Arne was now. Probably in a cell in the Politigaarden, being interrogated. Perhaps Peter Flemming would do the questioning – espionage was his department. Would Arne talk? Not at first, Harald felt sure. Arne would not crumble immediately. But would he have the strength to hold out? Harald had always felt there was a part of Arne he did not fully know. What if he were tortured? How long would it be before he betrayed Harald?

There was a commotion from the back staircase, and Betsy's latest client, the drunk, fell down the stairs. Betsy followed him, picked him up, and walked him through the door and up the outside steps.

She returned with another client, this one a respectable middle-aged man in a grey suit that was old but neatly pressed. He looked as if he had worked all his life in a bank and never got promoted. As they crossed the room, Betsy said to Harald: 'Where's Lou?'

'Gone to see a man for me.'

She stopped and came over to the bar, leaving the bank clerk looking embarrassed in the middle of the room. 'Don't get involved with Lou, he's a bastard.'

'I've got no choice.'

'Then take a tip.' She lowered her voice. 'Don't trust him a single inch.' She wagged her finger like a schoolteacher. 'Watch your back, for God's sake.' Then she went upstairs with the man in the worn suit.

At first Harald felt annoyed with her for being so sure he could not take care of himself. Then he told himself not to be stupid. She was right – he was out of his depth. He had never dealt with people like Luther, and he had no idea how to protect himself.

*Don't trust him*, Betsy had said. Well, he had only given the man ten crowns. He could not see how Luther could cheat him at this stage, though later he might take a larger sum then fail to deliver.

*Watch your back.* Be prepared for treachery. Harald could not think how Luther could betray him, but were there any precautions he could take? It occurred to him that he was trapped in this bar, with no back door. Maybe he should leave and watch the entrance from a distance. There might be some safety in unpredictable behaviour.

He swallowed the last of his beer and went out with a wave to the barman.

He walked along the quay, in the twilight, to where a big grain ship was tied up with hawsers as thick as his arm. He sat on the domed top of a steel capstan and turned to face the club. He could see the entrance clearly, and he thought he would probably recognize

Luther. Would Luther spot him here? He thought not, for he would be hard to see against the dark bulk of the ship. That was good. It put Harald in control. When Luther returned, if all seemed well, Harald would go back into the bar. If he smelled a rat he would vanish. He settled down to wait.

After ten minutes, a police car appeared.

It came along the quayside very fast, but with no siren. Harald stood up. His instinct was to run, but he realized that would call attention to him, and he forced himself to sit down again and keep very still.

The car pulled up sharply outside the jazz club.

Two men got out. One, the driver, wore a police uniform. The other was in a light-coloured suit. Peering at him in the dim light, Harald recognized the face, and gasped. It was Peter Flemming.

The two cops went into the club.

Harald was about to hurry away when another figure appeared, slouching along the cobblestones with a familiar gait. It was Luther. He stopped a few yards from the police car and leaned against the wall, like an idle bystander waiting to see what would happen.

Presumably he had told the police of Harald's planned flight to Sweden. No doubt he hoped to be paid for the tip-off. How wise Betsy had been – and what a good thing Harald had acted on her advice.

The police came out of the club after a few minutes. Peter Flemming talked to Luther. Harald could hear the voices, for they both spoke angrily, but he was too far away to make out the words. However, it seemed that Peter was reprimanding Luther, who kept throwing his hands in the air in a gesture of helpless frustration.

After a while the two policemen drove away, and Luther went inside.

Harald walked quickly away, shaken by his narrow escape. He found his motorcycle and drove off in the last of the twilight. He would spend the night in the ruined monastery at Kirstenslot.

Then what would he do?

* * *

Harald told Karen the whole story the following evening.

They sat on the floor in the disused church, while evening darkened outside and the draped shapes and boxes around them turned to ghosts in the twilight. She sat with her legs crossed, like a schoolgirl, and hiked the skirt of her silk evening gown above her knees, for comfort. Harald lit her cigarettes, and felt he was becoming intimate with her.

He told her about getting into the base on Sande, then pretending to be asleep while the soldier searched his parents' house. 'You've got such nerve!' she exclaimed. He was pleased by her admiration, and glad she could not see the dampness in his eyes as he explained that his father had told a lie to save him.

He explained Heis's deduction that there would be a major air raid at the next full moon, and his reasons for thinking the film had to get to London before then.

When he related how a police sergeant had answered the door of Jens Toksvig's house, she interrupted him. 'I got a warning,' she said.

'What do you mean?'

'A stranger came up to me at the railway station and told me the police knew where Arne was. This man was a cop himself, in the traffic department, but he happened to have overheard something, and he wanted to let us know because he was sympathetic.'

'Didn't you warn Arne?'

'Yes, I did! I knew he was with Jens, so I looked Jens up in the phone book then went to his house. I saw Arne and told him what had happened.'

It sounded a bit odd to Harald. 'What did Arne say?'

'He told me to leave first, and said he was going to get out immediately after me – but obviously he left it too late.'

'Or your warning was a ruse,' Harald mused.

'What do you mean?' she said sharply.

'Maybe your policeman was lying. Suppose he wasn't sympathetic at all. He might have followed you to Jens's place and arrested Arne the minute you left.'

'That's ridiculous – policemen don't do things like that!'

Harald realized that once again he had run up against Karen's faith in the integrity and good will of those around her. Either she was credulous or he was unduly cynical – he was not sure which. It reminded him of her father's belief that the Nazis would not harm Danish Jews. He wished he thought they were right. 'What did the man look like?'

'Tall, handsome, heavy, red hair, nice suit.'

'A kind of oatmeal tweed?'

'Yes.'

That settled it. 'He's Peter Flemming.' Harald did not feel bitter towards Karen: she had thought she was saving Arne. She was the victim of a clever ruse. 'Peter is more of a spy than a policeman. I know his family, back on Sande.'

'I don't believe you!' she said hotly. 'You've got too much imagination.'

He did not want to argue with her. It pierced his heart to know that his brother was in custody. Arne should never have got involved in deception. There was no slyness in his nature. Harald wondered grievingly if he would ever see his brother again.

But there were more lives at stake. 'Arne won't be able to get this film to England.'

'What are you going to do with it?'

'I don't know. I'd like to take it myself, but I can't figure out how.' He told her about the jazz club and Betsy and Luther. 'And perhaps it's just as well that I can't get to Sweden. I'd probably be jailed for not having the right papers.' It was part of the Swedish government's neutrality agreement with Hitler's Germany that Danes who travelled illegally to Sweden would be arrested. 'I don't mind taking a risk, but I need a better-than-even chance of success.'

'There must be a way – how was Arne going to do it?'

'I don't know, he didn't tell me.'

'That was silly.'

'In retrospect, perhaps, but he probably thought the fewer people who knew, the safer he would be.'

'Someone must know.'

'Well, Poul must have had a means of communication with the British – but it's in the nature of these things that they're kept secret.'

They were silent for a while. Harald felt depressed. Had he risked his life for nothing?

'Have you heard any news?' he asked her. He missed his radio.

'Finland declared war on the Soviet Union. So did Hungary.'

'Vultures scenting death,' Harald said bitterly.

'It's so maddening to be sitting here helpless while the filthy Nazis are conquering the world. I just wish there was something we could do.'

Harald touched the film canister in his trousers pocket. 'This would make a difference, if I could get it to London in the next ten days. A big difference.'

Karen glanced at the Hornet Moth. 'It's a pity that thing won't fly.'

Harald looked at the damaged undercarriage and the torn fabric. 'I might be able to repair it. But I've only had one lesson, I couldn't pilot it.'

Karen looked thoughtful. 'No,' she said slowly. 'But I could.'

# TWENTY

Arne Olufsen proved surprisingly resistant to interrogation.

Peter Flemming questioned him on the day of his arrest, and again on the following day, but he pretended to be innocent and revealed no secrets. Peter was disappointed. He had expected the fun-loving Arne to break as easily as a champagne glass.

He had no more luck with Jens Toksvig.

He considered arresting Karen Duchwitz, but he felt sure she was peripheral to the case. Besides, she was more use to him roaming around freely. She had already led him to two spies.

Arne was the prime suspect. He had all the connections: he knew Poul Kirke, he was familiar with the island of Sande, he had an English fiancée, he had gone to Bornholm which was so close to Sweden, and he had shaken off his police tail.

The arrest of Arne and Jens had restored Peter in General Braun's favour. But now Braun wanted to know more: how the spy ring worked, who else was in it, what means they used to communicate with England. Peter had arrested a total of six spies, but none of them had talked. The case would not be wound up until one of them cracked and revealed all. Peter had to break Arne.

He planned the third interrogation carefully.

At four o'clock on Sunday morning he burst into Arne's cell with two uniformed policemen. They woke Arne by shining a torch in his eyes and yelling, then pulled him out of bed and marched him along the corridor to the interrogation room.

Peter sat on the only chair, behind a cheap table, and lit a cigarette. Arne looked pale and frightened in his prison pyjamas. His left leg was bandaged and strapped from mid-thigh to shin, but he could stand upright – Peter's two bullets had damaged muscles but had not broken any bones.

Peter said: 'Your friend Poul Kirke was a spy.'

'I didn't know that,' Arne replied.

'Why did you go to Bornholm?'

'For a little holiday.'

'Why would an innocent man on holiday evade police surveillance?'

'He might dislike being followed around by a lot of nosey flatfoots.' Arne had more spirit than Peter had expected, despite the early hour and the rude awakening. 'But, as it happens, I didn't notice them. If, as you say, I evaded surveillance, I did it unintentionally. Perhaps your people are just bad at their job.'

'Rubbish. You deliberately shook off your tail. I know, I was part of the surveillance team.'

Arne shrugged. 'That doesn't surprise me, Peter.

You were never very bright as a kid. We were at school together, remember? In fact we were best friends.'

'Until they sent you off to Jansborg, where you learned to disrespect the law.'

'No. We were friends until our families quarrelled.'

'Because of your father's malice.'

'I thought it was over your father's tax fiddle.'

This was not going the way Peter planned it. He switched his line. 'Whom did you meet on Bornholm?'

'No one.'

'You walked around for days and never spoke to anyone?'

'I picked up a girl.'

Arne had not mentioned this in previous interrogations. Peter felt sure it was untrue. Maybe he could catch Arne out. 'What was her name?'

'Annika.'

'Surname?'

'I didn't ask.'

'When you came back to Copenhagen, you went into hiding.'

'Hiding? I was staying with a friend.'

'Jens Toksvig – another spy.'

'He didn't tell me that.' He added sarcastically: 'These spies are a bit secretive.'

Peter was dismayed that Arne had not been more weakened by his time in the cells. He was sticking to his story, which was unlikely but not impossible. Peter began to fear that Arne might never talk. He told himself this was just a preliminary skirmish. He pressed on. 'So you had no idea the police were searching for you?'

'No.'

'Not even when a policeman chased you in the Tivoli Garden?'

'That must have been someone else. I've never been chased by a policeman.'

Peter let the sarcasm sound in his voice. 'You didn't happen to see any of the one thousand posters of your face that have been put up around the city?'

'I must have missed them.'

'Then why did you change your appearance?'

'Did I change my appearance?'

'You shaved off your moustache.'

'Someone told me I looked like Hitler.'

'Who?'

'The girl I met on Bornholm, Anne.'

'You said her name was Annika.'

'I called her Anne for short.'

Tilde Jespersen came in with a tray. The smell of hot toast made Peter's mouth water. He trusted it was having the same effect on Arne. Tilde poured tea. She smiled at Arne and said: 'Would you like some?'

He nodded.

Peter said: 'No.'

Tilde shrugged.

This little exchange was an act. Tilde was pretending to be nice in the hope that Arne would warm to her.

Tilde brought in another chair and sat down to

drink her tea. Peter ate some buttered toast, taking his time. Arne had to stand and watch them.

When Peter had finished eating, he resumed the questioning. 'In Poul Kirke's office, I found a sketch of a military installation on the island of Sande.'

'I'm shocked,' Arne said.

'If he had not been killed, he would have sent those sketches to the British.'

'He might have had an innocent explanation for them, had he not been shot down by a trigger-happy fool.'

'Did you make those drawings?'

'Certainly not.'

'Sande is your home. Your father is pastor of a church there.'

'It's your home, too. Your father runs a hotel where off-duty Nazis get drunk on aquavit.'

Peter ignored that. 'When I met you in St Paul's Gade, you ran away. Why?'

'You had a gun. If not for that, I would have punched your ugly head, the way I did behind the post office twelve years ago.'

'I knocked you down behind the post office.'

'But I got up again.' Arne turned to Tilde with a smile. 'Peter's family and mine have been at loggerheads for years. That's the real reason he's arrested me.'

Peter ignored that. 'Four nights ago, there was a security alert at the base. Something disturbed the guard dogs. The sentries saw someone running across the dunes in the direction of your father's church.' As

Peter talked, he watched Arne's face. So far, Arne did not look surprised. 'Was that you running across the dunes?'

'No.'

Arne was telling the truth, Peter felt. He continued: 'Your parents' home was searched.' Peter saw a flicker of fear in Arne's eyes: he had not known about this. 'The guards were looking for a stranger. They found a young man asleep in bed, but the pastor said it was his son. Was that you?'

'No. I haven't been home since Whitsun.'

Once again, Peter thought he was telling the truth.

'Two nights ago, your brother Harald returned to Jansborg Skole.'

'From which he was expelled because of your malice.'

'He was expelled because he disgraced the school!'

'By daubing a joke on a wall?' Once again Arne turned to Tilde. 'The police superintendent had decided to release my brother without charges – but Peter went to his school and insisted they expel him. You see how much he hates my family?'

Peter said: 'He broke into the chemistry lab and used the darkroom to develop a film.'

Arne's eyes widened visibly. Clearly this was news to him. He was rattled, at last.

'Fortunately, he was discovered by another boy. I learned of this from the boy's father, who happens to be a loyal citizen and a believer in law and order.'

'A Nazi?'

'Was it your film, Arne?'

'No.'

'The head teacher says the film consisted of photographs of naked women, and claims he confiscated it and burned it. He's lying, isn't he?'

'I have no idea.'

'I believe the photographs were of the military installation on Sande.'

'Do you?'

'They were your pictures, weren't they?'

'No.'

Peter felt he was at last beginning to intimidate Arne, and he pressed his advantage. 'Next morning, a young man called at Jens Toksvig's house. One of our officers answered the door – a middle-aged sergeant, not one of the force's intellectual giants. The boy pretended to have come to the wrong address, looking for a doctor, and our man was gullible enough to believe him. But it was a lie. The young man was your brother, wasn't he?'

'I'm quite sure he was not,' Arne said, but he looked frightened.

'Harald was bringing you the developed film.'

'No.'

'That evening, a woman in Bornholm, who called herself Hilde, telephoned Jens Toksvig's house. Didn't you say you had picked up a girl called Hilde?'

'No, Anne.'

'Who is Hilde?'

'Never heard of her.'

'Perhaps it was a false name. Could she have been your fiancée, Hermia Mount?'

'She's in England.'

'There you are mistaken. I have been talking to the Swedish immigration authorities.' It had been hard to force them to cooperate, but in the end Peter had got the information he wanted. 'Hermia Mount flew in to Stockholm ten days ago, and has not yet departed.'

Arne feigned surprise, but the act was unconvincing. 'I know nothing of that,' he said, too mildly. 'I haven't heard from her for more than a year.'

If that had been true, he would have been astonished and shocked to learn that she had certainly been in Sweden and possibly in Denmark. He was definitely lying now. Peter continued: 'The same night – this is the day before yesterday – a young man nicknamed Schoolboy went to a waterfront jazz club, met with a small-time criminal called Luther Gregor, and asked for help to escape to Sweden.'

Arne looked horrified.

Peter said: 'It was Harald, wasn't it?'

Arne said nothing.

Peter sat back. Arne was badly shaken now, but overall he had put up an ingenious defence. He had explanations for everything Peter threw at him. Worse, he was cleverly turning the personal hostility between them to his advantage, claiming that his arrest had been motivated by malice. Frederik Juel might be gullible enough to believe that. Peter was worried.

Tilde poured tea into a mug and gave it to Arne without consulting Peter. Peter said nothing: this was all part of the prearranged scenario. Arne took the mug in a shaky hand and drank thirstily.

Tilde spoke in a kindly voice. 'Arne, you're in over your head. This isn't just about you any more. You've involved your parents, your fiancée and your young brother. Harald is in deep trouble. If this goes on, he'll end up hanged as a spy – and it will be your fault.'

Arne held the mug in both hands, saying nothing, looking bewildered and scared. Peter thought he might be weakening.

'We can make a deal with you,' Tilde went on. 'Tell us everything, and both you and Harald will escape the death penalty. You don't have to take my word for that – General Braun will be here in a few minutes, and he will guarantee that you'll live. But first you have to tell us where Harald is. If you don't, you'll die, and so will your brother.'

Doubt and fear crossed Arne's face. There was a long silence. At last Arne seemed to come to a resolution. He reached out and put the mug on the tray. He looked at Tilde, then turned his gaze to Peter. 'Go to Hell,' he said quietly.

Peter sprang to his feet, furious. 'You're the one who's going to Hell!' he shouted. He kicked his chair over backwards. 'Don't you understand what's happening to you?'

Tilde got to her feet and left quietly.

'If you don't talk to us, you'll be turned over to the Gestapo,' Peter went on angrily. '*They* won't give you tea and ask polite questions. They'll pull out your fingernails, and light matches under the soles of your feet. They'll fasten electrodes to your lips, and throw cold water over you to make the shocks more excruciating. They'll strip you naked and beat you with hammers. They'll smash the bones of your ankles and kneecaps so that you can never walk again, and then they'll carry on beating you, keeping you alive and conscious and screaming. You'll beg and plead with them to let you die, but they won't – not until you talk. And you will talk. Get that into your head. In the end, *everyone talks.*'

White-faced, Arne said quietly: 'I know.'

Peter was taken aback by the poise and resignation behind the fear. What did it mean?

The door opened and General Braun came in. It was now six o'clock, and Peter had been expecting him: his appearance was part of the scenario. Braun was the picture of cold efficiency in his crisp uniform with his holstered pistol. As always, his damaged lungs made his voice a gentle near-whisper. 'Is this the man to be sent to Germany?'

Arne moved fast, despite his injury.

Peter was looking the other way, towards Braun, and he saw only a blur as Arne reached for the tea tray. The heavy earthenware teapot flew through the air and struck the side of Peter's head, splashing tea over his face. When he had dashed the liquid from his eyes he saw Arne charge into Braun. Arne moved clumsily on his wounded leg, but he knocked the general over. Peter sprang to his feet, but he was too slow. In the second for which Braun lay still on the floor, gasping, Arne unbuttoned the general's holster and snatched out the pistol.

He swung the gun toward Peter, holding it two-handed.

Peter froze. The gun was a 9mm Luger. It held eight rounds of ammunition in the grip magazine – but was it loaded? Or did Braun wear it just for show?

Arne remained in a sitting position but pushed himself backward until he was up against the wall.

The door was still open. Tilde stepped inside, saying: 'What—?'

'Stay still!' Arne barked.

Peter asked himself urgently how familiar Arne was with weapons. He was a military officer, but in the air force he might not have had much practice.

As if to answer the unspoken question, Arne switched off the safety catch on the left side of the pistol with a deliberate movement that everyone could see.

Behind Tilde, were the two uniformed policemen who had escorted Arne from his cell. None of the four policemen was carrying a gun. They did not bring weapons into the cell area. It was a strict regulation imposed to prevent prisoners doing exactly what Arne had just done. But Braun did not consider himself subject to the regulations, and no one had had the nerve to ask him to hand in his weapon.

Now Arne had them all at his mercy.

Peter said: 'You can't get away, you know. This is the largest police station in Denmark. You've got the drop on us, but there are dozens of armed police outside. You can't get past them all.'

'I know,' Arne said.

There was that ominous note of resignation again.

Tilde said: 'And would you want to kill so many innocent Danish policemen?'

'No, I wouldn't.'

It all began to make sense. Peter remembered Arne's words when Peter had shot him: *You stupid pig, you should have killed me.* That fitted with the fatalistic attitude Arne had displayed since his arrest. He feared he was going to betray his friends – perhaps even his brother.

Suddenly Peter knew what was going to happen next. Arne had figured out that the only way to be completely safe was to be dead. But Peter wanted Arne to be tortured by the Gestapo and to reveal his secrets. He could not let Arne die.

Despite the gun pointed straight at him, Peter dashed at Arne.

Arne did not shoot him. Instead, he jerked back the gun and pressed its nose into the soft skin under his chin.

Peter flung himself on Arne.

The gun barked once.

Peter struck it from Arne's hand, but he was too late. A gush of blood and brain sprayed from the top of Arne's head, making a fan-shaped stain on the pale wall behind him. Peter fell on Arne, and some of the mess splashed on Peter's face. He rolled away and scrambled to his feet.

Arne's face was strangely unchanged. The damage was all behind, and he still had the ironic smile he had worn as he put the gun to his throat. After a moment, he fell sideways, the smashed back of his skull leaving a red smear on the wall. His body hit the floor with a lifeless thud. He lay still.

Peter wiped his face with his sleeve.

General Braun got to his feet, struggling for breath.

Tilde bent down and picked up the pistol.

They all looked at the body.

'Brave man,' said General Braun.

# TWENTY-ONE

When Harald woke up, he knew that something wonderful had happened, but for a moment he could not recall what it was. He lay on the ledge in the apse of the church, with Karen's blanket around him and Pinetop the cat curled up against his chest, and waited for his memory to work. It seemed to him that the wonderful event was interwoven with something worrying, but he was so excited that he did not care about the danger.

It all came back in a rush: Karen had agreed to fly him to England in the Hornet Moth.

He sat upright suddenly, displacing Pinetop, who leaped to the floor with an indignant yowl.

The danger was that they might both be caught, arrested, and killed. What made him happy, despite that, was that he would be spending hours alone with Karen. Not that he thought anything romantic would happen. He realized she was out of his league. But he could not help how he felt about her. Even if he was never going to kiss her, he was thrilled at the thought of how long they would be together. It was not just the journey, though that would be the climax. Before they could take off they would have to spend days working on the aircraft.

But the whole plan depended on whether he could repair the Hornet Moth. Last night, with only a flashlight for illumination, he had not been able to inspect it thoroughly. Now, with the rising sun shining through the high windows over the apse, he could assess the magnitude of the task.

He washed at the cold tap in the corner, pulled on his clothes, and began his examination.

The first thing he noticed was a long piece of stout rope tied to the undercarriage. What was that for? He thought for a minute, then realized it was for moving the aircraft when the engine was off. With the wings folded, it might be difficult to find a point at which to push the machine, but the rope would enable someone to pull it around like a cart.

Just then, Karen arrived.

She was casually dressed in shorts and sandals, showing off her long, strong legs. Her curly hair was freshly washed and stood out around her head in a coppery cloud. Harald thought angels must look like that. What a tragedy it would be if she died in the adventure that was ahead of them.

It was too early to talk of dying, he told himself. He had not even begun to repair the aircraft. And, in the clear light of morning, it looked a more daunting task.

Like Harald, Karen was pessimistic this morning. Yesterday she had been excited by the prospect of adventure. Today she took a more gloomy view. 'I've been thinking about mending this thing,' she said.

'I'm not sure it can be done, especially in ten days – nine, now.'

Harald felt the onset of the stubborn mood that always came over him when someone told him he could not do something. 'We'll see,' he said.

'You've got that look,' she observed.

'What?'

'The look that says you don't want to hear what's being said.'

'I haven't got a look,' he said tetchily.

She laughed. 'Your teeth are clenched, your mouth is turned down at the corners, and you're frowning.'

He was forced to smile, and in truth he was pleased that she noticed his expression.

'That's better,' she said.

He began to study the Hornet Moth with an engineer's eye. When he had first seen it, he had thought its wings were broken, but Arne had explained that they were folded back for easy storage. Harald looked at the hinges by which they were attached to the fuselage. 'I think I could refit the wings,' he said.

'That's easy. Our instructor, Thomas, did it every time he put the aircraft away. It only takes a few minutes.' She touched the nearer wing. 'The fabric is in a bad state, though.'

The wings and the fuselage were made of wood covered with a fabric that had been treated with some kind of paint. On the upper surface, Harald could see the stitches where the fabric was attached to the ribs with thick thread. The paint was cracked and crazed, and the fabric was torn in places. 'It's only superficial damage,' Harald said. 'Does it matter?'

'Yes. The rips in the fabric might interfere with the air flow over the wings.'

'So we need to patch them. I'm more worried about the undercarriage.'

The aircraft had been in some kind of accident, probably an awkward landing such as Arne had described. Harald knelt down to look more closely at the damaged landing gear. The solid steel stub axle appeared to have two prongs that fitted into a V-shaped strut. The V-strut was made of oval steel tube, and both arms of the V had creased and buckled at their weakest point, presumably just beyond the ends of the stub axle. They looked as if they would easily break. A third strut, that looked to Harald like a shock absorber, appeared undamaged. Nevertheless, the undercarriage was clearly too weak for a landing.

'I did that,' Karen said.

'You crashed?'

'I landed in a crosswind and swerved sideways. The wing tip hit the ground.'

It sounded terrifying. 'Were you scared?'

'No, I just felt such a fool, but Tom said it's not uncommon in a Hornet Moth. In fact he confessed he had done it himself once.'

Harald nodded. That fitted with what Arne had said. But there was something in the way she spoke about Thomas the instructor that made him feel jealous. 'Why was it never repaired?'

'We don't have the facilities here.' She waved at the

workbench and the tool rack. 'Tom could do minor repairs, and he was good with the engine, but this isn't a metalwork shop, and we have no welding gear. Then Daddy had a minor heart attack. He's fine, but it meant he would never get a pilot's licence, and he lost interest in learning to fly. So the work never got done.'

That was discouraging, Harald thought. How was he going to do metalwork? He walked to the tail and examined the wing that had hit the ground. 'It doesn't seem to be fractured,' he said. 'I can easily repair the tip.'

'You can't tell,' she said gloomily. 'One of the wooden spars inside might have been overloaded. There's no way to be sure just by looking at the outside. And if a wing is weakened, the plane will crash.'

Harald studied the tailplane. Its rear half was hinged, and moved up and down: this was the elevator, he recalled. The upright rudder moved right and left. Looking more closely, he saw that they were controlled by wire cables that emerged from the fuselage. But the cables had been cut and removed. 'What happened to the wire?' he said.

'I remember it being taken to repair some other machine.'

'That's going to be a problem.'

'Only the last ten feet of each cable is missing – as far forward as the turnbuckle behind the access panel under the fuselage. The rest was too difficult to get at.'

'All the same, that's forty feet, and you can't buy cables – no one can get spare parts for anything. No doubt that's why they were cannibalized in the first place.' Harald was beginning to feel overwhelmed by misgivings, but he deliberately spoke cheerfully. 'Well, let's see what else is wrong.' He moved to the nose. He found two catches on the right side of the fuselage, turned them, and opened the cowling, which was made of a thin metal that felt like tin but was probably aluminium. He studied the engine.

'It's a four-cylinder in-line layout,' Karen said.

'Yes, but it seems to be upside-down.'

'By comparison with a car engine, yes. The crankshaft is at the top. That's to raise the level of the propeller for ground clearance.'

Harald was surprised by her expertise. He had never met a girl who knew what a crankshaft was. 'What was this Tom like?' he said, trying hard to keep the note of suspicion out of his voice.

'He was a great teacher, patient but encouraging.'

'Did you have a love affair with him?'

'Please! I was fourteen!'

'I bet you had a crush on him.'

She was miffed. 'I suppose you think that's the only reason a girl would learn about engines.'

Harald did think that, but he said: 'No, no, I just noticed that you talked about him in a fond way. None of my business. The engine is air-cooled, I see.' There was no radiator, but the cylinders had cooling fins.

'I think all aero-engines are, to save weight.'

He moved to the other side and opened the right

cowling. All the fuel and oil hoses seemed to be firmly attached, and there were no outward signs of damage. He unscrewed the oil cap and checked the dipstick. There was still a little oil in the tank. 'It looks OK,' he said. 'Let's see if it starts.'

'It's easier with two people. You can sit inside while I swing the propeller.'

'Won't the battery be flat after all these years?'

'There's no battery. The electricity comes from two magnetos which are driven by the engine itself. Let's get into the cabin and I'll show you what to do.'

Karen opened the door then let out a squeal and fell back – into Harald's arms. It was the first time he had touched her body, and an electric thrill went through him. She seemed hardly to notice that they were hugging, and he felt guilty for enjoying a fortuitous embrace. He hastily set her upright and detached himself. 'Are you all right?' he said. 'What happened?'

'Mice.'

He opened the door again. Two mice jumped through the gap and ran down his trousers to the floor. Karen made a disgusted noise.

There were holes in the cloth upholstery of one seat, and Harald guessed they had nested in the stuffing. 'That problem is quickly solved,' he said. He made a kissing sound with his lips, and Pinetop appeared, hoping for food. Harald picked the cat up and handed him into the cabin.

Pinetop suddenly became energized. He darted from one side of the little cockpit to the other, and

Harald thought he saw a mouse tail disappear into the hole under the left-hand seat through which a copper pipe ran. Pinetop leaped on to the seat, then on to the luggage shelf behind, without catching a mouse. Then he investigated the holes in the upholstery. There he found a baby mouse, and began to eat it with great delicacy.

On the luggage shelf, Harald noticed two small books. He reached into the cabin and picked them up. They were manuals, one for the Hornet Moth and one for the Gipsy Major engine that powered it. He was delighted. He showed them to Karen.

'But what about the mice?' she said. 'I hate them.'

'Pinetop chased them off. In future, I'll leave the cabin doors open, so he can get in and out. He'll keep them away.' Harald opened the Hornet Moth manual.

'What's he doing now?'

'Pinetop? Oh, he's eating the babies. Look at these diagrams, this is great!'

'Harald!' she yelled. 'That's disgusting! Go and stop him!'

He was taken aback. 'What's the matter?'

'It's revolting!'

'It's natural.'

'I don't care if it is.'

'What's the alternative?' Harald said impatiently. 'We have to get rid of the nest. I could dig the babies out with my hands, and throw them into the bushes, but Pinetop would still eat them, unless the birds got them first.'

'It's so cruel.'

'They're *mice*, for God's sake!'

'How can you not understand? Can't you see that I hate it!'

'I do understand, I just think it's silly—'

'Oh, you're just a stupid engineer who thinks about how things work and never about how people feel.'

Now he was wounded. 'That's not true.'

'It is,' she said, and she stamped off.

Harald was astonished. 'What the hell was that all about?' he said aloud. Did she really believe he was a stupid engineer who never thought about how people felt? It was very unfair.

He stood on a box to look out of one of the high windows. He saw Karen marching off up the drive towards the castle. She seemed to change her mind, and veered off into the woods. Harald thought of following her, then decided not to.

On the first day of their great collaboration, they had had a row. What chance was there that they could fly to England?

He returned to the aircraft. He might as well try to start the engine. If Karen backed out, he would find another pilot, he told himself.

The instructions were in the manual.

*Chock the wheels and put handbrake hard on.*

He could not find the chocks, but he dragged two boxes of junk across the floor and pushed them hard up against the wheels. He located the handbrake lever in the left-hand door and checked that it was fully engaged. Pinetop was sitting on the seat, licking his paws, wearing a sated look. 'The lady thinks you're disgusting,' Harald told him. The cat looked disdainful and hopped out of the cabin.

*Turn on petrol (control in cabin).*

He opened the door and leaned into the cabin. It was small enough for him to reach the controls without climbing in. The fuel gauge was partly hidden between the two seat backs. Next to it was a knob in a slot. He moved it from 'Off' to 'On'.

*Flood carburetter by actuating the lever on either side of the engine pumps. Flow of petrol through the jet is then caused by operating the tickler of the carburetter.*

The left cowling was still open, and he immediately spotted the two fuel pumps, each with a small lever sticking out. The carburetter tickler was harder to identify, but he eventually guessed it was a ring-pull with a spring-back mechanism. He pulled the ring and worked one of the levers up and down. He had no way of telling whether what he was doing was having any effect. For all he knew, the tank might be dry.

He felt dejected now that Karen had gone. Why was he so clumsy with her? He was desperately keen to be friendly and charming and do whatever it took to please her, but he could not figure out what she wanted. Why could girls not be more like engines?

*Put throttle in 'shut' position, or nearly so.*

He hated manuals that could not make up their minds. Should the throttle be closed, or slightly open? He found the control, a lever in the cabin just forward of the left door. Thinking back to his flight in a Tiger Moth two weeks ago, he recalled that Poul Kirke had set the throttle at about half an inch from the 'Off' end. The Hornet Moth ought to be similar. It had an engraved scale graduated from one to ten, where the Tiger Moth had nothing. Guessing, Harald set the throttle at one.

*Put switches in 'on' position.*

There was a pair of switches on the dashboard marked simply 'On' and 'Off'. Harald guessed they must operate the twin magnetos. He put them on.

*Swing airscrew.*

Harald stood at the front and grasped one of the blades of the propeller. He pulled it down. It was very stiff, and he had to put all his strength into moving it. When finally it turned, it gave a sharp click then stopped.

He turned it again. This time it moved more easily. It clicked again.

The third time, he gave it a vigorous heave, hoping the engine would fire.

Nothing happened.

He tried again. The propeller moved easily, and clicked each time, but the engine remained silent and still.

Karen came in. 'Won't it start?' she said.

He looked at her in surprise. He had not expected to see her again today. He was elated, but replied in a matter-of-fact tone. 'Too early to say – I've only just begun.'

She seemed contrite. 'I'm sorry I stormed off.'

This was a new aspect of her. He would have guessed she was too proud to apologize. 'That's all right,' he said.

'It was just the thought of the cat eating the baby mice. I couldn't stand it. I know it's foolish to think about mice when men like Poul are losing their lives.'

That was how Harald saw it, but he did not say so. 'Pinetop's gone now, anyway.'

'I'm not surprised the engine won't start,' she said, reverting to practical problems – just as he did when embarrassed, he thought. 'It hasn't been turned over for at least three years.'

'It might be a fuel problem. Over a couple of winters, water must have condensed in the tank. But oil floats, so the fuel will lie on top. We might be able to drain off the water.' He consulted the manual again.

'We should turn off the switches, for safety,' Karen said. 'I'll do it.'

Harald learned from the manual that there was a panel on the underside of the fuselage that gave access to the fuel drain plug. He took a screwdriver from the tool rack then lay on the floor and wriggled under the aircraft to unscrew the panel. Karen lay beside him and he handed her the screws. She smelled good, a mixture of warm skin and shampoo.

When the panel came off, Karen handed him an adjustable spanner. The drain plug was awkwardly placed, being slightly to one side of the access hole. This was the kind of fault that made Harald long to be in charge, so that he could force lazy designers to do things properly. When his hand was in the gap, he could no longer see the drain plug, so he had to work blind.

He turned the plug slowly but, when it opened, he was startled by the sudden spurt of freezing liquid on to his hand. He withdrew his hand quickly, banging his numbed fingers on the edge of the access hole and, to his intense irritation, he dropped the plug.

With dismay he heard it roll down the fuselage. Fuel poured from the drain. He and Karen quickly wriggled out of the way of the gush. Then there was nothing they could do except watch until the system was empty and the church reeked of petroleum.

Harald cursed Captain de Havilland and the careless British engineers who had designed the aircraft. 'Now we've got no fuel,' he said bitterly.

'We could syphon some out of the Rolls-Royce,' Karen suggested.

'That's not aeroplane fuel.'

'The Hornet Moth runs on car petrol.'

'Does it? I didn't realize that.' Harald perked up again. 'Right. Let's see if we can get that drain plug back.' He guessed the plug had rolled back until it stopped up against a cross-member. He put his arm into the hole, but could not reach far enough. Karen got a wire brush from the work bench and retrieved it with that. Harald replaced the plug in the drain.

Next they had to take fuel from the car. Harald found a funnel and a clean bucket, while Karen used a pair of heavy pliers to cut a length off a garden hose. They pulled the cover off the Rolls-Royce. Karen undid the fuel cap and fed the hose into the tank.

Harald said: 'Shall I do that?'

'No,' she said. 'My turn.'

He guessed she wanted to prove she could do dirty work, especially after the mice incident, so he stood back and watched.

Karen put the end of the hose between her lips and sucked. When the petrol came into her mouth she quickly directed the hose into the bucket, while at the same time grimacing and spitting. Harald watched the grotesque expressions on her face. Miraculously, she was no less beautiful when screwing up her eyes and pursing her lips. She caught his gaze and said: 'What are you staring at?'

He laughed and said: 'You, of course – you're so pretty when you're spitting.' He realized immediately that he had revealed more of his feelings than he wanted to, and he waited for a sharp retort, but she just laughed.

He had only said she was pretty, of course. That was not news to her. But he had said it affectionately, and girls always noticed tones of voice, especially when you did not want them to. If she had been annoyed, she would have shown it with a disapproving look or an impatient toss of her head. But, on the contrary, she had seemed pleased – almost, he thought, as if she were glad he was fond of her.

He felt he had crossed a bridge.

The bucket filled up and the hose ran dry. They had emptied the tank of the car. There was only a gallon or so of petrol in the bucket, Harald guessed, but it was plenty for testing the engine. He had no idea where they would get enough fuel to cross the North Sea.

Harald carried the bucket over to the Hornet Moth. He flipped open the access cover and pulled the petrol cap. It had a hook to fix it to the lip of the filler neck. Karen held the funnel while Harald poured the fuel into the tank.

'I don't know where we're going to get any more,' Karen said. 'We certainly can't buy it.'

'How much do we need?'

'The tank takes thirty-five gallons. But that's another problem. The Hornet Moth's range is six hundred miles – in ideal conditions.'

'And it's about that distance to Britain.'

'So if conditions are less than perfect – for example, if we have head winds, which is not unlikely . . .'

'We'll come down in the sea.'

'Exactly.'

'One problem at a time,' said Harald. 'We haven't started the engine yet.'

Karen knew what to do. 'I'll flood the carburettor,' she said.

Harald turned on the fuel.

Karen worked the priming mechanism until fuel dribbled on the floor, then called: 'Mags on.'

Harald switched on the magnetos and checked that the throttle was still at the just-open position.

Karen grasped the propeller and pulled it down. Again there was a sharp click. 'Hear that?' she said.

'Yes.'

'It's the impulse starter. That's how you know it's working, by the click.' She swung the propeller a second time, then a third. Finally she gave it a mighty heave and stepped smartly back.

The engine gave a shocking bark which echoed around the church, then it died.

Harald cheered.

Karen said: 'What are you so pleased about?'

'It fired! There can't be much wrong.'

'It didn't start, though.'

'It will, it will. Try again.'

She swung the propeller again, but with the same result. The only change was that Karen's cheeks became attractively flushed with the effort.

After a third try, Harald turned the switches off. 'The fuel is flowing freely now,' he said. 'It sounds to me as if the problem is with the ignition. We need some tools.'

'There's a tool kit.' Karen reached into the cabin and lifted a cushion to reveal a large locker under the seat. She took out a canvas bag with leather straps.

Harald opened the bag and took out a spanner with a cylindrical head on a swivelling joint, designed to operate around corners. 'A universal spark plug spanner,' he said. 'Captain de Havilland did something right.'

There were four spark plugs on the right side of the engine. Harald removed one and examined it. There was oil on the points. Karen took a lace-edged handkerchief from the pocket of her shorts and wiped the plug clean. She found a feeler gauge in the tool kit and checked the gap. Then Harald replaced the plug. They repeated the process with the other three.

'There are four more on the other side,' Karen said.

Although the engine had only four cylinders, there were two magnetos, each operating its own set of spark plugs – a safety measure, Harald presumed. The left side plugs were harder to get at, behind two cooling baffles which first had to be removed.

When all the plugs had been checked, Harald removed the Bakelite caps over the contact breakers and checked the points. Finally, he removed the distributor cap from each magneto in turn, and wiped out the inside with Karen's handkerchief, which had now become a filthy rag.

'We've done all the obvious things,' he said. 'If it doesn't start now, we've got serious trouble.'

Karen primed the engine again then turned the propeller slowly three times. Harald opened the cabin door and threw the magneto switches. Karen gave the propeller a final heave and stepped back.

The engine turned over, barked, and hesitated. Harald, standing by the door with his head in the cabin, pushed the throttle forward. The engine roared to life.

Harald whooped with triumph as the propeller turned, but he could hardly hear his own voice over the noise. The sound of the engine bounced off the church walls and made a deafening racket. He saw Pinetop's tail disappear through a window.

Karen came up to him, her hair blowing wildly in the slipstream from the propeller. In his exuberance, Harald hugged her. 'We did it!' he yelled. She hugged

him back, to his intense pleasure, then said
something. He shook his head, to indicate that he
could not hear her. She came delightfully close to him
and spoke into his ear. He felt her lips brush his
cheek. He could hardly think of anything except how
easy it would be to kiss her now. 'We should turn it
off, before someone hears!' she shouted.

Harald remembered that this was not a game, and
that the purpose of repairing the aircraft was to fly a
dangerous secret mission. He put his head inside the
cabin, moved the throttle back to the closed position,
and switched off the magnetos. The engine stopped.

When the noise died away, the inside of the church
should have been silent, but it was not. A strange
sound came from outside. At first, Harald thought his
ears were still registering the din of the engine, but
gradually he realized it was something else. Still he
could not credit what he heard, for it sounded like
the tramp of marching feet.

Karen stared at him, bewilderment and fear
showing on her face.

They both turned and ran to the windows. Harald
leaped on the box he used for looking out over the
high sills. He gave his hand to Karen, who jumped up
beside him. They looked out together.

A troop of about thirty soldiers in German uniform
was marching up the drive.

At first he assumed they were coming for him, but
he quickly saw that they were in no shape for a
manhunt. Most of them appeared to be unarmed.
They had a heavy wagon drawn by four weary horses,

loaded with what looked like camping gear. They marched past the monastery and continued up the drive. 'What the hell is this?' he said.

'They mustn't get in here!' Karen said.

They both looked around the interior of the church. The main entrance, at the western end, consisted of two enormous wooden doors. This was the way the Hornet Moth must have come in, with its wings folded back. Harald had also driven his bike through there. It had a huge old lock on the inside with a giant key, plus a wooden bar that rested in brackets.

There was only one other entrance, the small side door that led in from the cloisters. This was the one Harald normally used. It had a lock, but Harald had never seen a key. There was no bar.

'We could nail the small door shut, then come in and out through the windows like Pinetop,' Karen said.

'We have a hammer and nails . . . we need a piece of wood.'

In a room full of junk it should have been easy to find a stout plank but, to Harald's disappointment, there was nothing suitable. In the end he prised one of the shelves from the wall above the workbench. He placed it diagonally across the door and nailed it firmly to the door frame.

'A couple of men could break it down without much effort,' he said. 'But at least no one can walk in casually and stumble over our secret.'

'They might look through the windows, though,'

Karen said. 'They would only have to find something to stand on.'

'Let's conceal the propeller.' Harald grabbed the canvas cover they had removed from the Rolls-Royce. Together they draped it over the nose of the Hornet Moth. It reached far enough to cover the cabin.

They stood back. Karen said: 'It still looks like an aircraft with its nose covered and its wings folded back.'

'To you, yes. But you already know what it is. Someone looking in through the window is just going to see a junk room.'

'Unless he happens to be an airman.'

'That wasn't the Luftwaffe out there, was it?'

'I don't know,' she said. 'I'd better go and find out.'

# TWENTY-TWO

Hermia had lived more years in Denmark than England, but suddenly it was a foreign country. The familiar streets of Copenhagen had a hostile air, and she felt she stood out. She hurried like a fugitive down streets where she had walked as a child, hand-in-hand with her father, innocent and carefree. It was not just the checkpoints, the German uniforms, and the grey-green Mercedes cars. Even the Danish police made her jumpy.

She had friends here, but she did not contact them. She was afraid of bringing more people into danger. Poul had died, Jens had presumably been arrested and she did not know what had happened to Arne. She felt cursed.

She was exhausted and stiff from her overnight ferry trip, and racked with worry about Arne. Excruciatingly aware of the hours ticking by toward the full moon, she forced herself to move with the utmost caution.

The home of Jens Toksvig in St Paul's Gade was one of a row, all single storey, with front doors that gave immediately on to the pavement. Number fifty-three appeared empty. No one went to the door except the postman. On the previous day, when Hermia telephoned from Bornholm, it had been occupied by at least one policeman, but the guard must have been withdrawn.

Hermia also observed the neighbours. On one side was a dilapidated house occupied by a young couple with a child – the kind of people who might be too absorbed in their own life to take an interest in their neighbours. But in the freshly painted and neatly curtained house on the other side was an older woman who looked out of the window frequently.

After watching for three hours, Hermia went to the neat house and knocked.

A plump woman of about sixty years came to the door in an apron. Looking at the little suitcase Hermia was carrying, she said: 'I never buy anything on the doorstep.' She smiled in a superior way, as if her refusal was a mark of social distinction.

Hermia smiled back. 'I've been told that number fifty-three might be available to rent.'

The neighbour's attitude changed. 'Oh?' she said with interest. 'Looking for a place to live, are you?'

'Yes.' The woman was as nosey as Hermia had hoped. Indulging her, Hermia said: 'I'm getting married.'

The woman's glance went automatically to Hermia's left hand, and Hermia showed her the engagement ring. 'Very nice. Well, I must say, it would be a relief to have a respectable family next door, after the goings-on.'

'Goings-on?'

She lowered her voice. 'It was a nest of Communist spies.'

'No, really?'

The woman folded her arms over her corseted bosom. 'They were arrested last Wednesday, the whole pack of them.'

Hermia felt a chill of fear, but she made herself keep up the pretence of idle gossip. 'Goodness! How many?'

'I couldn't say, exactly. There was the tenant, young Mr Toksvig, who I wouldn't have taken for a wrongdoer, though he wasn't always as respectful to his elders as he might have been, then lately an airman seemed to be living there, a nice-looking boy, though he never said much; but there were all sorts in and out of the place, mostly military types.'

'And they were arrested on Wednesday?'

'On that very pavement, where you see Mr Schmidt's spaniel cocking his leg against the lamp post, there was a shooting.'

Hermia gasped, and her hand flew to her mouth. 'Oh, no!'

The old woman nodded, pleased with this reaction to her story, not suspecting that she might be speaking of the man Hermia loved. 'A plain-clothes policeman shot one of the Communists.' She added superfluously: 'With a gun.'

Hermia was so afraid of what she might learn that she could hardly speak. She forced out three words: 'Who was shot?'

'I didn't actually see it myself,' the woman said with

infinite regret. 'I happened to be over at my sister's house in Fischer's Gade, borrowing a knitting pattern for a cardigan. It wasn't Mr Toksvig himself, that I can say for sure, because Mrs Eriksen in the shop saw it, and she said it was a man she didn't know.'

'Was he . . . killed?'

'Oh, no. Mrs Eriksen thought he might have been wounded in the leg. Anyhow, he cried out when the ambulance men lifted him on to the stretcher.'

Hermia felt sure it was Arne who had been shot. She seemed to feel the pain of a bullet wound herself. She was breathless and dizzy. She needed to get away from this awful old busybody who told the tragic story with such relish. 'I must be going,' she said. 'What a dreadful thing to happen.' She turned away.

'Anyway, I should think the place will be to rent, before too long,' the woman said to her back.

Hermia walked away, paying no attention.

She turned corners at random until she came to a café, where she sat down to gather her thoughts. A hot cup of ersatz tea helped her recover from the shock. She had to find out for sure what had happened to Arne and where he was now. But first she needed somewhere to spend the night.

She got a room at a cheap hotel near the waterfront. It was a sleazy place, but her bedroom door had a stout lock. At about midnight, a slurred voice outside asked if she would like a little drink, and she got up to jam the door with a tilted chair.

She spent most of the night awake, wondering if Arne had been the man shot in St Paul's Gade. If so, how badly was he hurt? If not, had he been arrested with the others, or was he still at large? Whom could she ask? She could contact Arne's family, but they probably would not know, and it would scare them to death to be asked whether he had been shot. She knew many of his friends, but the only ones likely to know what had happened were dead, or in custody, or in hiding.

In the early hours of the morning, it occurred to her that there was one person who was almost certain to know if Arne had been arrested: his commanding officer.

At first light, she went to the railway station and caught a train to Vodal.

As the train crawled south, stopping at every sleepy village, she thought of Digby. By now he would be back in Sweden, waiting impatiently on the quay at Kalvsby for her to arrive with Arne and the film. The fisherman would come back alone, and tell Digby that Hermia had not appeared at their rendezvous. Digby would not know whether she had been captured or merely delayed. He would be as distraught about her as she was about Arne.

The flying school had a desolate feel. There were no aircraft on the field and none in the sky. A few machines were being serviced and, in one of the hangars, some trainees were being shown the innards of an engine. She was directed to the headquarters building.

She had to give her real name, for there were people here who knew her. She asked to see the base commander, adding: 'Tell him I'm a friend of Arne Olufsen's.'

She knew she was taking a risk. She had met Squadron Leader Renthe, and remembered him as a tall, thin man with a moustache. She had no idea what his politics were. If he happened to be pro-Nazi, she could be in trouble. He might phone the police and report an Englishwoman asking questions. But he was fond of Arne, as so many people were, so she was hoping that for Arne's sake he would not betray her. Anyway, she was going to take the chance. She had to find out what had happened.

She was admitted immediately, and Renthe recognized her. 'My God – you're Arne's fiancée!' he said. 'I thought you'd gone back to England.' He hurried to close the door behind her – a good sign, she thought, for if he wanted privacy that suggested he was not going to alert the police, at least not immediately.

She decided to offer no explanation of why she was in Denmark. Let him draw his own conclusions. 'I'm trying to find out where Arne is,' she said. 'I fear he may be in trouble.'

'It's worse than that,' said Renthe. 'You'd better sit down.'

Hermia remained standing. 'Why?' she cried. 'Why sit down? What's happened?'

'He was arrested last Wednesday.'

'Is that all?'

'He was shot and wounded while trying to escape from the police.'

'So it was him.'

'I beg your pardon?'

'A neighbour told me one of them had been shot. How is he?'

'Please do sit down, my dear.'

Hermia sat down. 'It's bad, isn't it?'

'Yes.' Renthe hesitated. Then, in a low voice, he said slowly: 'I'm dreadfully sorry to have to tell you that I'm afraid Arne is dead.'

She cried out in anguish. In her heart she had known this might be so, but the possibility of losing him had been too dreadful to think about. Now that it had come, she felt as if she had been struck by a train. 'No,' she said. 'It's not true.'

'He died in police custody.'

'What?' With an effort, she made herself listen.

'He died at police headquarters.'

A terrible possibility entered her mind. 'Did they torture him?'

'I don't think so. It seems that, in order to avoid revealing information under torture, he took his own life.'

'Oh, God!'

'He sacrificed himself to protect his friends, I'd guess.'

Renthe looked blurred, and Hermia realized she was seeing him through tears which were streaming down her face. She fumbled for a handkerchief, and Renthe passed her his own. She wiped her face, but the tears kept coming.

Renthe said: 'I've only just heard. I've got to phone Arne's parents and tell them.'

Hermia knew them well. She found the steely pastor difficult to deal with: it seemed he could relate to people only by dominating them, and subservience did not come easily to Hermia. He loved his sons, but expressed his love by laying down rules. What Hermia remembered most vividly about Arne's mother was that her hands were always chapped from being in water too much, washing clothes and preparing vegetables and scrubbing floors. Thinking of them drew Hermia's thoughts away from her own loss, and she felt a surge of compassion. They would be distraught. 'How dreadful for you to be the bearer of such news,' she said to Renthe.

'Indeed. Their firstborn son.'

That made her think of the other son, Harald. He was fair where Arne was dark, and they were different in other ways: Harald was more serious, somewhat intellectual, with little of Arne's easy charm, but likeable in his own way. Arne had said he was going to talk to Harald about ways to sneak into the base on Sande. How much did Harald know? Had he got involved?

Her mind was turning to practical matters, but she felt hollow. The state of shock she was in would permit her to carry on with her life, but she felt as if she would never be whole again. 'What else did the police tell you?' she asked Renthe.

'Officially, they would say only that he had died while giving information, and that "No other person is thought to have been involved," which is their euphemism for suicide. But a friend at the

Politigaarden told me Arne did it to avoid being turned over to the Gestapo.'

'Did they find anything in his possession?'

'What do you mean?'

'Such as photographs?'

Renthe stiffened. 'My friend didn't say so, and it's dangerous for you and me to even discuss such a possibility. Miss Mount, I was fond of Arne, and for his sake I would like to do anything I can for you, but please remember that as an officer I have sworn loyalty to the King, whose orders to me are to cooperate with the occupying power. Whatever my personal opinions might be, I can't countenance espionage – and, if I thought someone was involved in such activity, it would be my duty to report the facts.'

Hermia nodded. It was a clear warning. 'I appreciate your frankness, Squadron Leader.' She stood up, wiping her face. She remembered that the handkerchief was his, and said: 'I'll launder this, and send it back to you.'

'Don't even think about it.' He came around his desk and put his hands on her shoulders. 'I really am most dreadfully sorry. Please accept my deepest sympathy.'

'Thank you,' she said, and she left.

As soon as she was out of the building, the tears came again. Renthe's handkerchief was a wet rag. She would not have thought she had so much fluid in her. Seeing everything through a watery screen, she made her way somehow to the railway station.

The hollow calm came back as she considered

where to go next. The mission that had killed Poul and Arne was not done. She still had to get photographs of the radar equipment on Sande before the next full moon. But now she had an additional motive: revenge. Completion of the task would be the most painful retribution she could inflict upon the men who had driven Arne to his death. And she found a new asset to help her. She no longer cared for her own safety. She felt ready to take any risk. She would walk down the streets of Copenhagen with her head held high, and woe betide anyone who tried to stop her.

But what, exactly, would she do?

Arne's brother might be the key. Harald would probably know whether Arne had returned to Sande before the police got him, and he might even know whether Arne had had photographs in his possession when he was arrested. Furthermore, she thought she knew where to find Harald.

She took a train back to Copenhagen. It travelled so slowly that by the time she got to the city it was too late for another journey. She went to bed in her flophouse, with the door locked against amorous drunks, and cried herself to sleep. On the following morning she got the first train to the suburban village of Jansborg.

The newspaper she bought at the station had the headline HALF WAY TO MOSCOW. The Nazis had made astonishing leaps. In only a week they had taken Minsk and were in sight of Smolensk, two hundred miles inside Soviet territory.

The full moon was eight days away.

She told the school secretary that she was Arne Olufsen's fiancée, and she was shown in to Heis's office immediately. The man who had been responsible for the education of Arne and Harald made her think of a giraffe in spectacles, looking down a long nose at the world below. 'So you're Arne's wife-to-be,' he said amiably. 'How very nice to meet you.'

He appeared to have no knowledge of the tragedy. Without preamble, Hermia said: 'Haven't you heard the news?'

'News? I'm not sure I have . . .'

'Arne is dead.'

'Oh, my goodness me!' Heis sat down heavily.

'I thought you might have heard.'

'No. When did it happen?'

'Early yesterday, at police headquarters in Copenhagen. He took his own life to avoid interrogation by the Gestapo.'

'How very dreadful.'

'Does this mean that his brother doesn't know yet?'

'I've no idea. Harald is no longer here.'

She was surprised. 'Why not?'

'I'm afraid he was expelled.'

'I thought he was a star pupil!'

'Yes, but he misbehaved.'

Hermia did not have time to discuss schoolboy transgressions. 'Where is he now?'

'Back at his parents' home, I presume.' Heis frowned. 'Why do you ask?'

'I'd like to talk to him.'

Heis looked thoughtful. 'About anything in particular?'

Hermia hesitated. Caution dictated that she say nothing to Heis about her mission, but his last two questions suggested to her that he knew something. She said: 'Arne may have had something of mine in his possession when he was arrested.'

Heis was pretending that his questions were casual, but he was gripping the edge of his desk hard enough to turn his knuckles white. 'May I ask what?'

She hesitated again, then took a chance. 'Some photographs.'

'Ah.'

'That means something to you?'

'Yes.'

Hermia wondered whether Heis would trust her. For all he knew, she could have been a detective posing as Arne's fiancée. 'Arne died for those photos,' she said. 'He was trying to get them to me.'

Heis nodded, and seemed to come to a decision. 'After Harald had been expelled, he returned to the school at night and broke into the photographic darkroom in the chemistry lab.'

Hermia gave a sigh of satisfaction. Harald had developed the film. 'Did you see the pictures?'

'Yes. I have been telling people they were photographs of young ladies in risqué poses, but that's just a story. The pictures were of a military installation.'

Hermia was thrilled. The photos had been taken.

The mission had succeeded to that extent. But where was the film now? Had there been time for Harald to give it to Arne? If so, the police had it now, and Arne's sacrifice had been for nothing. 'When did Harald do this?'

'Last Thursday.'

'Arne was arrested on Wednesday.'

'So Harald still has your photographs.'

'Yes.' Hermia's spirits lifted. Arne's death had not been futile. The crucial film was still in circulation, somewhere. She stood up. 'Thank you for your help.'

'You're going to Sande?'

'Yes. To find Harald.'

'Good luck,' said Heis.

# TWENTY-THREE

The German army had a million horses. Most divisions included a veterinary company, dedicated to healing sick and wounded beasts, finding fodder, and catching runaways. One such company had now been billeted on Kirstenslot.

It was the worst possible stroke of luck for Harald. The officers were living in the castle, and about a hundred men were bedded down in the ruined monastery. The old cloisters, adjacent to the church where Harald had his hideout, had been turned into a horse hospital.

The army had been persuaded not to use the church itself. Karen had pleaded with her father to negotiate this, saying she did not want the soldiers to damage the childhood treasures that were stored there. Mr Duchwitz had pointed out to the commanding officer, Captain Kleiss, that the junk in the church left little usable room anyway. After a glance through a window – Harald being absent, warned away by Karen – Kleiss had agreed to its remaining locked up. As a quid pro quo, he had requested three rooms in the castle for offices, and the deal had been struck.

The Germans were polite, friendly – and curious. On top of all the difficulties Harald faced repairing the Hornet Moth, he now had to do everything under the noses of the soldiers.

He was undoing the nuts that held the buckled wishbone axle. His plan was to detach the damaged section, then sneak past the soldiers and go to Farmer Nielsen's workshop. If Nielsen would let him, he would repair it there. Meanwhile, the intact third leg, with the shock absorber, would hold the weight of the aircraft while stationary.

The wheel brake was probably damaged, but Harald was not going to worry about brakes. They were used mainly when taxiing, and Karen had told him she could manage without them.

As he worked, Harald kept glancing up at the windows, expecting at any moment to see the face of Captain Kleiss looking in. Kleiss had a big nose and a thrusting chin, which gave him a belligerent look. But no one came, and after a few minutes Harald had the V-shaped strut in his hand.

He stood on a box to look through a window. The eastern end of the church was partly obscured by a chestnut tree that was now in full leaf. There seemed to be no one in the immediate vicinity. Harald pushed the strut through the window and dropped it on the ground outside, then jumped after it.

Beyond the tree, he could see the wide lawn in front of the castle. The soldiers had pitched four large tents and parked their vehicles there, jeeps and horse boxes and a fuel tanker. A few men were visible, passing from one tent to another, but it was afternoon, and most of the company were away on missions, taking horses to and from the railway station, negotiating with farmers for hay, or treating sick horses in Copenhagen and other towns.

He picked up the strut and walked quickly into the wood.

As he turned the corner of the church, he saw Captain Kleiss.

The captain was a big man with an aggressive air, and he was standing with his arms crossed and his legs apart, talking to a sergeant. They both turned and looked straight at Harald.

Harald suffered the sudden nausea of fear. Was he to be caught so early? He stopped, wanting to turn back, then realized that to run away would be incriminating. He hesitated then walked forward, conscious that his behaviour looked guilty, and that he was carrying part of the undercarriage of an aeroplane. He had been caught red-handed, and all he could do was try to bluff it out. He tried to hold the strut in a casual way, as he might carry a tennis racket or a book.

Kleiss addressed him in German. 'Who are you?'

He swallowed, trying to remain calm. 'Harald Olufsen.'

'And what's that you've got?'

'This?' Harald could hear his own heartbeat. He tried desperately to think of a plausible lie. 'It's, um . . .' He felt himself blush, then was saved by inspiration. 'Part of the mower assembly from a reaping machine.' It occurred to him that an uneducated Danish farm boy would not speak such good German, and he wondered anxiously whether Kleiss was subtle enough to spot the anomaly.

Kleiss said: 'What's wrong with the machine?'

'Er, it ran over a boulder and buckled the frame.'

Kleiss took the strut from him. Harald hoped he did not know what he was looking at. Horses were the man's business, and there was no reason why he should be able to recognize part of the undercarriage of an aircraft. Harald stopped breathing, waiting for Kleiss's verdict. At last the man gave him back the strut. 'All right, on your way.'

Harald walked into the woods.

When he was out of sight, he stopped and leaned against a tree. That had been an awful moment. He thought he might vomit, but managed to suppress the reaction.

He pulled himself together. There might be more such moments. He would have to get used to it.

He walked on. The weather was warm but cloudy, a summer combination dismally familiar in Denmark, where no place was far from the sea. As he approached the farm, he wondered how angry old Nielsen was that he had left without warning after working only one day.

He found Nielsen in the farmyard staring truculently at a tractor with steam pouring from its engine.

Nielsen gave him a hostile glare. 'What do you want, runaway?'

That was a bad start. 'I'm sorry I left without explanation,' Harald said. 'I was called home to my parents' place quite suddenly, and I didn't have time to speak to you before I left.'

Nielsen did not ask what the emergency had been. 'I can't afford to pay unreliable workers.'

That made Harald hopeful. If money was what the mean old farmer was concerned about, he could keep it. 'I'm not asking you to pay me.'

Nielsen only grunted at that, but he looked a shade less malign. 'What do you want, then?'

Harald hesitated. This was the difficult bit. He did not want to tell Nielsen too much. 'A favour,' he said.

'What sort?'

Harald showed him the strut. 'I'd like to use your workshop to repair a part from my motorcycle.'

Nielsen looked at him. 'By Christ, you've got a nerve, lad.'

I know that, Harald thought. 'It's really important,' he pleaded. 'Perhaps you could do that instead of paying me for the day I worked.'

'Perhaps I could.' Nielsen hesitated, obviously reluctant to do anything helpful, but his parsimony got the better of him. 'All right, then.'

Harald concealed his elation.

Nielsen added: 'If you fix this damn tractor first.'

Harald cursed under his breath. He did not want to waste time on Nielsen's tractor when he had such a short time to repair the Hornet Moth. But it was only a boiling radiator. 'All right,' he said.

Nielsen stomped off to find something else to grumble about.

The tractor soon ran out of steam, and Harald was able to look at the engine. He immediately saw that a hose had perished where it was clamped to a pipe, allowing water to leak out of the cooling system. There was no chance of getting a replacement hose, of course, but fortunately the existing one had some slack in it, so he was able to cut off the rotten end and reattach the hose. He got a bucket of hot water from the farmhouse kitchen and refilled the radiator – it was damaging to run cold water through an overheated engine. Finally he started the tractor to make sure the clamp held. It did.

At last he went into the workshop.

He needed some thin sheet steel to reinforce the fractured part of the axle strut. He already knew where to get it. There were four metal shelves on the wall. He took everything off the top shelf and rearranged the items on the three lower shelves. Then he lifted the top shelf down. Using Nielsen's metal shears, he trimmed off the flanged edges of the shelf, then cut four strips.

He would use these as splints.

He put one strip in a vice and hammered it into a rough curve to fit over the oval tube of the strut. He did the same with the other three strips. Then he welded them in place over the dents in the strut.

He stood back to look at his work. 'Unsightly, but effective,' he said aloud.

Tramping back through the woods to the castle, he could hear the sounds of the army camp: men calling to one another, engines revving, horses whinnying. It was early evening, and the soldiers would have returned from their day's duties. He wondered whether he would have trouble getting back into the church unnoticed.

He approached the monastery from the back. At the north side of the church, a young private was leaning against the wall, smoking a cigarette. Harald nodded to him, and the soldier said in Danish: 'Good day, I am Leo.'

Harald tried to smile. 'I'm Harald, nice to meet you.'

'Would you like a cigarette?'

'Thank you, another time, I'm in a hurry.'

Harald walked around to the side of the church. He had found a log and rolled it under one of the windows. Now he stood on it and looked into the church. He passed the wishbone strut through the glassless window and dropped it on to the box that stood below the window on the inside. It bounced off the box and fell to the floor. Then he wriggled through.

A voice said: 'Hello!'

His heart stopped, then he saw Karen. She was at the tail, partly concealed by the aircraft, working on the wing with the damaged tip. Harald picked up the axle strut and went to show it to her.

Then a voice said in German: 'I thought this place was empty!'

Harald spun around. The young private, Leo, was looking in through the window. Harald stared at him aghast, cursing his luck. 'It's a storeroom,' he said.

Leo wriggled through the window and dropped to the floor. Harald shot a glance back to the tail of the aircraft. Karen had vanished. Leo looked around, seeming curious rather than suspicious.

The Hornet Moth was covered from propeller to cabin, and the wings were folded back, but the fuselage was visible, and the tail fin could be made out at the far side of the church. How observant was Leo?

Luckily, the soldier seemed more interested in the Rolls-Royce. 'Nice car,' he said. 'Is it yours?'

'Unfortunately not,' said Harald. 'The motorcycle is mine.' He held up the axle strut from the Hornet Moth. 'This is for my sidecar. I'm trying to fix it up.'

'Ah!' Leo showed no sign of scepticism. 'I'd like to help you, but I don't know anything about machinery. Horseflesh is my specialty.'

'Of course.' They were about the same age, and Harald felt sympathy for the lonely young man far from home. But he wished all the same that Leo would go before he saw too much.

A shrill whistle sounded. 'Supper time,' Leo said.

Thank God, Harald thought.

'It was a pleasure talking to you, Harald. I look forward to seeing you again.'

'Me, too.'

Leo stood on the box and pulled himself out through the window.

'Jesus,' Harald said aloud.

Karen emerged from behind the tail of the Hornet Moth, looking shaken. 'That was a nasty moment.'

'He wasn't suspicious, he just wanted to talk.'

'God preserve us from friendly Germans,' she said with a smile.

'Amen.' He loved it when she smiled. It was like the sun coming up. He looked at her face as long as he dared.

Then he turned to the wing she had been working on. She was repairing the rips, he saw. He went closer and stood next to her. She was dressed in old corduroy trousers that looked as if they had been worn for gardening, and a man's shirt with the sleeves rolled. 'I'm gluing patches of linen over the damaged areas,' she explained. 'When the glue is dry, I'll paint over the patches to make them airtight.'

'Where did you get the material, and the glue, and the paint?'

'From the theatre. I fluttered my eyelashes at a set builder.'

'Good for you.' It was obviously easy for her to get men to do anything she wanted. He was jealous of the set builder. 'What do you do at the theatre all day, anyway?' he said.

'I'm understudying the lead in *Les Sylphides*.'

'Will you get to dance it on stage?'

'No. There are two casts, so both the other dancers would have to fall ill.'

'Shame. I'd love to see you.'

'If the impossible happens, I'll get you a ticket.' She

returned her attention to the wing. 'We have to make sure there are no internal fractures.'

'That means we have to examine the wooden spars under the fabric.'

'Yes.'

'Well, now that we've got the material to repair rips, I suppose we could cut an inspection panel in the fabric and just look inside.'

She looked dubious. 'OK . . .'

He did not think a knife would easily cut the treated linen, but he found a sharp chisel on the tool shelf. 'Where should we cut?'

'Near the struts.'

He pressed the chisel into the surface. Once the initial breach had been made, the chisel cut the fabric relatively easily. Harald made an L-shaped incision and folded back a flap, making a sizable opening.

Karen pointed a flashlight into the hole, then put her face down and peered inside. She took her time looking around, then withdrew her head and put her arm in. She grasped something and shook vigorously. 'I think we're in luck,' she said. 'Nothing shifts.'

She stepped back and Harald took her place. He reached inside, grasped a strut, and pushed and pulled it. The entire wing moved, but he felt no weakness.

Karen was pleased. 'We're making progress,' she said. 'If I can finish the work on the fabric tomorrow, and you can bolt the axle strut back on, the airframe will be complete, except for the missing cables. And we've still got eight days to go.'

'Not really,' Harald said. 'We probably need to reach England at least twenty-four hours before the raid, for our information to have any effect. That brings it down to seven. To arrive on the seventh day, we need to leave the previous evening and fly overnight. So we really have six days at the most.'

'Then I'll have to finish the fabric tonight.' She looked at her watch. 'I'd better show up at the house for dinner, but I'll come back as soon as I can.'

She put away the glue and washed her hands at the sink, using soap she had brought from the house for Harald. He watched her. He was always sorry when she left. He thought he would like to be with her all day, every day. He guessed that was the feeling that made people want to get married. Did he want to marry Karen? It seemed like a foolish question. Of course he did. He had no doubt. He sometimes tried to imagine the two of them after ten years, fed up with one another and bored, but it was impossible. Karen would never be boring.

She dried her hands on a scrap of towel. 'What are you so thoughtful about?'

He felt himself blush. 'Wondering what the future holds.'

She gave him a startlingly direct look, and for a moment he felt she could read his mind; then she looked away. 'A long flight across the North Sea,' she said. 'Six hundred miles without landfall. So we'd better be sure this old kite can make it.'

She went to the window and stood on the box.

'Don't look – this is an undignified manoeuvre for a lady.'

'I won't, I swear,' he said with a laugh.

She pulled herself up. Breaking his promise cheerfully, he watched her rear as she wriggled through. Then she dropped out of sight.

He turned his attention back to the Hornet Moth. It should not take long to reattach the braced axle strut. He found the nuts and bolts where he had left them, on the work bench. He knelt by the wheel, fitted the strut in place, and began to attach the bolts that held it to the fuselage and the wheel mounting.

Just as he was finishing, Karen came back in, much sooner than expected.

He smiled, pleased at her early return, then saw that she looked distraught. 'What's happened?' he said.

'Your mother telephoned.'

Harald was angry. 'Damn! I shouldn't have told her where I was going. Who did she speak to?'

'My father. But he told her you definitely weren't here, and she seems to have believed him.'

'Thank God.' He was glad he had decided not to tell Mother he was living in the disused church. 'What did she want, anyway?'

'There's bad news.'

'What?'

'It's about Arne.'

Harald realized, with a guilty start, that in the last few days he had hardly given a thought to his brother, languishing in jail. 'What's happened?'

'Arne is . . . he's dead.'

At first Harald could not take it in. 'Dead?' he said as if he did not understand the meaning of the word. 'How could that be?'

'The police say he took his own life.'

'Suicide?' Harald had the feeling the world was crumbling around him, the walls of the church collapsing and the trees in the park falling over and the castle of Kirstenslot blowing away in a strong wind. 'Why would he do that?'

'To avoid interrogation by the Gestapo, Arne's commanding officer told her.'

'To avoid . . .' Harald saw immediately what that meant. 'He was afraid he wouldn't be able to withstand the torture.'

Karen nodded. 'That was the implication.'

'If he had talked, he would have betrayed me.'

She was silent, neither agreeing with him nor contradicting him.

'He killed himself to protect me.' Harald suddenly needed Karen to confirm his inference. He took her by the shoulders. 'I'm right, am I not?' he shouted. 'That must be it! He did it for me! Say something, for God's sake.'

At last she spoke. 'I think you're right,' she whispered.

In an instant Harald's anger was transformed into grief. It swamped him, and he lost control. Tears flooded his eyes, and his body shook with sobs. 'Oh, God,' he said, and he covered his wet face with his hands. 'Oh, God, this is awful.'

He felt Karen's arms enfold him. Gently, she drew his head down to her shoulder. His tears soaked into her hair and ran down her throat. She stroked his neck and kissed his wet face.

'Poor Arne,' Harald said, his voice choked by sorrow. 'Poor Arne.'

'I'm sorry,' Karen murmured. 'My darling Harald, I'm so sorry.'

# TWENTY-FOUR

In the middle of the Politigaarden, Copenhagen's police headquarters, was a spacious circular courtyard open to the sunshine. It was ringed by an arcade with classical double pillars in a perfect repeating pattern. To Peter Flemming, the design stood for the way order and regularity permitted the light of truth to shine in on human wickedness. He often wondered whether the architect had intended that, or had just thought a courtyard might look nice.

He and Tilde Jespersen stood in the arcade, leaning against a pair of pillars, smoking cigarettes. Tilde wore a sleeveless blouse that showed the smooth skin of her arms. She had fine blonde hair on her forearms. 'The Gestapo have finished with Jens Toksvig,' he told her.

'And?'

'Nothing.' He felt exasperated, and he shook his shoulders as if to shrug off the feeling of frustration. 'He has told everything he knows, of course. He is one of the Nightwatchmen, he passed information to Poul Kirke, and he agreed to shelter Arne Olufsen when Arne was on the run. He also said that this whole project had been organized by Arne's fiancée, Hermia Mount, who is with MI6 back in England.'

'Interesting – but it doesn't get us anywhere.'

'Exactly. Unfortunately for us, Jens doesn't know who sneaked into the base on Sande, and he has no knowledge of the film Harald developed.'

Tilde drew in smoke. Peter watched her mouth. She seemed to be kissing the cigarette. She inhaled, then blew smoke out through her nostrils. 'Arne killed himself to protect someone,' she said. 'I assume that person has the film.'

'His brother Harald either has it or has passed it to someone else. Either way, we have to talk to him.'

'Where is he?'

'At the parsonage on Sande, I assume. It's the only home he's got.' He looked at his watch. 'I'm catching a train in an hour.'

'Why not phone?'

'I don't want to give him the chance to run away.'

Tilde looked troubled. 'What will you say to the parents? Don't you think they might blame you for what happened to Arne?'

'They don't know I was there when Arne shot himself. They don't even know I arrested him.'

'I suppose not,' she said dubiously.

'Anyway, I don't give a shit what they think,' Peter said impatiently. 'General Braun hit the roof when I told him that the spies may have photographs of the base on Sande. God knows what the Germans have there but it's deadly secret. And he blames me. If that film leaves Denmark, I don't know what he'll do to me.'

'But you're the one who uncovered the spy ring!'

'And I almost wish I hadn't.' He dropped his cigarette end and stamped on it, grinding it with the sole of his shoe. 'I'd like you to come to Sande with me.'

Her clear blue eyes gave him an appraising look. 'Of course, if you want my help.'

'And I'd like you to meet my parents.'

'Where would I stay?'

'I know a small hotel in Morlunde, quiet and clean, that I think would suit you.' His father owned a hotel, of course, but that was too close to home. If Tilde stayed there, the entire population of Sande would know what she was doing every minute of the day.

Peter and Tilde had not spoken about what had happened in his apartment, even though it was six days ago. He was not sure what to say. He had felt driven to do it, to have sex with Tilde in front of Inge, and Tilde had gone along with it, sharing his passion and seeming to understand his need. Afterwards, she had seemed troubled, and he had driven her home and left her with a goodnight kiss.

They had not repeated it. Once was enough to prove whatever he had to prove. He had gone to Tilde's apartment the following evening, but her son had been awake, asking for drinks of water and complaining of bad dreams, and Peter had left early. Now he saw the trip to Sande as a chance to get her alone.

But she seemed to hesitate. She asked another practical question: 'What about Inge?'

'I'll get the nursing agency to provide twenty-four-hour cover, as I did when we went to Bornholm.'

'I see.'

She looked across the courtyard, considering, and he studied her profile: the small nose, the bow-shaped mouth, the determined chin. He remembered the overwhelming thrill of possessing her. Surely she could not have forgotten that. He said: 'Don't you want to spend a night together?'

She turned to him with a smile. 'Of course I do,' she said. 'I'd better go and pack a case.'

\* \* \*

On the following morning, Peter woke up in the Oesterport Hotel in Morlunde. The Oesterport was a respectable establishment but its owner, Erland Berten, was not married to the woman who called herself Mrs Berten. Erland had a wife in Copenhagen who would not give him a divorce. No one in Morlunde knew this except Peter Flemming, who had discovered it by chance, while investigating the murder of one Jacob Berten, who was no relation. Peter had let Erland know he had found out about the real Mrs Berten, but had otherwise kept the news to himself, knowing that the secret gave him power over Erland. Now he could rely on Erland's discretion. Whatever happened between Peter and Tilde in the Oesterport Hotel, Erland would tell no one.

However, Peter and Tilde had not slept together in the end. Their train had been delayed, and had finally arrived in the middle of the night, long after the last ferry to Sande. Weary and bad-tempered after the frustrating journey, they had checked in to separate single rooms and grabbed a couple of hours' sleep. Now they were going to catch the first ferry of the morning.

He dressed quickly then went and tapped on Tilde's door. She was putting on a straw hat, looking in the mirror over the fireplace as she adjusted it. He kissed her cheek, not wanting to spoil her make-up.

They walked down to the harbour. A local policeman and a German soldier asked them for their identity cards as they boarded the ferry. The checkpoint was new. Peter guessed it was an additional security precaution brought in by the Germans because of the spies' interest in Sande. But it could be useful to Peter, too. He showed his police badge and asked them to write down the names of everyone visiting the island over the next few days. It would be interesting to see who came to Arne's funeral.

On the other side of the channel, the hotel's horse-drawn taxi was waiting for them. Peter told the driver to take them to the parsonage.

The sun was edging up over the horizon, gleaming off the little windows of the low houses. There had been rain overnight, and the coarse grass of the sand dunes glistened with droplets. A light breeze ruffled the surface of the sea. The island seemed to have put on its best clothes for Tilde's visit. 'What a pretty place,' she said. He was glad she liked it. He pointed out the sights as they drove: the hotel, his father's house – the largest on the island – and the military base that was the target of the spy ring.

Approaching the parsonage, Peter noticed that the door to the little church stood open, and he heard a piano. 'That might be Harald,' he said. He heard the excitement in his own voice. Could it be this easy? He coughed, and made his voice deeper and calmer. 'Let's see, shall we?'

They dismounted from the buggy. The driver said: 'What time shall I come back, Mr Flemming?'

'Wait here, please,' Peter said.

'I've got other customers—'

'Just wait!'

The driver muttered something under his breath.

Peter said: 'If you're not here when I come out, you're fired.' The driver looked sulky, but he stayed put.

Peter and Tilde entered the church. At the far end of the room a tall figure was seated at the piano. He had his back to the door, but Peter knew the broad shoulders and domed head. It was Bruno Olufsen, Harald's father.

Peter winced with disappointment. He was hungry for this arrest. He must be careful not to let his need take control.

The pastor was playing a slow hymn tune in a minor key. Peter glanced at Tilde and saw that she looked sorrowful. 'Don't be fooled,' he murmured. 'The old tyrant is as hard as gunmetal.'

The verse ended and Olufsen began another. Peter was not willing to wait. 'Pastor!' he said loudly.

The pastor did not stop playing immediately, but finished the line, and let the music hang in the air for a moment. Finally he turned around. 'Young Peter,' he said in a flat voice.

Peter was momentarily shocked to see that the pastor seemed to have aged. His face was lined with weariness and his blue eyes had lost their icy glitter. After an instant of surprise, Peter said: 'I'm looking for Harald.'

'I didn't imagine this was a condolence call,' the pastor said coldly.

'Is he here?'

'Is this an official inquiry?'

'Why do you ask? Is Harald involved in some wrongdoing?'

'Certainly not.'

'I'm glad to hear it. Is he in the house?'

'No. He's not on the island. I don't know where he went.'

Peter looked at Tilde. This was a letdown – but, on the other hand, it suggested that Harald was guilty. Why else would he disappear? 'Where do you think he might be?'

'Go away.'

Arrogant as ever – but this time the pastor was not going to get away with it, Peter thought with relish. 'Your elder son killed himself because he was caught spying,' he said harshly.

The pastor flinched as if Peter had struck him.

Peter heard Tilde gasp beside him, and realized he had shocked her by his cruelty, but he pressed on.

'Your younger son may be guilty of similar crimes. You're in no position to act high and mighty with the police.'

The pastor's normally proud face looked hurt and vulnerable. 'I've told you that I don't know where Harald is,' he said dully. 'Do you have any other questions?'

'What are you hiding?'

The pastor sighed. 'You're one of my flock, and if you come to me for spiritual help I won't turn you away. But I will not speak to you for any other reason. You're arrogant and cruel, and as near worthless as one of God's creatures can be. Get out of my sight.'

'You can't throw people out of the church – it doesn't belong to you.'

'If you want to pray, you're welcome here. Otherwise, go away.'

Peter hesitated. He did not want to submit to being thrown out, but he knew he had been defeated. After a moment he took Tilde's arm and led her outside. 'I told you he was hard,' he said.

Tilde seemed shaken. 'I think the man is in pain.'

'No doubt. But was he telling the truth?'

'Obviously Harald has gone into hiding – which means almost certainly that he has the film.'

'So we have to find him.' Peter reflected on the conversation. 'I wonder if his father really doesn't know where he is.'

'Have you ever known the pastor to lie?'

'No – but he might make an exception to protect his son.'

Tilde made a dismissive gesture. 'We're not going to get anything out of him, either way.'

'I agree. But we're on the right track, that's the main thing. Let's try the mother. She at least is made of flesh and blood.'

They went to the house. Peter steered Tilde to the back. He tapped on the kitchen door and went in without waiting for an answer, as was usual on the island.

Lisbeth Olufsen was sitting at the kitchen table, doing nothing. Peter had never in his life seen her idle: she was always cooking or cleaning. Even in church she was busy, straightening rows of chairs, putting out hymn books or gathering them up, stoking the peat boiler that warmed the big room in winter. Now she sat looking at her hands. The skin was cracked and raw in places, like a fisherman's.

'Mrs Olufsen?'

She turned her face to him. Her eyes were red and her cheeks were drawn. After a moment, she recognized him. 'Hello, Peter,' she said expressionlessly.

He decided to take a softer approach with her. 'I'm sorry about Arne.'

She nodded vaguely.

'This is my friend Tilde. We work together.'

'Pleased to meet you.'

He sat at the table and nodded to Tilde to do the same. Perhaps a simple, practical question would bring Mrs Olufsen out of her daze. 'When is the funeral?'

She thought for a moment, then answered: 'Tomorrow.'

That was better.

'I've spoken to the pastor,' Peter said. 'We saw him in the church.'

'His heart is broken. He doesn't show it to the world, though.'

'I understand. Harald must be dreadfully upset, too.'

She glanced at him and looked quickly down at her hands again. It was the briefest of looks, but Peter read fear and deceit in it. She muttered: 'We haven't spoken to Harald.'

'Why is that?'

'We don't know where he is.'

Peter could not tell whether she was lying from moment to moment, but he felt sure of her intention to deceive. It angered him that the pastor and his wife, who pretended to be morally superior to others, should deliberately hide the truth from the police. He raised his voice. 'You'd be well advised to cooperate with us!'

Tilde put a restraining hand on his arm and looked an inquiry at him. He nodded for her to go ahead. She said: 'Mrs Olufsen, I'm sorry to have to tell you that Harald may have been involved in the same illegal activities as Arne.'

Mrs Olufsen looked frightened.

Tilde continued: 'The longer he goes on, the worse trouble he'll be in when finally we catch up with him.'

The old woman shook her head from side to side, looking distressed, but she said nothing.

'If you would help us find him, you'd be doing the best thing for him.'

'I don't know where he is,' she repeated, but less firmly.

Peter sensed weakness. He stood up and leaned across the kitchen table, pushing his face into hers. 'I saw Arne die,' he said gratingly.

Mrs Olufsen's eyes widened in horror.

'I saw your son put the gun to his own throat and pull the trigger,' he went on.

Tilde said: 'Peter, no—'

He ignored her. 'I saw his blood and brains spatter the wall behind him.'

Mrs Olufsen cried out with shock and grief.

She was about to crack, Peter saw with satisfaction. He pressed his advantage. 'Your elder son was a spy and a criminal, and he met a violent end. They that live by the sword shall die by the sword, that's what the Bible says. Do you want the same to happen to your other son?'

'No,' she whispered. 'No.'

'Then tell me where he is!'

The kitchen door burst open and the pastor strode in. 'You filth,' he said.

Peter straightened up, startled but defiant. 'I'm entitled to question—'

'Get out of my house.'

Tilde said: 'Let's go, Peter.'

'I still want to know—'

'Now!' the pastor roared. 'Leave now!' He advanced around the table.

Peter backed away. He knew he should not allow himself to be shouted down. He was on legitimate police business and he had a right to ask questions. But the towering presence of the pastor scared him, despite the gun under his jacket, and he found himself reversing steadily to the door.

Tilde opened it and went out.

'I haven't finished with you two,' Peter said feebly as he backed through the doorway.

The pastor slammed the door in his face.

Peter turned away. 'Damned hypocrites,' he said. 'The pair of them.'

The buggy was waiting. 'To my father's house,' Peter said, and they got in.

As they drove away, he tried to put the humiliating scene out of his mind and concentrate on his next steps. 'Harald must be living somewhere,' he said.

'Obviously.' Tilde's tone was curt, and he guessed she was distressed by what she had just witnessed.

'He's not at school and he's not at home, and he has no relations except for some cousins in Hamburg.'

'We could circulate a picture of him.'

'We'll have trouble finding one. The pastor doesn't believe in photos – they're a sign of vanity. You didn't see any pictures in that kitchen, did you?'

'What about a school photo?'

'Not a Jansborg tradition. The only picture of Arne we could find was the one in his army record. I doubt there's a photo of Harald anywhere.'

'So what's our next move?'

'I think he's staying with friends – don't you?'

'Makes sense.'

She would not look at him. He sighed. She was in a bad mood with him. So be it. 'This is what you do,' he said in a tone of command. 'Call the Politigaarden. Send Conrad to Jansborg Skole. Get a list of the home addresses of all the boys in Harald's class. Then have someone call at each house, ask a few questions, snoop around a bit.'

'They must be all over Denmark. It would take a month to visit them all. How much time do we have?'

'Very little. I don't know how long it will take for Harald to figure out a way to get the film to London, but he's a cunning young villain. Use local police where necessary.'

'Very well.'

'If he's not staying with friends, he must be hiding out with another member of the spy ring. We're going to stay for the funeral and see who shows up. We'll check out every mourner. One of them must know where Harald is.'

The buggy slowed as it approached the entrance to Axel Flemming's house. Tilde said: 'Do you mind if I go back to the hotel?'

His parents were expecting them for lunch, but Peter could see that Tilde was not in the mood. 'All right.' He tapped the driver on the shoulder. 'Go to the ferry dock.'

They drove in silence for a while. As they approached the dock, Peter said: 'What will you do at the hotel?'

'In fact I think I should return to Copenhagen.'

That made him angry. As the horse stopped at the quayside, he said: 'What the hell is wrong with you?'

'I didn't like what just happened.'

'We had to do it!'

'I'm not sure.'

'It was our duty to try to make those people tell what they knew.'

'Duty isn't everything.'

She had said that during their argument about Jews, he recalled. 'That's just playing with words. Duty is what you have to do. You can't make exceptions. That's what's wrong with the world.'

The ferry was in dock. Tilde got down from the buggy. 'It's just life, Peter, that's all.'

'It's why we have crime! Wouldn't you rather live in a world where everyone did their duty? Just imagine it! Well-behaved people in smart uniforms getting things done, with no slacking, no lateness, no half-measures. If all crimes were punished and no excuses accepted there would be a lot less for the police to do!'

'Is that really what you want?'

'Yes – and if I ever get to be chief of police, and the Nazis are still running things, that's what it will be like! What's wrong with that?'

She nodded, but did not answer his question. 'Goodbye, Peter,' she said.

As she walked away he shouted after her: 'Well? What's wrong with it?' But she boarded the ferry without turning around.

# PART FOUR

# TWENTY-FIVE

Harald knew the police were looking for him.

His mother had phoned Kirstenslot again, ostensibly to tell Karen the date and time of Arne's funeral. During the conversation, she had said she had been questioned by the police about Harald's whereabouts. 'But I don't know where he is, so I couldn't tell them,' she had said. It was a warning, and Harald admired his mother for having the courage to send it and the shrewdness to figure out that Karen could probably deliver it.

Despite the warning, he had to go to the flying school.

Karen purloined some of her father's old clothes, so that Harald would not have to wear his distinctive school blazer. He put on a marvellously lightweight sports jacket from America and a linen cap, and wore sunglasses. He looked more like a millionaire playboy than a fugitive spy as he got on the train at Kirstenslot. Nevertheless he was nervous. He felt trapped in the railway carriage. If a policeman accosted him he could not run away.

In Copenhagen he walked the short distance from the Vesterport suburban station to the main line station without seeing a single police uniform. A few minutes later he was on another train to Vodal.

On the way, he thought about his brother. Everyone had thought Arne unsuited to Resistance work: too playful, too careless, perhaps not brave enough. And in the end he had turned out to be the greatest hero of all. The thought brought tears to Harald's eyes behind the sunglasses.

Squadron Leader Renthe, commanding officer of the flying school, reminded him of his old headmaster, Heis. Both men were tall and thin and long-nosed. Because of the resemblance, Harald found it difficult to lie to Renthe. 'I've come to, er, pick up my brother's effects,' he said. 'Personal stuff. If that's all right.'

Renthe did not appear to notice his embarrassment. 'Of course,' he said. 'One of Arne's colleagues, Hendrik Janz, has packed everything up. There's just a suitcase and a duffle bag.'

'Thanks.' Harald did not want Arne's effects, but he had needed an excuse to come here. What he was really after was about fifty feet of steel cable to replace the missing control cables of the Hornet Moth. And this was the only place he could think of where he might get it.

Now that he was here, the task seemed more daunting than it had from a distance. He felt a wave of mild panic. Without the cable, the Hornet Moth could not fly. Then he thought again of the sacrifice his brother had made, and told himself to stay calm. If he kept a cool head, he might find a way.

'I was going to send the bags to your parents,' Renthe added.

'I'll do it.' Harald wondered whether he could confide in Renthe.

'I only hesitated because I thought perhaps they should go to his fiancée.'

'Hermia?' Harald said, surprised. 'In England?'

'Is she in England? She was here three days ago.'

Harald was astonished. 'What was she doing here?'

'I assumed she had taken Danish citizenship and was living here. Otherwise, her presence in Denmark would have been illegal, and I would have been obliged to report her visit to the police. But obviously she would not have come here if that had been the case. She would know, wouldn't she, that as an army officer I'm obliged to report anything illegal to the police.' He looked hard at Harald and added: 'Do you see what I mean?'

'I think I do.' Harald realized he was being given a message. Renthe suspected that he and Hermia were involved in espionage with Arne, and he was warning Harald not to say anything about it to him. He obviously sympathized, but was not willing to break any rules. Harald stood up. 'You've made things very clear – thank you.'

'I'll get someone to show you to Arne's quarters.'

'No need – I can find my way.' He had seen Arne's room two weeks before, when he was here for a flight in a Tiger Moth.

Renthe shook his hand. 'My deepest condolences.'

'Thank you.'

Harald left the headquarters building and walked along the single road that connected all the low buildings that made up the base. He moved slowly, taking a good look inside the hangars. There was not much activity. What was there to do at an air base where the aircraft could not fly?

He felt frustrated. The cable he needed must be here, somewhere. All he had to do was find out where, and get hold of it. But it was not that simple.

In one hangar he saw a Tiger Moth completely dismantled. The wings were detached, the fuselage stood on trestles, the engine on a stand. His hopes rose. He walked in through the giant doorway. A mechanic in overalls was sitting on an oil can, drinking tea from a big mug. 'Amazing,' Harald said to him. 'I've never seen one taken to pieces like that.'

'Has to be done,' the man replied. 'Parts wear out, and you can't have them failing in mid-air. On aircraft, everything has to be perfect. Otherwise you fall out of the sky.'

Harald found that a sobering thought. He was planning to cross the North Sea in an aircraft that had not been looked at by a mechanic for years. 'So you replace everything?'

'Everything that moves, yes.'

Harald thought optimistically that this man might be able to give him what he wanted. 'You must get through a lot of spares.'

'That's right.'

'There's what, a hundred feet of control cables in each aircraft?'

'A Tiger Moth requires one hundred and fifty-nine feet of ten-hundredweight cable.'

And that's what I need, Harald thought with mounting excitement. But once again he hesitated to ask, for fear of giving himself away to someone unsympathetic. He looked around. He had vaguely imagined that aeroplane parts would be lying around for anyone to pick up. 'So, where do you keep it all?'

'Stores, of course. This is the army. Everything in its place.'

Harald grunted with exasperation. If only he could have seen a length of cable and picked it up casually ... but it was pointless to wish for easy solutions. 'Where's the store?'

'Next building along.' The mechanic frowned. 'Why all the questions?'

'Idle curiosity.' Harald guessed he had pushed this man far enough. He should move on before arousing serious suspicion. He gave a sketchy wave and turned away. 'Nice talking to you.'

He walked to the next building and stepped inside. A sergeant sat behind a counter, smoking and reading a newspaper. Harald saw a photograph of Russian soldiers surrendering, and the headline: STALIN TAKES CONTROL OF SOVIET DEFENCE MINISTRY.

Harald studied the rows of steel shelves that stretched out on the other side of the counter. He felt like a child in a sweet shop. Here was everything he could want, from washers to entire engines. He could build a whole aircraft out of these parts.

And one entire section was given over to miles of

cable of different kinds, all neatly wound on wooden cylinders like cotton reels.

Harald was delighted. He had learned exactly where the cable was. Now he had to figure out how to get his hands on it.

After a moment, the sergeant looked up from the newspaper. 'Yes?'

Could the man be bribed? Yet again, Harald hesitated. He had a pocketful of money, given to him for this purpose by Karen. But he did not know how to phrase an offer. Even a corrupt warehouseman might be offended by a crass proposal. He wished he had thought more about his approach. But he had to do it. 'Can I ask you something?' he said. 'All these spare parts – is there any way that someone, a civilian I mean, could buy, or—'

'No,' the sergeant said abruptly.

'Even if the price was, you know, not a major consideration—'

'Absolutely not.'

Harald did not know what else to say. 'If I've given offence . . .'

'Forget it.'

At least the man had not called the police. Harald turned away.

The door was solid wood with three locks, he noted as he left. It would not be easy to break in to this warehouse. Perhaps he was not the first civilian to realize that scarce components might be found in military stores.

Feeling defeated, he made his way to the officers'

quarters and found Arne's room. As Renthe had promised, there were two bags neatly lined up at the foot of the bed. The room was otherwise bare.

It struck Harald as pathetic that his brother's life could be packed into two bags, and that his room should then bear no trace of his existence. The thought brought tears to his eyes again. But the important thing was what a man left behind in the minds of others, he told himself. Arne would always live in Harald's memory – teaching him to whistle, making their mother laugh like a schoolgirl, combing his glossy hair in a mirror. He thought of the last time he had seen his brother, sitting on the tiled floor of the disused church in Kirstenslot, weary and scared but determined to fulfil his mission. And, once again, he saw that the way to honour Arne's memory was to finish the job he had started.

A corporal looked in at the door and said: 'Are you related to Arne Olufsen?'

'His brother. My name is Harald.'

'Benedikt Vessell, call me Ben.' He was a man in his thirties with a friendly grin that showed tobacco-stained teeth. 'I was hoping to run into someone from the family.' He fished in his pocket and pulled out money. 'I owe Arne forty crowns.'

'What for?'

The corporal looked sly. 'Well, don't say a word, I run a little book on the horse races, and Arne picked a winner.'

Harald took the money, not knowing what else to do. 'Thank you.'

'Is that all right, then?'

Harald did not really understand the question. 'Of course.'

'Good.' Ben looked furtive.

It crossed Harald's mind that the sum owed might have been more than forty crowns. But he was not going to argue. 'I'll give it to my mother,' he said.

'Deepest sympathy, son. He was a good sort, your brother.'

The corporal obviously was not a rule keeper. He seemed the type who would murmur 'Don't say a word' quite frequently. His age suggested he was a career soldier, but his rank was lowly. Perhaps he put his energies into illegal activities. He probably sold pornographic books and stolen cigarettes. Maybe he could solve Harald's problem. 'Ben,' Harald said. 'Can I ask you something?'

'Anything at all.' Ben took a tobacco pouch from his pocket and began to hand-roll a cigarette.

'If a man wanted, for private purposes, to get hold of fifty feet of control cable for a Tiger Moth, do you know of any way it could be done?'

Ben looked at him through narrowed eyes. 'No,' he said.

'Say, the person had a couple of hundred crowns to pay for it.'

Ben lit his cigarette. 'This is to do with what Arne was arrested for, isn't it?'

'Yes.'

Ben shook his head. 'No, lad, it can't be done. Sorry.'

'Never mind,' Harald said lightly, though he was bitterly disappointed. 'Where can I find Hendrik Janz?'

'Two doors along. If he's not in his room, try the canteen.'

Harald found Hendrik seated at a small desk, studying a book on meteorology. Pilots had to understand the weather, to know when it was safe to fly and if there was a storm coming. 'I'm Harald Olufsen.'

Hendrik shook his hand. 'Damn shame about Arne.'

'Thank you for packing up his stuff.'

'Glad to be able to do something.'

Did Hendrik approve of what Arne had done? Harald needed some indication before sticking his neck out. He said: 'Arne did what he thought was right for his country.'

Hendrik immediately looked wary. 'I know nothing of that,' he said. 'To me he was a reliable colleague and a good friend.'

Harald was dismayed. Hendrik obviously was not going to help him steal the cable. What was he going to do?

'Thanks again,' he said. 'Goodbye.'

He returned to Arne's room and picked up the bags. He was at a loss to know what else to do. He could not leave without the cable he needed – but how could he take it? He had tried everything.

Maybe there was another place he could get cable. But he could not think where. And he was running out of time. The full moon was six days away. That meant he had only four days left to work on the aircraft.

He left the building and headed for the gate, carrying the bags. He was going to return to Kirstenslot – but for what purpose? Without the cable, the Hornet Moth would not fly. He wondered how he was going to tell Karen he had failed.

As he passed the stores building, he heard his name called. 'Harald!'

A truck was parked to one side of the warehouse, and Ben stood half-concealed by the vehicle, beckoning. Harald hurried over.

'Here,' said Ben, and he held out a thick coil of steel cable. 'Fifty feet, and a bit extra.'

Harald was thrilled. 'Thank you!'

'Take it, for God's sake, it's heavy.'

Harald took the cable and turned away.

'No, no!' Ben said. 'You can't walk through the gate with that in your hand, for Christ's sake! Put it in one of the bags.'

Harald opened Arne's suitcase. It was full.

Ben said: 'Give me that uniform, quick.'

Harald took out Arne's uniform and replaced it with the coil.

Ben picked up the uniform. 'I'll get rid of this, don't worry. Now clear off!'

Harald shut the case and reached into his pocket. 'I promised you two hundred crowns—'

'Keep the money,' Ben said. 'And good luck to you, son.'

'Thanks!'

'Now get lost! I never want to see you again.'

'Right,' said Harald, and he walked rapidly away.

* * *

Next morning, Harald stood outside the castle in the grey gleam of dawn. It was half past three. In his hand he held a four-gallon oil can, empty and clean. The tank of the Hornet Moth would take thirty-five gallons of petrol, just under nine canfuls. There was no legitimate way to get fuel, so Harald was going to steal it from the Germans.

He had everything else he needed. The Hornet Moth required only a few more hours of work and it would be ready to take off. But its fuel tank was empty.

The kitchen door opened quietly and Karen stepped out. She was accompanied by Thor, the old red setter that made Harald smile because it looked so much like Mr Duchwitz. Karen paused on the doorstep, staring around warily, like a cat when there are strangers in the house. She wore a chunky green sweater that concealed her figure, and the old brown corduroys that Harald thought of as her gardening trousers. But she looked wonderful. She called me darling, he said to himself, hugging the memory. She called me darling.

She smiled brilliantly, dazzling him. 'Good morning!'

Her voice seemed dangerously loud. He put a finger on his lips for quiet. It would be safer to remain completely silent. There was nothing to discuss: they had made their plan last night, sitting on the floor in the disused church, eating chocolate cake from the Kirstenslot pantry.

Harald led the way into the woods. Under cover, they walked half the length of the park. When they drew level with the soldiers' tents, they peeked cautiously from the bushes. As expected, they saw a single man on guard duty, standing outside the mess tent, yawning. At this hour, everyone else was asleep. Harald was relieved to have his expectations fulfilled.

The veterinary company's fuel supply came from a small petrol tanker that was parked a hundred yards from the tents – no doubt as a safety precaution. The separation would be helpful to Harald, though he wished it were greater. The tanker had a hand pump, he had already observed, and there was no locking mechanism.

The truck was parked alongside the drive that led to the castle door, so that vehicles could approach it on a hard surface. The hose was on the drive side, for convenience. In consequence, the bulk of the truck shielded anyone using it from view by the encampment.

Everything was as expected, but Harald hesitated. It seemed madness to steal petrol from under the noses of the soldiers. But it was dangerous to think too much. Fear could paralyse. Action was the antidote. Without further reflection he broke cover, leaving Karen and the dog behind, and walked quickly across the damp grass to the tanker.

He took the nozzle from its hook and fed it into his

can, then reached for the pump lever. As he pulled it down, there was a gurgling sound from inside the tank, and the noise of petrol sloshing into the can. It seemed very loud, but perhaps not loud enough to be heard by the sentry a hundred yards away.

He glanced anxiously back at Karen. As agreed, she was watching from the screen of vegetation, ready to alert Harald if anyone approached.

The can filled quickly. He screwed on the cap and picked it up. It was heavy. He returned the nozzle tidily to its hook then hurried back to the trees. Once out of sight, he paused, grinning triumphantly at Karen. He had stolen four gallons of petrol and got away with it. The plan was working!

Leaving her there, he cut through the woods to the monastery. He had already opened the big church door so that he could slip in and out. It would have been too awkward and time-consuming to pass the heavy can through the high window. He stepped inside. With relief, he put down the can. He popped open the access panel and undid the petrol cap of the Hornet Moth. He fumbled awkwardly because his fingers were numb from carrying the heavy can, but he got the cap open. He emptied the can into the aircraft's tank, replaced both caps to minimize the smell of fuel, and went out.

While he was filling the can for the second time, the sentry decided to make a patrol.

Harald could not see the man, but knew something was wrong when Karen whistled. He looked up to see her emerging from the wood with Thor at her heel.

He let go of the hand pump and dropped to his knees to look under the tanker and across the lawn. He saw the soldier's boots approaching.

They had foreseen this problem and prepared for it. Still on his knees, Harald watched Karen stroll across the grass. She met up with the sentry while he was still fifty yards away from the tanker. The dog amiably sniffed the man's crotch. Karen took out cigarettes. Would the sentry be friendly, and smoke with a pretty girl? Or would he be a stickler for routine, and ask her to walk her dog somewhere else while he continued his patrol? Harald held his breath. The sentry took a cigarette, and they lit up.

The soldier was a small man with a bad complexion. Harald could not hear their words, but he knew what Karen was saying: she could not sleep, she felt lonely, she wanted someone to talk to. 'Don't you think he might be suspicious?' Karen had said while discussing this plan last night. Harald had assured her that the victim would enjoy being flirted with far too much to question her motives. Harald had not been as certain as he pretended, but to his relief the sentry was fulfilling his prediction.

He saw Karen point to a tree stump a little way off and then lead the soldier to it. She sat down, placing herself so that the sentry had to have his back to the tanker if he wanted to sit next to her. Now, Harald knew, she would be saying that the local boys were so dull, she liked to talk to men who had travelled a little and seen the world, they seemed more mature. She patted the surface beside her to encourage him. Sure enough, he sat down.

Harald resumed pumping.

He filled the can and hurried into the woods. Eight gallons!

When he returned, Karen and the sentry were in the same positions. While he refilled the can, he calculated how long he needed. Filling the can took about a minute, the walk to the church about two, pouring the petrol into the Hornet Moth another minute, the return journey another two. Six minutes for the round trip, then, making fifty-four minutes for nine canfuls. Assuming he would tire towards the end, call it an hour.

Could the sentry be kept chatting that long? The man had nothing else to do. The soldiers rose at five thirty, still more than an hour away, and began their duties at six. Assuming the British did not invade Denmark in the next hour, the sentry had no reason to stop talking to a pretty girl. But he was a soldier, under military discipline, and he might feel it his duty to patrol.

All Harald could do was hope for the best, and hurry.

He took the third canful to the church. Twelve gallons already, he thought optimistically; more than two hundred miles – a third of the way to England.

He continued his shuttle. According to the manual he had found in the cockpit, the DH87B Hornet Moth should fly 632 miles on a full tank. That figure assumed no wind. The distance to the English coast, as best he could reckon it from the atlas, was about 600 miles. The margin of safety was nowhere near enough. A head wind would reduce their mileage and bring them down in the sea. He would take a full can of petrol in the cabin, he decided. That would add seventy miles to the Hornet Moth's range, assuming he could figure out a way to top up the tank in flight.

He pumped with his right hand and toted with his left, and both arms were aching by the time he emptied the fourth canful into the aircraft. Returning for the fifth, he saw that the sentry was standing up, as if preparing to move off, but Karen still had him talking. She laughed at something the man said, and slapped his shoulder playfully. It was a coquettish gesture that was most uncharacteristic of her, but all the same Harald felt a pang of jealousy. She never slapped his shoulder playfully.

But she had called him darling.

He carried the fifth and sixth canfuls, and felt he was two thirds of the way to the English coast.

Whenever he felt scared, he thought of his brother. It was difficult, he found, to accept that Arne was dead. He kept thinking about whether his brother would approve of what he was doing, what he would say when Harald told him about some aspect of his plans, how he would be amused or sceptical or impressed. In that way, Arne was still part of Harald's life.

Harald did not believe in the obstinately irrational fundamentalism of his father. Talk of heaven and hell seemed mere superstition to him. But now he saw that in a way dead people lived on in the minds of those who had loved them, and that was a kind of afterlife. Any time his resolution weakened, he recalled that Arne had given everything for this mission, and felt an impulse of loyalty that gave him strength – even though the brother to whom he owed that loyalty was no more.

Returning to the church with the seventh canful, he was seen.

As he approached the church door, a soldier in underwear emerged from the cloisters. Harald froze, the can of petrol in his hand as incriminating as a hot gun. The soldier, half asleep, walked to a bush and began to urinate and yawn at the same time. Harald saw that it was Leo, the young private who had been so intrusively friendly three days ago.

Leo caught his eye, was startled to find himself observed, and looked guilty. 'Sorry,' he mumbled.

Harald guessed it was against the rules to pee in the bushes. They had dug a latrine behind the monastery, but it was a long walk, and Leo was being lazy. Harald tried to smile reassuringly. 'Don't worry,' he said in German. But he could hear the tremor of fear in his own voice.

Leo did not seem to notice it. Readjusting his clothing, he frowned. 'What's in the can?'

'Water, for my motorcycle.'

'Oh.' Leo yawned. Then he jerked a thumb at the bush. 'We're not supposed to . . .'

'Forget it.'

Leo nodded, and stumbled away.

Harald stepped into the church. He paused a moment, closing his eyes, getting over the tension. Then he poured the fuel into the Hornet Moth.

As he approached the petrol tanker for the eighth time, he saw that his plan was beginning to fall apart. Karen was walking away from the tree stump, back towards the woods. She gave the sentry a friendly wave, so they must have parted on good terms, but Harald guessed the man had some duty he was obliged to perform. However, he was walking away from the tanker, towards the mess tent, so Harald felt able to carry on, and he refilled the can.

As he carried it into the woods, Karen caught up with him and murmured: 'He has to light the kitchen stove.'

Harald nodded and hurried on. He poured the eighth canful into the aircraft's tank and returned for the ninth. The sentry was nowhere to be seen, and Karen gave him the thumbs-up sign to indicate that he could go ahead. He filled the can for the ninth time and returned to the church. As he had calculated, this brought the level to the brim, with some left over. But he needed an extra canful to carry in the cabin. He returned for the last time.

Karen stopped him at the edge of the wood and pointed. The sentry was standing beside the petrol tanker. Harald saw with dismay that, in his hurry, he had forgotten to return the nozzle to its hook, and the petrol hose dangled untidily. The soldier looked up and down the park with a puzzled frown, then returned the nozzle to its proper place. He remained standing there for a while. He took out cigarettes, put one in his mouth, and opened a box of matches; then moved away from the tanker before striking his match.

Karen whispered to Harald: 'Haven't you got enough petrol yet?'

'I need one more can.'

The sentry was strolling away with his back to the lorry, smoking, and Harald decided to take a chance. He walked fast across the grass. To his dismay, he found that the tanker did not quite conceal him from the soldier's angle of view. Nevertheless he put the nozzle in the can and started to pump, knowing he would be seen if the man chanced to turn around. He filled the can, replaced the nozzle, screwed the cap on the can and walked away.

He was almost at the woods when he heard a shout.

He pretended to be deaf and walked on without turning around or increasing his pace.

The sentry shouted again, and Harald heard running boots.

He passed into the trees. Karen appeared. 'Get out of sight!' she whispered. 'I'll head him off.'

Harald darted into a patch of shrubbery. Lying flat, he wriggled under a rambling bush, dragging the can with him. Thor tried to follow him, thinking this was a game. Harald smacked him sharply on the nose, and the dog retreated, his feelings hurt.

Harald heard the sentry say: 'Where's that man?'

'You mean Christian?' Karen said.

'Who is he?'

'One of the gardeners. You're terribly handsome when you're cross, Ludie.'

'Never mind that, what was he doing?'

'Treating diseased trees with the stuff in that can, something that kills those ugly mushroom growths you see on tree trunks.'

That was inventive of her, Harald thought, even if she's forgotten the German word for fungicide.

'This early?' Ludie said sceptically.

'He told me the treatment works best when it's cool.'

'I saw him walking away from the petrol tanker.'

'Petrol? What would Christian do with petrol? He doesn't have a car. I expect he was taking a short cut across the lawn.'

'Hm.' Ludie was still uneasy. 'I haven't noticed any diseased trees.'

'Well, look at this.' Harald heard them take a few paces. 'See that growing out of the bark like a great big wart? It would kill the tree unless Christian treated it.'

'I suppose it would. Well, please tell your servants to keep clear of the encampment.'

'I will, and I apologize. I'm sure Christian meant no harm.'

'Very well.'

'Goodbye, Ludie. Perhaps I'll see you tomorrow morning.'

'I'll be here.'

'Bye.'

Harald waited a few minutes, then he heard Karen say: 'All clear.'

He crawled out from the bush. 'You were brilliant!'

'I'm becoming such a good liar, it's worrying.'

They walked towards the monastery – and suffered another shock.

As they were about to leave the shelter of the woods, Harald saw Per Hansen, the village policeman and local Nazi, standing outside the church.

He cursed. What the hell was Hansen doing here? And at this time of the morning?

Hansen was standing still, legs apart and arms folded, looking across the park at the military encampment. Harald put a restraining hand on Karen's arm, but he was too late to stop Thor, who instantly sensed the hostility Karen felt. The dog erupted from the woods at a run, made for Hansen, stopped at a safe distance, and barked. Hansen looked scared and angry, and his hand went to the holstered gun at his belt.

Karen whispered: 'I'll deal with him.' Without waiting for Harald to reply she went forward and whistled to the dog. 'Come here, Thor!'

Harald put down his can of petrol, dropped to a crouch, and watched through the leaves.

Hansen said to Karen: 'You should keep that dog under control.'

'Why? He lives here.'

'It's aggressive.'

'He barks at intruders. It's his job.'

'If it attacks a member of the police force, it might be shot.'

'Don't be ridiculous,' Karen said, and Harald could not help observing that she displayed all the arrogance of her wealth and social position. 'What are you doing, snooping around my garden at the crack of dawn?'

'I'm on official business, young lady, so you mind your manners.'

'Official business?' she said sceptically. Harald guessed she was pretending to be incredulous in order to get more information out of him. 'What business?'

'I'm looking for someone called Harald Olufsen.'

Harald murmured: 'Oh, shit.' He had not been expecting this.

Karen was shocked, but she managed to cover up. 'Never heard of him,' she said.

'He's a school friend of your brother's, and he's wanted by the police.'

'Well, I can't be expected to know all my brother's schoolmates.'

'He's been to the castle.'

'Oh? What does he look like?'

'Male, eighteen years old, six feet one inch, fair hair and blue eyes, probably wearing a blue school blazer with a stripe on the sleeve.' Hansen sounded as if he were reciting something he had memorized from a police report.

'He sounds terribly attractive, apart from the blazer, but I don't recall him.' Karen was maintaining her air of careless disdain, but Harald could see the tension and worry on her face.

'He's been here twice at least,' Hansen said. 'I've seen him myself.'

'I must have missed him. What's his crime, failing to return a library book?'

'I don't – that is, I can't say. I mean, it's a routine inquiry.'

Hansen obviously did not know what the crime was, Harald thought. He must be asking on behalf of some other policeman – Peter Flemming, presumably.

Karen was saying: 'Well, my brother has gone to Aarhus, and there's no one staying here now – apart from a hundred soldiers, of course.'

'Last time I saw Olufsen, he had a very dangerous-looking motorcycle.'

'Oh, *that* boy,' Karen said, pretending to remember. 'He was expelled from school. Daddy won't let him come here any more.'

'No? Well, I think I'll have a word with your father anyway.'

'He's still asleep.'

'I'll wait.'

'As you please. Come on, Thor!' Karen walked away, and Hansen continued up the drive.

Harald waited. Karen approached the church, turned to check that Hansen was not watching her, then slipped through the door. Hansen walked up the drive towards the castle. Harald hoped he would not stop to talk to Ludie, and discover that the sentry had seen a tall blond man behaving suspiciously near the petrol tanker. Fortunately, Hansen walked past the encampment and eventually disappeared behind the castle, presumably heading for the kitchen door.

Harald hurried to the church and slipped inside. He put the last can of petrol down on the tiled floor.

Karen closed the big door, turned the key in the lock, and dropped the bar into place. Then she turned to Harald. 'You must be exhausted.'

He was. Both arms hurt, and his legs ached from hurrying through the woods with a heavy weight. As soon as he relaxed, he felt slightly nauseated from the petrol fumes. But he was ecstatically happy. 'You were wonderful!' he said. 'Flirting with Ludie as if he were the most eligible bachelor in Denmark.'

'He's two inches shorter than me!'

'And you completely fooled Hansen.'

'Not difficult, that.'

Harald picked up the can again and put it in the cabin of the Hornet Moth, stowing it on the luggage shelf behind the seats. He closed the door and turned around to see Karen standing right behind him, grinning broadly. 'We did it,' she said.

'My God, we did.'

She put her arms around him and looked at him expectantly. It was almost as if she wanted him to kiss her. He thought of asking, then decided to be more decisive. He closed his eyes and leaned forward. Her lips were soft and warm. He could have stayed that way, motionless, enjoying the touch of her lips, for a long time, but she had other ideas. She broke contact, then kissed him again. She kissed his upper lip, then the lower, then his chin, then his lips again. Her mouth was busily playful, exploring. He had never kissed like this before. He opened his eyes and was startled to see that she was looking at him with bright merriment in her eyes.

'What are you thinking?' she said.

'Do you really like me?'

'Of course I do, stupid.'

'I like you, too.'

'Good.'

He hesitated, then said: 'As a matter of fact, I love you.'

'I know,' she said, and she kissed him again.

# TWENTY-SIX

Walking through the centre of Morlunde in the bright light of a summer morning, Hermia Mount was in more danger than she had been in Copenhagen. People in this small town knew her.

Two years before, after she and Arne had become engaged, he had brought her to his parents' home on Sande. She had been to church, watched a football match, visited Arne's favourite bar, and gone shopping with Arne's mother. It broke her heart to remember that happy time.

But the consequence was that plenty of local people would remember the Olufsen boy's English fiancée, and there was a serious danger she would be recognized. If that happened, people would start talking, and before long the police would hear.

This morning she wore a hat and sunglasses, but still she felt perilously conspicuous. All the same, she had to take the risk.

She had spent the previous evening in the town centre, hoping to run into Harald. Knowing how much he loved jazz, she had gone first to the Club Hot, but it was closed. She had not found him in any of the bars and cafés where young people gathered. It had been a wasted evening.

This morning she was going to his home.

She had thought of telephoning, but it was hazardous. If she gave her real name she risked being overheard and betrayed. If she gave a false name, or called anonymously, she might spook Harald and cause him to flee. She had to visit in person.

This would be even more risky. Morlunde was a town, but on the small island of Sande every resident knew all the others. She could only hope that islanders might take her for a holidaymaker, and not look too closely. She had no better option. The full moon was five days away.

She made her way to the harbour, carrying her small suitcase, and boarded the ferry. At the top of the gangway stood a German soldier and a Danish policeman. She showed her papers in the name of Agnes Ricks. The documents had already passed three inspections, but nevertheless she suffered a shiver of fear as she offered the forgeries to the two uniformed men.

The policeman studied her identity card. 'You're a long way from home, Miss Ricks.'

She had prepared her cover story. 'I'm here for the funeral of a relative.' It was a good pretext for a long journey. She was not sure when Arne's interment was scheduled, but there was nothing suspicious about a family member arriving a day or two early, especially given the hazards of wartime travel.

'That would be the Olufsen funeral.'

'Yes.' Hot tears came to her eyes. 'I'm a second cousin, but my mother was very close to Lisbeth Olufsen.'

The policeman sensed her grief, despite the sunglasses, and he said gently: 'My condolences.' He handed the papers back. 'You're in plenty of time.'

'Am I?' That suggested it was today. 'I wasn't sure, I couldn't get through on the telephone to check.'

'I believe the service is at three o'clock this afternoon.'

'Thank you.'

Hermia went forward and leaned on the rail. As the ferry chugged out of the harbour, she looked across the water to the flat, featureless island and recalled her first visit. She had been shocked to see the cold, unadorned rooms where Arne had grown up, and to meet his stern parents. It was a mystery how that solemn family had produced someone as much fun as Arne.

She was a somewhat severe person herself, or so her colleagues seemed to think. In that way she had played a role in Arne's life similar to that of his mother. She had made him punctual, and discouraged him from getting drunk, while he had taught her to relax and have fun. She had once said to him: 'There's a time and place for spontaneity,' and he had laughed about it all day.

She had returned to Sande once more, for the Christmas festival. It had seemed more like Lent. For the Olufsens, Christmas was a religious event, not a bacchanal. Yet she had found the holiday enjoyable in its quiet way, doing crossword puzzles with Arne, getting to know Harald, eating Mrs Olufsen's plain food, and walking along the cold beach in a fur coat, hand in hand with her lover.

She had never imagined returning here for his funeral.

She longed to go to the service, but she knew it was impossible. Too many people would see her and recognize her. There might even be a police detective present, studying the faces. After all, if Hermia could figure out that Arne's mission was being carried on by someone else, the police could make the same deduction.

In fact, she now realized, the funeral was going to delay her by some hours. She would have to wait until after the service before going to the house. Beforehand there would be neighbours in the kitchen preparing food, parishioners in the church arranging flowers, and an undertaker fussing about timings and pallbearers. It would be almost as bad as the service itself. But afterwards, as soon as the mourners had had their tea and smorrebrod, they would all depart, leaving the immediate family to grieve alone.

It meant she would have to kill time now, but caution was everything. If she could get the film from Harald this evening she could catch the first train to Copenhagen in the morning, sail to Bornholm tomorrow night, cross to Sweden the following day, and be in London twelve hours later, with two days to go before the full moon. It was worth wasting a few hours.

She disembarked on to the quay at Sande and walked to the hotel. She could not go into the building, for fear she might encounter someone who remembered her, so she walked on to the beach. It was not really sunbathing weather – there was patchy cloud, and a cool breeze off the water – but the old-fashioned striped bathing huts had been wheeled out, and a few people were splashing in the waves or picnicking on the sand. Hermia was able to find a sheltered dip in the dunes and disappear into the holiday scene.

She waited there while the tide came in and a horse from the hotel pulled the wheeled bathing huts back up the beach. She had spent so much of the last two weeks sitting and waiting.

She had met Arne's parents a third time, on their once-a-decade trip to Copenhagen. Arne had taken them all to the Tivoli Garden and had been his most debonair, amusing self, charming waitresses, making his mother laugh, even getting his dour father to reminisce about schooldays at Jansborg. A few weeks later the Nazis had come and Hermia had left the country, ignominiously she felt, in a closed train with a crowd of diplomats from countries hostile to Germany.

And now she was back, seeking out a deadly secret, risking her life and the lives of others.

She left her position at half past four. The parsonage was ten miles from the hotel, a brisk walk of two and a half hours, so she would arrive at seven. She felt sure all the guests would have left by then, and she would find Harald and his parents sitting quietly in the kitchen.

The beach was not deserted. Several times on her long walk she encountered people. She gave them a wide berth, letting them assume she was an unfriendly holidaymaker, and no one recognized her.

At last she saw the outlines of the low church and the parsonage. The thought that this had been Arne's home struck her with sadness. There was no one in sight. As she came nearer, she saw the fresh grave in the little cemetery.

With a full heart, she crossed the churchyard and stood by the grave of her fiancé. She took off her sunglasses. There were lots of flowers, she observed: people were always touched by the death of a young man. Grief took hold of her, and she began to shake with sobs. Tears streamed down her face. She fell to her knees and took a handful of the piled-up earth, thinking of his body lying below. I doubted you, she said in her mind, but you were the bravest of us all.

At last the storm abated and she was able to stand up. She wiped her face dry with her sleeve. She had work to do.

When she turned away, she saw the tall figure and domed head of Arne's father, standing a few yards off, watching her. He must have approached silently, and waited for her to rise. 'Well, Hermia,' he said. 'God bless you.'

'Thank you, pastor.' She wanted to hug him, but he was not a hugging man, so she shook his hand.

'You arrived too late for the funeral.'

'That was intentional. I can't afford to be seen.'

'You'd better come into the house.'

Hermia followed him across the rough grass. Mrs Olufsen was in the kitchen, but for once she was not at the sink. Hermia guessed that neighbours had cleared up after the wake and washed the dishes. Mrs Olufsen was sitting at the kitchen table in a black dress and hat. When she saw Hermia she burst into tears.

Hermia hugged her, but her compassion was distracted. The person she wanted was not in the room. As soon as she decently could, she said: 'I was hoping to see Harald.'

'He's not here,' said Mrs Olufsen.

Hermia had a dreadful feeling that this long and dangerous journey would turn out to have been for nothing. 'Didn't he come to the funeral?'

She shook her head tearfully.

Curbing her exasperation as best she could, Hermia said: 'So where is he?'

The pastor said: 'You'd better sit down.'

She forced herself to be patient. The pastor was used to being obeyed. She would not get anywhere by defying his will.

Mrs Olufsen said: 'Will you have a cup of tea? It's not the real thing, of course.'

'Yes, please.'

'And a sandwich? There's such a lot left over.'

'No, thank you.' Hermia had had nothing all day, but she was too tense to eat. 'Where is Harald?' she said impatiently.

'We don't know,' said the pastor.

'How come?'

The pastor looked ashamed, a rare expression on his face. 'Harald and I had harsh words. I was as stubborn as he. Since then, the Lord has reminded me how precious is the time a man spends with his sons.' A tear rolled down his lined face. 'Harald left in anger, refusing to say where he was going. Five days later he returned, just for a few hours, and there was something of a reconciliation. On that occasion, he told his mother he was going to stay at the home of a school mate, but when we telephoned, they said he was not there.'

'Do you think he is still angry with you?'

'No,' said the pastor. 'Well, perhaps he is, but that's not why he has disappeared.'

'What do you mean?'

'My neighbour, Axel Flemming, has a son in the Copenhagen police.'

'I remember,' Hermia said. 'Peter Flemming.'

Mrs Olufsen put in: 'He had the nerve to come to the funeral.' Her tone was uncharacteristically bitter.

The pastor went on: 'Peter claims that Arne was a spy for the British, and Harald is continuing his work.'

'Ah.'

'You don't seem surprised.'

'I won't lie to you,' Hermia said. 'Peter is right. I asked Arne to take photographs of the military base here on the island. Harald has the film.'

Mrs Olufsen cried: 'How could you? Arne is dead because of that! We lost our son and you lost your fiancé! How could you?'

'I'm sorry,' Hermia whispered.

The pastor said: 'There's a war, Lisbeth. Many young men have died fighting the Nazis. It's not Hermia's fault.'

'I have to get the film from Harald,' Hermia said. 'I have to find him. Won't you help me?'

Mrs Olufsen said: 'I don't want to lose my other son! I couldn't bear it!'

The pastor took her hand. 'Arne was working against the Nazis. If Hermia and Harald can finish the job he started, his death will have some meaning. We have to help.'

Mrs Olufsen nodded. 'I know,' she said. 'I know. I'm just so scared.'

Hermia said: 'Where did Harald say he was going?'

Mrs Olufsen answered. 'Kirstenslot. It's a castle outside Copenhagen, the home of the Duchwitz family. The son, Josef, is at school with Harald.'

'But they say he's not there?'

She nodded. 'But he's not far away. I spoke to Josef's twin sister, Karen. She's in love with Harald.'

The pastor said incredulously: 'How do you know that?'

'By the sound of her voice when she spoke about him.'

'You didn't mention it to me.'

'You would have said I couldn't possibly tell.'

The pastor smiled ruefully. 'Yes, I would.'

Hermia said: 'So you think Harald is in the vicinity of Kirstenslot, and Karen knows where he is?'

'Yes.'

'Then I'll have to go there.'

The pastor took a watch out of his waistcoat pocket. 'You've missed the last train. You'd better stay the night. I'll take you to the ferry first thing in the morning.'

Hermia's voice dropped to a whisper. 'How can you be so kind? Arne died because of me.'

'The Lord giveth, and the Lord taketh away,' said the pastor. 'Blessed be the name of the Lord.'

# TWENTY-SEVEN

The Hornet Moth was ready to fly.

Harald had installed the new cables from Vodal. His final task had been the punctured tyre. He had used the car jack from the Rolls-Royce to lift the aircraft, then he had taken the wheel to the nearest garage and paid a mechanic to repair the tyre. He had devised a method of refuelling in flight, knocking out a cabin window and passing a hose through it and into the petrol filler pipe. Finally he had unfolded the wings, fixing them in flying position with the simple steel pins provided. Now the aircraft filled the width of the church.

He looked outside. It was a calm day, with a light wind, and patchy low cloud that would serve to hide the Hornet Moth from the Luftwaffe. They would go tonight.

His stomach clenched with anxiety when he thought of it. Simply circling the Vodal training school in a Tiger Moth had seemed like a hair-raising adventure. Now he was planning to fly hundreds of miles over the open sea.

An aircraft such as this should hug the coast, so that it could glide to land in case of trouble. Flying to

England from here, it was theoretically possible to follow the coastlines of Denmark, Germany, Holland, Belgium and France. But Harald and Karen would be many miles out to sea, well away from German-occupied land. If anything went wrong, they would have nowhere to go.

Harald was still worrying when Karen slipped through the window, carrying a basket like Little Red Riding Hood. His heart leaped with pleasure at the sight of her. All day, as he worked on the aircraft, he had thought about the way they had kissed early this morning, after stealing the petrol. He kept touching his lips with his fingertips to bring back the memory.

Now she looked at the Hornet Moth and said: 'Wow.'

He was pleased to have impressed her. 'Pretty, isn't it?'

'But you can't get it through the door like that.'

'I know. I'll have to fold the wings again, then unfold them outside.'

'So why have you rigged them now?'

'For practice. I'll be able to do it faster the second time.'

'How fast?'

'I'm not sure.'

'What about the soldiers? If they see us . . .'

'They'll be asleep.'

She looked solemn. 'We're ready, aren't we?'

'We're ready.'

'When shall we go?'

'Tonight, of course.'

'Oh, my God.'

'Waiting just increases the chance that we'll be found out before we get away.'

'I know, but . . .'

'What?'

'I suppose I just didn't think it would come so quickly.' She took a package out of her basket and handed it to him absent-mindedly. 'I brought you some cold beef.' She fed him every night.

'Thanks.' He studied her carefully. 'You're not having second thoughts, are you?'

She shook her head decisively. 'No. I'm just remembering that it's three years since I sat in a pilot's seat.'

He went over to the work bench and selected a small hatchet and a ball of stout cord. He stowed them in the locker under the dashboard of the aircraft.

Karen said: 'What are they for?'

'If we come down in the sea, I figure the aircraft will sink, because of the weight of the engine. But the wings on their own would float. So if we could chop the wings off, we could lash them together for a makeshift raft.'

'In the North Sea? I think we'd die of cold before long.'

'It's better than drowning.'

She shivered. 'If you say so.'

'We ought to take some biscuits and a couple of bottles of water.'

'I'll get some from the kitchen. Speaking of water

. . . we're going to be in the air for more than six hours.'

'So?'

'How do we pee?'

'Open the door and hope for the best.'

'That's all right for you.'

He grinned. 'Sorry.'

She looked around and picked up a handful of old newspapers. 'Put these inside.'

'What for?'

'In case I have to pee.'

He frowned. 'I don't see how . . .'

'Pray that you never have to find out.'

He put the newspapers on the seat.

'Do we have any maps?' she asked.

'No. I assumed we would just fly west until we see land, and that will be England.'

She shook her head. 'It's quite difficult to know where you are in the air. I used to get lost just flying around here. Suppose we get blown off course? We could come down in France by mistake.'

'My God, I didn't think of that.'

'The only way to check your position is to compare the terrain features below you with a map. I'll see what we've got in the house.'

'OK.'

'I'd better go and get all the stuff we need.' She slipped out through the window again, carrying the empty basket.

Harald was too tense to eat the beef she had

brought him. He began to refold the wings. The process was quick, by design: the intention was that the gentleman owner would do this every night, and garage the aircraft alongside the family car.

To prevent the upper wing fouling the cabin roof when the wings were folded, the inner section of the trailing edge was hinged to swing up out of the way. So Harald's first step was to unlock the hinged sections and push them up.

On the underside of each upper wing was stowed a brace, called a jury strut, which Harald detached then fixed between the inner ends of the upper and lower wings, to prevent their collapsing together.

The wings were held in the flying position by L-shaped sliding pins in the front spars of all four wings. On the upper wings, the pin was locked in place by the jury strut, which Harald had now removed, so all he had to do was turn the pin through ninety degrees and pull it forward about four inches.

The pins on the lower wings were locked in place by leather straps. Harald undid the strap on the left wing, then turned the pin and pulled it.

As soon as it came free, the wing started to move.

Harald realized he should have expected this. In its parked position, with its tail on the ground, the aircraft was tilted, with its nose in the air; and now the heavy double wing was swinging backwards by force of gravity. He grabbed at it, terrified that it would crash against the fuselage and cause damage. He tried to seize the leading edge of the lower wing, but it was too thick for him to get a grasp. 'Hell!' he cried. He stepped forward, chasing the wing, and grabbed at the steel rigging wires between upper and lower wings. He got a purchase, and slowed the swing, then the wire bit into the skin of his hand. He cried out and automatically let go. The wing swivelled back and came to rest with a painful thud against the fuselage.

Cursing his carelessness, Harald went to the tail, took hold of the lower wing tip in both hands, and swung it out so that he could check for damage. To his intense relief there seemed to be none. The trailing edges of the upper and lower wings were intact, and the fuselage was unmarked. Nothing was broken but the skin of Harald's right hand.

Licking the blood from his hand, he went to the right side. This time he braced the lower wing with a tea-chest full of old magazines, so that it could not move. He pulled the pins, then walked around the wing, shoved the chest out of the way, and held the wing, allowing it to swing slowly back into the folded position.

Karen came back.

'Did you get everything?' Harald said anxiously.

She dropped her basket on the floor. 'We can't go tonight.'

'What?' He felt cheated. He had got scared for nothing. 'Why not?' he said angrily.

'I'm dancing tomorrow.'

'*Dancing?*' He was outraged. 'How can you put that before our mission?'

'It's really special. I told you I've been understudying the lead role. Half the company has gone down with some kind of gastric illness. There are two casts, but the leads in both are sick, so I've been called in. It's a great piece of luck!'

'Damn bad luck, it seems to me.'

'I'll be on the main stage at the Royal Theatre, and guess what? The King will be there!'

He ran his fingers through his hair distractedly. 'I can't believe you're saying this.'

'I reserved a ticket for you. You can pick it up at the box office.'

'I'm not going.'

'Don't be so grumpy! We can fly tomorrow night, after I dance. The ballet isn't on again for another week after that, and one of the other two is sure to be better by then.'

'I don't care about the damn ballet – what about the war? Heis reckoned the RAF must be planning a massive air raid. They need our photographs before then! Think of the lives at stake!'

She sighed, and her voice softened. 'I knew you would feel this way, and I thought about forgoing the opportunity, but I just can't. Anyway, if we fly tomorrow, we'll be in England three days before the full moon.'

'But we'll be in deadly danger here for an extra twenty-four hours!'

'Look, no one knows about this plane – why would they find out tomorrow?'

'It's possible.'

'Oh, don't be so childish, anything's *possible*.'

'Childish? The police are looking for me, you know

that. I'm a fugitive and I want to get out of this country as soon as I can.'

Now she was getting angry. 'You really ought to understand how I feel about this performance.'

'Well, I don't.'

'Look, I might die in this damn plane.'

'So might I.'

'While I'm drowning in the North Sea, or freezing to death on your makeshift raft, I'd like to be able to think that before I died I achieved my life's ambition, and danced wonderfully on the stage of the Royal Danish Theatre in front of the King. Can't you understand that?'

'No, I can't!'

'Then you can go to Hell,' she said, and she went out through the window.

Harald stared after her. He was thunderstruck. A minute passed before he moved. Then he looked inside the basket she had brought. There were two bottles of mineral water, a packet of crackers, a flashlight, a spare battery and two spare bulbs. There were no maps, but she had put in an old school atlas. He picked up the book and opened it. On the end-paper was written, in a girlish hand: 'Karen Duchwitz, Class 3.'

'Oh, Hell,' he said.

# TWENTY-EIGHT

Peter Flemming stood on the quay at Morlunde, watching the last ferry of the day come in from Sande, waiting for a mystery woman.

He had been disappointed, though not really surprised, that Harald had not shown up yesterday for his brother's funeral. Peter had carefully scrutinized all the mourners. Most were islanders whom Peter had known since childhood. It was the others who interested him. After the service, taking tea in the parsonage, he had spoken to all the strangers. There were a couple of old school pals, some army buddies, friends from Copenhagen, and the headmaster of Jansborg Skole. He had ticked their names on the list given him by the policeman on the ferry. And he noticed one name not ticked: Miss Agnes Ricks.

Returning to the ferry dock, he had asked the policeman if Agnes Ricks had gone back to the mainland. 'Not yet,' the man had said. 'I'd remember her. She's a bit of all right.' He grinned and cupped his hands over his chest to signify large breasts.

Peter had gone to his father's hotel and learned that no Agnes Ricks had checked in.

He was intrigued. Who was Miss Ricks and what was

she doing? Instinct told him she had some connection with Arne Olufsen. Perhaps it was wishful thinking. But she was the only lead he had.

He was too conspicuous loitering at the quay on Sande, so he crossed to the mainland and made himself unobtrusive at the large commercial harbour there. However, Miss Ricks did not appear. Now, as the ferry docked for the last time until morning, Harald retired to the Oesterport Hotel.

There was a phone in a little booth in the hotel lobby, and he used it to call Tilde Jespersen at home in Copenhagen.

'Was Harald at the funeral?' she said immediately.

'No.'

'Damn.'

'I checked out the mourners. No clues there. But there's one more lead I'm following up, a Miss Agnes Ricks. What about you?'

'I've spent the day on the phone to local police stations all over the country. I've got men checking on each of Harald's classmates. I should hear from all of them tomorrow.'

'You walked off the job,' he said with an abrupt change of subject.

'It wasn't a normal job, though, was it?' She was obviously prepared for this.

'Why not?'

'You took me because you wanted to sleep with me.'

Peter ground his teeth. He had compromised his own professionalism by having sex with her, and now

489

he could not admonish her. Angrily, he said: 'Is that your excuse?'

'It's not an excuse.'

'You said you disliked the way I interrogated the Olufsens. That's not a reason for a police officer to run away.'

'I didn't run away from the job. I just didn't want to sleep with a man who could do that.'

'I was just doing my duty!'

Her voice changed. 'Not quite.'

'What do you mean?'

'It would be all right if you had been tough just for the sake of getting the job done. I could respect that. But you liked what you were doing. You tortured the pastor and bullied his wife, and you enjoyed it. Their grief gave you satisfaction. I can't get into bed with a man like that.'

Peter hung up.

He spent much of the night awake, thinking about Tilde. Lying in bed, angry with her, he imagined himself slapping her. He would have liked to go to her apartment, and pull her out of bed in her nightgown, and punish her. In his fantasy she pleaded for mercy, but he ignored her cries. Her gown became torn in the struggle, and he became aroused and raped her. She screamed and fought him off, but he held her down. Afterwards, she begged forgiveness with tears in her eyes, but he left her without a word.

Eventually he fell asleep.

In the morning he went to the dock to meet the first ferry from Sande. He looked hopefully at the salt-caked boat as it steamed into the dock. Agnes Ricks was his only hope. If she turned out to be innocent, he was not sure what to do next.

A handful of passengers disembarked. Peter's plan had been to ask the policeman if one of them was Miss Ricks, but there was no need. He immediately noticed, among the men in work clothes headed for the early shift at the cannery, a tall woman wearing sunglasses and a headscarf. As she came closer, he realized he knew her. He saw black hair escaping from under the scarf, but it was the large, curved nose that gave her away. She walked with a confident, mannish stride, he observed, and he remembered noticing that gait when he first met her, two years before.

She was Hermia Mount.

She looked thinner and older than the woman who had been introduced as Arne Olufsen's fiancée back in 1939, but Peter had no doubt.

'You treacherous bitch, I've got you,' he said with profound satisfaction.

Anxious that she might recognize him, he put on heavy-rimmed glasses and pulled his hat forward to cover the distinctive red of his hair. Then he followed her to the station, where she bought a ticket to Copenhagen.

After a long wait they boarded an old, slow, coal-burning train that meandered across Denmark from west to east, stopping at half-timbered stations in seaweed-smelling resorts and sleepy market towns. Peter sat in a first-class carriage, fidgeting with impatience. Hermia was in the next carriage, in a third-class seat. She could not get away from him while they were on the train, but on the other hand he could make no progress until she got off.

It was mid-afternoon when the train pulled into Nyborg, on the central island of Fyn. From here they had to transfer to a ferry across the Great Belt to Zealand, the largest island, where they would board another train to Copenhagen.

Peter had heard talk of an ambitious plan to replace the ferry with a huge bridge twelve miles long. Traditionalists liked the numerous Danish ferries, saying their slow progress was part of the country's relaxed attitude to life, but Peter would have liked to scrap them all. He had a lot to do; he preferred bridges.

While waiting for the ferry, he found a phone and called Tilde at the Politigaarden.

She was coolly professional. 'I haven't found Harald, but I've got a clue.'

'Good!'

'Twice in the last month he's visited Kirstenslot, the home of the Duchwitz family.'

'Jews?'

'Yes. The local policeman recalls meeting him. He says Harald had a steam-driven motorcycle. But he swears Harald is not there now.'

'Make double sure. Go there yourself.'

'I was planning to.'

He wanted to talk to her about what she had said yesterday. Did she really mean that she could not sleep with him again? But he could not think of a way to raise the subject, so he kept talking about the case. 'I found Miss Ricks. She's Hermia Mount, Arne Olufsen's fiancée.'

'The English girl?'

'Yes.'

'Good news!'

'It is.' Peter was glad Tilde had not lost her enthusiasm for the case. 'She's on her way to Copenhagen now, and I'm following her.'

'Isn't there a chance she'll recognize you?'

'Yes.'

'In case she tries to give you the slip, why don't I meet the train?'

'I'd rather you go to Kirstenslot.'

'Maybe I can do both. Where are you?'

'Nyborg.'

'You're at least two hours away.'

'More. This train is torpid.'

'I can drive out to Kirstenslot, snoop around for an hour, and still meet you at the station.'

'Good,' he said. 'Do it.'

# TWENTY-NINE

When Harald cooled down, he saw that Karen's decision to postpone their flight for a day was not completely mad. He put himself in her place by imagining that he had been offered the chance to perform an important experiment with the physicist Neils Bohr. He might have delayed the escape to England for the sake of such an opportunity. Perhaps he and Bohr together would change mankind's understanding of how the universe worked. If he were going to die, he would like to know he had done something like that.

Nevertheless he spent a tense day. He checked everything on the Hornet Moth twice. He studied the instrument panel, familiarizing himself with the gauges so that he could help Karen. The panel was not illuminated, for the aircraft was not designed to be used at night, so they would have to shine the torch on the dials to read the instruments. He practised folding and unfolding the wings, improving his time. He tried out his in-flight refuelling system, pouring a little petrol through the hose that led from the cabin, through the smashed-out window, into the tank. He watched the weather, which was fine, with patchy cloud and a light breeze. A three-quarter moon rose late in the afternoon. He put on clean clothes.

He was lying on his ledge bed, stroking Pinetop the cat, when someone rattled the big church door.

Harald sat upright, putting Pinetop on the floor, and listened.

He heard the voice of Per Hansen. 'I told you it was locked.'

A woman replied: 'All the more reason to look inside.'

The voice was authoritative, Harald noted fearfully. He pictured a woman in her thirties, attractive but businesslike. Obviously she was with the police. Presumably she had sent Hansen to look for Harald at the castle yesterday. Clearly she had not been satisfied with Hansen's inquiries and had come herself today.

Harald cursed. She would probably be more thorough than Hansen. It would not take her long to find a way into the church. There was nowhere for him to hide except the trunk of the Rolls-Royce, and any serious searcher was sure to open that.

Harald was afraid he might already be too late to exit by his usual window, which was just around the corner from the main door. But there were windows all around the curved chancel, and he quickly made his escape through one of those.

When he hit the ground, he looked around warily. This end of the church was only partly concealed by trees, and he might have been seen by a soldier; but he was in luck, and no one was nearby.

He hesitated. He wanted to get away, but he needed

to know what happened next. He flattened himself against the wall of the church and listened. He heard Hansen's voice say: 'Mrs Jespersen? If we stand on that log we could get through the window.'

'No doubt that's why the log is there,' the woman replied crisply. She was obviously a lot smarter than Hansen. Harald had a dreadful feeling she was going to learn everything.

He heard the scrape of feet on the wall, a grunt from Hansen as, presumably, he squeezed himself through the window, then a thud as he hit the tiled floor of the church. A lighter thud followed a few seconds afterwards.

Harald crept around the side of the church, stood on the log, and peeped through the window.

Mrs Jespersen was a pretty woman of about thirty, not fat but well rounded, smartly dressed in practical clothes, a blouse and skirt with flat shoes and a sky-blue beret over her blonde curls. As she was not in uniform, she must be a detective, Harald deduced. She carried a shoulder bag which presumably had a gun in it.

Hansen was red-faced from the exertion of getting through the window, and he looked harassed. Harald guessed the village policeman was finding it a strain dealing with the quick-thinking detective.

She looked first at the bike. 'Well, here's the motorcycle you told me about. I see the steam engine. Ingenious.'

'He must have left it here,' Hansen said in a

defensive tone. Obviously he had told the detective that Harald had gone away.

But she was not convinced. 'Perhaps.' She moved to the car. 'Very nice.'

'It belongs to the Jew.'

She ran a finger along the curve of a mudguard and looked at the dust. 'He hasn't been out in it for a while.'

'Of course not – its wheels are off.' Hansen thought he had caught her out, and looked pleased.

'That doesn't mean much – wheels can be put on quickly. But it's difficult to fake a layer of dust.'

She crossed the room and picked up Harald's discarded shirt. He groaned inwardly. Why had he not put it away somewhere? She sniffed it.

Pinetop appeared from somewhere and rubbed his head against Mrs Jespersen's leg. She stooped to stroke him. 'What are you after?' she said to the cat. 'Has someone been feeding you?'

Nothing could be hidden from this woman, Harald saw with dismay. She was too thorough. She moved to the ledge where Harald slept. She picked up his neatly folded blanket, then put it down again. 'Someone's living here,' she said.

'Perhaps it's a vagrant.'

'And perhaps it's Harald fucking Olufsen.'

Hansen looked shocked.

She turned to the Hornet Moth. 'What have we here?' Harald watched in despair as she pulled off the cover. 'I do believe it's an aeroplane.'

That's the end, Harald thought. It's all over now.

Hansen said: 'Duchwitz used to have a plane, I remember now. He hasn't flown it for years, though.'

'It's not in bad condition.'

'It's got no wings!'

'The wings are folded back – that's how they got it through the door.' Reaching inside the cabin, she moved the control stick, looking at the tailplane at the same time, seeing the elevator move. 'The controls seem to work.' She peered at the fuel gauge. 'The tank is full.' Looking around the little cabin, she added: 'And there's a four-gallon can behind the seat. And the locker contains two bottles of water and a packet of biscuits. Plus an axe, a ball of good strong cord, a flashlight, and an atlas – with no dust on any of them.'

She withdrew her head from the cabin and looked at Hansen. 'Harald is planning to fly.'

'Well, I'm damned,' said Hansen.

The wild thought of killing them both occurred to Harald. He was not sure he could kill another human being in any circumstances, but he immediately realized he could not overpower two armed police officers with his bare hands, and he dismissed the thought.

Mrs Jespersen became very brisk. 'I have to go into Copenhagen. Inspector Flemming, who's in charge of this case, is coming in by train. Given the way the railways are nowadays, he could arrive any time in the next twelve hours. When he does, we'll come back.

We'll arrest Harald, if he's here, and set a trap for him if he's not.'

'What do you want me to do?'

'Stay here. Find a vantage point in the woods, and watch the church. If Harald appears, don't speak to him, just phone the Politigaarden.'

'Aren't you going to send someone to help me?'

'No. We mustn't do anything to scare Harald off. If he sees you, he won't panic – you're just the village policeman. But a couple of strange cops might spook him. I don't want him to run away and hide somewhere. Now that we've tracked him down, we mustn't lose him again. Is that clear?'

'Yes.'

'On the other hand, if he tries to fly that plane, stop him.'

'Arrest him?'

'Shoot him, if you have to – but don't for God's sake let him take off.'

Harald found her matter-of-fact tone absolutely terrifying. If she had been over-dramatic, he might not have felt so scared. But she was an attractive woman speaking calmly about practicalities – and she had just told Hansen to shoot him if necessary. Until this moment, Harald had not confronted the possibility that the police might simply kill him. Mrs Jespersen's quiet mercilessness shook him.

'You can open this door, to save me scrambling through the window again,' she said. 'Lock it up when I've gone, so that Harald won't suspect anything.'

Hansen turned the key and removed the bar, and they went out.

Harald jumped to the ground and retreated around the end of the church. Moving away from the building, he stood behind a tree and watched from a distance as Mrs Jespersen walked to her car, a black Buick. She looked at her reflection in the car's window and adjusted her sky-blue beret in a very feminine gesture. Then she reverted to cop mode, shook hands briskly with Hansen, got into the car and drove away fast.

Hansen came back, and disappeared from Harald's view, screened by the church.

Harald leaned against the trunk of the tree for a moment, thinking. Karen had promised to come to the church as soon as she got home from the ballet. If she did that she might find the police waiting for her. And how would she explain what she was doing? Her guilt would be obvious.

Harald had to head her off somehow. Thinking about the best way to intercept her and warn her, he decided the simplest thing would be to go to the theatre. That way he could be sure he would not miss her.

He felt a moment of anger towards her. If they had taken off last night they might be in England now. He had warned her that she was putting them both in danger, and now he had been proved right. But recriminations were fruitless. It was done, and he had to deal with the consequences.

Unexpectedly, Hansen came walking around the

corner of the church. He saw Harald and stopped dead.

They were both astonished. Harald had thought Hansen had gone back into the church to lock up. Hansen, for his part, could not have imagined that his quarry was so close. They stared at each other for a paralysed moment.

Then Hansen reached for his gun.

Mrs Jespersen's words flashed through Harald's mind: 'Shoot him, if you have to.' Hansen, a village constable, had probably never shot at anyone in his life. But he might jump at the chance.

Harald reacted instinctively. Without thought for the consequences, he rushed at Hansen. As Hansen drew his pistol from the holster, Harald cannoned into him. Hansen was thrown back, and hit the church wall with a thud, but he did not lose his grip on the gun.

He raised the gun to point it. Harald knew he had only a fraction of a second to save himself. He drew back his fist and hit Hansen on the point of the chin. The blow had the force of desperation behind it. Hansen's head jerked back and hit the brickwork with a sound like the crack of a rifle. His eyes rolled up, his body slumped, and he fell to the ground.

Harald was dreadfully afraid the man was dead. He knelt beside the unconscious body. He saw immediately that Hansen was breathing. Thank God, he thought. It was horrifying to think he might have killed a man – even a vicious fool such as Hansen.

The fight had lasted only a few seconds, but had it

been observed? He looked across the park to the soldiers' encampment. A few men were walking around, but no one was looking Harald's way.

He stuffed Hansen's gun into his pocket then lifted the limp body. Slinging it over his shoulder in a fireman's lift, he hurried around the church to the main door, which was still open. His luck held, and no one saw him.

He put Hansen down, then quickly closed and locked the church door. He got the cord out of the cabin of the Hornet Moth and tied Hansen's feet together. He rolled the man over and tied his hands behind his back. Then he picked up his discarded shirt, stuffed half of it in Hansen's mouth so the man could not cry out, and tied string around Hansen's head so that the gag would not fall out.

Finally he put Hansen in the boot of the Rolls-Royce and closed the lid.

He looked at his watch. He still had time to get to the city and warn Karen.

He lit the boiler on his motorcycle. He might well be seen driving out of the church, but there was no longer any time for caution.

However, he could get into trouble with a policeman's gun making a bulge in his pocket. Not knowing what to do with the pistol, he opened the right door of the Hornet Moth and put it on the floor, where no one would see it unless they got in the aircraft and trod on it.

When the motorcycle engine had a head of steam he opened the doors, drove the bike out, locked up from inside and exited by the window. He was lucky, and saw no one.

He drove into the city, keeping a nervous eye out for policemen, and parked at the side of the Royal Theatre. A red carpet led up to the entrance, and he recalled that the King was attending this performance. A notice informed him that *Les Sylphides* was the last of three ballets on the programme. A crowd of well-dressed people stood on the steps with drinks, and Harald gathered that he had arrived during the interval.

He went to the stage door, where he encountered an obstacle. The entrance was guarded by a uniformed commissionaire. 'I need to speak to Karen Duchwitz,' Harald said.

'Out of the question,' the commissionaire told him. 'She's about to go on stage.'

'It's really important.'

'You'll have to wait until afterwards.'

Harald could see that the man was immovable. 'How long is the ballet?'

'About half an hour, depending how fast the orchestra play.'

Harald remembered that Karen had left a ticket for him at the box office. He decided he would watch her dance.

He went into the marble foyer, got his ticket, and entered the auditorium. He had never been in a theatre before, and he gazed in wonder at the lavish gilded decoration, the rising tiers of the circle, and the rows of red plush seats. He found his place in the fourth row and sat down. There were two German officers in uniform immediately in front of him. He checked his watch. Why did the ballet not start? Every minute brought Peter Flemming nearer.

He picked up a programme that had been left on the seat beside him and flicked through it, looking for Karen's name. She was not on the cast list, but a slip of paper which fell out of the booklet said that the prima ballerina was indisposed and her place would be taken by Karen Duchwitz. It also revealed that the lone male dancer in the ballet would also be played by an understudy, Jan Anders, presumably because the principal man had also fallen victim to the gastric illness that had spread through the cast. This must be a worrying moment for the company, Harald thought, the leading roles being taken by students when the King was in the audience.

A few moments later he was startled to see Mr and Mrs Duchwitz take their seats two rows in front of him. He should have known they would not miss their daughter's big moment. At first he worried that they would see him. Then he realized it no longer mattered. Now that the police had found his hiding-place, he did not need to keep it secret from anyone else.

He remembered guiltily that he was wearing Mr Duchwitz's American sports jacket. It was fifteen years old, according to the tailor's label in the inside pocket, but Karen had not actually asked her father's permission to take it. Would Pa Duchwitz recognize it? Harald told himself he was foolish even to think about it. Being accused of stealing a jacket was the least thing he had to worry about.

He touched the roll of film in his pocket and wondered if there was any chance he and Karen could still escape in the Hornet Moth. A lot depended on Peter Flemming's train. If it came in early, Flemming and Mrs Jespersen would be back at Kirstenslot before Harald and Karen. Perhaps they could avoid getting caught, but it was hard to see how they could get access to the aircraft with the police watching over it. On the other hand, with Hansen out of the way there was no guard on the aircraft at the moment. If Flemming's train did not get in until the early hours of the morning, perhaps there was a chance they could yet take off.

Mrs Jespersen did not know that Harald had seen her. She thought she had plenty of time. That was the only thing in Harald's favour.

When would the damn show start?

After everyone was seated in the auditorium, the King came into the royal box. The audience stood up. It was the first time Harald had seen King Christian X in person, but the face was familiar from photographs, the downturned moustache giving it a permanently grim expression that was appropriate to the monarch of an occupied country. He was in evening dress and stood very upright. In pictures the King always wore some kind of hat, and now Harald saw for the first time that he was losing his hair.

When the King sat, the audience followed suit, and the lights went down. At last, Harald thought.

The curtain rose on twenty or more women motionless in a circle and one man standing at the twelve o'clock position. The dancers, all dressed in white, posed in a pale blueish light like moonlight, and the bare stage disappeared into dark shadows at its edges. It was a dramatic opening, and Harald was fascinated despite his worries.

The music played a slow, descending phrase, and the dancers moved. The circle widened, leaving four people motionless upstage, the man and three women. One of the women lay on the ground as if asleep. A slow waltz began.

Where was Karen? All the girls were in identical dresses, with tight bodices that left their shoulders bare, and full skirts that billowed as they danced. It was a sexy outfit, but the atmospheric lighting made them all look the same, and Harald could not tell which was Karen.

Then the sleeping one moved, and he recognized Karen's red hair. She glided to the centre of the stage. Harald was taut with anxiety, fearing she would do something wrong and spoil her great day; but she seemed assured and controlled. She began to dance on the tips of her toes. It looked painful, and made Harald wince, but she seemed to float. The company formed patterns around her, lines and circles. The audience was silent and still, captivated by her, and Harald's heart filled with pride. He was glad she had decided to do this, no matter what the consequences.

The music changed key and the male dancer

moved. As he leaped across the stage, Harald thought he seemed uncertain and remembered that he, too, was an understudy, Anders. Karen had danced with confidence, making every move seem effortless, but there was tension in the boy's movements that gave his dancing a sense of risk.

The dance closed with the slow phrase that had opened it, and Harald realized there was no story, the dances would be as abstract as the music. He checked his watch. Only five minutes had passed.

The ensemble dispersed and reformed in new configurations that framed a series of solo dances. All the music seemed to be in three-four time, and very melodic. Harald, who loved the discords of jazz, found it almost too sweet.

The ballet fascinated him, but nevertheless his mind wandered to the Hornet Moth, and Hansen tied up in the boot of the Rolls, and Mrs Jespersen. Could Peter Flemming have found the only punctual train in Denmark? If so, had he and Mrs Jespersen gone to Kirstenslot yet? Had they found Hansen? Were they already lying in wait? How could Harald check? Perhaps he would approach the monastery through the woods, in the hope of spotting any ambush.

Karen began a solo dance, and he found himself more tense about her than about the police. He need not have worried: she was relaxed and self-possessed, swirling and tiptoeing and leaping as happily as if she were making it up as she went along. He was astonished at how she could perform some vigorous step, running or jumping across the stage, then come to an abrupt stop in a perfectly graceful pose, as if she had no inertia. She seemed to flout the laws of physics.

Harald became even more nervous when Karen began a dance with Jan Anders. It was called a *pas de deux*, he thought, although he was not sure how he knew that. Anders kept lifting her dramatically high in the air. Her skirt would billow up, showing her fabulous legs. Anders would hold her up, sometimes with one hand, while he struck a pose or moved around the stage. Harald feared for her safety, but again and again she came down with ease and grace. Nevertheless Harald was relieved when the *pas de deux* ended and the ensemble began. He checked his watch again. This must be the last dance, thank God.

Anders performed several spectacular leaps during the last dance, and reprised some of his lifts with Karen. Then, as the music built to a climax, disaster struck.

Anders lifted Karen again, then held her in the air with his hand in the small of her back. She stretched out parallel to the ground. Her legs curved forward with pointed toes, and her arms reached backwards over her head, making an arch. They held the pose for a moment. Then Anders slipped.

His left foot shot out from under him. He staggered and fell flat on his back. Karen tumbled to the stage beside him, landing on her right arm and leg.

The audience gasped with horror. The other dancers rushed to the two fallen figures. The music played on for a few bars then died away. A man in black trousers and a black sweater came on from the wings.

Anders got to his feet, holding his elbow, and Harald saw that he was crying. Karen tried to get up but fell back. The figure in black made a gesture, and the curtain came down. The audience burst into excited chatter.

Harald realized he was standing up.

He saw Mr and Mrs Duchwitz, two rows in front of him, get to their feet and push urgently along the row, excusing themselves to the people they were passing. They were obviously intending to go backstage. Harald decided to do the same.

It was painfully slow getting out of the row of seats. In his anxiety, he had to restrain himself from simply walking along everyone's knees. But he reached the aisle at the same time as the Duchwitzes. 'I'm coming with you,' he said.

'Who are you?' said her father.

Her mother answered the question. 'It's Josef's friend Harald, you've met him before, Karen is sweet on him, let him come.'

Mr Duchwitz grunted assent. Harald had no idea how Mrs Duchwitz knew that Karen was 'sweet' on him, but he was relieved to be accepted as part of the family.

As they reached the exit, the audience fell silent. The Duchwitzes and Harald turned at the door. The curtain had come up. The stage was empty but for the man in black.

'Your majesty, ladies and gentlemen,' he began. 'By

good fortune, the company doctor was in the audience tonight.' Harald guessed that everyone associated with the ballet company would want to be present for a royal performance. 'The doctor is already backstage, and is examining our two principals. He has told me that neither appears to be gravely injured.'

There was a scatter of applause.

Harald was relieved. Now that he knew she was going to be all right, he thought for the first time about how the accident might affect their escape. Even if they could get at the Hornet Moth, would Karen be able to fly it?

The man in black resumed. 'As you know from your programme, both lead roles were played by understudies tonight, as were many of the other parts. Nevertheless, I hope you agree with me that they all danced wonderfully well, and gave a superb performance almost to the very end. Thank you.'

The curtain came down, and the audience applauded. It came up again to reveal the cast, minus Karen and Anders, and they took a bow.

The Duchwitzes went out, and Harald followed.

They hurried to the stage door. An usher took them to Karen's dressing room.

She was sitting with her right arm in a sling. She looked stunningly beautiful in the creamy-white gown, with her shoulders bare and the rise of her breasts showing above the bodice. Harald felt breathless, and did not know whether the cause was anxiety or desire.

The doctor was kneeling in front of her, wrapping a bandage around her right ankle.

Mrs Duchwitz rushed to Karen, saying: 'My poor baby!' She put her arms around Karen and hugged her. It was what Harald would have liked to do.

'Oh, I'm all right,' Karen said, though she looked pale.

Mr Duchwitz spoke to the doctor. 'How is she?'

'She's fine,' the man said. 'She's sprained her wrist and ankle. They'll be painful for a few days, and she must take it easy for at least two weeks, but she'll get over it.'

Harald was relieved that her injuries were not serious, but his immediate thought was: Can she fly?

The doctor fastened the bandage with a safety pin and stood up. He patted her bare shoulder. 'I'd better go and see Jan Anders. He didn't fall as hard as you, but I'm a bit worried about his elbow.'

'Thank you, doctor.'

His hand lingered on her shoulder, to Harald's annoyance. 'You'll dance as wonderfully as ever, don't you worry.' He left.

Karen said: 'Poor Jan, he can't stop crying.'

Harald thought Anders should be shot. 'It was his fault – he dropped you!' he said indignantly.

'I know, that's why he's so upset.'

Mr Duchwitz looked at Harald with irritation. 'What are you doing here?'

Once again it was his wife who answered. 'Harald has been living at Kirstenslot.'

Karen was shocked. 'Mother, how did you know?'

'Do you think nobody noticed how the leftovers disappeared from the kitchen every night? We mothers aren't stupid, you know.'

Mr Duchwitz said: 'But where does he sleep?'

'In the disused church, I expect,' his wife replied. 'That would be why Karen was so keen to keep it locked.'

Harald was horrified that his secret had been so easily unveiled. Mr Duchwitz was looking angry but, before he could explode, the King walked in.

Everyone fell silent.

Karen tried to stand up, but he stopped her. 'My dear girl, please stay just where you are. How do you feel?'

'It hurts, your majesty.'

'I'm sure it does. But no permanent damage, I gather?'

'That's what the doctor said.'

'You danced divinely, you know.'

'Thank you, sir.'

The King looked inquiringly at Harald. 'Good evening, young man.'

'I'm Harald Olufsen, your majesty, a school friend of Karen's brother.'

'Which school?'

'Jansborg Skole.'

'Do they still call the headmaster Heis?'

'Yes – and his wife Mia.'

'Well, be sure to take good care of Karen.' He turned to the parents. 'Hello, Duchwitz, it's good to see you again. Your daughter is marvellously talented.'

'Thank you, your majesty. You remember my wife, Hanna.'

'Of course.' The King shook her hand. 'This is very worrying for a mother, Mrs Duchwitz, but I'm sure Karen will be all right.'

'Yes, your majesty. The young heal fast.'

'Indeed they do! Now, then, let's have a look at the poor fellow who dropped her.' The King moved to the door.

For the first time, Harald noticed the King's companion, a young man who was assistant, or bodyguard, or perhaps both. 'This way, sir,' said the young man, and he held the door.

The King went out.

'Well!' said Mrs Duchwitz in a thrilled voice. 'How very charming!'

Mr Duchwitz said: 'I suppose we'd better get Karen home.'

Harald wondered when he would get a chance to speak to her alone.

Karen said: 'Mother will have to help me out of this dress.'

Mr Duchwitz moved to the door, and Harald followed him, not knowing what else to do.

Karen said: 'Before I change, do you mind if I have a word alone with Harald?'

Her father looked irritated, but her mother said: 'All right – just be quick.' They left the room, and Mrs Duchwitz closed the door.

'Are you really all right?' Harald asked Karen.

'I will be when you've kissed me.'

513

He knelt beside the chair and kissed her lips. Then, unable to resist the temptation, he kissed her bare shoulders and her throat. His lips travelled downwards, and he kissed the swell of her breasts.

'Oh, my goodness, stop, it's too nice,' she said.

Reluctantly, Harald drew back. He saw that the colour had returned to her face, and she was breathless. He was amazed to think his kisses had done that.

'We have to talk,' she said.

'I know. Are you fit to fly the Hornet Moth?'

'No.'

He had feared as much. 'Are you sure?'

'It hurts too much. I can't even open a damn door. And I can hardly walk, so I couldn't possibly operate the rudder with my feet.'

Harald buried his face in his hands. 'Then it's all over.'

'The doctor said it would only hurt for a few days. We could go as soon as I feel better.'

'There's something I haven't told you yet. Hansen came snooping around again tonight.'

'I wouldn't worry about him.'

'This time he was with a woman detective, Mrs Jespersen, who is a lot cleverer. I listened to their conversation. She went into the church and figured out everything. She guessed that I'm living there and that I'm planning to escape in the aircraft.'

'Oh, no! What did she do?'

'Went to fetch her boss, who happens to be Peter Flemming. She left Hansen on guard and told him to shoot me if I try to take off.'

'To *shoot* you? What are you going to do?'

'I knocked Hansen out and tied him up,' Harald said, not without a touch of pride.

'Oh, my God! Where is he now?'

'In the boot of your father's car.'

She found that funny. 'You fiend!'

'I thought we had just one chance. Peter is on a train and she didn't know when he would get in. If you and I could have got back to Kirstenslot tonight before Peter and Mrs Jespersen, we could still have taken off. But now that you can't fly . . .'

'We could still do it.'

'How?'

'You can be the pilot.'

'I can't – I've only had one lesson!'

'I'll talk you through everything. Poul said you had a natural talent for it. And I could operate the control stick with my left hand some of the time.'

'Do you really mean it?'

'Yes!'

'All right.' Harald nodded solemnly. 'That's what we'll do. Just pray for Peter's train to be late.'

# THIRTY

Hermia had spotted Peter Flemming on the ferry.

She saw him leaning on the rail, looking at the sea, and recalled a man with a ginger moustache and a smart tweed suit on the platform at Morlunde. No doubt several people from Morlunde were travelling all the way to Copenhagen, as she was, but the man looked vaguely familiar. The hat and glasses put her off for a while, but eventually her memory dredged him up: Peter Flemming.

She had met him with Arne, in the happy days. The two men had been boyhood friends, she seemed to recall, then had fought when their families quarrelled.

Now Peter was a cop.

As soon as she remembered that, she realized he must be following her. She felt a chill of fear like a cold wind.

She was running out of time. The full moon was three nights away, and she still had not found Harald Olufsen. If she got the film from him tonight, she was not sure how she could get it home in time. But she was not going to give up – for the sake of Arne's memory, for the sake of Digby, and for all the airmen risking their lives to stop the Nazis.

But why had Peter not arrested her already? She was a British spy. What was he up to? Perhaps, like her, Peter was looking for Harald.

When the ferry docked, Peter followed her on to the Copenhagen train. As soon as the train got going, she walked along the corridor, and spotted him in a first-class compartment.

She returned to her seat, worried. This was a very bad development. She must not lead Peter to Harald. She had to throw him off.

She had plenty of time to think about how. The train was delayed repeatedly, and got into Copenhagen at ten o'clock in the evening. By the time it pulled into the station, she had made a plan. She would go into the Tivoli Garden and lose Peter in the crowd.

As she left the train, she glanced back along the platform and saw Peter stepping down from the first-class carriage.

She walked at a normal pace up the stairs from the platform, through the ticket barrier and out of the station. It was dusk. The Tivoli Garden was a few steps from the station. She went to the main entrance and bought a ticket. 'Closing at midnight,' the vendor warned her.

She had come here with Arne in the summer of 1939. It had been a festival night, and fifty thousand people had crammed into the park to watch the fireworks. Now the place was a sad version of its former self, like a black-and-white photograph of a bowl of fruit. The paths still wound charmingly between flower beds, but the fairy lights in the trees had been switched off, and the paths were illuminated by special low-intensity lamps to conform with blackout regulations. The air raid shelter outside the Pantomime Theatre added a dismal touch. Even the bands seemed muted. Most dismaying for Hermia, the crowds were not as dense, making it easier for someone to follow her.

She stopped, pretending to watch a juggler, and glanced back. She saw Peter close behind her, buying a glass of beer from a stall. How was she going to shake him off?

She moved into a crowd around an open-air stage on which an operetta was being sung. She pushed her way through to the front then out at the far side but, when she walked on, Peter was still behind her. If this went on much longer, he would realize she was trying to lose him. Then he might cut his losses and arrest her.

She began to feel frightened. She circled the lake and came to an open-air dance floor where a large orchestra was playing a foxtrot. There were at least a hundred couples dancing energetically, and many more watching. Hermia at last felt something of the atmosphere of the old Tivoli. Seeing a good-looking young man standing alone at the side, she was inspired. She went up to him and turned on her biggest smile. 'Would you like to dance with me?' she said.

'Of course!' He took her in his arms and they were off. Hermia was not a good dancer, but she could get by with a competent partner. Arne had been superb, stylish and masterful. This man was confident and decisive.

'What's your name?' he said.

She almost told him, then stopped herself at the last minute. 'Agnes.'

'I am Johan.'

'I'm very happy to meet you, Johan, and you foxtrot wonderfully.' She looked back to the path and saw Peter watching the dancers.

Inconveniently, the tune came to an abrupt end. The dancers applauded the orchestra. Some couples left the floor and others came on. Hermia said: 'Another dance?'

'It would be my pleasure.'

She decided to level with him. 'Listen, there's a horrid man following me and I'm trying to get away from him. Will you steer us all the way over to the far side?'

'How exciting!' He looked across the floor to the spectators. 'Which one is it? That fat man with the red face?'

'No. The one in the light brown suit.'

'I see him. He's quite handsome.'

The band struck up a polka. 'Oh, dear,' said Hermia. The polka was difficult, but she had to try.

Johan was expert enough to make it easier for her. He could also converse at the same time. 'The man who is bothering you – is he a complete stranger, or someone you know?'

'I have met him before. Take me to the far end, by the orchestra – that's right.'

'Is he your boyfriend?'

'No. I'm going to leave you in a minute, Johan. If he runs after me, will you trip him up, or something?'

'If you wish.'

'Thank you.'

'I think he is your husband.'

'Absolutely not.' They were close to the orchestra. Johan steered her to the edge of the dance floor. 'Perhaps you are a spy, and he is a policeman hoping to catch you stealing military secrets from the Nazis.'

'Something like that,' she said gaily, and she slipped from his arms.

She walked quickly off the floor and around the bandstand into the trees. She ran across the grass until she came to another path, then she made for a side exit. She looked back: Peter was not behind her.

She left the park and hurried to the suburban railway station across the street from the main line terminus. She bought a ticket for Kirstenslot. She felt exhilarated. She had shaken Peter off.

There was no one on the platform with her but an attractive woman in a sky-blue beret.

# THIRTY-ONE

Harald approached the church cautiously.

There had been a shower, and the grass was wet, but the rain had stopped. A light breeze blew the clouds along, and a three-quarter moon shone brightly through the gaps. The shadow of the bell tower came and went with the moonlight.

He saw no strange cars parked nearby, but that did not much reassure him. The police would have concealed their vehicles if they were serious about setting a trap.

There were no lights anywhere in the ruined monastery. It was midnight, and the soldiers were in bed, all but two: the sentry in the park outside the mess tent, and a veterinary nurse on duty in the horse hospital.

Harald listened outside the church. He heard a horse snort in the cloisters. With utmost caution, he stood on the log and peeped over the windowsill.

He could see the vague outlines of the car and the aircraft in the dim reflected moonlight. There could be someone hiding in there, lying in wait.

He heard a muffled grunt and a thud. The noise was repeated after a minute, and he guessed it was

Hansen, struggling with his bonds. Harald's heart leaped with hope. If Hansen was still tied up, that meant Mrs Jespersen had not yet returned with Peter. There was still a chance Harald and Karen could take off in the Hornet Moth.

He slipped through the window and padded across the floor to the aircraft. He got the flashlight out of the cabin and shone it around the church. There was no one here.

He opened the boot of the car. Hansen was still tied and gagged. Harald checked the knots. They were holding firm. He closed the boot again.

He heard a loud whisper: 'Harald! Is that you?'

He shone the torch on the windows and saw Karen looking through.

She had been brought home in an ambulance. Her parents had ridden with her. Before they parted, at the theatre, she had promised to slip out of the house as soon as she could, and join him in the church if the coast was clear.

He turned off the torch, then opened the big church door for her. She limped in, wearing a fur coat over her shoulders and carrying a blanket. He put his arms around her gently, careful of her right arm in its sling, and hugged her. For a brief moment he thrilled to the warmth of her body and the scent of her hair.

Then he returned to practicalities. 'How do you feel?'

'I hurt like hell, but I'll live.'

He looked at her coat. 'Are you cold?'

'Not yet, but I will be at five thousand feet over the North Sea. The blanket is for you.'

He took the blanket from her and held her good hand. 'Are you ready to do this?'

'Yes.'

He kissed her softly. 'I love you.'

'I love you, too.'

'Do you? You've never said that before.'

'I know – I'm telling you now in case I don't survive this trip,' she said in her usual matter-of-fact tone. 'You're the best man I've ever met, by a factor of ten. You're brainy, but you never put people down. You're gentle and kind, but you've got courage enough for an army.' She touched his hair. 'You're even nice-looking, in a funny way. What more could I want?'

'Some girls like a man to be well dressed.'

'Good point. We can fix that, though.'

'I'd like to tell you why I love you, but the police could get here any minute.'

'That's all right, I know why, it's because I'm wonderful.'

Harald opened the cabin door and tossed the blanket in. 'You'd better get on board now,' he said. 'The less we have to do once we're outside in plain view, the more chance we have of getting away.'

'OK.'

He saw that it was going to be difficult for her to get into the cabin. He dragged a box over, and she stood on it, but then she could not put her injured foot inside. Getting in was awkward anyway – the cabin was more cramped than the front seat of a small car –

and it seemed impossible with two injured limbs. Harald realized he would have to lift her in.

He picked her up with his left arm under her shoulders and his right under her knees, then he stood on the box and eased her into the passenger seat on the right-hand side of the cabin. That way, she could operate the Y-shaped central control stick with her good left hand, and Harald, beside her in the pilot's seat, would be able to use his right.

'What's this on the floor?' she said, reaching down.

'Hansen's gun. I didn't know what else to do with it.' He closed the door. 'Are you OK?'

She slid the window open. 'I'm fine. The best place to take off will be along the drive. The wind is just right, but blowing towards the castle, so you're going to have to push the aircraft all the way to the door of the castle, then turn it around to take off into the wind.'

'OK.'

He opened the church doors wide. Next he had to get the aircraft out. Fortunately it had been parked intelligently, pointing directly at the door. There was a length of rope firmly tied to the undercarriage which, Harald had surmised when he first saw it, was used to pull the aircraft. He got a firm grasp on the rope and heaved.

The Hornet Moth was heavier than he had thought. As well as its engine, it was carrying thirty-nine gallons of petrol plus Karen. That was a lot to pull.

To overcome its inertia, Harald managed to rock the aircraft on its wheels, get a rhythm going, then heave it into motion. Once it was moving, the strain was less, but it was still heavy. With considerable effort he pulled it out of the church into the park and got it as far as the drive.

The moon came from behind a cloud. The park was lit up almost like day. The aircraft was in full view of anyone who looked in the right direction. Harald had to work fast.

He undid the catch holding the left wing against the fuselage and swung the wing into position. Next, he flipped down the foldaway flap at the inner end of the upper wing. That held the wing in place while he moved around the wing to the front edge. There he turned the lower wing pin and eased it into its slot. It seemed to catch against an obstruction. He had encountered this problem when practising. He wiggled the wing gently, and that enabled him to slide the pin home. He locked it with the leather strap. He repeated the exercise with the upper wing pin, locking it by stowing the jury strut.

It had taken him three or four minutes. He looked across the park to the soldiers' encampment. The sentry had seen him and was walking over.

He went through the same procedure with the right wing. By the time he had finished, the sentry was standing behind him, watching. It was friendly Leo. 'What are you doing?' he said curiously.

Harald had a story ready. 'We're going to take a photograph. Mr Duchwitz wants to sell the aircraft because he can't get fuel for it.'

'Photography? At night?'

'It's a moonlight shot, with the castle in the background.'

'Does my captain know?'

'Oh, yes, Mr Duchwitz spoke to him, and Captain Kleiss said there would be no problem.'

'Oh, good,' Leo said, then he frowned again. 'It's strange that the captain didn't tell me about it, though.'

'He probably didn't think it was important.' Harald realized he was probably on a loser. If the German military were careless, they would not have conquered Europe.

Leo shook his head. 'A sentry must be briefed on any unusual events scheduled to take place during his watch,' he said as if repeating from a rule book.

'I'm sure Mr Duchwitz wouldn't have told us to do this without speaking to Captain Kleiss.' Harald leaned on the tailplane, pushing.

Seeing him struggle to move the tail, Leo helped him. Together they swung the back around in a quarter-circle so that the aircraft was facing along the drive.

Leo said: 'I'd better check with the captain.'

'If you're sure he won't mind being woken up.'

Leo looked doubtful and worried. 'Perhaps he's not asleep yet.'

Harald knew that the officers slept in the castle. He thought of a way to delay Leo and speed up his own task. 'Well, if you've got to go all the way to the castle, you could help me move this crate.'

'OK.'

'I'll take the left wing, you take the right.'

Leo shouldered his rifle and leaned on the metal strut between the upper and lower wings. With the two of them pushing, the Hornet Moth moved more easily.

\*   \*   \*

Hermia caught the last train of the evening from the Vesterport station. It pulled into Kirstenslot after midnight.

She was not sure what to do when she reached the castle. She did not want to call attention to herself by banging on the door and waking the household. She might have to wait until morning before asking for Harald. That would mean spending the night in the open. But that would not kill her. On the other hand, if there were lights on in the castle she might find someone with whom she could have a discreet word, a servant perhaps. And she was nervous about losing precious time.

One other person got off the train with her. It was the woman in the sky-blue beret.

She suffered a moment of fear. Had she made a mistake? Could this woman be following her, having taken over from Peter Flemming?

She would just have to check.

Outside the darkened station she stopped and opened her suitcase, pretending to search for something. If the woman were tailing her she, too, would have to find a pretext for waiting.

The woman came out of the station and walked past her without hesitating.

Hermia continued to fumble in her case while watching from the corner of her eye.

The woman walked briskly to a black Buick parked nearby. Someone was sitting at the wheel, smoking. Hermia could not see the face, just the glow of the cigarette. The woman got in. The car started up and pulled away.

Hermia breathed easier. The woman had spent the evening in the city, and her husband had come to the station to drive her home. False alarm, Hermia thought with relief.

She started walking.

\* \* \*

Harald and Leo pushed the Hornet Moth along the drive, past the petrol tanker from which Harald had stolen fuel, all the way to the courtyard in front of the castle, then turned it into the wind. Leo ran inside to wake Captain Kleiss.

Harald had only a minute or two.

He took the torch from his pocket, switched it on, and held it in his mouth. He turned the catches on the left side of the fuselage nose and opened the cowling. 'Fuel on?' he called.

'Fuel on,' Karen called back.

Harald tugged on the pull-ring of the tickler and worked the lever of one of the two fuel pumps to flood the carburettor. He closed the cowling and secured the catches. Taking the torch from his mouth, he called: 'Throttle set and mags on?'

'Throttle set, mags on.'

He stood in front of the aircraft and swung the propeller. Imitating what he had seen Karen do, he turned it a second time, then a third. Finally he gave it a vigorous heave and stepped smartly back.

Nothing happened.

He cursed. There was no time to deal with snags.

He repeated the procedure. Something was wrong, he thought even as he tried it. Before, when he turned the propeller, something had happened that was not happening now. He tried desperately to remember what it was.

Once again the engine failed to start.

In a flash of recollection he realized what was missing. There was no click when he turned the propeller. He recalled Karen telling him that the click was the impulse starter. Without that, there would be no spark.

He ran to her open window. 'There's no click!' he said.

'Magneto jam,' she said calmly. 'It often happens. Open the right cowling. You'll see the impulse starter between the magneto and the engine. Give it a sharp tap with a stone or something. That usually does the trick.'

He opened the right cowling and shone his torch on the engine. The impulse starter was a flat metal cylinder. He scanned the ground at his feet. There were no stones. 'Give me something from the tool kit,' he said to Karen.

She found the kit and handed him a spanner. He tapped the impulse starter.

A voice behind him called: 'Stop that right now.'

He turned to see Captain Kleiss, dressed in uniform trousers and a pyjama jacket, striding across the courtyard towards him, with Leo close behind. Kleiss was not armed, but Leo had a rifle.

Harald stuffed the spanner into his pocket, closed the cowling, and moved to the nose.

'Stand away from that aircraft!' Kleiss shouted. 'This is an order!'

Suddenly Karen's voice rang out. 'Stop right where you are or I'll shoot you dead!'

Harald saw her arm sticking out of the window, pointing Hansen's pistol straight at Kleiss.

Kleiss stopped, and so did Leo.

Whether Karen knew how to fire the thing, Harald had no idea – but nor did Kleiss.

'Drop the rifle on the ground, Leo,' said Karen.

Leo dropped his weapon.

Harald reached for the propeller and swung it.

It turned with a loud, deeply satisfying click.

* * *

Peter Flemming drove to the castle ahead of Hermia, with Tilde Jespersen in the passenger seat beside him. 'We'll park out of sight, and watch what she does when she gets here,' he said.

'OK.'

'About what happened on Sande—'

'Please don't speak of it.'

He suppressed his anger. 'What, never?'

'Never.'

He wanted to strangle her.

The car's headlights showed a small village with a church and a tavern. Just beyond the village they approached a grand entrance.

'I'm sorry, Peter,' Tilde said. 'I made a mistake, but it's over. Let's just be friends and colleagues.'

He felt he did not care about anything any more. 'To Hell with that,' he said, and turned into the castle grounds.

On the right of the drive was a ruined monastery. 'That's odd,' Tilde said. 'The church doors are wide open.'

Peter hoped there would be some action to take his mind off Tilde's rejection. He stopped the Buick and turned off the engine. 'Let's have a look.' He took a flashlight out of the glove box.

They got out of the car and went into the church. Peter heard a muffled grunt followed by a thud. It seemed to come from the Rolls-Royce car that was standing on blocks in the middle of the room. He opened the boot and shone his torch on a policeman, bound and gagged.

'Is this your man Hansen?' he said.

Tilde said: 'The aeroplane isn't here! It's gone!'

At that moment, they heard an aircraft engine start.

\* \* \*

The Hornet Moth roared into life and seemed to lean forward as if eager to go.

Harald walked quickly to where Kleiss and Leo stood. He picked up the rifle and held it menacingly, putting on an air of confidence that he did not feel. He backed away from them slowly and walked around the spinning propeller to the left side door. He reached for the handle, flung open the door, and threw the rifle on to the luggage shelf behind the seats.

As he climbed in, a sudden movement made him glance past Karen out of the far window. He saw Captain Kleiss throw himself forward, towards the aircraft, and dive to the ground. There was a bang, deafening even over the noise of the engine, as Karen fired Hansen's pistol. But Harald could see that the window frame prevented her bringing her wrist low enough, and her shot missed the captain.

Kleiss rolled under the fuselage, came up the other side, and jumped on the wing.

Harald tried to slam the door, but Kleiss was in the way. The captain grabbed Harald by the lapels and tried to pull him out of his seat. Harald struggled, trying to dislodge Kleiss's grip. Karen was holding the pistol in her left hand and could not turn around, in the cramped cabin, to get a shot at Kleiss. Leo came running up but, because of the door and the wing, he was unable to get close enough to join in the fight.

Harald pulled the spanner from his pocket and lashed out with all his might. The sharp end of the tool hit Kleiss under the eye, drawing blood, but he held on.

Karen reached past Harald and thrust the throttle lever all the way forward. The engine roared louder and the aircraft moved forward. Kleiss lost his balance. He flung one arm out, but held on to Harald with the other.

The Hornet Moth moved faster, bumping over the grass. Harald hit Kleiss again, and this time he cried out, let go, and fell to the ground.

Harald slammed the door.

He reached for the control column in the centre, but Karen said: 'Leave the stick to me – I can do it left handed.'

The aircraft was pointing down the drive but, as soon as it began to pick up speed, it veered off to the right. 'Use the rudder pedals!' Karen shouted. 'Keep it in a straight line!'

Harald pushed the left pedal to bring the aircraft back on to the drive. Nothing happened, so he pressed it with all his might. After a moment, the aircraft swung all the way over to the left. It crossed the drive and plunged into the long grass on the other side.

She yelled: 'There's a lag, you have to anticipate.'

He understood what she meant. It was like steering a boat, only worse. He pushed with his right foot to bring the aircraft back then, as soon as it began to turn, he corrected with his left foot. This time it did not swing so wildly. As it came back to the drive he managed to line it up.

'Now keep it like that,' Karen shouted.

The aircraft accelerated.

At the far end of the drive, a car's headlights came on.

\* \* \*

Peter Flemming thrust the gearstick into first and floored the pedal. Just as Tilde was opening the passenger door to get in, the car jerked away. She let go of the door with a cry and fell back. Peter hoped she had broken her neck.

He steered along the drive, letting the passenger door flap. When his engine started to scream he changed up into second. The Buick gathered speed.

In his headlights he saw a small biplane rolling down the drive, coming straight at him. Harald Olufsen was in that plane, he felt sure. He was going to stop Harald, even if it killed them both.

He changed up into third.

\* \* \*

Harald felt the Hornet Moth tilt as Karen pushed the stick forward, bringing the tail up. He shouted: 'Do you see that car?'

'Yes – is he trying to ram us?'

'Yes.' Harald was staring along the drive, concentrating on keeping the aircraft on a straight course with the rudder pedals. 'Can we take off in time to fly over him?'

'I'm not sure—'

'You have to make up your mind!'

'Get ready to turn if I say!'

'I'm ready!'

The car was dangerously close. Harald could see they were not going to lift over it. Karen yelled: 'Turn!'

He pressed the left pedal. The aircraft, responding less sluggishly at higher speed, swung sharply off the drive – too sharply: he feared his undercarriage repair job might not stand the strain. He corrected quickly.

Out of the corner of his eye he saw the car turn the same way, still aiming to ram the Hornet Moth. It was a Buick, he saw, just like the one in which Peter Flemming had driven him to Jansborg Skole. It turned sharply, trying to maintain a collision course with the aircraft.

But the aircraft had a rudder, whereas the car was steered by its wheels, and this made a difference on the wet grass. As soon as the Buick hit the grass it went into a skid. As it slid sideways, the moonlight momentarily caught the face of the man behind the wheel, fighting for control, and Harald recognized Peter Flemming.

The aircraft wobbled and straightened out. Harald saw that he was about to crash into the petrol tanker. He stamped on the left pedal, and the right wingtip of the Hornet Moth missed the truck by inches.

Peter Flemming was not so lucky.

Glancing back, Harald saw the Buick, completely out of control, slide with terrible inevitability towards the tanker. It smashed into the truck at top speed. There was a booming explosion, and a second later the entire park was lit up with a yellow glow. Harald tried to see if the tail of the Hornet Moth might have caught fire, but it was impossible to look directly behind, so he just hoped for the best.

The Buick was a furnace.

'Steer the aircraft!' Karen yelled at him. 'We're about to take off!'

He returned his attention to the rudder. He saw that he was heading for the mess tent. He pressed the right pedal to miss it.

When they were on a straight course again the aircraft accelerated.

* * *

Hermia had begun to run when she heard the aero engine start up. As she came into the grounds of Kirstenslot she saw a dark car, very like the one at the station, tearing along the drive. As she watched, it went into a skid and crashed into a truck parked alongside the drive. There was a terrific explosion, and both car and truck burst into flame.

She heard a woman cry: 'Peter!'

In the fire's light she saw the woman in the blue beret. Everything fell into place. The woman *had* been following her. The man waiting in the Buick had been Peter Flemming. They had not needed to follow her, because they knew where she was going. They had come to the castle ahead of her. Then what?

She saw a small biplane rolling across the grass, looking as if it was about to take off. Then she saw the woman in the blue beret kneel down, pull a gun from her shoulder bag, and aim at the aircraft.

What was happening here? If the woman in the beret was a colleague of Peter Flemming's, the pilot must be on the side of the angels, Hermia deduced. It could even be Harald, escaping with the film in his pocket.

She had to stop the woman shooting the aircraft down.

\*   \*   \*

The park was lit up by the flames from the petrol tanker, and in the brightness Harald saw Mrs Jespersen aim a gun at the Hornet Moth.

There was nothing he could do. He was heading straight for her and, if he turned to one side or the other, he would merely present her with a better target. He gritted his teeth. The bullets might pass through the wings or the fuselage without causing serious damage. On the other hand they might disable the engine, damage the controls, hole the petrol tank, or kill him or Karen.

Then he saw a second woman runnning across the grass, carrying a suitcase. 'Hermia!' he shouted in astonishment as he recognized her. She hit Mrs Jespersen over the head with her case. The detective fell sideways and dropped her gun. Hermia hit her again, then grabbed the gun.

Then the aircraft passed over them and Harald realized it had left the ground.

Looking up, he saw that it was about to crash into the bell tower of the church.

# THIRTY-TWO

Karen thrust the Y-shaped control column sharply to the left, banging it against Harald's knee. The Hornet Moth banked as it climbed, but Harald could see that the turn was not sharp enough, and the aircraft was going to hit the bell tower.

'Left rudder!' Karen screamed.

He remembered that he, too, could steer. He jammed his left foot down hard on the pedal and immediately felt the aircraft bank more steeply. Still he felt sure the right wing would smash into the brickwork. The aircraft came around with excruciating slowness. He braced himself for the crash. The wingtip missed the tower by inches.

'Jesus Christ,' he said.

The gusty wind made the aircraft buck like a pony. Harald felt they could fall out of the sky at any second. But Karen continued the climbing turn. Harald gritted his teeth. The aircraft came around a hundred and eighty degrees. At last, when it was heading back over the castle, she straightened out. As they gained altitude, the aircraft steadied, and Harald recalled Poul Kirke saying there was more turbulence near the ground.

He looked down. Flames still flickered in the petrol tanker, and by their light he could see the soldiers emerging from the monastery in their nightwear. Captain Kleiss was waving his arms and shouting orders. Mrs Jespersen lay still, apparently out cold. Hermia Mount was nowhere to be seen. At the door of the castle, a few servants stood looking up at the aircraft.

Karen pointed to a dial on the instrument panel. 'Keep an eye on this,' she said. 'It's the turn-and-slip indicator. Use the rudder to hold the needle straight upright, at the twelve o'clock position.'

Bright moonlight came through the transparent roof of the cabin, but it was not enough to read the instruments. Harald shone the torch on the dial.

They continued to climb, and the castle shrank behind them. Karen kept looking to left and right as well as ahead, although there was nothing much to see but the moonlit Danish landscape.

'Fasten your lap strap,' she said. He saw that hers was done up. 'It will save you banging your head on the cabin roof if the ride gets bumpy.'

Harald fastened his belt. He began to believe that they had escaped. He allowed himself to feel triumphant. 'I thought I was going to die,' he said.

'So did I – several times!'

'Your parents will go out of their minds with worry.'

'I left them a note.'

'That's more than I did.' He had not thought of it.

'Let's just stay alive, that will make them happy.'

He touched her cheek. 'How do you feel?'

'A bit feverish.'

'You've got a temperature. You should sip water.'

'No, thanks. We've got a six-hour flight ahead of us, and no bathroom. I don't want to have to pee on a newspaper in front of you. It could be the end of a beautiful friendship.'

'I'll close my eyes.'

'And fly the aircraft with your eyes shut? Forget it. I'll be all right.'

She was being jocular, but he was anxious about her. He felt shattered by what they had been through, and she had done all the same things with a sprained ankle and a sprained wrist. He hoped she would not pass out.

'Look at the compass,' she said. 'What's our course?'

He had examined the compass while the aircraft was in the church, and knew how to read it. 'Two hundred and thirty.'

Karen banked right. 'I figure our heading for England is two-fifty. Tell me when we're on course.'

He shone the torch on the compass until it showed the right course, then said: 'That's it.'

'Time?'

'Twelve-forty.'

'We should write all this down, but we didn't bring pencils.'

'I don't think I'll forget any of it.'

'I'd like to get above this patchy cloud,' she said. 'What's our altitude?'

Harald shone the torch on the altimeter. 'Four thousand seven hundred feet.'

'So this cloud is at about five thousand.'

A few moments later the aircraft was engulfed by what looked like smoke, and Harald realized they had entered the cloud.

'Keep the light on the airspeed indicator,' Karen said. 'Let me know if our speed changes.'

'Why?'

'When you're flying blind, it's difficult to keep the aircraft in the correct attitude. I could put the nose up or down without realizing it. But if that happens we'll know because our speed will increase or decrease.'

He found it unnerving to be blind. This must be how accidents happen, he thought. An aircraft could easily hit the side of a mountain in cloud. Fortunately there were no mountains in Denmark. But if another aircraft happened to be flying through the same cloud, neither pilot would know until it was too late.

After a couple of minutes, he found that enough moonlight was penetrating the cloud for him to see it swirling against the windows. Then, to his relief, they emerged, and he could see the Hornet Moth's moon shadow on the cloud below.

Karen eased the stick forward to level out. 'See the rev counter?'

Harald shone the torch. 'It says two thousand, two hundred.'

'Bring the throttle smoothly back until it drops to nineteen hundred.'

Harald did as she said.

'We use power to change our altitude,' she explained. 'Throttle forward, we go up; throttle back, we go down.'

'So how do we control our speed?'

'By the attitude of the aircraft. Nose down to go faster, nose up to go slower.'

'Got it.'

'But never lift the nose too sharply, or you will stall. That means you lose lift, and the aircraft falls out of the sky.'

Harald found that a terrifying thought. 'What do you do then?'

'Put the nose down and increase the revs. It's easy – except that your instinct tells you to pull the nose up, and that makes it worse.'

'I'll remember that.'

Karen said: 'Take the stick for a while. See if you can fly straight and level. All right, you have control.'

He grasped the control stick in his right hand.

She said: 'You're supposed to say: "I have control." That's so that the pilot and copilot never get into a situation where each thinks the other is flying the aircraft.'

'I have control,' he said, but he did not feel it. The Hornet Moth had a life of its own, turning and dipping with air turbulence, and he found himself using all his powers of concentration to keep the wings level and the nose in the same position.

Karen said: 'Do you find that you're constantly pulling back on the stick?'

'Yes.'

'That's because we've used some fuel and changed the aircraft's centre of gravity. Do you see that lever by the top forward corner of your door?'

He glanced up briefly. 'Yes.'

'That's the elevator trim lever. I set it all the way forward for take-off, when the tank was full and the tail was heavy. Now the aircraft needs to be retrimmed.'

'How do we do that?'

'Simple. Ease your grip on the stick. You feel it wanting to go forward of its own accord?'

'Yes.'

'Move the trim lever back. You'll find less need for constant back pressure on the stick.'

She was right.

'Adjust the trim lever until you no longer need to pull on the stick.'

Harald drew the lever back gradually. Before he knew it, the control column was pressing back on his hand. 'Too much,' he said. He pushed the trim lever forward a fraction. 'That's about right.'

'You can also trim the rudder, by moving the knob in that toothed rack at the bottom of the instrument panel. When the aircraft is correctly trimmed, it should fly straight and level with no pressure on the controls.'

Harald took his hand off the column experimentally. The Hornet Moth continued to fly level.

He returned his hand to the stick.

The cloud below them was not continuous, and at intervals they were able to see through gaps to the moonlit earth below. Soon they left Zealand behind and flew over the sea. Karen said: 'Check the altimeter.'

He found it difficult to look down at the instrument panel, feeling instinctively that he needed to concentrate on flying the aircraft. When he tore his gaze away from the exterior, he saw that they had reached seven thousand feet. 'How did that happen?' he said.

'You're holding the nose too high. It's natural. Unconsciously, you're afraid of hitting the ground, so you keep trying to climb. Dip the nose.'

He pushed the stick forward. As the nose came down, he saw another aircraft. It had large crosses on its wings. Harald felt sick with fear.

Karen saw it at the same time. 'Hell,' she said. 'The Luftwaffe.' She sounded as scared as Harald felt.

'I see it,' Harald said. It was to their left and down, a quarter of a mile or so away, and climbing towards them.

She took the stick and put the nose sharply down. 'I have control.'

'You have control.'

The Hornet Moth went into a dive.

Harald recognized the other aircraft as a Messerschmitt Bf110, a twin-engined night fighter with a distinctive double-finned tailplane and long, greenhouse-like cockpit canopy. He remembered

Arne talking about the Bf110's armament with a mixture of fear and envy: it had cannons and machine guns in the nose, and Harald could see the rear machine guns poking up from the back end of the canopy. This was the aircraft used to shoot down Allied bombers after the radio station on Sande had detected them.

The Hornet Moth was completely defenceless.

Harald said: 'What are we going to do?'

'Try to get back into that cloud layer before he gets within range. Damn, I shouldn't have let you climb so high.'

The Hornet Moth was diving steeply. Harald glanced at the airspeed indicator and saw that they had reached one hundred and thirty knots. It felt like the downhill stretch of a roller-coaster. He realized he was grasping the edge of his seat. 'Is this safe?' he said.

'Safer than being shot.'

The other aircraft came rapidly closer. It was much faster than the Moth. There was a flash and a rattle of gunfire. Harald had been expecting the Messerschmitt to fire on them, but he could not restrain a yell of shock and fear.

Karen turned right, trying to spoil the gunner's aim. The Messerschmitt flashed past below. The gunfire stopped, and the Hornet Moth's engine droned on. They had not been hit.

Harald recalled Arne saying that it was difficult for a fast aircraft to shoot at a slow one. Perhaps that had saved them.

As they turned, he looked out of the window and saw the fighter receding into the distance. 'I think he's out of range,' he said.

'Not for long,' Karen replied.

Sure enough, the Messerschmitt was turning. The seconds dragged by as the Hornet Moth dived toward the protection of the cloud and the fast-moving fighter swept through a wide turn. Harald saw that their airspeed had reached one hundred and sixty. The cloud was tantalizingly close – but not close enough.

He saw the flashes and heard the bangs as the fighter opened up. This time the aircraft were closer and the fighter had a better angle of attack. To his horror he saw a jagged rip appear in the fabric of the lower left wing. Karen shoved the stick over and the Hornet Moth banked.

Then, suddenly, they were plunged into cloud.

The gunfire stopped.

'Thank God,' Harald said. Although it was cold, he was sweating.

Karen pulled back on the stick and brought them out of the dive. Harald shone the torch on the altimeter and watched the needle slow its anticlockwise movement and steady at just above five thousand feet. The airspeed returned gradually to the normal cruising speed of eighty knots.

She banked the aircraft again, changing direction, so that the fighter would not be able to overtake them simply by following their previous course.

'Bring the revs down to about sixteen hundred,' she said. 'We'll get just below this cloud.'

'Why not stay in it?'

'It's difficult to fly in cloud for long. You get disoriented. You don't know up from down. The instruments tell you what's happening but you don't believe them. It's how a lot of crashes happen.'

Harald found the lever in the dark and drew it back.

'Was it just luck that the fighter turned up?' Karen said. 'Maybe they can see us with their radio beams.'

Harald frowned, thinking. He was glad to have a puzzle to take his mind off the danger they were in. 'I doubt it,' he said. 'Metal interferes with radio waves, but I don't think wood or linen does. A big aluminium bomber would reflect the beams back to their aerials, but only our engine would do that, and it's probably too small to show up on their detectors.'

'I hope you're right,' she said. 'If not, we're dead.'

They came out below the cloud. Harald increased the revs to nineteen hundred, and Karen pulled the stick back.

'Keep looking around,' Karen said. 'If we see him again, we have to go up fast.'

Harald did as she said, but there was not much to see. A mile ahead, the moon was shining through a gap in the clouds, and Harald could make out the irregular geometry of fields and woodland. They must be over the large central island of Fyn, he thought. Nearer, a bright light moved perceptibly across the dark landscape, and he guessed it was a railway train or a police car.

Karen banked right. 'Look up to your left,' she said.

Harald could see nothing. She banked the other way, and looked up out of her window. 'We have to watch every angle,' she explained. He noticed that she was getting hoarse with the constant shouting over the noise of the engine.

The Messerschmitt appeared ahead.

It dropped out of the cloud a quarter of a mile in front of them, dimly revealed by moonlight reflected off the ground, heading away. 'Full power!' Karen shouted, but Harald had already done it. She jerked back on the stick to lift the nose.

'Maybe he won't even see us,' Harald said optimistically, but his hopes were immediately dashed as the fighter went into a steep turn.

The Hornet Moth took several seconds to respond to the controls. At last they began to rise towards the cloud. The fighter came around in a wide circle and pitched up to follow their climb. As soon as he was lined up, he fired.

Then the Hornet Moth was in the cloud.

Karen changed direction immediately. Harald cheered. 'Dodged him again!' he said. But his underlying fear gave a brittle tone to the triumph in his voice.

They climbed through the cloud. When the glow of moonlight began to illuminate the swirling mist around them, Harald realized they were near the top of the cloud layer. 'Throttle back,' Karen said. 'We'll have to stay in the cloud as long as we can.' The aircraft levelled. 'Watch that airspeed indicator,' she said. 'Make sure I'm not climbing or diving.'

'OK.' He checked the altimeter, too. They were at five thousand eight hundred feet.

Just then the Messerschmitt appeared only yards away.

It was slightly lower and to the right, heading across their path. For a split-second, Harald saw the terrified face of the German pilot, his mouth opening in a shout of horror. They were all an inch from death. The fighter's wing passed under the Hornet Moth, missing the undercarriage by a hair.

Harald trod on the left rudder pedal and Karen jerked back on the control stick, but the fighter was already gone from view.

Karen said: 'My God, that was close.'

Harald stared into the swirling cloud, expecting the Messerschmitt to appear. A minute went by, then another. Karen said: 'I think he was as scared as us.'

'What do you think he'll do?'

'Fly above and below the cloud for a while, hoping we'll pop out. With luck, our courses will diverge, and we'll lose him.'

Harald checked the compass. 'We're going north,' he said.

'I went off-heading in all that dodging about,' she said. She banked left, and Harald helped with the rudder. When the compass read two-fifty he said: 'Enough,' and she straightened up.

They came out of the cloud. They both scanned the sky in all directions, but there were no other aircraft.

'I feel so tired,' Karen said.

'It's not surprising. Let me take control. Rest for a while.'

Harald concentrated on flying straight and level. The endless minor adjustments started to become instinctive.

'Keep an eye on the dials,' Karen warned him. 'Watch the air speed indicator, the altimeter, the compass, the oil pressure and the fuel gauge. When you're flying, you're supposed to check all the time.'

'OK.' He forced himself to look at the dashboard every minute or two and he found, contrary to what his instincts told him, that the aircraft did not fall to earth as soon as he did so.

'We must be over Jutland now,' Karen said. 'I wonder how far north we strayed?'

'How can we tell?'

'We'll have to fly low as we cross the coast. We should be able to identify some terrain features and establish our position on the map.'

The moon was low on the horizon. Harald checked his watch and was astonished to see that they had been flying for almost two hours. It seemed like a few minutes.

'Let's take a look,' said Karen after a while. 'Pull the revs back to fourteen hundred and dip the nose.' She found the atlas and studied it by the light of the torch. 'We'll have to go lower,' she said. 'I can't see the land well enough.'

Harald brought the aircraft down to three thousand feet, then two. The ground was visible in the moonlight, but there were no distinguishing elements, just fields. Then Karen said: 'Look – is that a town ahead?'

Harald peered down. It was hard to tell. There were no lights because of the blackout – which had been imposed precisely in order to make towns hard to see from the air. But the ground ahead certainly seemed to have a different texture in the moonlight.

Suddenly, small burning lights began to appear in the air. 'What the hell is that?' Karen yelled.

Was someone aiming fireworks at the Hornet Moth? Fireworks had been banned since the invasion.

Karen said: 'I've never seen tracer bullets, but—'

'Shit, is that what they are?' Without waiting for instructions, Harald pushed the throttle forward all the way and lifted the nose to gain altitude.

As he did so, searchlights came on.

There was a bang and something exploded nearby. 'What was that?' Karen cried.

'I think it must have been a shell.'

'Someone's firing at us?'

Harald suddenly realized where they were. 'This must be Morlunde! We're right over the port defences!'

'Turn!'

He banked.

'Don't climb too steeply,' she said. 'You'll stall.'

Another shell burst above them. Searchlight beams scythed the darkness all around. Harald felt as if he were lifting the aircraft by will power.

They came around one hundred and eighty degrees. Harald straightened out and continued to climb. Another shell exploded, but it was behind them. He began to feel they might yet survive.

The firing stopped. He turned again, flying on their original heading, still climbing.

A minute later they passed over the coast.

'We're leaving the land behind,' he said.

She made no reply, and he turned to see that her eyes were closed.

He glanced back at the coastline disappearing behind him in the moonlight. 'I wonder if we'll ever see Denmark again,' he said.

# THIRTY-THREE

The moon set, but for a while the sky was clear of cloud, and Harald could see stars. He was grateful for them, as they were the only way he could tell up from down. The engine gave a reassuringly constant roar. He flew at five thousand feet and eighty knots. There was less turbulence than he remembered from his first flight, and he wondered whether that was because he was over the sea, or because it was night – or both. He kept checking his heading by the compass, but he did not know how much the Hornet Moth might be blown off course by wind.

He took his hand off the control stick and touched Karen's face. Her cheek was burning. He trimmed the aircraft to fly straight and level, then took a bottle of water from the locker under the dashboard. He poured some on his hand then dabbed her forehead to cool her. She was breathing normally, though her breath was hot on his hand. She seemed to be in a feverish sleep.

When he returned his attention to the outside world, he saw that dawn was breaking. He checked his watch: it was just after three o'clock in the morning. He must be half way to England.

By the faint light, he saw cloud ahead. There seemed to be no top or bottom to it, so he flew into it. There was also rain, and the water stayed on the windscreen. Unlike a car, the Hornet Moth had no windscreen wipers.

He remembered what Karen had said about disorientation, and resolved not to make any sudden moves. However, staring constantly into swirling nothingness was strangely hypnotic. He wished he could talk to Karen, but he felt she needed sleep after what she had been through. He lost track of the passage of time. He started to imagine shapes in the cloud. He saw a horse's head, the bonnet of a Lincoln Continental, and the moustached face of Neptune. Ahead of him, at eleven o'clock and a few feet below, he saw a fishing boat, with sailors on deck gazing up at him in wonderment.

That was no illusion, he realized, snapping back to full consciousness. The mist had cleared and he was seeing a real boat. He looked at the altimeter. Both hands pointed up. He was at sea level. He had lost altitude without noticing.

Instinctively, he pulled the stick back, lifting the nose, but as he did so he heard Karen's voice in his head saying: 'But never lift the nose too sharply, or you will stall. That means you lose lift, and the aircraft falls out of the sky.' He realized what he had done, and remembered how to correct it, but he was not sure he had time. The aircraft was already losing altitude. He put the nose down and pushed the throttle all the way forward. He was level with the fishing boat as he passed it. He risked pulling the nose up a fraction. He waited for the wheels to hit the waves. The aircraft flew on. He pulled the nose up a little more. He risked a glance at the altimeter. He was climbing. He let out a long breath.

'Pay attention, you fool,' he said aloud. 'Stay awake.'

He continued climbing. The cloud dissipated, and he emerged into a clear morning. He checked his watch. It was four o'clock. The sun was about to rise. Looking up through the transparent roof of the cabin, he could see the North Star to his right. That meant his compass was accurate, and he was still heading west.

Frightened of getting too close to the sea, he climbed for half an hour. The temperature dropped, and cold air came in through the window he had smashed out for his improvised fuel line. He wrapped the blanket around himself for warmth. At ten thousand feet, he was about to level off when the engine coughed.

At first he could not figure out what the noise was. The engine sound had been steady for so many hours that he had ceased to hear it.

Then it came again, and he realized the engine had misfired.

He felt as if his heart had stopped. He was about two hundred miles from land in any direction. If the engine failed now, he would come down in the sea.

It coughed again.

'Karen!' he shouted. 'Wake up!'

She slept on. He took his hand off the stick and shook her shoulder. 'Karen!'

Her eyes opened. She appeared better for her sleep, calmer and less flushed, but a look of fear came over her face as soon as she heard the engine. 'What's happening?'

'I don't know!'

'Where are we?'

'Miles from anywhere.'

The engine continued to cough and splutter.

'We may have to land in the sea,' Karen said. 'What's our altitude?'

'Ten thousand feet.'

'Is the throttle fully open?'

'Yes, I was climbing.'

'That's the problem. Bring it back half way.'

He pulled the throttle back.

Karen said: 'When the throttle is on full, the engine draws air from outside, rather than from within the engine compartment, so it's colder – at this altitude, cold enough to form ice in the carburettor.'

'What can we do?'

'Descend.' She took the stick and pushed it forward. 'As we go down, the air temperature should rise, and the ice will melt – eventually.'

'If it doesn't . . .'

'Look for a ship. If we can splash down near one, we may be rescued.'

Harald scanned the sea from horizon to horizon, but he could see no shipping.

With the engine misfiring they had little thrust and

lost altitude rapidly. Harald took the axe from the locker, ready to carry out his plan of hacking off a wing to use as a float. He put the bottles of water in his jacket pockets. He did not know if they would survive in the sea long enough to die of thirst.

He watched the altimeter. They came down to a thousand feet, then five hundred. The sea looked black and cold. There was still no shipping in sight.

A weird calm settled over Harald. 'I think we're going to die,' he said. 'I'm sorry I got you into this.'

'We're not finished yet,' she said. 'See if you can give me a few more revs, so that we don't splash down too hard.'

Harald pushed the throttle forward. The engine note rose. It missed, fired, and missed again.

Harald said: 'I don't think—'

Then the engine seemed to catch.

It roared steadily for several seconds, and Harald held his breath; then it misfired again. Finally it burst into a steady roar. The aircraft began to climb.

Harald realized they were both cheering.

The revs rose to nineteen hundred without missing a beat. 'The ice melted!' Karen said.

Harald kissed her. It was quite difficult. Although they were shoulder to shoulder and thigh to thigh in the cramped cabin, it was awkward to turn in the seat, especially with a lap strap on. But he managed it.

'That was nice,' she said.

'If we survive this, I'm going to kiss you every day for the rest of my life,' he said happily.

'Really?' she said. 'The rest of your life could be a long time.'

'I hope so.'

She looked pleased. Then she said: 'We should check the fuel.'

Harald twisted in his seat to look at the gauge between the seat backs. It was difficult to read, having two scales, one for use in the air and the other for on the ground when the aircraft was tilted.

But they both read near to Empty.

'Hell, the tank is almost dry,' Harald said.

'There's no land in sight.' She looked at her watch. 'We've been in the air five and a half hours, so we're probably still half an hour from land.'

'That's all right, I can top up the tank.' He unbuckled his lap strap and turned awkwardly to kneel on his seat. The petrol can stood on the luggage shelf behind the seats. Beside it was a funnel and one end of a length of garden hose. Before take-off, Harald had broken the window and passed the hose through the hole, lashing the other end to the petrol inlet in the side of the fuselage.

But now he could see the outside end of the hose flapping in the slipstream. He cursed.

Karen said: 'What's the matter?'

'The hose has worked loose in flight. I didn't tie it tight enough.'

'What are we going to do? We have to refuel!'

Harald looked at the petrol can, the funnel, the hose, and the window. 'I've got to put the hose into the filler neck. And it can't be done from in here.'

'You can't go outside!'

'What will it do to the aircraft if I open the door?'

'My God, it's like a giant airbrake. It will slow us down and turn us left.'

'Can you cope with that?'

'I can maintain air speed by putting the nose down. I suppose I could press down on the right rudder pedal with my left foot.'

'Let's try it.'

Karen put the aircraft into a gentle dive, then put her left foot on the right rudder pedal. 'OK.'

Harald opened the door. The aircraft immediately veered sharply to the left. Karen pushed down on the right rudder pedal, but they continued to turn. She eased the stick over to the right and banked, but the aircraft still went left. 'It's no good, I can't hold it!' she cried.

Harald closed the door. 'If I smash these windows out, that will almost halve the area of wind resistance,' he said. He took the spanner from his pocket. The windows were made of some kind of celluloid that was tougher than glass, but he knew it was not unbreakable, for he had knocked out a rear window two days ago. He drew back his right arm as far as he could and hit the window hard, and the celluloid shattered. He tapped the remaining material out of the frame.

'Ready to try again?'

'Just a minute – we need more air speed.' She leaned across and pushed the throttle open, then eased the trim lever forward an inch. 'OK.'

Harald opened the door.

Once again the aircraft veered left, but this time less sharply, and Karen seemed to be able to correct with the rudder.

Kneeling on the seat, Harald put his head out of the door. He could see the end of the hose flapping around the petrol access cover. Holding the door open with his right shoulder, he stretched out his right arm and grasped the hose. Now he had to feed it into the tank. He could see the open access panel but not the filler neck. He got the end of the hose positioned roughly over the panel, but the length of rubber in his hand constantly flopped around with the movement of the aircraft, and he could not get the end into the pipe. It was like trying to thread a needle in a hurricane. He tried for several minutes, but it became more hopeless as his hand got colder.

Karen tapped his shoulder.

He drew his hand back into the cabin and closed the door.

'We're losing altitude,' she said. 'We need to climb.' She pulled the stick back.

Harald blew on his hand to warm it. 'I can't do it this way,' he told her. 'I can't get the hose into the pipe. I need to be able to hold the other end of the tube.'

'How?'

He thought for a minute. 'Maybe I can put one foot out of the door.'

'Oh, God.'

'Let me know when we've gained enough altitude.'

After a couple of minutes she said: 'OK, but be ready to close the door as soon as I tap your shoulder.'

Facing backwards with his left knee on the seat, Harald put his right foot out through the door and on to the reinforced strip on the wing. Holding his lap strap with his left hand for security, he leaned out and grasped the hose. He ran his hand along its length until he was holding the tip. Then he leaned out farther to put the end into the pipe.

The Hornet Moth hit an air pocket. The aircraft bucked in the air. Harald lost his balance and thought he was going to fall off the wing. He jerked hard on the hose and his lap strap at the same time, trying to stay upright. The other end of the hose, inside the cabin, broke free of the string holding it. As it came loose, Harald involuntarily let go of it. The slipstream whisked it away.

Shaking with fear, he eased back into the cabin and closed the door.

'What happened?' she said. 'I couldn't see!'

For a moment he was unable to reply. When he had recovered, he said: 'I dropped the hose.'

'Oh, no.'

He checked the fuel gauge. 'We're running on empty.'

'I don't know what we can do!'

'I'll have to stand on the wing and pour the petrol in directly from the can. It will take two hands – I can't hold a four-gallon can with one hand, it's too heavy.'

'But you won't be able to hold on.'

'You'll have to hold my belt with your left hand.' Karen was strong, but he was not sure she could take his weight if he slipped. However, there was no alternative.

'Then I won't be able to move the control stick.'

'We'll just have to hope you don't need to.'

'All right, but let's gain more altitude.'

He looked around. There was no land in sight.

Karen said: 'Warm your hands. Put them under my coat.'

He turned, still kneeling on the seat, and pressed his hands to her waist. Under the fur coat she was wearing a light summer sweater.

'Put them under my sweater. Go on, feel my skin, I don't mind.'

She was hot to his touch.

He kept his hands there as they climbed. Then the engine missed. 'We're out of fuel,' Karen said.

The engine caught again, but he knew she was right. 'Let's do it,' he said.

She trimmed the aircraft. Harald unscrewed the cap of the four-gallon can, and the tiny cabin filled with the unpleasant smell of petrol, despite the wind blowing in at the broken windows.

The engine missed again and began to falter.

Harald lifted the can. Karen took hold of his belt. 'I've got you tight,' she said. 'Don't worry.'

He opened the door and put his right foot out. He moved the can to the seat. He put his left foot out, so that he was standing on the wing and leaning inside the cabin. He was absolutely terrified.

He lifted the can and stood upright on the wing. He made the mistake of looking beyond the trailing edge of the wing to the sea below. His stomach lurched with nausea. He almost dropped the can. He closed his eyes, swallowed, and got himself under control.

He opened his eyes, resolving not to look down. He leaned over the petrol inlet. His belt tightened over his stomach as Karen took the strain. He tilted the can.

The constant movement of the aircraft made it impossible to pour straight, but after a few moments he got the knack of compensating. He leaned forwards and back, relying on Karen to keep him safe.

The engine continued to misfire for a few seconds, then returned to normal.

He wanted desperately to get back inside, but they needed fuel to reach land. The petrol seemed to flow as slowly as honey. Some blew away in the air flow, and more spilled around the access plate and was wasted, but most of it seemed to go into the pipe.

At last the can was empty. He dropped it into the air and gratefully grabbed the door frame with his left hand. He eased himself back into the cabin and closed the door.

'Look,' said Karen, pointing ahead.

In the far distance, right on the horizon, was a dark shape. It was land.

'Hallelujah,' he said softly.

'Just pray that it's England,' Karen said. 'I don't know how far we might have been blown off course.'

It seemed to take a long time, but eventually the dark shape turned green and became a landscape. Then it resolved into a beach, a town with a harbour, an expanse of fields, and a range of hills.

'Let's take a closer look,' Karen said.

They descended to two thousand feet to examine the town.

'I can't tell whether it's France or England,' Harald said. 'I've never been to either place.'

'I've been to Paris and London, but neither of them looks like this.'

Harald checked the fuel gauge. 'We're going to have to land soon anyway.'

'But we need to know whether we're in enemy territory.'

Harald glanced up through the roof and saw two aircraft. 'We're about to find out,' he said. 'Look up.'

They both stared at the two small aircraft that were rapidly approaching from the south. As they came closer, Harald stared at their wings, waiting for the markings to become distinct. Would they turn out to be German crosses? Had all this been for nothing?

The aircraft came closer, and Harald saw that they were Spitfires with RAF roundels. This was England.

He let out a whoop of triumph. 'We made it!'

The aircraft came closer and flew either side of the Hornet Moth. Harald could see the pilots, staring at them. Karen said: 'I hope they don't think we're enemy spies and shoot us down.'

It was dreadfully possible. Harald tried to think of some way of telling the RAF they were friendly. 'Flag of truce,' he said. He pulled off his shirt and pushed it out of the broken window. The white cotton fluttered in the wind.

It seemed to do the trick. One of the Spitfires moved in front of the Hornet Moth and waggled its wings. Karen said: 'That means "Follow me," I think. But I haven't got enough fuel.' She looked at the landscape below. 'Sea breeze from the east, to judge by the smoke from that farmhouse. I'll come down in that field.' She put the nose down and turned.

Harald looked anxiously at the Spitfires. After a moment they turned and began to circle, but maintained their altitude, as if watching to see what would happen next. Perhaps they had decided that a Hornet Moth could not be much of a threat to the British Empire.

Karen came down to a thousand feet and flew downwind past the field she had chosen. There were no obstructions visible. She turned into the wind for landing. Harald operated the rudder, helping keep the aircraft in a straight line.

When they were twenty feet above the grass, Karen said: 'Throttle all the way back, please.' Harald pulled the lever back. She lifted the nose of the aircraft gently with the stick. When it seemed to Harald that they were almost touching the ground, they continued to fly for fifty yards or more. Then there was a bump as the wheels made contact with the earth.

The aircraft slowed down in a few seconds. As it came to a halt, Harald looked through the broken window and saw, just a few yards away, a young man on a bicycle, watching from a pathway alongside the field, staring at them open-mouthed.

'I wonder where we are?' Karen said.

Harald called out to the bicyclist. 'Hello there!' he said in English. 'What is this place?'

The young man looked at him as if he had come from outer space. 'Well,' he said at last, 'it's not the bloody airport.'

# EPILOGUE

Twenty-four hours after Harald and Karen landed in England, the photographs Harald had taken at the radar station on Sande had been printed, enlarged, and pinned up on one wall of a big room in a grand building in Westminster. Some had been marked with arrows and notes. In the room were three men in RAF uniforms, examining the pictures and talking in low, urgent voices.

Digby Hoare ushered Harald and Karen into the room and closed the door, and the officers turned around. One of them, a tall man with a grey moustache, said: 'Hello, Digby.'

'Good morning, Andrew,' Digby said: 'This is Air Vice Marshal Sir Andrew Hogg. Sir Andrew, may I present Miss Duchwitz and Mr Olufsen.'

Hogg shook Karen's left hand, as her right was still in a sling. 'You're an exceptionally brave young woman,' he said. He spoke English with a clipped accent that made him sound as if he had something in his mouth, and Harald had to listen hard to understand him. 'An experienced pilot would hesitate to cross the North Sea in a Hornet Moth,' Hogg added.

'To tell the truth, I had no idea how dangerous it was when I set off,' she replied.

Hogg turned to Harald. 'Digby and I are old friends. He's given me a full report on your debriefing, and frankly I can't tell you how important this information is. But I want you to go over again your theory about how these three pieces of apparatus work together.'

Harald concentrated, retrieving from his memory the English words he needed. He pointed to the general shot he had taken of the three structures. 'The large aerial rotates steadily, as if constantly scanning the skies. But the smaller ones tilt up and down and side to side, and it seemed to me they must be tracking aircraft.'

Hogg interrupted him to say to the other two officers: 'I sent a radio expert on a reconnaissance flight over the island this morning at dawn. He picked up waves of two point four metres wavelength, presumably emanating from the big Freya, and also fifty centimetre waves, presumably from the smaller machines, which must be Wurtzburgs.' He turned back to Harald. 'Carry on, please.'

'So I guessed that the large machine gives long-range warning of the approach of bombers. Of the smaller machines, one tracks a single bomber, and the other tracks the fighter sent up to attack it. That way, a controller could direct a fighter to the bomber with great accuracy.'

Hogg turned to his colleagues again. 'I believe he's right. What do you think?'

One of them said: 'I'd still like to know the meaning of *himmelbett*.'

Harald said: '*Himmelbett?* That's the German word for one of those beds . . .'

'A four-poster bed, we call it in English,' Hogg told him. 'We've heard that the radar equipment operates in a *himmelbett*, but we don't know what that means.'

'Oh!' said Harald. 'I've been wondering how they would organize things. This explains it.'

The room went quiet. 'Does it?' said Hogg.

'Well, if you were in charge of German air defence, it would make sense to divide your borders up into blocks of air space, say five miles wide and twenty miles deep, and assign a set of three machines to each block . . . or *himmelbett*.'

'You might be right,' Hogg said thoughtfully. 'That would give them an almost impenetrable defence.'

'If the bombers fly side by side, yes,' said Harald. 'But if you made your RAF pilots fly in line, and sent them all through one single *himmelbett*, the Luftwaffe would be able to track only one bomber, and the others would have a much better chance of getting through.'

Hogg stared at him for a long moment. Then he looked at Digby, and at his two colleagues, then back at Harald.

'Like a stream of bombers,' Harald said, not sure they understood.

The silence stretched out. Harald wondered if there was something wrong with his English. 'Do you see what I mean?' he said.

'Oh, yes,' said Hogg at last. 'I see exactly what you mean.'

\* \* \*

On the following morning Digby drove Harald and Karen out of London to the north-east. After three hours they arrived at a country house that had been commandeered by the air force as officers' quarters. They were each given a small room with a cot, then Digby introduced them to his brother, Bartlett.

In the afternoon they all went with Bart to the nearby RAF station where his squadron was based. Digby had arranged for them to attend the briefing, telling the local commander it was part of a secret intelligence exercise; and no further questions were asked. They listened as the commanding officer explained the new formation the pilots would use for that night's raid – the bomber stream.

Their target was Hamburg.

The same scene was repeated, with different targets, on airfields up and down eastern England. Digby told Harald that more than six hundred bombers would take part in tonight's desperate attempt to draw some of the Luftwaffe's strength back from the Russian front.

The moon rose a few minutes after six o'clock in the evening, and the twin engines of the Wellingtons began to roar at eight. On the big blackboard in the operations room, take-off times were noted beside the code letter for each aircraft. Barty was piloting G for George.

As night fell, and the wireless operators reported in from the bombers, their positions were marked on a big map table. The markers moved ever closer to Hamburg. Digby smoked one anxious cigarette after another.

The lead aircraft, C for Charlie, reported that it was under attack from a fighter, then its transmissions stopped. A for Able approached the city, reported heavy flak, and dropped incendiaries to light the target for the bombers following.

When they began to drop their bombs, Harald thought of his Goldstein cousins in Hamburg, and hoped they would be safe. As part of his school work last year he had had to read a novel in English, and he had chosen *War in the Air* by H. G. Wells, which had given him a nightmare vision of a city under attack from the air. He knew this was the only way to defeat the Nazis, but all the same he dreaded what might happen to Monika.

An officer came over to Digby and said in a quiet voice that they had lost radio contact with Bart's aircraft. 'It may just be a wireless problem,' he said.

One by one, the bombers called in to report that they were heading back – all but C for Charlie and G for George.

The same officer came over to say: 'The rear gunner of F for Freddie saw one of ours go down. He doesn't know which, but I'm afraid it sounds like G for George.'

Digby buried his face in his hands.

The counters representing the aircraft moved back

across the map of Europe on the table. Only 'C' and 'G' remained over Hamburg.

Digby made a phone call to London, then said to Harald: 'The bomber stream worked. They're estimating a lower level of losses than we've had for a year.'

Karen said: 'I hope Bart's all right.'

In the early hours, the bombers began to come back in. Digby went outside, and Karen and Harald joined him, watching the big aircraft land on the runway and disgorge their crews, tired but jubilant.

When the moon went down, they were all back but Charlie and George.

Bart Hoare never did come home.

\* \* \*

Harald felt low as he undressed and put on the pyjamas Digby had loaned him. He should have been jubilant. He had survived an incredibly dangerous flight, given crucial intelligence to the British, and seen the information save the lives of hundreds of airmen. But the loss of Bart's aircraft, and the grief on Digby's face, reminded Harald of Arne, who had given his life for this, and Poul Kirke, and the other Danes who had been arrested and would almost certainly be executed for their parts in the triumph; and all he could feel was sadness.

He looked out of the window. Dawn was breaking. He drew the flimsy yellow curtains across the little window and got into bed. He lay there, unable to sleep, feeling bad.

After a while Karen came in. She, too, was wearing borrowed pyjamas, with the sleeves and the trousers rolled to shorten them. Her face was solemn. Without speaking, she climbed into bed next to him. He held her warm body in his arms. She pressed her face into his shoulder and began to cry. He did not ask why. He felt sure she had been having the same thoughts as he. She cried herself to sleep in his arms.

After a while he drifted into a doze. When he opened his eyes again, the sun was shining through the thin curtains. He gazed in wonderment at the girl in his arms. He had often daydreamed about sleeping with her, but he had never foreseen it quite like this.

He could feel her knees, and one hip that dug into his thigh, and something soft against his chest that he thought might be a breast. He watched her face as she slept, studying her lips, her chin, her reddish eyelashes, her eyebrows. He felt as if his heart would burst with love.

Eventually she opened her eyes. She smiled at him and said: 'Hello, my darling.' Then she kissed him.

After a while, they made love.

\* \* \*

Three days later, Hermia Mount appeared.

Harald and Karen walked into a pub near the Palace of Westminster, expecting to meet Digby, and there she was, sitting at a table with a gin-and-tonic in front of her.

'But how did you get home?' Harald asked her.

'Last time we saw you, you were hitting Detective Constable Jespersen over the head with your suitcase.'

'There was so much confusion at Kirstenslot that I was able to slip away before anyone noticed me,' Hermia said. 'I walked into Copenhagen under cover of darkness and reached the city at sunrise. Then I came out the way I had gone in: Copenhagen to Bornholm by ferry, then a fishing boat across to Sweden, and a plane from Stockholm.'

Karen said: 'I'm sure it wasn't as easy as you make it sound.'

Hermia shrugged. 'It was nothing compared with your ordeal. What a journey!'

'I'm very proud of you all,' said Digby, though Harald thought, by the fond look on his face, that he was especially proud of Hermia.

Digby looked at his watch. 'And now we have an appointment with Winston Churchill.'

An air raid warning sounded as they were crossing Whitehall, so they met the prime minister in the underground complex known as the Cabinet War Rooms. Churchill sat at a small desk in a cramped office. On the wall behind him was a large-scale map of Europe. A single bed covered with a green quilt stood against one wall. He was dressed in a chalk stripe suit and had taken off the jacket, but he looked immaculate.

'So you're the lass who flew the North Sea in a Tiger Moth,' he said to Karen, shaking her left hand.

'A Hornet Moth,' she corrected him. The Tiger

Moth was an open aircraft. 'I think we might have frozen to death in a Tiger Moth.'

'Ah, yes, of course.' He turned to Harald. 'And you're the lad who invented the bomber stream.'

'One of those ideas that came out of a discussion,' he said with some embarrassment.

'That's not the way I heard the story, but your modesty does you credit.' Churchill turned to Hermia. 'And you organized the whole thing. Madam, you're worth two men.'

'Thank you, sir,' she said, although Harald could tell by her wry smile that she did not think that was much of a compliment.

'With your help, we have forced Hitler to withdraw hundreds of fighter aircraft from the Russian Front and bring them back for the defence of the Fatherland. And, partly thanks to that success, it may interest you to know that I have today signed a co-belligerency pact with the Union of Soviet Socialist Republics. Britain no longer stands alone. We have as an ally one of the world's greatest powers. Russia may be bowed, but she is by no means beaten.'

'My God,' said Hermia.

Digby murmured: 'It will be in tomorrow's papers.'

'And what are you two young people thinking of doing next?' Churchill asked.

'I'd like to join the RAF,' Harald said immediately. 'Learn to fly properly. Then help to free my country.'

Churchill turned to Karen. 'And you?'

'Something similar. I'm sure they won't let me be a

pilot, even though I can fly much better than Harald. But I'd like to join the women's air force, if there is one.'

'Well,' said the prime minister, 'we have an alternative to suggest to you.'

Harald was surprised.

Churchill nodded to Hermia, who said: 'We want you both to go back to Denmark.'

It was the one thing Harald had not been expecting. 'Go back?'

Hermia went on: 'First, we'd send you on a training course – quite long, six months. You'd learn radio operation, the use of codes, handling firearms and explosives, and so on.'

Karen said: 'For what purpose?'

'You'd parachute into Denmark equipped with radio sets, weapons, and false papers. Your task would be to start a new Resistance movement, to replace the Nightwatchmen.'

Harald's heart beat faster. It was a remarkably important job. 'I had my heart set on flying,' he said. But the new idea was even more exciting – though dangerous.

Churchill intervened. 'I've got thousands of young men who want to fly,' he said brusquely. 'But so far we haven't found anyone who could do what we're asking of you two. You're unique. You're Danish, you know the country, you speak the language as natives, which you are. And you have proved yourselves quite extraordinarily courageous and resourceful. Let me put it this way: if you don't do it, it won't be done.'

It was hard to resist the force of Churchill's will – and Harald did not really want to. He was being offered the chance to do what he had longed for, and he was thrilled at the prospect. He looked at Karen. 'What do you think?'

'We'd be together,' she said, as if that was the most important thing for her.

'Then you'll go?' said Hermia.

'Yes,' said Harald.

'Yes,' said Karen.

'Good,' said the prime minister. 'Then that's settled.'

# Afterword

The Danish resistance eventually became one of the most successful underground movements in Europe. It provided a continuous flow of military intelligence to the Allies, undertook thousands of acts of sabotage against the occupying forces, and provided secret routes by which almost all Denmark's Jews escaped from the Nazis.

# Acknowledgments

As always, I was helped in my research by Dan Starer of Research for Writers, New York City (*dstarer@researchforwriters.com*). He put me in touch with most of the people named below.

Mark Miller of de Havilland Support Ltd was my consultant on Hornet Moth planes, what goes wrong with them, and how to repair them. Rachel Lloyd of the Northamptonshire Flying School did her best to teach me to fly a Tiger Moth. Peter Gould and Walt Kessler also helped in this area, as did my flying friends Ken Burrows and David Gilmour.

My guide to all things Danish was Erik Langkjaer. For details of life in wartime Denmark I'm also grateful to Claus Jessen, Bent Jorgensen, Kurt Hartogsen, Dorph Petersen, and Soren Storgaard.

For help with life at a Danish boarding school I thank Klaus Eusebius Jakobsen of Helufsholme Skole og Gods, Erik Jorgensen of the Birkerod Gymnasium, and Helle Thune of Bagsvaerd Kostkole og Gymnasium, all of whom welcomed me to their schools and patiently answered my questions.

I'm grateful for information from Hanne Harboe of the Tivoli Garden, Louise Lind of the Stockholm

Postmuseum, Anita Kempe, Jan Garnert and K.V. Tahvanainen of the Stockholm Telemuseum, Hans Schroder of the Flyvevabnets Bibliotek, Anders Lunde of the Dansk Boldspil-Union, and Henrik Lundbak of the Museum of Danish Resistance in Copenhagen.

Jack Cunningham told me about the Admiralty Cinema, and Neil Cook of HOK International gave me photographs of it. Candice DeLong and Mike Condon helped with weapons. Josephine Russell told me what it was like to be a student ballerina. Titch Allen and Pete Gagan helped with antique motorcycles.

I'm grateful to my editors and agents: Amy Berkower, Leslie Gelbman, Phyllis Grann, Neil Nyren, Imogen Tate, and Al Zuckerman.

Finally, I thank members of my family for reading outlines and drafts: Barbara Follett, Emanuele Follett, Marie-Claire Follett, Richard Overy, Kim Turner, and Jann Turner.

# PAPER MONEY

# Introduction

This book was written in 1976, immediately before *Eye of the Needle*, and I think it is the best of my unsuccessful books. It was published under the pseudonym Zachary Stone, as was *The Modigliani Scandal*, because the books are similar: they lack a central character, but feature several groups of characters whose stories are linked and share a common climax.

In *Paper Money* the links are less fortuitous, for the book is supposed to show how crime, high finance, and journalism are corruptly interconnected. The ending is rather sombre by comparison with *The Modigliani Scandal* – in fact it is almost a tragedy. However, it is the differences and similarities between *Paper Money* and *Eye of the Needle* that are most instructive. (Readers who want the cake, not the recipe, should skip this and go straight to Chapter One.) The plot of *Paper Money* is the cleverest I have ever devised, and the small sales of the book convinced me that clever plots satisfy authors more than readers. The plot of *Eye of the Needle* is of course very simple – in fact it can be written down in three paragraphs, as indeed I did write it when I first thought of it. *Eye of the Needle* has only three or four main characters whereas *Paper Money* has a dozen or so. Yet with its complex plot and large cast, *Paper Money* is only half the length of *Eye of the Needle*. As a writer I have always had to struggle against a tendency to underwrite, and in *Paper Money* you see me struggling in vain. Consequently the many characters are painted in brisk, bold brushstrokes, and the book lacks the feeling of detailed personal involvement with the private lives of the characters that readers demand of a best seller.

One of the strengths of the book is its form. The action takes place during a single day in the life of a London evening newspaper (I worked for such a newspaper in 1973 and 1974) and each chapter chronicles one hour of that day in three or four scenes describing both what happens at the news desk and what happens in the stories the paper is covering (or missing). *Eye of the Needle* has an even more rigid structure, although nobody to my knowledge has ever noticed it: there are six parts, each with six chapters (except for the last part, which has seven), the first chapter in each part dealing with the spy, the second with the spy catchers, and so on until the sixth, which always tells of the international military consequences of what has gone before. Readers do not notice such things – and why should they? – but still I suspect that regularity, and even symmetry, contribute to what they perceive as a well-told story.

The other feature *Paper Money* shares with *Eye of*

*the Needle* is a wealth of good minor characters – tarts, thieves, half-witted children, working-class wives, and lonely old men. In subsequent books I have not done this, for it only diverts from the main characters and their story; yet I often wonder whether I am being too clever.

Today I am not as sure as I was in 1976 of the links between crime, high finance, and journalism; but I think this book is true to life in another way. It presents a detailed picture of the London that I knew in the seventies, with its policemen and crooks, bankers and call girls, reporters and politicians, its shops and slums, its roads and its river. I loved it, and I hope you will too.

# Six a.m.

# Chapter One

It was the luckiest night of Tim Fitzpeterson's life.

He thought this the moment he opened his eyes and saw the girl, in bed beside him, still sleeping. He did not move, for fear of waking her; but he looked at her, almost furtively, in the cold light of the London dawn. She slept flat on her back, with the absolute relaxation of small children. Tim was reminded of his own Adrienne when she was little. He put the unwelcome thought out of his mind.

The girl beside him had red hair, fitting her small head like a cap, showing her tiny ears. All her features were small: nose, chin, cheekbones, dainty teeth. Once, in the night, he had covered her face with his broad, clumsy hands, pressing his fingers gently into the hollows of her eyes and her cheeks, opening her soft lips with his thumbs, as if his skin could feel her beauty like the heat from a fire.

Her left arm lay limply outside the coverlet, which was pushed down to reveal narrow, delicate shoulders and one shallow breast, its nipple soft in slumber.

They lay apart, not quite touching, although he could feel the warmth of her thigh close to his. He looked away from her, up at the ceiling, and for a

3

moment he let the sheer joy of remembered forni-
cation wash over him like a physical thrill; then he
got up.

He stood beside the bed and looked back at her.
She was undisturbed. The candid morning light made
her no less lovely, despite tousled hair and the untidy
remains of what had been elaborate make-up. Day-
break was less kind to Tim Fitzpeterson, he knew.
That was why he tried not to wake her: he wanted to
look in a mirror before she saw him.

He went naked, padding across the dull green living
room carpet to the bathroom. In the space of a few
moments he saw the place as if for the first time,
and found it hopelessly unexciting. The carpet was
matched by an even duller green sofa, with fading
flowered cushions. There was a plain wooden desk,
of the kind to be found in a million offices; an elderly
black-and-white television set; a filing cabinet; and a
bookshelf of legal and economic textbooks plus
several volumes of *Hansard*. He had once thought it
so dashing to have a London pied-à-terre.

The bathroom had a full-length mirror – bought
not by Tim, but by his wife, in the days before she
had totally retired from town life. He looked in it
while he waited for the bath to fill, wondering what
there was about this middle-aged body that could
drive a beautiful girl of – what, twenty-five? – into a
frenzy of lust. He was healthy, but not fit; not in the
sense with which that word is used to describe men
who do exercises and visit gymnasia. He was short,

and his naturally broad frame was thickened by a little superfluous fat, particularly on the chest, waist, and buttocks. His physique was okay, for a man of forty-one, but it was nothing to excite even the most physical of women.

The mirror became obscured by steam, and Tim got into the bath. He rested his head and closed his eyes. It occurred to him that he had had less than two hours of sleep, yet he felt quite fresh. His upbringing would have him believe that pain and discomfort, if not actual illness, were the consequences of late nights, dancing, adultery, and strong drink. All those sins together ought to bring down the wrath of God.

No: the wages of sin were sheer delight. He began to soap himself languidly. It had started at one of those appalling dinners: grapefruit cocktail, overdone steak and *bombe* no *surprise* for three hundred members of a useless organization. Tim's speech had been just another exposition of the Government's current strategy, emotionally weighted to appeal to the particular sympathies of the audience. Afterwards he had agreed to go somewhere else for a drink with one of his colleagues – a brilliant young economist – and two faintly interesting people from the audience.

The venue turned out to be a nightclub which would normally have been beyond Tim's means; but someone else had paid the entrance. Once inside, he began to enjoy himself, so much so that he bought a bottle of champagne with his credit card. More people had joined their group: a film company executive

Tim had vaguely heard of; a playwright he hadn't; a left-wing economist who shook hands with a wry smile and avoided shop talk; and the girls.

The champagne and the floor show inflamed him slightly. In the old days, he would at this point have taken Julia home and made love to her roughly – she liked that, just occasionally. But now she no longer came to town, and he no longer went to nightclubs; not normally.

The girls had not been introduced. Tim started to talk to the nearest, a flat-chested redhead in a long dress of some pale colour. She looked like a model, and said she was an actress. He expected that he would find her boring, and that she would reciprocate. That was when he got the first intimation that tonight would be special: she seemed to find him fascinating.

Their close conversation gradually isolated them from the rest of the party, until someone suggested another club. Tim immediately said he would go home. The redhead caught his arm and asked him not to; and Tim, who was being gallant to a beautiful woman for the first time in twenty years, instantly agreed to go along.

He wondered, as he got out of the bath, what they had talked about for so long. The work of a Junior Minister in the Department of Energy was hardly cocktail-party conversation: when it was not technical, it was highly confidential. Perhaps they had discussed politics. Had he told wry anecdotes about senior politicians, in the deadpan tone which was his only way of being humorous? He could not remember. All he could recall was the way she had sat, with every part of her body angled devotedly towards him: head, shoulders, knees, feet; a physical attitude that was at once intimate and teasing.

He wiped steam off the shaving mirror and rubbed his chin speculatively, sizing up the task. He had very dark hair, and his beard, if he were to grow it, would be thick. The rest of his face was, to say the least, ordinary. The chin was receding, the nose sharply pointed with twin white marks either side of the bridge where spectacles had rested for thirty-five years, the mouth not small but a little grim, the ears too large, the forehead intellectually high. No character could be read there. It was a face trained to conceal thoughts, instead of displaying emotion.

He switched on the shaver and grimaced to bring all of his left cheek into view. He was not even ugly. Some girls had a thing about ugly men, he had heard – he was in no position to verify such generalizations about women – but Tim Fitzpeterson did not even fit into that dubiously fortunate category.

But perhaps it was time to think again about the categories he fitted into. The second club they had visited had been the kind of place he would never knowingly have entered. He was no music-lover, and if he had liked it his taste would not have included the blaring, insistent row which drowned conversation in The Black Hole. Nevertheless, he had danced to it – the jerky, exhibitionist dancing that seemed to be *de rigueur* there. He enjoyed it, and thought he acquitted himself well enough; there were no amused glances from the other patrons, as he feared there might be. Perhaps that was because many of them were his age.

The disc jockey, a bearded young man in a T-shirt improbably printed with the words 'Harvard Business School', capriciously played a slow ballad, sung by an American with a heavy cold. They were on the small dance floor at the time. The girl came close to him and wound her arms around him. Then he knew she meant it; and he had to decide whether he was equally serious. With her hot, lithe body clinging to him as closely as a wet towel, he made up his mind very quickly. He bent his head – she was slightly shorter than he – and murmured into her ear: 'Come and have a drink at my flat.'

He kissed her in the taxi – *there* was something he had not done for many years! The kiss was so luscious, like a kiss in a dream, that he touched her breasts, wonderfully small and hard under the loose gown; and after that they found it difficult to restrain themselves until they reached home.

The token drink was forgotten. We must have got into bed in less than a minute, Tim thought smugly. He finished shaving and looked around for cologne. There was an old bottle in the wall cabinet.

He went back to the bedroom. She was still asleep. He found his dressing gown and cigarettes and sat in the upright chair by the window. I was pretty terrific in bed, he thought. He knew he was kidding himself:

*she* had been the activist, the creative one. On her initiative they had done things which Tim could not suggest to Julia after fifteen years in the same bed.

Yes, Julia. He gazed unseeing from the first-floor window, across the narrow street to the red-brick Victorian school, its meagre playground painted with the fading yellow lines of a netball court. He still felt the same about Julia: if he had loved her before, he loved her now. This girl was different. But wasn't that what fools always told themselves before embarking on an affair?

Let's not be hasty, he told himself. For her this might be a one-night stand. He could not assume she would want to see him again. Yet he wanted to decide where his aims lay before asking her what the options were: government had taught him to brief himself before meetings.

He had a formula for the approach to complex issues. First, what have I got to lose?

Julia, again: plump, intelligent, contented; her horizons contracting inexorably with every year of motherhood. There had been a time when he lived for her: he bought the clothes she liked, he read novels because she was interested in novels, and his political successes pleased him all the more because they pleased her. But the centre of gravity of his life had shifted. Now Julia held sway only over trivia. She wanted to live in Hampshire, and it did not matter to him, so they lived there. She wanted him to wear check jackets, but Westminster chic demanded sober suits, so he wore dark, faintly patterned greys and navy blues.

When he analysed his feelings, he found there was not a lot to tie him to Julia. A little sentiment, perhaps; a nostalgic picture of her, with her hair in a pony-tail, doing the jive in a tapered skirt. Was that love or something? He doubted it.

The girls? That was something else. Katie, Penny and Adrienne: only Katie was old enough to understand love and marriage. They did not see much of him, but he took the view that a little father-love goes a long way, and is a great deal better than no father at all. There was no room for debate there: his opinion was fixed.

And there was his career. A divorce might not harm a Junior Minister, but it could ruin a man higher up. There had never been a divorced Prime Minister. Tim Fitzpeterson wanted that job.

So there was a lot to lose – in fact, all he held dear. He turned his gaze from the window to the bed. The girl had rolled onto her side, facing away. She was right to have her hair short – it emphasized the slender neck and pretty shoulders. Her back tapered sharply to a small waist, then disappeared beneath a crumpled sheet. Her skin was faintly tanned.

There was so much to gain. 'Joy' was a word Tim had little use for, but it entered his thoughts now. If he had known joy before, he could not remember when. Satisfaction, yes: in the writing of a sound, comprehensive report; in the winning of one of those countless small battles in committees and in the House of Commons; in a book that was correct or a wine that was right. But the savagely chemical pleasure he had with this girl was new.

There; those were the pros and cons. The formula said, now add them up and see which is greater. But this time the formula would not work. Tim had acquaintances who said it never did. Perhaps they were right. It might be a mistake to think that reasons could be counted like pound notes: he was reminded, curiously, of a phrase from a college philosophy lecture, 'the bewitchment of our intelligence by means of language'. Which is longer – an aeroplane or a one-act play? Which do I prefer – satisfaction or joy? His thinking was getting woolly. He made a disgusted noise, then looked quickly at the bed to see whether he had disturbed her. She slept on. Good.

Out in the street, a grey Rolls-Royce pulled up at the kerb a hundred yards away. Nobody got out. Tim looked more closely, and saw the driver open a newspaper. A chauffeur, perhaps, picking someone up at six-thirty? A businessman who had travelled overnight and arrived too early? Tim could not read the number plate. But he could see that the driver was a big man; big enough to make the interior of the car seem as cramped as a Mini.

He turned his mind back to his dilemma. What do we do in politics, he thought, when we face two forceful but conflicting demands? The answer came immediately: we choose a course of action which, really or apparently, meets both needs. The parallel was obvious. He would stay married to Julia and have an affair with this girl. It seemed a very political solution, and it pleased him.

He lit another cigarette and thought about the future. It was a pleasant pastime. There would be many more nights here at the flat; the occasional weekend in a small hotel in the country; perhaps even a fortnight in the sun, on some discreet little beach in North Africa or the West Indies. She would be sensational in a bikini.

Other hopes paled beside these. He was tempted by the thought that his early life had been wasted; but he knew the idea to be extravagant. Not wasted, then; but it was as if he had spent his youth working out long-division sums and never discovered differential calculus.

He decided to talk to her about the problem and his solution. She would say it could not be done, and he would tell her that making compromises work was his special talent.

How should he begin? 'Darling, I want to do this again, often.' That seemed all right. What would she say? 'So would I,' or: 'Call me at this number,' or: 'Sorry, Timmy, I'm a one-night girl.'

No, not that; it wasn't possible. Last night had been good for her, too. He was special for her. She had said so.

He stood up and put out his cigarette. I'll go over to the bed, he thought; and I'll pull the blankets off her gently, and look at her nakedness for a few moments; then I'll lie beside her, and kiss her belly, and her thighs, and her breasts, until she wakes; and then I'll make love to her again.

He looked away from her and out of the window, savouring the anticipation. The Rolls was still there, like a grey slug in the gutter. For some reason it bothered him. He put it out of his mind, and went over to wake the girl.

# Chapter Two

Felix Laski did not have much money, despite the fact that he was very rich. His wealth took the form of shares, land, buildings, and occasionally more nebulous assets like half a film script or one third of an invention for making instant potato chips. Newspapers were fond of saying that if all his riches were turned into cash, he would have so many millions of pounds; and Laski was equally fond of pointing out that to turn his riches into cash would be close to impossible.

He walked from Waterloo railway station to the City, because he believed that laziness caused heart attacks in men of his age. This concern with his health was foolish, for he was as fit a fifty-year-old as could be found within the Square Mile. Just short of six feet tall, with a chest like the stern of a battleship, he was about as vulnerable to cardiac arrest as a young ox.

He cut a striking figure, walking across Blackfriars Bridge in the brittle sunshine of the early morning. His clothes were expensive, from the blue silk shirt to the handmade shoes; by City standards he was a dandy. This was because every man in the village

where Laski had been born wore cotton dungarees
and a cloth cap; now good clothes gave him a buzz
by reminding him of what he had left behind.

The clothes were part of his image, which was that
of a buccaneer. His deals usually involved risk, or
opportunism, or both; and he took care that from
the outside they looked sharper than they were. A
reputation for having the magic touch was worth
more than a merchant bank.

It was the image that had seduced Peters. Laski
thought about Peters as he walked briskly past St
Paul's Cathedral towards their rendezvous. A small,
narrow-minded man, his expertise was in the movement of cash: not credit, but physical funds, paper
money. He worked for the Bank of England, the
ultimate source of legal tender. His job was to arrange
for the creation and destruction of notes and coins.
He did not make policy – that was done at a higher
level, perhaps in the Cabinet – but he knew how many
fivers Barclays Bank needed before they did.

Laski had first met him at the cocktail-party opening of an office block built by a discount house. Laski
went to such affairs for no reason other than to meet
people like Peters, who might one day come in useful.
Five years later, Peters became useful. Laski phoned
him at the Bank, and asked him to recommend a
numismatist to advise on a fictitious purchase of old
coins. Peters announced that he was a collector, in a
small way, and that he would look at them himself, if
Laski wished. Splendid, Laski said, and rushed out to

get the coins. Peters advised him to buy. Suddenly, they were friends.

(The purchase became the foundation of a collection which was now worth double what Laski had paid for it. That was incidental to his purpose, but he was inordinately proud of it.)

It turned out that Peters was an early riser, partly because he liked it, but also because money was moved around in the mornings, and so the bulk of his work needed to be done before nine o'clock. Laski learned that it was Peters' custom to drink coffee in a particular café at around six-thirty each day, and he began to join him, at first occasionally, and then regularly. Laski pretended to be an early riser himself, and joined in Peters' praise of the quiet streets and the crisp morning air. In truth he liked to get up late, but he was prepared to make a lot of sacrifices if there was half a chance of this far-fetched scheme coming off.

He turned in to the café, breathing hard. At his age, even a fit man was entitled to blow after a long walk. The place smelled of coffee and fresh bread. The walls were hung with plastic tomatoes and water-colours of the proprietor's home town in Italy. Behind the counter, a woman in overalls and a long-haired youth were making mountains of sandwiches ready for the hundreds of people who would snatch a bite at their desks this lunch-time. A radio was on somewhere, but it was not loud. Peters was already there, at a window seat.

Laski bought coffee and a *leberwurst* sandwich and sat down opposite Peters, who was eating doughnuts

– he seemed to be one of those people who never put on weight. Laski said: 'It's going to be a fine day.' His voice was deep and resonant, like an actor's, with just a trace of some East European accent.

Peters said: 'Beautiful. And I shall be in my garden by four-thirty.'

Laski sipped coffee and looked at the other man. Peters had very short hair and a small moustache, and his face looked pinched. He had not yet started work, and he was already looking forward to going home; Laski thought that tragic. He felt a momentary pang of compassion for Peters and all the other little men for whom work was a means instead of an end.

'I like my work,' Peters said, as if reading Laski's mind.

Laski covered his surprise. 'But you like your garden better.'

'In this weather, yes. Do you have a garden... Felix?'

'My housekeeper tends the window boxes. I'm not a man of hobbies.' Laski reflected on Peters' hesitant use of his Christian name. The man was slightly awe-struck, he decided. Good.

'No time, I suppose. You must work very hard.'

'So people tell me. It's just that I prefer to spend the hours between six p.m. and midnight making fifty thousand dollars than watching actors pretend to kill each other on television.'

Peters laughed. 'The most imaginative brain in the City turns out to have no imagination.'

'I don't follow that.'

'You don't read novels or go to the cinema, either, do you?'

'No.'

'You see? You've got a blind spot – you can't empathize with fiction. It's true of many of the most enterprising businessmen. The incapacity seems to go with heightened acumen, like a blind man's hypersensitive hearing.'

Laski frowned. Being analysed put him at a disadvantage. 'Maybe,' he said.

Peters seemed to sense his discomfort. 'I'm fascinated by the careers of great entrepreneurs,' he said.

'So am I,' Laski said. 'I'm all in favour of pinching other people's brainwaves.'

'What was your first coup, Felix?'

Laski relaxed. This was more familiar territory. 'I suppose it was Woolwich Chemicals,' he said. 'That was a small pharmaceuticals manufacturer. After the war they set up a small chain of High Street chemists' shops, with the object of guaranteeing their markets. The trouble was, they knew all about chemistry and nothing about retailing, and the shops ate up most of the profits made by the factory.

'I was working for a stockbroker at the time, and I'd made a little money playing the market. I went to my boss and offered him a half-share in the profits if he would finance the deal. We bought the company, and immediately sold the factory to ICI for almost as much as we paid for the shares. Then we closed the shops and sold them one by one – they were all in prime sites.'

'I'll never understand this sort of thing,' Peters said. 'If the factory and the shops were worth so much, why were the shares cheap?'

'Because the enterprise was losing money. They hadn't paid a dividend for years. The management didn't have the guts to cash in their chips, so to speak. We did. Everything in business is courage.' He started to eat his sandwich.

'It's fascinating,' Peters said. He looked at his watch. 'I must go.'

'Big day?' Laski said lightly.

'Today's one of *the* days – and that always means headaches.'

'Did you solve that problem?'

'Which?'

'Routes.' Laski lowered his voice a fraction. 'Your security people wanted you to send the convoy a different way each time.'

'No.' Peters was embarrassed: it had been indiscreet of him to tell Laski about that dilemma. 'There is really only one sensible way to get there. However . . .' He stood up.

Laski smiled and kept his voice casual. 'So today's big shipment goes by the old direct route.'

Peters put a finger to his lips. 'Security,' he said.

'Sure.'

Peters picked up his raincoat. 'Good-bye.'

'I'll see you tomorrow,' Laski said, smiling broadly.

# Chapter Three

Arthur Cole climbed the steps from the station, his breath rattling unhealthily in his chest. A gust of warm air came up from the bowels of the Underground, wrapped itself snugly around him, and blew away. He shivered slightly as he emerged into the street.

The sunshine took him by surprise – it had hardly been dawn when he boarded the train. The air was chilled and sweet. Later it would become poisonous enough to knock out a policeman on point duty. Cole remembered the first time that had happened: the story had been an *Evening Post* exclusive.

He walked slowly until his breathing eased. Twenty-five years in newspapers have ruined my health, he thought. In truth, any industry would have done the same, for he was prone to worry and to drink, and his chest was weak; but it comforted him to blame his profession.

Anyway, he had given up smoking. He had been a non-smoker for – he looked at his watch – one hundred and twenty-eight minutes, unless he counted the night, in which case it was eight hours. He had already passed several moments of risk: immediately after the alarm clock went off at four-thirty (he usually smoked one on the WC); driving away from his house, at the moment when he got into top gear and turned on the radio ready for the five o'clock news; accelerating down the first fast stretch of the A12 as his large Ford hit its stride; and waiting on a cold, open-air tube station in East London for the earliest train of the day.

The BBC's five o'clock bulletin had not cheered him. It had had all his attention as he drove, for the route was so familiar that he negotiated the bends and roundabouts automatically, from memory. The lead story came from Westminster: the latest industrial relations bill had been passed by Parliament, but the majority had been narrow. Cole had caught the story the previous night on television. That meant the morning papers would certainly have it, which in turn meant that the *Post* could do nothing with it unless there were developments later in the day.

There was a story about the Retail Price Index. The source would be official government statistics, which would have been embargoed until midnight: again, the mornings would have it.

It was no surprise to learn that the car workers' strike was still on – it would hardly have been settled overnight.

Test cricket in Australia solved the sports editor's problem, but the score was not sufficiently sensational for the front page.

Cole began to worry.

He entered the *Evening Post* building and took the lift. The newsroom occupied the entire first floor. It was a huge, I-shaped open-plan office. Cole entered at the foot of the I. To his left were the typewriters and telephones of the copytakers, who would type out stories dictated over the phone; to the right, the filing cabinets and bookshelves of specialist writers – political, industrial, crime, defence, and more. Cole walked up the stem of the I, through rows of desks belonging to ordinary common-or-garden reporters, to the long news desk which divided the room in two. Behind it was the U-shaped sub-editors' table, and beyond that, in the crosspiece of the I, was the sports department – a semi-independent kingdom, with its own editor, reporters, and subs. Cole occasionally showed curious relatives around the place; he always told them: 'It's supposed to work like a production line. Usually it's more like a bun fight.' It was an exaggeration, but it always got a laugh.

The room was brightly lit, and empty. As deputy news editor, Cole had a section of the news desk to himself. He opened a drawer and took out a coin, then walked to the vending machine in Sport and punched buttons for instant tea with milk and sugar. A teleprinter chattered to life, breaking the silence.

As Cole walked back to his desk with his paper cup, the far door bumped open. A short, grey-haired figure came in, wearing a bulky parka and cycle clips. Cole waved and called: 'Morning, George.'

# Paper Money

'Hello, Arthur. Cold enough for you?' George began to take off his coat. The body inside it was small and thin. Despite his age, George's title was Head Lad: he was chief of the office's team of messengers. He lived in Potters Bar and cycled to work. Arthur thought that an astonishing feat.

Arthur put down his tea, shrugged out of his raincoat, turned on the radio, and sat down. The radio began to murmur. He sipped tea and gazed straight ahead. The newsroom was scruffy – chairs were scattered randomly, newspapers and sheets of copy paper littered the desks, and redecoration had been postponed in last year's economy drive – but the scene was too familiar to register. Cole's mind was on the first edition, which would be on the streets in three hours.

Today's paper would have sixteen pages. Fourteen of the first edition's pages already existed as semicylindrical metal plates on the press downstairs. They contained advertising, features, television programmes, and news written in such a way that its age would – it was hoped – be overlooked by the reader. That left the back page for the sports editor and the front page for Arthur Cole.

Parliament, a strike, and inflation – they were all yesterday stories. There was not much he could do with them. Any of them could be dressed up with a today intro, like 'Cabinet Ministers today held an inquest on the Government's narrow escape...' There was one of those for every situation. Yesterday's disaster became today's news story with 'Dawn today revealed the full horror . . .' Yesterday's murder benefited from 'Detectives today searched London for the man who . . .' Arthur's problem had given birth to scores of clichés. In a civilized society, he thought, when there was no news there would be no newspapers. It was an old thought, and he brushed it out of his mind impatiently.

Everyone accepted that the first edition was rubbish three days out of six. But that gave no comfort, because it was the reason Arthur Cole had the job of producing that edition. He had been deputy news editor for five years. Twice during that period the news editor's chair had fallen vacant, and both times a younger man than Cole had been promoted. Someone had decided that the number two job was the limit of his capabilities. He disagreed.

The only way he could demonstrate his talent was by turning out an excellent first edition. Unfortunately, how good the edition was depended largely upon luck. Cole's strategy was to aim for a paper which was consistently slightly better than the opposition's first edition. He thought he was succeeding: whether anyone upstairs had noticed, he had no idea; and he would not let himself worry about it.

George came up behind him and dumped a pile of newspapers on his desk. 'Young Stephen's reported sick again,' he grumbled.

Arthur smiled. 'What is it – a hangover or a runny nose?'

'Remember what they used to tell us? "If you can walk, you can work." Not this lot.'

Arthur nodded.

'Am I right?' George said.

'You're right.' The two of them had been Lads together on the *Post*. Arthur had got his NUJ card after the war. George, who had not been called up, had remained a messenger.

George said: 'We were keen. We *wanted* to work.'

Arthur picked up the top newspaper from the pile. This was not the first time George had complained about his staff, nor the first time Arthur had commiserated with him. But Arthur knew what was wrong with the Lads of today. Thirty years ago, a smart Lad could become a reporter; nowadays, that road was closed. The new system had a double impact: bright youngsters stayed at school instead of becoming messengers; and those who did become messengers knew they had no prospects, so they did as little work as they could get away with. But Arthur could not say this to George, because it would call attention to the fact that Arthur had done so much better than his old colleague. So he agreed that the youth of today were rotten.

George seemed disposed to persist with his grouse. Arthur cut him off by saying: 'Anything on the overnight wire?'

'I'll get it. Only I've got to do all the papers myself—'

'I'd better see the wire copy first.' Arthur turned away. He hated to pull rank. He had never learned to do it naturally, perhaps because he took no pleasure in it. He looked at the *Morning Star*: they had led with the industry bill.

It was unlikely that there would be any national news on the teletype yet; it was too early. But foreign news came in sporadically during the night, and more often than not it included one story which could be the splash, in a pinch. Most nights there was a major fire, a multiple murder, a riot, or a coup somewhere in the world. The *Post* was a London paper and did not like to lead with foreign news unless it was sensational; but it might be better than 'Cabinet Ministers today held an inquest . . .'

George dumped a sheet of paper several feet long on his desk. Not cutting the sheet into individual stories was his way of showing displeasure. He probably wanted Arthur to complain, so that he could point out how much work there was for him to do with the early Lad off sick. Arthur fumbled in his desk for scissors, and began to read.

He went through a political story from Washington, a Test Match report, and a Middle East round-up. He was halfway through a minor Hollywood divorce when the phone rang. He picked it up and said: 'Newsdesk.'

'I've got an item for your gossip column.' It was a man's voice, with a broad Cockney accent.

Cole was instantly sceptical. This was not the voice

of a man who would have inside information on the love lives of the aristocracy. He said: 'Good. Would you like to tell me your name?'

'Never mind about that. Do you know who Tim Fitzpeterson is?'

'Of course.'

'Well, he's making a fool of himself with a redhead. She must be twenty years younger than him. Do you want his phone number?'

'Please.' Cole wrote it down. He was interested now. If a Minister's marriage had broken up, it would make a good story, not just a gossip item. 'Who's the girl?' he said.

'Calls herself an actress. Truth is, she's a brass. Just give him a ring right away, and ask him about Dizi Disney.' The line went dead.

Cole frowned. This was a little odd: most tipsters wanted money, especially for news of this kind. He shrugged. It was worth checking out. He would give it to a reporter later on.

Then he changed his mind. Innumerable stories had been lost for ever by being put aside for a few minutes. Fitzpeterson might leave for the House, or his Whitehall office. And the informant had said: 'Give him a ring right away.'

Cole read the number off his notebook and dialled.

# Seven a.m.

# Chapter Four

'Have you ever watched yourself doing it in the mirror?' she had asked; and when Tim admitted he had not, she insisted they try it. They were standing in front of the full-length glass in the bathroom when the phone rang. The noise made Tim jump, and she said: 'Ouch! Careful.'

He wanted to ignore it, but the intrusion of the outside world took away his desire. He left her, and went into the bedroom. The phone was on a chair underneath a pile of her clothes. He found it and lifted the receiver. 'Yes?'

'Mr Fitzpeterson?' It was the voice of a middle-aged man with a London accent. He sounded slightly asthmatic.

'Yes. Who is that?'

'*Evening Post*, sir. I'm sorry to call you so early. I have to ask you whether it's true you're getting divorced.'

Tim sat down heavily. For a moment he was unable to speak.

'Are you there, sir?'

'Who the devil told you that?'

'The informant mentioned a woman called Dizi Disney. Do you know her?'

'I've never heard of her.' Tim was regaining his composure. 'Don't wake me up in the morning with idle rumours.' He put the phone down.

The girl came into the bedroom. 'You look quite white,' she said. 'Who was it?'

'What's your name?' he snapped.

'Dizi Disney.'

'Jesus Christ.' His hands were trembling. He clenched his fists and stood up. 'The papers have got hold of a whisper that I'm getting divorced!'

'They must hear that sort of thing about famous people all the time.'

'They mentioned your name!' He slammed one fist into the palm of his other hand. 'How could they find out so quickly? What am I going to do?'

She turned her back on him and put her panties on.

He stared out of the window. The grey Rolls was still there, but now it was empty. He wondered where the driver had gone. The stray thought annoyed him. He tried to assess the situation coolly. Someone had seen him leave a club with the girl, and phoned the information to a reporter. The informant had built the incident up for dramatic effect. But Tim was sure no one had seen them enter the flat together.

'Listen,' he said. 'Last night you said you weren't feeling well. I took you out of the club and got a taxi. The cab dropped me off then took you home. All right?'

'Whatever you say,' she said uninterestedly.

Her attitude infuriated him. 'For God's sake, this involves you!'

'I think my part in it is over.'

'What does that mean?'

There was a knock at the door.

Tim said: 'Oh, Jesus, no.'

The girl zipped up her dress. 'I'll go.'

'Don't be such a damn fool.' He grabbed her arm. 'You mustn't be seen here, don't you understand? Stay here in the bedroom. I'll open the door. If I have to ask them in, just keep quiet until they go.'

He put on his underwear shorts and struggled into his dressing gown as he crossed the living room. There was a tiny hall, and a front door with a peephole. Tim swung the flap aside and put an eye to the glass.

The man outside looked vaguely familiar. He had the face of a boxer. Broad-shouldered and well built, he would have been a heavyweight. He wore a grey coat with a velvet collar. Tim put his age at late twenties. He did not look like a newspaper reporter.

Tim unbolted the door and opened it. 'What is it?' he said.

Without speaking, the man pushed Tim aside, stepped in, and closed the door behind him. He walked into the living room.

Tim took a deep breath and tried not to panic. He followed the man. 'I'm going to call the police,' he said.

The man sat down. He called: 'Are you in there, Dizi?'

The girl came to the bedroom door.

33

The man said: 'Make us a cup of tea, girl.'

'Do you know him?' Tim asked her incredulously.

She ignored him and went into the kitchen.

The man laughed. 'Know me? She works for me.'

Tim sat down. 'What is this all about?' he said weakly.

'All in good time.' The man looked around. 'I can't say you've got a nice place here, because you haven't. I expected you to have something a bit flash, know what I mean? By the way, in case you haven't recognized me, I'm Tony Cox.' He stuck out his hand. Tim ignored it. Cox said: 'Please yourself.'

Tim was remembering – the face and the name were familiar. He thought Cox was a fairly wealthy businessman, but he could not recall what his business was. He thought he had seen the man's picture in a newspaper – something to do with raising money for boys' clubs in the East End.

Cox jerked his head towards the kitchen. 'Did you enjoy her?'

'For God's sake,' Tim said.

The girl came in, carrying two mugs on a tray. Cox asked her: 'Did he enjoy it?'

'What do you think?' she said sourly.

Cox took out his wallet and counted out some notes. 'Here you are,' he said to her. 'You done a good job. Now you can fuck off.'

She took the money and put it in a handbag. She said: 'You know, Tone, I think the thing I like most about you is your beautiful manners.' She went out without looking at Tim.

Tim thought: I've made the biggest mistake of my life.

As the girl left, the door slammed.

Cox winked. 'She's a good girl.'

'She's the lowest form of human life,' Tim spat.

'Now, don't be like that. She's just a good actress. She might have got into films if I hadn't of found her first.'

'I presume you're a ponce.'

Anger flashed in Cox's eyes, but he controlled it. 'You'll regret that little joke,' he said mildly. 'All you need to know about me and Dizi is that she does what I tell her to. If I say "Keep your mouth shut," she does. And if I say "Tell the nice man from the *News of the World* how Mr Fitzpeterson seduced you," she will. Know what I mean?'

Tim said: 'I suppose it was you who contacted the *Evening Post.*'

'Don't worry! Without confirmation, they can't do a thing. And only three people can confirm the story: you, Dizi, and me. You're not going to say anything, Dizi's got no will of her own, and I can keep a secret.'

Tim lit a cigarette. He was finding his confidence again. Cox was just a working-class hoodlum, despite his velvet collar and his grey Rolls-Royce. Tim had the feeling he could handle the man. He said: 'If this is blackmail, you're on to a loser. I haven't any money.'

'Quite warm in here, isn't it?' Cox stood up and took his coat off. 'Well,' he resumed, 'if you haven't got money, we'll have to think of something else you can give me.'

Tim frowned. He was lost again.

Cox continued: 'In the last few months, half a dozen or so companies have put in bids for drilling rights in a new oil field called Shield, right?'

Tim was astonished. Surely this crook could not be connected with any of those respectable companies? He said: 'Yes, but it's too late for me to influence the result – the decision has been made. It will be announced this afternoon.'

'Don't jump to conclusions. I know it's too late to change it. But you can tell me who's won the licence.'

Tim stared. Was that all he wanted? It was too good to be true! He said: 'What possible use could you have for that sort of information?'

'None, really. I'm going to trade it for another piece of information. I've got a deal going with this gent, see. He doesn't know how I get my inside dope, and he doesn't know what I do with the stuff he tells me. That way he keeps his nose clean. Know what I mean? Now, then: who gets the licence?'

It was so easy, Tim thought. Two words, and the nightmare would be over. A breach of confidence like this could ruin his career: but then, if he did not do it, his career was finished anyway.

Cox said: 'If you're not sure what to do, just think of the headlines. "The Minister and the Actress. He wouldn't make an honest woman of me, showgirl weeps." Remember poor old Tony Lambton?'

'Shut up,' Tim said. 'It's Hamilton Holdings.'

Cox smiled. 'My friend will be pleased,' he said. 'Where's the phone?'

Tim jerked a thumb. 'Bedroom,' he said wearily.

Cox went into the room, and Tim closed his eyes. How naïve he had been, to think that a young girl like Dizi could fall head over heels in love with someone like him. He was a patsy in some elaborate scheme which was much bigger than petty blackmail.

He could hear Cox speaking. 'Laski? It's me. Hamilton Holdings. You got that? Announcement this afternoon. Now, what about your end?' There was a pause. 'Today? Terrific. You've made my day, pal. And the route?' Another pause. 'What do you mean, you *think* it's the usual? You're supposed – okay, okay. So long.'

Tim knew of Laski – he was an ageing City whiz kid – but he was emotionally too exhausted to feel appropriately astonished. He could believe anything of anyone now.

Cox came back in. Tim stood up. Cox said: 'Well, a successful little morning, one way and another. And don't feel too bad about it. After all, it was the best night's nooky you'll ever have.'

'Are you going to leave now, please?' Tim said.

'Well, there is one more little matter to discuss. Give us your dressing gown.'

'Why?'

37

'I'll show you. Come on.'

Tim was too battered to argue. He slipped the robe off his shoulders and handed it over. He stood in his shorts, waiting.

Cox threw the garment to one side. 'I want you to remember that word "ponce",' he said. Then he punched Tim in the stomach.

Tim turned away and doubled over in agony. Cox reached out, grabbed his genitals in one huge hand, and squeezed. Tim tried to scream, but he had no breath. His mouth gaped in a soundless howl as he tried desperately to suck air.

Cox let go and kicked him. Tim toppled to the floor. He curled up there, and his eyes flooded with tears. He had no pride, no dignity left. He said: 'Please don't hurt me any more.'

Tony Cox smiled and put his coat on. 'Not just yet,' he said. Then he went away.

# Chapter Five

The Hon. Derek Hamilton woke up with a pain. He lay in bed with his eyes shut while he traced the discomfort to his abdomen, examined it, and graded it bad but not incapacitating. Then he recalled last night's dinner. Asparagus mousse was harmless; he had refused seafood pancakes; his steak had been well done; he had taken cheese in preference to apple tart. A light white wine, coffee with cream, brandy—

Brandy. Damn, he should stick to port.

He knew how the day would go. He would do without breakfast, and by mid-morning the hunger would be as bad as the ulcer pain, so he would eat something. By lunch-time the hunger would be back and the ulcer would be worse. During the afternoon some trivial thing would irritate him beyond all reason, he would yell at his staff, and his stomach would ball into a knot of pain which made him incapable of thinking at all. He would go home and take too many pain killers. He would sleep, wake with a headache, eat dinner, take sleeping pills, and go to bed.

At least he could look forward to bedtime.

He rolled over, yanked open the drawer of the

bedside table, found a tablet, and put it in his mouth. Then he sat up and picked up his cup of tea. He sipped, swallowed, and said: 'Good morning, dear.'

'Morning.' Ellen Hamilton sat on the edge of the twin bed, wearing a silk robe, perching her cup on one slender knee. She had brushed her hair already. Her nightwear was as elegant as the rest of her large wardrobe, despite the fact that only he ever saw it, and he was not interested. That did not matter, he surmised: it was not that she wanted men to desire her – only that she should be able to think of herself as desirable.

He finished his tea and swung his legs to the floor. His ulcer protested at the sudden movement, and he winced with pain.

Ellen said: 'Again?'

He nodded. 'Brandy last night. Ought to know better.'

Her face was expressionless. 'I suppose it has nothing to do with yesterday's half-year results.'

He heaved himself to his feet and walked slowly across the expanse of oyster-coloured carpet to the bathroom. The face he saw in the mirror was round and red, balding, with rolls of fat under the jaw. He examined his morning beard, pulling the loose skin this way and that to make the bristles stand up. He began to shave. He had done this every day for the last forty years, and still he found it tiresome.

Yes, the half-year results were bad. Hamilton Holdings was in trouble.

# Paper Money

When he had inherited Hamilton Printing from his father it had been efficient, successful, and profitable. Jasper Hamilton had been a printer – fascinated by typefaces, keen on the new technology, loving the oily smell of the presses. His son was a businessman. He had taken the flow of profits from the works and diverted it into more businesses – wine importing, retailing, publishing, paper mills, commercial radio. This had achieved its primary purpose of turning income into wealth and thereby avoiding tax. Instead of Bibles and paperbacks and posters, he had concerned himself with liquidity and yields. He had bought up companies and started new enterprises, building an empire.

The continuing success of the original business disguised the flimsiness of the superstructure for a long time. But when the printing complex weakened, Hamilton discovered that most of his other businesses were marginal; that he had underestimated the capital investment needed to nurse them to maturity; and that some of them were very long-term indeed. He sold forty-nine per cent of his equity in each of the companies, then transferred his stock to a holding company and sold forty-nine per cent of that. He raised more money, and negotiated an overdraft running into seven figures. The borrowing kept the organization alive, but the interest – rising fast through the decade – ate up what little profit there was.

Meanwhile, Derek Hamilton cultivated an ulcer.

The rescue programme had been inaugurated almost a year ago. Credit had been tightened in an attempt to reduce the overdraft; costs had been cut by every means possible from cancellation of advertising campaigns to utilization of print-roll off-cuts for stationery. Hamilton was running a tight ship now; but inflation and the economic slump ran faster. The six-month results had been expected to show the world that Hamilton Holdings had turned the corner. Instead they demonstrated further decline.

He patted his face dry with a warm towel, splashed on cologne, and returned to the bedroom. Ellen was dressed, sitting in front of the mirror, making up her face. She always managed to dress and undress while her husband was out of the bedroom: it occurred to him that he had not seen her naked for years. He wondered why. Had she run to seed, the fifty-five-year-old skin wrinkling and the once-firm flesh sagging? Would nakedness destroy the illusion of desirability? Perhaps; but he suspected something more complex. It was obscurely connected with the way his own body had aged, he thought, as he climbed into his cavernous underpants. She was always decently clad; therefore he never lusted after her; therefore she never had to reveal how undesirable *she* found *him*. Such a combination of deviousness and sensitivity would be characteristic.

She said: 'What are you going to do?'

The question caught him off balance. He thought at first that she must know what he was thinking, and be referring to that; then he realized she was continuing the conversation about the business. He fastened his braces, wondering what to tell her. 'I'm not sure,' he said eventually.

She peered closely into the mirror, doing something to her eyelashes. 'Sometimes I wonder what you want out of life.'

He stared at her. Her upbringing had taught her to be indirect and never to ask personal questions, for seriousness and emotion spoiled parties and caused ladies to faint. It would have cost her considerable effort to enquire about the purpose of someone's existence.

He sat on the edge of his bed and spoke to her back. 'I must cut out brandy, that's all.'

'I'm sure you know it has nothing to do with what you eat and drink.' She applied lipstick, contorting her mouth to spread it evenly. 'It began nine years ago, and your father died ten years ago.'

'I've got printing ink in my blood.' The response came formally, like a catechism. The conversation would have seemed dislocated to an eavesdropper, but they knew its logic. There was a code: the death of his father meant his assumption of control of the business; his ulcer meant his business problems.

She said: 'You *haven't* got ink in your veins. Your father had, but *you* can't stand the smell of the old works.'

'I inherited a strong business, and I want to bequeath to my sons an even stronger one. Isn't that what people of our class are supposed to do with their lives?'

'Our sons aren't interested in what we leave them. Michael is building his own business from scratch, and all Andrew wants to do is vaccinate the whole of the African continent against chicken pox.'

He could not tell how serious she was now. The things she was doing to her face made her expression unreadable. No doubt it was deliberate. Almost everything she did was deliberate.

He said: 'I have a duty. I employ more than two thousand people, and many more jobs are directly dependent upon the health of my companies.'

'I think you've done your duty. You kept the firm going during a time of crisis – not everyone managed that. You've sacrificed your health to it; and you've given it ten years of your life, and ... God knows what else.' Her voice dropped on the final phrase, as if at the last minute she regretted saying it.

'Should I give it my pride as well?' he said. He carried on dressing, tying a tight little knot in his tie. 'I've turned a jobbing printer's into one of the thousand biggest companies in the country. My business is worth five times what my father's was. I put it together, and I have to make it work.'

'You have to do better than your father.'

'Is that such a poor ambition?'

'Yes!' Her sudden vehemence was a shock. 'You should want good health, and long life, and – and my happiness.'

'If the company was prosperous, perhaps I could sell it. As things are, I wouldn't get its asset value.' He looked at his watch. 'I must go down.'

He descended the broad staircase. A portrait of his father dominated the hall. People often thought it was Derek at fifty. In fact it was Jasper at sixty-five. The phone on the hall stand shrilled as he passed. He ignored it: he did not take calls in the morning.

He went into the small dining room – the large one was reserved for parties, which were rare these days. The circular table was laid with silver cutlery. An elderly woman in an apron brought in half a grapefruit in a bone china dish.

'Not today, Mrs Tremlett,' he told her. 'Just a cup of tea, please.' He picked up the *Financial Times*.

The woman hesitated, then put the dish down in Ellen's place. Hamilton glanced up. 'Just take it away, will you?' he said irritably. 'Serve Mrs Hamilton's breakfast when Mrs Hamilton comes down, and not before, please.'

'Very good,' Mrs Tremlett murmured. She took the grapefruit away.

When Ellen came in she picked up the argument where they had left it. 'I don't think it matters whether you get five million or five hundred thousand for the company. Either way we'd be better off than we are now. Since we don't live comfortably, I fail to see the point of being comfortably off.'

He put down the paper and looked at her. She was wearing an original tailored suit in a cream-coloured fabric, with a printed silk blouse and handmade shoes. He said: 'You have a pleasant home, with a small staff. You've friends here, and a social life in town when you care to take advantage of it. This morning you're wearing several hundred pounds' worth of clothes, and you'll probably go no farther than the village. Sometimes I wonder what *you* want out of life.'

She blushed – a rare event. 'I'll tell you,' she began.

There was a knock at the door, and a good-looking man came in, wearing an overcoat and carrying a cap. 'Good morning, sir, madam,' he said. 'If we're to catch the seven forty-five, sir . . .'

Hamilton said: 'All right, Pritchard. Just wait in the hall.'

'Very good, sir. May I ask if you'll be using the car today, madam?'

Hamilton looked at Ellen. She kept her eyes on her dish as she said: 'I expect so, yes.'

Pritchard nodded and went out.

Hamilton said: 'You were about to tell me what you want out of life.'

'I don't think it's a breakfast-table subject, especially when you're rushing to catch a train.'

'Very well.' He stood up. 'Enjoy your drive. Don't go too fast.'

'What?'

'Drive carefully.'

'Oh. Oh, Pritchard drives me.'

He bent to kiss her cheek, but she turned her face to him and kissed his lips. When he pulled away, her face was flushed. She held his arm and said: 'I want you, Derek.'

He stared at her.

'I want us to spend a long, contented retirement together,' she went on, speaking hurriedly. 'I want you to relax, and eat the right food, and grow healthy and slim again. I want the man who came courting in an open-top Riley, and the man who came back from the war with medals and married me, and the man who held my hand when I bore my children. I want to love *you.*'

He stood nonplussed. She had never been like this with him, never. He felt hopelessly incapable of dealing with it. He did not know what to say, what to do, where to look. He said: 'I . . . must catch the train.'

She regained her composure quickly. 'Yes. You must hurry.'

He looked at her a moment longer, but she would not meet his eyes. He said: 'Um . . . good-bye.'

She nodded dumbly.

He went out. He put on his hat in the hall, then let Pritchard open the front door for him. The dark-blue Mercedes stood on the gravel drive, gleaming in the sunshine. Pritchard must wash it every morning before I get up, Hamilton thought.

The conversation with Ellen had been most peculiar, he decided, as they drove to the railway station. Through the window he watched the play of sunlight on the already-browning leaves, and ran over the key scenes in his mind. *I want to love you*, she had said, with the emphasis on *you*. Talking of the things he had sacrificed for the business, she had said *and God knows what else*.

*I want to love you, not someone else.* Was that what she meant? Had he lost the fidelity of his wife, as well as his health? Perhaps she simply wanted him to think she might be having an affair. That was more like Ellen. She dealt in subtleties. Cries for help were not her style.

After the six-month results, he needed domestic problems like a creditors' meeting.

There was something else. She had blushed when Pritchard asked if she would be using the car; then, hastily, she had said *Pritchard drives me*.

Hamilton said: 'Where do you take Mrs Hamilton, Pritchard?'

'She drives herself, sir. I make myself useful around the house – there's always plenty—'

'Yes, all right,' Hamilton interrupted. 'This isn't a time-and-motion study. I was only curious.'

'Sir.'

His ulcer stabbed him. Tea, he thought: I should drink milk in the morning.

# Chapter Six

Herbert Chieseman switched on the light, silenced the alarm clock, turned up the volume of the radio which had been playing all night, and pressed the rewind button of the reel-to-reel tape recorder. Then he got out of bed.

He put the kettle on, and stared out of the studio apartment window while he waited for the seven-hour tape to return to the start. The morning was clear and bright. The sun would be strong later, but now it was chilly. He put on trousers and a sweater over the underwear he had worn in bed, and stepped into carpet slippers.

His home was a single large room in a north London Victorian house which was past its best. The furniture, the Ascot heater, and the old gas cooker belonged to the landlord. The radio was Herbert's. His rent included the use of a communal bathroom and – most important – exclusive use of the attic.

The radio dominated the room. It was a powerful VHF receiver, made from parts he had carefully selec-ted in half a dozen shops along Tottenham Court Road. The aerial was in the roof loft. The tape deck was also homemade.

He poured tea into a cup, added condensed milk from a tin, and sat at his work table. Apart from the electronic equipment, the table bore only a telephone, a ruled exercise book, and a ballpoint pen. He opened the book at a clean page and wrote the date at the top in a large, cursive script. Then he reduced the volume of the radio and began to play the night's tape at high speed. Each time a high-pitched squeal indicated that there was speech on the recording, he slowed the reel with his finger until he could distinguish the words.

'... car proceed to Holloway Road, the bottom end, to assist PC ...'

'... Ludlow Road, West Five, a Mrs Shaftesbury – sounds like a domestic, Twenty-One ...'

'... Inspector says if that Chinese is still open he'll have chicken fried rice with chips ...'

'... Holloway Road get a move on, that PC's in trouble ...'

Herbert stopped the tape and made a note.

'... reported burglary of a house – that's near Wimbledon Common, Jack ...'

'... Eighteen, do you read ...'

'... any cars Lee area free to assist Fire Brigade at twenty-two Feather Street ...'

Herbert made another note.

'... Eighteen, do you read ...'

'... I don't know, give her an aspirin ...'

'... assault with a knife, not serious ...'

'... where the hell have you been, Eighteen ...'

Herbert's attention strayed to the photograph on

the mantelpiece above the boarded-in fireplace. The picture was flattering: Herbert had known this, twenty years ago, when she had given it to him; but now he had forgotten. Oddly, he did not think of her as she really had been, any more. When he remembered her he visualized a woman with flawless skin and hand-tinted cheeks, posing before a faded panorama in a photographer's studio.

'... theft of one colour television and damage to a plate-glass window ...'

He had been the first among his circle of friends to 'lose the wife', as they would put it. Two or three of them had suffered the tragedy since: one had become a cheerful drunkard, another had married a widow. Herbert had buried his head in his hobby, radio. He began listening to police broadcasts during the day when he did not feel well enough to go to work, which was quite often.

'... Grey Avenue, Golders Green, reported assault ...'

One day, after hearing the police talk about a bank raid, he had telephoned the *Evening Post*. A reporter had thanked him for the information and taken his name and address. The raid had been a big one – a quarter of a million pounds – and the story was on the front page of the *Post* that evening. Herbert had been proud to have given them the tip-off, and told the story in three pubs that night. Then he forgot about it. Three months later he got a cheque for fifty pounds from the newspaper. With the cheque was a statement which read: 'Two shot in £250,000 raid' and gave the date of the robbery.

'. . . leave it out, Charlie, if she won't make a complaint, forget it . . .'

The following day Herbert had stayed at home and phoned the *Post* every time he picked something up on the police wavelength. That afternoon he got a call from a man who said he was deputy news editor, who explained just what the paper wanted from people like Herbert. He was told not to report an assault unless a gun was used or someone was killed; not to bother with burglaries unless the address was in Belgravia, Chelsea, or Kensington; not to report robberies except when weapons were used or very large amounts of cash stolen.

'. . . proceed to twenty-three, Narrow Road, and wait . . .'

He got the idea quickly, because he was not stupid, and the *Post*'s news values were far from subtle. Soon he realized he was earning slightly more on his 'sick' days than when he went to work. What was more, he preferred listening to the radio to making boxes for cameras. So he gave in his notice, and became what the newspaper called an earwig.

'. . . better give me that description now . . .'

After he had been working full-time on the radio for a few weeks the deputy news editor came to his house – it was before he moved to the studio apartment – to talk to him. The newspaperman said Herbert's work was very useful to the paper, and how would he like to work for them exclusively? That would mean Herbert would phone tips only to the *Post*, and not to other papers. But he would get a weekly retainer to make up for the loss of income. Herbert did not say that he never had phoned any other papers. He accepted the offer graciously.

'. . . sit tight and we'll get you some assistance in a few minutes . . .'

Over the years he had improved both his equipment and his understanding of what the newspaper wanted. He learned that they were grateful for more or less anything early in the morning, but as the day wore on they became more choosy, until by about three p.m. nothing less than murder in the street or large-scale robbery with violence interested them. He also discovered that the paper, like the police, was a lot less interested in a crime done to a coloured man in a coloured area. Herbert thought this quite reasonable, since he, as an *Evening Post* reader, was not much interested in what the wogs did to each other in their own parts of London; and he surmised, correctly, that the reason the *Post* was not interested was simply that people like Herbert who bought the *Post* weren't interested. And he learned to read between the lines of police jargon: knew when an assault was trivial or a complaint domestic; heard the note of urgency in the operations-room sergeant's voice when a call for assistance was desperate; discovered how to switch his mind off when they decided to read out great lists of stolen-car numbers over the air.

The speeded-up sound of his own alarm clock came out of the big speaker, and he turned the deck off. He increased the volume on the radio, then dialled the *Post*'s number. He sipped his tea while he waited for an answer.

'*Post*, g'morning.' It was a man's voice.

'Copytakers, please,' Herbert said. There was another pause.

'Copy.'

'Hello. Chieseman here, timing at oh seven fifty-nine.'

There was a clatter of typewriters in the background. 'Hello, Bertie. Anything doing?'

'Seems to have been a quiet night,' Herbert said.

# Eight a.m.

# Chapter Seven

Tony Cox stood in a phone booth on the corner of Quill Street, Bethnal Green, with the receiver to his ear. He was perspiring inside the warm coat with the velvet collar. In his hand he held the end of a chain which was attached to the collar of the dog outside. The dog was sweating, too.

The phone at the other end of the line was answered, and Tony pressed a coin into the slot.

A voice said: 'Yes?' in the tone of one who is not really accustomed to these new-fangled telephones.

Tony spoke curtly. 'It's today. Get it together.' He hung up without giving his name or waiting for an answer.

He strode off along the narrow pavement, pulling the dog behind him. It was a pedigree boxer with a trim, powerful body, and Tony continually had to yank at the chain to make it keep pace. The dog was strong, but its master was a great deal stronger.

The doors of the old terraced houses gave directly on to the street. Tony stopped at the one outside which was parked the grey Rolls-Royce. He pushed the house door open. It was never locked, for the occupants had no fear of thieves.

There was a smell of cooking in the little house. Pulling the dog behind him, Tony went into the kitchen and sat on a chair. He unhooked the chain from the dog's collar and sent it away with a hefty slap on the rump. He stood up and took off his coat.

A kettle was warming on the gas cooker, and there was sliced bacon on a piece of greaseproof paper. Tony opened a drawer and took out a kitchen knife with a ten-inch blade. He tested the edge with his thumb, decided it needed sharpening, and went out into the yard.

There was an old grinding wheel in the lean-to shed. Tony sat beside it on a wooden stool and worked the treadle, the way he had seen the old man do it years ago. It made Tony feel good to do things the way his father had. He pictured him: a tall man, and handsome, with wavy hair and glittering eyes, making sparks with the grinder while his children shrieked with laughter. He had been a stallholder in a street market, selling china and saucepans, calling his wares in that strong, carrying voice. He used to make a performance of pretending to needle the grocer next to him, shouting: 'There y'are, I just sold a pot for half a nicker. How many spuds d'you sell afore you take ten bob?' He could spot a strange woman yards away, and would use his good looks shamelessly. 'I tell you what, darling—' this to a middle-aged woman in a hairnet '—we don't get many beautiful young girls down this end of the market, so I'm going to sell you this at a loss and hope you'll come back.

Look at it – solid copper bottom, if you'll pardon the word, and it's my last one; I've made my profit on the rest, so you can have it for two quid, half what I paid for it, just because you made an old man's heart beat faster, and take it quick afore I change my mind.'

Tony had been shocked by the speed at which the old man changed after the one lung went. His hair turned white, the cheeks sank between the bones, and the fine voice went high and whining. The stall was rightfully Tony's, but by then he had his own sources of income, so he had let it go to young Harry, his dumb brother, who had married a beautiful White-chapel girl with the patience to learn how to talk with her hands. It took guts for a dumb man to run a market stall, writing on a blackboard when he needed to speak to the customers, and keeping in his pocket a plain postcard bearing the word THANKS in capital letters to flash when a sale was made. But he ran it well, and Tony lent him the money to move into a proper shop and hire a manager, and he made a success of that, too. Guts – they ran in the family.

The kitchen knife was sharp enough. He tested it and cut his thumb. Holding it to his lips, he went into the kitchen.

His mother was there. Lillian Cox was short and a little overweight – her son had inherited the tendency to plumpness without the shortness – and she had much more energy than the average sixty-three-year-old. She said: 'I'm doing you a bit of fried bread.'

'Lovely.' He put the knife down and found a

bandage. 'Take care with that knife – I done it a bit too sharp.'

She fussed over his cut, then, making him hold it under the cold tap and count to one hundred, then putting on antiseptic cream, and gauze, and finally a roll of bandage held with a safety pin. He stood still and let her do what she wished.

She said: 'Ah, but you're a good boy to sharpen the knives for me. Where you been so early, anyhow?'

'Took the dog up the park. And I had to ring someone up.'

She made a disgusted noise. 'I don't know what's wrong with the phone in the parlour, I'm sure.'

He leaned over the cooker to sniff the frying bacon. 'You know how it is, Mum. The Old Bill listen to that one.'

She put a teapot in his hand. 'Go in there and pour the tea out, then.'

He took the pot into the living room and put it down on a mat. The square table was laid with an embroidered cloth, cutlery for two, salt and pepper and sauce bottles.

Tony sat nearest the fireplace, where the old man used to sit. From there he reached into the sideboard and took out two cups and two saucers. He pictured the old man again, overseeing mealtimes with the back of his hand and a good deal of rhyming slang. 'Get your chalks off the Cain,' he would bark if they put their arms on the table. The only thing Tony held against him was the way he treated Mum. Being so handsome and that, he had a few women on the side, and at times he would spend his money buying them gin instead of bringing it home. Those times, Tony and his brother would go up the Smithfield market, stealing scraps from under the tables to sell to the soap factory for a few coppers. And he never went in the Army – but then, a lot of wide boys went on the trot in wartime.

'What are you going to do – go back to sleep, or pour that tea out?' Lillian put a plate in front of Tony and sat down opposite him. 'Never mind, I'll do it now.'

Tony picked up his cutlery, holding his knife like a pencil, and began to eat. There were sausages, two fried eggs, a mess of canned tomatoes, and several slices of fried bread. He took a mouthful before reaching for the brown sauce. He was hungry after his morning's exertions.

His mother passed him his tea. She said: 'I don't know, we was never afraid to use the phone when your father was alive, God rest his soul. He was careful to stay out of the way of the Old Bill.'

Tony thought they had had no phone in his father's day, but he let that pass. He said: 'Yeah. He was so careful, he died a pauper.'

'But an honest one.'

'Was he?'

'You know bloody well he was, and never let me hear you say no different.'

'I don't like you to swear, Mum.'

'You shouldn't provoke me.'

Tony ate silently and finished quickly. He emptied his teacup and began to unwrap a cigar.

His mother picked up his cup. 'More tea?'

He looked at his watch. 'No, thanks. I've got a couple of things to do.' He set fire to the cigar and stood up. 'That's set me up lovely, that breakfast.'

She narrowed her eyes. 'Are you having a tickle?'

This annoyed him. He blew smoke into the air. 'Who needs to know?'

'It's your life. Go on, then, I'll see you later. Mind you look after yourself.'

He looked at her a moment longer. Although she gave in to him, she was a strong woman. She had led the family since the old man went: mending marriages, borrowing from one son to lend to another, giving advice, using her disapproval as a powerful sanction. She had resisted all efforts to move her from Quill Street to a nice little bungalow in Bournemouth, suspecting – rightly – that the old house and its memories were a potent symbol of her authority. Once, there had been queenly arrogance in her high-bridged nose and pointed chin; now, she was regal but resigned, like an abdicated monarch; knowing she was wise to release the reins of power, but regretting it all the same. Tony realized that this was why she needed him: he was king now, and having him to live with her kept her close to the throne. He loved her for needing him. No one else needed him.

She stood up. 'Well, are you going?'

# Paper Money

'Yes.' He realized he had been lost in thought. He put an arm around her shoulders and squeezed briefly. He never kissed her. 'Ta-ta, Mum.' He picked up his coat, patted the dog, and went out.

The interior of the Rolls was hot. He pressed the button that lowered the window before settling himself in the leather seat and pulling away.

He took pleasure in the car as he threaded it through the narrow East End streets. Its shameless luxury, in contrast with the mean streets and undignified old houses, told the story of Tony Cox's life. People looked at the car – housewives, paperboys, working men, villains – and said to each other: 'There's Tony Cox. He did well.'

He flicked cigar ash through the open window. He *had* done well. He had bought his first car for six pounds when he was sixteen years old. The blank Ministry of Transport certificate had cost him thirty shillings on the black market. He filled in the blanks and resold the car for eighty pounds.

Before long he had a used car lot which he gradually turned into a legitimate business. Then he sold it, with the stock, for five thousand pounds, and went into the long firm racket.

He used the five thousand to open a bank account, giving as a reference the name of the man who had bought the car lot. He told the bank manager his real name, but gave a false address – the same false address he had given the purchaser of the car business.

He took a lease on a warehouse, paying three

# Ken Follett

months' rent in advance. He bought small quantities of radio, television, and hi-fi equipment from manufacturers and resold it to shops in London. He paid suppliers on the dot, and his bank account was busy. Within a couple of months he was making a small loss, and had a reputation for credit-worthiness.

At that point he made a series of very large orders. Small manufacturers to whom he had promptly paid a couple of bills of five hundred pounds each were glad to supply him with three or four thousand pounds' worth of goods on the same credit terms: he looked like becoming a good customer.

With a warehouse full of expensive electronic gadgetry for which he had paid nothing, he held a sale. Record players, colour television sets, digital clocks, tape decks, amplifiers, and radios went for knockdown prices, sometimes as little as half their retail value. In two days the warehouse was empty and Tony Cox had three thousand pounds in cash in two suitcases. He locked the warehouse and went home.

He shivered in the front seat of the warm car as he remembered. He would never take risks like those again. Suppose one of the suppliers had got wind of the sale? Suppose the bank manager had seen Tony in a pub a few days later?

He still did the occasional long firm, but these days he used front men, who took long holidays in Spain as soon as the axe fell. And *nobody* saw Tony's face.

However, his business interests had diversified. He owned property in Central London which he let to young ladies at extremely high rents; he ran night-clubs; he even managed a couple of pop groups. Some of his projects were legitimate, some criminal; some were a mixture, and others were on the nebulous borderline between the two, where the law is unsure of itself but respectable businessmen with reputations to worry about fear to tread.

The Old Bill knew about him, of course. There were so many grasses about nowadays that nobody could become a respected villain without his name going into a file at Scotland Yard. But getting evidence was the problem, especially with a few detectives around who were prepared to warn Tony in advance of a raid. The money he spent in that direction was never skimped. Every August there were three or four police families in Benidorm on Tony's money.

Not that he trusted them. They were useful, but they were all telling themselves that one day they would repay their debt of loyalty by turning him in. A bent copper was still, ultimately, a copper. So all transactions were cash; no books were kept, except in Tony's head; all jobs were done by his cronies on verbal instructions.

Increasingly, he played even safer by simply acting as a banker. A draftsman would get some inside information and dream up a plan; then he would recruit a villain to organize the equipment and manpower. The two of them would then come to Tony and tell him the plan. If he liked it, he would lend them the money for bribes, guns, motor cars, explosives, and anything else they needed. When they had done the job they would repay the loan five or six times over out of the proceeds.

Today's job was not so simple. He was draftsman as well as banker for this one. It meant he had to be extra careful.

He stopped the car in a back street and got out. Here the houses were larger – they had been built for foremen and craftsmen rather than dockers and labourers – but they were no more sound than the hovels of Quill Street. The concrete facings were cracking, the wooden window frames were rotten, and the front gardens were smaller than the boot of Tony's car. Only about half of them were lived in: the rest were warehouses, offices, or shops.

The door Tony knocked on bore the sign 'Billiards and Snooker' with most of the 'and' missing. It was opened immediately and he stepped inside.

He shook hands with Walter Burden then followed him upstairs. A road accident had left Walter with a limp and a stammer, depriving him of his job as a docker. Tony had given him the managership of the billiards hall, knowing that the gesture – which cost Tony nothing – would be rewarded by increased respect among East Enders and undying loyalty on Walter's part.

Walter said: 'Want a cup of tea, Tony?'

'No, thanks, Walter, I just had my breakfast.' He looked around the first-floor hall with a proprietorial air. The tables were covered, the linoleum floor swept, the cues racked neatly. 'You keep the place nice.'

'Only doing my job, Tone. You looked after me, see.'

'Yeah.' Cox went to the window and looked down on the street. A blue Morris 1100 was parked a few yards away on the opposite side of the road. There were two people in it. Tony felt curiously satisfied: he had been right to take this precaution. 'Where's the phone, Walter?'

'In the office.' Walter opened a door, ushered Tony in, and closed it, staying outside.

The office was tidy and clean. Tony sat at the desk and dialled a number.

A voice said: 'Yeah?'

'Pick me up,' Tony said.

'Five minutes.'

Tony hung up. His cigar had gone out. When things made him nervous, he let his smoke go out. He relit it with a gold Dunhill, then went out.

He showed himself at the window again. 'All right, mate, I'm off,' he said to Walter. 'If one of the young detective-constables in the blue car takes it into his head to knock on the door, don't answer it. I'll be about half an hour.'

'Don't w-worry. You can rely on me, you know that.' Walter nodded his head like a bird.

'Yeah, I know.' Tony touched the old man's shoulder briefly, then went to the back of the hall. He opened the door and trotted rapidly down the fire escape.

He picked his way around a rusting baby carriage, a sodden mattress, and three fifths of an old car. Weeds sprouted stubbornly in the cracked concrete of the yard. A grubby cat scampered out of his way. His Italian shoes got dirty.

A gate led from the yard to a narrow lane. Tony walked to the end of the lane. As he got there, a small red Fiat with three men in it drew up at the kerb. Tony got in and sat in the empty seat in the back. The car pulled away immediately.

The driver was Jacko, Tony's first lieutenant. Beside Jacko was Deaf Willie, who knew more about explosives now than he had twenty years ago when he lost his left eardrum. In the back with Tony was Peter 'Jesse' James, whose two obsessions were firearms and girls with fat bottoms. They were good men; all permanent members of Tony's firm.

Tony said: 'How's the boy, Willie?

Deaf Willie turned his good ear towards Tony. 'What?'

'I said, how's young Billy?'

'Eighteen today,' Willie said. 'He's the same, Tone. He'll never be able to look after hisself. The social worker told us to think about putting him in a home.'

Tony tutted sympathetically. He went out of his way to be kind to Deaf Willie's half-witted son; mental illness frightened him. 'You don't want to do that.'

Willie said: 'I said to the wife, what does a social

worker know? This one's a girl of about twenty. Been to college. Still, she don't push herself.'

Jacko broke in impatiently. 'We're all set, Tony. The lads are there, the motors are ready.'

'Good.' Tony looked at Jesse James. 'Shooters?'

'Got a couple of shotguns and an Uzi.'

'A what?'

Jesse grinned proudly. 'It's a nine-millimetre machine pistol. Israeli.'

'Stroll on,' Tony muttered.

Jacko said: 'Here we are.'

Tony took a cloth cap from his pocket and fixed it on his head. 'You've put the lads indoors, have you?'

'Yes,' Jacko said.

'I don't mind them knowing it's a Tony Cox job, but I don't want them to be able to say they saw me.'

'I know.'

The car pulled into a scrap yard. It was a remarkably tidy yard. The shells of cars were piled three high in orderly lines, and component parts were stacked neatly round about: pillars of tyres, a pyramid of rear axles, a cube of cylinder blocks.

Near the gateway were a crane and a long car transporter. Farther in, a plain blue Ford van with double rear wheels stood next to the yard's heavy-duty oxy-acetylene cutting gear.

The car stopped and Tony got out. He was pleased. He liked things neat. The other three stood around, waiting for him to do something. Jacko lit a cigarette.

Tony said: 'Did you fix the owner of the yard?'

Jacko nodded. 'He made sure the crane, the transporter, and the cutting gear were here. But he doesn't know what they're for, and we've tied him up, just for the sake of appearances.' He started to cough.

Tony took the cigarette out of Jacko's mouth and dropped it in the mud. 'Those things make you cough,' he said. He took a cigar from his pocket. 'Smoke this and die old.'

Tony walked back towards the yard gate. The three men followed. Tony trod gingerly around potholes and swampy patches, past a stack of thousands of lead-acid accumulators, between mounds of drive shafts and gearboxes, to the crane. It was a smallish model, on caterpillar tracks, capable of lifting a car, a van, or a light truck. He unbuttoned his overcoat and climbed the ladder to the high cab.

He sat in the operator's seat. The all-round windows enabled him to see the whole of the yard. It was triangular in plan. One side was a railway viaduct, its brick arches filled in by storerooms. A high wall on the adjacent side separated the yard from a playground and a bomb site. The road ran along the front of the yard, curving slightly as it followed the bend of the river a few yards beyond. It was a wide road, but little used.

In the lee of the viaduct was a hut made of old wooden doors supporting a tar-paper roof. The men would be in there, huddled around an electric fire, drinking tea and smoking nervously.

Everything was right. Tony felt elation rise in his

belly as instinct told him it would work. He climbed out of the crane.

He deliberately kept his voice low, steady and casual. 'This van doesn't always go the same route. There are lots of ways from the City to Loughton. But this place is on most of the routes, right? They got to pass here unless they want to go via Birmingham or Watford. Now, they do go daft ways occasionally. Today might be one of those days. So, if it doesn't come off, just give the lads a bonus and send them home until next time.'

Jacko said: 'They all know the score.'

'Good. Anything else?'

The three men were silent.

Tony gave his final instructions. 'Everybody wears a mask. Everybody wears gloves. Nobody speaks.' He looked to each man in turn for acknowledgement. Then he said: 'Okay, take me back.'

There was no conversation as the red Fiat wound its way through the little streets to the lane behind the billiard hall.

Tony got out, then leaned on the front passenger door and spoke through the open window. 'It's a good plan, and if you do right, it will work. There's a couple of wrinkles you don't know about – safeguards, inside men. Keep calm, do good, and we'll have it away.' He paused. 'And don't shoot nobody with that bleeding tommy-gun, for fuck's sake.'

He walked up the lane and entered the billiard hall by the back door. Walter was playing billiards at one of the tables. He straightened up when he heard the door.

'All right, Tone?'

Tony went to the window. 'Did pally stay put?' He could see the blue Morris in the same place.

'Yes. They've been smoking theirself to death.'

It was fortunate, Tony thought, that the law did not have enough manpower to watch him at night as well as in the day. The nine-to-five surveillance was quite useful, for it permitted him to establish alibis without seriously restricting his activities. One of these days they would start following him twenty-four hours a day. But he would have plenty of advance notice of that.

Walter jerked a thumb at the table. 'Fancy a break?'

'No.' Tony left the window. 'I got a busy day.' He went down the stairs, and Walter hobbled after him.

'Ta-ta, Walter,' he said as he went out into the street.

'So long, Tony,' Walter said. 'God bless you, boy.'

# Chapter Eight

The newsroom came to life suddenly. At eight o'clock it had been as still as a morgue, the quietness broken only by inanimate sounds like the stuttering of the teleprinter and the rustle of the newspapers Cole was reading. Now three copytakers were pounding the keys, a Lad was whistling a pop song, and a photographer in a leather coat was arguing with a sub-editor about a football match. The reporters were drifting in. Most of them had an early-morning routine, Cole had observed: one bought tea, another lit a cigarette, another turned to page three of the *Sun* to look at the nude; each using an habitual crutch to help him start the day.

Cole believed in letting people sit down for a few minutes before setting them to work: it made for an atmosphere of order and cool-headedness. His news editor, Cliff Poulson, had a different approach. Poulson, with his froglike green eyes and Yorkshire accent, liked to say: 'Don't take your coat off, lad.' His delight in snap decisions, his perpetual hurry, and his brittle air of bonhomie created a frenetic atmosphere. Poulson was a speed freak. Cole did not reckon a story had ever missed an edition because someone took a minute out to think about it.

Kevin Hart had been here for five minutes now. He was reading the *Mirror*, with one hip perched on the edge of a desk, the trousers of his striped suit falling gracefully. Cole called out to him. 'Give the Yard a ring, please, Kevin.' The young man picked up a telephone.

The Bertie Chieseman tips were on his desk: a thick wad of copy. Cole looked around. Most of the reporters were in. It was time to get them working. He sorted through the tips, impaling some on a sharp metal spike, handing others to reporters with brief instructions. 'Anna, a PC got into trouble in the Holloway Road – ring the nearest nick and find out what it was all about. If it's drunks, forget it. Joe, this fire in the East End – check with the Brigade. A burglary in Chelsea, Phillip. Look up the address in Kelly's Directory in case anyone famous lives there. Barney – "Police pursued and arrested an Irishman after calling at a house in Queenstown Street, Camden." Ring the Yard and ask them if it's anything to do with the IRA.'

An internal phone beeped and he lifted it. 'Arthur Cole.'

'What have you got for me, Arthur?'

Cole recognized the voice of the picture editor. He said: 'At the moment, it looks as though the splash will be last night's vote in the Commons.'

'But that was on the television yesterday!'

'Did you call to ask me things or tell me things?'

'I suppose I'd better have somebody at Downing Street for a today picture of the Prime Minister. Anything else?'

'Nothing that isn't in the morning papers.'

'Thank you, Arthur.'

Cole hung up. It was poor, to be leading on a yesterday story. He was doing his best to update it – two reporters were ringing around for reactions. They were getting backbench MPs to shoot off their mouths, but no Ministers.

A middle-aged reporter with a pipe called out: 'Mrs Poulson just rang. Cliff won't be in today. He's got Delhi belly.'

Cole groaned. 'How did he catch that in Orpington?'

'Curry supper.'

'Okay.' That was clever, Cole thought. It looked like being the dullest day for news in the month, and Poulson was off sick. With the assistant news editor on holiday, Cole was on his own.

Kevin Hart approached the desk. 'Nothing from the Yard,' he said. 'It's been quiet all night.'

Cole looked up. Hart was about twenty-three and very tall, with curly fair hair which he wore long. Cole suppressed a spasm of irritation. 'That is ridiculous,' he said. 'Scotland Yard never has a completely quiet night. What's the matter with that Press Bureau?'

'We ought to do a story – "London's first crime-free night for a thousand years," ' Hart said with a grin.

His levity annoyed Cole. 'Never be satisfied with that kind of reply from the Yard,' he said coldly.

Hart flushed. It embarrassed him to be lectured like a cub reporter. 'I'll ring them back, shall I?'

'No,' said Cole, seeing that he had made his point. 'I want you to do a story. You know this new oil field in the North Sea?'

Hart nodded. 'It's called Shield.'

'Yes. Later on the Energy Minister is going to announce who has got the licence to develop it. Do a holding piece to run until we get the announcement. Background, what the licence will mean to the people who are bidding, how the Minister makes up his mind. This afternoon we can sling your piece out and leave a hole in the paper for the real news.'

'Okay.' Hart turned away and made for the library. He knew he was being given a dumb job as a kind of punishment, but he took his medicine gracefully, Cole thought. He stared at the boy's back for a moment. He got on Cole's nerves, with his long hair and his suits. He had rather too much self-confidence – but then, reporters needed a lot of cheek.

Cole stood up and went to the sub-editors' table. The deputy chief sub had in front of him the wire service story about the passing of the Industry Bill and the new stuff Cole's reporters had come up with. Cole looked over his shoulder. On a scratch pad he had written:

# Paper Money

## REBEL MPs TOLD
## 'JOIN THE LIBS'

The man scratched his beard and looked up. 'What do you think?'

'It looks like a story about Women's Lib,' Cole said. 'I hate it.'

'So do I.' The sub tore the sheet off the pad, crumpled it, and tossed it in a metal bin. 'What else is new?'

'Nothing. I've only just given out the tips.'

The bearded man nodded and glanced reflexively at the clock hanging from the ceiling in front. 'Let's hope we get something decent for the second.'

Cole leaned over him and wrote on the pad:

## REBEL MPs TOLD
## 'JOIN LIBERALS'

He said: 'It makes more sense, but it's the same count.'

The sub grinned. 'Want a job?'

Cole went back to his desk. Annela Sims came up and said: 'The Holloway Road incident came to nothing. A bunch of rowdies, no arrests.'

Cole said: 'Okay.'

Joe Barnard put down the phone and called: 'There's not a lot to this fire, Arthur. Nobody hurt.'

'How many people living there?' Cole said automatically.

'Two adults, three children.'

'So, it's a family of five escaped death. Write it.'

Phillip Jones said: 'The burgled flat seems to belong to Nicholas Crost, quite a well-known violinist.'

'Good,' Cole said. 'Ring Chelsea nick and find out what was taken.'

'I did already,' Phillip grinned. 'There's a Stradivarius missing.'

Cole smiled. 'Good boy. Write it, then get down there and see if you can interview the heartbroken maestro.'

The phone rang, and Cole picked it up.

Although he would not have admitted it, he was thoroughly enjoying himself.

# Nine a.m.

# Chapter Nine

Tim Fitzpeterson was dry of tears, but the weeping had not helped. He lay on the bed, his face buried in the damp pillow. To move was agony. He tried not to think at all, his mind turning away thoughts like an innkeeper with a full house. At one point his brain switched off completely, and he dozed for a few moments, but the escape from pain and despair was brief, and he woke up again.

He did not rise from the bed because there was nothing he wanted to do, nowhere he could go, nobody he felt he could face. All he could do was think about the promise of joy that had been so false. Cox had been right when he said so coarsely, 'It was the best night's nooky you'll ever have.' Tim could not quite banish the flashing memories of her slim, writhing body; but now they had a dreadfully bitter taste. She had shown him Paradise then slammed the door. She, of course, had been faking ecstasy; but there had been nothing simulated about Tim's own pleasure. A few hours ago he had been contemplating a new life, enhanced by the kind of sexual love he had forgotten existed. Now it was hard to see any point at all in tomorrow.

He could hear the noise of the children in the playground outside, shouting and shrieking and quarrelling; and he envied them the utter triviality of their lives. He pictured himself as a schoolboy, in a black blazer and short grey trousers, walking three miles of Dorset country lanes to get to the one-class primary school. He was the brightest pupil they had ever had, which was not saying much. But they taught him arithmetic and got him a place at the grammar school, and that was all he needed.

He had flourished in the grammar school, he remembered. He had been the leader of the gang, the one who organized playground games and classroom rebellions. Until he got his glasses.

There: he had been trying to remember when in his life he had felt despair like this; and now he knew. It had been the first day he wore his glasses to school. The members of his gang had been at first dismayed, then amused, then scornful. By playtime he was being followed by a crowd chanting 'Four-eyes'. After lunch he tried to organize a football match, but John Willcott said: 'It's not your game.' Tim put his spectacles in their case and punched Willcott's head; but Willcott was big, and Tim, who normally dominated by force of personality, was no fighter. Tim ended up staunching a bloody nose in the cloakroom while Willcott picked teams.

He tried to make a comeback during History, by flicking inky paper pellets at Willcott under the nose of Miss Percival, known as Old Percy. But the normally indulgent Percy decided to have a clampdown that day, and Tim was sent to the headmaster for six of the best. On the way home he had another fight, lost again, and tore his blazer; his mother took the money for a new one out of the nest egg Tim was saving to buy a crystal radio kit, setting him back six months. It was the blackest day of young Tim's life, and his leadership qualities remained stifled until he went to college and joined the Party.

A lost fight, a torn blazer, and six of the best: he could wish for problems like that now. A whistle blew in the playground outside the flat, and the noise of the children ceased abruptly. I could end my troubles that quickly, Tim thought; and the idea appealed.

What was I living for yesterday? he wondered. Good work, my reputation, a successful government; none of these things seemed to matter today. The school whistle meant it was past nine o'clock. Tim should have been chairing a committee meeting to discuss the productivity of different kinds of power station. How could I ever have been interested in anything so meaningless? He thought of his pet project, a forecast of the energy needs of British industry through to the year 2000. He could summon no enthusiasm for it. He thought of his daughters, and dreaded the idea of facing them. Everything turned to ashes in his mouth. What did it matter who would win the next election? Britain's fortunes were determined by forces outside its leaders' control. He had always known it was a game, but he no longer wanted the prizes.

There was nobody he could talk to, nobody. He imagined the conversation with his wife: 'Darling, I've been foolish and disloyal. I was seduced by a whore, a beautiful, supple girl, and blackmailed . . .' Julia would freeze on him. He could see her face, taking on a rigid look of distaste as she withdrew from emotional contact. He would reach out to her with his hand, and she would say: 'Don't touch me.' No, he could not tell Julia; not until he was sure his own wounds had healed – and he did not think he could survive that long.

Anyone else? Cabinet colleagues would say: 'Good God, Tim, old chap – I'm terribly sorry . . .' and immediately begin to map out a fallback position for the time when it got out. They would take care not to be associated with anything he sponsored, not to be seen with him too often; might even make a morality speech to establish Puritan credentials. He did not hate them for what he knew they would do: his prognosis was based on what *he* would do in that situation.

His agent had come close to being a friend, once or twice. But the man was young; he could not know how much depended upon fidelity in a twenty-year-old marriage; he would cynically recommend a thorough cover-up and overlook the damage already done to a man's soul.

His sister, then? An ordinary woman, married to a carpenter, she had always envied Tim a little. She would wallow in it. Tim could not contemplate that.

# Paper Money

His father was dead, his mother senile. Was he that short of friends? What had he done with his life, to be left with no one who would love him right or wrong? Perhaps it was that that kind of commitment was two-way, and he had been careful to see that there was nobody he wouldn't be able to abandon if they became a liability.

There was no support to be had. Only his own resources were available. What do we do, he thought wearily, when we lose the election by a landslide? Regroup, draw up the scenario for the years of opposition, start hacking away at the foundations, use our anger and our disappointment as fuel for the fight. He looked inside himself for courage, and hatred, and bitterness, to enable him to deny the victory to Tony Cox; and found only cowardice and spite. At other times he had lost battles and suffered humiliation, but he was a man, and men had the strength to struggle on, didn't they?

His strength had always come from a certain image of himself: a civilized man, steadfast, trustworthy, loyal, and courageous; able to win with pride and lose with grace. Tony Cox had shown him a new picture; naïve enough to be seduced by an empty-headed girl; weak enough to betray his trust at the first threat of blackmail; frightened enough to crawl on the floor and beg for mercy.

He screwed up his eyes tightly, but still the image invaded his mind. It would be with him for the rest of his life.

But that need not be long.

At last he moved. He sat on the edge of the bed, then stood up. There was blood, his blood, on the sheet, a disgraceful reminder. The sun had moved around the sky, and now shone brightly through the window. Tim would have liked to close the window, but the effort was too much. He hobbled out of the bedroom, and went through the living room into the kitchen. The kettle and the teapot were where *she* had left them after making tea. She had spilled a few leaves carelessly over the Formica counter top, and she had not bothered to put the bottle of milk back into the little fridge.

The first-aid kit was in a high, locked cupboard, where small children could not reach. Tim pulled a stool across the Marley-tiled floor and stood on it. The key was on top of the cupboard. He unlocked the door and took down an old biscuit tin with a picture of Durham Cathedral on the lid.

He got off the stool and put the tin down. Inside he found bandages, a roll of bandage, scissors, antiseptic cream, gripe water for babies, a displaced tube of Ambre Solaire, and a large, full bottle of sleeping tablets. He took out the tablets and replaced the lid. Then he found a glass in another cupboard.

He kept *not* doing things: not putting the milk away, not clearing up the spilled tea leaves, not replacing the first-aid tin, not closing the door of the crockery cupboard. There was no need, he had to keep reminding himself.

He took the glass and the tablets into the living room and put them on his desk. The desk was bare except for a telephone: he always cleared it when he finished working.

He opened the cupboard beneath the television set. Here was the drink he had planned to offer her. There was whisky, gin, dry sherry, a good brandy, and an untouched bottle of *eau de vie prunes* that someone had brought back from the Dordogne. Tim chose the gin, although he did not like it.

He poured some into the glass on the desk, then sat down in the upright chair.

He did not have the will to wait, perhaps years, for the revenge which would restore his self-respect. However, right now he could not harm Cox without doing worse damage to himself. Exposing Cox would expose Tim.

But the dead feel no pain.

He could destroy Cox, and then die.

In the circumstances it seemed the only thing to do.

# Chapter Ten

Derek Hamilton was met at Waterloo Station by another chauffeur, this time in a Jaguar. The Chairman's Rolls-Royce had gone in the economy drive: sadly, the unions had not appreciated the gesture. The chauffeur touched his cap and held the door, and Hamilton got in without speaking.

As the car pulled away he made a decision. He would not go straight to the office. He said: 'Take me to Nathaniel Fett – do you know where it is?'

The chauffeur said: 'Yes, sir.'

They crossed Waterloo Bridge and turned into Aldwych, heading for the City. Hamilton and Fett had both gone to Westminster School: Nathaniel Fett senior had known that his son would not suffer for his Jewishness there, and Lord Hamilton had believed that the school would not turn his son into an upper-class twit – his Lordship's phrase.

The two boys had superficially similar backgrounds. Both had wealthy, dynamic fathers and beautiful mothers; both were from intellectual households where politicians came to dinner; both grew up surrounded by good paintings and unlimited books. Yet, as the friendship grew, and the two young men went to Oxford – Fett to Balliol, Hamilton to Magdalen – the Hamilton house had suffered by the comparison. Derek came to see his own father's intellect as shallow. Old man Fett would tolerantly discuss abstract painting, communism, and be-bop jazz, then tear them to pieces with surgical accuracy. Lord Hamilton held the same conservative views, but expressed them in the thundering clichés of a House of Lords speech.

Derek smiled to himself in the back of the car. He had been too hard on his father; perhaps sons always were. Few men had known more about political skirmishing: the old man's cleverness had given him real power, whereas Nathaniel's father had been too wise ever to wield real influence in affairs of state.

Nathaniel had inherited that wisdom and made a career of it. The stockbroking firm which had been owned by six generations of firstborn sons named Nathaniel Fett had been changed, by the seventh, into a merchant bank. People had always gone to Nathaniel for advice, even at school. Now he advised on mergers, share issues, and take-overs.

The car pulled up. Hamilton said: 'Wait for me, please.'

The offices of Nathaniel Fett were not impressive – the firm had no need to prove itself rich. There was a small nameplate outside a street door near the Bank of England. The entrance was flanked by a sandwich shop on one side and a tobacconist's on the other. A casual observer might have taken it for a small, and none-too-prosperous, insurance or shipping company; but he would not have known how far the premises to either side were occupied by the one firm.

The inside was comfortable, rather than opulent, with air conditioning, concealed lighting, and carpets which had aged well and stopped short of the walls. The same casual observer might have thought that the paintings hanging on the walls were expensive. He would have been right and wrong: they were expensive, but they were not hanging on the walls. They were set into the brickwork behind armoured glass – only the false frames actually hung on top of the wallpaper.

Hamilton was shown straight in to Fett's ground-floor office. Nathaniel was sitting in a club chair reading the *Financial Times*. He stood up to shake hands.

Hamilton said: 'I've never seen you sitting at that desk. Is it just for decoration?'

'Sit down, Derek. Tea, coffee, sherry?'

'A glass of milk, please.'

'If you would, Valerie.' Fett nodded to his secretary and she went out. 'The desk – no, I never use it. Everything I write is dictated; nothing I read is too heavy to hold in my hands; why should I sit at a desk like a clerk in Dickens?'

'So it is for decoration.'

'It's been here longer than I. Too big to get out through the door and too valuable to chop up. I think they built the place around it.'

Hamilton smiled. Valerie brought in his milk and

went out again. He sipped and studied his friend. Fett and his office matched: both were small but not dwarfish, dark but not gloomy, relaxed without being frivolous. The man had heavy-rimmed glasses and brilliantined hair. He wore a club tie, a mark of social acceptability: it was the only Jewish thing about him, Hamilton thought wryly.

He put his glass down and said: 'Were you reading about me?'

'Just skimming. A predictable reaction. Ten years ago, results like that from a company like Hamilton would have made waves from audio shares to zinc prices. Today, it's just another conglomerate in trouble. There's a word for it: recession.'

Hamilton sighed. 'Why do we do it, Nathaniel?'

'I beg your pardon?' Fett was startled.

He shrugged. 'Why do we overwork, lose sleep, risk fortunes?'

'And get ulcers.' Fett smiled, but a subtle change had come over his demeanour. His eyes narrowed behind the pebble-lensed spectacles, and he smoothed the bristly hair at the back of his head in a gesture Hamilton recognized to be defensive. Fett was retreating into his role as a careful adviser, a friendly counsel with an objective viewpoint. But his reply was measuredly casual. 'To make money. What else?'

Hamilton shook his head. His friend always had to be beckoned twice before stepping into deeper water. 'Sixth-form economics,' he said derisively. 'I would have made more profit if I'd sold my inheritance and put it into the Post Office. Most people who own large businesses could live very comfortably for the rest of their lives by doing that. Why do we conserve our fortunes, and try to enlarge them? Is it greed, or power, or adventure? Are we all compulsive gamblers?'

Fett said: 'I suppose Ellen has been saying this kind of thing to you.'

Hamilton laughed. 'You're right, but it pains me that you think I'm incapable of such ponderings on my own.'

'Oh, I don't doubt you mean it. It's just that Ellen has a way of saying what you are thinking. All the same, you wouldn't be repeating these things to me if they hadn't struck a chord.' He paused. 'Derek, be careful not to lose Ellen.'

They stared at one another for a moment, then they both looked away. There was silence. They had reached the limit of intimacy permitted by their friendship.

Eventually Fett said: 'We might get a cheeky bid in the next few days.'

Hamilton was surprised. 'Why?'

'Someone might think he can pick you up at a bargain price while you're depressed and panicked by the interim results.'

'What would your advice be, then?' Hamilton asked thoughtfully.

'It depends on the offer. But I'd probably say "Wait." We should know today whether you've won the oil-field licence.'

'Shield.'

'Yes. Win that, and your shares will strengthen.'

'We're still a poor prospect for profits.'

'But ideal material for an asset stripper.'

'Interesting,' Hamilton mused. 'A gambler would make the bid today, before the Minister's announcement. An opportunist would do it tomorrow, if we win the licence. A genuine investor would wait until next week.'

'And a wise man would say no to all of them.'

Hamilton smiled. 'Money isn't everything, Nathaniel.'

'Good lord!'

'Is that so heretical?'

'Not at all.' Fett was amused, and his eyes sparkled behind the spectacles. 'I've known it for years. What surprises me is that *you* should say it.'

'It surprises me, too.' Hamilton paused. 'A matter of curiosity: do you think we'll get the licence?'

'Can't say.' Suddenly the broker's face was unreadable again. 'Depends whether the Minister believes it should go to an already-profitable company as a bonus, or to an ailing one as a lifebelt.'

'Hm. Neither, I suspect. Remember, we only head the syndicate: it's the total package that counts. The Hamilton section, in control, provides City contacts and management expertise. We'll *raise* the development money, rather than supply it out of our own pocket. Others in the team offer engineering skills, oil experience, marketing facilities, and so on.'

'So you've a good chance.'

Hamilton smiled again. 'Socrates.'

'Why?'

'He always made people answer their own questions.' Hamilton lifted his heavy frame out of the chair. 'I must go.'

Fett walked to the door with him. 'Derek, about Ellen – I hope you don't mind my saying . . .'

'No.' They shook hands. 'I value your judgement.'

Fett nodded, and opened the door. 'Whatever you do, don't panic.'

'Okey-dokey.' As he went out, Hamilton realized that he had not used *that* expression for thirty years.

# Chapter Eleven

Two motor-cycle police parked their machines either side of the rear entrance to the bank. One of them produced an identity card and held it flat against the small window beside the door. The man inside read the card carefully, then picked up a red telephone and spoke into it.

A black van without markings drove between the motor-cycles and stopped with its nose to the door. The side windows of its cab were fitted with wire mesh internally, and the two men inside wore police-type uniforms with crash helmets and transparent visors. The body of the van had no windows, despite the fact that there was a third man in there.

Two more police bikes drew up behind the van, completing the convoy.

The steel door to the building lifted smoothly and noiselessly, and the van pulled in. It was in a short tunnel, brightly lit by fluorescent tubes. Its way was blocked by another door identical with the first. The van stopped and the door behind closed. The police motor-cyclists remained in the street.

The van driver wound his window down and spoke

through the wire mesh into a microphone on a stand. 'Morning,' he said cheerfully.

There was a large plate-glass window in one wall of the tunnel. Behind the window, which was bullet-proof, a bright-eyed man in shirtsleeves spoke into another microphone. His amplified words resonated in the confined space. 'Code word, please.'

The driver, whose name was Ron Biggins, said: 'Obadiah.' The Controller who had set up today's run was a deacon in a Baptist church.

The shirtsleeved man pressed a large red button in the white-painted wall behind him, and the second steel door slid upward. Ron Biggins muttered: 'Miserable sod,' and eased the van forward. Again the steel door closed behind it.

It was now in a windowless room in the bowels of the building. Most of the floor space was occupied by a turntable. The room was otherwise empty. Ron steered carefully onto the marked tracks and switched off his engine. The turntable jerked, and the van moved slowly through 180 degrees then stopped.

The rear doors were now opposite the lift in the far wall. As Ron watched in his wing mirror, the lift doors parted and a bespectacled man in a black jacket and striped trousers emerged. He carried a key, holding it out in front of him as if it were a torch or a gun. He unlocked the van's rear doors, then they were opened from the inside. The third guard got out.

Two more men came out of the lift, carrying between them a formidable metal box the size of a suitcase. They loaded it into the van and went back for more.

Ron looked around. The room was bare, apart from its two entrances, three parallel lines of fluorescent lights, and a vent for the air conditioning. It was small, and not quite rectangular. Ron guessed that few of the people who worked at the bank would know it was there at all. The lift presumably went only to the vault, and the steel door to the street had no apparent connection with the main entrance around the corner.

The guard who had been inside, Stephen Younger, came around to the left-hand side of the van; and Ron's co-driver, Max Fitch, lowered his window. Stephen said: 'Big one today.'

'Makes no difference to us,' Ron said sourly. He looked back at his mirror. The loading was finished.

Stephen said to Max: 'The gaffer here likes Westerns.'

'Yeah?' Max was interested. He had not been here before, and the clerk in striped trousers did not look like a John Wayne fan. 'How do you know?' he asked.

'Watch. Here he comes.'

The clerk came to Ron's window and said: 'Move 'em out!'

Max spluttered and tried to cover his laughter. Stephen went around to the back of the van and got in. The clerk locked him in.

The three bank employees disappeared into the lift. Nothing happened for two or three minutes; then the steel door lifted. Ron fired the engine and drove into the tunnel. They waited for the inner door to close and the outer one to open. Just before they pulled away, Max said into the microphone: 'So long, Laughing Boy.'

The van emerged into the street.

The motor-cycle escort was ready. They took up their positions, two in front and two behind, and the convoy headed east.

At a large road junction in East London, the van turned onto the A11. It was watched by a large man in a grey coat with a velvet collar, who immediately went into a phone booth.

Max Fitch said: 'Guess who I just saw.'

'No idea.'

'Tony Cox.'

Ron's expression was blank. 'Who's he when he's at home?'

'Used to be a boxer. Good, he was. I saw him knock out Kid Vittorio at Bethnal Green Baths, it must be ten years ago. Hell of a boy.'

Max really wanted to be a detective, but he had failed the police force intelligence test and gone into security. He read a great deal of crime fiction, and consequently laboured under the delusion that the CID's most potent weapon was logical deduction. At home he did things like finding a lipstick-smeared cigarette butt in the ashtray and announcing grandly that he had reason to believe that Mrs Ashford from next door had been in the house.

He shifted restlessly in his seat. 'Them cases are

what they keep old notes in, aren't they?'

'Yes,' Ron said.

'So we must be going to the destruction plant in Essex,' Max said proudly. 'Right, Ron?'

Ron was staring at the outriders in front of the van and frowning. As the senior member of the team, he was the only one who got told where they were going. But he was not thinking of the route, or the job, or even Tony Cox the ex-boxer. He was trying to figure out why his eldest daughter had fallen in love with a hippie.

# Chapter Twelve

Felix Laski's office in Poultry did not display his name anywhere. It was an old building, standing shoulder-to-shoulder with two others of different design. Had he been able to get planning permission to knock it down and build a skyscraper, he could have made millions. Instead it stood as an example of the way his wealth was locked up. But he reckoned that, in the long term, sheer pressure would blow the lid off planning restrictions; and he was a patient man where business was concerned.

Almost all of the building was sublet. Most of the tenants were minor foreign banks who needed an address near Threadneedle Street, and their names were well displayed. People tended to assume that Laski had interests in the banks, and he encouraged this error in every way short of outright lying. Besides, he did own one of the banks.

The furnishings inside were adequate but cheap: solid old typewriters, shop-soiled filing cabinets, second-hand desks, and the threadbare minimum of carpet. Like every successful man in middle age, Laski liked to explain his achievement in aphorisms: a favourite was 'I never spend money. I invest.' It was truer than most dicta of its kind. His one home, a small mansion in Kent, had been rising in value since he bought it shortly after the war; his meals were often expense-account affairs with business prospects; and even the paintings he owned – kept in a safe, not hung on walls – had been bought because his art dealer said they would appreciate. To him, money was like the toy bank notes in Monopoly: he wanted it, not for what it could buy, but because it was needed to play the game.

Still, his lifestyle was not uncomfortable. A primary-school teacher, or the wife of an agricultural labourer, would have thought he lived in unpardonable luxury.

The room he used as his own office was small. There was a desk bearing three telephones, a swivel chair behind it, two more chairs for callers, and a long, upholstered couch against the wall. The bookshelf beside the wall safe held scores of weighty volumes on taxation and company law. It was a room without a personality: no photographs of loved ones on the desk, no pictures on the walls, no foolish plastic pen holder given by a well-meaning grandchild, no ashtray brought home from Clovelly or stolen from the Hilton.

Laski's secretary was an efficient, overweight girl who wore her skirts too short. He often told people: 'When they were giving out sex appeal, Carol was elsewhere getting extra rations of brains.' That was a good joke, an English joke, the kind directors told each other in the executive canteen. Carol had arrived at nine twenty-five to find her boss's 'out' tray full of work which had not been there last night. Laski liked to do things like that: it impressed the staff and helped to counteract envy. Carol had not touched the papers until she had made him coffee. He liked that, too.

He was sitting on the couch, hidden behind *The Times*, with the coffee near him on the arm of the chair, when Ellen Hamilton came in.

She closed the door silently and tiptoed across the carpet, so that he did not see her until she pushed the newspaper down and looked at him over it. The sudden rustle made him jump with shock.

She said: 'Mr Laski.'

He said: 'Mrs Hamilton!'

She lifted her skirt to her waist and said: 'Kiss me good morning.'

Under the skirt she wore old-fashioned stockings with no panties. Laski leaned forward and rubbed his face in the crisp, sweet-smelling pubic hair. His heart beat a little faster, and he felt delightfully wicked, the way he had the first time he kissed a woman's vulva.

He sat back and looked up at her. 'What I like about you is the way you manage to make sex seem dirty,' he said. He folded the newspaper and dropped it to the floor.

She lowered her skirt and said: 'Sometimes I just get the hots.'

He smiled knowingly, and let his eyes roam her

body. She was about fifty, and very slender, with small, pointed breasts. Her ageing complexion was saved by a deep suntan which she nourished all winter under an ultraviolet lamp. Her hair was black, straight, and well cut; and the grey hairs which appeared from time to time were swiftly obliterated in an expensive Knightsbridge salon. She wore a cream-coloured outfit: very elegant, very expensive, and very English. He ran his hand up the inside of her thigh, under the perfectly tailored skirt. With intimate insolence his fingers probed between her buttocks. He wondered whether anyone would believe that the demure wife of the Hon. Derek Hamilton went around with no panties on just so that Felix Laski could feel her arse any time he wanted to.

She wriggled pleasurably, then moved slightly away and sat down beside him on the couch where, during the last few months, she had fulfilled some of his weirdest sexual fantasies.

He had intended Mrs Hamilton to be a minor character in his grand scenario, but she had turned out to be a very enjoyable bonus.

He had met her at a garden party. The hosts were friends of the Hamiltons', not of his; but he got an invitation by pretending a financial fancy for the host's company, a light-engineering group. It was a hot day in July. The women wore summer dresses and the men, linen jackets; Laski had a white suit. With his tall, distinguished figure and faintly foreign looks, he cut quite a dash, and he knew it.

There was croquet for the older guests, tennis for the young people, and a pool for the children. The hosts provided endless champagne and strawberries with cream. Laski had done his homework on the host – even his pretences were thorough – and he knew they could hardly afford it. Yet he had been invited reluctantly, and only because he had more or less asked. Why should a couple who were short of money give a pointless party for people they did not need? English society baffled him. Oh, he knew its rules, and understood their logic; but he would never know why people played the game.

The psychology of middle-aged women was something he understood much more profoundly. He took Ellen Hamilton's hand with just a hint of a bow, and saw a twinkle in her eye. That, and the fact that her husband was gross while she remained beautiful, was enough to tell him that she would respond to flirtation. A woman like her was sure to spend a great deal of time wondering whether she could still excite a man's lust. She might also be wondering whether she would ever know sexual pleasure again.

Laski proceeded to play the European charmer like an outrageous old ham. He fetched chairs for her, summoned waiters to top up her glass, and touched her discreetly but frequently: her hand, her arm, her shoulders, her hip. There was no point in subtlety, he felt: if she wanted to be seduced, he might as well give the message of his availability as clearly as possible; and if she did not want to be seduced, nothing he could do would change her mind.

When she had finished her strawberries – he ate none: to refuse mouth-watering food was a mark of class – he began to guide her away from the house. They moved from group to group, lingering where the conversation interested them, passing on quickly from social gossip. She introduced him to several people, and he was able to introduce her to two stock-brokers he knew slightly. They watched the children splashing around, and Laski said in her ear: 'Did you bring your bikini?' She giggled. They sat in the shade of a mature oak and looked at the tennis players, who were boringly professional. They walked along a gravel path which wound through a small landscaped wood; and when they were out of sight, he took her face in his hands and kissed her. She opened her mouth to him, and ran her hands up inside his jacket, and dug her fingers into his chest with a force that surprised him; then she pulled away and looked furtively up and down the path.

Quickly he said: 'Have dinner with me? Soon?'

'Soon,' she said.

Then they walked back to the party and split up. She left without saying good-bye to him. The next day he took a suite at a hotel in Park Lane, and there he gave her dinner and champagne, then he took her to bed. It was in the bedroom that he discovered how wrong he had been about her. He expected her to be hungry, but easily satisfied. Instead, he found that her sexual tastes were at least as bizarre as his own. Over the next few weeks they did everything that two people can do to one another, and when they ran out of ideas Laski made a phone call and another woman arrived to open up a whole new series of permutations. Ellen did everything with the delighted thoroughness of a child in a fairground where all the rides are suddenly free.

He looked at her, sitting beside him on the couch in his office, as he remembered; and he felt suffused with a sentiment which he thought people would probably call love.

He said to her: 'What do *you* like about *me*?'

'What an egocentric question!'

'I told you what I like about you. Come on, satisfy my ego. What is it?'

She looked down at his lap. 'I give you three guesses.'

He laughed. 'Would you like coffee?'

'No, thank you. I'm going shopping. I just came in for a quick feel.'

'You're a shameless old baggage.'

'What a funny thing to say.'

'How is Derek?'

'Another funny thing to say. He's depressed. Why do you ask?'

Laski shrugged. 'The man interests me. How could he possess a prize like Ellen Hamilton, then let her slip through his fingers?'

She looked away. 'Talk about something else.'

'All right. Are you happy?'

She smiled again. 'Yes. I only hope it will last.'

'Why shouldn't it?' he said lightly.

'I don't know. I meet you, and I fuck like ... like ...'

'Like a bunny.'

'What?'

'Fuck like a bunny. This is the correct English expression.'

She opened her mouth and laughed. 'You old fool. I love you when you're being all Prussian and correct. I know you only do it to amuse me.'

'So: we meet, and we fuck like bunnies, and you don't think it can last.'

'You can't deny the whole thing has an air of impermanence.'

'Would you have it otherwise?' he asked carefully.

'I don't know.'

It was the only answer she could give, he realized. She added: 'Would you?'

He chose his words. 'This is the first time I have had occasion to reflect upon the permanence or otherwise of our relationship.'

'Stop talking like the Chairman's Annual Report.'

'If you will stop talking like the heroine of a romantic novelette. Speaking of Chairmen's Reports, I suppose that is what Derek is depressed about.'

'Yes. He thinks it's his ulcer that makes him feel bad, but I know better.'

'Would he sell the company, do you think?'

'I wish he would.' She looked at Laski sharply. 'Would you buy it?'

'I might.'

She stared at him for a long moment. He knew that she was evaluating what he had said, weighing possibilities, considering his motives. She was a clever woman.

She decided to let it pass. 'I must go,' she said. 'I want to be home for lunch.'

They stood up. He kissed her mouth, and ran his hands all over her body with sensual familiarity. She put a finger into his mouth, and he sucked it.

'Goodbye,' she said.

'I'll call you,' Laski told her.

Then she was gone. Laski went to the bookcase and stared unseeingly at the spine of *The Directory of Directors*. She had said, *I only hope it will last*, and he needed to think about that. She had a way of saying things that made him think. She was a subtle woman. What did she want, then – marriage? She had said she did not know what she wanted, and although she could hardly have said anything else, he had a feeling she was sincere. So, what do I want? he thought. Do I want to marry her?

He sat down behind his desk. He had a lot to do. He pressed the intercom and spoke to Carol. 'Ring the Department of Energy for me, and find out exactly when – I mean what *time* – they plan to announce the name of the company that won the licence for the Shield oil field.'

'Certainly,' she said.

'Then ring Fett and Co. for me. I want Nathaniel Fett, the boss.'

'Right.'

He flipped the switch up. He thought again: do I want to marry Ellen Hamilton?

Suddenly he knew the answer, and it astonished him.

# Ten a.m.

# Chapter Thirteen

The editor of the *Evening Post* was under the illusion that he belonged to the ruling class. The son of a railway clerk, he had climbed the social ladder very fast in the twenty years since he left school. When he needed reassurance, he would remind himself that he was a director of Evening Post Ltd, and an opinion former; and that his income placed him in the top nine per cent of heads of households. It did not occur to him that he would never have become an opinion former were it not that his opinions coincided exactly with those of the newspaper's proprietor; nor that his directorship was in the proprietor's gift; nor that the ruling class is defined by wealth, rather than income. And he had no idea that his ready-to-wear suit by Cardin, his shaky plum-in-the-mouth accent, and his four-bedroom executive home in Chislehurst marked him plainly, in the jaundiced eyes of cynics like Arthur Cole, as a poor boy made good: more plainly than if he had worn a cloth cap and cycle clips.

Cole arrived in the editor's office on the dot of ten o'clock, with his tie straightened, his thoughts marshalled, and his list typed out. He realized instantly that that was an error. He should have burst in two minutes late in his shirtsleeves, to give the impression he had reluctantly torn himself away from the hot seat in the newsroom powerhouse for the purpose of giving less essential personnel a quick rundown on what was going on in really important departments. But then, he always thought of these things too late: he was no good at office politics. It would be interesting to watch how other executives made their entrance into the morning conference.

The editor's office was trendy. The desk was white and the easy chairs came from Habitat. Vertical venetian blinds shaded the blue carpet from sunlight, and the aluminium-and-melamine bookcases had smoked-glass doors. On a side table were copies of all the morning papers, and a pile of yesterday's editions of the *Evening Post*.

He sat behind the white desk, smoking a thin cigar and reading the *Mirror*. The sight made Cole yearn for a cigarette. He popped a peppermint into his mouth as a substitute.

The others came in in a bunch: the picture editor, in a tight-fitting shirt, with shoulder-length hair many women would envy; the sports editor, in a tweed jacket and lilac shirt; the features editor, with a pipe and a permanent slight grin; and the circulation manager, a young man in an immaculate grey suit who had started out selling encyclopedias and risen to this lofty height in only five years. The dramatic last-minute entrance was made by the chief sub-editor, the paper's designer; a short man with close-cropped hair, wearing braces. There was a pencil behind his ear.

When they were all seated, the editor tossed the *Mirror* onto the side table and pulled his chair closer to his desk. He said: 'No first edition yet?'

'No.' The chief sub looked at his watch. 'We lost eight minutes because of a web break.'

The editor switched his gaze to the circulation manager. 'How does that affect you?'

He, too, was looking at his watch. 'If it's only eight minutes, and if you can catch up by the next edition, we can wear it.'

The editor said: 'We seem to have a web break every bloody day.'

'It's this bog-paper we're printing on,' the chief sub said.

'Well, we have to live with it until we start to make a profit again.' The editor picked up the list of news stories Cole had put on his desk. 'There's nothing here to start a circulation boom, Arthur.'

'It's a quiet morning. With luck we'll have a Cabinet crisis by midday.'

'And they're two-a-penny with this bloody government.' The editor continued to read the list. 'I like this Stradivarius story.'

Cole ran down the list, speaking briefly about each item. When he had finished, the editor said: 'And not a splash among 'em. I don't like to lead all day on politics. We're supposed to cover "every facet of the Londoner's day", to quote our own advertising. I don't suppose we can make this Strad a million-pound violin?'

'It's a nice idea,' Cole said. 'But I don't suppose it's worth that much. Still, we'll try it on.'

The chief sub said: 'If it won't work in sterling, try the million-*dollar* violin. Better still, the million-dollar fiddle.'

'Good thinking,' the editor said. 'Let's have a library picture of a similar fiddle, and interviews with three top violinists about how they would feel if they lost their favourite instrument.' He paused. 'I want to go big on the oil-field licence, too. People are interested in this North Sea oil – it's supposed to be our economic salvation.'

Cole said: 'The announcement is due at twelve-thirty. We're getting a holding piece meanwhile.'

'Careful what you say. Our own parent company is one of the contenders, in case you didn't know. Remember that an oil well isn't instant riches – it means several years of heavy investment first.'

'Sure,' Cole nodded.

The circulation manager turned to the chief sub. 'Let's have street placards on the violin story, and this fire in the East End—'

The door opened noisily, and the circulation manager stopped speaking. They all looked up to see Kevin Hart standing in the doorway, looking flushed and excited. Cole groaned inwardly.

Hart said: 'I'm sorry to interrupt, but I think this is the big one.'

'What is it?' the editor said mildly.

'I just took a phone call from Timothy Fitzpeterson, a Junior Minister in the—'

'I know who he is,' the editor said. 'What did he say?'

'He claims he's being blackmailed by two people called Laski and Cox. He sounded pretty far gone. He—'

The editor interrupted again. 'Do you know his voice?'

The young reporter looked flustered. He had obviously been expecting instant panic, not a cross-examination. 'I've never spoken to Fitzpeterson before,' he said.

Cole put in: 'I had a fairly nasty anonymous tip about him this morning. I checked it out – he denied it.'

The editor grimaced. 'It stinks,' he said. The chief sub nodded agreement. Hart looked crestfallen.

Cole said: 'All right, Kevin, we'll discuss it when I come out.'

Hart went out and closed the door.

'Excitable fellow,' the editor commented.

Cole said: 'He's not stupid, but he's got a lot to learn.'

'So teach him,' the editor said. 'Now, what's lined up on the picture desk?'

# Chapter Fourteen

Ron Biggins was thinking about his daughter. In this, he was at fault: he should have been thinking about the van he was driving, and its cargo of several hundred thousand pounds' worth of paper money – soiled, torn, folded, scribbled-on, and fit only for the Bank of England's destruction plant in Loughton, Essex. But perhaps his distraction was forgivable: for a man's daughter is more important than paper money; and when she is his only daughter, she is a queen; and when she is his only *child*, well, she just about fills his life.

After all, Ron thought, a man spends his life bringing her up, in the hope that when she comes of age he can hand her over to a steady, reliable type who will look after her the way her father did. Not some drunken, dirty, longaired, pot-smoking, unemployed *fucking layabout—*

'What?' said Max Fitch.

Ron snapped back into the present. 'Did I speak?'

'You were muttering,' Max told him. 'You got something on your mind?'

'I just might have, son,' Ron said. I just might have

118

murder on my mind, he thought, but he knew he did not mean it. He accelerated slightly to keep the regulation distance between the van and the motor cyclists. He had nearly taken the young swine by the throat, though, when he had said, 'Me and Judy thought we might live together, like, for a while, see how it goes, see?' It had been as casual as if he were proposing to take her to a matineé. The man was twenty-two years of age, five years older than Judy – thank God she was still a minor, obliged to obey her father. The boyfriend – his name was Lou – had sat in the parlour, looking nervous, in a nondescript shirt, grubby jeans held up with an elaborate leather belt like some medieval instrument of torture, and open sandals which showed his filthy dirty feet. When Ron asked what he did for a living, he said he was an unemployed poet, and Ron suspected the lad was taking the mickey.

After the remark about living together, Ron threw him out. The rows had been going on ever since. First, he had explained to Judy that she must not live with Lou because she ought to save herself for her husband; whereupon she laughed in his face and said she had already slept with him at least a dozen times, when she was supposed to be spending the night with a girlfriend in Finchley. He said he supposed she was going to say she was in the pudding club; and she said he should not be so stupid, she had been on the pill since her sixteenth birthday, when her mother had taken her up to the family planning clinic. That was when Ron came near to hitting his wife for the first time in twenty years of marriage.

Ron got a pal in the police force to check out Louis Thurley, aged twenty-two, unemployed, of Barracks Road, Harringey. The Criminal Records Office had turned up two convictions: one for possession of cannabis resin at the Reading pop festival, and one for stealing food from Tesco's in Muswell Hill. That information should have finished it. It did convince Ron's wife, but Judy just said that she knew all about both incidents. Pot shouldn't be an offence, she declared, and as far as the theft was concerned, Ron and his friends had simply sat on the supermarket floor eating pork pies off the shelf until they got arrested. They had done it because they believed food should be free, and because they were hungry and broke. She seemed to think their attitude was totally reasonable.

Unable to make her see sense, Ron had finally forbidden her to go out in the evening. She had taken it calmly. She would do as he said, and in four months' time, when she was eighteen, she would move into Lou's studio apartment with his three mates and the girl they all shared.

Ron was defeated. He had been obsessed by the problem for eight days, and still he could see no way to rescue his daughter from a life of misery – for that was what it meant, without a shadow of doubt. Ron had seen it happen. A young girl marries a wrong 'un. She goes out to work while he sits at home watching the racing on television. He does a bit of villainy from time to time to keep himself in beer and smokes. She has a few babies, he gets nicked and goes inside for a stretch, and suddenly the poor girl is trying to bring up a family on the Assistance with no husband.

He would give his life for Judy – he *had* given her eighteen years of it – and all she wanted to do was throw away everything Ron stood for and spit in his eye. He would have wept, if he could remember how.

He could not get it out of his mind, so he was still thinking about it at 10:16 a.m. this day. That was why he did not notice the ambush sooner. But his lack of concentration made little difference to what happened in the next few seconds.

He turned under a railway arch into a long, curving road which had the river on its left-hand side and a scrap yard on the right. It was a mild, clear day, and so, as he followed the gentle bend, he had no difficulty in seeing the large car transporter, piled high with battered and crushed vehicles, reversing with difficulty into the scrap yard gate.

At first it looked as though the truck would be out of the way by the time the convoy reached it. But the driver obviously did not have the angle of approach quite right, for he pulled forward again, completely blocking the road.

The two motor cycles in front braked to a halt, and Ron drew the van up behind them. One cyclist heaved his machine onto its stand and jumped up on the footplate of the cab to shout at the driver. The truck's engine was revving noisily, and black smoke poured from its exhaust in clouds.

'Report an unscheduled stop,' Ron said. 'Let's work the routine like the book says.'

Max picked up the radio microphone. 'Mobile to Obadiah Control.'

Ron was looking at the truck. It carried an odd assortment of vehicles. There was an elderly green van with 'Coopers Family Butcher' painted on the side; a crumpled Ford Anglia with no wheels; two Volkswagen Beetles piled one on top of the other; and, on the upper rack, a large white Australian Ford with a coachline and a new-looking Triumph. The whole thing looked a bit unsteady, especially the two Beetles in a rusty embrace, like a pair of copulating insects Ron looked back at the cab: the motor cyclist was making signs at the driver to get out of the convoy's way.

Max repeated: 'Mobile to Obadiah Control. Come in, please.'

We must be quite low, Ron thought, this close to the river. Maybe reception is bad. He looked again at the cars on the transporter, and realized that they were not roped down. That really was dangerous. How far had the transporter travelled with its load of unsecured scrap?

Suddenly he understood. 'Give the Mayday!' he yelled.

Max stared at him. 'What?'

Something hit the roof of the van with a clang. The

truck driver jumped out of his cab onto the motor cyclist. Several men in stocking masks swarmed over the scrap yard wall. Ron glanced in his wing mirror and saw the two motor cyclists behind the van being knocked from their machines.

The van lurched and then, incomprehensibly, seemed to rise in the air. Ron looked to his right and saw the arm of a crane reaching over the wall to his roof. He snatched the microphone from a bemused Max as one of the masked men ran towards the van. The man lobbed something small and black, like a cricket ball, at the windshield.

The next second passed slowly, in a series of pictures, like a film seen frame by frozen frame: a crash helmet flying through the air; a wooden club landing on someone's head; Max grabbing the gear stick as the van tilted; Ron's own thumb pressing the talk button on the microphone as he said 'Obadiah Mayd—'; the small bomb that looked like a cricket ball hitting the windshield and exploding, sending toughened glass fragments into the air in a shower; and then the physical blow as the shock wave hit and the quiet darkness of unconsciousness.


Sergeant Wilkinson heard the call sign 'Obadiah' from the currency shipment, but he ignored it. It had been a busy morning, with three major traffic hold-ups, a cross-London chase after a hit-and-run driver, two serious accidents, a warehouse fire, and an impromptu demonstration in Downing Street by a group of anarchists. When the call came in he was taking a cup of instant coffee and a ham roll from a young West Indian girl and saying: 'What does your husband think about you coming to work with no bra?'

The girl, who had a large bust, said: 'He doesn't notice,' and giggled.

Constable Jones, on the other side of the console, said: 'There you are, Dave, take the hint.'

Wilkinson said: 'What are you doing tonight?'

She laughed, knowing he was not serious. 'Working,' she said.

The radio said: 'Mobile to Obadiah Control. Come in, please.'

Wilkinson said: 'Another job? What?'

'I'm a go-go dancer in a pub.'

'Topless?'

'You'll have to come along and see, won't you?' the girl said, and she pushed her trolley on.

The radio said: 'Mayd—' then there was a muffled bang, like a burst of static, or an explosion.

The grin faded rapidly from Wilkinson's young face. He flicked a switch and spoke into the microphone. 'Obadiah Control, come in, Mobile.'

There was no reply. Wilkinson called to his supervisor, putting a note of urgency into his voice. 'Guvnor!'

Inspector 'Harry' Harrison came across to Wilkinson's position. A tall man, he had been running his hands through his thinning hair, and now he looked more distraught than he was. He said: 'Everything under control, Sergeant?'

'I think I caught a Mayday from Obadiah, guv.'

Harrison snapped: 'What do you mean, *think*?'

Wilkinson had not made sergeant by admitting his mistakes. He said: 'Distorted message, sir.'

Harrison picked up the mike. 'Obadiah Control to Mobile, do you read? Over.' He waited, then repeated the message. There was no reply. He said to Wilkinson: 'A distorted message, then they go off the air. We've got to treat it as a hijack. That's all I need.' He had the air of a man to whom Fate has been not merely unjust but positively vindictive.

Wilkinson said: 'I didn't get a location.'

They both turned to look at the giant map of London on the wall.

Wilkinson said: 'They took the river route. Last time they checked in was at Aldgate. Traffic's normal, so they must be somewhere like, say, Dagenham.'

'Great,' Harrison said sarcastically. He thought for a moment. 'Put out an all-cars alert. Then detach three from East London patrols and send them on a search. Alert Essex, and make sure those idle sods know how much bloody money is in that van. All right, on your bike.'

Wilkinson began to make the calls. Harrison stood behind him for a few moments, deep in thought. 'We should get a call before too long – someone must have seen it happen,' he muttered. He thought a bit more. 'But then, if chummy is clever enough to knock the radio out before the boys can call in, he's clever enough to do the job somewhere quiet.' There was a longer pause. Finally Harrison said: 'Personally, I don't think we stand a sodding chance.'

It was going like a dream, Jacko thought. The currency van had been hoisted over the wall and gently set down beside the cutting gear. The four police motor cycles had been tossed aboard the transporter, which had then reversed into the yard. The riders now lay in a neat line, each of them handcuffed hand and foot, and the yard gates were shut.

Two of the boys, wearing goggles over their stocking masks, made a man-sized hole in the side of the currency van while another plain blue van was backed up. A large rectangle of steel fell away, and a uniformed guard jumped out with his hands above his head. Jesse handcuffed him and made him lie down beside the police escort.

The cutting gear was wheeled away rapidly, and two more men got into the currency van and began to pass the chests out. They were put straight into the second van.

Jacko cast an eye over the prisoners. They had all been bashed about a bit, but not seriously. All were conscious. Jacko was perspiring under the mask, but he dare not take it off.

There was a shout from the cabin of the crane, where one of the boys was keeping watch. Jacko looked up. At the same time, he heard the sound of a siren.

He looked around. It couldn't be true! The whole idea was that they should knock the guards out before they had time to radio for help. He cursed. The men were looking to him for guidance.

The transporter had backed behind a pile of tyres, so the white motor cycles could not be seen. The two vans and the crane looked innocent enough. Jacko shouted: 'Everybody get under cover!' Then he remembered the prisoners. No time to drag them out of the way. His eye lit upon a tarpaulin. He pulled it over the five bodies, then dived behind a skip.

The siren came nearer. The car was travelling very fast. He heard the squeal of tyres as it swung under the railway arch, then the scream of the engine as the car touched seventy in third before changing up. The sound got louder, then suddenly the pitch of the siren dropped and the noise began to recede. Jacko breathed a sigh of relief, then heard the second siren. He yelled: 'Stay down!'

The second car passed, and he heard a third. There was the same squeal under the arch, the same third-gear burst after the corner – but this time the car slowed outside the gate.

Everything seemed very quiet. Jacko's face was unbearably hot under the nylon. He felt he was going to suffocate. He heard a sound like policeman's boots scraping on the gate. One of them must be climbing up to have a look over. Suddenly Jacko remembered that there were two more guards in the cab of the van. He hoped to Christ they didn't come round just now.

What was the copper up to? He hadn't climbed right over, but he hadn't fallen back, either. If they came in for a good look, it would all be up. No, don't panic, he thought, ten of us can see to a carful of wollies. But it would take time, and they might have left one in the car, who could radio for reinforcements—

Jacko could almost feel all that money slipping through his fingers. He wanted to risk a peep around the side of the skip, but he told himself there was no point: he would know when they left by the sound of the car.

*What were they doing?*

He looked again at the currency van. Jesus, one of the blokes was moving. Jacko hefted his shotgun. It was going to come to a fight. He whispered: 'Oh, bollocks.'

There was a noise from the van – a hoarse yell. Jacko scrambled to his feet and stepped around the skip with his gun ready.

There was nobody there.

Then he heard the car pull away with a screech of tyres. Its siren started up again and faded into the distance.

Deaf Willie emerged from behind the rusty shell of a Mercedes taxi. Together, they went towards the van. Willie said: 'Jolly good fun, ain't it?'

'Yes,' Jacko said sourly. 'Better than watching the

bloody television.' They looked inside the van. The driver was groaning, but he did not look badly hurt. 'Out you come, Grandad,' Jacko said through the broken window. 'Tea break's over.'

The voice had a calming effect on Ron Biggins. Until then he had been dazed and panicky. He did not seem to be hearing properly, there was a pain in his head, and when he put his hand up to his face he touched something sticky.

The sight of a man in a stocking mask was curiously bracing. It was all very clear. An extremely efficient raid – in fact, Ron was somewhat awed by the smoothness of the operation. They had known the route, and the timing, of the currency van's trip. He began to feel angry. No doubt a percentage of the haul would find its way into the secret bank account of a corrupt detective. Like most police and security workers, he hated bent coppers even more than villains.

The man who had called him Grandad opened the door, reaching through the shattered glass of the side window to operate the internal lock. Ron got out. The movement hurt him.

The man was young – Ron could distinguish long hair underneath the stocking. He wore jeans and carried a shotgun. He gave Ron a contemptuous push and said: 'Hands out, neatly together, Pop. You can go to hospital in a minute.'

The pain in Ron's head seemed to grow with his

anger. He fought down an urge to kick out at something, and made himself remember how he was supposed to behave during a raid: *Don't resist, cooperate with them, give them the money. We're insured for it, your own life is more valuable to us, don't be a hero.*

He began to breathe hard. In his concussed mind he confused the young man holding the shotgun with the corrupt detective and with Lou Thurley, panting and groaning on top of innocent, virginal Judy, in some verminous bed at a dingy studio apartment; and suddenly he realized that it was this man who had messed up his, Ron's, life, and that maybe a hero was what he needed to be to win back the respect of his only child; and that no-goods like this corrupt detective wearing a stocking mask in bed with Judy and carrying a shotgun was the kind who always messed it up for good people like Ron Biggins; so he took two steps forward and punched the astonished young man's nose, and the man stumbled and pulled both triggers of his gun, shooting not Ron, but another masked man beside him, who screamed blood and fell down; and Ron stared, horrified, at the blood until the first man hit him over the head very hard with the metal barrel of the gun, and Ron passed out again.

Jacko knelt beside Deaf Willie and pulled the shreds of stocking away from the older man's face. Willie's face was a dreadful mess, and Jacko went pale. Jacko and his like usually inflicted wounds upon their victims and one another with blunt instruments; consequently Jacko had never seen gunshot wounds before. And since in-house training in first aid was not one of the perks in Tony Cox's management training scheme, Jacko did not really know what to do. But he was capable of quick thinking.

He looked up. The others were standing around, staring. Jacko yelled: 'Get on with it, you dozy bastards!' They jumped.

He bent closer to Willie and said: 'Can you hear me, mate?'

Willie's face twisted, but he was unable to speak.

Jesse knelt on Willie's other side. 'We got to get him to hospital,' he said.

Jacko was ahead of him. 'I need a hot car,' he said. He pointed to a blue Volvo parked nearby. 'Whose is that?'

'It belongs to the owner of the yard,' Jesse said.

'Perfect. Help me get Willie in there.'

Jacko took his shoulders and Jesse his legs. They carried him to the car, whimpering, and put him on the backseat. The keys were in the ignition.

One of the men called from the currency truck: 'All done, Jacko.'

Jacko would have struck the man for using his name, but he was preoccupied. He said to Jesse: 'Know where you're going?'

'Yes, but you're supposed to come with me.'

'Never mind. I'll get Willie to hospital somehow, and meet you at the farm. Tell Tony what happened.

Now, drive *slow*, don't shoot the lights, pull up at zebra crossings, do it like it was a bleeding driving test, okay?'

'Yes,' Jesse said. He ran back to the getaway van and tested the rear doors. They were locked. He stripped the brown paper off the number plates – its purpose had been to stop the guards getting the number; Tony Cox thought of everything – and got behind the wheel.

Jacko started the Volvo. Someone opened the yard gate. The rest of the men were already getting into their own cars and peeling off their gloves and masks. Jesse pulled out in the van and turned right. Jacko followed him out and went the opposite way.

As he accelerated down the street, he glanced at his watch: ten twenty-seven. The whole thing had taken eleven minutes. Tony was right: he had said they would be away and clear in the time it takes a squad car to get from Vine Street nick to the Isle of Dogs. It had been a beautiful job, except for poor Deaf Willie. Jacko hoped he would live to spend his share.

He was approaching the hospital. He had figured out the way he would play it, but he needed Willie to be out of sight. He said: 'Will? Can you get on the floor?' There was no response. Jacko glanced back. Willie's eyes were such a mess that words like 'open' and 'shut' no longer applied. But the poor sod must be unconscious. Jacko reached behind and pulled the body off the seat onto the floor. It fell with a painful bump.

He steered into the hospital grounds and parked in

the car park. He got out of the car and followed signs for Casualty. Just inside the entrance he found a pay phone. He opened the directory and found the number of the hospital.

He dialled, thumbed a coin into the slot, and asked for Casualty. A phone on a desk near where he stood buzzed twice, and the sister picked it up.

She said: 'One moment, please,' and laid the receiver on the desk. She was a plump woman in her forties wearing a crisply starched uniform and a harassed air. She wrote a few words in a book, then picked the phone up again.

'Casualty, can I help you?'

Jacko spoke quietly, watching the sister's face. 'There is a man with shotgun wounds in the back of a blue Volvo car in your car park.'

The portly nurse paled. 'You mean here?'

Jacko was angry. 'Yes, you dozy old cow, in your own hospital. Now get off your bum and go and get him!' He was tempted to slam the phone down, but he stopped himself and pressed the cradle instead: if he could see the sister, then she could see him. He held the dead phone to his ear while she put hers down, got to her feet, summoned a nurse, and went out into the car park.

Jacko went farther into the hospital and left by another exit. He looked across from the main gate and saw a stretcher being carried across the car park. He had done all he could for Willie.

Now he needed another car.

# Chapter Fifteen

Felix Laski liked the office of Nathaniel Fett. It was a comfortable room with unobtrusive decor, a good place in which to do business. It had none of the gimmicks Laski used in his own office to give him advantage, like a desk by the window so that his own face was in shadow, or the low, unsteady visitors' chairs, or the priceless bone china coffee cups which people were terrified of dropping. Fett's office had the atmosphere of a club for company chairmen: no doubt it was deliberate. Laski noticed two things as he shook Fett's long, narrow hand: first, that there was a large, apparently little-used desk; and second, that Fett wore a club tie. The tie was a curious choice for a Jew, he reflected; then, on second thoughts, he decided it was not curious at all. Fett wore it for the same reason Laski wore a beautifully tailored Savile Row pinstriped suit: as a badge which said I, too, am an Englishman. So, Laski thought; even after six generations of banking Fetts, Nathaniel is still a little insecure. It was a piece of information which could be used.

Fett said: 'Sit down, Laski. Would you like coffee?'

'I drink coffee all day. It's bad for the heart. No, thank you.'

'A drink?'

Laski shook his head. Refusing hospitality was one of his ways of putting a host at a disadvantage. He said: 'I knew your father quite well, until he retired. His death was a loss. This is said of so many people, but in his case it is true.'

'Thank you.' Fett sat back in a club chair opposite Laski and crossed his legs. His eyes were inscrutable behind the thick glasses. 'It was ten years ago,' he added.

'So long? He was much older than I, of course, but he knew that, like his ancestors, I came from Warsaw.'

Fett nodded. 'The first Nathaniel Fett crossed Europe with a bag of gold and a donkey.'

'I did the same journey on a stolen Nazi motor cycle and a suitcase full of worthless Reichsmarks.'

'Yet your rise was so much more meteoric.'

It was a put-down, Laski realized: Fett was saying *We may be jumped-up Polish Jews, but we're not half as jumped-up as you.* The stockbroker was Laski's match at this game; and with those spectacles to hide his expression he did not need the light behind him. Laski smiled. 'You're like your father. One never knew what he was thinking.'

'You haven't yet given me anything to think about.'

'Ah.' So the small talk is over, Laski thought. 'I'm sorry my phone call was a little mysterious. It was good of you to see me at short notice.'

'You said you had a seven-figure proposal to put to one of my clients: how could I *not* see you? Would you like a cigar?' Fett got up and proffered a box from a side table.

Laski said: 'Thank you.' He lingered a little too long over his choice; then, as his hand descended to take a cigar, he said: 'I want to buy Hamilton Holdings from Derek Hamilton.'

The timing was perfect, but Fett showed no flicker of surprise. Laski had hoped he might drop the box. But, of course, Fett had known Laski would choose that moment to drop the bombshell; had created the moment for just that purpose.

He closed the box and gave Laski a light without speaking. He sat down again and crossed his legs. 'Hamilton Holdings, for seven figures.'

'Exactly one million pounds. When a man sells his life's work, he is entitled to a nice round figure.'

'Oh, I see the psychology of your approach,' Fett said lightly. 'This is not entirely unexpected.'

'What?'

'I don't mean we expected *you*. We expected somebody. The time is ripe.'

'The bid is substantially more than the value of the shares at current prices.'

'The margin is about right,' Fett said.

Laski spread his hands, palms upwards, in a gesture of appeal. 'Let's not fence,' he said. 'It's a high offer.'

'But less than what the shares will be worth if Derek's syndicate gets the oil well.'

'Which brings me to my only condition. The offer depends upon the deal being done this morning.'

Fett looked at his watch. 'It's almost eleven. Do you really think this could be done – even assuming Derek's interested – in one hour?'

Laski tapped his briefcase. 'I have all the necessary documents drawn up.'

'We could hardly read them—'

'I also have a letter of intent containing heads of agreement. That will satisfy me.'

'I should have guessed you would be prepared.' Fett considered for a moment. 'Of course, if Derek *doesn't* get the oil well, the shares will probably go down a bit.'

'I am a gambler,' Laski smiled.

Fett continued: 'In which case, you will sell off the company's assets and close down the unprofitable branches.'

'Not at all,' Laski lied. 'I think it could be profitable in its present form with new top management.'

'You're probably right. Well, it's a sensible offer; one that I'm obliged to put to the client.'

'Don't play hard to get. Think of the commission on a million pounds.'

'Yes,' Fett said coldly. 'I'll ring Derek.' He picked up a phone from a coffee table and said: 'Derek Hamilton, please.'

Laski puffed at his cigar and concealed his anxiety.

'Derek, it's Nathaniel. I've got Felix Laski with me. He's made an offer.' There was a pause. 'Yes, we did, didn't we? One million in round figures. You would . . . all right. We'll be here. What? Ah . . . I see.'

He gave a faintly embarrassed laugh. 'Ten minutes.' He put the phone down. 'Well, Laski, he's coming over. Let's read those documents of yours while we're waiting.'

Laski could not resist saying: 'He's interested, then.'

'He could be.'

'He said something else, didn't he?'

Fett gave the embarrassed little laugh again. 'I suppose there's no harm in telling you. He said that if he gives you the company by midday, he wants the money in his hand by noon.'

# Eleven a.m.

# Chapter Sixteen

Kevin Hart found the address the news desk had given him and parked on a yellow line. His car was a two-year-old Rover with a V8 engine, for he was a bachelor, and the *Evening Post* paid Fleet Street salaries, so he was a good deal wealthier than most men aged twenty-two. He knew this, and he took pleasure in it; and he was not old enough discreetly to conceal that pleasure, which was why men like Arthur Cole disliked him.

Arthur had been very ratty when he came out of the editor's conference. He had sat behind the news desk, given out a batch of assignments in the usual way, then called Kevin and told him to come around to his side of the desk and sit down: a sure sign that he was about to be given what the reporters called a bollocking.

Arthur had surprised him by talking, not about the way he had barged into the conference, but about the story. He had asked: 'What was the voice like?'

Kevin said: 'Middle-aged man, Home Counties accent. He was choosing his words. Maybe too carefully – he might have been drunk, or distressed.'

'That's not the voice I heard this morning,' Arthur mused. 'Mine was younger, and Cockney. What did yours say?'

Kevin read from his shorthand. 'I am Tim Fitzpeterson, and I am being blackmailed by two people called Laski and Cox. I want you to crucify the bastards when I'm gone.'

Arthur shook his head in disbelief. 'That all?'

'Well, I asked what they were blackmailing him with, and he said, "God, you're all the same," and put the phone down on me.' Kevin paused, expecting a rebuke. 'Was that the wrong question?'

Arthur shrugged. 'It was, but I can't think of a right one.' He picked up the phone and dialled, then handed the receiver to Kevin. 'Ask him if he's phoned us in the last half hour.'

Kevin listened for a moment, then cradled the handset. 'Busy signal.'

'No help.' Arthur patted his pockets, looking for cigarettes.

'You're giving it up,' said Kevin, recognizing the symptoms.

'So I am.' Arthur began to chew his nails. 'You see, the blackmailer's biggest hold over a politician is the threat to go to the newspapers. Therefore, the blackmailers wouldn't ring us and give us the story. That would be throwing away their trump card. By the same token, since the papers are what the victim fears, he wouldn't ring us and say he was being blackmailed.' With the air of one who comes to a final conclusion, he finished: 'That's why I think the whole thing is a hoax.'

Kevin took it for a dismissal. He stood up. 'I'll get back to the oil story.'

'No,' Arthur said. 'We've got to check it out. You'd better go round there and knock on his door.'

'Oh, good.'

'But next time you think of interrupting an editor's conference, sit down and count to one hundred first.'

Kevin could not suppress a grin. 'Sure.'

But the more he thought about it, the less chance he gave the story of standing up. In the car he had tried to recall what he knew of Tim Fitzpeterson. The man was a low-profile moderate. He had a degree in economics, and was reputed to be clever, but he just did not seem to be sufficiently lively or imaginative a person to provide blackmailers with any raw material. Kevin recalled a photograph of Fitzpeterson and family – a plain wife and three awkward girls – on a Spanish beach. The politician had worn a dreadful pair of khaki shorts.

At first sight, the building outside which Kevin now stood seemed an unlikely love nest. It was a dirty grey thirties block in a Westminster back street. Had it not been so close to Parliament, it would have become a slum by now. As he entered, Kevin saw that the landlords had upgraded the place with a lift and a hall porter: no doubt they called the flats 'luxury service apartments'.

It would be impossible, he thought, to keep a wife

and three children here; or, at least, a man like Fitzpeterson would think it impossible. It followed that the flat was a pied-à-terre, so Fitzpeterson might have homosexual orgies or pot parties here after all.

Stop speculating, he told himself; you'll know in a minute.

There was no avoiding the hall porter. His cubbyhole faced the single lift across a narrow lobby. A cadaverous man with a sunken, white face, he looked for all the world as if he were chained to the desk and never allowed to see the light of day. As Kevin approached, the man put down a book called *How to Make Your Second Million* and removed his glasses.

Kevin pointed to the book. 'I'd like to know how to make my first.'

'Nine,' said the porter in a patiently bored voice.

'What?'

'You're the ninth person to say that.'

'Oh. Sorry.'

'Then you ask why I'm reading it, and I say a resident lent it to me, and you say you'd like to make friends with that resident. Now that we've got all that out of the way, what can I do for you?'

Kevin knew how to deal with smart alecks. Pander, pander, he told himself. Aloud, he said: 'What number's Mr Fitzpeterson in?'

'I'll ring him for you.' The porter reached for the house phone.

'Just a minute.' Kevin brought out his wallet and

selected two notes. 'I'd like to surprise him.' He winked, and laid the money on the counter.

The man took the money and said loudly: 'Certainly, sir, as you're his brother. Five C.'

'Thanks.' Kevin crossed to the lift and pressed the button. The conspiratorial wink had done the trick more than the bribe, he guessed. He got into the lift, pressed the button for the fifth floor, then held the doors open. The porter was reaching for the house phone. Kevin said: 'A surprise. Remember?' The porter picked up his book without replying.

The lift creaked upwards Kevin felt a familiar, physical sensation of anticipation. He always did just before knocking on a door for a story. The feeling was not unpleasant, but it was invariably mixed with a trace of worry that he might not score.

The top-floor landing was graced with a token square of thin nylon carpet and a few fading watercolours, tasteless but inoffensive. There were four flats, each with a bell, a letter-box and a peephole. Kevin found 5C, took a deep breath, and rang the bell.

There was no answer. After a while he rang again, then put his ear to the door to listen. He could hear nothing. The tension drained out of him, leaving him a little depressed.

Wondering what to do, he walked across the landing to the tiny window and looked out. There was a school across the road. A class of girls played netball in the playground. From where he was, Kevin could not tell whether they were old enough for him to lust after.

He went back to Fitzpeterson's door and leaned on the bell. The noise of the lift arriving startled him. If it was a neighbour, maybe he could ask—

The sight of a tall young policeman emerging from the lift shocked him. He felt guilty. But, to his surprise, the constable saluted him.

'You must be the gentleman's brother,' the policeman said.

Kevin thought fast. 'Who told you that?' he said.

'The porter.'

Kevin came at him fast with another question. 'And why are you here?'

'Just checking he's all right. He didn't turn up for a meeting this morning, and his phone's off the hook. They ought to have bodyguards, you know, but they won't, these Ministers.' He looked at the door. 'No answer?'

'No.'

'Any reason you know of he might have been . . . well, ill? Upset? Called away?'

Kevin said: 'Well, he rang me up this morning and sounded distressed. That's why I came.' It was a very dangerous game he was playing, he knew; but he had not lied yet, and anyway it was too late to back out.

The policeman said: 'Perhaps we should get the key from the porter.'

Kevin did not want that. He said: 'I wonder if we should break the door down. My God, if he's ill in there . . .'

The policeman was young and inexperienced, and

the prospect of breaking a door down seemed to appeal to him. He said: 'It could be as bad as that, you think?'

'Who knows? For the sake of a door . . . the Fitzpetersons are not a *poor* family.'

'No, sir.' He needed no more encouragement. He put his shoulder to the door experimentally. 'One good shove . . .'

Kevin stood close to him, and the two men hit the door simultaneously. They made more noise than impact. Kevin said: 'It's not like this in the movies,' then bit his tongue – the remark was inappropriately flippant.

The policeman seemed not to notice. He said: 'Once more.'

This time they both put all their weight into it. The doorpost splintered and the female half of the lock came free, falling to the floor as the door flew open.

Kevin let the policeman go in first. As he followed him into the hall, the man said: 'No smell of gas.'

'All-electric flats,' Kevin said, guessing.

There were three doors off the tiny hall. The first led into a small bathroom, where Kevin glimpsed a row of toothbrushes and a full-length mirror. The second stood open, revealing a kitchen which looked as if it might have been searched recently. They went through the third door, and saw Fitzpeterson immediately.

He sat in an upright chair at his desk, his head in

his arms, as if he had fallen asleep over his work. But there was no work on his desk: just the phone, a glass, and an empty bottle. The bottle was small, and made of brown glass, with a white cap and a white label bearing handwriting – the kind of bottle chemists use to dispense sleeping pills.

For all his youth, the policeman acted commendably fast. He said: 'Mr Fitzpeterson, sir!' very loudly; and without pause crossed the room and thrust his hand inside the dressing gown to feel the prone man's heart. Kevin stood very still for a moment. At last the policeman said: 'Still alive.'

The young constable seemed to take command. He waved Kevin towards Fitzpeterson. 'Talk to him!' he said. Then he took a radio from his breast pocket and spoke into it.

Kevin took the politician's shoulder. The body felt curiously dead under the dressing gown. 'Wake up! Wake up!' he said.

The policeman finished on the radio and joined him. 'Ambulance any minute,' he said. 'Let's walk him.'

They took an arm each and tried to make the unconscious man walk. Kevin said: 'Is this what you're supposed to do?'

'I bloody well hope so.'

'Wish I'd paid attention at my first-aid classes.'

'You and me both.'

Kevin was itching to get to a phone. He could see the headline: I SAVE MINISTER'S LIFE. He was not a callous young man, but he had long known that the story which made his name would probably be a tragedy for someone else. Now that it had happened he wanted to use it before it slipped through his fingers. He wished the ambulance would hurry.

There was no reaction from Fitzpeterson to the walking treatment. The policeman said: 'Talk to him. Tell him who you are.'

This was getting a bit near the bone. Kevin swallowed hard and said: 'Tim, Tim! It's me.'

'Tell him your name.'

Kevin was saved by an ambulance in the street. He shouted over the noise of the siren: 'Let's get him onto the landing, ready.'

They dragged the limp body out through the door. As they waited by the lift, the policeman felt Fitzpeterson's heart again. 'Struth, I can't feel nothing,' he said.

The lift arrived, and two ambulance men emerged. The elder took a quick look and said: 'Overdose?'

'Yes,' the policeman said.

'No stretcher, then, Bill. Keep him standing.'

The policeman said to Kevin: 'Do you want to go with him?'

It was the last thing Kevin wanted to do. 'I should stay here and use the phone,' he said.

The ambulance men were in the elevator, supporting Fitzpeterson between them. 'We're off,' the elder said, and pressed the button.

The policeman got out his radio again, and Kevin

went back into the flat. The phone was on the desk, but he did not want the copper listening in. Maybe there was an extension in the bedroom.

He went through. There was a grey Trimphone on a little chipboard bedside unit. He dialled the *Post*.

'Copy, please ... Kevin Hart here. Government Minister Tim Fitzpeterson was rushed to hospital today after attempting to commit suicide point paragraph. I discovered the comatose body of the Energy Ministry's oil supremo after he had told me comma in a hysterical phone call comma that he was being blackmailed point par. The Minister ...' Kevin tailed off.

'You still there?' the copytaker demanded.

Kevin was silent. He had just noticed the blood on the crumpled sheets beside him, and he felt ill.

# Chapter Seventeen

What do I get out of my work? Derek Hamilton had been asking himself this question all morning, while the drugs wore off and the pain of his ulcer became sharper and more frequent. Like the pain, the question surfaced at moments of stress. Hamilton had begun badly, in a meeting with a finance director who had proposed a schedule of expenditure cuts amounting to a fifty-per-cent shutdown of the entire operation. The plan was no good – it would have helped cash flow and destroyed profitability – but Hamilton could see no alternatives, and the dilemma had made him angry. He had yelled at the accountant: 'I ask you for solutions and you tell me to close up the bloody shop!' Such behaviour towards senior management was quite intolerable, he knew. The man would certainly resign, and might not be dissuaded. Then his secretary, an elegant unflappable married woman who spoke three languages, had bothered him with a list of trivia, and he had shouted at her, too. Being what she was, she probably thought it part of her job to take that kind of maltreatment, but that was no excuse, he thought.

And each time he cursed himself, and his staff, and

his ulcer, he found himself wondering: What am I doing here?

He ran over possible answers as the car took him the short distance between his office and Nathaniel Fett's. Money as an incentive could not be dismissed quite as easily as he sometimes pretended. It was true that he and Ellen could live comfortably on his capital, or even the interest on his capital. But his dreams went beyond a comfortable life. Real success in business would mean a million-pound yacht, and a villa in Cannes, and a grouse moor of his own, and the chance to buy the Picassos he liked instead of just looking at reproductions in glossy books. Such were his dreams: or such they had been – it was now probably too late. Hamilton Holdings would not make sensational profits in his lifetime.

As a young man he had wanted power and prestige, he supposed. In that he had failed. There was no prestige in being chairman of an ailing company, no matter how big; and his power was rendered worthless by the strictures of the accountants.

He was not sure what people meant when they talked about job satisfaction. It was an odd expression, calling to mind a picture of a craftsman making a table from a piece of wood, or a farmer leading a herd of plump lambs to market. Business was not like that: even if one were moderately successful, there would always be new frustrations. And for Hamilton there was nothing other than business. Even if he had wanted to, he had not the ability to make tables or breed sheep, write textbooks or design office blocks.

He thought again about his sons. Ellen had been right: neither of them was counting on the inheritance. If asked for their counsel, they would certainly say: 'It's yours – spend it!' Nevertheless, it went against his instincts to dispose of the business which had made his family rich. Perhaps, he thought, I should disobey my instinct – following it has not made me happy.

For the first time he wondered what he would do if he did not have to go to the office. He had no interest in village life. Walking to the pub with a dog on a lead, like his neighbour Colonel Quinton, would bore Hamilton. Newspapers would hold no interest – he only read the business pages now, and if he had no business even they would be dull. He was fond of his garden, but he could not see himself spending all day digging weeds and forking in fertilizer.

What were the things we used to do, when we were young? It seemed, in retrospect, that Ellen and he had spent an awful lot of time doing absolutely nothing. They had gone for long drives in his two-seater, sometimes meeting friends for a picnic. Why? Why get in a car, go a long way, eat sandwiches and come back? They had gone to shows and to restaurants, but that was in the evening. Yet there had always seemed to be too few free days for them to spend together.

Well, it might be time for him and Ellen to start rediscovering each other. And a million pounds would buy some of his dreams. They could have a villa –

perhaps not in Cannes, but somewhere in the Sud. He could buy a yacht big enough for the Mediterranean and small enough for him to drive himself. The grouse moor was out of the question, but there might be enough left for one or two decent paintings.

This Laski fellow was buying a headache. However, headaches seemed to be his speciality. Hamilton knew a little about him. The man had no background, no education, no family; but he had brains and cash, and in hard times those things counted for more than good breeding. Perhaps Laski and Hamilton Holdings deserved each other.

It was an odd thing Hamilton had said to Nathaniel Fett: 'Tell Laski that if I sell him my company by midday, I want the money in my hand by noon.' How eccentric, to ask for cash on the nail like the proprietor of a Glasgow liquor store. But he knew why he had done it. The effect had been to take the decision out of his hands: if Laski could produce the money, the deal would be done; if not, not. Incapable of making up his mind, Hamilton had tossed a ha'penny.

Suddenly he hoped fervently that Laski would be able to raise the cash. Derek Hamilton wanted never to go back to the office.

The car drew up outside Fett's place, and he got out.

# Chapter Eighteen

The beauty of being an earwig, Bertie Chieseman had found, was that you could do almost anything while you were listening to the police radio. And the tragedy of it, from his point of view, was that there was nothing much he wanted to do.

Already this morning he had swept the carpet – a process of raising dust only for it to fall again soon afterwards – while the airwaves were filled with uninteresting messages about traffic in the Old Kent Road. He had also shaved at the sink in the corner, using a safety razor and hot water from the Ascot; and fried a single rasher of bacon on the cooker in the same room for his breakfast. He ate very little.

He had called the *Evening Post* only once since his first report at eight o'clock: to tip them off about an ambulance call to a block of flats in Westminster. The name of the patient had not been mentioned over the air, but Bertie had surmised from the address that it might, just possibly, be someone important. It was up to the news desk to phone ambulance headquarters and ask the name; and if headquarters had been told, they would pass the information on. Often the ambulance men did not make their report until the patient was in the hospital. Bertie occasionally talked to reporters, and he always asked them questions about how they used the information he gave them, and turned it into stories. He was quite well informed about the mechanics of journalism.

Apart from that and the traffic, there had been only shoplifting, petty vandalism, a couple of accidents, a small demonstration in Downing Street, and one mystery.

The mystery was in East London, but that was about all Bertie knew. He had heard an all-cars alert, but the subsequent message had been uninformative: the cars were asked to look out for a plain blue van with a certain registration number. It might simply have been hijacked with a cargo of cigarettes, or it might be driven by someone the police wanted to question, or it might have been in a robbery. The word 'Obadiah' had been used; Bertie did not know why. Immediately after the alert, three cars had been detached from regular patrol to search for the van. That meant very little.

The fuss might be over nothing at all – perhaps even some Flying Squad inspector's runaway wife; Bertie had known it to happen. On the other hand, it could be big. He was waiting for more information.

The landlady came up while he was cleaning his frying pan with warm water and a rag. He dried his hands on his sweater and got out the rent book. Mrs Keeney, in an apron and curlers, stared in awe at the radio equipment, although she saw it every week.

Bertie gave her the money and she signed the book. Then she handed him a letter.

'I don't know why you don't have some nice music on,' she said.

He smiled. He had not told her what he used the radio for, as it was against the law to listen to police radio. 'I'm not very musical,' he said.

She shook her head resignedly, and went out. Bertie opened the letter. It was his monthly cheque from the *Evening Post*. He had had a good spell: the cheque was for five hundred pounds. Bertie paid no tax. He found it difficult to spend all his money. The job compelled him to live fairly simply. He spent every evening in pubs, and on Sundays he went out in the car, his one luxury, a bright new Ford Capri. He went to all sorts of places, like a tourist: he had been to Canterbury Cathedral, Windsor Castle, Beaulieu, St Albans, Bath, Oxford; he visited safari parks, stately homes, ancient monuments, historic towns, racetracks and funfairs with equal enjoyment. He had never had so much money in his life. There was enough to buy everything he wanted, and a little left over to save.

He put the cheque in a drawer and finished cleaning the frying pan. As he was putting it away the radio crackled, and a sixth sense told him to listen carefully.

'That's right, blue Bedford six-wheeler. Alpha Charlie London two oh three Mother. Has it what? Distinguishing marks? Yes, if you look inside you'll notice it has a most unusual feature – six large boxes of used notes.'

Bertie frowned. The radio operator at headquarters was being funny, obviously; but what he said implied that the missing van was carrying a large sum of money. That sort of van did not go missing accidentally. It must have been hijacked.

Bertie sat down at his table and picked up the phone.

# Chapter Nineteen

Felix Laski and Nathaniel Fett stood up when Derek Hamilton entered the room. Laski, the would-be buyer, and Hamilton, the vendor, shook hands briefly, like boxers before a fight. Laski realized with a shock that he and Hamilton were wearing identical suits: dark blue with a pinstripe. They even had the same six-button double-breasted jacket without vents. But Hamilton's gross body took away any elegance the style had. On him, the most beautiful suit would look like a length of cloth wrapped around a jelly. Laski knew, without looking in a mirror, that his own suit appeared to be much more expensive.

He told himself not to feel superior. The wrong attitude could ruin a negotiation. He said: 'Nice to see you again, Hamilton.'

Hamilton nodded. 'How do you do, Mr Laski.' The chair squeaked as he sat down.

The use of 'Mr' did not escape Laski. Hamilton would only employ the unadorned surname with his equals.

Laski crossed his legs and waited for Fett, the broker, to open the proceedings. He studied Hamilton out of the corner of his eye. The man might have been handsome in his youth, he decided: he had a high forehead, a straight nose, and bright blue eyes. Right now he looked relaxed, with his hands folded in his lap. Laski thought: He had made up his mind already.

Fett said: 'For the record, Derek owns five hundred and ten thousand shares in Hamilton Holdings, Limited, a public company. Another four hundred and ninety thousand are owned by various parties, and there are no unissued shares. Mr Laski, you offer to buy those five hundred and ten thousand shares for the sum of one million pounds, on condition the deed of sale is dated today and signed at twelve noon.'

'Or that a letter to that intent is so dated and signed.'

'Quite so.'

Laski tuned out as Fett continued to enunciate formalities in a dry monotone. He was thinking that Hamilton probably deserved to lose his wife. A woman as vivacious and highly sexed as Ellen was entitled to a full-blooded love life: her husband had no right to let himself run to seed.

Here I am, he thought, stealing the man's wife and taking away his life's work, and still he can make me squirm by calling me Mister.

'As I see it,' Fett was concluding, 'the deal can be done just as Mr Laski has outlined it. The documents are satisfactory. There remains only the larger question of whether, and under what conditions, Derek will sell.' He sat back with the air of one who has completed a ritual.

Hamilton looked at Laski. 'What are your plans for the group?' he asked.

Laski suppressed a sigh. There was no point to any kind of cross-examination. He was quite free to tell Hamilton a pack of lies. He did just that. 'The first step would be a large capital injection,' he said. 'Then an improvement in management services, a shake-out at top level in the operating companies, and some streamlining in low-performance sectors.' Nothing could have been farther from the truth, but if Hamilton wanted to read the script from the top, Laski was happy to go along with it.

'You've chosen a crucial moment at which to make your offer.'

'Not really,' Laski said. 'The oil well, if it happens, will be a bonus. What I'm buying is a fundamentally sound group which is going through a bad patch. I shall make it profitable without meddling with its infrastructure. That happens to be my particular talent.' He smiled self-consciously. 'Despite my reputation, I'm interested in running real industries, not trading in equities.'

He caught a hostile glance from Fett: the broker knew he was lying. 'So why the twelve o'clock deadline?'

'I think the price of Hamilton shares will go up unreasonably if you get the licence. This could be my last chance for some time of buying at a sensible price.'

'Fair enough,' Hamilton said, taking the initiative away from Fett. 'But I, too, have set a deadline. How do you feel about that?'

'Quite happy,' Laski lied. In truth he was desperately worried. Hamilton's wish to see the money 'in his hand' at the time the deal was signed, was unexpected. Laski had planned to pay a deposit today and the balance when final contracts were exchanged. But although Hamilton's stipulation was eccentric, it was perfectly reasonable. Once the letter had been signed Laski was able to trade in the shares, either selling them or using them to raise a loan. What he planned was to use the shares – at their oil-inflated price – to raise the money to pay for the original purchase.

But he had fallen into the pit he had dug. He had tempted Hamilton with a fast deal, and the old man had gone for it too well. Laski did not know what he was going to do, for he did not have a million pounds – he would have been scraping the barrel for the one-hundred-thousand deposit. But he did know what he was *not* going to do: he would not let this deal slip through his fingers.

'Quite happy,' he repeated.

Fett said: 'Derek, perhaps now is the time you and I should have a few minutes together—'

'I don't think so,' Hamilton interrupted. 'Unless you plan to tell me that this deal is riddled with pitfalls?'

'Not at all.'

'In that case –' Hamilton turned to Laski ' – I accept.'

Laski stood up and shook Hamilton's hand. The

fat man was mildly embarrassed by the gesture, but it was one Laski believed in. Men like Hamilton could always find escape clauses in a contract, but they could not bear to renege on a handshake.

Laski said: 'The funds are in the Cotton Bank of Jamaica – London branch, of course. I imagine this presents no problem.' He drew a cheque-book from his pocket.

Fett frowned. It was a very small bank, but perfectly respectable. He would have preferred a cheque drawn on a clearing bank, but he could hardly object at this stage without seeming obstructive: Laski knew he would feel like this.

Laski wrote the cheque and handed it to Hamilton. 'It's not often a man pockets a million pounds,' he said.

Hamilton seemed to become jovial. He smiled: 'It's not often a man spends it.'

Laski said: 'When I was ten years old our rooster died, and I went with my father to market to buy a new one. It cost the equivalent of ... oh, three pounds. But my family had saved for a year to accumulate that money. More heart searching went into the purchase of that rooster than any financial deal I have ever done, this one included.' He smiled, knowing they were uneasy to hear this story, and not caring. 'A million pounds is nothing, but a rooster can save a whole family from starvation.'

Hamilton mumbled: 'Very true.'

Laski reverted to his normal image. 'Let me call the

bank to warn them that this cheque is on its way.'

'Surely.' Fett took him to the door and pointed. 'That room is empty. Valerie will give you a line.'

'Thank you. When I return, we can sign the letters.' Laski went into the little room and picked up the phone. When he heard the dialling tone, he looked out of the room to make sure Valerie was not listening. She was at the filing cabinet. Laski dialled.

'Cotton Bank of Jamaica.'

'Laski here. Give me Jones.'

There was a pause.

'Good morning, Mr Laski.'

'Jones, I've just signed a cheque for a million pounds.'

At first there was no reply. Then Jones said: 'Jesus. You haven't got it.'

'All the same, you will clear the cheque.'

'But what about Threadneedle Street?' The banker's voice was rising in pitch. 'We don't have enough cash on deposit at the bank!'

'We'll cross that bridge when we come to it.'

'Mr Laski. This bank cannot authorize one million pounds to be transferred from its account at the Bank of England to another account at the Bank of England, because this bank does not have one million pounds on deposit at the Bank of England. I don't think I can make the situation plainer.'

'Jones, who owns the Cotton Bank of Jamaica?'

Jones drew in his breath loudly. 'You do, sir.'

'Quite.' Laski put the phone down.

# Twelve Noon

# Chapter Twenty

Peter 'Jesse' James was perspiring. The midday sun was unseasonably strong, and the wide glass windscreen of the van magnified its heat, so that the rays burned his naked, meaty forearms and scorched the legs of his trousers. He was awful hot.

As well as that, he was terrified.

Jacko had told him to drive slowly. The advice was superfluous. A mile from the scrap yard he had run into heavy traffic; and it had been bumper-to-bumper since then, across half of south London. He could not have hurried if he had wanted to.

He had both of the van's sliding side doors open, but this did not help. There was no wind when the vehicle was stationary, and all he got when he moved was a light breeze of warm exhaust smoke.

Jesse believed driving ought to be an adventure. He had been in love with cars since he stole his first motor – a Zephyr-Zodiac with customized fins – at the age of twelve. He liked to race away from traffic lights, double-declutch on bends, and scare the hell out of Sunday drivers. When another motorist dared to sound his horn, Jesse would yell curses and shake his fist, and fantasize about shooting the bastard through the head. In his own car he kept a pistol in the glove compartment. It had never been used.

But driving was no fun when you had a fortune in stolen money in the back. You had to accelerate gradually and brake evenly, give the old slowing-down signal when you pulled up, refrain from over-taking, and give way to pedestrians at road junctions. It occurred to him that there was such a thing as suspiciously good behaviour: an intelligent copper, seeing a youngish bloke in a van poodling along like an old dear on a driving test, might well smell a rat.

He came to yet another junction on the intermin-able South Circular Road. The light turned from green to amber. Jesse's instinct was to push his foot to the floor and race the signal. He gave a weary sigh, flap-ped his arm out of the window like a fool, and came to a careful stop.

He should try not to worry – nervous people made mistakes. He ought to forget the money, think about something else. He had driven thousands of miles through the exasperating traffic of London without ever being stopped by the law: why should today be different? Even the Old Bill couldn't *smell* hot money.

The lights changed and he pulled forward. The road narrowed into a shopping centre where delivery trucks lined the kerb and a series of pedestrian cross-ings slowed the flow of cars. The narrow pavements were thronged with shoppers and obstructed by several hawkers flogging substandard costume jewel-lery and ironing-board covers.

# Paper Money

The women were wearing summery clothes – there was something to be said for the hot weather. Jesse started to watch the tight T-shirts, the delightfully loose-fitting frocks and the bare knees as he crawled forward a few yards at a time. He liked girls with big bottoms, and he scanned the crowds for a suitable specimen to undress with his eyes.

He spotted her a good fifty yards away. She was wearing a blue nylon sweater and tight white trousers. She probably thought she was overweight, but Jesse would have told her otherwise. She had a nice, old-fashioned bra which made her tits look like torpedoes; and her high-waisted slacks flared out over big hips. Jesse peered at her, hoping to see her tits wobble. They did.

What he would like to do, was to stand behind her, and pull her trousers down slowly, then—

The car in front moved forward twenty yards, and Jesse followed it. It was a brand-new Marina with a vinyl roof. Maybe he would get one with his share of the takings. The line of cars stopped again. Jesse pulled the handbrake and looked for the plump girl.

He did not pick her up until the traffic was moving off again. As he let the clutch in he saw her, looking in the window of a shoe shop, her back to him. The trousers were so tight that he could see the hem of her panties, two diagonal lines pointing to the fork of her thighs. He loved it when you could see their panties under the trousers: it turned him on almost as much as a bare bum. Then I'd slide her panties down, he thought, and—

There was a crash of steel on steel. The van stopped with a bump, throwing Jesse forward against the steering wheel. The doors slid shut with a double bang. He knew, before he looked, what he had done; and the taste of fear made him feel sick.

The Marina in front had stopped sooner than it needed to, and Jesse, wrapped up in the plump girl with the tight trousers, had gone straight into its back.

He got out of the van. The driver of the saloon car was already inspecting the damage. He looked up at Jesse, his face red with anger. 'You mad bastard,' he spat. 'What are you – blind, or stupid?' He had a Lancashire accent.

Jesse ignored him and looked at the bumpers of the two vehicles, folded together in a steel kiss. He made an effort to keep calm. 'Sorry, pal. My fault.'

'Sorry! You people should be banned from the ruddy road.'

Jesse stared at the man. He was short and portly, and wore a suit. His round face was a picture of righteous indignation. He had the quick aggressiveness of small people, and their characteristic backward tilt of the head. Jesse hated him instantly. He looked like a sergeant-major. Jesse would have liked to punch his face; or better, shoot him through the forehead.

'We all make mistakes,' he said with forced amiability. 'Let's just give each other our names and everything, and get on. It's only a little bump. Don't make a national disaster of it.'

It was the wrong thing to say. The short man became even redder. 'You're not getting off that lightly,' he said.

The traffic in front had moved on, and drivers behind were getting impatient. Several of them sounded their horns. One man got out of his car.

The Marina driver was writing the number of the van in a little notebook. That type of man always does have a little notebook and pencil in his jacket pocket, Jesse thought.

He closed the book. 'This is bloody careless driving. I'm going to ring the police.'

The driver from behind said: 'How about moving this little lot out the way, so the rest of us can get on?'

Jesse sensed an ally. 'Nothing I'd rather do, mate, but this fellow wants to call in Kojak on the case.'

The portly man wagged a finger. 'I know your type – drive like a hooligan and let the insurance pay. I'm having you up, Sonny Jim.'

Jesse took a step forward, clenching his fists; then stopped himself. He was getting panicky. 'The police have got enough to do,' he pleaded.

The other man's eyes narrowed. He had seen Jesse's fear. 'We'll let them decide whether they've got better things to do.' He looked around, and spotted a phone booth. 'You stop here.' He turned away.

Jesse grabbed his shoulder. He was scared now. He said: 'This is nothing to do with the police!'

The man turned and knocked Jesse's hand away. 'Get off, you young punk—'

Jesse seized him by the lapels and pulled him onto his toes. 'I'll give you punk . . .' Suddenly he became conscious of the crowd that had gathered, looking on with interest. There were about a dozen people. He stared at them. They were mostly housewives with shopping bags. The girl with the tight trousers was at the front. He realized he was doing all the wrong things.

He decided to get out of it.

He let the aggrieved man go and got into the van. The man stared at him disbelievingly.

Jesse restarted the stalled engine and backed up. There was a wrenching sound as the vehicles parted. He could see that the Marina's bumper hung loose, and its rear-light cluster was smashed. Fifty quid to put right, and a tenner if you do the work yourself, he thought wildly.

The portly man moved in front of the van and stood there like Neptune, waving an officious finger. 'You stay right here!' he shouted. The crowd was growing as the row became more spectacular. There was a lull in the oncoming traffic, and the cars behind began to pull out past the accident.

Jesse found first gear and revved the engine. The man stood his ground. Jesse engaged the clutch with a jerk, and the van shot forward.

Too late, the portly man dived towards the kerb. Jesse heard a dull thud from the nearside wing as he swung out. A car behind braked with a squeal of tyres. Jesse changed up and tore away without looking back.

The street seemed narrow and oppressive, traplike, as he hurtled along, ignoring pedestrian crossings, swerving and braking. He tried desperately to think. He had screwed it all up. The whole tickle had gone beautifully, and Jesse James had pranged the getaway motor. A vanload of paper money blown on a fifty-nicker crunch. Arseholes.

Stay cool, he told himself. It wasn't a blowout until he was locked up. There was still time, if only he could *think*.

He slowed the van and turned off the main road. There was no point in attracting attention again. He threaded his way through a series of back streets while he figured it out.

What would happen now? A bystander would phone the police, especially as he had knocked down the portly man. The van's number was in the little notebook; besides, somebody in the crowd would have noted it too. It would be reported as a hit-and-run, and the number would go out over the air to patrol cars. Anything from three minutes to fifteen to get that far. Another five minutes, and they would broadcast a description of Jesse. What was he wearing? Blue trousers and an orange shirt. Arseholes.

What would Tony Cox say, if he were here to be asked? Jesse recalled the guvnor's fleshy face and heard his voice. *Tell yourself what the problem is, right?*

Jesse said aloud: 'The police have got my number and description.'

*Think what you'd have to do to solve the problem.*

'What the hell can I do, Tone? Change my number plate and my appearance?'

*Then do it, right?*

Jesse frowned. Tony's analytical thinking only went so far. Where the hell could he get number plates, and how could he fit them?

Of course, it was easy.

He found his way to a main road and drove along until he came to a garage. He pulled on to the forecourt. Quad stamps, he thought: jolly good show. There was a repair shop behind the pumps. A tanker was discharging on the far side.

The attendant approached, cleaning his spectacles on an oily rag. 'Five quids' worth,' Jesse said. 'Where's the khasi?'

'Round the side.'

Jesse followed the jerked thumb. A rough concrete path led alongside the garage. He found a broken door marked 'Gents' and went past it.

Behind the garage was a small patch of waste ground where newish cars in for repair jostled with rusty doors, buckled wings, and discarded machinery. Jesse could not see what he was looking for.

The back entrance to the repair shop gaped open beside him, big enough to drive a bus through. There was no point in being furtive. He walked in.

It took a moment to adjust to the gloom after the

sunlight outside. The air smelled of engine oil and ozone. A Mini was on a ramp at head height, its entrails hanging down obscenely. The front end of an articulated truck was wired up to a Krypton tester. A Jaguar on chocks had its wheels off. There was no one about. He looked at his wristwatch: they would be having their dinner. He looked around.

He spotted the things he needed.

A pair of red-and-white trade plates stood on an oil drum in a corner. He crossed the floor and picked them up. He looked around again, and stole two more things: clean overalls hanging on a peg in the brick wall, and a length of dirty string off the floor.

A voice said: 'Looking for something, brother?'

Jesse jerked around, his heart in his mouth. A black mechanic in a grimy overall stood on the far side of the shop, leaning on the gleaming white wing of the Jaguar, his mouth full of food. His Afro haircut shifted as he chewed. Jesse tried to cover the trade plates with the overalls. 'The khasi,' he said. 'Want to change my clothes.' He held his breath.

The mechanic pointed. 'Outside,' he said. He swallowed, and took another bite out of a Scotch egg.

'Thanks.' Jesse hurried out.

'Any time,' the mechanic called after him. Jesse realized the man had an Irish accent. Irish spades? That was a new one.

The pump attendant was waiting beside the van. Jesse climbed in and threw the overalls and their contents over the seat into the back. The attendant looked curiously at the bundle. Jesse said: 'My overalls were hanging out the back door. It must be filthy. How much?'

'We generally charge a fiver for five quids' worth. I didn't notice it.'

'Nor did I, for fifty bleeding miles. I did say five quids' worth, didn't I?'

'That's what you said. No charge for the bog.'

Jesse gave him a five-pound note and pulled away rapidly.

He was a little off his route now, which was good. The area was quieter than the places he had travelled through earlier. There were oldish detached houses on either side, set back from the road. Horse-chestnut trees lined the pavements. He saw a Green Line bus stop.

He needed a quiet lane in which to perform the switch. He checked his watch again. It must be fifteen minutes since the accident. There was no time left for finesse.

He took the next turning. The street was called Brook Avenue. All the houses were semis. He needed somewhere less exposed, for Christ's sake! He could not switch plates in full view of sixty nosy housewives.

He took another turn, and another – and found a service road behind a little row of shops. He pulled in and stopped. There were garages and garbage cans, and the back doors through which goods were delivered to the stores. It was the best he could hope for.

# Paper Money

He climbed over the seat into the back of the van. It was very hot. He sat on one of the money chests and pulled the overalls up his legs. Jesus, he was nearly there: give me a couple more minutes, he thought – it was almost a prayer.

He stood up, bending over, and shrugged into the garment. If I'd blown it, Tony would have slit my throat, he thought. He shuddered. Tony Cox was a hard bastard. He had a bit of a kink about punishment.

Jesse zipped up the overalls. He knew about eye-witness descriptions. The police would by now be looking for a very big, vicious-looking character with desperate eyes, wearing an orange shirt and jeans. Anyone actually looking at Jesse would just see a mechanic.

He picked up the trade plates. The string had gone – he must have dropped it. He looked around the floor. Damn, there was *always* a piece of rope floating around on the floor of a van! He opened the toolbox and found a length of oily string tied around the jack.

He got out and went to the front of the van. He worked carefully, afraid to botch the job by hurrying. He tied the red-and-white trade plate over the original number plate, just as garages usually did when taking a commercial vehicle for a road test. He stood back and examined his work. It looked fine.

He went to the rear of the van and repeated the job on the back plate. It was done. He breathed more easily.

'Changing the plates, then?'

Jesse jumped and turned. His heart sank. The voice belonged to a policeman.

For Jesse it was the last straw. He could think of no more wrinkles, no more plausible lies, no more ruses. His instincts deserted him. He did not have a single thing to say.

The copper walked towards him. He was quite young, with ginger sideburns and a freckled nose. 'Trouble?'

Jesse was amazed to see him smile. A ray of hope penetrated his petrified brain. He found his tongue. 'Plates worked loose,' he said. 'Just tightened them up.'

The copper nodded. 'I used to drive one of these,' he said conversationally. 'Easier than driving a car. Lovely jobs.'

It crossed Jesse's mind that the man might be playing a sadistic cat-and-mouse game, knowing perfectly well that Jesse was the driver of the hit-and-run van, but pretending ignorance so as to shock him at the last minute.

'Easy when they're running right,' he said. The sweat on his face felt cold.

'Well, you've done it now. On your way, you're blocking the road.'

Like a sleepwalker, Jesse climbed into the cab and started the engine. Where was the copper's car? Did he have his radio switched off? Had the overalls and the trade plates fooled him?

If he were to walk around to the front of the van

and see the dent made by the bumper of the Marina—

Jesse eased his foot off the clutch and drove slowly along the service road. He stopped at the end and looked both ways. In his wing mirror, he saw the policeman at the far end getting into a patrol car.

Jesse pulled into the road and the patrol car was lost from view. He wiped his brow. He was trembling.

'Gawd, stone the crows,' he breathed.

# Chapter Twenty-One

Evan Jones was drinking whisky before lunch for the first time in his life. There was a reason. He had a Code, and he had broken it – also for the first time. He was explaining this to his friend, Arny Matthews, but he was not doing too well, for he was unused to whisky, and the first double was already reaching his brain.

'It's my upbringing, see,' he said in his musical Welsh accent. 'Strict chapel. We lived by the Book. Now, a man can exchange one Code for another, but he can't shake the habit of obedience. See?'

'I see,' said Arny, who did not see at all. Evan was manager of the London branch of the Cotton Bank of Jamaica, and Arny was a senior actuary at Fire and General Marine Insurance, and they lived in adjoining mock-Tudor houses in Woking, Surrey. Their friendship was shallow, but permanent.

'Bankers have a Code,' Evan continued. 'Do you know, it caused quite a stir when I told my parents I wanted to be a banker. In South Wales the grammar-school boys are expected to become teachers, or ministers, or Coal Board clerks, or trade union officials – but not bankers.'

'My mother didn't even know what an actuary was,' said Arny sympathetically, missing the point.

'I'm not talking about the principles of good banking – the law of the least risk, the collateral to more-than-cover the loan, higher interest for longer term – I don't mean all that.'

'No.' Arny now had no idea what Evan did mean. But he sensed that Evan was going to be indiscreet, and like everyone in the City he enjoyed the indiscretions of others. 'Have another?' He picked up the glasses.

Evan nodded assent, and watched Arny go to the bar. The two of them often met in the lounge of Pollard's before catching the train home together. Evan liked the plush seats, and the quiet, and the faintly servile barmen. He had no time for the newer kind of pub that was springing up in the Square Mile: trendy, crowded cellars with loud music for the long-haired whiz kids in their three-piece suits and gaudy ties, drinking lager in pints or Continental aperitifs.

'I'm talking about integrity,' Evan resumed when Arny came back. 'A banker can be a fool, and survive, if he's straight; but if he hasn't got integrity . . .'

'Absolutely.'

'Now, take Felix Laski. There's a man totally without integrity.'

'This is the man who's taken you over.'

'To my everlasting regret, yes. Shall I tell you how he got control?'

Arny leaned forward in his seat, holding a cigarette halfway to his lips. 'Okay.'

'We had a customer called South Middlesex Properties. They were tied up with a discounting outfit we knew, and we wanted an outlet for a lot of long-term money. The loan was too big for the property company, really, but the collateral was vast. To cut a long story short, they defaulted on the loan.'

'But you had the property,' Arny said. 'Surely the title deeds were in your vault.'

'Worthless. What we had were copies – and so did several other creditors.'

'Straightforward fraud.'

'Indeed, although somehow they managed to make it look like mere incompetence. However, we were in a hole. Laski bailed us out in exchange for a majority holding.'

'Shrewd.'

'Shrewder than you think, Arny. Laski practically controlled South Middlesex Properties. Mind you, he wasn't a director. But he had shares, and he was employed by them as a consultant, and the management was weak . . .'

'So he bought into the Cotton Bank with the money he'd borrowed and defaulted on.'

'Looks like it, doesn't it?'

Arny shook his head. 'I find that very hard to credit.'

'You wouldn't if you knew the bugger.' Two men in solicitors' stripes sat at the next table with half-pints of beer, and Evan lowered his voice. 'A man totally without integrity,' he repeated.

'What a stroke to pull.' There was a note of admiration in Arny's voice. 'You could have gone to the newspapers – if it's true.'

'Who the hell would publish it, other than *Private Eye*? But it's true, boy. There is no depth to which that man will not sink.' He took a large swallow of whisky. 'You know what he's done today?'

'It couldn't be worse than the South Middlesex deal,' Arny goaded him.

'Couldn't it? Ha!' Evan's face was slightly flushed now, and the glass trembled in his hand. He spoke slowly and deliberately. 'He has instructed me – instructed, mind you – to clear a rubber cheque for a million pounds.' He set down his glass with a flourish.

'But what about Threadneedle Street?'

'My exact words to him!' The two solicitors looked around, and Evan realized he had shouted. He spoke more quietly. 'My *very* words. You'll never believe what he said. He said: "Who owns the Cotton Bank of Jamaica?" Then he put the phone down on me.'

'So what did you do?'

Evan shrugged. 'When the payee phoned up, I said the cheque was good.'

Arny whistled. 'What *you* say makes no difference. It's the Bank of England who have to make the transfer. And when they discover that you haven't got a million—'

'I told him all that.' Evan realized he was close to tears, and felt ashamed. 'I have never, in thirty years of banking, since I started behind the counter of Barclays Bank in Cardiff, passed a rubber cheque. Until today.' He emptied his glass and stared at it gloomily. 'Have another?'

'No. You shouldn't, either. Will you resign?'

'Must do.' He shook his head from side to side. 'Thirty years. Come on, have another.'

'No,' Arny said firmly. 'You should go home.' He stood up and took Evan's elbow.

'All right.'

The two men walked out of the wine bar and into the street. The sun was high and hot. Lunch-hour queues were beginning to form at cafés and sandwich shops. A couple of pretty secretaries walked by eating ice-cream cones.

Arny said: 'Lovely weather, for the time of year.'

'Beautiful,' Evan said lugubriously.

Arny stepped off the kerb and hailed a taxi. The black cab swerved across and pulled up with a squeal.

Evan said: 'Where are you going?'

'Not me. You.' Arny opened the door and said to the driver: 'Waterloo Station.'

Evan stumbled in and sat down on the back seat.

'Go home before you get too drunk to walk,' Arny said. He shut the door.

Evan opened the window. 'Thanks,' he said.

'Home's the best place.'

Evan nodded. 'I wish I knew what I'm going to tell Myfanwy.'

\*

# Paper Money

Arny watched the cab disappear, then walked towards his office, thinking about his friend. Evan was finished as a banker. A reputation for honesty was made slowly and lost quickly in the City. Evan would lose his as surely as if he had tried to pick the pocket of the Chancellor of the Exchequer. He might get a decent pension out of it, but he would never get another job.

Arny was secure, if hard up: quite the opposite of Evan's plight. He earned a respectable salary, but he had borrowed money to build an extension to his lounge, and he was having difficulty with the payments. He could see a way to earn out of Evan's misfortune. It felt disloyal. However, he reasoned, Evan could suffer no more.

He went into a phone booth and dialled a number.

The pips went and he thumbed in a coin. '*Evening Post*?'

'Which department?'

'City Editor.'

There was a pause, then a new voice said: 'City desk.'

'Mervyn?'

'Speaking.'

'This is Arnold Matthews.'

'Hello, Arny. What goes on?'

Arny took a deep breath. 'The Cotton Bank of Jamaica is in trouble.'

# Chapter Twenty-Two

Doreen, the wife of Deaf Willie, sat stiffly upright in the front of Jacko's car, clutching a handbag in her lap. Her face was pale, and her lips were twisted into a strange expression compounded of fury and dread. She was a large-boned woman, very tall with broad hips, and tending to plumpness because of Willie's liking for chips. She was also poorly dressed, and this was because of Willie's liking for brown ale. She stared straight ahead, and spoke to Jacko out of the side of her mouth.

'Who've took him up the hospital, then?'

'I don't know, Doreen,' Jacko lied. 'Perhaps it was a job, and they didn't want to let on who, you know. All I know is, I get a phone call, Deaf Willie's up the hospital, tell his missus, bang.' He made a slamming-the-phone-down gesture.

'Liar,' Doreen said evenly.

Jacko fell silent.

In the back of the car, Willie's son, Billy, stared vacantly out of the window. With his long, awkward body he was cramped in the small space. Normally he enjoyed travelling in cars, but today his mother was very tense, and he knew something bad had happened. Just what it was, he was not sure: things were confusing. Ma seemed to be cross with Jacko, but Jacko was a friend. Jacko had said that Dad was up the hospital, but not that he was ill; and indeed, how could he be? For he had been well when he left the house early this morning.

The hospital was a large brick building, faintly Gothic, which had once been the residence of the Mayor of Southwark. Several flat-roofed extensions had been built in the grounds, and tarmacadamed car parks had obliterated the rest of the lawns.

Jacko stopped near the entrance to Casualty. No one spoke as they got out of the car and walked across to the door. They passed an ambulance man with a pipe in his mouth, leaning against an anti-smoking poster on the side of his vehicle.

They went from the heat of the car park into the cool of the hospital. The familiar antiseptic smell caused a nauseous surge of fear in Doreen's stomach. Green plastic chairs were ranged around the walls, and a desk was placed centrally, opposite the entrance. Doreen noticed a small boy nursing a glass cut, a young man with his arm in an improvised sling, and a girl with her head in her hands. Somewhere nearby a woman moaned. Doreen felt panicky.

The West Indian nurse at the desk was speaking into a telephone. They waited for her to finish, then Doreen said: 'Have you had a William Johnson brought in here this morning?'

The nurse did not look at her. 'Just a minute,

please.' She made a note on a scribbling pad, then glanced up as an ambulance arrived outside. She said: 'Would you sit down, please?' She came around the desk and walked past them to the door.

Jacko moved away, as if to sit down, and Doreen snatched at his sleeve. 'Stay here!' she commanded. 'I'm not waiting bloody hours – I'm stopping here until she tells me.'

They watched as a stretcher was brought in. The prone figure was wrapped in a bloody blanket. The nurse escorted the bearers through a pair of swing doors.

A plump white woman in sister's uniform arrived through another door, and Doreen waylaid her. 'Why can't I find out whether my husband's here?' she said shrilly.

The sister stopped, and took the three of them in at a glance. The black nurse came back in.

Doreen said: 'I asked her and she wouldn't tell me.'

The sister said: 'Nurse, why were these people not attended to?'

'I thought the road-accident case with two severed limbs looked sicker than this lady.'

'You did the right thing, but there's no need for witticism.' The plump sister turned to Doreen. 'What is your husband's name?'

'William Johnson.'

The sister looked in a register. 'That name isn't here.' She paused. 'But we do have an unidentified patient. Male, white, medium build, middle-aged, with gunshot wounds to the head.'

Jacko said: 'That's him.'

Doreen said: 'Oh, my God!'

The sister picked up the phone. 'You'd better see him, to find out whether he is your husband.' She dialled a single number and waited for a moment. 'Oh, Doctor, this is Sister Rowe in Casualty. I have a woman here who may be the wife of the gunshot patient. Yes. I will . . . we'll meet you there.' She hung up and said: 'Please follow me.'

Doreen fought back despair as they trod the linoleum corridor floors through the hospital. She had dreaded this ever since the day, fifteen or more years ago, when she had discovered she had married a villain. She had always suspected it; Willie had told her he was in business, and she asked no more questions because in the days when they were courting a girl who wanted a husband learned not to come on strong. But it was never easy to keep secrets in marriage. There had been a knock at the door, when little Billy was still in nappies, and Willie had looked out of the front window and seen a copper. Before answering the door he said to Doreen: 'Last night, there was a poker game here: me, and Scotch Harry, and Tom Webster, and old Gordon. It started at ten, and went on till four in the morning.' Doreen, who had been up half the night in an empty house, trying to get Billy to sleep, had nodded dumbly; and when the Old Bill asked her, she said what Willie had told her to say. Since then she had worried.

When it's only a suspicion, you can tell yourself not to worry; but when you *know* your husband is out there somewhere breaking into a factory or a shop or even a bank, you can't help wondering if he'll ever come home.

She was not sure why she was so full of rage and fear. She did not love Willie, not in any familiar sense of the word. He was a pretty lousy husband: always out at night, bad with money, and a poor lover. The marriage had varied from tolerable to miserable. Doreen had two miscarriages, then Billy; after that they stopped trying. They stuck together because of Billy, and she did not suppose they were the only couple to do *that*. Not that Willie shouldered much of the burden of bringing up a handicapped child, but it seemed to make him just guilty enough to stay married. The boy loved his father.

No, Willie, I don't love you, she thought. But I want you and I need you; I like to have you there in bed, and sitting next to me watching television, and doing your pools at the table; and if *that* was called love, I'd say I love you.

They had stopped walking, and the sister was speaking. 'I'll call you in when Doctor's ready,' she said. She disappeared into a ward, closing the door behind her.

Doreen stared hard at the blank, cream-painted wall, trying not to wonder what was behind it. She had done this once before, after the Componiparts payroll job. But then it had been different: they had come to the house saying 'Willie's up the hospital, but he's all right – just stunned.' He had put too much gelignite on the safe door, and had lost all hearing in one ear. She had gone to the hospital – a different one – and waited; but she had known he was okay.

After that job she had tried, for the first and only time, to make him go straight. He had seemed willing, until he got out of hospital and was faced with the prospect of actually doing something about it. He sat around the house for a few days, then when he ran out of money he did another job. Later he let it slip that Tony Cox had taken him on the firm. He was proud, and Doreen was furious.

She hated Tony Cox ever afterwards. Tony knew it, too. He had been at their home, once, eating a plate of chips and talking to Willie about boxing, when suddenly he looked up at Doreen and said: 'What you got against me, girl?'

Willie looked worried and said: 'Go easy, Tone.'

Doreen tossed her head and said: 'You're a villain.'

Tony laughed at that, showing a mouthful of half-chewed chips. Then he said: 'So's your husband – didn't you know?' After that they went back to talking about boxing.

Doreen never had quick answers for clever people like Tony, so she said no more. Her opinion made no difference to anything, anyway. It would never occur to Willie that the fact that she disliked someone was a reason for not bringing him to the house. It was Willie's house, even if Doreen had to pay the rent out of her income from the mail-order catalogue every other week.

It was a Tony Cox job that Willie had been on today. Doreen had got that from Jacko's wife – Willie wouldn't tell her. If Willie dies, she thought, I swear to God I'll swing for that Tony Cox. Oh, God, let him be all right—

The door opened and the sister put her head out. 'Would you like to come in, please?'

Doreen went first. A short, dark-skinned doctor with thick black hair stood near the door. She ignored him and went straight to the bedside.

At first she was confused. The figure on the high, metal-framed bed was covered to the neck in a sheet, and from the chin to the top of the head in bandages. She had been expecting to see a face, and know instantly whether it was Willie. For a moment she did not know what to do. Then she knelt down and gently pulled back the sheet.

The doctor said: 'Mrs Johnson, is this your husband?'

She said: 'Oh, God, Willie, what have they done?' Her head fell slowly forward until her brow rested on her husband's bare shoulder.

Distantly, she heard Jacko say: 'That's him. William Johnson.' He went on to give Willie's age and address. Doreen became aware that Billy was standing close to her. After a few moments the boy put his hand on her shoulder. His presence forced her to deny grief, or at least postpone it. She composed her features and stood up.

The doctor looked grave. 'Your husband will live,' he said.

She put her arm around her son. 'What have they done to him?'

'Shotgun pellets. Close range.'

She was gripping Billy's shoulder very hard. She was *not* going to cry. 'But he'll be all right?'

'I said he'll live, Mrs Johnson. But we may not be able to save his eyesight.'

'What?'

'He's going to be blind.'

Doreen shut her eyes tight and screamed: 'No!'

They were all around her, very quickly; they had been expecting hysterics. She fought them off. She saw Jacko's face in front of her, and she shouted: 'Tony Cox done this, you bastard!' She hit Jacko. 'You bastard!'

She heard Billy sob, and she calmed down immediately. She turned to the boy and pulled him to her, hugging him. He was several inches taller than she. 'There, there, Billy,' she murmured. 'Your Dad's alive, be glad of that.'

The doctor said: 'You should go home, now. We have a phone number where we can reach you . . .'

'I'll take her,' Jacko said. 'It's my phone, but I live close.'

Doreen detached herself from Billy and went to

the door. The sister opened it. Two policemen stood outside.

Jacko said: 'What's this, then?' He sounded outraged.

The doctor said: 'We are obliged to inform the police in cases like this.'

Doreen saw that one of the police was a woman. She was seized with the urge to blurt out the fact that Willie had been shot on a Tony Cox job: that would screw Tony. But she had acquired the habit of deceiving the police during fifteen years of marriage to a thief. And she knew, as soon as the thought crossed her mind, that Willie would never forgive her for squealing.

She could not tell the police. But, suddenly, she knew who she could tell.

She said: 'I want to make a phone call.'

# One p.m.

# Chapter Twenty-Three

Kevin Hart ran up the stairs and entered the news-room of the *Evening Post*. A Lad in a Brutus shirt and platform shoes walked past him, carrying a pile of newspapers: the one o'clock edition. Kevin snatched one off the top and sat down at a desk.

His story was on the front page.

The headline was: GOVT. OIL BOSS COLLAPSES. Kevin stared for a moment at the delightful words 'By Kevin Hart.' Then he read on.

Junior Minister Mr Tim Fitzpeterson was found unconscious at his Westminster flat today.

An empty bottle of pills was found beside him.

Mr Fitzpeterson, a Department of Energy Minister responsible for oil policy, was rushed to the hospital in an ambulance.

I called at his flat to interview him at the same time as PC Ron Bowler, who had been sent to check after the Minister failed to appear at a committee meeting.

We found Mr Fitzpeterson slumped at his desk. An ambulance was called immediately.

A Department of Energy spokesman said: 'It appears that Mr Fitzpeterson took an accidental overdose. A full enquiry is to be made.'

Tim Fitzpeterson is 41. He has a wife and three daughters.

A hospital spokesman said later: 'He is off the critical list.'

Kevin read the whole thing through again, hardly able to believe what he was reading. The story he had dictated over the phone had been rewritten beyond recognition. He felt empty and bitter. This was to have been his moment of glory, and some spineless sub-editor had soured it.

What about the anonymous tip that Fitzpeterson had a girlfriend? What about the call from the man himself, claiming he was being blackmailed? Newspapers were supposed to tell the truth, weren't they?

His anger grew. He had not entered the business to become a mindless hack. Exaggeration was one thing – he was quite prepared to turn a drunken brawl into a gang war for the sake of a story on a slow day – but suppression of important facts, especially concerning politicians, was not part of the game.

If a reporter couldn't insist on the truth, who the hell could?

He stood up, folded the newspaper, and walked across to the news desk.

Arthur Cole was putting a phone down. He looked up at Kevin.

Kevin thrust the paper under his nose. 'What's this, Arthur? We've got a blackmailed politician committing suicide, and the *Evening Post* says it's an accidental overdose.'

Cole looked past him. 'Barney,' he called. 'Here a minute.'

Kevin said: 'What's going on, Arthur?'

Cole looked at him. 'Oh, fuck off, Kevin,' he said.

Kevin stared at him.

Cole said to the reporter called Barney: 'Ring Essex police and find out whether they've been alerted to look for the getaway van.'

Kevin turned away, dumbfounded. He had been ready for discussion, argument, even a row; but not for such a casual dismissal. He sat down again, on the far side of the room, with his back to the news desk, staring blindly at the paper. Was this what provincial diehards had known when they warned him about Fleet Street? Was this what the nutcase lefties at college had meant when they said the Press was a whore?

It's not as if I'm a lousy idealist, he thought. I'll defend our prurience and our sensationalism, and I'll say with the best of them that the people get the papers they deserve. But I'm not a total cynic, not yet, for God's sake. I believe we're here to discover the truth, and then to print it.

He began to wonder whether he really wanted to be a journalist. It was dull most of the time. There was the occasional high, when something went right, a story turned good and you got a by-line; or when a big story broke, and six or seven of you got on to the phones at once in a race with the opposition and with each other – something like that was going on now, a currency raid, but Kevin was out of it. But nine tenths of your time was spent waiting: waiting for detectives to come out of police stations, waiting for juries to return verdicts, waiting for celebrities to arrive, waiting just for a story to break.

Kevin had thought that Fleet Street would be different from the Midlands evening paper he had joined when he left university. He had been content, as a trainee reporter, to interview dim, self-important councilmen, to publish the exaggerated complaints of council house tenants, and to write stories about amateur dramatics, lost dogs, and waves of petty vandalism. He had occasionally done things he was quite proud of: a series about the problems of the town's immigrants; a controversial feature on how the Town Hall wasted money; coverage of a lengthy and complex planning inquiry. The move to Fleet Street, he had fondly imagined, would mean doing the important stories on a national level and dropping the trivia entirely. He had found instead that all the serious topics – politics, economics, industry, the arts – were handled by specialists; and that the line for those specialist jobs was a long line of bright, talented people just like Kevin Hart.

He needed a way to shine – something which would make the *Post*'s executives notice him and say: 'Young Hart is good – are we making the most of him?'

# Paper Money

One good break could do it: a hot tip, an exclusive interview, a spectacular piece of initiative.

He had thought he had found that something today, and he had been wrong. Now he wondered whether it would ever happen.

He stood up and went to the Gents'. What else can I do? he thought. I could always go into computers, or advertising, or public relations, or retail management. But I want to leave newspapers as a success, not a failure.

While he was washing his hands, Arthur Cole came in. The older man spoke to Kevin over his shoulder. To Kevin's astonishment, he said: 'Sorry about that, Kevin. You know how it gets on that news desk sometimes.'

Kevin pulled down a length of towel. He was not sure what to say.

Cole moved across to the washbasin. 'No hard feelings?'

'I'm not offended,' Kevin said. 'I don't mind you swearing. I wouldn't care if you called me the biggest bastard on earth.' He hesitated. This was not what he wanted to say. He stared in the mirror for a moment, then took the plunge. 'But when my story appears in the paper without half of the facts, I start to wonder if I ought to become a computer programmer.'

Cole filled the basin with cold water and splashed some on his face. He fumbled for the towel and wiped himself dry. 'You ought to know this, but I'll tell you anyway,' he began. 'The story we put in the paper consisted of what we *know*, and only what we know. We *know* Fitzpeterson was found unconscious and rushed to hospital, and we *know* there was an empty bottle beside him, because you saw all that. You were in the right place at the right time, which, incidentally, is an important talent for a reporter to have. Now, what else do we know? We know we got an anonymous tip that the man had spent the night with a whore; and that someone phoned up claiming to be Fitzpeterson and saying he was being blackmailed by Laski and Cox. Now, if we print those two facts, we cannot but imply that they are connected with the overdose; indeed, that he took the overdose because he was being blackmailed over the whore.'

Kevin said: 'But that implication is *so* obvious that surely we're deceiving people if we don't print it!'

'And what if the calls were hoaxes, the tablets were indigestion pills, and the man's in a diabetic coma? And we've ruined his career?'

'Isn't that a bit unlikely?'

'You bet. Kevin, I'm ninety per cent sure that the truth is the way your original story read. But we're not here to print our suspicions. Now, let's get back to work.'

Kevin followed Arthur through the door and across the newsroom. He felt like the heroine in the movie who says: 'I'm so confused, I don't know *what* to do!' He was half inclined to think that Arthur was right; but he also felt that things should not be that way.

# Paper Money

A phone rang at an unattended desk, and Kevin picked it up. 'Newsroom.'

'Are you a reporter?' It was a woman's voice.

'Yes, madam. My name is Kevin Hart. How can I help you?'

'My husband's been shot and I want justice.'

Kevin sighed. A domestic shooting meant a court case, which in turn meant there was no way the paper could do much of a story. He guessed that the woman was going to tell him who had shot her husband and ask him to print it. But it was juries who decided who shot whom, not newspapers. Kevin said: 'Tell me your name, please?'

'Doreen Johnson, five Yew Street, east one. My Willie was shot on this currency job.' The woman's voice cracked. 'He's been blinded.' She started to shout. 'It was a Tony Cox job, so just print that!' The line went dead.

Kevin put the phone down slowly, trying to take it in.

This was turning out to be one hell of a day for phone calls.

He picked up his notebook and went to the news desk.

Arthur said: 'Got something?'

'Don't know,' Kevin told him. 'A woman phoned up. Gave me her name and address. She said her husband was on the currency raid, that he was shot in the face and blinded, and that it was a Tony Cox job.'

Arthur stared. 'Cox?' he said. '*Cox?*'

Someone called: 'Arthur!'

Kevin looked up, annoyed at the interruption. The voice belonged to Mervyn Glazier, the paper's City editor, a stocky young man in battered suede shoes and a sweat-stained shirt.

Glazier came nearer and said: 'I may have a story for your pages this afternoon. Possible collapse of a bank. It's called the Cotton Bank of Jamaica, and it's owned by a man called Felix Laski.'

Arthur and Kevin stared at one another.

Arthur said: 'Laski? *Laski?*'

Kevin said: 'Jesus Christ.'

Arthur frowned, scratched his head, and said wonderingly: 'What the hell is going on?'

# Chapter Twenty-Four

The blue Morris was still tailing Tony Cox. He spotted it in the car park of the pub when he came out. He hoped they would not play silly buggers and breathalyse him: he had drunk three pints of lager with his smoked-salmon sandwiches.

The detectives pulled out of the exit a few seconds behind the Rolls. Tony was not concerned. He had lost them once today, and he could do it again. The simplest way would have been to find a fast stretch of road and put his foot down. However, he would prefer that they did not know they had lost him, just like this morning.

It would not be difficult.

He crossed the river and entered the West End. As he picked his way through the traffic he wondered about the Old Bill's motives in following him around. It was partly a simple case of making a nuisance of themselves, he was sure. What did the briefs call it? Harassment. They figured that if they tailed him long enough he would get impatient or careless and do something stupid. But that was only the justification: the real motive probably lay in Scotland Yard politics. Perhaps the Assistant Commissioner (Crime) had

threatened to take the Tony Cox firm away from CI
and give it to the Flying Squad, so CI had laid on the
surveillance in order to be able to say they were doing
something.

So long as they did not get all serious about it,
Tony did not mind. They had got serious once, a few
years ago. At that time Tony's firm had been under
the eagle eye of the CID at West End Central. Tony
had had a close understanding with the detective-
inspector working on his case. One week the DI had
refused his usual money, and warned Tony that the
game was over. The only way Tony had been able to
square it had been to sacrifice some of his soldiers.
He and the DI had set up five middle-management
villains on extortion charges. The five had gone to
jail, the Press had praised the CID for breaking the
gang's hold on London, and business had gone on as
usual. Sadly, that DI later went down himself, for
planting cannabis on a student: a sorry end to a promising career, Tony felt.

He pulled into a multistorey car park in Soho. He
paused at the entry, spending a long time taking his
ticket from the machine, and watched the blue Morris
in his mirrors. One of the detectives jumped out of
the car and ran across the road to cover the pedestrian
exit. The other found a parking space on a meter a
few yards away – a position from which he could
see cars coming out of the building. Tony nodded,
satisfied.

He drove up to the first floor and stopped the Rolls

beside the office. Inside he found a young man he did
not know.

He said: 'I'm Tony Cox. I want you to park mine
and get me one of your long-stay motors – one that's
not likely to be picked up today.'

The man frowned. He had frizzy, untidy hair and
oil-stained jeans with frayed bottoms. He said: 'I can't
do that, mate.'

Tony tapped his foot impatiently. 'I don't like
saying things twice, son. *I'm Tony Cox.*'

The young man laughed. He stood up, putting
down a comic, and said: 'I don't care who you are,
you—'

Tony hit him in the stomach. His large fist landed
with a soft thump. It was like punching a feather
pillow. The attendant doubled over, moaning and
gasping for air.

'I'm short of time, boy,' Tony said.

The office door opened. 'What's going on?' An
older man in a baseball cap entered. 'Oh, it's you,
Tony. Having trouble?'

'Where have you been – smoking in the bog?' Tony
said harshly. 'I want a car that can't be traced to me,
and I'm in a hurry.'

'No problem,' the older man said. He took a bunch
of keys from a hook on the asbestos wall. 'Got a nice
Granada, in here for a fortnight. Three-litre automatic, a nice bronze colour—'

'I don't give a toss what colour it is.' Tony took
the keys.

'Over there.' The man pointed. 'I'll park yours.'

Tony went out of the office and got into the Granada. He put on the safety belt and pulled away. He paused beside his own car, which the man in the cap was now sitting in.

'What's your name?' Tony said.

'I'm Davy Brewster, Tony.'

'All right, Davy Brewster.' Tony reached for his wallet and took out two ten-pound notes. 'Make sure the kid keeps his mouth shut, okay?'

'No problem. Thanks very much.' Davy took the money.

Tony pulled away. As he drove, he put on sunglasses and his cloth cap. When he emerged into the street, the blue Morris was away to his right. He put his right elbow on the window ledge, covering his face, and steered with his left hand. The second detective, on Tony's left, had his back to the road so that he could see the pedestrian exit. The man was pretending to look in the window of a religious bookshop.

Tony looked in his mirror as he accelerated away. Neither of them had seen him.

'Easy,' Tony said aloud. He drove south.

The car was quite pleasant, with automatic gears and power-assisted steering. It had a tape deck. Tony sorted through the cassettes, found a Beatles album, and put it on. Then he lit a cigar.

In less than an hour he would be at the farm, counting the money.

Felix Laski had been well worth cultivating, Tony

thought. They had met in the restaurant of one of Tony's clubs. The Cox casinos served the best food in London. They had to. Tony's motto was: if you serve peanuts, you get monkeys for customers. He wanted rich people in his gambling clubs, not yobboes asking for draft bitter and five penn'orth of chips. He did not like fancy food himself, but on the night he met Laski he was eating a vast, rare T-bone steak at a table near the financier's.

The chef was pinched from Prunier's. Tony did not know what he did to the steaks, but the result was sensational. The tall, elegant man at the next table had caught his eye: a fine-looking man for his age. He was with a young girl whom Tony instantly marked as a tart.

Tony had finished his steak, and was tucking into a mountain of trifle, when the accident happened. The waiter was serving Laski with cannelloni, and somehow a half-full bottle of claret got knocked over. The tart squealed and jumped out of the way, and a few drops of wine spattered Laski's brilliant white shirt.

Tony acted immediately. He stood up, dropping his napkin on the table, and summoned three waiters and the maître d'hôtel. He spoke first to the waiter who had caused the mess. 'Go and get changed. Pick up your cards on Friday.' He turned to the others. 'Bernardo, a cloth. Giulio, another bottle of wine. Monsieur Charles, another table, and no bill for this gentleman.' Finally he spoke to the diners. 'I'm the proprietor, Tony Cox. Please have your dinner on the house, with my apologies, and I hope you'll have the most expensive dishes on the menu, beginning with a bottle of Dom Perignon.'

Laski spoke then. 'These things can't be helped.' His voice was deep and faintly accented. 'But it is nice to have such a generous, old-fashioned apology.' He smiled.

'It missed my dress,' the tart said. Her accent confirmed Tony's guess about her profession: she came from the same part of London as he did.

The maître d'hôtel said: 'M'sieur Cox, the house is full. There is no other table.'

Tony pointed to his own table. 'What's wrong with that one? Clear it, quickly.'

'Please don't,' Laski said. 'We wouldn't like to deprive you.'

'I insist.'

'Then, please join us.'

Tony looked at them both. The tart obviously didn't like the idea. Was the gent just being polite, or did he mean it? Well, Tony had almost finished, so if it didn't work out he could leave the table quite soon.

'I don't want to intrude—'

'You won't be,' Laski said. 'And you can tell me how to win at roulette.'

'Right-oh,' Tony said.

He stayed with them all evening. He and Laski got on famously, and it was made clear early on that what the girl thought did not count. Tony told stories of villainy in the world of gambling clubs, and Laski matched him, anecdote for anecdote, with tales of Stock Exchange sharp practice. It transpired that Laski was not a gambler, but that he liked to bring people to the club. When they went into the casino he bought fifty pounds' worth of chips and gave them all to the girl. The evening ended when Laski, by now quite drunk, said: 'I suppose I should take her home and screw her.'

After that they met several times – never by arrangement – in the club, and always ended up getting drunk together. After a while Tony let the other man know that he was gay, and Laski did nothing about it, from which Tony concluded that the financier was a tolerant heterosexual.

It pleased Tony to know that he could befriend someone of Laski's class. The scene in the restaurant was the easiest bit, and it was well rehearsed: the grand gestures, the posture of command, the heavy courtesy, and a conscious moderating of his accent. But to maintain the acquaintance with someone as brainy, as rich, and as used to moving in near-aristocratic circles as Laski was, seemed quite an achievement.

It was Laski who made the first move towards a deeper relationship. They had been bragging-drunk in the early hours of a Sunday morning, and Laski had been talking about the power of money. 'Given enough money,' he said, 'I can find out anything in the City – right down to the combination of the lock on the vault in the Bank of England.'

Tony said: 'Sex is better.'

'What do you mean?'

'Sex is a better weapon. I can find out anything in London, using sex.'

'Now that I doubt,' said Laski, whose sexual urges were well under control.

Tony shrugged. 'All right. Challenge me.'

That was when Laski made his move. 'The development licence for the Shield oil field. Find out who's got it – before the government makes the announcement.'

Tony saw the gleam in the financier's eye, and guessed that the whole conversation had been planned. 'Why don't you ask me something difficult?' he countered. 'Politicians and civil servants are much too easy.'

'It will do,' Laski smiled.

'Okay. But I've got to challenge you, too.'

Laski's eyes narrowed. 'Go on.'

Tony said the first thing that came into his head. 'Find out the schedule for deliveries of used notes to the currency destruction plant of the Bank of England.'

'It won't even cost me money,' Laski said confidently.

And that was how it had started. Tony grinned as he drove the Ford through south London. He did not know how Laski had managed to keep his half of the bargain; but Tony's side had been a doddle. Who has the information we want? The Minister. What's he like? The next thing to a virgin – a faithful husband. Is he getting his oats from the wife? Not much. Will he fall for the oldest trick in the game? Like a dream.

The tape ended, and he turned it over. He wondered how much money had been in the currency van – a hundred grand? Maybe even a quarter of a million. Much more than that would be embarrassing. You couldn't walk into Barclays Bank with sacks full of used fivers without arousing suspicion. About a hundred and fifty grand would be ideal. Five gees for each of the boys, a few more for expenses, and about fifty thousand surreptitiously added to the takings of various legitimate businesses tonight. Gambling clubs were very useful for concealing illicit income.

The boys knew what to do with five grand. Pay off a few debts, buy a secondhand car, put a few hundred in each of two or three bank accounts, give the wife a new coat, lend the mother-in-law a couple of bob, spend a night in the pub, and bang, it was all gone. But give them twenty thousand and they started to get silly ideas. When unemployed labourers and freelance odd-job men were heard to talk about villas in the South of France, the law began to get suspicious.

Tony grinned at himself. I should worry about having too much money, he thought. Problems of success are the kind I like. Don't count your chicks before you've laid them, Jacko sometimes said. The van might be full of worn-out halfpennies for melting down.

Now *that* would be a chuckle.

He was nearly there. He started to whistle.

# Chapter Twenty-Five

Felix Laski sat in his office, watching a television screen and tearing a buff envelope into narrow strips. The closed-circuit TV was the modern equivalent of the tickertape; and Laski felt like the worried broker in an old movie about the 1929 crash. The set continuously screened market news and price movements in equities, commodities, and currency. There had been no mention of the oil licence. Hamilton shares had dropped five points on yesterday, and trading was moderate.

He finished demolishing the envelope and dropped the scraps into a metal waste-paper basket. The oil licence should have been announced an hour ago.

He picked up the blue phone and dialled 123. 'At the third stroke, the time will be one forty-seven, and fifty seconds.' The announcement was more than an hour late. He dialled the Department of Energy and asked for the Press Office. A woman told him: 'The Secretary of State has been delayed. The Press conference will begin as soon as he arrives, and the announcement will be made immediately he opens the conference.'

The hell with your delays, Laski thought: I've got a fortune riding on this.

He pressed the intercom. 'Carol?' There was no reply. He bellowed: 'Carol!'

The girl poked her head around the door. 'I'm sorry, I was at the filing cabinet.'

'Get me some coffee.'

'Certainly.'

He took from his 'in' tray a file headed: Precision Tubing – Sales Report, 1st Quarter. It was a piece of routine espionage on a firm he was thinking of taking over. He had a theory that capital equipment tended to do well when a slump was bottoming out. But does Precision have the capacity for expansion? he wondered.

He looked at the first page of the report, winced at the sales director's indigestible prose, and tossed the file aside. When he took a gamble and lost, he could accept it with equanimity. What threw him was something going wrong for unknown reasons. He knew he would not be able to concentrate on anything until the Shield business was settled.

He fingered the sharp crease of his trousers, and thought about Tony Cox. He had taken to the young hoodlum, despite his obvious homosexuality, because he sensed what the English called a kindred spirit. Like Laski, Cox had come from poverty to wealth on determination, opportunism, and ruthlessness. Also like Laski, he tried in small ways to take the edge off his lower-class manners: Laski was doing it better, but only because he had been practising longer. Cox wanted to be like Laski, and he would make it – by

the time he was in his fifties, he would be a distinguished, grey-haired City gent.

Laski realized he did not have a single sound reason
for trusting Cox. There was his instinct, of course,
which told him the young man was honest with
people he knew: but the Tony Coxes of this world
were practised deceivers. Had he simply invented the
whole thing about Tim Fitzpeterson?

The television set screened the Hamilton Holdings
price again: it was down another point. Laski wished
they wouldn't use that damn computer typeface, all
horizontal and vertical lines: it strained his eyes. He
began to calculate what he stood to lose if Hamilton
did not get the licence.

If he could sell the 510,000 shares right now, he
would have lost only a few thousand pounds. But
it would not be possible to dump the lot at the market
value. And the price was still slipping. Say a loss of
twenty thousand at the outside. And a psychological
setback – damage to his reputation as a winner.

Was there anything else at risk? What Cox planned
to do with the information Laski had supplied was
certain to be criminal. However, since Laski did not
actually know about it, he could not be convicted of
conspiracy.

There was still Britain's Official Secrets Act – mild
by East European standards, but a formidable piece
of legislation. It was illegal to approach a civil servant
and get from him confidential data. Proving that Laski
had done that would be difficult, but not impossible.

He had asked Peters whether he had a big day ahead, and Peters had said: 'One of *the* days.' Then Laski had said to Cox: 'It's today.' Well, if Cox and Peters could be persuaded to testify, then Laski would be convicted. But Peters did not even know he had given away a secret, and nobody would think of asking him. Suppose Cox was arrested? The British police had ways of squeezing information out of people, even if they did not use baseball bats. Cox might say he got the information from Laski, then they would check Laski's movements on the day, and they might discover he had taken coffee with Peters . . .

It was a pretty distant possibility. Laski was more worried about finishing off the Hamilton deal.

The phone rang. Laski answered: 'Yes?'

'It's Threadneedle Street – Mr Ley,' Carol said.

Laski tutted. 'It's probably about the Cotton Bank. Put him on to Jones.'

'He's been through to the Cotton Bank, and Mr Jones has gone home.'

'Gone home? All right, I'll take it.'

He heard Carol say: 'I have Mr Laski for you now.'

'Laski?' The voice was high-pitched, the accent an aristocratic drawl.

'Yes.'

'Ley here, Bank of England.'

'How are you?'

'Good afternoon. Now look here, old chap—' Laski rolled his eyes at this phrase '—you've made out rather a large cheque to Fett and Company.'

Laski paled. 'My God, have they presented it already?'

'Yes, well, I rather gathered the ink was still wet. Now the thing is, it's drawn on the Cotton Bank, as you obviously know, and the poor little Cotton Bank can't cover it. Do you follow me?'

'Of course I follow you.' The bloody man was talking as if to a child. Nothing annoyed Laski more. 'Clearly, my instructions as to the arrangements for providing these funds have not been followed. However, perhaps I can plead that my staff might well have thought they had a little time to spare.'

'Mmm. It's nice, really, to have the funds ready before you sign the damn thing, you know, just to be safe, don't you think?'

Laski thought fast. Damn, this need not have happened if the announcement had been made on time. And where the devil was Jones? 'You may have guessed that the cheque is payment for a controlling interest in Hamilton Holdings. I should think those shares would stand as security—'

'Oh, dear me, no,' Ley interrupted. 'That really wouldn't do. The Bank of England is not in business to finance speculation on the stock market.'

Maybe not, Laski thought; but if the announcement had been made, and you knew that Hamilton Holdings now had an oil well, you wouldn't be making this fuss. It occurred to him that perhaps they did know, and Hamilton had not got the oil well; hence the phone call. He felt angry. 'Look, you're a bank,' he said. 'I'll pay you the rate for twenty-four-hour money—'

'The Bank is not accustomed to being in the money market.'

Laski raised his voice. 'You know damn well I can cover that cheque with ease, given a little time! If you return it, my reputation is gone. Are you going to ruin me for the sake of a lousy million overnight and a foolish tradition?'

Ley's voice went very cold. 'Mr Laski, our traditions exist specifically for the purpose of ruining people who sign cheques they cannot honour. If this draft cannot be cleared today, I shall ask the payee to re-present. That means, in effect, that you have an hour and a half in which to make a cash deposit of one million pounds at Threadneedle Street. Good day.'

'Damn you,' Laski said, but the line was dead. He cradled the receiver, cracking the plastic of the phone. His mind raced. There had to be a way of raising a million instantly . . . didn't there?

His coffee had arrived while he was on the phone. He had not noticed Carol come in. He sipped it, and made a face.

'Carol!' he shouted.

She opened the door. 'Yes?'

Red-faced and trembling, he threw the delicate china cup into the metal waste-paper basket, where it shattered noisily. He bellowed: 'The bloody coffee is cold!'

The girl turned around and fled.

# Two p.m.

# Chapter Twenty-Six

Young Billy Johnson was looking for Tony Cox, but he kept forgetting this.

He had got out of the house quite fast after they all returned from the hospital. His mother was doing a lot of screaming, there were a few policemen hanging around, and Jacko had been carted off to the station to help with inquiries. The neighbours and relatives who kept dropping in added to the confusion. Billy liked quiet.

Nobody seemed disposed to get his lunch or pay him any attention, so he ate a packet of ginger biscuits and went out the back way, telling Mrs Glebe from three doors down that he was going up to his auntie's to watch her colour television.

He had been getting things sorted out as he walked. Walking helped him to think. When he found himself baffled, he could look at the cars and the shops and the people for a while, to rest his mind.

He went towards his auntie's at first, until he remembered that he did not really want to go there; he had only said that to stop Mrs Glebe from making trouble. Then he had to think where he *was* going. He stopped, looking in the window of a record shop, painstakingly reading the names on the gaudy sleeves, and trying to match them to songs he had heard on the radio. He had a record player, but he never had any money to buy records, and his parents' taste did not suit him. Ma liked soppy songs, Pa liked brass bands, and Billy liked rock-and-roll. The only other person he knew who liked rock-and-roll was Tony Cox—

That was it. He was looking for Tony Cox.

He headed in what he thought was roughly the direction for Bethnal Green. He knew the East End very well – every street, every shop, all the bomb sites, patches of waste ground, canals and parks – but he knew it in bits. He passed a demolition site, and remembered that Granny Parker had lived there, and had sat stubbornly in her front room while the old houses on either side had been torn down, until she had caught pneumonia and died, relieving the London Borough of Tower Hamlets of the problem of what to do about her. Billy had followed the story with interest: it was like something on the television. Yes, he knew every particle of the East London land-scape; but he could not connect them together in his mind. He knew Commercial Road and he knew Mile End Road, but he did not know that they met at Aldgate. Despite this, he could almost always find his way home, even if sometimes it took longer than he expected; and if he really got lost the Old Bill would run him back to the house in a squad car. All the coppers knew his pa.

# Paper Money

By the time he got to Wapping, he had forgotten his destination again; but he thought he was probably going to see the ships. He got in through a hole in a fence: the same hole he had used with Snowy White and Tubby Toms that day when they caught a rat and the others told Billy to take it home to his Ma, because she would be pleased and cook it for tea. She had not been pleased, of course: she jumped in the air and dropped a bag of sugar and screamed, and later she cried and said they shouldn't make fun of Billy. People often played tricks on him, but he did not mind, because it was nice to have pals.

He wandered around for a while. He had the feeling that there used to be more ships here, in the days when he was little. Today he could see only one. It was a big one, quite low in the water, with a name on the side which he could not read. The men were running a pipe from the ship to a warehouse.

He stood watching for a while, then asked one of the men: 'What's in it?'

The man, who wore a cloth cap and a waistcoat, looked at him. 'Wine, mate.'

Billy was surprised. 'In the ship? All wine? Full?'

'Yes, mate. Château Morocco, vintage about last Thursday.' All the men laughed at this, but Billy did not understand it. He laughed all the same. The men worked on for a while, then the one he had spoken to said: 'What are you doing here, anyway?'

Billy thought for a moment, then said: 'I've forgot.'

The man looked hard at him, and mumbled something to one of the others. Billy heard part of the reply: '—might fall in the bleeding drink.' The first man went inside the warehouse.

After a while, a docks' policeman came along. He said to the men: 'Is this the lad?' They nodded, and the copper addressed Billy. 'Are you lost?'

'No,' Billy said.

'Where are you going?'

Billy was about to say he was not going anywhere, but that seemed the wrong answer. Suddenly he remembered. 'Bethnal Green.'

'All right, come with me and I'll set you on the right road.'

Always willing to take the line of least resistance, Billy walked alongside the copper to the dock gate.

'Where do you live, then?' the man asked.

'Yew Street.'

'Does your mother know where you are?'

Billy decided that the policeman was another Mrs Glebe, and that a lie was called for. 'Yes. I'm going up my auntie's.'

'Sure you know the way?'

'Yes.'

They were at the gate. The copper looked at him speculatively, then made up his mind. 'All right, then, off you go. Don't wander around the docks no more – you're safer to stop outside.'

'Thanks,' Billy said. When in doubt, he thanked people. He walked off.

It was getting easier to remember. Pa was up the

hospital. He was going to be blind, and it was Tony Cox's fault. Billy knew one blind man – well, two, if you counted Squint Thatcher, who was blind only when he went up West with his accordion. But really blind, there was only Hopcraft, who lived alone in a smelly house on the Isle of Dogs and carried a white stick. Would Pa have to wear sunglasses and walk very slowly, tapping the kerb with a stick? The thought upset Billy.

People usually thought he was incapable of getting upset, because he never shed tears. That was how they found out he was different, when he was a baby: he used to hurt himself and not cry. Ma sometimes said: 'He do feel things, but he don't never show it.'

Pa used to say that Ma got upset often enough for two, anyway.

When really awful things happened, like the rat joke that Snowy and Tubby played, Billy found he got all boiled up inside, and he *wanted* to do something drastic, like scream, but it just never happened.

He had killed the rat, and that had helped. He had held it with one hand, and with the other banged it on the head with a brick until it stopped wriggling.

He would do something like that to Tony Cox.

It occurred to him that Tony was bigger than a rat – indeed, bigger than Billy. That baffled him, so he put it out of his mind.

He stopped at the end of a street. The corner house had a shop downstairs – one of the old shops, where they sold lots of things. Billy knew the owner's daughter, a pretty girl with long hair called Sharon. A couple of years ago she let him feel her tits, but then she ran away from him and would not speak to him any more. For days afterwards he had thought of nothing else but the small round mounds under her blouse, and the way he felt when he touched them. Eventually he had realized that the experience was one of those nice things that never happen twice.

He went into the shop. Sharon's mother was behind the counter, wearing candy-striped nylon overalls. She did not recognize Billy.

He smiled and said: 'Hello.'

'Can I help you?' She was uneasy.

Billy said: 'How's Sharon?'

'Fine, thanks. She's out at the moment. Do you know her?'

'Yes.' Billy looked around the shop, at the assortment of food, hardware, books, fancy goods, tobacco, and confectionery. He wanted to say, She let me feel her tits once, but he knew that would not be right. 'I used to play with her.'

It seemed to be the answer the woman wanted: she looked relieved. She smiled, and Billy saw that her teeth were brown-stained, like his father's. She said: 'Can I serve you with something?'

There was a clatter of shoes on stairs, and Sharon came into the shop from the door behind the counter. Billy was surprised: she looked much older. Her hair was short, and her tits were quite big, wobbling under a T-shirt. She had long legs in tight jeans. She called: 'Bye, Mum.' She was rushing out.

Billy said: 'Hello, Sharon!'

She stopped and stared at him. Recognition flickered in her face. 'Oh, hi, Billy. Can't stop.' Then she was gone.

Her mother looked embarrassed. 'I'm sorry – I forgot she was upstairs still—'

'It's all right. I forget a lot of things.'

'Well, can I serve you with something?' the woman repeated.

'I want a knife.'

It had popped into Billy's head from nowhere, but he knew straight away that it was right. There was no point in banging a strong man like Tony Cox on the head with a stone – he would just hit you back. So you had to knife him in the back, like an Indian.

'For yourself, or your mother?'

'Me.'

'What's it for?'

Billy knew he shouldn't tell her that. He frowned, and said: 'Cutting things. String, and that.'

'Oh.' The woman reached into the window display, and pulled out a knife in a sheath, like Boy Scouts had.

Billy took all the money out of his trouser pocket. Money was something he was not good about – he always let the shopkeeper take however much was needed.

Sharon's mother looked and said: 'But you've only got eight pence.'

'Is it enough?'

She sighed. 'No, I'm sorry.'

'Well, can I have some bubblegum, then?'

The woman put the knife back in the window and took a packet of gum from a shelf. 'Six pence.'

Billy offered his handful of money, and the woman took some coins.

'Thanks,' Billy said. He went out into the street and opened the packet. He liked to put it all in his mouth at once. He walked on, chewing with enjoyment. For the moment, he had forgotten where he was going.

He stopped to watch some men digging a hole in the pavement. The tops of their heads were level with Billy's feet. He saw, with interest, that the wall of the trench changed colour as it went down. First there was the pavement, then some black stuff like tar, then loose brown earth, then wet clay. In the bottom lay a pipe made of clean new concrete. Why did they put pipes under the pavement? Billy had no idea. He leaned over and said: 'Why are you putting a pipe under the pavement?'

A workman looked up at him and said: 'We're hiding it from the Russians.'

'Oh.' Billy nodded, as if he understood. After a moment he moved on.

He felt hungry, but there was something he had to do before he went home for lunch. Lunch? He had eaten a packet of biscuits because Pa was up the hospital. That had something to do with why he was here in Bethnal Green, but he could not quite make the connection.

He turned a corner, looked at the road name on a sign tacked high up on a wall, and saw that he was in Quill Street. Now he remembered. This was where Tony Cox lived – at number nineteen. He would knock on the door—

No. He didn't know why, but he felt sure he ought to creep in by the back door. There was a lane behind the terrace. Billy walked along it until he came to the back of Tony's house.

All the taste was gone from his bubblegum, so he took it out of his mouth and threw it away before quietly unlatching the back gate and walking stealthily in.

# Chapter Twenty-Seven

Tony Cox drove slowly along the rutted mud track, out of consideration for his own comfort rather than for the owner of the 'borrowed' car. The lane, which had no name, led from a B-road to a farmhouse with a barn. The barn, the empty, dilapidated house, and the acre of infertile land surrounding them, were owned by a company called Land Development Ltd; which was in turn owned by a compulsive gambler who owed Tony Cox a lot of money. The barn was occasionally used to store job lots of fire-damaged goods bought at rock-bottom prices, so it was not unusual for a van and a car to draw up in the farmyard.

The five-bar gate at the end of the lane was open, and Tony drove in. There was no sign of the blue van, but Jesse was leaning against the farmhouse wall, smoking a cigarette. He came across to open the car door for Tony.

'It haven't gone smooth, Tony,' he said immediately.

Tony got out of the car. 'Is the money here?'

'In the van.' Jesse jerked his head toward the barn. 'But it never went smooth.'

'Let's get inside – it's too hot out here.' Tony heaved

Paper Money

the barn door open and stepped in. Jesse followed
him. A quantity of packing cases occupied one third
of the floor area. Tony read the labels on a couple:
they contained surplus Forces uniforms and coats.
The blue van stood opposite the door. Tony noticed
that trade plates had been tied over the original
number plates with string.

'What have you been playing at?' he asked incredulously.

'Oh, blimey, Tony, wait till you hear what I've had
to do.'

'Well bloody tell me then!'

'Well, I had a prang, see – nothing much, just a
little bump. But the geezer gets out of his car and
wants to call the police. So I pisses off, don't I. But
he stands in the way and I hits him.'

Tony cursed softly.

Now fear showed in Jesse's face. 'Well, I knew the
law would be looking for me, didn't I. So I stops at
this garage, goes round the back to the khasi, and
nicks a set of trade plates and these overalls.' He
nodded eagerly, as if to lend his own approval to his
actions. 'Then I come on here.'

Tony stared at him in amazement, then burst out
laughing. 'You mad bastard!' he chuckled.

Jesse looked relieved. 'I done the best thing for it,
though, didn't I?'

Tony's laughter subsided. 'You mad bastard,' he
repeated. 'Here you are, with a fortune in hot money
in the van, and you stop—' his chest heaved, and he

wheezed with renewed laughter'—you stop at a garage and nick a pair of overalls!'

Jesse smiled too, not from amusement but out of the pleasure of a fear removed. Then he became serious again. 'There is proper bad news, though.'

'Gorblimey, what else?'

'The van driver tried to be a hero.'

'You never killed him?' Tony said anxiously.

'No, just knocked him on the head. But Jacko's shooter went off in the fracas—' he pronounced it frackarse '—and Deaf Willie got hit. In the boat race. He's bad, Tone.'

'Oh, balls.' Tony sat down suddenly on an old three-legged stool. 'Oh, poor old Willie. Did they take him up the hospital, did they?'

Jesse nodded. 'That's why Jacko's not here. He's took him. Whether he got there alive ...'

'That bad?'

Jesse nodded.

'Oh, balls.' He was silent for a while. 'He don't get no luck, Deaf Willie. The one ear's gone already, and his boy's a mental case, and his wife looks like Henry Cooper – and now this.' He clicked his tongue in sorrow. 'We'll give him a double share, but it won't mend his head.' He got up.

Jesse opened the van, relieved that he had managed to convey the bad news without suffering Tony's wrath.

Tony rubbed his hands together. 'Right, let's have a look at what we got.'

# Paper Money

There were nine grey steel chests in the back of the van. They looked like squat metal suitcases, each with handles at both ends, each secured by a double lock. They were heavy. The two men unloaded them, one by one, and lined them up in the centre of the barn. Tony looked at them greedily. His expression showed an almost sensual pleasure. He said: 'It's like Ali Baba and the forty bloody thieves, mate.'

Jesse was taking plastic explosive, wires and detonators out of a duffle bag in a corner of the barn. 'I wish Willie was here to do the bang-bangs.'

Tony said: 'I wish he was here, full stop.'

Jesse prepared to blow open the chests. He stuck the jellylike explosive all around the locks, attached detonators and wires, and connected each tiny bomb to the plunger-type trigger.

Watching him, Tony said: 'You seem to know what you're doing.'

'I've seen Willie do it often enough.' He grinned. 'Maybe I can become the firm's peterman—'

'Willie ain't dead,' Tony interrupted gruffly. 'Not so far as we know.'

Jesse picked up the trigger and, trailing wires, took it outside. Tony followed him.

Tony said: 'Drive the van outside, in case of the petrol going up, know what I mean?'

'There's no danger—'

'You've never done a peter before, and I'm not taking the risk.'

'Okay.' Jesse closed the rear doors and backed the

van into the farmyard. Then he opened the bonnet and used crocodile clips to connect the trigger with the van's battery.

He said: 'Hold your breath,' and pressed the plunger.

There was a muffled bang.

The two men went back inside. The chests stood in line with their tops hanging open at odd, twisted angles.

'You done a good job,' Tony said.

The chests were neatly and tightly packed. The bundles of notes were stacked twenty across, ten wide, and five deep: one thousand bundles per chest. Each bundle contained one hundred notes. That made one hundred thousand notes per chest.

The first six chests contained ten-shilling notes, obsolete and worthless.

Tony said: 'Jesus H. Christ.'

The next contained oncers, but it was not quite full. Tony counted eight hundred bundles. The last chest but one also contained one-pound notes, and it was full. Tony said: 'That's better. Just about right.'

The last chest was packed solid with tenners.

Tony muttered: 'Gawd help us.'

Jesse's eyes were wide. 'How much is it, Tony?'

'One million, one hundred and eighty thousand pounds sterling, my son.'

Jesse gave a whoop of delight. 'We're rich! We're lousy with it!'

Tony's face was sombre. 'I suppose we could burn all the tenners.'

'What are you talking about?' Jesse looked at him as if he were mad. 'What do you mean, burn them? You going potty?'

Tony turned around and gripped Jesse's arm, squeezing hard. 'Listen. If you go into the Rose and Crown, ask for a half of bitter and a meat pie, and pay with a tenner; and if you do that every day for a week; what will they all think?'

'They'll think I've had a tickle. You're hurting my arm, Tone.'

'And how long would it take for one of those dirty little snouts in there to get round the nick and spill it? Five minutes?' He let go. 'It's too much, Jess. Your trouble is, you don't think. This much money, you've got to keep it somewhere – and if it's kept somewhere, the Old Bill can find it.'

Jesse found this point of view too radical to digest. 'But you can't throw money away.'

'You're not listening to me, are you? They've got Deaf Willie, right? Their driver will connect Willie with the raid, right? And they know Willie's on my firm, so they know we done the job, right? You bet your life they'll be up your place tonight, slitting the mattresses and digging up the potato patch. Now, five grand in oncers might be your life savings, but fifty grand in tenners gotta be incriminating, right?'

'I never thought of it that way,' Jesse said.

'The word for it is overkill.'

'I suppose you can't put that much money in the Abbey National. Anybody can have a good night at the dogs, but if you got too much, it proves you've had a tickle, see?' Jesse was explaining it back to Tony, as if to demonstrate that he understood. 'That's it, ain't it?'

'Yes.' Tony had lost interest in the lecture. He was trying to think of a foolproof way of disposing of hot money in large quantity.

'And you can't walk into Barclays Bank with over a million nicker and ask to open a savings account, can you?'

'You're getting it,' Tony said sarcastically. Suddenly he looked sharply at Jesse. 'Ah, but who *can* walk into the bank with a pile of money and not arouse suspicion?'

Jesse was lost. 'Well, nobody can.'

'You reckon?' Tony pointed to the packing cases of surplus Forces clothes. 'Open a couple of those boxes. I want you dressed as a Royal Navy seaman. I've just had a bloody clever idea.'

# Chapter Twenty-Eight

An editor's conference in the afternoon was rare. The editor sometimes said: 'The mornings are fun, the afternoons are work.' Up until lunch-time, his efforts were expended in the production of a newspaper. By two o'clock it was too late to do anything significant: the content of the paper was more or less determined, most of the day's editions had been printed and distributed, and the editor turned his brain to what he called administrative sludge. But he had to be around, in case something came up which required a top-level decision. Arthur Cole believed that such a thing had come up.

Cole, the deputy news editor, sat opposite the editor's oversize white desk. On Cole's left was the reporter Kevin Hart; on his right was Mervyn Glazier, City editor.

The editor finished signing a pile of letters and looked up. 'What have we got?'

Cole said: 'Tim Fitzpeterson will live, the oil announcement's been delayed, the currency van raiders got away with more than a million, and England are all out for seventy-nine.'

'And?'

'And there's something going on.'

The editor lit a cigar. If the truth were known, he quite liked to have his administrative sludge interrupted by something exciting like a story. 'Go on.'

Cole said: 'You remember Kevin came in during the morning conference, a little overexcited about a phone call allegedly from Tim Fitzpeterson.'

The editor smiled indulgently. 'If young reporters don't get excited, what the hell will they be like when they get old?'

'Well, it's possible Kevin was right to say it was the big one. Remember the names of the people allegedly blackmailing Fitzpeterson? Cox and Laski.' Cole turned to Hart. 'Okay, Kevin.'

Hart uncrossed his legs and leaned forward. 'Another phone call, this time from a woman who gave her name and address. She said that her husband, William Johnson, had been on the currency van raid, that he had been shot and blinded, and that it was a Tony Cox job.'

The editor said: '*Tony* Cox! Did you follow it up?'

'There is a William Johnson in the hospital with shotgun wounds to the face. And there's a detective beside his bed, waiting for him to come round. I went to see the wife, but she wouldn't speak.'

The editor, who had once been a crime reporter, said: 'Tony Cox is a very big fish. I'd believe anything of him. Not at all a nice man. Go on.'

Cole said: 'The next bit is Mervyn's.'

'There's a bank in trouble,' the City editor said.

'The Cotton Bank of Jamaica – it's a foreign bank with a branch in London. Does a lot of UK business. Anyway, it's owned by a man called Felix Laski.'

'How do we know?' the editor asked. 'That it's in trouble, I mean.'

'Well, I got a tip from a contact. I rang Threadneedle Street to check it out. Of course, they won't give a straight answer, but the noises they made tended to confirm the tip.'

'Tell me exactly what was said.'

Glazier pulled out his pad. He could write shorthand at 150 words per minute, and his notes were always immaculate. 'I spoke to a man called Ley, who is most likely to be dealing with it. I happen to know him, because—'

'Skip the commercial, Mervyn,' the editor interrupted. 'We all know how good your contacts are.'

Glazier grinned. 'Sorry. First, I asked him if he knew anything about the Cotton Bank of Jamaica. He said: "The Bank of England knows a good deal about every bank in London."'

'I said: "Then you'll know just how viable the Cotton Bank is at the moment."'

'He said: "Of course. Which is not to say that I'm going to tell you."'

'I said: "They're about to go under – true or false?"'

'He said: "Pass."'

'I said: "Come on, Donald, this isn't *Mastermind* – it's people's money."'

'He said: "You know I can't talk about that sort

of thing. Banks are our customers. We respect their trust."

'I said: "I am going to print a story saying that the Cotton Bank is about to fold. Are you or are you not telling me that such a story would be false?"

'He said: "I'm telling you to check your facts first." That's about it.' Glazier closed his notebook. 'If the bank was okay, he would have said so.'

The editor nodded. 'I have never liked that kind of reasoning, but in this case you're probably right.' He tapped his cigar on a large glass ashtray. 'Where does it get us?'

Cole summed up. 'Cox and Laski blackmail Fitz-peterson. Fitzpeterson tries to kill himself. Cox does a raid. Laski goes bust.' He shrugged. 'There's something going on.'

'What do you want to do?'

'Find out. Isn't that what we're here for?'

The editor got up and went to the window, as if to make time in which to consider. He made a small adjustment to his blinds, and the room became slightly brighter. Slats of sunshine appeared on the rich blue carpet, picking out the sculptured pattern. He returned to his desk and sat down.

'No,' he said. 'We're going to leave it, and I'm going to tell you why. One: we can't predict the collapse of a bank, because our prediction on its own would be enough to cause that collapse. Just to ask questions about the bank's viability would set the City all a-tremble.

'Two: we can't try to detect the perpetrators of a currency raid. That's the police force's job. Anyway, anything we discover can't be printed for fear of prejudicing a trial. I mean, if we know it's Tony Cox, the police must know; and the law says that if we know an arrest is imminent or likely, the story becomes *sub judice*.

'Three: Tim Fitzpeterson is not going to die. If we blunder around London asking about his sex life, before you know it there will be questions in Parliament about *Evening Post* reporters scouring the country for dirt on politicians. We leave that sort of thing to the Sunday rags.'

He laid his hands on his desk, palms down. 'Sorry, boys.'

Cole got up. 'Okay, let's get back to work.'

The three journalists left. When they got back to the newsroom, Kevin Hart said: 'If he was editor of *The Washington Post*, Nixon would still be winning elections on a law-and-order ticket.'

Nobody laughed.

# Three p.m.

# Chapter Twenty-Nine

'I have Smith and Bernstein for you, Mr Laski.'

'Thank you, Carol. Put him on. Hello, George?'

'Felix, how are you?'

Laski put a smile into his voice. It was not easy. 'On top of the world. Has your service improved any?' George Bernstein played tennis.

'Not a bit. You know I was teaching George junior to play?'

'Yes.'

'Now he beats me.'

Laski laughed. 'And how's Rachel?'

'No thinner. We were talking about you last night. She said you ought to be married. I said: "Didn't you know? Felix is gay." She said: "Gay? So why can't happy people be married?" I said: "No, I mean he's a homosexual, Rachel." She dropped her knitting. She believed me, Felix! Would you credit it?'

Laski forced another laugh. He was not sure how much longer he could keep this up. 'I'm thinking about it, George.'

'Marriage? Don't do it! Don't do it! Is that what you called to say?'

'No, that's just a little thought hovering around in the back of my mind.'

'So what can I tell you?'

'It's a little thing. I want a million pounds for twenty-four hours, and I thought I'd put the business your way.' Laski held his breath.

There was a short silence. 'A million. For how long has Felix Laski been in the money market?'

'Since I found out how to make a real profit overnight.'

'Let me in on the secret, will you?'

'All right. After you lend me the money. No kidding, George: can you do it?'

'Sure we can. What's your collateral?'

'Uh – surely you don't normally ask for collateral against twenty-four-hour money?' Laski's fist tightened on the phone until the knuckles bulged whitely.

'You're right. And we don't normally lend sums like this to banks like yours.'

'Okay. My collateral is five hundred and ten thousand shares in Hamilton Holdings.'

'Just a minute.'

There was a silence. Laski pictured George Bernstein: a thickset man with a large head, a big nose, and a permanent broad grin; sitting at an old desk in a poky office with a view of St Paul's; checking figures in the *Financial Times*, his fingers playing lightly over the keys of a desktop computer.

Bernstein came back on the line. 'At today's price it's not nearly enough, Felix.'

'Oh, come on, this is a formality. You know I'm not going to screw you. This is me – Felix – your friend.' He wiped his brow with his sleeve.

'I'd like to do it, but I've got a partner.'

'Your partner is sleeping so heavily there's a rumour he's dead.'

'A deal like this would wake him if he was in his grave. Try Larry Wakely, Felix. He might do something for you.'

Laski had already tried Larry Wakely, but he did not say so. 'I will. How about a game this weekend?'

'Love to!' The relief in Bernstein's voice was obvious. 'Saturday morning at the club?'

'Ten pounds a game?'

'It'll break my heart to take your money.'

'Look forward to it. Good-bye, George.'

'Take care.'

Laski closed his eyes for a moment, letting the phone dangle from his hand. He had known that Bernstein would not lend him the money: he was just trying anything now. He rubbed his face with his fingers. He was not beaten yet.

He depressed the cradle and got a purring tone. He dialled with a chewed pencil.

The number rang for a long time. Laski was about to dial again when it answered. 'Department of Energy.'

'Press Office,' Laski said.

'Trying to connect you.'

Another woman's voice. 'Press Office.'

'Good afternoon,' Laski said. 'Can you tell me when the Secretary of State is going to make the announcement about the oil—'

'The Secretary of State has been delayed,' the woman interrupted. 'Your news desk has been told, and there is a full explanation on the PA wire.' She hung up.

Laski sat back in his chair. He was running scared, and he did not like it. It was his role to dominate situations such as this: he liked to be the only one in the know, the manipulator who had everyone else running around trying to figure out what was going on. Going cap in hand to money-lenders was not his style.

The phone rang again. Carol said: 'A Mr Hart on the line.'

'Am I supposed to know him?'

'No, but he says it's in connection with the money the Cotton Bank needs.'

'Put him on. Hello, Laski here.'

'Good afternoon, Mr Laski.' It was the voice of a young man. 'I'm Kevin Hart of the *Evening Post*.'

Laski was startled. 'I thought she said— Never mind.'

'The money the Cotton Bank needs. Yes, well, a bank in trouble needs money, doesn't it?'

Laski said: 'I don't think I want to talk to you, young man.'

Before Laski could hang up, Hart said: 'Tim Fitzpeterson.'

Laski paled. 'What?'

'Do the Cotton Bank's troubles have anything to do with the attempted suicide of Tim Fitzpeterson?'

How the hell did they know? Laski's mind raced. Maybe they didn't know. They might be guessing – flying a kite, they called it; pretending to know something in order to see whether people would deny it. Laski said: 'Does your editor know you're making this call?'

'Um – of course not.'

Something in the reporter's voice told Laski he had struck a chord of fear. He pressed the point home. 'I don't know what kind of game you're playing, young man, but if I hear any more about all this nonsense, I'll know from where the rumours originated.'

Hart said: 'What is your relationship with Tony Cox?'

'Who? Good-bye, young man.' Laski put the phone down.

He looked at his wristwatch: it was a quarter past three. There was no way he could raise a million pounds in fifteen minutes. It looked as if it was all over.

The bank was going to go under; Laski's reputation was to be destroyed; and he would probably be involved in criminal proceedings. He contemplated leaving the country, this afternoon. He would be able to take nothing with him. Start all over again, in New York or Beirut? He was too old. If he stayed, he would be able to salvage enough from his empire to live on for the rest of his life. But what the hell kind of a life would it be?

He swivelled around in his chair and looked out of the window. The day was cooling; after all, it was not summer. The high buildings of the City were casting long shadows, and both sides of the street below were shaded. Laski watched the traffic and thought about Ellen Hamilton.

Today, of all days, he had decided to marry her. It was a painful irony. For twenty years he could have had his pick of women: models, actresses, debs, even princesses. And when at last he chose one, he went broke. A superstitious man would take that as a sign that he should not marry.

The option might no longer be open to him. Felix Laski, millionaire playboy, was one thing; Felix Laski, bankrupt ex-convict, was quite another. He was sure his relationship with Ellen was not the kind of love that could survive that level of disaster. Their love was a sensual, self-indulgent, hedonistic thing, quite different from the eternal devotion of the *Book of Common Prayer*.

At least, that was how it always had been. Laski had theorized that the permanent affection might come, later, from simply living together and sharing things; after all, the near-hysterical lust that had brought them together was sure to fade, in time.

I shouldn't be theorizing, he thought: at my age I should know.

This morning, the decision to marry her had seemed

like a choice he could make coolly, lightly, even cynically, figuring what he would get out of it as if it were just another stock market coup. But now that he was no longer in command of the situation, he realized – and the thought hit him like a physical blow – that he needed her quite desperately. He *wanted* eternal devotion: he wanted someone to care about him, and to like his company, and to touch his shoulder with affection as she passed his chair; someone who would always be there, someone who would say 'I love you', someone who would share his old age. He had been alone all his life: it was quite long enough.

Having admitted that much to himself, he went farther. If he could have her, he would cheerfully see his empire crumble, the Hamilton Holdings deal collapse, his reputation destroyed. He would even go to gaol with Tony Cox if he thought she would be waiting when he got out.

He wished he had never met Tony Cox.

Laski had imagined it would be easy to control a two-bit hoodlum like Cox. The man might be enormously powerful inside his own little world, but he surely could not touch a respectable businessman. Maybe not: but when that businessman went into partnership – however informal – with the hoodlum, he ceased to be respectable. It was Laski, not Cox, who was compromised by the association.

Laski heard the office door open, and swung around in his chair to see Tony Cox walk in.

Laski stared open-mouthed. It was like seeing a ghost.

Carol scuttled in behind Cox, worrying him like a terrier. She said to Laski: 'I asked him to wait, but he wouldn't – he just walked in!'

'All right, Carol, I'll deal with it,' Laski said.

The girl went out and shut the door.

Laski exploded. 'What the devil are you doing here? Nothing could be more dangerous! I've already had the newspapers on, asking me about you and about Fitzpeterson – did you know he tried to kill himself?'

'Calm down. Keep your hair on,' Cox told him.

'Calm down? The whole thing is a disaster! I've lost everything, and if I'm seen with you I'll end up in gaol—'

Cox took a long stride forward, grabbed Laski by the throat, and shook him. 'Shut your mouth,' he growled. He threw him backwards in his chair. 'Now, listen. I want your help.'

'No way,' Laski muttered.

'Shut up! I want your help, and you're going to give it, or I'll make bloody sure you do go to gaol. Now you know I done this job this morning – a currency van.'

'I know no such thing.'

Cox ignored that. 'Well, I've got nowhere to hide the money, so I'm going to put it in your bank.'

'Don't be ridiculous,' Laski said lightly. Then he frowned. 'How much is it?'

'Just over a million.'

'Where?'

'Outside in the van.'

Laski jumped to his feet. 'You've got a million pounds in stolen money, outside here in a fucking *van*?'

'Yes.'

'You are insane.' Laski's thoughts were racing. 'What form is the money in?'

'Assorted used notes.'

'Are they in the original containers?'

'I'm not that daft. They've been transferred to packing cases.'

'Serial numbers out of sequence?'

'You're getting the idea slowly. If you don't get a move on they'll tow the van away for parking on a yellow line.'

Laski scratched his head. 'How will you carry it into the vault?'

'I got six of the boys out there.'

'I can't let six of your roughnecks carry all that money into my vault! The staff will suspect—'

'They're in uniform – Navy surplus jackets, trousers, shirts and ties. They look like security guards, Felix. If you want to play twenty questions, leave it till afterwards, eh?'

Laski decided. 'All right, get moving.' He ushered Cox out and followed him as far as Carol's desk. 'Ring down to the vault,' he told the girl. 'Tell them to prepare to take in a consignment of cash immediately. I will be dealing with the paperwork personally. And give me an outside line on my phone.'

He strode back into his office, picked up the phone, and dialled the Bank of England. He looked at his watch. It was three twenty-five. He got through to Mr Ley.

'It's Laski here,' he said.

'Ah, yes?' The banker was cautious.

Laski forced himself to sound calm. 'I've sorted out this little problem, Ley. The necessary cash is in my vault. Now I can arrange delivery immediately, as you suggested earlier; or you can inspect today and take delivery tomorrow.'

'Um.' Ley thought for a moment. 'I don't think either will be necessary, Laski. It would rather throw us to have to count so much money this late in the afternoon. If you can deliver first thing in the morning, we'll clear the cheque tomorrow.'

'Thank you.' Laski decided to rub salt in the wound. 'I'm sorry to have irritated you so much, earlier today.'

'Perhaps I was a little brusque. Goodbye, Laski.'

Laski hung up. He was still thinking fast. He reckoned he could drum up about a hundred thousand in cash overnight. Cox could probably equal that from his clubs. They could swap that cash for two hundred thousand of the stolen notes. It was just another precaution: if *all* the notes he delivered tomorrow were too worn to be reissued, someone might wonder at the coincidence of a theft one day and a deposit the next. A leavening of good-condition currency would allay that suspicion.

# Paper Money

He seemed to have covered everything. He allowed himself to relax for a moment. I've done it again, he thought: I've won. A laugh of sheer triumph escaped from his throat.

Now to supervise the details. He had better go down to the vault to provide reassurance to his no-doubt bemused staff. And he wanted to see Cox and his crew off the premises fast.

Then he would phone Ellen.

# Chapter Thirty

Ellen Hamilton had been at home almost all day. The shopping trip she had told Felix about was invented: she just needed an excuse for going to see him. She was a very bored woman. The trip to London had not taken long: on her return she had changed her clothes, redone her hair, and taken much longer than necessary to prepare a lunch of cottage cheese, salad, fruit, and black coffee without sugar. She had washed her dishes, scorning the dishwasher for so few items and sending Mrs Tremlett upstairs to vacuum-clean. She watched the news and a soap opera on television; began to read an historical novel, and put it down after five pages; went from room to room in the house tidying things that did not need to be tidied; and went down to the pool for a swim, changing her mind at the last minute.

Now she stood naked on the tiled floor of the cool summerhouse, her swimsuit in one hand and her dress in the other, thinking: If I can't make up my mind whether or not to go swimming, how will I ever summon the will-power to leave my husband?

She dropped the clothes and let her shoulders sag. There was a full-length mirror on the wall, but she did not look in it. She took care of her appearance out of scruple, not vanity: she found mirrors quite resistible.

She wondered what it would be like to swim in the nude. Such things had been unheard-of when she was young: besides, she had always been inhibited. She knew this, and did not fight it, for she actually liked her inhibitions – they gave to her lifestyle a shape and constancy which she needed.

The floor was deliciously cool. She was tempted to lie down and roll over, enjoying the feel of the cold tiles on her hot skin. She calculated the risk of Pritchard or Mrs Tremlett walking in on her, and decided it was too great. She got dressed again.

The summerhouse was quite high up. From its door one could see most of the grounds – there were nine acres. It was a delightful garden, created at the beginning of the last century; eccentrically landscaped and planted with dozens of different species of trees. It had given her much pleasure, but lately it had palled, like everything else.

The place was at its best in the cool of the afternoon. A light breeze set Ellen's printed cotton dress flapping like a flag. She walked past the pool into a copse, where the leaves filtered the sunlight and made shifting patterns on the dry earth.

Felix said she was uninhibited, but of course he was wrong. She had simply made an area in her life where constancy was sacrificed for the sake of joy. Besides, it was no longer gauche to have a lover, provided one was discreet; and she was extremely discreet.

The trouble was, she liked the taste of freedom. She realized that she was at a dangerous age. The women's magazines she flicked through (but never actually read) were constantly telling her that this was when a woman added up the years she had left, decided they were shockingly few, and determined to fill them with all the things she had missed so far. The trendy, liberated young writers warned her that disappointment lay in that direction. How would they know? They were just guessing, like everyone else.

She suspected it was nothing to do with age. When she was seventy she would be able to find a lively nonagenarian to lust after her, if at that age she still cared. Nor was it anything to do with the menopause, which was well behind her. It was simply that every day she found Derek a little less attractive and Felix a little more. It had reached the point where the contrast was too much to bear.

She had let both of them know what the situation was, in her indirect manner. She smiled as she recalled how thoughtful each had looked after she had delivered her veiled ultimatums. She knew her men: each would analyse what she had said, understand after a while, and congratulate himself on his perspicacity. Neither would know he was being threatened.

She emerged from the copse and leaned on a fence at the edge of a field. The pasture was shared by a donkey and an old mare: the donkey was there for the grandchildren and the mare because she had once been Ellen's favourite hunter. It was all right for them – they did not know they were getting old.

She crossed the field and climbed the embankment to the disused railway line. Steam engines had puffed along here when she and Derek were gay young socialites, dancing to jazz music and drinking too much champagne, giving parties they could not really afford. She walked along between the rusty lines, jumping from sleeper to sleeper, until something small and furry ran out from under the rotting black wood and scared her. She scampered down the bank and walked back towards the house, following the stream through rough woodland. She did not want to be a gay young thing again; but she still wanted to be in love.

Well, she had laid her cards on the table, as it were, with both men. Derek had been told that his work was edging his wife out of his life, and that he would have to change his ways if he was to keep her. Felix had been warned that she would not be his fancy piece for ever.

Both men might bow to her will, which would leave her still with the problem of choice. Or they might both decide they could do without her, in which case there would be nothing for her to do except to become *désolée*, like a girl in a novel by Françoise Sagan; and she knew that would not suit her.

Well, suppose they both were prepared to do as she wished: whom would she choose? As she rounded the corner of the house she thought: Felix, probably.

She realized with a shock that the car was in the drive, and Derek was getting out of it. Why was he home so early? He waved to her. He seemed happy.

She ran to him across the gravel and, full of guilt, she kissed him.

# Chapter Thirty-One

Kevin Hart should have been worrying, but somehow he could not summon up the energy.

The editor had quite explicitly told them not to investigate the Cotton Bank. Kevin had disobeyed, and Laski had asked: 'Does your editor know you are making this call?' The question was often asked by outraged interviewees, and the answer was always an unworried No – unless, of course, the editor had forbidden the call. So, if Laski should take it into his head to ring the editor – or even the Chairman – Kevin was in trouble.

So why wasn't he worried?

He decided that he did not care for his job as much as he had this morning. The editor had good reasons for killing the story, of course; there were always good reasons for cowardice. Everyone seemed to accept that 'It's against the law' was a final argument; but the great newspapers of the past had always broken the laws: laws at once harsher and more strictly applied than those of today. Kevin believed that newspapers should publish and be sued, or even arrested. It was easy for him to believe this, for he was not an editor.

So he sat in the newsroom, close to the news desk, sipping machine tea and reading his own paper's gossip column, composing the heroic speech he would like to have made to the editor. It was the fag-end of the day as far as the paper was concerned. Nothing less than a major assassination or a multiple-death disaster would get in the paper now. Half the reporters – those on eight-hour shifts – had gone home. Kevin worked ten hours, four days a week. The industrial correspondent, having taken eight pints of Guinness at lunch, was asleep in a corner. A lone typewriter clacked desultorily as a girl reporter in jeans wrote an undated story for tomorrow's first edition. The copytakers were arguing about football and the sub-editors were composing joke captions for spiked pictures, laughing uproariously at each other's wit. Arthur Cole was pacing up and down, resisting the temptation to smoke and secretly hoping for a fire at Buckingham Palace. Every so often he would stop and leaf through the sheets of copy impaled on his spike, as if worrying that he might have overlooked the big story of the day.

After a while Mervyn Glazier sauntered across from his own small kingdom. His shirt was hanging out. He sat down beside Kevin, lighting a steel-stemmed pipe and resting one scuffed shoe on the rim of the wastepaper basket.

'The Cotton Bank of Jamaica,' he said by way of preamble. He spoke quietly.

Kevin grinned. 'Have you been a naughty boy, too?'

Mervyn shrugged. 'I can't help it if people ring me up with information. Anyway, if the bank ever was in danger, it's out now.'

'How do you know?'

'My tight-lipped contact at Threadneedle Street. "I have looked more closely at the Cotton Bank since your call, and I find it to be in excellent financial health." Unquote. In other words, it's been quietly rescued.'

Kevin finished his tea and crumpled the plastic-paper cup noisily. 'So much for that.'

'I also hear, from a quite separate source not a million miles from the Council of the Stock Exchange, that Felix Laski has bought a controlling share in Hamilton Holdings.'

'He can't be short of a few bob, then. Is the Council interested?'

'No. They know, and they don't mind.'

'Do you think we made a big fuss over nothing?'

Mervyn shook his head slowly. 'By no means.'

'Nor do I.'

Mervyn's pipe had gone out. He tapped it into the waste-paper basket. The two journalists looked helplessly at each other for a moment, then Mervyn got up and went away.

Kevin returned his attention to the gossip column, but he could not concentrate. He read a paragraph four times without understanding it, then gave up.

Some large piece of skulduggery had gone on today, and he itched to know what it was; the more so because he felt so close to understanding it.

Arthur called him. 'Sit behind here while I go to the lav, will you?'

Kevin walked around the news desk and took a seat behind the news editor's bank of telephones and switchboards. It gave him no thrill: he had the job because, at this time of day, it hardly mattered. He was just the nearest idle man.

Idleness was inevitable on newspapers, Kevin mused. The staff had to be sufficiently many to cope on a big day, so they were bound to be too many on a normal day. On some papers they gave you silly jobs to do just to keep you busy: writing stories from publicity handouts and local government press releases, stuff that would never get in the paper. It was demoralizing, time-wasting work, and only the more insecure of newspaper executives demanded it.

A lad came across from the teleprinter room, carrying a Press Association story on a long sheet of paper. Kevin took it from him and glanced at it.

He read it with a growing sense of shock and elation.

A syndicate headed by Hamilton Holdings today won the licence to drill for oil in the last North Sea oil field, Shield.

The Secretary of State for Energy, Mr Carl Wrightment, announced the name of the winning contender at a Press conference overshadowed by the sudden illness of his Junior Minister, Mr Tim Fitzpeterson.

The announcement was expected to provide a much-needed fillip to the ailing shares of the Hamilton print group, whose half-year results, published yesterday, were disappointing.

Shield is estimated to hold oil reserves which could ultimately amount to half a million barrels a week.

The Hamilton group's partners in the syndicate include Scan, the engineering giant, and British Organic Chemicals.

After making the announcement Mr Wrightment added: 'It is with sadness that I have to tell you of the sudden illness of Tim Fitzpeterson, whose work on the Government's oil policy has been so invaluable.'

Kevin read the story three times, hardly able to believe its implications. Fitzpeterson, Cox, Laski, the raid, the bank crisis, the take-over – all leading in a great, frightening circle, back to Tim Fitzpeterson.

'It can't be that,' he said aloud.

'What have you got?' Arthur's voice came from behind him. 'Is it worth a fudge?' The fudge was what the public called the Stop Press.

Kevin passed him the story and vacated his chair. 'I think,' he said slowly, 'that story will persuade the editor to change his mind.'

Arthur sat down to read. Kevin watched him eagerly. He wanted the older man to react; to jump up and shout 'Hold the front page!' or something; but Arthur stayed cool.

Eventually he dropped the sheet of paper on the desk. He looked coldly at Kevin. 'So what?' he said.

'Isn't it obvious?' Kevin said excitedly.

'No. Tell me.'

'Look. Laski and Cox blackmail Fitzpeterson into telling them who has won the Shield licence. Cox, maybe with Laski's help, raids the currency van and gets a million pounds. Cox gives the money to Laski, who uses it to buy the company that got the oil licence.'

'So what would you like us all to do about it?'

'For Christ's sake! We could drop hints, or mount an investigation, or tell the police – at least tell the police! We're the only people who know it all – we can't let the bastards get away with it!'

'Don't you know anything?' Arthur said bitterly.

'What do you mean?'

Arthur's voice was as sombre as the grave. 'Hamilton Holdings is the parent company of the *Evening Post*.' He paused, then looked Kevin in the eye. 'Felix Laski is your new boss.'

# Four p.m.

# Chapter Thirty-Two

They sat down in the small dining room, on either side of the little circular table, and he said: 'I've sold the company.'

She smiled, and said calmly: 'Derek, I'm so glad.' Then, against her will, tears came to her eyes, and her icy self-control weakened and crumbled for the first time since the birth of Andrew. She saw, through the tears, the shock in his expression as he realized how much it meant to her. She stood up and opened a cupboard, saying: 'I think this calls for a drink.'

'I got a million pounds for it,' he said, knowing she was not interested.

'Is that good?'

'As it happens, yes. But more importantly, it's enough to keep us comfortably well off for as long as we're likely to live.'

She made gin-and-tonic for herself. 'Would you like a drink?'

'Perrier, please. I've decided to go on the wagon for a bit.'

She gave him his drink and sat opposite him again. 'What made you decide?'

'No single thing. Talking to you, and talking to

Nathaniel.' He sipped his mineral water. 'Talking to you, mainly. The things you said about our lifestyle.'

'When does it become final?'

'It already has. I shan't go back to the office, ever.' He looked away from her, out through the French windows across the lawn. 'I resigned at twelve noon, and I haven't felt the ulcer since. Isn't that marvellous?'

'Yes.' She followed his gaze, and saw the sun shining redly through the branches of her favourite tree, the Scots pine. 'Have you made any plans?'

'I thought we could do that together.' He smiled directly at her. 'But I shall get up late; and eat three small meals a day, always at the same times; and watch television; and see whether I can remember how to paint.'

She nodded. She felt awkward; they both did. Suddenly there was a new relationship between them, and they were feeling their way, unsure what to say or how to behave. For him, the situation was simple: he had made the sacrifice she asked, given her his soul; and now he wanted her to acknowledge it, to accept the gift with some gesture. But for her, that gesture would mean letting Felix go out of her life. I can't do it, she thought; and the words rang in her head like the echoing syllables of a curse.

He said: 'What would you like us to do?'

It was as if he knew of her dilemma, and wanted to force her hand, to make her talk about the two of them as a unit. 'I would like us to take a long time deciding,' she said.

'Good idea.' He got to his feet. 'I'm going to change my clothes.'

'I'll come up with you.' She picked up her drink and followed him. He looked surprised, and in truth she too was a little shocked: it was thirty years since they had been in the habit of watching one another undress.

They went through the hall and climbed the main staircase together. He panted with the effort, and said: 'In six months' time I shall be running up here.' He was looking to the future with so much pleasure; she with so much dread. For him, life was beginning again. If only he had done this before she met Felix!

He held the bedroom door open for her, and her heart missed a beat. This had once been a ritual; a sign between them; a lovers' code. It had started when they were young. She had noticed that he became almost embarrassingly courteous to her when he felt lustful, and she said as a joke: 'You only open doors for me when you want to make love.' Then, of course, they thought of sex every time he opened a door for her, and it became his way of letting her know he wanted it. One felt the need of such signals in those days: nowadays she felt quite happy about saying to Felix: 'Let's do it on the floor.'

Did Derek remember? Was he now telling her that this was the acknowledgment he wanted? It had been years; and he was so gross. Was it possible?

He went into the bathroom and turned on the taps. She sat at her dressing table and brushed her hair. In the mirror she watched him come out of the bathroom and begin to take off his clothes. He still did it the same way: first shoes, then trousers, then jacket. He had told her, once, that this was the way it had to be; for the trousers went on the hanger before the jacket, and the shoes had to come off before the trousers would. She had told him how peculiar a man looked in his shirt, tie, and socks. They had both laughed.

He removed his tie and unbuttoned his shirt collar with a sigh of relief. Collars always bothered him. Perhaps he need not wear them buttoned any more.

He took off his shirt, then his socks, then his vest, and finally his underwear shorts. Then he caught her eye in the mirror. There was something close to defiance in his gaze, as if he were saying: 'This is what an old man looks like, so you'd better get used to it.' She met his eyes for a moment, then looked away. He went into the bathroom, and she heard the surge of the water as he climbed into the bath.

Now that he was out of sight she felt freer to think, as if before he might have overheard her thoughts. Her dilemma had been posed in the most brutal way: could she, or could she not, face the thought of sex with Derek? A few months ago she might have – no, not 'might', but 'would', and eagerly – but since then she had touched the firm, muscular body of Felix, and rediscovered her own body in the sheer physicality of their relationship.

She forced herself to visualize Derek's naked body: the thick neck, the fatty breasts with tufts of grey-white hair at the nipples, the huge belly with its arrow of hair widening to the groin, and there – well, at least he and Felix were much the same there.

She imagined herself in bed with Derek, and thought of how he would touch her, and kiss her, and what she would do to him – and suddenly she realized she *could* do it, and take pleasure in it, because of what it meant: Felix's fingers might be skilful and knowing, but Derek's were the hands she had held for years; she might scratch Felix's shoulders in passion, but she knew she could lean on Derek's; Felix had dashing good looks, but in Derek's face there were years of kindness and comfort, of compassion and understanding.

Perhaps she loved Derek. And perhaps she was just too old to change.

She heard him stand up in the bath, and she panicked. She had not had enough time; she was not yet ready to make an irrevocable decision. She could not, right here and now, accept the thought of never having Felix inside her again. It was too soon.

She must talk to Derek. She must change the subject; break his mood and hers. What could she say? He stepped out of the bath: now he would be towelling himself, and in a moment he would be here.

She called out: 'Who bought the company?'

His reply was inaudible; and at that moment, the phone rang.

As she crossed the room to pick it up, she repeated: 'Who bought the company?' She lifted the receiver.

Derek shouted: 'A man called Felix Laski. You've met him. Remember?'

She stood frozen, with the phone to her ear, not speaking. It was too much to take in: the implications, the irony, the treachery.

The voice from the telephone said in her ear: 'Hello, hello?'

It was Felix.

She whispered: 'Oh, God, no.'

'Ellen?' he said. 'Is that you?'

'Yes.'

'I've a lot I want to talk to you about. Can we meet?'

She stammered: 'I – I don't think so.'

'Don't be like that.' His deep, Shakespearian voice was like the music from a cello. 'I want you to marry me.'

'Oh, God!'

'Ellen, speak to me. Will you marry me?'

Suddenly she knew what she wanted, and with the realization came the beginning of calm. She took a deep breath. 'No, I most certainly will not,' she said.

She hung up the phone, and stood staring at it for several moments.

Slowly and deliberately, she took off all her clothes and placed them in a neat pile on a chair.

Then she got into bed and lay waiting for her husband.

# Chapter Thirty-Three

Tony Cox was a happy man. He played the radio as he drove slowly home through the streets of East London in the Rolls. He was thinking how well everything had gone, and he was forgetting what had happened to Deaf Willie. He drummed his fingers on the steering wheel in time to a pop song with a bouncy beat. It was cooler now. The sun was low, and there were streamers of high white clouds in the blue sky. The traffic was getting heavier as the rush hour approached, but Tony had all the patience in the world this evening.

It *had* gone well, in the end. The boys had had their shares, and Tony had explained how the rest of the money had been hidden in a bank, and why. He had promised them another payout in a couple of months' time, and they had been happy.

Laski had accepted the stolen money more readily than Tony expected. Maybe the crafty sod thought he could embezzle some of it: just let him try. The two of them would have to cook up some scheme for concealing the true nature of any withdrawals Tony made from the funds. That couldn't be difficult.

Tonight, nothing could be difficult. He wondered

what to do with the evening. Perhaps he would go to a gay bar and pick up a friend for the night. He would dress up, put on some fancy jewellery, and stuff a roll of tenners into his pocket. He would find a boy a couple of years younger than himself, and shower him with kindness: a wonderful meal, a show, champagne – then back to the Barbican flat. He would knock the boy about a bit, just to soften him up, and then . . .

It would be a good night. In the morning the boy would go away with his pockets full of money, bruised but happy. Tony enjoyed making people happy.

On impulse, he pulled up outside a corner shop and went in. It was a newsagent's, with bright modern decor and new racking along the walls for magazines and books. Tony asked for the biggest box of chocolates in the shop.

The young girl behind the counter was fat, spotty and cheeky. She reached up for the chocolates, letting her nylon overalls ride up almost to her bottom. Tony looked away.

'Who's the lucky lady, then?' the girl asked him.

'My mum.'

'Pull the other one.'

Tony paid and got out fast. There was nothing more revolting than a revolting woman.

As he drove away he thought: really, with a million pounds I should do something more than just going out for a night on the town. But there was nothing else he wanted. He could buy a house in Spain, but he got too hot out there. He had enough cars; world cruises bored him; he did not want a mansion in the country; there was nothing he collected. It made him laugh when he thought of it this way: he had become a millionaire in a day, and the only thing he could think of to buy was a three-pound box of chocolates.

The money *was* security, though. If he went through a bad patch – even if, God forbid, he did a stretch – he could look after the boys more or less indefinitely. Running the firm could be expensive at times. There were about twenty blokes in all, and each of them looked to him for a few quid every Friday, whether they had had a tickle or not. He sighed. Yes, his responsibilities would weigh less heavily now. It was worth it for that.

He pulled up outside his mother's house. The dashboard clock said four thirty-five. Ma would have tea ready soon: perhaps a bit of cheese on toast, or a plate of baked beans; then some fruit cake or Battenberg; and tinned pears with Ideal milk to finish off. Or she might have got him his favourite – crumpets and jam. He would eat again later tonight. He had always had a good appetite.

He entered the house and closed the front door behind him. The hall was untidy. The vacuum cleaner stood unattended halfway up the stairs, a raincoat had fallen from the hall stand on to the tiled floor, and there was some kind of mess by the kitchen door. It looked as if Ma had been called away suddenly: he hoped there wasn't bad news.

He picked up the raincoat and hung it on a hook. The dog was out, too; there was no welcoming bark.

He went into the kitchen, and stopped with one foot still in the hall.

The mess was awful. At first he could not figure out what it was. Then he smelled the blood.

It was everywhere: walls, floor, ceiling; all over the fridge, the cooker, and the draining board. The stench of the abattoir filled his nostrils, and he felt sick. But where had it all come from? What had caused it? He looked around wildly for some clue, but there was nothing; just the blood.

He crossed the kitchen in two big, squelching strides, and flung open the back door.

Then he understood.

His dog lay on her back in the middle of the little concrete yard. The knife was still in her – the same knife he had sharpened too much this morning. Tony knelt beside the mutilated corpse. The body looked shrunken, like a balloon with a leak.

A string of soft, blasphemous curses came from Tony's lips. He stared at the multiple cuts, and the bits of cloth between the dog's bared teeth, and whispered: 'You put up a fight, girl.'

He went to the garden gate and looked out, as if the killer might still be there. All he could see was a large pink wad of chewed bubblegum on the ground, casually thrown away by a child.

Obviously, Ma had been out when it happened, which was a mercy. Tony decided to clear up before she got back.

He got a spade from the outhouse. Between the yard and the garden gate was a small patch of poor soil which the old man used to cultivate intermittently. Now it was overgrown. Tony took off his jacket, marked out a small square of ground, and began to dig.

The grave did not take him long. He was strong, and angry too. He trod the spade viciously and thought about what he would do to the killer if he ever found him. And he would find him. The bastard had done it out of spite, and when people did things like that they had to boast about it, either before or afterwards, otherwise they would have proved their point to nobody but themselves, and that was never enough. He knew the type. Somebody would hear something, and tell one of the boys in the hope of a reward.

It crossed his mind that the Old Bill might be behind it. It was unlikely: this was not their style. Who, then? He had plenty of enemies, but none of them possessed both the hatred and the guts to do a number like this. When Tony met somebody with much front he usually hired the bloke.

He wrapped the dead dog in his jacket and placed the bundle gently in the hole. He shovelled the earth in and made the surface even with the flat of the spade. You didn't say prayers for dogs, did you? No.

He went back into the kitchen. The mess was awful. There was no way he could clean it up alone. Ma would be back any minute – it was a bloody miracle she had stayed out this long. He had to have help. He decided to ring his sister-in-law.

He went through the kitchen, trying not to spread the blood around. It seemed an awful lot of blood, even for a boxer dog.

He went into the parlour to use the phone, and there she was.

She must have been trying to reach the phone. A thin trail of blood led from the door to the body, lying stretched full length on the carpet. She had been stabbed only once, but the cut had been fatal.

The look of horror frozen on Tony's face changed slowly as his features contorted, like a squeezed cushion, into an expression of despair. He raised his arms slowly upwards and pressed his palms against his cheeks. His mouth opened.

At last words came, and he roared like a bull. 'Ma!' he cried. 'Oh God, Ma!'

He fell to his knees beside the body and cried: huge, loud, racking sobs, like the cries of a child in tot misery.

Outside in the street a crowd gathered aroun parlour window, but no one dared to come in.